BLUE MARS

Kim Stanley Robinson was born in 1952. After several years of travelling and working in different parts of the world, he has now returned to his beloved California. One of the finest science fiction writers to emerge in recent years, Robinson has won many awards in his career, including the Nebula, Asimov, John W. Campbell, Locus and World Fantasy Awards. His previous books include the critically acclaimed *The Wild Shore*, *The Gold Coast*, *Pacific Edge*, *Escape from Kathmandu*, and the first volume in his stunning new series, *Red Mars*.

Mars has always been an obsession for Stan. Ever since the Viking and Mariner probes were sent out, he has been researching the planet, in close contact with NASA and the Mars Underground Organisation, for what he regards as his most important work – the Mars trilogy. In all, these books have taken seventeen years of meticulous planning and investigation.

By the same author

Voyager

KIM STANLEY ROBINSON

Blue Mars

HarperCollins*Publishers*

Voyager
An imprint of HarperCollins*Publishers*
77–85 Fulham Palace Road,
Hammersmith, London W6 8JB

The *Voyager* World Wide Web site address is
http://www.harpercollins.co.uk/voyager

This paperback edition 1996
3 5 7 9 8 6 4

First published in Great Britain by *Voyager* 1996

Copyright © Kim Stanley Robinson 1996

ISBN 0 586 21391 0

Set in Aldus
Rowland Phototypesetting Limited
Bury St Edmunds, Suffolk

Printed and bound in Great Britain by
Caledonian International Book Manufacturing Ltd, Glasgow

For Lisa, David and Timothy

CONTENTS

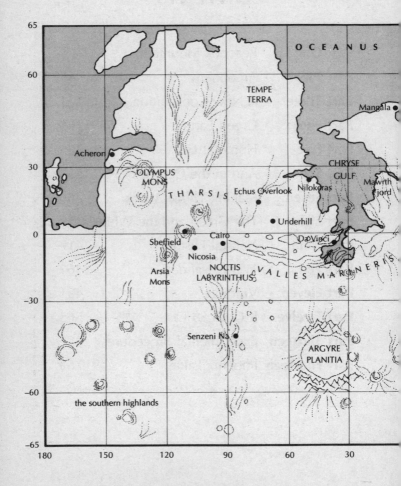

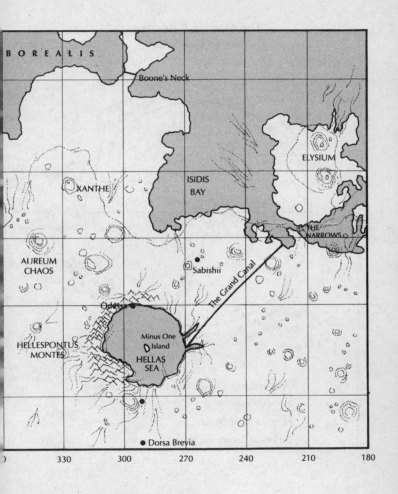

The Martian Calendar
Year 1 (20278AD)

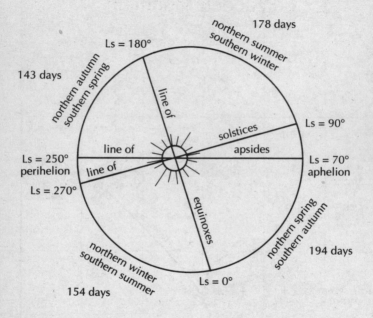

178 days

northern summer
southern winter

Ls = 180°

143 days

northern autumn
southern spring

line of solstices

Ls = 90°

line of apsides

Ls = 250°
perihelion

line of

Ls = 70°
aphelion

Ls = 270°

equinoxes

northern spring
southern autumn

194 days

northern winter
southern summer

154 days

Ls = 0°

669 total Martian days in 1 Martian year

24 months =

21 months at 28 days

3 months (every eighth) at 27 days

PART ONE

Peacock Mountain

Mars is free now. We're on our own. No one tells us what to do.

Ann stood at the front of the train as she said this.

But it's so easy to backslide into old patterns of behaviour. Break one hierarchy and another springs up to take its place. We will have to be on guard for that, because there will always be people trying to make another Earth. The areophany will have to be ceaseless, an eternal struggle. We will have to think harder than ever before what it means to be Martian.

Her listeners sat slumped in chairs, looking out of the windows at the terrain flowing by. They were tired, their eyes were scoured. Red-eyed Reds. In the harsh dawn light everything looked new, the windswept land outside bare except for a khaki scree of lichen and scrub. They had kicked all Earthly power off Mars, it had been a long campaign, capped by months of furious action; they were tired.

We came from Earth to Mars, and in that passage there was a certain purification. Things were easier to see, there was a freedom of action that we had not had before. A chance to express the best part of ourselves. So we acted. We are making a better way to live.

This was the myth, they had all grown up with it. Now as Ann told it to them again, the young Martians stared through her. They had engineered the revolution; they had fought all over Mars, and pushed the Terran police into Burroughs; then they had drowned Burroughs, and chased the Terrans up to Sheffield, on Pavonis Mons. They still had to force the enemy out of Sheffield, up the space cable and back to Terra; there was work still to be done. But in the successful evacuation of Burroughs they had won a great victory, and some of the blank faces staring at Ann or out of the window seemed to want a break, a moment for triumph. They were all exhausted.

Hiroko will help us, a young man said, breaking the silence of the train's levitation over the land.

Ann shook her head. *Hiroko is a Green,* she said, *the original Green.*

Hiroko invented the areophany, the young native countered.

3

That's her first concern: Mars. She will help us, I know. I met her. She told me.

Except she's dead, someone else said.

Another silence. The world flowed under them.

Finally a tall young woman stood up and walked down the uisle, and gave Ann a hug. The spell was broken; words were abandoned; they got to their feet and clustered in the open space at the front of the train, around Ann, and hugged her, or shook her hand – or simply touched her, Ann Clayborne, the one who had taught them to love Mars for itself, who had led them in the struggle for its independence from Earth. And though her bloodshot eyes were still fixed, gazing through them at the rocky battered expanse of the Tyrrhena Massif, she was smiling. She hugged them back, she shook their hands, she reached up to touch their faces. It will be all right, she said. We will make Mars free. And they said yes, and congratulated each other. On to Sheffield, they said. Finish the job. Mars will show us how.

Except she's not dead, the young man objected. I saw her last month in Arcadia. She'll show up again. She'll show up somewhere.

At a certain moment before dawn the sky always glowed the same bands of pink as in the beginning, pale and clear in the east, rich and starry in the west. Ann watched for this moment as her companions drove them west, toward a mass of black land rearing into the sky – the Tharsis bulge, punctuated by the broad cone of Pavonis Mons. As they rolled uphill from Noctis Labyrinthus they rose above most of the new atmosphere; the air pressure at the foot of Pavonis was only 180 millibars, and then as they drove up the eastern flank of the great shield volcano it dropped under 100 millibars, and continued to fall. Slowly they ascended above all visible foliage, crunching over dirty patches of wind-carved snow; then they ascended above even the snow, until there was nothing but rock, and the ceaseless thin cold winds of the jetstream. The bare land looked just as it had in the prehuman years, as if they were driving back up into the past.

It wasn't so. But something fundamental in Ann Clayborne warmed at the sight of this ferric world, stone on rock in the perpetual wind, and as the Red cars rolled up the mountain all their occupants grew as rapt as Ann, the cabins falling silent as the sun cracked the distant horizon behind them.

Then the slope they ascended grew less steep, in a perfect sine curve, until they were on the flat land of the round summit plateau. Here they saw tent towns ringing the edge of the giant caldera, clustered in particular around the foot of the space elevator, some thirty kilometres to the south of them.

They stopped their cars. The silence in the cabins had shifted from reverent to grim. Ann stood at one upper cabin window, looking south toward Sheffield, that child of the space elevator: built because of the elevator, smashed flat when the elevator fell, built again with the elevator's replacement. This was the city she had come to destroy, as thoroughly as Rome had Carthage; for she meant to bring down the replacement cable too, just as they had the first one in 2061. When they did that, much of Sheffield would again be flattened. What remained would be located uselessly on the peak of a high volcano, above most of the atmosphere; as time passed the surviving structures would be abandoned and dismantled for salvage, leaving only the tent foundations, and perhaps a weather station, and, eventually, the long sunny silence of a mountain summit. The salt was already in the ground.

A cheerful Tharsis Red named Irishka joined them in a small rover, and led them through the maze of warehouses and small tents surrounding the intersection of the equatorial piste with the one circling the rim. As they followed her she described for them the local situation. Most of Sheffield and the rest of the Pavonis rim settlements were already in the hands of the Martian revolutionaries. But the space elevator and the neighbourhood surrounding its base complex were not, and there lay the difficulty. The revolutionary forces on Pavonis were mostly poorly equipped militias, and they did not necessarily share the same agenda. That they had succeeded as far as they had was due to many factors: surprise, the control of Martian space, several strategic victories, the support of the great majority of the Martian population, the unwillingness of the United Nations Transitional Authority to fire on civilians, even when they were making mass demonstrations in the streets. As a result the UNTA security forces had retreated from all over Mars to regroup in Sheffield, and now most of them were in elevator cars, going up to Clarke, the ballast asteroid and space station at the top of the elevator; the rest were jammed into the neighbourhood surrounding the elevator's massive base complex, called the Socket. This district consisted of elevator support facilities, industrial warehouses, and the hostels, dormitories and restaurants needed to house and feed the port's workforce. 'Those are coming in useful now,' Irishka said, 'because even so they're squeezed in like trash in a compactor, and if there hadn't been food and shelter they would probably have tried a breakout. As it is things are still tense, but at least they can live.'

It somewhat resembled the situation just resolved in Burroughs, Ann thought. Which had turned out fine. It only took someone willing to act and the thing would be done – UNTA evacuated to Earth, the cable brought down, Mars's link to Earth truly broken.

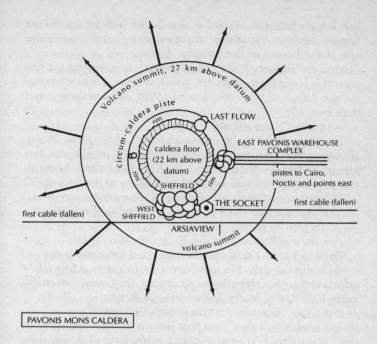

Volcano summit, 27 km above datum

circum-caldera piste

rim

rim

rim

rim

LAST FLOW

caldera floor
(22 km above
datum)

SHEFFIELD

EAST PAVONIS WAREHOUSE
COMPLEX

pistes to Cairo,
Noctis and points east

WEST
SHEFFIELD

THE SOCKET

first cable (fallen)

first cable (fallen)

ARSIAVIEW

volcano summit

PAVONIS MONS CALDERA

So Irishka led them through the jumble that was East
Pavonis, and their little caravan came to the rim of the caldera,
where they parked their rovers. To the south on the western
edge of Sheffield they could just make out the elevator cable,
a line that was barely visible, and then only for a few kilometres out of its twenty-four thousand. Nearly invisible, in
fact, and yet its existence dominated every move they made,
every discussion – every thought they had, almost, speared
and strung out on that black thread connecting them to Earth.

When they were settled in their camp Ann called her son
Peter on the wrist. He was one of the leaders of the revolution
on Tharsis, and had directed the campaign against UNTA that

had left its forces contained in the Socket and its immediate neighbourhood. A qualified victory at best, but it made Peter one of the heroes of the previous month.

Now he answered the call and his face appeared on her wrist. He looked quite like her, which she found disconcerting. He was absorbed, she saw, concentrating on something other than her call.

'Any news?' she asked.

'No. We appear to be at something of an impasse. We're allowing all of them caught outside free passage into the elevator district, so they've got control of the train station and the south rim airport, and the subway lines from those to the Socket.'

'Did the planes that evacuated them from Burroughs come here?'

'Yes. Apparently most of them are leaving for Earth. It's very crowded in there.'

'Are they going back to Earth, or into Mars orbit?'

'Back to Earth. I don't think they trust orbit any more.'

He smiled at that. He had done a lot in space, aiding Sax's efforts and so on. Her son the spaceman, the Green. For many years they had scarcely spoken to each other.

Ann said, 'So what are you going to do now?'

'I don't know. I don't see that we can take the elevator, or the Socket either. It just wouldn't work. Even if it did, they could always bring the elevator down.'

'So?'

'Well — ' He looked suddenly concerned. 'I don't think that would be a good thing. Do you?'

'I think it should come down.'

Now he looked annoyed. 'Better stay out of the fall line then.'

'I will.'

'I don't want anyone bringing it down without a full discussion,' he told her sharply. 'This is important. It should be a decision made by the whole Martian community. I think we need the elevator, myself.'

'Except we have no way to take possession of it.'

'That remains to be seen. Meanwhile, it's not something for you to take into your own hands. I heard what happened in Burroughs, but it's different here, you understand? We decide strategy together. It needs to be discussed.'

'It's a group that's very good at that,' Ann said bitterly.

Everything was always thoroughly discussed and then always she lost. It was past time for that. Someone had to act. But again Peter looked as if he were being taken from his real work. He thought he would be making the decisions about the elevator, she could see that. Part of a more general feeling of ownership of the planet, no doubt, the birthright of the nisei, displacing the First Hundred and all the rest of the issei. If John had lived that would not have been easy, but the king was dead, long live the king – her son, king of the nisei, the first true Martians.

But king or not, there was a Red army now converging on Pavonis Mons. They were the strongest military operation left on the planet, and they intended to complete the work begun when Earth had been hit by its great flood. They did not believe in consensus or compromise, and for them, knocking down the cable was killing two birds with one stone: it would destroy the last police stronghold, and it would also sever easy contact between Earth and Mars, a primary Red goal. No, knocking down the cable was the obvious thing to do.

But Peter did not seem to know this. Or perhaps he did not care. Ann tried to tell him, but he just nodded, muttering, 'Yeah yeah, yeah yeah.' So arrogant, like all the Greens, so blithe and stupid with all their prevaricating, their dealing with Earth, as if you could ever get anything from such a leviathan. No. It was going to take direct action, as in the drowning of Burroughs, as in all the acts of sabotage that had set the stage for the revolution. Without those the revolution wouldn't even have begun, or if it had it would have been crushed immediately, as in 2061.

'Yeah yeah. We'd better call a meeting then,' Peter said, looking as annoyed at her as she felt at him.

'Yeah yeah,' Ann said heavily. Meetings. But they had their uses; people could assume they meant something, while the real work went on elsewhere.

'I'll try to set one up,' Peter said. She had got his attention at last, she saw; but there was an unpleasant look on his face, as if he had been threatened. 'Before things get out of hand.'

'Things are already out of hand,' she told him, and cut the connection.

*　　*　　*

9

She checked the news on the various channels, Mangalavid, the Reds' private nets, the Terran summaries. Though Pavonis and the elevator were now the focus of everyone on Mars, the physical convergence on the volcano was only partial. It appeared to her that there were more Red guerrilla units on Pavonis than the Green units of Free Mars and their allies; but it was hard to be sure. Kasei and the most radical wing of the Reds, called the Kakaze ('fire wind'), had recently occupied the north rim of Pavonis, taking over the train station and tent at Lastflow. The Reds Ann had travelled with, most of them from the old Red mainstream, discussed moving around the rim and joining the Kakaze, but decided in the end to stay in East Pavonis. Ann observed this discussion silently but was glad at the result, as she wanted to keep her distance from Kasei and Dao and their crowd. She was pleased to stay in East Pavonis.

Many Free Mars troops were staying there as well, moving out of their cars into the abandoned warehouses. East Pavonis was becoming a major concentration of revolutionary groups of all kinds; and a couple of days after her arrival, Ann went in and walked over compacted regolith to one of the biggest warehouses in the tent, to take part in a general strategy session.

The meeting went about as she expected. Nadia was at the centre of the discussion, and it was useless talking to her now. Ann just sat on a chair against the back wall, watching the rest of them circle the situation. They did not want to say what Peter had already admitted to her in private: there was no way to get UNTA off the space elevator. Before they conceded that they were going to try to talk the problem out of existence.

Late in the meeting, Sax Russell came over to sit by her side.

'A space elevator,' he said. 'It could be . . . used.'

Now, Ann was not the least bit comfortable talking to Sax. She knew that he had suffered brain damage at the hands of UNTA security, and had taken a treatment that had changed his personality; but somehow this had not helped at all; it only made things very strange, in that sometimes he seemed to her to be the same old Sax, as familiar as a much-hated brother;

while at other times he did indeed seem like a completely different person, inhabiting Sax's body. These two contrary impressions oscillated rapidly, even sometimes co-existed; just before joining her, as he had talked with Nadia and Art, he had looked like a stranger, a dapper old man with a piercing glare, talking in Sax's voice and Sax's old style. Now as he sat next to her, she could see that the changes to his face were utterly superficial. But though he looked familiar the stranger was now inside him – for here was a man who halted and jerked as he delved painfully after what he was trying to say, and then as often as not came out with something scarcely coherent.

'The elevator is a, a device. For . . . raising up. A . . . a *tool*.'

'Not if we don't control it,' Ann said to him carefully, as if instructing a child.

'Control . . .' Sax said, thinking over the concept as if it was entirely new to him. 'Influence? If the elevator can be brought down by anyone who really wants to, then . . .' He trailed away, lost in his thoughts.

'Then what?' Ann prompted.

'Then it's controlled by all. Consensual existence. It's obvious?'

It was as if he were translating from a foreign language. This was not Sax; Ann could only shake her head, and try gently to explain. The elevator was the conduit for the metanationals to reach Mars, she told him. It was in the possession of the metanats now, and the revolutionaries had no means to kick their police forces off of it. Clearly the thing to do in such a situation was to bring it down. Warn people, give them a schedule, and then do it. 'Loss of life would be minimal, and what there was would be pretty much the fault of anyone so stupid as to stay on the cable, or the equator.'

Unfortunately Nadia heard this from the middle of the room, and she shook her head so violently that her cropped grey locks flew out like a clown's ruff. She was still very angry with Ann over Burroughs, for no good reason at all, and so Ann glared at her as she walked over to them and said curtly, 'We need the elevator. It's our conduit to Terra just as much as it's their conduit to Mars.'

'But we don't need a conduit to Terra,' Ann said. 'It's not a

11

physical relationship for us, don't you see? I'm not saying we don't need to have an influence on Terra, I'm not an isolationist like Kasei or Coyote. I agree we need to try to work on them. But it's not a *physical* thing, don't you see? It's a matter of ideas, of talk, and perhaps a few emissaries. It's an *information exchange*. At least it is when it's going right. It's when it gets into a physical thing – a resource exchange, or mass emigration, or police control – that's when the elevator becomes useful, even necessary. So if we took it down we would be saying, we will deal with you on *our* terms, and not yours.'

It was so obvious. But Nadia shook her head, at what Ann couldn't imagine.

Sax cleared his throat, and in his old periodic table style said, 'If we can bring it down, then in effect it is as if it already were down,' blinking and everything. Like a ghost suddenly there at her side, the voice of the terraforming, the enemy she had lost to time and time again – Saxifrage Russell his own self, same as ever. And all she could do was make the same arguments she always had, the losing arguments, feeling the words' inadequacy right in her mouth.

Still she tried. 'People act on what's there, Sax. The metanat directors and the UN and the governments will look up and see what's there, and act accordingly. If the cable's gone they just don't have the resources or the time to mess with us right now. If the cable's here, then they'll want us. They'll think, well, we could do it. And there'll be people screaming to try.'

'They can always come. The cable is only a fuel-saver.'

'A fuel-saver which makes mass transfers possible.'

But now Sax was distracted, and turning back into a stranger. No one would pay attention to her for long enough. Nadia was going on about control of orbit and safe conduct passes and the like.

The strange Sax interrupted Nadia, having never heard her, and said, 'We've promised to . . . help them out.'

'By sending them more metals?' Ann said. 'Do they really need those?'

'We could . . . take people. It might help.'

Ann shook her head. 'We could never take enough.'

He frowned. Nadia saw they weren't listening to her, returned to the table. Sax and Ann fell into silence.

Always they argued. Neither conceded anything, no compromises were made, nothing was ever accomplished. They argued using the same words to mean different things, and scarcely even spoke to one another. Once it had been different, very long ago, when they had argued in the same language, and understood each other. But that had been so long ago she couldn't even remember when exactly it was. In Antarctica? Somewhere. But not on Mars.

'You know,' Sax said in a conversational tone, again very unSaxlike but in a different way, 'it wasn't the Red militia that caused the Transitional Authority to evacuate Burroughs and the rest of the planet. If guerrillas had been the only factor then the Terrans would have gone after us, and they might well have succeeded. But those mass demonstrations in the tents made it clear that almost everyone on the planet was against them. That's what governments fear the most; mass protests in the cities. Hundreds of thousands of people going into the streets to reject the current system. That's what Nirgal means when he says political power comes out of the look in people's eye. And not out of the end of a gun.'

'And so?' Ann said.

Sax gestured at the people in the warehouse. 'They're all Greens.'

The others continued debating. Sax watched her like a bird.

Ann got up and walked out of the meeting, into the strangely unbusy streets of East Pavonis. Here and there militia bands held posts on street corners, keeping an eye to the south, toward Sheffield and the cable terminal. Happy, hopeful, serious young natives. There on one corner a group was in an animated discussion, and as Ann passed them a young woman, her face utterly intent, flushed with passionate conviction, cried out, 'You can't just do what you want!'

Ann walked on. As she walked she felt more and more uneasy, without knowing why. This is how people change – in little quantum jumps when struck by outer events – no intention, no plan. Someone says 'the look in people's eye', and the phrase is suddenly conjoined with an image: a face glowing with passionate conviction, another phrase: you can't just do what you want! And so it occurred to her (the look on that young woman's face!) that it was not just the cable's

13

fate they were deciding – not just 'should the cable come down', but 'how do we decide things?' That was the critical postrevolutionary question, perhaps more important than any single issue being debated, even the fate of the cable. Up until now, most people in the underground had operated by a working method which said *if we don't agree with you we will fight you*. That attitude was what had drawn people into the underground in the first place, Ann included. And once used to that method, it was hard to get away from it. After all, they had just proved that it worked. And so there was the inclination to continue to use it. She felt that herself.

But political power . . . say it did come out of the look in people's eye. You could fight forever, but if people weren't behind you . . .

Ann continued to think about that as she drove down into Sheffield, having decided to skip the farce of the afternoon strategy session in East Pavonis. She wanted to have a look at the seat of the action.

It was curious how little seemed to have changed in the day-to-day life of Sheffield. People still went to work, ate in restaurants, talked on the grass of the parks, gathered in the public spaces in this most crowded of tent towns. The shops and restaurants were jammed. Most businesses in Sheffield had belonged to the metanats, and now people read on their screens long arguments over what to do – what the employees' new relationship to their old owners should be – where they should buy their raw materials, where they should sell – whose regulations they ought to obey, whose taxes they ought to pay. All very confusing, as the screen debates and nightly news vids and wrist nets indicated.

In the plaza devoted to the food market, however, things looked as they always did. Food was already mostly grown and distributed by co-ops; ag networks were in place, the greenhouses on Pavonis were still producing, and so in the market things ran as usual, goods paid for with UNTA dollars or with credit. Except once or twice Ann saw sellers in their aprons shouting red-faced at customers, who shouted right back, arguing over some point of government policy. As Ann passed by one of these arguments, which were no different than those going on among the leaders in East Pavonis, the disputants all stopped and stared at her. She had been recognized. The vegetable seller said loudly, 'If you Reds would lay off they would just go away!'

'Ah come on,' someone retorted. 'It isn't her doing it.'

So true, Ann thought as she walked on.

A crowd stood waiting for a tram to come. The transport systems were still running, ready for autonomy. The tent itself was functioning, which was not something to be taken for granted, though clearly most people did; but every tent's operators had their task obvious before them. They mined their raw materials themselves, mostly out of the air; their solar collectors and nuclear reactors were all the power they needed. So the tents were physically fragile, but if left alone, they could very well become politically autonomous; there was no reason for them to be owned, no justification for it.

So the necessities were served. Daily life plodded on, barely perturbed by revolution.

Or so it seemed at first glance. But there in the streets also were armed groups, young natives in threes and fours and fives, standing on street corners. Revolutionary militias around their missile launchers and remote sensing dishes – Green or Red, it didn't matter, though they were almost certainly Greens. People eyed them as they walked by, or stopped to chat and find out what they were doing. Keeping an eye on the Socket, the armed natives said. Though Ann could see that they were functioning as police as well. Part of the scene, accepted, supported. People grinned as they chatted; these were *their* police, they were fellow Martians, here to protect them, to guard Sheffield for them. People wanted them there, that was clear. If they hadn't, then every approaching questioner would have been a threat, every glance of resentment an attack; which eventually would have forced the militias from the street corners into some safer place. People's faces, staring in concert; this ran the world.

So Ann brooded over the next few days. And even more so after she took a rim train in the direction opposite to Sheffield, counterclockwise to the north arc of the rim. There Kasei and Dao and the Kakaze were occupying apartments in the little tent at Lastflow. Apparently they had forcibly evicted some noncombatant residents, who naturally had trained down to Sheffield in fury, demanding to be reinstated in their homes, and reporting to Peter and the rest of the Green leaders that the Reds had set up truck-drawn rocket-launchers on the north rim, with the rockets aimed at the elevator and Sheffield more generally.

So Ann walked out into Lastflow's little station in a bad mood, angry at the Kakaze's arrogance, as stupid in its way as the Greens'. They had done well in the Burroughs campaign, seizing the dyke very visibly to give everyone a warning, then taking it on themselves to breach the dyke after all the other revolutionary factions had gathered on the heights to the south, ready to rescue the city's civilian population while the metanat security were forced to retreat. The Kakaze had seen what had been needed and they had done it, without getting bogged down in debate. Without their decisiveness everyone would still be gathered around Burroughs, and the metanats no doubt organizing a Terran expeditionary force to relieve them. It had been a perfectly delivered coup.

Now it seemed that success had gone to their head.

Lastflow had been named after the depression it occupied, a fanshaped lava flow extending more than a hundred kilometres down the northeast flank of the mountain. It was the only blemish in what was otherwise a flawlessly circular summit cone and caldera, and clearly it had come very late in the volcano's history of eruptions. Standing down in the depression, one's view of the rest of the summit was cut off – it was like being in a shallow hanging valley, with little visible in any direction – until one walked out to the drop-off at rim's edge, and saw the huge cylinder of the caldera coring the planet, and on the far rim the skyline of Sheffield, looking like a tiny Manhattan over forty kilometres away.

The curtailed view perhaps explained why the depression had been one of the last parts of the rim to be developed. But now it was filled by a fair-sized tent, six kilometres in diameter and a hundred metres high, heavily reinforced as all tents up here had to be. The settlement had been home mostly to commuter labourers in the rim's many industries. Now the rimfront district had been taken over by the Kakaze, and just outside the tent stood a fleet of large rovers, no doubt the ones that had caused the rumours about rocket-launchers.

As Ann was led to the restaurant that Kasei had made his headquarters, she was assured by her guides that this was indeed the case; the rovers did haul rocket-launchers, which were ready to flatten UNTA's last refuge on Mars. Her guides were obviously happy about this, and happy also to be able to tell her about it, happy to meet her and guide her around. A varied bunch – mostly natives, with some Terran newcomers and oldtimers, of all ethnic backgrounds. Among them were a few faces Ann recognized: Etsu Okakura, Al-Khan, Yussuf. A lot of young natives unknown to her stopped them at the restaurant door to shake her hand, grinning enthusiastically. The Kakaze: they were, she had to admit to herself, the wing of the Reds for which she felt the least sympathy. Angry ex-Terrans or idealistic young natives from the tents, their stone eye-teeth dark in their smiles, their eyes glittering as they got this chance to meet her, as they spoke of *kami*, the need for purity, the intrinsic value of rock, the rights of the planet, and so on. In short, fanatics. She shook their hands and nodded, trying not to let her discomfort show.

Inside the restaurant Kasei and Dao were sitting by a window, drinking dark beer. Everything in the room stopped on Ann's entrance, and it took a while for people to be introduced, for Kasei and Dao to welcome her with hugs, for meals and conversations to resume. They got her something to eat from the kitchen. The restaurant workers came out to meet her; they were Kakaze as well. Ann waited until they were gone and people had gone back to their tables, feeling impatient and awkward. These were her spiritual children, the media were always saying; she was the original Red; but in truth they made her uncomfortable.

Kasei, in excellent spirits, as he had been ever since the revolution began, said, 'We're going to bring down the cable in about a week.'

'Oh you are!' Ann said. 'Why wait so long?'

Dao missed her sarcasm. 'It's a matter of warning people,

so they have time to get off the equator.' Though normally a sour man, today he was as cheery as Kasei.

'And off the cable too?'

'If they feel like it. But even if they evacuate it and give it to us, it's still coming down.'

'How? Are those really rocket-launchers out there?'

'Yes. But those are there in case they come down and try to retake Sheffield. As for bringing down the cable, breaking it here at the base isn't the way to do it.'

'The control rockets might be able to adjust to disruptions at the bottom,' Kasei explained. 'Hard to say what would happen, really. But a break just above the areosynchronous point would decrease damage to the equator, and keep New Clarke from flying off as fast as the first one did. We want to minimize the drama of this, you know, avoid any martyrs we can. Just demolition of a building, you know. Like a building past its usefulness.'

'Yes,' Ann said, relieved at this sign of good sense. But it was curious how hearing her idea expressed as someone else's plan disturbed her. She located the main source of her concern: 'What about the others – the Greens? What if they object?'

'They won't,' Dao said.

'They are!' Ann said sharply.

Dao shook his head. 'I've been talking to Jackie. It may be that some of the Greens are truly opposed to it, but her group is just saying that for public consumption, so that they look moderate to the Terrans, and can blame the dangerous stuff on radicals out of their control.'

'On us,' Ann said.

They both nodded. 'Just like with Burroughs,' Kasei said with a smile.

Ann considered it. No doubt it was true. 'But some of them are genuinely opposed. I've been arguing with them about it, and it's no publicity stunt.'

'Uh huh,' Kasei said slowly.

Both he and Dao watched her.

'So you'll do it anyway,' she said at last.

They continued to watch her. She saw all of a sudden that they would no more do what she told them to do than would boys ordered about by a senile grandmother. They were humouring her. Figuring out how they could best put her to use.

'We have to,' Kasei said. 'It's in the best interest of Mars. Not just for Reds, but all of us. We need some distance between us and Terra, and the gravity well re-establishes that distance. Without it we'll be sucked down into the maelstrom.'

It was Ann's argument, it was just what she had been saying in the meetings in East Pavonis. 'But what if they try to stop you?'

'I don't think they can,' Kasei said.

'But if they try?'

The two men glanced at each other. Dao shrugged.

So, Ann thought, watching them. They were willing to start a civil war.

People were still coming up the slopes of Pavonis to the summit, filling up Sheffield, East Pavonis, Lastflow and the other rim tents. Among them were Michel, Spencer, Vlad, Marina and Ursula; Mikhail and a whole brigade of Bogdanovists; Coyote, on his own; a group from Praxis; a large train of Swiss; rover caravans of Arabs, both Sufi and secular; natives from other towns and settlements on Mars. All coming up for the endgame. Everywhere else on Mars, the natives had consolidated their control; all the physical plants were being operated by local teams, in co-operation with Séparation de L'Atmosphère. There were some small pockets of metanat resistance, of course, and there were some Kakaze out there systematically destroying terraforming projects; but Pavonis was clearly the crux of the remaining problem – either the endgame of the revolution or, as Ann was beginning to fear, the opening moves of a civil war. Or both. It would not be the first time.

So she went to the meetings, and slept poorly at night, waking from troubled sleep, or from naps in the transit between one meeting and the next. The meetings were beginning to blur: all contentious, all pointless. She was getting tired, and the broken sleep did not help. She was nearly one hundred and fifty years old, after all, and had not had a gerontological treatment in twenty-five years, and she felt weary all through, all the time. So she watched from a well of growing indifference as the others chewed over the situation. Earth was still in disarray; the great flood was indeed proving to be the ideal trigger mechanism for which General Sax had waited. Sax felt no remorse for taking advantage of Earth's trouble, Ann could see; he never thought once about the many deaths the flood had caused down there. She could read his face thought by thought as he talked about it – what would be the point of remorse? The flood was an accident, a geological catastrophe like an ice age or a meteor impact. No one should waste time feeling remorse for it, not even if they were taking advantage of it for their own purposes. Best to take what good one possibly could from the chaos and disorder, and not worry. All this was right on Sax's face as he discussed what they should do next vis à vis Earth. Send a delegation, he suggested. Diplomatic mission, personal appearance, something about throwing things together; incoherent on the surface, but she could read him like a brother, this old enemy! Well, Sax – the old Sax anyway – was nothing if not rational. Therefore easy to read. Easier than the young fanatics of the Kakaze, now that she thought of it.

And one could only meet him on his own ground, speak to him on his own terms. So she sat across from him in the meetings and tried to concentrate, even though her mind seemed to be hardening somehow, petrifying inside her head. Round and round the arguments went: what to do on Pavonis? Pavonis Mons, Peacock Mountain. Who would ascend the Peacock Throne? There were potential Shahs everywhere – Peter, Nirgal, Jackie, Zeyk, Kasei, Maya, Nadia, Mikhail, Ariadne, the invisible Hiroko . . .

Now someone was invoking the Dorsa Brevia conference as the framework for discussion they should use. All very well, but without Hiroko among them the moral centre was gone, the one person in all Martian history, apart from John Boone, to whom everyone would defer. But Hiroko and John were gone, along with Arkady, and Frank, who would have come in useful now, if he had been on her side, which he wouldn't have been. All gone. And they were left with anarchy. Curious how at a crowded table those absent could be more visible than those present. Hiroko, for instance; people referred to her frequently; and no doubt she was somewhere in the outback, deserting them as usual in their hour of need. Pissing them out of the nest.

Curious too how the only child of their lost heroes, Kasei the son of John and Hiroko, should be the most radical leader there, a disquieting man even though he was on her side. There he sat, shaking his grey head at Art, a small smile twisting his mouth. He was nothing like either John or Hiroko – well, he had some of Hiroko's arrogance, some of John's simplicity. The worst of both. And yet he was a power, he did what he wanted, and a lot of people followed him. But he was not like his parents had been.

And Peter, sitting just two seats away from Kasei, was nothing like her or Simon. It was hard to see what blood relationships meant; nothing, obviously. Though it did twist her heart to hear Peter speak, as he argued with Kasei and opposed the Reds at every point, making a case for some kind of interplanetary collaborationism. And never in these sessions addressing her, or even looking at her. It was perhaps intended as some kind of courtesy – I will not argue with you in public. But it looked like a slight – I will not argue with you because you don't matter.

He continued to argue for keeping the cable, and agreed with Art about the Dorsa Brevia document, naturally, given the Green majority that had existed then and persisted now. Using Dorsa Brevia as a guide would assure the cable's survival. Meaning the continued presence of the United Nations Transitional Authority. And indeed some of them around Peter were talking about 'semi-autonomy' in relation to Terra, instead of independence, and Peter went along with that; it made her sick. And all without meeting her eye. It was Simonlike, somehow, a kind of silence. It made her angry.

'We have no reason to talk about long-term plans until we have solved the cable problem,' she said, interrupting him and earning a very black look indeed, as if she had broken an understanding; but there was no understanding, and why should they not argue, when they had no real relationship – nothing but biology . . .

Art claimed that the UN was now saying that it would be willing to agree to Martian semi-autonomy, as long as Mars remained in 'close consultation' with Earth, and an active aid in Earth's crisis. Nadia said she was in communication with Derek Hastings, who was now up in New Clarke. Hastings had abandoned Burroughs without a bloody battle, it was true, and now she claimed he was willing to compromise. No doubt; his next retreat would not be so easy, nor would it take him to a very pleasant place, for despite all the emergency action, Earth was now a world of famine, plague, looting – breakdown of the social contract, which was so fragile after all. It could happen here too; she had to remember that fragility when she got angry enough, as now, to want to tell Kasei and Dao to abandon the discussions and fire away. If she did that it very likely would happen; a strange sensation of her own power came over her then, as she looked around the table at the anxious, angry, unhappy faces. She could tip the balance; she could knock this table right over.

Speakers were taking five-minute turns to make their case one way or the other. More were in favour of cutting the cable than Ann would have guessed, not just Reds, but representatives of cultures or movements that felt most threatened by the metanat order, or by mass emigration from Earth: Bedouins, the Polynesians, the Dorsa Brevia locals, some of the cannier natives. Still, they were in the minority. Not a tiny minority, but a minority. Isolationist versus interactive; yet another fracture to add to all the others rending the Martian independence movement.

Jackie Boone stood up and spoke for fifteen minutes in favour of keeping the cable, threatening anyone who wanted to bring it down with expulsion from Martian society. It was a disgusting performance, but popular, and afterward Peter stood and spoke in the same way, only slightly more subtly. It made Ann so angry that she stood up immediately after he had finished, to argue for bringing the cable down. This got her another poisonous look from Peter, but it scarcely registered – she talked in a white heat, forgetting all about the five-minute limit. No one tried to cut her off, and she went on and on, though she had no idea what she was going to say next, and no memory of what she had already said. Perhaps her subconscious had organized it all like a lawyer's brief – hopefully so – on the other hand, a part of her thought as her mouth ran

22

on, perhaps she was just saying the word *Mars* over and over again, or babbling, and the audience simply humouring her, or else miraculously comprehending her in a moment of glossolalic grace, invisible flames on their heads like caps of jewels – and indeed their hair looked to Ann like spun metal, the old men's bald pates like chunks of jasper, inside which all languages dead and living were understood equally; and for a moment they appeared all caught up together with her, all inside an epiphany of Red Mars, free of Earth, living on the primal planet that had been and could be again.

She sat down. This time it was not Sax who rose to debate with her, as it had been so many times before. In fact he was cross-eyed with concentration, looking at her open-mouthed, in an amazement that she could not interpret. They stared at each other, the two of them, eyes locked; but what he was thinking she had no idea. She only knew she had caught his attention at last.

This time it was Nadia who rebutted her, Nadia her sister, arguing slowly and calmly for interaction with Earth, for intervention in the Terran situation. She spoke of the need to compromise, the need to engage, influence, transform. It was deeply contradictory, Ann thought; because they were weak, Nadia was saying, they could not afford to offend, and therefore they must change all Terran social reality.

'But how!' Ann cried. 'When you have no fulcrum you can't move a world! No fulcrum, no lever, no force —'

'It isn't just Earth,' Nadia replied. 'There are going to be other settlements in the solar system. Mercury, Luna, the big outer moons, the asteroids. We've got to be part of all that. As the original settlement, we're the natural leader. An unbridged gravity well is just an obstruction to all that – a reduction in our ability to act, a reduction in our power.'

'Getting in the way of progress,' Ann said bitterly. 'Think what Arkady would have said to that. No, look. We had a chance here to make something different. That was the whole point. We still have that chance. Everything that increases the space within which we can create a new society is a good thing. Everything that reduces our space is a bad thing. Think about it!'

Perhaps they did. But it made no difference. Any number of elements on Earth were sending up their arguments for the cable – arguments, threats, entreaties. They needed help down there. Any help. Art Randolph continued energetically lobbying for the cable on behalf of Praxis, which was looking to Ann as if it would become the next transitional authority, metanationalism in its latest manifestation or disguise.

But the natives were being won over by them slowly, intrigued by the possibility of 'conquering Earth', unaware of how impossible this was, incapable of imagining Earth's vastness and immobility. One could tell them and tell them, but they would never be able to imagine it.

Finally it was time for an informal vote. It was representative voting, they had decided, one vote for each of the signatory groups to the Dorsa Brevia document, one vote also to all the interested parties that had arisen since then – new settlements in the outback, new political parties, associations, labs, companies, guerrilla bands, the several Red splinter groups. Before they started some generous naïve soul even offered the First Hundred a vote, and everyone there laughed at the idea that the First Hundred might be able to vote the same way on anything. The generous soul, a young woman from Dorsa Brevia, then proposed that each of the First Hundred be given an individual vote, but this was turned down as endangering the tenuous grasp they had on representative governance. It would have made no difference anyway.

So they voted to allow the space elevator to remain standing, for the time being – and in the possession of UNTA, down to and including the Socket, without contestation. It was like King Canute deciding to declare the tide legal after all, but no one laughed except Ann. The other Reds were furious. Ownership of the Socket was still being actively contested, Dao objected loudly, the neighbourhood around it was vulnerable and could be taken, there was no reason to back off like this, they were only trying to sweep a problem under the rug because it was hard! But the majority were in agreement. The cable should remain.

*　　*　　*

24

Ann felt the old urge: escape. Tents and trains, people, the little Manhattan skyline of Sheffield against the south rim, the summit basalt all torn and flattened and paved over ... There was a piste all the way around the rim, but the western side of the caldera was very nearly uninhabited. So Ann got in one of the smallest Red rovers, and drove around the rim counterclockwise, just inside the piste, until she came to a little meteorological station, where she parked the rover and went out through its lock, stiff in a walker that was much like the ones they had gone out in during the first years.

She was a kilometre or two away from the rim's edge. She walked slowly east toward it, stumbling once or twice before she started to pay proper attention. The old lava on the flat expanse of the broad rim was smooth and dark in some places, rough and lighter in others. By the time she approached the edge she was in full areologist mode, doing a boulder ballet she could sustain all day, attuned to every knob and crack underfoot. And this was a good thing, because near the rim's drop-off the land collapsed in a series of narrow curving ledges, the drops sometimes a step, sometimes taller than she was. And always the growing sense of empty air ahead, as the far side of the caldera and the rest of the great circle became visible. And then she was climbing down onto the last ledge, a bench only some five metres wide, with a curved back wall, shoulder-high: and below her dropped the great round chasm of Pavonis.

This caldera was one of the geological marvels of the solar system, a hole forty-five kilometres across and a full five kilometres deep, and almost perfectly regular in every way – circular, flat-floored, almost vertically walled – a perfect cylinder of space, cut into the volcano like a rock sampler's coring. None of the other three big calderas even approached this simplicity of form; Ascraeus and Olympus were complicated palimpsests of overlapping rings, while the very broad, shallow caldera of Arsia was roughly circular, but shattered in every way. Pavonis alone was a regular cylinder: the Platonic ideal of a volcanic caldera.

Of course from this wonderful vantage point she now had, the horizontal stratification of the interior walls added a lot of irregular detail, rust and black and chocolate and umber bands indicating variations in the composition of the lava deposits; and some bands were harder than those above and below, so that there were many arcuate balconies lining the wall at different elevations – isolated curving benches, perched on the side of the immense rock throat, most never visited. And the floor so flat. The subsidence of the volcano's magma chamber, located some one hundred and sixty kilometres below the mountain, had to have been unusually consistent; it had dropped in the same place every time. Ann wondered if it had been determined yet why that had been; if the magma chamber had been younger than the other big volcanoes, or smaller, or the lava more homogenous . . . Probably someone had investigated the phenomenon; no doubt she could look it up on the wrist. She tapped out the code for the *Journal of Areological Studies*, typed in *Pavonis*: 'Evidence of Strombolian explosive activity found in west Tharsis clasts'. 'Radial ridges in caldera and concentric graben outside the rim suggest late subsidence of the summit'. She had just crossed some of those graben. 'Release of juvenile volatiles into atmosphere calculated by radiometric dating of Lastflow mafics'.

She clicked off the wristpad. She no longer kept up with all the latest areology, she hadn't for years. Even reading the abstracts would have taken far more time than she had. And of course a lot of areology had been badly compromised by the terraforming project. Scientists working for the metanats had concentrated on resource exploration and evaluation, and had found signs of ancient oceans, of the early warm wet atmosphere, possibly even of ancient life; on the other hand radical Red scientists had warned of increased seismic activity, rapid subsidence, mass wasting, and the disappearance of even a single surface sample left in its primal condition. Political stress had skewed nearly everything written about Mars in the past hundred years. The *Journal* was the only publication Ann knew of which tried to publish papers delimiting their inquiries very strictly to reporting areology in the pure sense, concentrating on what had happened in the five billion years of solitude; it was the only publication Ann still read, or at least glanced at, looking through the titles and some of the abstracts, and the editorial material at the front; once or twice she had even sent in a letter concerning some detail or other, which they had printed without fanfare. Published by the university in Sabishii, the *Journal* was peer-reviewed by like-minded areologists, and the articles were rigorous, well-researched and with no obvious political point to their conclusions; they were simply science. The *Journal*'s editorials advocated what had to be called a Red position, but only in the most limited sense, in that they argued for the preservation of the primal landscape so that studies could be carried on without having to deal with gross contaminations. This had been Ann's position from the very start, and it was still where she felt most comfortable; she had moved from that scientific position into political activism only because it had been forced on her by the situation. This was true for a lot of areologists now supporting the Reds. They were her natural peer group, really – the people she understood, and with whom she sympathized.

But they were few; she could almost name them individually. The regular contributors to the *Journal* more or less. As for the rest of the Reds, the Kakaze and the other radicals, what they advocated was a kind of metaphysical position, a cult – they were religious fanatics, the equivalent of Hiroko's Greens, members of some kind of rock-worshipping sect. Ann had very little in common with them, when it came down to it; they formulated their Redness from a completely different worldview.

And given that there was that kind of fractionization among the Reds themselves, then what could one say about the Martian independence movement as a whole? Well. They were going to fall out. It was happening already.

Ann sat down carefully on the edge of the final bench. A good view. It appeared there was a station of some kind down there on the caldera floor, though from five thousand metres up, it was hard to be sure. Even the ruins of old Sheffield were scarcely visible – ah – there they were, on the floor under the new town, a tiny pile of rubble with some straight lines and plane surfaces in it. Faint vertical scorings on the wall above might have been caused by the fall of the city in '61. It was hard to say.

The tented settlements still on the rim were like toy villages in paperweights. Sheffield with its skyline, the low warehouses across from her to the east, Lastflow, the various smaller tents all around the rim . . . many of them had merged, to become a kind of greater Sheffield, covering almost 180° of the rim, from Lastflow around to the southwest, where pistes followed the fallen cable down the long slope of west Tharsis to Amazonis Planitia. All the towns and stations would always be tented, because at twenty-seven kilometres high the air would always be a tenth as thick as it was at the datum – or sea level, one could now call it. Meaning the atmosphere up here was still only thirty or forty millibars thick.

Tent cities forever; but with the cable (she could not see it) spearing Sheffield, development would certainly continue, until they had built a tent city entirely ringing the caldera, looking down into it. No doubt they would then tent the caldera itself, and occupy the round floor – add about fifteen hundred square kilometres to the city, though it was a question who would want to live at the bottom of such a hole, like living at the bottom of a mohole, rock walls rising up around you as if you were in some circular roofless cathedral . . . perhaps it would appeal to some. The Bogdanovists had lived in moholes for years, after all. Grow forests, build climbers' huts or rather millionaires' penthouses on the arcuate balcony ledges, cut staircases into the sides of the rock, install glass elevators that took all day to go up or down . . . rooftops, terraces, skyscrapers reaching up toward the rim, heliports on their flat round roofs, pistes, flying freeways . . . oh yes, the whole summit of Pavonis Mons, caldera and all, could be covered by the great world city, which was always growing, growing like a fungus over every rock in the solar system. Billions of people, trillions of people, quadrillions of people, all as close to immortal as they could make themselves . . .

She shook her head, in a great confusion of spirits. The radicals in Lastflow were not her people, not really, but unless they succeeded, the summit of Pavonis and everywhere else on Mars would become part of the great world city. She tried to concentrate on the view, she tried to feel it, the awe of the symmetrical formation, the love of rock hard under her bottom. Her feet hung over the edge of the bench, she kicked her heels against basalt; she could throw a pebble and it would fall five thousand metres. But she couldn't concentrate. She couldn't feel it. Petrification. So numb, for so long . . . She sniffed, shook her head, pulled her feet in over the edge. Walked back up to her rover.

She dreamed of the long run-out. The landslide was rolling across the floor of Melas Chasma, about to strike her. Everything visible with surreal clarity. Again she remembered Simon, again she groaned and got off the little dyke, going through the motions, appeasing a dead man inside her, feeling awful. The ground was vibrating —

She woke, by her own volition she thought – escaping, running away – but there was a hand, pulling hard on her arm.

'Ann, Ann, Ann.'

It was Nadia. Another surprise. Ann struggled up, disoriented. 'Where are we?'

'Pavonis, Ann. The revolution. I came over and woke you because a fight has broken out between Kasei's Reds and the Greens in Sheffield.'

The present rolled over her like the landslide in her dream. She jerked out of Nadia's grasp, groped for her shirt. 'Wasn't my rover locked?'

'I broke in.'

'Ah.' Ann stood up, still foggy, getting more annoyed the more she understood the situation. 'Now *what* happened?'

'They launched missiles at the cable.'

'They did!' Another jolt, further clearing away the fog. 'And?'

'It didn't work. The cable's defence systems shot them down. They've got a lot of hardware up there now, and they're happy to be able to use it at last. But now the Reds are moving into Sheffield from the west, firing more rockets, and the UN forces on Clarke are bombing the first launch sites, over on Ascraeus, and they're threatening to bomb every armed force down here. This is just what they wanted. And the Reds think it's going to be like Burroughs, obviously, they're trying to force the action. So I came to you. Look, Ann, I know we've been fighting a lot. I haven't been very, you know, patient, but look, this is just *too much*. Everything could fall apart at the last minute – the UN could decide the situation here is anarchy, and come up from Earth and try to take over again.'

'Where are they?' Ann croaked. She pulled on pants, went to the bathroom. Nadia followed her right in. This too was a surprise; in Underhill it might have been normal between them, but it had been a long long time since Nadia had followed her into a bathroom talking obsessively while Ann washed her face and sat down and peed. 'They're still based in Lastflow, but now they've cut the rim piste and the one to Cairo, and they're fighting in west Sheffield, and around the Socket. Reds fighting Greens.'

'Yes, yes.'

'So will you talk to the Reds, will you stop them?'

A sudden fury swept through Ann. *You drove them to this,*' she shouted in Nadia's face, causing Nadia to crash back into the door. Ann got up and took a step toward Nadia and yanked her trousers up, shouting still: 'You and your smug, stupid terraforming, it's all green green green green, with never a hint of compromise! It's just as much your fault as theirs, since they have no hope!'

'Maybe so,' Nadia said mulishly. She didn't care about that, it was the past and didn't matter; she waved it aside and would not be swerved from her point: 'But will you try?'

Ann stared at her stubborn old friend, at this moment almost youthful with fear, utterly focused and alive.

'I'll do what I can,' Ann said grimly. 'But from what you say, it's already too late.'

It was indeed too late. The rover camp Ann had been staying in was deserted, and when she got on the wrist and called around, she got no answers. So she left Nadia and the rest of them stewing in the East Pavonis warehouse complex, and drove her rover around to Lastflow, hoping to find some of the Red leaders based there. But Lastflow had been abandoned by the Reds, and none of the locals knew where they had gone. People were watching TVs in the stations and café windows, but when Ann looked too she saw no news of the fighting, not even on Mangalavid. A feeling of desperation began to seep into her grim mood; she wanted to do something but did not know how. She tried her wristpad again, and to her surprise Kasei answered on their private band. His face in the little image looked shockingly like John Boone's, so much so that in her confusion Ann didn't at first hear what he said. He looked so happy, it was John to the life!

'. . . had to do it,' he was telling her. Ann wondered if she had asked him about that. 'If we don't do something they'll tear this world apart. They'll garden it right to the tops of the big four.'

This echoed Ann's thoughts on the ledge enough to shock her again, but she collected herself and said, 'We've got to work within the framework of the discussions, Kasei, or else we'll start a civil war.'

'We're a minority, Ann. The framework doesn't care about minorities.'

'I'm not so sure. That's what we have to work on. And even if we do decide on active resistance, it doesn't have to be here and now. It doesn't have to be Martians killing Martians.'

'They're not Martian.' There was a glint in his eye, his expression was Hirokolike in its distance from the ordinary world. In that sense he was not like John at all. The worst of both parents; and so they had another prophet, speaking a new language.

'Where are you now?'

'West Sheffield.'

'What are you going to do?'

'Take the Socket, and then bring down the cable. We're the ones with the weapons and the experience. I don't think we'll have much trouble.'

'You didn't bring it down first try.'

'Too fancy. We'll just chop it down this time.'

'I thought that wasn't the way to do it.'

'It'll work.'

'Kasei, I think we need to negotiate with the Greens.'

He shook his head, impatient with her, disgusted that she had lost her nerve when push came to shove. 'After the cable is down we'll negotiate. Look Ann, I've gotta go. Stay out of the fall line.'

'Kasei!'

But he was gone. No one listened to her – not her enemies, not her friends, not her family – though she would have to call Peter. She would have to try Kasei again. She needed to be there in person, to get his attention as she had Nadia's – yes, it had come to that: to get their attention she had to shout right in their faces.

The possibility of getting blocked around East Pavonis kept her going west from Lastflow, circling counterclockwise as she had the day before, to come on the Red force from its rear, no doubt the best approach anyway. It was about a hundred and fifty kilometre drive from Lastflow to the western edge of Sheffield, and as she sped around the summit, just outside the piste, she spent the time trying to call the various forces on the mountain, with no success. Explosive static marked the fight for Sheffield, and memories of '61 erupted with these brutal bursts of white noise, frightening her; she drove the rover as fast as it would go, keeping it on the piste's narrow outside apron to make the ride smoother and faster – a hundred kilometres per hour, then faster – racing, really, to try to stave off the disaster of a civil war – there was a terrible dreamlike quality to it. And especially in that it was too late, too late. In moments like these she was always too late. In the sky over the caldera, starred clouds appeared instantaneously – explosions, without a doubt missiles fired at the cable and shot down in midflight, in white puffs like incompetent fireworks, clustered over Sheffield and peaking in the region of the cable, but puffing into existence all over the vast summit, then drifting off east on the jetstream. Some of those rockets were getting nailed a long way from their target.

Looking up at the battle overhead she almost drove into the first tent of west Sheffield, which was already punctured. As the town had grown westward new tents had attached to the previous ones like lobes of pillow lava; now the construction moraines outside the latest tent were littered with bits of framework, like shards of glass, and the tent fabric was missing in the remaining soccer-ball shapes. Her rover bounced wildly over a mound of basalt rubble; she braked, drove slowly up to the wall. The vehicle lock doors were stuck shut. She put on her suit and helmet, ducked into the rover's own lock, left the car. Heart pounding hard, she walked up to the city wall and climbed over it into Sheffield.

The streets were deserted. Glass and bricks and bamboo shards and twisted magnesium beams lay scattered on the streetgrass. At this elevation, tent failure caused flawed buildings to pop like balloons; windows gaped empty and dark, and here and there complete rectangles of unbroken windows lay scattered, like great clear shields. And there was a body, face frosted or dusted. There would be a lot of dead, people weren't used to thinking about decompression any more, it was an old settlers' worry. But not today.

Ann kept walking east. 'Look for Kasei or Dao or Marion or Peter,' she said to her wrist again and again. But no one replied.

She followed a narrow street just inside the southern wall of the tent. Harsh sunlight, sharp-edged black shadows. Some buildings had held, their windows in place, their lights on inside. No one to be seen in them, of course. Ahead, the cable was just visible, a black vertical stroke rising into the sky out of east Sheffield, like a geometric line become visible in their reality.

The Red emergency band was a signal transmitted in a rapidly varying wavelength, synchronized for everyone who had the current encryption. This system cut through some kinds of radio jamming very well; nevertheless Ann was surprised when a crow voice cawed from her wrist, 'Ann, it's Dao. Up here.'

He was actually in sight, waving at her from a doorway into a building's little emergency lock. He and a group of some twenty people were working with a trio of mobile rocket-launchers out in the street. Ann ran over to them, ducked into the doorway beside Dao. 'This has to stop!' she cried.

Dao looked surprised. 'We've almost got the Socket.'

'But what then?'

'Talk to Kasei about that. He's up ahead, going for Arsiaview.'

One of their rockets whooshed away, its noise faint in the thin air. Dao was back at it. Ann ran forward up the street, keeping as close as she could to the buildings siding it. It was obviously dangerous, but at that moment she didn't care if she were killed or not, so she had no fear. Peter was somewhere in Sheffield, in command of the Green revolutionaries who

33

had been there from the beginning. These people had been efficient enough to keep the UNTA security forces trapped on the cable and up on Clarke, so they were by no means the hapless pacifistic young native street demonstrators that Kasei and Dao seemed to have assumed they were. Her spiritual children, mounting an attack on her only actual child, in complete confidence that they had her blessing. As once they had. But now —

She struggled to keep running, her breath hard and ragged, the sweat beginning to flood through all over her skin. She hurried to the south tent wall, where she came on a little fleet of Red boulder cars, Turtle Rocks from the Acheron car manufactory. But no one inside them answered her calls, and when she looked closer she saw that their rock roofs were punctured by holes at their fronts, where the windshields would have been, underneath the rock overhang. Anyone inside them was dead. She ran on eastward, staying against the tent wall, heedless of debris underfoot, feeling a rising panic. She was aware that a single shot from anyone could kill her, but she had to find Kasei. She tried again over the wrist.

While she was at it, a call came in to her. It was Sax.

'It isn't logical to connect the fate of the elevator with terraforming goals,' he was saying, as if he was speaking to more people than just her. 'The cable could be tethered to quite a cold planet.'

It was the usual Sax, the all-too-Sax: but then he must have noticed she was on, because he stared owlishly into his wrist's little camera and said, 'Listen Ann, we can take history by the arm and break it – *make it.* Make it new.'

Her old Sax would never have said that. Nor chattered on at her, clearly distraught, pleading, visibly nerve-racked; one of the most frightening sights she had ever seen, actually: 'They love you, Ann. It's that that can save us. Emotional histories are the true histories. Watersheds of desire and devolution – *devotion.* You're the – the personification of certain values – for the natives. You can't escape that. You have to act with that. I did it in Da Vinci, and it proved – helpful. Now it's your turn. You must. You must – Ann – just this once you must join us all. Hang together or hang separately. Use your iconic value.'

34

So strange to hear such stuff from Saxifrage Russell. But then he shifted again, seemed to pull himself together: '. . . logical procedure is to establish some kind of equation for conflicting interests'. Just like his old self.

Then there was a beep from her wrist and she cut Sax off, and answered the incoming call. It was Peter, there on the Red coded frequency, a black expression on his face that she had never seen before.

'Ann!' He stared intently at his own wristpad. 'Listen, mother – I want you to stop these people!'

'Don't you mother me,' she snapped. 'I'm trying. Can you tell me where they are?'

'I sure as hell can. They've just broken into the Arsiaview tent. Moving through – it looks like they're trying to come up on the Socket from the south.' Grimly he took a message from someone off-camera. 'Right.' He looked back at her. 'Ann, can I patch you into Hastings up on Clarke? If you tell him you're trying to stop the Red attack, then he may believe that it's only a few extremists, and stay out of it. He's going to do what he has to to keep the cable up, and I'm afraid he's about to kill us all.'

'I'll talk to him.'

And there he was, a face from the deep past, a time lost to Ann she would have said; and yet he was instantly familiar, a thin-faced man, harried, angry, on the edge of snapping. Could anyone have sustained such enormous pressures for the past hundred years? No. It was just that kind of time, come back again.

'I'm Ann Clayborne,' she said, and as his face twisted even further, she added, 'I want you to know that the fighting going on down here does not represent Red party policy.'

Her stomach clamped as she said this, and she tasted chyme at the back of her throat. But she went on: 'It's the work of a splinter group, called the Kakaze. They're the ones who broke the Burroughs dyke. We're trying to shut them down, and expect to succeed by the end of the day.'

It was the most awful string of lies she had ever said. She felt as if Frank Chalmers had come down and taken over her mouth; she couldn't stand the sensation of such words on her tongue. She cut the connection before her face betrayed what

35

falsehoods she was vomiting. Hastings disappeared without having said a word, and his face was replaced by Peter's, who did not know she was back on line; she could hear him but his wristpad was facing a wall. 'If they don't stop on their own we'll have to do it ourselves, or else UNTA will and it'll all go to hell. Get everything ready for a counter-attack, I'll give the word.'

'Peter!' she said without thinking.

The picture on the little screen swung around, came onto his face.

'You deal with Hastings,' she choked out, barely able to look at him, traitor that he was. 'I'm going for Kasei.'

Arsiaview was the southernmost tent, filled now with smoke, which snaked overhead in long amorphous lines that revealed the tent's ventilation patterns. Alarms were ringing everywhere, loud in the still-thick air, and shards of clear framework plastic were scattered on the green grass of the street. Ann stumbled past a body curled just like the figures modelled in ash in Pompeii. Arsiaview was narrow but long, and it was not obvious where she should go. The whoosh of rocket-launchers led her eastward toward the Socket, the magnet of the madness – like a monopole, discharging Earth's insanity onto them.

There might be a plan revealed here; the cable's defences seemed to be capable of handling the Reds' lightweight missiles, but if the attackers thoroughly destroyed Sheffield and the Socket, then there would be nothing for UNTA to come down to, and so it would not matter if the cable remained swinging overhead. It was a plan that mirrored the one used to deal with Burroughs.

But it was a bad plan. Burroughs was down in the lowlands, where there was an atmosphere, where people could live outside, at least for a while. Sheffield was high, and so they were back in the past, back in '61 when a broken tent meant the end for everyone in it exposed to the elements. At the same time most of Sheffield was underground, in many stacked floors against the wall of the caldera. Undoubtedly most of the population had retreated down there, and if the fighting tried to follow them it would be impossible, a nightmare. But up on the surface where fighting was possible, people were exposed to fire from the cable above. No, it wouldn't work. It wasn't even possible to see what was happening. There were more explosions near the Socket, static over the intercom, isolated words as the receiver caught bits of other coded frequencies cycling through: '— taken Arsiaview*pkkkkkk* — ' 'We need the AI back but I'd say X axis three two two, Y axis eight*pkkkkk* — '

Then another barrage of missiles must have been launched at the cable, for overhead Ann caught sight of an ascending line of brilliant explosions of light, no sound to them at all; but after that, big black fragments rained down on the tents around her, crashing through the invisible fabrics or smashing onto the invisible framework, then falling the last distance onto the buildings like the dropped masses of wrecked vehicles, loud despite the thin air and the intervening tents, the ground vibrating and jerking under her feet. It went on for minutes, with the fragments falling farther outward all the time, and any second in all those minutes could have brought death down on her. She stood looking up at the dark sky, and waited it out.

Things stopped falling. She had been holding her breath, and she breathed. Peter had the Red code, and so she called his number and tapped in a patch attempt, heard only static. But as she was turning down the volume in her earphones, she caught some garbled half-phrases – Peter, describing Red movements to Green forces, or perhaps even to UNTA. Who could then fire rockets from the cable defence systems down onto them. Yes, that was Peter's voice, bits of it all cut with static. Calling the shots. Then it was only static.

At the base of the elevator brief flashes of explosive light transformed the lower part of the cable from black to silver, then back to black again. Every alarm inside Arsiaview began ringing or howling. All the smoke whipped away toward the east end of the tent. Ann got into a north-south alley and leaned back against the east wall of a building, flat against concrete. No windows on the alley. Booms, crashes, wind. Then the silence of near airlessness.

She got up and wandered through the tent. Where did one

go when people were being killed? Find your friends if you can. If you can tell who they are.

She collected herself and continued looking for Kasei's group, going to where Dao had said they would be, and then trying to think where they would go next. Outside the city was a possibility; but having come inside they might try for the next tent to the east, try to take them one by one, decompress them, force everyone below and then move on. She stayed on the street paralleling the tent wall, jogging along as fast as she could. She was in good shape but this was ridiculous, she couldn't catch her breath, and she was soaking the inside of her suit with sweat. The street was deserted, eerily silent and still, so that it was hard to believe she was in the middle of a battle, and impossible to believe she would ever find the group for which she was looking.

But there they were. Up ahead, in the streets around one of the triangular parks – figures in helmets and suits, carrying automatic weapons and mobile missile-launchers, firing at unseen opponents in a building fronted with chert. The red circles on their arms, Reds —

A blinding flash and she was knocked down. Her ears roared. She was at the foot of a building, pressed against its polished stone side. Jaspilite: red jasper and iron oxide, in alternating bands. Pretty. Her back and bottom and shoulder hurt, and her elbow. But nothing was agonizing. She could move. She crawled around, looked back up to the triangle park. Things were burning in the wind, the flames little oxygen-starved orange spurts, going out already. The figures there were cast about like broken dolls, limbs akimbo, in positions no bones could hold. She got up and ran to the nearest knot of them, drawn by a familiar grey-haired head that had come free of its helmet. That was Kasei, only son of John Boone and Hiroko Ai, one side of his jaw bloody, his eyes open and sightless. He had taken her too seriously. And his opponents not seriously enough. His pink stone eye-tooth lay there exposed by his wound, and seeing it Ann choked and turned away. The waste. All three of them dead now.

She turned back and crouched, unclipped Kasei's wristpad. It was likely that he had a direct access band to the Kakaze, and when she was back in the shelter of an obsidian building marred by great white shatter-stars, she tapped in the general call code, and said, 'This is Ann Clayborne, calling all Reds. All Reds. Listen, this is Ann Clayborne. The attack on Sheffield has failed. Kasei is dead, along with a lot of others. More attacks here won't work. They'll cause the full UNTA security force to come back down onto the planet again.' She wanted to say how stupid the plan had been in the first place, but she choked back the words. 'Those of you who can, get off the mountain. Everyone in Sheffield, get back to the west and get out of the city, and off the mountain. This is Ann Clayborne.'

Several acknowledgements came in, and she half-listened to them as she walked west, back through Arsiaview toward her rover. She made no attempt to hide; if she was killed she was killed, but now she didn't believe it would happen; she walked under the wings of some dark covering angel, who kept her from death no matter what happened, forcing her to witness the deaths of all the people she knew and all the planet she loved. Her fate. Yes; there was Dao and his crew, all dead right where she had left them, lying in pools of their own blood. She must have just missed it.

And there, down a broad boulevard with a line of linden trees in its centre, was another knot of bodies – not Reds – they wore green headbands, and one of them looked like Peter, it was his back – she walked over weak-kneed, under a compulsion, as in a nightmare, and stood over the body and finally circled it. But it was not Peter. Some tall young native with shoulders like Peter's, poor thing. A man who would have lived a thousand years.

She moved on carelessly. She came to her little rover without incident, got in and drove to the train terminal at the west end of Sheffield. There a piste ran down the south slope of Pavonis, into the saddle between Pavonis and Arsia. Seeing it, she conceived a plan, very simple and basic, but workable because of that. She got on the Kakaze band and made her recommendations as though they were orders. Run away, disappear. Go down into South Saddle, then around Arsia on the western slope above the snowline, there to slip into the upper end of Aganippe Fossa, a long straight canyon that contained a hidden Red refuge, a cliff dwelling in the northern wall.

There they could hide and hide and start another long underground campaign, against the new masters of the planet. UNOMA, UNTA, metanat, Dorsa Brevia – they were all Green.

She tried calling Coyote, and was somewhat surprised when he answered. He was somewhere in Sheffield as well, she could tell; lucky to be alive no doubt, a bitter furious expression on his cracked face.

Ann told him her plan; he nodded.

'After a time they'll need to get farther away,' he said.

Ann couldn't help it: 'It was stupid to attack the cable!'

'I know,' Coyote said wearily.

'Didn't you try to talk them out of it?'

'I did.' His expression grew blacker. 'Kasei's dead?'

'Yes.'

Coyote's face twisted with grief. 'Ah, God. Those bastards.'

Ann had nothing to say. She had not known Kasei well, or liked him much. Coyote on the other hand had known him from birth, back in Hiroko's hidden colony, and from boyhood had taken him along on his furtive expeditions all over Mars. Now tears coursed down the deep wrinkles on Coyote's cheeks, and Ann clenched her teeth.

'Can you get them down to Aganippe?' she asked. 'I'll stay and deal with the people in East Pavonis.'

Coyote nodded. 'I'll get them down as fast as I can. Meet at West Station.'

'I'll tell them that.'

'The Greens will be mad at you.'

'Fuck the Greens.'

Some part of the Kakaze sneaked into the west terminal of Sheffield, in the light of a smoky dull sunset: small groups wearing blackened dirty walkers, their faces white and frightened, angry, disoriented, in shock. Wasted. Eventually there were three or four hundred of them, sharing the day's bad news. When Coyote slipped in the back, Ann rose and spoke in a voice just loud enough to carry to all of them, aware as she never had been in her life of her position as the first Red; of what that meant, now. These people had taken her seriously and here they were, beaten and lucky to be alive, with dead friends everywhere in the town east of them.

'A direct assault was a bad idea,' she said, unable to help herself. 'It worked in Burroughs, but that was a different kind of situation. Here it failed. People who might have lived a thousand years are dead. The cable wasn't worth that. We're going to go into hiding and wait for our next chance, our next real chance.'

There were hoarse objections to this, angry shouts: 'No! No! Never! Bring down the cable!'

Ann waited them out. Finally she raised a hand, and slowly they went silent again.

'It could backfire all too easily if we fight the Greens now. It could give the metanats an excuse to come in again. That would be far worse than dealing with a native government. With Martians we can at least talk. The environmental part of the Dorsa Brevia agreement gives us some leverage. We'll just have to keep working as best we can. Start somewhere else. Do you understand?'

This morning they wouldn't have. Now they still didn't want to. She waited out the protesting voices, stared them down. The intense, cross-eyed glare of Ann Clayborne . . . A lot of them had joined the fight because of her, back in the days when the enemy was the enemy, and the underground an actual working alliance, loose and fractured but with all its elements more or less on the same side . . .

They bowed their heads, reluctantly accepting that if Clayborne was against them, their moral leadership was gone. And without that – without Kasei, without Dao – with the bulk of the natives Green, and firmly behind the leadership of Nirgal and Jackie, and Peter the traitor . . .

'Coyote will get you off Tharsis,' Ann said, feeling sick. She left the room, walked through the terminal and out of the lock, back into her rover. Kasei's wristpad lay on the car's dashboard, and she threw it across the compartment, sobbed. She sat in the driver's seat and composed herself, and then started the car and went looking for Nadia and Sax and all the rest.

She drove sightlessly back around the caldera, clockwise this time. Eventually she found herself in East Pavonis, and there they were, all still in the warehouse complex; when she walked in the door they stared at her as if the attack on the cable had been her idea, as if she was personally responsible for everything bad that had happened, both on that day and throughout the revolution – just as they had stared at her after Burroughs, in fact. Peter was actually there, the traitor, and she veered away from him, and ignored the rest, or tried to, Irishka frightened, Jackie red-eyed and furious, her father killed this day after all, and though she was in Peter's camp and so partly responsible for the crushing response to the Red offensive, you could see with one look at her that someone would pay – but Ann ignored all that, and walked across the room to Sax – who was in his nook in the far corner of the big central room, sitting before a screen reading long columns of figures, muttering things to his AI. Ann waved a hand between his face and his screen and he looked up, startled.

Strangely, he was the only one of the whole crowd who did not appear to blame her. Indeed he regarded her with his head tilted to the side, with a birdlike curiosity that almost resembled sympathy.

'Bad news about Kasei,' he said. 'Kasei and all the rest. I'm glad that you and Desmond survived.'

She ignored that, and told him in a rapid undertone where the Reds were going, and what she had told them to do. 'I think I can keep them from trying any more direct attacks on the cable,' she said. 'And from most acts of violence, at least in the short term.'

'Good,' Sax said.

'But I want something for it,' she said. 'I want it and if I don't get it, I'll set them on you forever.'

'The soletta?' Sax asked.

She stared at him. He must have listened to her more often than she had thought. 'Yes.'

His eyebrows came together as he thought it over. 'It could cause a kind of ice age,' he said.

'Good.'

He stared at her as he thought about it. She could see him doing it, in quick flashes or bursts: ice age – thinner atmosphere – terraforming slowed – new ecosystems destroyed – perhaps compensate – greenhouse gases. And so on and so

42

forth. It was almost funny how she could read this stranger's face, this hated brother looking for a way out. He would look and look, but heat was the main driver of terraforming, and with the soletta gone, they would at least be restricted to Mars's normal level of sunlight, thus slowed to a more 'natural' pace. It was possible that the inherent stability of that approach even appealed to Sax's conservatism, such as it was.

'Okay,' he said.

'You can speak for these people?' she said, waving disdainfully at the crowd behind them, as if all her oldest companions were not among them, as if they were UNTA technocrats or metanat functionaries . . .

'No,' he said. 'I only speak for me. But I can get rid of the soletta.'

'You'd do it against their wishes?'

He frowned. 'I think I can talk them into it. If not, I know I can talk the Da Vinci team into it. They like challenges.'

'Okay.'

It was the best she could get from him, after all. She straightened up, still nonplussed. She hadn't expected him to agree. And now that he had, she discovered that she was still angry, still sick at heart. This concession – now that she had it, meant nothing. They would figure out other ways to heat things. Sax would make his argument using that point, no doubt. Give the soletta to Ann, he would say, as a way of buying off the Reds. Then forge on.

She walked out of the big room without a glance at the others. Out of the warehouses to her rover.

For a while she drove blindly, without any sense of where she was going. Just get away, just escape. Thus by accident she headed westward, and in short order she had to stop or run over the rim's edge.

Abruptly she braked the car.

In a daze she looked out the windshield. Bitter taste in her mouth, guts all knotted, every muscle tense and aching. The great encircling rim of the caldera was smoking at several points, chiefly from Sheffield and Lastflow, but also from a dozen other places as well. No sight of the cable over Sheffield – but it was still there, marked by a concentration of smoke around its base, lofting east on the thin, hard wind. Another peak banner, blown on the endless jetstream. Time was a wind sweeping them away. The plumes of smoke marred the dark sky, obscuring some of the many stars that shone in the hour before sunset. It looked as if the old volcano was waking again, rousing from its long dormancy and preparing to erupt. Through the thin smoke the sun was a dark red glowing ball, looking much like an early molten planet must have looked, its colour staining the shreds of smoke maroon and rust and crimson. Red Mars. But red Mars was gone, and gone for good. Soletta or not, ice age or not, the biosphere would grow and spread until it covered everything, with an ocean in the north, and lakes in the south, and streams, forests, prairies, cities and roads, oh she saw it all; white clouds raining mud on the ancient highlands, while the uncaring masses built their cities as fast as they could, the long run-out of civilization burying her world.

PART TWO

Areophany

To Sax it looked like that least rational of conflicts, civil war. Two parts of a group shared many more interests than disagreements, but fought anyway. Unfortunately it was not possible to force people to study cost-benefit analysis. Nothing to be done. Or – possibly one could identify a crux issue causing one or both sides to resort to violence. After that, try to defuse that issue.

Clearly in this case a crux issue was terraforming. A matter with which Sax was closely identified. This could be viewed as a disadvantage, as a mediator ought ideally to be neutral. On the other hand, his actions might speak symbolically for the terraforming effort itself. He might accomplish more with a symbolic gesture than anyone else. What was needed was a concession to the Reds, a real concession, the reality of which would increase its symbolic value by some hidden exponential factor. Symbolic value: it was a concept with which Sax was trying hard to come to grips. Words of all kinds gave him trouble now, so much so that he had taken to etymology to try to understand them better. A glance at the wrist: symbol, 'something that stands for something else', from the Latin symbolum, adopted from a Greek word meaning throw together. Exactly. It was alien to his understanding, this throwing together, a thing emotional and even unreal, and yet vitally important.

The afternoon of the battle for Sheffield, he called Ann on the wrist and got her briefly, and tried to talk to her, and failed. So he drove to the edge of the city's wreckage, not knowing what else to do, looking for her. It was very disturbing to see how much damage a few hours' fighting could do. Many years of work lay in smoking shambles, the smoke not fire-ash particulates for the most part but merely disturbed fines, old volcanic ash blown up and then torn east on the jetstream. The cable stuck out of the ruins like a black line of carbon nanotube fibres.

There was no sign of any further Red resistance. Thus no way of locating Ann. She was not answering her phone. So Sax returned to the warehouse complex in East Pavonis, feeling balked. He went back inside.

And then there she was, in the vast warehouse, walking through the others toward him as if about to plunge a knife in his heart. He sank in his seat unhappily, remembering an overlong sequence of unpleasant interviews between them. Most recently they had argued on the train ride out of Libya Station. He recalled her saying something about removing the soletta and the annular mirror; which would be a very powerful symbolic statement indeed. And he had never been comfortable with such a major element of the terraforming's heat input being so fragile.

So when she said, 'I want something for it,' he thought he knew what she meant, and suggested removing the mirrors before she could. This surprised her. It slowed her down, it took the edge off her terrible anger. Leaving something very much deeper, however – grief, despair – he could not be sure. Certainly a lot of Reds had died that day, and Red hopes as well. 'I'm sorry about Kasei,' he said.

She ignored that, and made him promise to remove the space mirrors. He did, meanwhile calculating the loss of light that would result, then trying to keep a wince off his face. Insolation would drop by about twenty per cent, a very substantial amount indeed. 'It will start an ice age,' he muttered.

'Good,' she said.

But she was not satisfied. And as she left the room, he could see by the set of her shoulders that his concession had done little if anything to comfort her. One could only hope her cohorts were more easily pleased. In any case it would have to be done. It might stop a civil war. Of course a great number of plants would die, mostly at the higher elevations, though it would affect every ecosystem to some extent. An ice age, no doubt about it. Unless they reacted very effectively. But it would be worth it, if it stopped the fighting.

It would have been easy just to cut the great band of the annular mirror and let it fly away into space, right out of the plane of the ecliptic. Same with the soletta: fire a few of its positioning rockets and it would spin away like a catherine wheel.

But that would be a waste of processed aluminium silicate, which Sax did not like to see. He decided to investigate the possibility of using the mirrors' directional rockets, and their reflectivity, to propel them elsewhere in the solar system. The soletta could be located in front of Venus, and its mirrors realigned so that the structure became a huge parasol, shading the hot planet and starting the process of freezing out its atmosphere; this was something that had been discussed in the literature for a long time, and no matter what other plans for terraforming Venus one had, this was the standard first step. Then having done that, the annular mirror would have to be placed in the corresponding polar orbit around Venus, as its reflected light helped to hold the soletta/parasol in its position against the push of solar radiation. So the two would still be put to use, and it would also be a gesture, another symbolic gesture, saying, *Look here – this big world might be terraformable too*. It wouldn't be easy, but it was possible. Thus some of the psychic pressure on Mars, 'the only other possible Earth', might be relieved. This was not logical, but it didn't matter; history was strange, people were not rational systems, and in the peculiar symbolic logic of the limbic system, it would be a sign to the people on Earth, a portent, a scattering of psychic seed, a throwing together. Look there! Go there! And leave Mars alone.

So he talked it over with the Da Vinci space scientists, who had effectively taken over control of the mirrors. The lab rats, people called them behind their backs, and his (though he heard anyway); the lab rats, or the saxaclones. Serious young native Martian scientists, in fact, with just the same variations of temperament as grad students and post-docs in any lab anywhere, any time; but the facts didn't matter. They worked with him and so they were the saxaclones. Somehow he had

49

become the very model of the modern Martian scientist; first as white-coated lab rat, then as full-blown mad scientist, with a crater-castle full of eager Igors, mad-eyed but measured in manner, little Mr Spocks, the men as skinny and awkward as cranes on the ground, the women drab in their protective non-coloration, their neuter devotion to Science. Sax was very fond of them. He liked their devotion to science, it made sense to him — an urge to understand things, to be able to express them mathematically. It was a sensible desire. In fact it often seemed to him that if everyone were a physicist then they would be very much better off. 'Ah, no, people like the idea of a flat universe because they find negatively curved space difficult to deal with.' Well, perhaps not. In any case the young natives at Da Vinci Crater were a powerful group, strange or not. At this point Da Vinci was in charge of a lot of the underground's technological base, and with Spencer fully engaged there, their production capability was staggering. They had engineered the revolution, if the truth were told, and were now in de facto control of Martian orbital space.

This was one reason why many of them looked displeased or at least nonplussed when Sax first told them about the removal of the soletta and annular mirror. He did it in a screen meeting, and their faces squinched into expressions of alarm: Captain, it is not logical. But neither was civil war. And the one was better than the other.

'Won't people object?' Aonia asked. 'The Greens?'

'No doubt,' Sax said. 'But right now we exist in, in anarchy. The group in East Pavonis is a kind of proto-government, perhaps. But we in Da Vinci control Mars space. And no matter the objections, this might avert civil war.'

He explained as best he could. They got absorbed in the technical challenge, in the problem pure and simple, and quickly forgot their shock at the idea. In fact giving them a technical challenge of that sort was like giving a dog a bone. They went away gnawing at the tough parts of the problem, and just a few days later they were down to the smooth polished gleam of procedure. Mostly a matter of instructions to AIs, as usual. It was getting to the point where having conceived a clear idea of what one wanted to do, one could just say to an AI, 'please do thus and such' – please spin the soletta and annular mirror into Venusian orbit, and adjust the slats of the soletta so that it becomes a parasol shielding the planet from all of its incoming insolation; and the AIs would calculate the trajectories and the rocket firings and the mirror angles necessary, and it would be done.

People were becoming too powerful, perhaps. Michel always went on about their godlike new powers, and Hiroko in her actions had implied that there should be no limit to what they tried with these new powers, ignoring all tradition. Sax himself had a healthy respect for tradition, as a kind of default survival behaviour. But the techs in Da Vinci cared no more for tradition than Hiroko had. They were in an open moment in history, accountable to no one. And so they did it.

Then Sax went to Michel. 'I'm worried about Ann.'

They were in a corner of the big warehouse on East Pavonis, and the movement and clangour of the crowd created a kind of privacy. But after a look around Michel said, 'Let's go outside.'

They suited up and went out. East Pavonis was a maze of tents, warehouses, manufactories, pistes, parking lots, pipelines, holding tanks, holding yards; also junkyards and scrapheaps, their mechanical detritus scattered about like volcanic ejecta. But Michel led Sax westward through the mess, and they came quickly to the caldera rim, where the human clutter was put into a new and larger context, a logarithmic shift that left the pharaonic collection of artefacts suddenly looking like a patch of bacterial growth.

At the very edge of the rim, the blackish speckled basalt cracked down in several concentric ledges, each lower than the last. A set of staircases led down these terraces, and the lowest was railed. Michel led Sax down to this terrace, where they could look over the side into the caldera. Straight down for five kilometres. The caldera's large diameter made it seem less deep than that; still it was an entire round country down there, far, far below. And when Sax remembered how small the caldera was proportional to the volcano entire, Pavonis itself seemed to bulk under them like a conical continent, rearing right up out of the planet's atmosphere into low space. Indeed

51

the sky was only purple around the horizon, and blackish overhead, with the sun a hard gold coin in the west, casting clean, slantwise shadows. They could see it all. The fines thrown up by the explosions were gone, everything returned to its normal telescopic clarity. Stone and sky and nothing more – except for the thread of buildings cast around the rim. Stone and sky and sun. Ann's Mars. Except for the buildings. And on Ascraeus and Arsia and Elysium, and even on Olympus, the buildings would not be there.

'We could easily declare everything above about eight kilometres a primal wilderness zone,' Sax said. 'Keep it like this forever.'

'Bacteria?' Michel asked. 'Lichen?'

'Probably. But do they matter?'

'To Ann they do.'

'But *why*. Michel? *Why* is she like that?'

Michel shrugged.

After a long pause he said, 'No doubt it is complex. But she was mistreated as a girl, did you know that?'

Sax shook his head. He tried to imagine what that meant.

Michel said, 'Her father died. Her mother married her stepfather when she was eight. From then on he mistreated her, until she was sixteen, when she moved to the mother's sister. I've asked her what the mistreatment consisted of, but she says she doesn't want to talk about it. Abuse is abuse, she said. She doesn't remember much anyway, she says.'

'I believe that.'

Michel waggled a gloved hand. 'We remember more than we think we do. More than we want to, sometimes.'

They stood there looking into the caldera.

'It's hard to believe,' Sax said.

Michel looked glum. 'Is it? There were fifty women in the First Hundred. Odds are more than one of them was abused by men in their lives. More like ten or fifteen, if the statistics are to be believed. Sexually violated, struck, mistreated . . . that's just the way it was.'

'It's hard to believe.'

'Yes.'

Sax recalled hitting Phyllis in the jaw, knocking her senseless with a single blow. There had been a certain satisfaction in that. He had needed to do it, though. Or so it had felt at the time.

'Everyone has their reasons,' Michel said, startling him. 'Or so they think.' He tried to explain – tried, in his usual Michel fashion, to make it something other than plain evil. 'At the base of human culture,' he said as he looked down into the country of the caldera, 'is a neurotic response to people's earliest psychic wounds. Before birth and during infancy people exist in a narcissistic oceanic bliss, in which the individual is the universe. Then some time in late infancy we come to the awareness that we are separate individuals, different from our mother and everyone else. This is a blow from which we never completely recover. There are several neurotic strategies used to try to deal with it. First, merging back into the mother. Then denying the mother, and shifting our ego ideal to the father – this strategy often lasts forever, and the people of that culture worship their king and their father god, and so on. Or the ego ideal might shift again, to abstract ideas, or to the brotherhood of men. There are names and full descriptions for all these complexes – the Dionysian, the Persean, the Apollonian, the Heraclean. They all exist, and they are all neurotic, in that they all lead to misogyny, except for the Dionysian complex.'

'This is one of your semantic rectangles?' Sax asked apprehensively.

'Yes. The Apollonian and the Heraclean complexes might describe Terran industrial societies. The Persean its earlier cultures, with strong remnants of course right up to this day. And they are all three patriarchal. They all denied the maternal, which was connected in patriarchy with the body and with nature. The feminine was instinct, the body, and nature; while the masculine was reason, mind, and law. And the law ruled.'

Sax, fascinated by so much throwing together, said only, 'And on Mars?'

'Well, on Mars it may be that the ego ideal is shifting back to the maternal. To the Dionysian again, or to some kind of post-Oedipal reintegration with nature, which we are still in the process of inventing. Some new complex that would not be so subject to neurotic over-investment.'

Sax shook his head. It was amazing how floridly elaborated a pseudo-science could get. A compensation technique, perhaps; a desperate attempt to be more like physics. But what they did not understand was that physics, while admittedly complicated, was always trying very hard to become simpler.

Michel, however, was continuing to elaborate. Correlated to patriarchy was capitalism, he was saying, a hierarchical system in which most men had been exploited economically, also treated like animals, poisoned, betrayed, shoved around, shot. And even in the best of circumstances under constant threat of being tossed aside, out of a job, poor, unable to provide for loved dependants, hungry, humiliated. Some trapped in this unfortunate system took out their rage at their plight on whomever they could, even if that turned out to be their loved ones, the people most likely to give them comfort. It was illogical, and even stupid. Brutal and stupid. Yes. Michel shrugged; he didn't like where this train of reasoning had led him. It sounded to Sax as if the implication was that many men's actions indicated that they were, alas, fairly stupid. And the limbic array got all twisted in some minds, Michel was going on, trying to veer away from that, to make a decent explanation. Adrenalin and testosterone were always pushing for a fight-or-flight response, and in some dismal situations a satisfaction circuit got established in the get hurt/hurt back axis, and then the men involved were lost, not only to fellow feeling but to rational self-interest. Sick, in fact.

Sax felt a little sick himself. Michel had explained away male evil in several different ways in no more than a quarter of an hour, and still the men of Earth had a lot to answer for. Marsmen were different. Although there had been torturers in Kasei Vallis, as he well knew. But they had been settlers from Earth. Sick. Yes, he felt sick. The young natives were not like that, were they? A Marsman who hit a woman or molested a child would be ostracized, excoriated, perhaps beaten up, he would lose his home, he would be exiled to the asteroids and never allowed back. Wouldn't he?

Something to look into.

Now he thought again of Ann. Of how she was: her manner, so obdurate; her focus on science, on rock. A kind of Apollonian

54

response, perhaps. Concentration on the abstract, denial of the body and therefore of all its pain. Perhaps.

'What would help Ann now, do you think?' Sax said.

Michel shrugged again. 'I have wondered that for years. I think Mars has helped her. I think Simon helped her, and Peter. But they have all been at some kind of distance. They don't change that fundamental no in her.'

'But she – she loves all this,' Sax said, waving at the caldera. 'She truly does.' He thought over Michel's analysis. 'It's not just a no. There's a yes in there as well. A love of Mars.'

'But if you love stones and not people,' Michel said, 'it's somehow a little . . . unbalanced? Or displaced? Ann is a great mind, you know —'

'I know —'

' — and she has achieved a great deal. But she does not seem content with it.'

'She doesn't like what's happening to her world.'

'No. But is that what she truly dislikes? Or dislikes the most? I'm not so sure. It seems displaced to me, again. Both the love and the hate.'

Sax shook his head. Astounding, really, that Michel could consider psychology any kind of science at all. So much of it consisted of throwing together. Of thinking of the mind as a steam engine, the mechanical analogy most ready to hand during the birth of modern psychology. People had always done that when they thought about the mind: clockwork for Descartes, geological changes for the early Victorians, computers or holography for the twentieth century, AIs for the twenty-first . . . and for the Freudian traditionalists, steam engines. Application of heat, pressure build-up, pressure displacement, venting, all shifted into repression, sublimation, the return of the repressed. Sax thought it unlikely steam engines were an adequate model for the human mind. The mind was more like – what? – an ecology – a fellfield – or else a jungle, populated by all manner of strange beasts. Or a universe, filled with stars and quasars and black holes. Well – a bit grandiose, that – really it was more like a complex collection of synapses and axons, chemical energies surging hither and yon, like weather in an atmosphere. That was better – weather – storm fronts of thought, high pressure zones, low pressure cells, hurricanes – the jetstreams of biological desires, always making their swift powerful rounds ... life in the wind. Well. Throwing together. In fact the mind was poorly understood.

'What are you thinking?' Michel asked.

'Sometimes I worry,' Sax admitted, 'about the theoretical basis of these diagnoses of yours.'

'Oh no, they are very well supported empirically, they are very precise, very accurate.'

'Both precise *and* accurate?'

'Well, what, they're the same, no?'

'No. In estimates of a value, accuracy means how far away you are from the true value. Precision refers to the window size of the estimate. A hundred plus or minus fifty isn't very precise. But if your estimate is a hundred plus or minus fifty, and the true value is a hundred and one, it's quite accurate, while still being not very precise. Often true values aren't really determinable, of course.'

Michel had a curious expression on his face. 'You're a very accurate person, Sax.'

'It's just statistics,' Sax said defensively. 'Every once in a while language allows you to say things precisely.'

'And accurately.'

'Sometimes.'

They looked down into the country of the caldera.

'I want to help her,' Sax said.

Michel nodded. 'You said that. I said I didn't know how. For her, you are the terraforming. If you are to help her, then terraforming has to help her. Do you think you can find a way that terraforming helps her?'

Sax thought about it for a while. 'It could get her outdoors. Outdoors without helmets, eventually without even masks.'

'You think she wants that?'

'I think everyone wants that, at some level. In the cerebellum. The animal, you know. It feels right.'

'I don't know if Ann is very well attuned to her animal feelings.'

Sax considered it.

Then the whole landscape darkened.

They looked up. The sun was black. Stars shone in the sky

56

around it. There was a faint glow around the black disc, perhaps the sun's corona.

Then a sudden crescent of fire forced them to look away. That was the corona; what they had seen before had probably been the lit exosphere.

The darkened landscape lightened again, as the artificial eclipse came to an end. But the whole sun that returned was distinctly smaller than what had shone just moments before. The old bronze button of the Martian sun! It was like a friend come back for a visit. The world was dimmer, all the colours of the caldera one shade darker, as if invisible clouds obscured the sunlight. A very familiar sight, in fact – Mars's natural light, shining on them again for the first time in twenty-eight years.

'I hope Ann saw that,' Sax said. He felt chilled, although he knew there had not been enough time for the air to have cooled, and he was suited up in any case. But there would be a chill. He thought grimly of the fellfields scattered all over the planet, up at the four or five kilometre elevation, and lower in the mid and high latitudes. Up at the edge of the possible, whole ecosystems would now start dying. Twenty per cent drop in insolation: it was worse than any Terran ice age, more like the darkness after the great extinction events – the KT event, the Ordovician, the Devonian, or the worst one of all, the Permian event two hundred and fifty million years ago, which killed up to ninety-five per cent of all the species alive at the time. Punctuated equilibrium; and very few species survived the punctuations. The ones that did were tough, or just lucky.

Michel said, 'I doubt it will satisfy her.'

This Sax fully believed. But for the moment he was distracted by thinking how best to compensate for the loss of the soletta's light. It would be better not to have any biomes suffering great losses. If he had his way, those fellfields were just something Ann was going to have to get used to.

It was Ls 123, right in the middle of the northern summer/southern winter, near aphelion, which along with higher elevation caused the south's winter to be much colder than the north's; temperatures regularly dipped to 230° K, not much warmer than the primal colds that had existed before their arrival. Now, with the soletta and annular mirror gone, temperatures would drop further still. No doubt the southern highlands were headed for a record winterkill.

On the other hand, a lot of snow had already fallen in the south, and Sax had gained a great respect for snow's ability to protect living things from cold and wind. The subnivean environment was quite stable. It could be that a drop in light, and subsequently in surface temperature, would not do that much harm to snowed-over plants, already shut down by their winter hardening. It was hard to say. He wanted to get into the field and see for himself. Of course it would be months or perhaps years before any difference would be quantifiable. Except in the weather itself, perhaps. And weather could be tracked merely by watching the meteorological data, which he was already doing, spending many hours in front of satellite pictures and weather maps, watching for signs. As were many other people, particularly meteorologists. It made for a useful diversion when people came by to remonstrate with him for removing the mirrors, an event so common in the week following the event that it became tiresome.

Unfortunately weather on Mars was so variable that it was difficult to tell if the removal of the big mirrors was affecting it or not. A very sad admission of the state of their understanding of the atmosphere, in Sax's opinion. But there it was. Martian weather was a violent, semi-chaotic system. In some ways it resembled Earth's, not surprising given that it was a matter of air and water moving around the surface of a spinning sphere: Coriolis forces were the same everywhere, and so here as on Earth there were tropical easterlies, temperate westerlies, polar easterlies, jetstream anchor points and so on; but that was almost all one could say for sure about Martian weather. Well – you could say that it was colder and drier in the south than in the north. That there were rainshadows downwind of high volcanoes or mountain chains. That it was warmer near the equator, colder at the poles. But this sort of obvious generalization was all that they could assert with confidence, except for some local patterns, although most of those were subject to lots of variation – more a matter of highly analysed statistics than lived experience. And with only fifty-two M-years on record, with the atmosphere thickening radically all the while, with water being pumped onto the surface, etc, etc, it was actually fairly difficult to say what normal or average conditions might be.

Meanwhile, Sax found it hard to concentrate there on East Pavonis. People kept interrupting him to complain about the mirrors, and the volatile political situation lurched along in storms as unpredictable as the weather's. Already it was clear that removing the mirrors had not placated all the Reds; there were sabotages of terraforming projects almost every day, and sometimes violent fights in defence of these projects. And reports from Earth, which Sax forced himself to watch for an hour a day, made it clear that some forces there were trying to keep things the way they had been before the flood, in sharp conflict with other groups trying to take advantage of the flood in the same way the Martian revolutionaries had, using it as a break point in history and a springboard to some new order, some fresh start. But the metanationals were not going to give up easily, and on Earth they were entrenched, the order of the day; they were in command of vast resources, and no mere seven-metre rise in sea level was going to push them off stage.

Sax switched off his screen after one such depressing hour, and joined Michel for supper out in his rover.

'There's no such thing as a fresh start,' he said as he put water on to boil.

'The Big Bang?' Michel suggested.

'As I understand it, there are theories suggesting that the – the clumpiness of the early universe was caused by the earlier – clumpiness of the previous universe, collapsing down into its Big Crunch.'

'I would have thought that would crush all irregularities.'

'Singularities are strange – outside their event horizons, quantum effects allow some particles to appear. Then the cosmic inflation blasting those particles out apparently caused small clumps to start and become big ones.' Sax frowned; he was sounding like the Da Vinci theory group. 'But I was referring to the flood on Earth. Which is not as complete an alteration of conditions as a singularity, by any means. In fact there must be people down there who don't think of it as a break at all.'

'True.' For some reason Michel was laughing. 'We should go down there and see, eh?'

As they finished eating their spaghetti Sax said, 'I want to get out in the field. I want to see if there are any visible effects of the mirrors going away.'

'You already saw one. That dimming of the light, when we were out on the rim . . .' Michel shuddered.

'Yes, but that only makes me more curious.'

'Well – we'll hold down the fort for you.'

As if one had physically to occupy any given space in order to be there. 'The cerebellum never gives up,' Sax said.

Michel grinned. 'Which is why you want to go out and see it in person.'

Sax frowned.

Before he left, he called Ann.

'Would you like to, to accompany me, on a trip to South Tharsis, to, to, to examine the upper boundary of the areobiosphere, together?'

She was startled. Her head was shaking back and forth as she thought it over – the cerebellum's answer, some six or seven seconds ahead of her conscious verbal response: 'No.' And then she cut the connection, looking somewhat frightened.

Sax shrugged. He felt bad. He saw that one of his reasons for going into the field had to do with getting Ann out there, showing her the fellfields himself. Showing her how beautiful they were. Talking to her. Something like that. His mental image of what he would say to her if he actually got her out there was fuzzy at best. Just show her. Make her *see* it.

Well, one couldn't make people see things.

He went to say goodbye to Michel. Michel's entire job was to make people see things. This was no doubt the cause of the frustration in him when he talked about Ann. She had been one of his patients for over a century now and still she hadn't changed, or even told him very much about herself. It made Sax smile a little to think of it. Though clearly it was vexing for Michel, who obviously loved Ann. As he did all his old friends and patients, including Sax. It was in the nature of a professional responsibility, as Michel saw it – to fall in love with all the objects of his 'scientific study'. Every astronomer loves the stars. Well, who knew. Sax reached out and clasped Michel's upper arm, who smiled happily at this unSaxlike behaviour, this 'change in thinking'. Love, yes; and how much more so when the object of study consisted of women known for years and years, studied with the intensity of pure science – yes, that would be a feeling. A great intimacy, whether they co-operated in the study or not. In fact they might even be more beguiling if they didn't co-operate, if they refused to answer any questions at all. After all if Michel wanted questions answered, answered at great length even when they weren't asked, he always had Maya, Maya the all-too-human, who led Michel on a hard steeplechase across the limbic array, including throwing things at him, if Spencer was to be believed. After that kind of symbolism, the silence of Ann might prove to be very endearing. 'Be careful,' Michel said: the happy scientist, with one of his areas of study standing before him, loved like a brother.

Sax took a solo rover and drove it down the steep, bare southern slope of Pavonis Mons, then across the saddle between Pavonis and Arsia Mons. He contoured around the great cone of Arsia Mons on its dry eastern side. After that he drove down the southern flank of Arsia, and of the Tharsis bulge itself, until he was on the broken highlands of Daedalia Planitia. This plain was the remnant of a giant ancient impact basin, now almost entirely erased by the uptilt of Tharsis, by lava from Arsia Mons, and by the ceaseless winds, until nothing was left of the impact basin except for a collection of areologists' observations and deductions, faint radial arrays of ejecta scrapes and the like, visible on maps but not in the landscape.

To the eye as one travelled over it, it looked like much of the rest of the southern highlands: rugged, bumpy, pitted, cracked land. A wild rockscape. The old lava flows were visible as smooth lobate curves of dark rock, like tidal swells fanning out and down. Wind streaks both light and dark marked the land, indicating dust of different weights and consistencies: there were light, long triangles on the southeast sides of craters and boulders, dark chevrons to the northwest of them, and dark splotches inside the many rimless craters. The next big dust storm would redesign all these patterns.

Sax drove over the low stone waves with great pleasure, down down up, down down up, reading the sand paintings of the dust streaks like a wind chart. He was travelling not in a boulder car, with its low, dark room and its cockroach scurry from one hiding place to the next, but rather in a big, boxy areologist's camper, with windows on all four sides of the third-storey driver's compartment. It was a very great pleasure indeed to roll along up there in the thin, bright daylight, down and up, down and up, down and up over the sand-streaked plain, the horizons very distant for Mars. There was no one to hide from; no one hunting for him. He was a free man on a free planet, and if he wanted to he could drive this car right around the world. Or anywhere he pleased.

The full impact of this feeling took him about two days'

drive to realize. Even then he was not sure that he comprehended it. It was a sensation of lightness, a strange lightness
that caused little smiles to stretch his mouth repeatedly for
no obvious reason. He had not been consciously aware, before,
of any sense of oppression or fear – but it seemed it had
been there – since 2061, perhaps, or the years right before it.
Sixty-six years of fear, ignored and forgotten but always there
– a kind of tension in the musculature, a small hidden dread
at the core of things. 'Sixty-six bottles of fear on the wall,
sixty-six bottles of fear! Take one down, pass it around, sixty-
five bottles of fear on the wall!'

Now gone. He was free, his world was free. He was driving
down the wind-etched tilted plain, and earlier that day snow
had begun to appear in the cracks, gleaming aquatically in a
way dust never did; and then lichen; he was driving down into
the atmosphere. And no reason, now, why his life ought not
to continue this way, puttering about freely every day in his
own world lab, and everybody else just as free as that!

It was quite a feeling.

Oh they could argue on Pavonis, and they most certainly
would. Everywhere in fact. A most extraordinarily contentious
lot they were. What was the sociology that would explain
that? Hard to say. And in any case they had co-operated despite
their bickering; it might have been only a temporary confluence of interests, but everything was temporary now – with
so many traditions broken or vanished, it left what John used
to called the necessity of creation; and creation was hard. Not
everyone was as good at creation as they were at complaining.

But they had certain capabilities now as a group, as a – a
civilization. The accumulated body of scientific knowledge was
growing vast indeed, and that knowledge was giving them an
array of powers that could scarcely be comprehended, even
in outline, by any single individual. But powers they were,
understood or not. Godlike powers, as Michel called them,
though it was not necessary to exaggerate them or confuse
the issue – they were powers in the material world, real but
constrained by reality. Which nevertheless might allow – it
looked to Sax as if they could – if rightly applied – make a
decent human civilization after all. After all the many centuries of trying. And why not? Why not? Why not pitch the

whole enterprise at the highest level possible? They could provide for everyone in an equitable way, they could cure disease, they could delay senescence until they lived for a thousand years, they could understand the universe from the Planck distance to the cosmic distance, from the Big Bang to the eskaton – all this was possible, it was technically achievable. And as for those who felt that humanity needed the spur of suffering to make it great, well they could go out and find anew the tragedies that Sax was sure would never go away, things like lost love, betrayal by friends, death, bad results in the lab. Meanwhile the rest of them could continue the work of making a decent civilization. They could do it! It was amazing, really. They had reached that moment in history when one could say it was possible. Very hard to believe, actually; it made Sax suspicious; in physics one became immediately dubious when a situation appeared to be somehow extraordinary or unique. The odds were against that, it suggested that it was an artefact of perspective, one had to assume that things were more or less constant and that one lived in average times – the so-called principle of mediocrity. Never a particularly attractive principle, Sax had thought; perhaps it only meant that justice had always been achievable; in any case, there it was, an extraordinary moment, right there outside his four windows, burnished under the light touch of the natural sun. Mars and its humans, free and powerful.

It was too much to grasp. It kept slipping out of his mind, then reoccurring to him, and surprised by joy he would exclaim, 'Ha! Ha!' The taste of tomato soup and bread; 'Ha!' The dusky purple of the twilight sky; 'Ha!' The spectacle of the dashboard instrumentation, glowing faintly, reflected in the black windows; 'Ha! Ha! Ha! My oh my.' He could drive anywhere he wanted to. No one told them what to do. He said that aloud to his darkened AI screen: 'No one tells us what to do!' It was almost frightening. Vertiginous. Ka, the yonsei would say. Ka, supposedly the little red people's name for Mars, from the Japanese *ka*, meaning fire. The same word existed in several other early languages as well, including proto-Indo-European; or so the linguists said.

Carefully he got in the big bed at the back of the compartment, in the hum of the rover's heating and electrical system, and he lay humming to himself under the thick coverlet that caught up his body's heat so fast, and put his head on the pillow and looked out at the stars.

The next morning a high pressure system came in from the northwest, and the temperature rose to 262° K. He had driven down to five kilometres above the datum, and the exterior air pressure was 230 millibars. Not quite enough to breathe freely, so he pulled on one of the heated surface suits, then slipped a small air tank over his shoulders, and put its mask over his nose and mouth, and a pair of goggles over his eyes.

Even so, when he climbed out of the outer lock door and down the steps to the sand, the intense cold caused him to sniffle and tear up, to the point of impeding his vision. The whistle of the wind was loud, though his ears were inside the hood of his suit. The suit's heater was up to the task, however, and with the rest of him warm, his face slowly got used to it.

He tightened the hood's drawstring and walked over the land. He stepped from flat stone to flat stone; here they were everywhere. He crouched often to inspect cracks, finding lichen and widely scattered specimens of other life: mosses, little tufts of sedge, grass. It was very windy. Exceptionally hard gusts slapped him four or five times a minute, with a steady gale between. This was a windy place much of the time, no doubt, with the atmosphere sliding south around the bulk of Tharsis in massed quantities. High pressure cells would dump a lot of their moisture at the start of this rise, on the western side; indeed at this moment the horizon to the west was obscured by a flat sea of cloud, merging with the land in the far distance, out there two or three kilometres lower in elevation, and perhaps sixty kilometres away.

Underfoot there were only bits of snow, filling some of the shaded crack systems and hollows. These snowbanks were so hard that he could jump up and down on them without leaving a mark. Windslab, partially melted and then refrozen. One scalloped slab cracked under his boots, and he found it was several centimetres thick. Under that it was powder, or granules. His fingers were cold, despite his heated gloves.

He stood again and wandered, mapless over the rock. Some of the deeper hollows contained ice pools. Around midday he descended into one of these and ate his lunch by the ice pool, lifting the air mask to take bites out of a grain and honey bar. Elevation 4·5 kilometres above the datum; air pressure 267 millibars. A high pressure system indeed. The sun was low in the northern sky, a bright dot surrounded by pewter.

The ice of the pool was clear in places, like little windows giving him a view of the black bottom. Elsewhere it was bubbled or cracked, or white with rime. The bank he sat on was a curve of gravel, with patches of brown soil and black dead vegetation lying on it in a miniature berm – the high-water mark of the pond, apparently, a soil shore above the gravel one. The whole beach was no more than four metres long, one wide. The fine gravel was an umber colour, piebald umber or . . . He would have to consult a colour chart. But not now.

The soil berm was dotted by pale green rosettes of tiny grass blades. Longer blades stood in clumps here and there. Most of the taller blades were dead, and light grey. Right next to the pond were patches of dark green succulent leaves, dark red at their edges. Where the green shaded into red was a colour he couldn't name, a dark lustrous brown stuffed some-how with both its constituent colours. He would have to call up a colour chart soon it seemed; lately when looking around outdoors he found that a colour chart came in handy about once a minute. Waxy almost-white flowers were tucked under some of these bi-coloured leaves. Further on lay some tangles, red-stalked, green-needled, like beached seaweed in miniature. Again that intermixture of red and green, right there in nature staring at him.

A distant wind-washed hum; perhaps the harping rocks, perhaps the buzz of insects. Black midges, bees . . . in this air they would only have to sustain about 30 millibars of CO_2, because there was so little partial pressure driving it into them, and at some point internal saturation was enough to hold any more out. For mammals that might not work so well. But they might be able to sustain 20 millibars, and with plant life flourishing all over the planet's lower elevations, CO_2 levels might drop to 20 millibars fairly soon; and then they could dispense with the air tanks and the facemasks. Set loose animals on Mars.

In the faint hum of the air he seemed to hear their voices, immanent or emergent, coming in the next great surge of *viriditas*. The hum of distant voices; the wind; the peace of this little pool on its rocky moor; the Nirgalish pleasure he took in the sharp cold . . . 'Ann should see this,' he murmured.

Then again, with the space mirrors gone, presumably everything he saw here was doomed. This was the upper limit of the biosphere, and surely with the loss of light and heat the upper limit would drop, at least temporarily, perhaps for good. He didn't like that; and it seemed possible there might be ways to compensate for the lost light. After all, the terraforming had been doing quite well before the mirrors' arrival; they hadn't been necessary. And it was good not to depend on something so fragile, and better to be rid of it now rather than later, when large animal populations might have died in the setback along with the plants.

Even so it was a shame. But the dead plant matter would only be more fertilizer in the end, and without the same kind of suffering as animals. At least so he assumed. Who knew how plants felt? When you looked closely at them, glowing in all their detailed articulation like complex crystals, they were as mysterious as any other life. And now their presence here made the entire plain, everything he could see, into one great fellfield, spreading in a slow tapestry over the rock; breaking down the weathered minerals, melding with them to make the first soils. A very slow process. There was a vast complexity in every pinch of soil; and the look of this fellfield was the loveliest thing he had ever seen.

To weather. This whole world was weathering. The first printed use of the word with that meaning had appeared in a book on Stonehenge, appropriately enough, in 1665. 'The weathering of so many Centuries of Years.' On this stone world. Weathering. Language as the first science, exact yet vague, or multivalent. Throwing things together. The mind as weather. Or being weathered.

There were clouds coming up over the nearby hillocks to

the west, their bottoms resting on a thermal layer as levelly as if pressing down on glass. Streamers like spun wool led the way east.

Sax stood up and climbed out of the pool's depression. Out of the shelter of the hole, the wind was shockingly strong – in it the cold intensified as if an ice age had struck full force that very second. Windchill factor, of course; if the temperature was 262° K, and the wind was blowing at about seventy kilometres an hour, with gusts much stronger, then the windchill factor would create a temperature equivalent of about 250° K. Was that right? That was very cold indeed to be out without a helmet. And in fact his hands were going numb. His feet as well. And his face was already without feeling, like a thick mask at the front of his head. He was shivering, and his blinks tended to stick together; his tears were freezing. He needed to get back to his car.

He plodded over the rockscape, amazed at the power of the wind to intensify cold. He had not experienced windchill like this since childhood, if then, and had forgotten how frigid one became. Staggering in the blasts, he climbed onto a low swell of the ancient lava and looked upslope. There was his rover – big, vivid green, gleaming like a spaceship – about two kilometres up the slope. A very welcome sight.

But now snow began to fly horizontally past him, giving a dramatic demonstration of the wind's great speed. Little granular pellets clicked against his goggles. He took off toward the rover, keeping his head down and watching the snow swirl over the rocks. There was so much snow in the air that he thought his goggles were fogging up, but after a painfully cold operation to wipe the insides, it became clear that the condensation was actually out in the air. Fine snow, mist, dust, it was hard to tell.

He plodded on. The next time he looked up, the air was so thick with snow that he couldn't see all the way to the rover. Nothing to do but press on. It was lucky the suit was well insulated and sewn through with heating elements, because even with the heat on at its highest power, the cold was cutting against his left side as if he were naked to the blast. Visibility extended now something like twenty metres, shifting rapidly depending on how much snow was passing by at the moment;

he was in an amorphously expanding and contracting bubble of whiteness, which itself was shot through with flying snow, and what appeared to be a kind of frozen fog or mist. It seemed likely he was in the storm cloud itself. His legs were stiff. He wrapped his arms around his torso, his gloved hands trapped in his armpits. There was no obvious way of telling if he was still walking in the right direction. It seemed as if he was on the same course he had been when visibility had collapsed, but it also seemed as if he had gone a long way toward the rover.

There were no compasses on Mars; there were, however, APS systems in his wristpad and back in the car. He could call up a detailed map on his wristpad and then locate himself and his car on it; then walk for a while and track his positions; then make his way directly toward the car. That seemed like a great deal of work – which brought it to him that his thinking, like his body, was being affected by the cold. It wasn't that much work, after all.

So he crouched down in the lee of a boulder and tried the method. The theory behind it was obviously sound, but the instrumentation left something to be desired; the wristpad's screen was only five centimetres across, so small that he couldn't see the dots on it at all well. Finally he spotted them, walked a while, and took another fix. But unfortunately his results indicated that he should be hiking at about a right angle to the direction he had been going.

This was unnerving to the point of paralysis. His body insisted that it had been going the right way; his mind (part of it, anyway) was pretty certain that it was better to trust the results on the wristpad, and assume that he had gone off course somewhere. But it didn't feel that way; the ground was still at a slope that supported the feeling in his body. The contradiction was so intense that he suffered a wave of nausea, the internal torque twisting him until it actually hurt to stand, as if every cell in his body was twisting to the side against the pressure of what the wristpad was telling him – the physiological effects of a purely cognitive dissonance, it was amazing. It almost made one believe in the existence of an internal magnet in the body, as in the pineal glands of migrating birds – but there was no magnetic field to speak of. Perhaps his skin was sensitive to solar radiation to the point of being able to pinpoint the sun's location, even when the sky was a thick dark grey everywhere. It had to be something like that, because the feeling that he was properly oriented was so strong!

Eventually the nausea of the disorientation passed, and in the end he stood and took off in the direction suggested by the wristpad, feeling horrible about it, listing a little uphill just to try and make himself feel better. But one had to trust instruments over instincts, that was science. And so he plodded on, traversing the slope, shading somewhat uphill, clumsier than ever. His nearly insensible feet ran into rocks that he did not see, even though they were directly beneath him; he stumbled time after time. It was surprising how thoroughly snow could obscure the vision.

After a while he stopped, and tried again to locate the rover by APS; and his wristpad map suggested an entirely new direction, behind him and to the left.

It was possible he had walked past the car. Was it? He did not want to walk back into the wind. But now that was the way to the rover, apparently. So he ducked his head down into the biting cold and persevered. His skin was in an odd state, itching under the heating elements crisscrossing his suit, numb everywhere else. His feet were numb. It was hard to walk. There was no feeling in his face; clearly frostbite was in the offing. He needed shelter.

He had a new idea. He called up Aonia, on Pavonis, and got her almost instantly.

'Sax! Where are you?'

'That's what I'm calling about!' he said. 'I'm in a storm on Daedalia! And I can't find my car! I was wondering if you would look at my APS and my rover's! And see if you can tell me which direction I should go!'

He put the wristpad right against his ear. 'Ka wow, Sax.' It sounded like Aonia was shouting too, bless her. Her voice was an odd addition to the scene. 'Just a second, let me check! . . . Okay! There you are! And your car too! What are you doing so far south? I don't think anyone can get to you very quickly! Especially if there's a storm!'

'There is a storm,' Sax said. 'That's why I called.'

'Okay! You're about three hundred and fifty metres to the west of your car.'

'Directly west?'

' — and a little south! But how will you orient yourself?'

Sax considered it. Mars's lack of a magnetic field had never struck him as such a problem before, but there it was. He could assume the wind was directly out of the west, but that was just an assumption. 'Can you check the nearest weather stations and tell me what direction the wind is coming from?' he said.

'Sure, but it won't be much good for local variations! Here, just a second, I'm getting some help here from the others.'

A few long icy moments passed.

'The wind is coming from west north west, Sax! So you need to walk with the wind at your back and a touch to your left!'

'I know. Be quiet now, until you see what course I'm making, and then correct it.'

He walked again, fortunately almost downwind. After five or six painful minutes his wrist beeped.

Aonia said, 'You're right on course!'

This was encouraging, and he carried on with a bit more speed, though the wind was penetrating through his ribs right to his core.

'Okay, Sax! Sax?'

'Yes!'

'You and your car are right on the same spot!'

But there was no car in view.

His heart thudded in his chest. Visibility was still some twenty metres; but no car. He had to get shelter fast. 'Walk in an ever-increasing spiral from where you are,' the little voice on the wrist was suggesting. A good idea in theory, but he couldn't bear to execute it; he couldn't face the wind. He stared dully at his black plastic wristpad console. No more help to be had there.

For a moment he could make out snowbanks, off to his left. He shuffled over to investigate, and found that the snow rested in the lee of a shoulder-high escarpment, a feature he did not remember seeing before, but there were some radial breaks in the rock caused by the Tharsis rise, and this must be one of them, protecting a snowbank. Snow was a tremendous insulator. Though it had little intrinsic appeal as shelter. But Sax knew mountaineers often dug into it to survive nights out. It got one out of the wind.

He stepped to the bottom of the snowbank, and kicked it with one numb foot. It felt like kicking rock. Digging a snow cave seemed out of the question. But the effort itself would warm him a bit. And it was less windy at the foot of the bank. So he kicked and kicked, and found that underneath a thick cake of windslab there was the usual powder. A snow cave might be possible after all. He dug away at it.

'Sax, Sax!' cried the voice from his wrist. 'What are you doing?'

'Making a snow cave,' he said. 'A bivouac.'

'Oh, Sax – we're flying in help! We'll be able to get in next morning no matter what, so hang on! We'll keep talking to you!'

'Fine.'

He kicked and dug. On his knees he scooped out hard granular snow, tossing it into the swirling flakes flying over him. It was hard to move, hard to think. He bitterly regretted walking so far from the rover, then getting so absorbed in the landscape around that ice pond. It was a shame to get killed when things were getting so interesting. Free but dead. There was a little hollow in the snow now, through an oblong hole in the windslab. Wearily he sat down and wedged himself back into the space, lying on his side and pushing back with his boots. The snow felt solid against the back of his suit, and warmer than the ferocious wind. He welcomed the shivering in his torso, felt a vague fear when it ceased. Being too cold to shiver was a bad sign.

Very weary, very cold. He looked at his wristpad. It was four p.m. He had been walking in the storm for just over three hours. He would have to survive another fifteen or twenty hours before he could expect to be rescued. Or perhaps in the morning the storm would have abated, and the location of the rover become obvious. One way or another he had to survive the night by huddling in a snow cave. Or else venture out again and find the rover. Surely it couldn't be far away. But until the wind lessened, he could not bear to be out looking for it.

He had to wait in the snow cave. Theoretically he could survive a night out, though at the moment he was so cold it was hard to believe that. Night temperatures on Mars still plummeted drastically. Perhaps the storm might lessen in the next hour, so that he could find the rover and get to it before dark.

He told Aonia and the others where he was. They sounded very concerned, but there was nothing they could do. He felt irritation at their voices.

It seemed many minutes before he had another thought. When one was chilled, blood flow was greatly reduced to the limbs – perhaps that was true for the cortex as well, the blood going preferentially to the cerebellum where the necessary work would continue right to the end.

More time passed. Near dark, it appeared. Should call out again. He was *too* cold – something seemed wrong. Advanced age, altitude, CO_2 levels – some factor or combination of factors was making it worse than it should be. He could die of exposure in a single night. Appeared in fact to be doing just that. Such a storm! Loss of the mirrors, perhaps. Instant ice age. Extinction event.

The wind was making odd noises, like shouts. Powerful gusts no doubt. Like faint shouts, howling, 'Sax! Sax! Sax!'

Had they flown someone in? He peered out into the dark storm, the snowflakes somehow catching the late light and tearing overhead like dim white static.

Then between his ice-crusted eyelashes he saw a figure emerge out of the darkness. Short, round, helmeted. 'Sax!' The sound was distorted, it was coming from a loudspeaker in the figure's helmet. Those Da Vinci techs were very resourceful people. Sax tried to respond, and found he was too cold to speak. Just moving his boots out of the hole was a stupendous effort. But it appeared to catch this figure's eye, because it turned and strode purposefully through the wind, moving like a skilful sailor on a bouncing deck, weaving this way and that through the slaps of the gusts. The figure reached him and bent down and grabbed Sax by the wrist, and he saw its face through the faceplate, as clear as through a window. It was Hiroko.

She smiled her brief smile and hauled him up out of his cave, pulling so hard on his left wrist that his bones creaked painfully.

'Ow!' he said.

Out in the wind the cold was like death itself. Hiroko pulled his left arm over her shoulder, and, still holding hard to his wrist just above the wristpad, she led him past the low escarpment and right into the teeth of the gale.

'My rover is near,' he mumbled, leaning hard on her and trying to move his legs fast enough to make steady plants of the foot. So good to see her again. A solid little person, very powerful as always.

'It's over here,' she said through her loudspeaker. 'You were pretty close.'

'How did you find me?'

'We were tracking you as you came down Arsia. Then today when the storm hit I checked you out, and saw you were out of your rover. After that I came out to see how you were doing.'

'Thanks.'

'You have to be careful in storms.'

Then they were standing before his rover. She let go of his wrist, and it throbbed painfully. She bonked her faceplate against his goggles. 'Go on in,' she said.

He climbed carefully up the steps to the rover's lock door; opened it; fell inside. He turned clumsily to make room for Hiroko, but she wasn't in the door. He leaned back out into the wind, looked around. No sight of her. It was dusk; the snow now looked black. 'Hiroko!' he cried.

No answer.

He closed the lock door, suddenly frightened. Oxygen deprivation – he pumped the lock, fell through the inside door into the little changing room. It was shockingly warm, the air a steamy blast. He plucked ineffectively at his clothes, made no progress. He went at it more methodically. Goggles and facemask off. They were coated with ice. Ah – possibly his air supply had been restricted by ice in the tube between tank and mask. He sucked in several deep breaths, then sat still through another bout of nausea. Pulled off his hood, unzipped the suit. It was almost more than he could do to get his boots off. Then the suit. His underclothes were cold and clammy. His hands were burning as if on fire. It was a good sign, proof that he was not substantially frostbitten; nevertheless it was agony.

His whole skin began to buzz with the same inflamed pain. What caused that, return of blood to capillaries? Return of sensation to chilled nerves? Whatever it was, it hurt almost unbearably. 'Ow!'

He was in excellent spirits. It was not just that he had been spared from death, which was nice; but that Hiroko was alive. Hiroko was alive! It was incredibly good news. Many of his friends had assumed all along that she and her group had slipped away from the assault on Sabishii, moving through that town's mound maze back out into their system of hidden refuges; but Sax had never been sure. There was no evidence to support the idea. And there were elements in the security forces perfectly capable of murdering a group of dissidents and disposing of their bodies. This, Sax had thought, was probably what had happened. But he had kept this opinion to himself, and reserved judgement. There had been no way of knowing for sure.

But now he knew. He had stumbled into Hiroko's path, and she had rescued him from death by freezing, or asphyxiation, whichever came first. The sight of her cheery, somehow impersonal face – her brown eyes – the feel of her body supporting him – her hand clamped over his wrist . . . he would have a bruise because of that. Perhaps even a sprain. He flexed his hand, and the pain in his wrist brought tears to his eyes, it made him laugh. Hiroko!

After a time the fiery return of sensation to his skin banked down. Though his hands felt bloated and raw, and he did not have proper control of his muscles, or his thoughts, he was basically getting back to normal. Or something like normal.

'Sax! Sax! Where are you? Answer us, Sax!'

'Ah. Hello there. I'm back in my car.'

'You found it? You left your snow cave?'

'Yes. I – I saw my car, in the distance, through a break in the snow.'

They were happy to hear it.

He sat there, barely listening to them babble, wondering why he had spontaneously lied. Somehow he was not comfortable telling them about Hiroko. He assumed that she would want to stay concealed; perhaps that was it. Covering for her . . .

He assured his associates that he was all right, and got off the phone. He pulled a chair into the kitchen and sat on it. Warmed soup and drank it in loud slurps, scalding his tongue. Frostbitten, scalded, shaky – slightly nauseous – once weeping – mostly stunned – despite all this, he was very, very happy. Sobered by the close call, of course, and embarrassed or even ashamed at his ineptitude, staying out, getting lost and so on – all very sobering indeed – and yet still he was happy. He had survived, and even better, so had Hiroko. Meaning no doubt that all of her group had survived with her, including the half-dozen of the First Hundred who had been with her from the beginning, Iwao, Gene, Rya, Raul, Ellen, Evgenia . . . Sax ran a bath and sat in the warm water, adding hotter water slowly as his body core warmed; and he kept returning to that wonderful realization. A miracle – well not a miracle of course – but it had that quality, of unexpected and undeserved joy.

When he found himself falling asleep in the bath he got out, dried off, limped on sensitive feet to his bed, crawled under the coverlet, and fell asleep, thinking of Hiroko. Of making love with her in the baths in Zygote, in the warm relaxed lubriciousness of their bathhouse trysts, late at night when everyone else was asleep. Of her hand clamped on his wrist, pulling him up. His left wrist was very sore. And that made him happy.

The next day he drove back up the great southern slope of Arsia, now covered with clean white snow to an amazingly high altitude, 10.4 kilometres above the datum to be exact. He felt a strange mix of emotions, unprecedented in their strength and flux, although they somewhat resembled the powerful emotions he had felt during the synaptic stimulus treatment he had taken after his stroke – as if sections of his brain were actively growing – the limbic system, perhaps, the home of the emotions, linking up with the cerebral cortex at last. He was alive, Hiroko was alive, Mars was alive; in the face of these joyous facts the possibility of an ice age was as nothing, a momentary swing in a general warming pattern, something like the almost-forgotten Great Storm. Although he did want to do what he could to mitigate it.

Meanwhile, in the human world there were still fierce conflicts going on everywhere, on both worlds. But it seemed to Sax that the crisis had somehow got beyond war. Flood, ice age, population boom, social chaos, revolution; perhaps things had become so bad that humanity had shifted into some kind of universal catastrophe rescue operation, or, in other words, the first phase of the postcapitalist era.

Or maybe he was just getting overconfident, buoyed by the events on Daedalia Planitia. His Da Vinci associates were certainly very worried, they spent hours onscreen telling him every little thing about the arguments ongoing in East Pavonis. But he had no patience for that. Pavonis was going to become a standing wave of argument, it was obvious. And the Da Vinci crowd, worrying so – that was simply them. At Da Vinci if someone even raised his voice two decibels people worried that things were getting out of control. No. After his experience on Daedalia, these things simply weren't interesting enough to engage him. Despite the encounter with the storm, or perhaps because of it, he only wanted to get back out into the country. He wanted to see as much of it as he could – to observe the changes wrought by the removal of the mirror – to talk to various terraforming teams about how to compensate for it. He called Nanao in Sabishii, and asked him if he could come visit and talk it over with the university crowd. Nanao was agreeable.

'Can I bring some of my associates?' Sax asked.

Nanao was agreeable.

And all of a sudden Sax found he had plans, like little Athenas jumping out of his head. What would Hiroko do about this possible ice age? That he couldn't guess. But he had a large group of associates in the labs at Da Vinci who had spent the last decades working on the problem of independence, building weapons and transport and shelters and the like. Now that was a problem solved, and there they were, and an ice age was coming. Many of them had come to Da Vinci from his earlier terraforming effort, and could be talked into returning to it, no doubt. But what to do? Well, Sabishii was four kilometres above the datum, and the Tyrrhena Massif went up to five. The scientists there were the best in the world at high altitude ecology. So: a conference. Another little utopia enacted. It was obvious.

That afternoon Sax stopped his rover in the saddle between Pavonis and Arsia, at the spot called Four Mountain View – a sublime place, with two of the continent-volcanoes filling the horizons to north and south, and then the distant bump of Olympus Mons off to the northwest, and on clear days (this one was too hazy) a glimpse of Ascraeus, in the distance just to the right of Pavonis. In this spacious, sere highland he ate his lunch, then turned east, and drove down toward Nicosia, to catch a flight to Da Vinci, and then on to Sabishii.

He had to spend a lot of screen time with the Da Vinci team and many other people on Pavonis, trying to explain this move, reconciling them to his departure from the warehouse meetings. 'I am in the warehouse in every sense that matters,' he said, but they wouldn't accept that. Their cerebellums wanted him there in the flesh, a touching thought in a way. 'Touching' – a symbolic statement that was nevertheless quite literal. He laughed, but Nadia came on and said irritably, 'Come on Sax, you can't give up just because things are getting sticky; in fact that's exactly when you're needed, you're General Sax now, you're the great scientist, you have to stay in the game.'

But Hiroko showed just how present an absent person could be. And he wanted to go to Sabishii.

'But what should we do?' Nirgal asked him, and others too in less direct ways.

The situation with the cable was at an impasse; on Earth there was chaos; on Mars there were still pockets of meta-national resistance, and other areas in Red control, where they were systematically tearing out all terraforming projects, and much of the infrastructure as well. There were also a variety of small revolutionary splinter movements that were taking this opportunity to assert their independence, sometimes over areas as small as a tent or a weather station.

'Well,' Sax said, thinking about all this as much as he could bear to, 'whoever controls the life support system is in charge.'

Social structure as life support system – infrastructure, mode of production, maintenance . . . he really ought to speak to the folks at Séparation de L'Atmosphère, and to the tentmakers. Many of whom had a close relation to Da Vinci. Meaning that in certain senses he himself was as much in charge as anyone. A bad thought.

'But what do you suggest we *do*?' Maya demanded; something in her voice made it clear she was repeating the question.

By now Sax was closing in on Nicosia, and impatiently he said, 'Send a delegation to Earth? Or convene a constitutional congress, and formulate a first approximation constitution, a working draft.'

Maya shook her head. 'That won't be easy, with this crowd.'

'Take the constitutions of the twenty or thirty most success-ful Terran countries,' Sax suggested, thinking out loud, 'and see how they work. Have an AI compile a composite document, perhaps, and see what it says.'

'How would you define most successful?' Art asked.

'Country Futures Index, Real Values Gauge, Costa Rica Comparisons – even Gross Domestic Product, why not?' Econ-omics was like psychology, a pseudo-science trying to hide that fact with intense theoretical hyper-elaboration. And Gross Domestic Product was one of those unfortunate measurement concepts, like inches or the British Thermal Unit, that ought to have been retired long before. But what the hell — 'Use

81

several different sets of criteria, human welfare, ecologic success, what have you.'

'But Sax,' Coyote complained, 'the very concept of the nation-state is a bad one. That idea by itself will poison all those old constitutions.'

'Could be,' Sax said. 'But as a starting point.'

'All this is just sidestepping the problem of the cable,' Jackie said.

It was strange how certain elements of the Greens were as obsessed by total independence as the radical Reds. Sax said, 'In physics I often bracket the problems I can't solve, and try to work around them and see if they don't get solved retroactively, so to speak. To me the cable looks like that kind of problem. Think of it as a reminder that Earth isn't going to go away.'

But they ignored that, arguing as they were over what to do about the cable, what they might do about a new government, what to do about the Reds who had apparently abandoned the discussion, and so on and so forth, ignoring all his suggestions and getting back to their ongoing wrangles. So much for General Sax in the postrevolutionary world.

Nicosia's airport was almost shut down, and yet Sax did not want to go into the town; he ended up flying to Da Vinci with some friends of Spencer's from Dawes's Forked Bay, flying a big new ultralight they had built just before the revolt, in anticipation of the freedom from the need for stealth. As the AI pilot floated the big silver-winged craft over the great maze of Noctis Labyrinthus, the five passengers sat in a chamber on the bottom of the fuselage which had a large clear floor, so that they could look over the arms of their chairs at the view below; in this case, the immense linked network of troughs which was the Chandelier. Sax stared down at the smooth plateaus that stood between the canyons, often islanded; they looked like nice places to live, somewhat like Cairo, there on the north rim, looking like a model town in a glass bottle.

The plane's crew started talking about Séparation de L'Atmosphère, and Sax listened closely. Although these people had been concerned with the revolution's armaments and with basic materials research, while 'Sep' as they called it had dealt with the more mundane world of mesocosm management, they still had a healthy respect for it. Designing strong tents and keeping them functioning was a task with very severe consequences for failure, as one of them said. Criticalities everywhere, and every day a potential adventure.

Sep was associated with Praxis, apparently, and each tent or covered canyon was run by a separate organization. They pooled information and shared roving consultants and construction teams. Since they deemed themselves necessary services, they ran on a co-operative basis – on the Mondragon plan, one said, non-profit version – though they made sure to provide their members with very nice living situations and lots of free time. 'They think they deserve it, too. Because when something goes wrong they have to act fast or else.' Many of the covered canyons had had close calls, sometimes the result of meteor strike or other drama, other times more ordinary mechanical failures. The usual format for covered canyons had the physical plant consolidated at the higher end of the canyon, and this plant sucked in the appropriate amounts of nitrogen, oxygen and trace gases from the surface winds. The proportions of gases and the pressure range they were kept at varied from mesocosm to mesocosm, but they averaged around 500 millibars, which gave some lift to the tent roofs, and was pretty much the norm for indoor spaces on Mars, in a kind of invocation of the eventual goal for the surface at the datum. On sunny days, however, the expansion of air inside the tents was very significant, and the standard procedures for dealing with it included simply releasing air back into the atmosphere, or else saving it by compressing it into huge container chambers hollowed out of the canyon cliffs. 'So one time I was in Dao Vallis,' one of the techs said, 'and the excess air chamber blew up, shattering the plateau and causing a big landslide that fell down onto Reull Gate and tore open the tent roof. Pressures dropped to the local ambient, which was about 260, and everything started to freeze, and they had the old emergency bulkheads,' which were clear curtains only a few molecules thick but very strong, as Sax recalled, 'and when they deployed automatically around the

83

break, this one woman got pinned to the ground by the super-sticky at the bottom of the bulkhead, with her head on the wrong side! We ran over to her and did some quick cut and paste and got her loose, but she almost died.'

Sax shivered, thinking of his own recent brush with cold; and 260 millibars was the pressure one would find on the peak of Everest. The others were already talking about other famous blowouts, including the time Hiranyagarbha's dome had fallen in its entirety under an ice rain, despite which no one had died.

Then they were descending over the great cratered high plain of Xanthe, coming down on the Da Vinci Crater floor's big sandy runway, which they had just started using during the revolution. The whole community had been preparing for years for the day when stealthing would become unnecessary, and now a big curve of copper-mirrored windows had been installed in the arc of the southern crater rim. There was a layer of snow in the bottom of the crater, which the central knob broke out of quite dramatically. It was possible they could arrange for a lake in the crater floor, with a central knob island, which would have as its horizon the circling cliffy hills of the crater rim. A circular canal could be built just under the rim cliffs, with radial canals connecting it to the inner lake; the resulting alternation of circular water and land would resemble Plato's description of Atlantis. In this configuration Da Vinci could support, in near self-sufficiency, some twenty or thirty thousand people, Sax guessed; and there were scores of craters like Da Vinci. A commune of communes, each crater a city-state of sorts, its polis fully capable of supporting itself, of deciding what kind of culture it might have; and then with a vote in a global council of some kind . . . No regional association larger than the level of the town, except for arrangements of local interchange . . . might it work?

Da Vinci made it seem as if it might. The south arc of the rim was alive with arcades and wedge-shaped pavilions and the like, now all shot through with sunlight. Sax toured the whole complex one morning, visiting one lab after the next, and congratulating the occupants on the success of their preparations for a smooth removal of UNTA from Mars. *Some political power came out of the end of a gun, after all, and* some out of the look in the eye; and the look in the eye changed depending on whether a gun was pointed at it or not. They had spiked the guns, these people, the saxaclones, and so they were in high spirits – happy to see him, and already looking for different work – back to basic research, or figuring out uses for the new materials that Spencer's alchemists were constantly churning out; or studying the terraforming problem.

They were also paying attention to what was going on in space and on Earth. A fast shuttle from Earth, contents unknown, had contacted them requesting permission to make an orbital insertion without a keg of nails being thrown in its way. So a Da Vinci team was now nervously working out security protocols, in heavy consultation with the Swiss embassy, which had taken an office in a suite of apartments at the northwest end of the arc. From rebels to administrators; it was an awkward transition.

'What political parties do we support?' Sax asked.

'I don't know. The usual array I guess.'

'No party gets much support. Whatever works, you know.'

Sax knew. That was the old tech position, held ever since scientists had become a class in society, a priest caste almost, intervening between the people and their power. They were apolitical, supposedly, like civil servants – empiricists, who only wanted things managed in a rational scientific style, the greatest good for the greatest number, which ought to be fairly simple to arrange, if people were not so trapped in emotions, religions, governments and other mass delusional systems of that sort.

The standard scientist politics, in other words. Sax had once tried to explain this outlook to Desmond, causing his friend for some reason to laugh prodigiously, even though it made perfect sense. Well, it was a bit naïve, therefore a bit comical, he supposed; and like a lot of funny things, it could be that it was hilarious right up to the moment it turned horrible, because it was an attitude that had kept scientists from going at politics in any useful way for centuries now; and dismal centuries they had been.

But now they were on a planet where political power came out of the end of a mesocosm aerating fan. And the people in charge of that great gun (holding the elements at bay) were at least partly in charge. If they cared to exercise the power.

Gently Sax reminded people of this when he visited them in their labs; and then to ease their discomfort with the idea of politics, he talked to them about the terraforming problem. And when he finally got ready to leave for Sabishii, about sixty of them were willing to come with him, to see how things were going down there. 'Sax's alternative to Pavonis,' he heard one of the lab techs describe the trip. Which was not a bad thought.

Sabishii was located on the western side of a five-kilometre high prominence called the Tyrrhena Massif, south of Jarry-Desloges Crater, in the ancient highlands between Isidis and Hellas, centred at longitude 275°, latitude 15° south. A reasonable choice for a tent town site, as it had long views to the west, and low hills backing it to the east, like moors. But when it came to living in the open air, or growing plants out in the rocky countryside, it was a bit high; in fact it was, if you excluded the very much larger bulges of Tharsis and Elysium, the highest region on Mars, a kind of bioregion island, which the Sabishiians had been cultivating for decades.

They proved to be severely disappointed by the loss of the big mirrors, one might even say thrown into emergency mode, an all-out effort to do what they could to protect the plants of the biome; but it was precious little. Sax's old colleague Nanao Nakayama shook his head. 'Winterkill will be very bad. Like ice age.'

'I'm hoping we can compensate for the loss of light,' Sax said. 'Thicken the atmosphere, add greenhouse gases – it's possible we could do some of that with more bacteria and suralpine plants, right?'

'Some,' Nanao said dubiously. 'A lot of niches are already full. The niches are quite small.'

They settled in over a meal to talk about it. All the techs from Da Vinci were there in the big dining hall of the Claw, and many Sabishiians were there to greet them. It was a long, interesting, friendly talk. The Sabishiians were living in the mound maze of their mohole, behind one talon of the dragon figure it made, so that they didn't have to look at the burned ruins of their city when they weren't working on it. The rebuilding was much reduced now, as most of them were out dealing with the results of the mirror loss. Nanao said to Tariki, in what was clearly the continuation of a long-standing argument, 'It makes no sense to rebuild it as a tent city anyway. We might as well wait, and build it open air.'

'That may be a long wait,' Tariki said, glancing at Sax. 'We're near the top of the viability atmosphere named in the Dorsa Brevia document.'

Nanao looked at Sax. 'We want Sabishii under any limit that is set.'

Sax nodded, shrugged; he didn't know what to say. The Reds would not like it. But if the viable altitude limit was raised a kilometre or so, it would give the Sabishiians this massif, and make little difference on the larger bulges – so it seemed to make sense. But who knew what they would decide on Pavonis? He said, 'Maybe we should focus now on trying to keep atmospheric pressures from dropping.'

They looked sombre.

Sax said, 'You'll take us out and show us the massif?'

They cheered up. 'Most happy.'

The land of the Tyrrhena Massif was what the areologists in Sax's day had called the 'dissected unit' of the southern highlands, which was much the same as the 'cratered unit', but further broken by small channel networks. The lower and more typical highlands surrounding the massif also contained areas of 'ridged unit' and 'hilly unit'. In fact, as quickly became obvious the morning they drove out onto the land, all aspects of the rough terrain of the southern highlands were on view, often all at once: cratered, broken, uneven, ridged, dissected and hilly land, the quintessential Noachian landscape. Sax and Nanao and Tariki sat on the observation deck of one of the Sabishii university rovers; they could see other cars carrying other colleagues, and there were teams out walking ahead of them. On the last hills before the horizon to the east, a few energetic people were fell-running. The hollows of the land were all lightly dusted with dirty snow. The massif was centred

15° south of the equator, and they got a fair bit of precipitation around Sabishii, Nanao said. The southeast side of the massif was drier, but here, the cloud masses pushed south over the ice in Isidis Planitia and climbed the slope and dropped their loads.

Indeed, as they drove uphill great waves of dark cloud rolled in from the northwest, pouring over them as if chasing the fell-runners. Sax shuddered, remembering his recent exposure to the elements; he was happy to be in a rover, and felt he would need only short walks away from it to be satisfied.

Eventually, however, they stopped on a high point in a low old ridge, and got out. They made their way over a surface littered with boulders and knobs, cracks, sand drifts, very small craters, breadloafed bedrock, scarps and alases, and the old shallow channels that gave the dissected unit its name. In truth there were deformational features of every kind to be seen, for the land here was four billion years old. A lot had happened to it, but nothing had ever happened to destroy it completely and clean the slate, so all four billion years were still there to be seen, in a veritable museum of rockscapes. It had been thoroughly pulverized in the Noachian, leaving regolith several kilometres deep, and craters and deformities that no aeolian stripping could remove. And during this early period the other side of the planet had had its lithosphere to a depth of six kilometres blasted into space by the so-called Big Hit; a fair amount of that ejecta had eventually landed in the south. That was the explanation for the Great Escarpment, and the lack of ancient highlands in the north; and one more factor in the extremely disordered look of this land.

Then also, at the end of the Hesperian had come the brief warm wet period, when water had occasionally run on the surface. These days most areologists thought that this period had been quite wet but not really very warm, annual averages of well under 273 still allowing for surface water sometimes, replenished by hydrothermal convection rather than precipitation. This period had lasted for only a hundred million years or so, according to current estimates, and it had been followed by billions of years of winds, in the arid cold Amazonian Age, which had lasted right up to the point of their arrival. 'Is there a name for the age starting with M-1?' Sax asked.

'The Holocene.'

And then lastly, everything had been scoured by two billion years of ceaseless wind, scoured so hard that the older craters were completely rimless, everything stripped by the relentless winds stratum by stratum, leaving behind a wilderness of rock. Not chaos, technically speaking, but wild, speaking its unimaginable age in polyglot profusion, in rimless craters and etched mesas, dips, hummocks, escarpments, and oh so many blocky pitted rocks.

Often they stopped the rover to walk around. Even small mesas seemed to tower over them. Sax found himself staying near their rover, but nevertheless he came upon all kinds of interesting features. Once he discovered a rover-shaped rock, cracked vertically all the way through. To the left of the block, off to the west, he had a view to a distant horizon, the rocky land out there a smooth yellow glaze. To the right, the waist-high wall of some old fault, pocked as if by cuneiform. Then a sand drift bordered by ankle-high rocks, some of them pyramidal dark basaltic ventifacts, others lighter, pitted, granulated rocks. There a balanced shattercone, big as any dolmen. There a sand tail. There a crude circle of ejecta, like an almost completely weathered Stonehenge. There a deep snake-shaped hollow – the fragment of a watercourse, perhaps – behind it another gentle rise – then a distant prominence like a lion's head. The prominence next to it was like the lion's body.

In the midst of all this stone and sand, plant life was unobtrusive. At least at first. One had to look for it, to pay close attention to colour, above all else to green, green in all its shades, but especially its desert shades – sage, olive, khaki and so on. Nanao and Tariki kept pointing out specimens he hadn't seen. Closer he looked, and closer again. Once attuned to the pale, living colours, which blended so well with the ferric land, they began to jump out from the rust and brown and umber and ochre and black of the rockscape. Hollows and cracks were likely places to see them, and near the shaded patches of snow. The closer he looked, the more he saw; and then, in one high basin, it seemed there were plants tucked everywhere. In that moment he understood; it was all fellfield, the whole Tyrrhena Massif.

Then, coating entire rockfaces, or covering the inside areas of drip catchments, were the dayglow greens of certain lichens, and the emerald or dark velvet greens of the mosses. Wet fur.

The diversicoloured palette of the lichen array; the dark green of pine needles. Bunched sprays of Hokkaido pines, fox-tail pines, Sierra junipers. Life's colours. It was somewhat like walking from one great roofless room to another, over ruined walls of stone. A small plaza; a kind of winding gallery; a vast ballroom; a number of tiny interlocked chambers; a sitting room. Some rooms held krummholz bansei against their low walls, the trees no higher than their nooks, gnarled by wind, cut along the top at the snow level. Each branch, each plant, each open room, as shaped as any bonsai – and yet effortless.

Actually, Nanao told him, most of the basins were inten-sively cultivated. 'This basin was planted by Abraham.' Each little region was the responsibility of a certain gardener or gardening group.

'Ah!' Sax said. 'And fertilized, then?'

Tariki laughed. 'In a manner of speaking. The soil itself has been imported, for the most part.'

'I see.'

This explained the diversity of plants. A little bit of culti-vation, he knew, had been done around Arena Glacier, where he had first encountered the fellfields. But here they had gone far beyond those early steps. Labs in Sabishii, Tariki told him, were trying their best to manufacture topsoil. A good idea; soil in fellfields appeared naturally at a rate of only a few centimetres a century. But there were reasons for this, and manufacturing soil was proving to be extremely difficult.

Still, 'We pick up a few million years at the start,' Nanao said. 'Evolve from there.' They hand-planted many of their specimens, it seemed, then for the most part left them to their fate, and watched what developed.

'I see,' Sax said.

He looked more closely yet. The clear dim light: it was true that each great open room displayed a slightly different array of species. 'These are gardens, then.'

'Yes . . . or things like that. Depends.'

Some of the gardeners, Nanao said, worked according to the precepts of Muso Soseki, others according to other Japanese Zen masters; others still to Fu Hsi, the legendary inventor of the Chinese system of geomancy called feng shui; others to Persian gardening gurus, including Omar Khayyám; or to Leopold or Jackson, or other early American ecologists, like the nearly forgotten biologist Oskar Schnelling; and so on.

These were influences only, Tariki added. As they did the work, they developed visions of their own. They followed the inclination of the land, as they saw that some plants prospered, and others died. Co-evolution, a kind of epigenetic development.

'Nice,' Sax said, looking around. For the adepts, the walk from Sabishii up onto the massif must have been an aesthetic journey, filled with allusions and subtle variants of tradition that were invisible to him. Hiroko would have called it areoformation, or the areophany. 'I'd like to visit your soil labs.'

'Of course.'

They returned to the rover, drove on. Late in the day, under dark threatening clouds, they came to the very top of the massif, which turned out to be a kind of broad, undulating moor. Small ravines were filled with pine needles, sheered off by winds so that they looked like the blades of grass on a well-mowed yard. Sax and Tariki and Nanao again got out of the car, walked around. The wind cut through their suits, and the late afternoon sun broke out from under the dark cloud cover, casting their shadows all the way out to the horizon. Up here on the moors there were many big masses of smooth, bare bedrock; looking around, the landscape had the red, primal look Sax remembered from the earliest years; but then they would walk to the edge of a small ravine, and suddenly be looking down into green.

Tariki and Nanao talked about ecopoesis, which for them was terraforming redefined, subtilized, localized. Transmuted into something like Hiroko's areoformation. No longer powered by heavy industrial global methods, but by the slow, steady, and intensely local process of working on individual patches of land. 'Mars is all a garden. Earth too for that matter. This is what humans have become. So we have to think about gardening, about that level of responsibility to the land. A human-Mars interface that does justice to both.'

Sax waggled a hand uncertainly. 'I'm used to thinking of Mars as a kind of wilderness,' he said, as he looked up the etymology of the word garden. French, Teutonic, Old Norse, *gard*, enclosure. Seemed to share origins with *guard*, or keeping. But who knew what the supposedly equivalent word in Japanese meant? Etymology was hard enough without translation thrown into the mix. 'You know – get things started, let loose the seeds, then watch it all develop on its own. Self-organizing ecologies, you know.'

'Yes,' Tariki said, 'but wilderness too is a garden now. A kind of garden. That's what it means to be what we are.' He shrugged, his forehead wrinkled; he believed the idea was true, but did not seem to like it. 'Anyway, ecopoesis is closer to your vision of wilderness than industrial terraforming ever was.'

'Maybe,' Sax said. 'Maybe they're just two stages of a process. Both necessary.'

Tariki nodded, willing to consider it. 'And now?'

'It depends on how we want to deal with the possibility of an ice age,' Sax said. 'If it's bad enough, kills off enough plants, then ecopoesis won't have a chance. The atmosphere could freeze back onto the surface, the whole process crash. Without the mirrors, I'm not confident that the biosphere is robust enough to continue growing. That's why I want to see those soil labs you have. It may be that industrial work on the atmosphere remains to be done. We'll have to try some modelling and see.'

Tariki nodded, and Nanao too. Their ecologies were being snowed under, right before their eyes; flakes drifted down through the transient bronze sunlight at this very moment, tumbling in the wind. They were open to suggestion.

Meanwhile, as throughout these drives, their young associates from Da Vinci and Sabishii were running over the massif together, and returning to Sabishii's mound maze babbling through the night about geomancy and areomancy, ecopoetics, heat exchange, the five elements, greenhouse gases, and so on. A creative ferment that looked to Sax very promising. 'Michel should be here,' he said to Nanao. 'John should be here. How he would love a group like this.'

And then it occurred to him: 'Ann should be here.'

So he went back to Pavonis, leaving the group in Sabishii talking things over.

Back on Pavonis everything was the same. More and more people, spurred on by Art Randolph, were proposing that they hold a constitutional congress. Write an at least provisional constitution, hold a vote on it, then establish the government described.

'Good idea,' Sax said. 'Perhaps a delegation to Earth as well.'

Casting seeds. It was just like on the moors; some would sprout, others wouldn't.

He went looking for Ann, but found she had left Pavonis – gone, people said, to a Red outpost in Tempe Terra, north of Tharsis. No one went there but Reds, they said.

After some thought Sax asked for Steve's help, and looked up the outpost's location. Then he borrowed a little plane from the Bogdanovists and flew north, past Ascraeus Mons on his left, then down Echus Chasma, and past his old headquarters at Echus Overlook, on top of the huge wall to his right.

Ann too had no doubt flown this route, and thus gone by the first headquarters of the terraforming effort. Terraforming . . . there was evolution in everything, even in ideas. Had Ann noticed Echus Overlook, had she even remembered that small beginning? No way of telling. That was how humans knew each other. Tiny fractions of their lives intersected or were known in any way to anybody else. It was very like living alone in the universe. Which was strange. A justification for living with friends, for marrying, for sharing rooms and lives as much as possible. Not that this made people truly intimate; but it reduced the sensation of solitude. So that one was still sailing solo through the oceans of the world, as in Mary Shelley's *The Last Man*, a book that had much impressed Sax as a youth, in which the eponymous hero at the conclusion occasionally saw a sail, joined another ship, anchored against a shore, shared a meal – then voyaged on, alone and solitary. An image of their lives; for every world was as empty as the one Mary Shelley had imagined, as empty as Mars had been in the beginning.

He flew past the blackened curve of Kasei Vallis without noting it at all.

The Reds had long ago hollowed out a rock the size of a city block, in a promontory that served as the last dividing wedge in the intersection of two of the Tempe Fossae, just south of Perepelkin Crater. Windows under overhangs gave them a view over both of the bare straight canyons, and the larger canyon they made after their confluence. Now all these fossae cut down what had become a coastal plateau; Mareotis and Tempe together formed a huge peninsula of ancient highlands, sticking far into the new ice sea.

Sax landed his little plane on the sandy strip on top of the promontory. From here the ice plains were not visible; nor could he spot any vegetation – not a tree, not a flower, not even a patch of lichen. He wondered if they had somehow sterilized the canyons. Just primal rock, with a dusting of frost. And nothing they could do about frost, unless they wanted to tent these canyons, to keep air out rather than in. 'Hmm,' Sax said, startled at the idea.

Two Reds let him in the lock door on the top of the promontory, and he descended the stairs with them. The shelter appeared to be nearly empty. Just as well. It was nice only to have to withstand the cold gazes of two young women leading him through the rough-hewn rock galleries of the refuge, rather than a whole gang. Interesting to see Red aesthetics. Very spare, as might be expected – not a plant to be seen – just different textures of rock: rough walls, rougher ceilings, contrasted to a polished basalt floor, and the glistening windows overlooking the canyons.

They came to a cliffside gallery that looked like a natural cave, no straighter than the nearly Euclidean lines of the canyon below. There were mosaics inlaid into the back wall, made of bits of coloured stone, polished and set against each other without gaps, forming abstract patterns that seemed almost to represent something, if only he could focus properly on them. The floor was a stone parquet of onyx and alabaster, serpentine and bloodstone. The gallery went on and on – big, dusty – the whole complex somewhat disused, perhaps. Reds preferred their rovers, and places like this no doubt had been seen as unfortunate necessities. Hidden refuge; with windows shuttered, one could have walked down the canyons right past the place and not known it was there; and Sax felt that this was not just to avoid the notice of the UNTA, but also to be unobtrusive before the land itself, to melt into it.

As Ann seemed to be trying to do, there in a stone window-seat. Sax stopped abruptly; lost in his thoughts, he had almost run into her, just as an ignorant traveller might have run into the shelter. A chunk of rock, sitting there. He looked at her closely. She looked ill. One didn't see that much any more, and the longer Sax looked at her, the more alarmed he became. She had told him, once, that she was no longer taking the longevity treatment. That had been some years before. And during the revolution she had burned like a flame. Now, with the Red rebellion quelled, she was ash. Grey flesh. It was an awful sight. She was somewhere around one hundred and fifty years old, like all the First Hundred left alive, and without the treatments . . . she would soon die.

Well. Strictly speaking, she was at the physiological equivalent of being seventy or so, depending on when she had last had the treatments. So not that bad. Perhaps Peter would know. But the longer one went between treatments, he had heard, the more problems cropped up, statistically speaking. It made sense. It was only wise to be prudent.

But he couldn't say that to her. In fact, it was hard to think what he could say to her.

Eventually her gaze lifted. She recognized him and shuddered, her lip lifting like a trapped animal's. Then she looked away from him, grim, stone-faced. Beyond anger, beyond hope.

'I wanted to show you some of the Tyrrhena Massif,' he said lamely.

She got up like a statue rising, and left the room.

Sax, feeling his joints creak with the pseudo-arthritic pain that so often accompanied his dealings with Ann, followed her.

He was trailed in his turn by the two stern-looking young women. 'I don't think she wants to talk to you,' the taller one informed him.

'Very astute of you,' Sax said.

Far down the gallery, Ann was standing before another window: spellbound, or else too exhausted to move. Or part of her did want to talk.

Sax stopped before her.

'I want to get your impressions of it,' he said. 'Your suggestions for what we might do next. And I have some, some, some areological questions. Of course it could be that strictly scientific questions aren't of interest to you any more — '

She took a step toward him and struck him on the side of the face. He found himself slumped against the gallery wall, sitting on his bottom. Ann was nowhere to be seen. He was being helped to his feet by the two young women, who clearly didn't know whether to cheer or groan. His whole body hurt, more even than his face, and his eyes were very hot, stinging slightly. It seemed he might cry before these two young idiots, who by trailing him were complicating everything enormously; with them around he could not yell or plead, he could not go on his knees and say Ann, please, forgive me. He couldn't.

'Where did she go?' he managed to say.

'She really, *really* doesn't want to talk to you,' the tall one declared.

'Maybe you should wait and try later,' the other advised.

'Oh shut up!' Sax said, suddenly feeling an irritation so vehement that it was like rage. 'I suppose you would just let her stop taking the treatment and kill herself!'

'It's her right,' the tall one pontificated.

'Of course it is. I wasn't speaking of rights. I was speaking of how a friend should behave when someone is suicidal. Not a subject you are likely to know anything about. Now help me find her.'

'You're no friend of hers.'

'I most certainly am.' He was on his feet. He staggered a little as he tried to walk in the direction he thought she had gone. One of the young women tried to take his elbow. He avoided the help and went on. There Ann was, in the distance, collapsed in a chair, in some kind of dining chamber, it seemed. He approached her, slowing like Apollo in Zeno's paradox.

She swivelled and glared at him.

'It's *you* who abandoned science, right from the start,' she snarled. 'So don't you give me that shit about not being interested in science!'

'True,' Sax said. 'It's true.' He held out both hands. 'But now I need advice. Scientific advice. I want to learn. And I want to show you some things as well.'

But after a moment's consideration she was up and off again, right past him, so that he flinched despite himself. He hurried after her; her gait was much longer than his, and she was moving fast, so that he had almost to jog. His bones hurt.

'Perhaps we could go out here,' Sax suggested. 'It doesn't matter where we go out.'

'Because the whole planet is wrecked,' she muttered.

'You must still go out for sunsets occasionally,' Sax persisted. 'I could join you for that, perhaps.'

'No.'

'Please, Ann.' She was a fast walker, and enough taller than him that it was hard to keep up with her and talk as well. He was huffing and puffing, and his cheek still hurt. 'Please, Ann.'

She did not answer, she did not slow down. Now they were walking down a hall between suites of living quarters, and Ann sped up to go through a doorway and slam the door behind her. Sax tried it; it was locked.

Not, on the whole, a promising beginning.

Hound and hind. Somehow he had to change things so that it was not a hunt, a pursuit. Nevertheless: 'I huff, I puff, I blow your house down,' he muttered. He blew at the door. But then the two young women were there, staring hard at him.

One evening later that week, near sunset, he went down to the changing room and suited up. When Ann came in he jumped several centimetres. 'I was just going out,' he stammered. 'Is that okay with you?'

'It's a free country,' she said heavily.

And they went out of the lock together, into the land. The young women would have been amazed.

*   *   *

97

He had to be very careful. Naturally, although he was out there with her to show to her the beauty of the new biosphere, it would not do to mention plants, or snow, or clouds. One had to let things speak for themselves. This was perhaps true of all phenomena. Nothing could be spoken for. One could only walk over the land, and let it speak for itself.

Ann was not gregarious. She barely spoke to him. It was her usual route, he suspected as he followed her. He was being allowed to come along.

It was perhaps permissible to ask questions: this was science. And Ann stopped often enough, to look at rock formations up close. It made sense at those times to crouch beside her, and with a gesture or a word ask what she was finding. They wore suits and helmets, even though the altitude was low enough to have allowed breathing with only the aid of a CO_2 filter mask. Thus conversations consisted of voices in the ear, as of old. Asking questions.

So he asked. And Ann would answer, sometimes in some detail. Tempe Terra was indeed the Land of Time, its basement material a surviving piece of the southern highlands, one of those lobes of it that stuck far into the northern plains – a survivor of the Big Hit. Then later Tempe had fractured extensively, as the lithosphere was pushed up from below by the Tharsis bulge to the south. These fractures included both the Mareotis Fossae and the Tempe Fossae surrounding them now.

The spreading land had cracked enough to allow some late-comer volcanoes to emerge, spilling over the canyons. From one high ridge they saw a distant volcano like a black cone dropped from the sky; then another, looking just like a meteor crater as far as Sax could see. Ann shook her head at this observation, and pointed out lava flows and vents, features all visible once they were pointed out, but not at all obvious under a scree of later ejecta rubble and (one had to admit it) a dusting of dirty snow, collecting like sand drifts in wind shelters, turning sand-coloured in the sunset light.

To see the landscape in its history, to read it like a text, written by its own long past; that was Ann's vision, achieved by a century's close observation and study, and by her own native gift, her love for it. Something to behold, really – something to marvel at. A kind of resource, or treasure – a love beyond science, or something into the realm of Michel's mystical science. Alchemy. But alchemists wanted to change things. A kind of oracle, rather. A visionary, with a vision just as powerful as Hiroko's, really. Less obviously visionary, perhaps, less spectacular, less active; an acceptance of what was there; love of rock, for rock's sake. For Mars's sake. The primal planet, in all its sublime glory, red and rust, still as death; dead; altered through the years only by matter's chemical permutations, the immense slow life of geophysics. It was an odd concept – abiologic life – but there it was, if one cared to see it, a kind of living, out there spinning, moving through the stars that burned, moving through the universe in its great systolic/diastolic movement, its one big breath, one might say. Sunset somehow made it easier to see that.

Trying to see things Ann's way. Glancing furtively at his wristpad, behind her back. Stone, from Old English *stán*, cognates everywhere, back to proto-Indo-European *sti*, a pebble. Rock, from medieval Latin *rocca*, origin unknown; a mass of stone. Sax abandoned the wristpad and fell away into a kind of rock reverie, open and blank. Tabula rasa, to the point where apparently he did not hear what Ann herself was saying to him; for she snorted and walked on. Abashed, he followed, and steeled himself to ignore her displeasure, and ask more questions.

There seemed to be a lot of displeasure in Ann. In a way this was reassuring; lack of affect would have been a very bad sign; but she still seemed quite emotional. At least most of the time. Sometimes she focused on the rock so intently it was almost like watching her obsessed enthusiasm of old, and he was encouraged; other times it seemed she was just going through the motions, doing areology in a desperate attempt to stave off the present moment; stave off history; or despair; or all of that. In those moments she was aimless, and did not stop to look at obviously interesting features they passed, and did not answer his questions about same. The little Sax had read about depression alarmed him; not much could be done, one needed drugs to combat it, and even then nothing was sure. But to suggest anti-depressants was more or less the same as suggesting the treatment itself; and so he could not speak of it. And besides, was despair the same as depression?

Happily, in this context, plants were pitifully few. Tempe was not like Tyrrhena, or even the banks of the Arena Glacier. Without active gardening, this was what one got. The world was still mostly rock.

On the other hand, Tempe was low in altitude, and humid, with the ice ocean just a few kilometres to the north and west. And various Johnny Appleseed flights had passed over the entire southern shoreline of the new sea – part of Biotique's efforts, begun some decades ago, when Sax had been in Burroughs. So there was some lichen to be seen, if you looked hard. And small patches of fellfield. And a few krummholz trees, half-buried in snow. All these plants were in trouble in this northern summer-turned-winter, except for the lichen of course. There was a fair bit of miniaturized fall colour already, there in the tiny leaves of the ground-hugging koenigia, and pygmy buttercup, and icegrass, and, yes, arctic saxifrage. The reddening leaves served as a kind of camouflage in the ambient redrock; often Sax didn't see plants until he was about to step on them. And of course he wasn't drawing attention to them anyway, so when he did stumble on one, he gave it a quick evaluative glance and walked on.

They climbed a prominent knoll overlooking the canyon west of the refuge, and there it was: the great ice sea, all orange and brass in the late light. It filled the lowland in a great sweep and formed its own smooth horizon, from southwest to northeast. Mesas of the fretted terrain now stuck out of the ice like sea stacks or cliff-sided islands. In truth this part of Tempe was going to be one of the most dramatic coastlines on Mars, with the lower ends of some fossae filling to become long fjords or lochs. And one coastal crater was right at sea level, and had a break in its sea side, making it a perfect round bay some fifteen kilometres wide, with an entry channel about two kilometres across. Farther south, the fretted terrain at the foot of the Great Escarpment would create a veritable Hebrides of an archipelago, many of the islands visible from the cliffs of the mainland. Yes, a dramatic coastline. As one could see already, looking at the broken sheets of sunset ice.

But of course this was not to be noted. No mention at all of the ice, the jagged bergs jumbled on the new shoreline. The bergs had been formed by some process Sax wasn't aware of, though he was curious – but it could not be discussed. One could only stand in silence, as if having stumbled into a cemetery.

Embarrassed, Sax kneeled to look at a specimen of Tibetan rhubarb he had almost stepped on. Little red leaves, in a floret from a central red bulb.

Ann was looking over his shoulder. 'Is it dead?'

'No.' He pulled off a few dead leaves from the exterior of the floret, showed her the brighter ones beneath. 'It's hardening for the winter already. Fooled by the drop in light.' Then Sax went on, as if to himself: 'A lot of the plants will die, though. The thermal overturn,' which was when air temperatures turned colder than the ground temperatures, 'came more or less overnight. There won't be much chance for hardening. Thus lots of winterkill. Plants are better at handling it than animals would have been. And insects are surprisingly good, considering they're little containers of liquid. They have supercooling cryoprotectants. They can stand whatever happens, I think.'

Ann was still inspecting the plant, and so Sax shut up. It's alive, he wanted to say. Insofar as the members of a biosphere depend on each other for existence, it is part of your body. How can you hate it?

But then again, she wasn't taking the treatment.

The ice sea was a shattered blaze of bronze and coral. The sun was setting, they would have to get back. Ann straightened and walked away, a black silhouette, silent. He could speak in her ear, even now when she was a hundred metres away, then two hundred, a small black figure in the great sweep of the world. He did not; it would have been an invasion of her privacy, almost of her thoughts. But how he wondered what those thoughts were. How he longed to say Ann, Ann, what are you thinking? Talk to me, Ann. Share your thoughts.

The intense desire to talk with someone, sharp as any pain; this was what people meant when they talked about love. Or rather; this was what Sax would acknowledge to be love. Just the super-heightened desire to share thoughts. That alone. Oh Ann, please talk to me.

*   *   *

But she did not talk to him. On her the plants seemed not to have had the effect they had had on him. She seemed truly to abominate them, these little emblems of her body, as if viriditas were no more than a cancer that the rock must suffer. Even though in the growing piles of wind-drifted snow, plants were scarcely visible any more. It was getting dark, another storm was sweeping in, low over the black-and-copper sea. A pad of moss, a lichened rockface; mostly it was rock alone, just as it had ever been. Nevertheless.

Then as they were getting back into the refuge lock, Ann fell in a faint. On the way down she hit her head on the door-jamb. Sax caught her body as she was landing on a bench against the inner wall. She was unconscious, and Sax half-carried her, half-dragged her all the way into the lock. Then he pulled the outer door shut, and when the lock was pumped, pulled her through the inner door into the changing room. He must have been shouting over the common band, because by the time he got her helmet off, five or six Reds were there in the room, more than he had seen in the refuge so far. One of the young women who had so impeded him, the short one, turned out to be the medical person of the station, and when they got Ann up onto a rolling table that could be used as a gurney, this woman led the way to the refuge's medical clinic, and there took over. Sax helped where he could, getting Ann's walker boots off her long feet with shaking hands. His pulse rate – he checked his wristpad – was a hundred and forty-five beats a minute – and he felt hot, even light-headed.

'Has she had a stroke?' he said. 'Has she had a stroke?'

The short woman looked surprised. 'I don't think so. She fainted. Then struck her head.'

'But why did she faint?'

'I don't know.'

She looked at the tall young woman, who sat next to the door. Sax understood that they were the senior authorities in the refuge. 'Ann left instructions for us not to put her on any kind of life support mechanism, if she were ever incapacitated like this.'

'No,' Sax said.

'Very explicit instructions. She forbade it. She wrote it down.'

'You put her on whatever it takes to keep her alive,' Sax

said, his voice harsh with strain. Everything he had said since Ann's collapse had been a surprise to him; he was a witness to his actions just as much as they were. He heard himself say, 'It doesn't mean you have to keep her on it, if she doesn't come around. It's just a reasonable minimum, to make sure she doesn't go for nothing.'

The doctor rolled her eyes at this distinction, but the tall woman sitting in the doorway looked thoughtful.

Sax heard himself go on: 'I was on life support for some four days, as I understand it, and I'm glad no one decided to turn it off. It's her decision, not yours. Anyone who wants to die can do it without having to make a doctor compromise her Hippocratic oath.'

The doctor rolled her eyes even more disgustedly than before. But with a glance at her colleague, she began to pull Ann onto the life support bed; Sax helped her; and then she was turning on the medical AI, and getting Ann out of her walker. A rangy old woman, now breathing with an oxygen mask over her face. The tall woman stood and began to help the doctor, and Sax went and sat down. His own physiological symptoms were amazingly severe, marked chiefly by heat all through him, and a kind of incompetent hyperventilation; and an ache that made him want to cry.

After a time the doctor came over. Ann had fallen into a coma, she said. It looked like a small heart rhythm abnormality had caused her to faint in the first place. She was stable at the moment.

Sax sat in the room. Much later the doctor returned. Ann's wristpad had recorded an episode of rapid irregular heartbeat, at the time she fainted. Now there was still a small arrhythmia. And apparently anoxia, or the blow to the head, or both, had initiated a coma.

Sax asked what a coma was, and felt a sinking feeling when the doctor shrugged. It was a catch-all term, apparently, for unconscious states of a certain kind. Pupils fixed, body insensitive, and sometimes locked into decorticate postures. Ann's left arm and leg were twisted. And unconsciousness of course. Sometimes odd vestiges of responsiveness, clenching hands and the like. Duration of coma varied widely. Some people never came out of them.

Sax looked at his hands until the doctor left him alone. He sat in the room until everyone else was gone. Then he got up and stood at Ann's side, looking down at her masked face. Nothing to be done. He held her hand; it did not clench. He held her head, as he had been told Nirgal had held his when he was unconscious. It felt like a useless gesture.

He went to the AI screen, and called up the diagnostic program. He called up Ann's medical data, and ran back the heart monitor data from the incident in the lock. A small arrhythmia, yes; rapid, irregular pattern. He fed the data into the diagnostic program, and looked up heart arrhythmia on his own. There were a lot of aberrant cardiac rhythm patterns, but it appeared that Ann might have a genetic predisposition to suffer from a disorder called long QT syndrome, named for a characteristic abnormal long wave in the electrocardiogram. He called up Ann's genome, and instructed the AI to run a search in the relevant regions of chromosomes three, seven and eleven. In the gene called HERG, in her chromosome seven, the AI identified a small mutation: one reversal of adenine-thymine and guanine-cytosine. Small, but HERG contained instructions for the assembly of a protein that served as a potassium ion channel in the surface of heart cells, and these ion channels acted as a switch to turn off contracting heart cells. Without this brake the heart could go arrhythmic, and beat too fast to pump blood effectively.

Ann also appeared to have another problem, with a gene on chromosome three called SCN5A. This gene encoded a different regulatory protein, which provided a sodium ion channel on the surface of heart cells. This channel functioned as an accelerator, and mutations here could add to the problem of rapid heartbeat. Ann had a CG bit missing.

These genetic conditions were rare, but for the diagnostic AI, that was not an issue. It contained a symptomology for all known problems, no matter how rare. It seemed to consider Ann's case to be fairly straightforward, and it listed the treatments that existed to counteract the problems presented by the condition. There were a lot of them.

One of the treatments suggested was the recoding of the problem genes, in the course of the standard gerontological treatments. Persistent gene recodings through several longevity treatments should erase the cause of the problem right at the root, or rather in the seed. It seemed strange that this hadn't been done already, but then Sax saw that the recommendation was only about two decades old; it came from a period after the last time Ann had taken the treatments.

For a long time Sax sat there, staring at the screen. Much later he got up. He began to inspect the Reds' medical clinic, instrument by instrument, room by room. The nursing attendants let him wander; they thought he was distraught.

This was a major Red refuge, and it seemed likely to him that one of the rooms might contain the equipment necessary to administer the gerontological treatments. Indeed it was so. A small room at the back of the clinic appeared to be devoted to the process. It didn't take much: a bulky AI, a small lab, the stock proteins and chemicals, the incubators, the MRIs, the IV equipment. Amazing, when you considered what it did. But that had always been true. Life itself was amazing: simple protein sequences only, at the start, and yet here they were.

So. The main AI had Ann's genome record. But if he ordered this lab to start synthesizing her DNA strands for her (adding the recodings of HERG and SCN5A) the people here would surely notice. And then there would be trouble.

He went back to his tiny room to make a coded call to Da Vinci. He asked his associates there to start the synthesis, and they agreed without any questions beyond the technical ones. Sometimes he loved those saxaclones with all his heart.

After that it was back to waiting. Hours passed; more hours; more hours. Eventually several days had passed, with no change in Ann. The doctor's expression grew blacker and blacker, though she said nothing more about unhooking Ann. But it was in her eye. Sax took to sleeping on the floor in Ann's room. He grew to know the rhythm of her breathing. He spent a lot of time with a hand cradling her head, as Michel had told him Nirgal had done with him. He very much doubted that this had ever cured anybody of anything, but he did it anyway. Sitting for so long in such a posture, he had occasion to think about the brain plasticity treatments that Vlad and Ursula had administered to him after his stroke. Of course a stroke was a very different thing to a coma. But a change of mind was not necessarily a bad thing, if one's mind was in pain.

More days passed without a change, each day slower and blanker and more fearful than the one before. The incubators in the Da Vinci labs had long since cooked up a full set of corrected Ann-specific DNA strands, and anti-sense reinforcers, and glue-ons – the whole gerontological package, in its latest configuration.

So one night he called up Ursula, and had a long consultation with her. She answered his questions calmly, even as she struggled with the idea of what he wanted to do. 'The synaptic stimulus package we gave you would produce too much synaptic growth in undamaged brains,' she said firmly. 'It would alter personality to no set pattern.' Creating madmen like Sax, her alarmed look said.

Sax decided to skip the synaptic supplements. Saving Ann's life was one thing, changing her mind another. Random change was not the goal anyway. Acceptance was. Happiness – Ann's true happiness, whatever that might be – now so far away, so hard to imagine. He ached to think of it. It was extraordinary how much physical pain could be generated by thought alone – the limbic system a whole universe in itself, suffused with pain, like the dark matter that suffused everything in the universe.

'Have you talked to Michel?' Ursula asked.

'No. Good idea.'

He called Michel, explained what had happened, and what he had in mind to do. 'My God, Sax,' Michel said, looking shocked. But in only a few moments he was promising to come. He would get Desmond to fly him to Da Vinci to pick up the treatment supplies, and then fly on up to the refuge.

So Sax sat in Ann's room, a hand to her head. A bumpy skull; no doubt a phrenologist would have had a field day.

Then Michel and Desmond were there, his brothers, standing beside him. The doctor was there too, escorting them, and the tall woman and others as well; so everything had to be communicated by looks, or the absence of looks. Nevertheless everything was perfectly clear. Desmond's face was if anything too clear. They had Ann's longevity package with them. They only had to wait their chance.

106

Which came quite soon; with Ann settled into her coma, the situation in the little hospital was routine. The effects of the longevity treatment on a coma, however, were not fully known; Michel had scanned the literature, and the data were sparse. It had been tried as an experimental treatment in a few unresponsive comas before, and had been successful in rousing victims almost half the time. Because of that Michel now thought it was a good idea.

And so, soon after their arrival, the three of them got up in the middle of the night, and tiptoed past the sleeping attendant in the medical centre's anteroom. Medical training had had its usual effect, and the attendant was sound asleep, though awkwardly propped in her chair. Sax and Michel hooked Ann up to the IVs, and stuck the needles in the veins on the backs of her hands, working slowly, carefully, precisely. Quietly. Soon she was hooked up, the IVs were flowing, the new protein strands were in her bloodstream. Her breathing grew irregular, and Sax felt hot with fear. He groaned silently. It was comforting to have Michel and Desmond here, each holding an arm as if supporting him, keeping him from falling; but he wished desperately for Hiroko. This was what she would have done, he was certain of it. Which made him feel better. Hiroko was one of the reasons he was doing this. Still he longed for her support, her physical presence, he wished she would show up to help him like she had on Daedalia Planitia. To help Ann. She was the expert at this kind of radically irresponsible human experimentation, this would have been small potatoes to her . . .

When the operation was finished, they took out the IV needles and put the equipment away. The attendant slept on, mouth open, looking like the girl she was. Ann was still unconscious, but breathing easier, Sax felt. More strongly.

The three men stood looking down at Ann together. Then they slipped out, and tiptoed back down the hall to their rooms. Desmond was dancing on his toes like a fool, and the other two shushed him. They got back in their beds but couldn't sleep; and couldn't talk; and so lay there silently, like brothers in a big house, late at night, after a successful expedition out into the nocturnal world.

The next morning the doctor came in. 'Her vital signs are better.'

107

The three men expressed their pleasure at this.

Later, down in the dining hall, Sax had a strong urge to tell Michel and Desmond about his encounter with Hiroko. The news would mean more to these two than anyone else. But something in him was afraid to do it. He was afraid of seeming overwrought, perhaps even delusional. That moment when Hiroko had left him at the rover, and walked off into the storm – he didn't know what to think of that. In his long hours with Ann he had done some thinking, and some research, and he knew now that Terran climbers alone at high altitude, suffering from oxygen loss, not infrequently hallucinated companion climbers. Some kind of doppelganger figure. Rescue by anima. And his air tube had been partially clogged.

He said, 'I thought this was what Hiroko would have done.'

Michel nodded. 'It's bold, I'll hand you that. It has her style. No, don't misunderstand me – I'm glad you did it.'

'About fucking time, if you ask me,' said Desmond. 'Someone should have tied her down and made her take the treatment years ago. Oh my Sax, my Sax —' he laughed happily. 'I only hope she doesn't come to as crazy as you did.'

'But Sax had a stroke,' Michel said.

'Well,' Sax said, concerned to set the record straight, 'actually I was somewhat eccentric before.'

His two friends nodded, mouths pursed. They were in high spirits, though the situation was still unresolved. Then the tall doctor came in; Ann had come out of her coma.

Sax felt that his stomach was still too contracted by tension to take in food, but he noted that he was disposing of a pile of buttered toast quite handily. Wolfing it down, in fact.

'But she's going to be very angry at you,' Michel said.

Sax nodded. It was, alas, probable. Likely, even. A bad thought. He did not want to be struck by her again. Or worse, denied her company.

'You should come with us to Earth,' Michel suggested. 'Maya and I are going with the delegation, and Nirgal.'

'There's a delegation going to Earth?'

'Yes, someone suggested it, and it seems like a good idea. We need to have some representatives right there on Earth talking to them. And by the time we get back from that, Ann will have had time to think it over.'

'Interesting,' Sax said, relieved at the mere suggestion of an escape from the situation. In fact it was almost frightening how quickly he could think of ten good reasons for going to Earth. 'But what about Pavonis, and this conference they're talking about?'

'We can stay part of that by video.'

'True.' It was just what he had always maintained.

The plan was attractive. He did not want to be there when Ann woke up. Or rather, when she found out what he had done. Cowardice, of course. But still. 'Desmond, are you going?'

'Not a fucking chance.'

'But you say Maya is going too?' Sax asked Michel.

'Yes.'

'Good. The last time I, I, I tried to save a woman's life, Maya killed her.'

'What? What – Phyllis? You saved Phyllis's life?'

'Well – no. That is to say, I did, but I was also the one who put her in danger in the first place. So I don't think it counts.' He tried to explain what had happened that night in Burroughs, with little success. It was fuzzy in his own mind, except for certain vivid horrible moments. 'Never mind. It was just a thought. I shouldn't have spoken. I'm . . .'

'You're tired,' Michel said. 'But don't worry. Maya will be away from the scene here, and safely under our eye.'

Sax nodded. It was sounding better all the time. Give Ann some time to cool off; think it over; understand. Hopefully. And it would be very interesting of course to see conditions on Earth at first hand. Extremely interesting. So interesting that no rational person could pass up the opportunity.

PART THREE

A New Constitution

Ants came to Mars as part of the soil project, and soon they were everywhere, as is their way. And so the little red people encountered ants, and they were amazed. These creatures were just the right size to ride; it was like the Native Americans meeting the horse. Tame the things and they would run wild.

Domesticating the ant was no easy matter. The little red scientists had not believed such creatures were even possible, because of surface area-to-volume constraints, but there they were, clumping around like intelligent robots, so the little red scientists had to explain them. To get some help they climbed up into the humans' reference books, and read up on ants. They learned about the ants' pheromones, and they synthesized the ones they needed to control the soldier ants of a particularly small docile red species, and after that, they were in business. Little red cavalry. They charged around everywhere on antback, having a fine old time, twenty or thirty of them on each ant, like pashas on elephants. Look close at enough ants and you'll see them, right there on top.

But the little red scientists continued to read the texts, and learned about human pheromones. They went back to the rest of the little red people, awestruck and appalled. Now we know why these humans are such trouble, they reported. Humans have no more will than these ants we are riding around on. They are giant meat ants.

The little red people tried to comprehend such a travesty of life.

Then a voice said, No they're not, to all of them at once. The little red people talk to each other telepathically, you see, and this was like a telepathic loudspeaker announcement. Humans are spiritual beings, this voice insisted.

How do you know? the little red people asked telepathically. Who are you? Are you the ghost of John Boone?

I am the Gyatso Rimpoche, the voice answered. The eighteenth reincarnation of the Dalai Lama. I am travelling the Bardo in search of my next reincarnation. I've looked everywhere on Earth, but I've had no luck, and I decided to look

113

somewhere new. Tibet is still under the thumb of the Chinese, and they show no signs of letting up. The Chinese, although I love them dearly, are hard bastards. And the other governments of the world long ago turned their backs on Tibet. So no one will challenge the Chinese. Something needs to be done. So I came to Mars.

Good idea, the little red people said.

Yes, the Dalai Lama agreed, but I must admit I am having a hard time finding a new body to inhabit. For one thing there are very few children anywhere. Then also it does not look as if anyone is interested. I looked in Sheffield but everyone was too busy talking. I went to Sabishii but everyone there had their heads stuck in the dirt. I went to Elysium but everyone had assumed the lotus position and could not be roused. I went to Christianopolis but everyone there had other plans. I went to Hiranyagarbha but everyone there said we've already done enough for Tibet. I've gone everywhere on Mars, to every tent and station, and everywhere people are just too busy. No one wants to be the nineteenth Dalai Lama. And the Bardo is getting colder and colder.

Good luck, the little red people said. We've been looking ever since John died and we haven't even found anyone worth talking to, much less living inside. These big people are all messed up.

The Dalai Lama was discouraged by this response. He was getting very tired, and could not last much longer in the Bardo. So he said, What about one of you?

Well, sure, the little red people said. We'd be honoured. Only it will have to be all of us at once. We do everything like that together.

Why not, said the Dalai Lama, and he transmigrated into one of the little red specks, and that same instant he was there in all of them, all over Mars. The little red people looked up at the humans crashing around above them, a sight which before they had tended to regard as some kind of bad widescreen movie, and now they found they were filled with all the compassion and wisdom of the eighteen previous lives of the Dalai Lama. They said to each other, Ka wow, these people really are messed up. We thought it was bad before, but look at that, it's even worse than we thought. They're lucky they

114

can't read each other's minds or they'd kill each other. That must be why they're killing each other – they know what they're thinking themselves, and so they suspect all the others. How ugly. How sad.

They need your help, the Dalai Lama said inside them all. Maybe you can help them.

Maybe, the little red people said. They were dubious, to tell the truth. They had been trying to help humans ever since John Boone died, they had set up whole towns in the porches of every ear on the planet, and talked continuously ever since, sounding very much like John had, trying to get people to wake up and act decently, and never with any effect at all, except to send a lot of people to ear, nose and throat specialists. Lots of people on Mars thought they had tinnitus, but no one ever understood their little red people. It was enough to discourage anyone.

But now the little red people had the compassionate spirit of the Dalai Lama infusing them, and so they decided to try one more time. Perhaps it will take more than whispering in their ears, the Dalai Lama pointed out, and they all agreed. We'll have to get their attention some other way.

Have you tried your telepathy on them? the Dalai Lama asked.

Oh no, they said. No way. Too scary. The ugliness might kill us on the spot. Or at least make us real sick.

Maybe not, the Dalai Lama said. Maybe if you blocked off your reception of what they thought, and just beamed your thoughts at them, it would be all right. Just send lots of good thoughts, like an advice beam. Compassion, love, agreeableness, wisdom, even a little common sense.

We'll give it a try, the little red people said. But we're all going to have to shout at the top of our telepathic voices, all in chorus, because these folks just aren't listening.

I've faced that for nine centuries now, the Dalai Lama said. You get used to it. And you little ones have the advantage of numbers. So give it a try.

And so all the little red people all over Mars looked up and took a deep breath.

Art Randolph was having the time of his life.

Not during the battle for Sheffield, of course – that had been a disaster, a breakdown of diplomacy, the failure of everything Art had been trying to do – a miserable few days, in fact, during which he had run around sleeplessly trying to meet with every group he thought might help defuse the crisis, and always with the feeling that it was somehow his fault, that if he had done things right it would not have happened. The fight went right to the brink of torching Mars, as in 2061; for a few hours on the afternoon of the Red assault, it had teetered.

But fallen back. Something – diplomacy, or the realities of battle (a defensive victory for those on the cable), common sense, sheer chance – something had tipped things back from the edge.

And with that nightmare interval past, people had returned to East Pavonis in a thoughtful mood. The consequences of failure had been made clear. They needed to agree on a plan. Many of the radical Reds were dead, or escaped into the outback, and the moderate Reds left in East Pavonis, while angry, were at least there. It was a very uncomfortable and uncertain period. But there they were.

So once again Art began flogging the idea of a constitutional congress. He ran around under the big tent through warrens of industrial warehouses and storage zones and concrete dormitories, down broad streets crowded with a museum's worth of heavy vehicles, and everywhere he urged the same thing: constitution. He talked to Nadia, Nirgal, Jackie, Zeyk, Maya, Peter, Ariadne, Rashid, Tariki, Nanao, Sung and H. X. Borazjani. He talked to Vlad and Ursula and Marina, and to the Coyote. He talked to a few score young natives he had never met before, all major players in the recent unrest; there were so many of them it began to seem like a textbook demonstration of the polycephalous nature of mass social movements. And to every head of this new hydra Art made the same case: 'A constitution would legitimate us to Earth, and it would give us a framework for settling disputes among ourselves. And we're all gathered here, we could start right away. Some people have plans ready to look at.' And with the events of the past week fresh in their minds, people would nod and say, 'Maybe so,' and wander off thinking about it.

Art called up William Fort and told him what he was doing, and got an answer back later the same day. The old man was at a new refugee town in Costa Rica, looking just as distracted as always. 'Sounds good,' he said. And after that Praxis people were checking with Art daily to see what they could do to help organize things. Art became busier than he had ever been, doing what the Japanese there called *nema-washi*, the preparations for an event: starting strategy sessions for an organizing group, revisiting everyone he had spoken to before, trying, in effect, to talk to every individual on Pavonis Mons. 'The John Boone method,' Coyote commented with his cracked laugh. 'Good luck!'

Sax, packing his few belongings for the diplomatic mission to Earth, said, 'You should invite the, the United Nations.'

Sax's adventure in the storm had knocked him back a bit; he tended to stare around at things, as if stunned by a blow to the head. Art said gently, 'Sax, we just went to a lot of trouble to kick their butts off this planet.'

'Yes,' Sax said, staring at the ceiling. 'But now co-opt them.'

'Co-opt the UN!' Art considered it. Co-opt the United Nations: it had a certain ring to it. It would be a challenge, diplomatically speaking.

Just before the ambassadors left for Earth, Nirgal came to the Praxis offices to say goodbye. Embracing his young friend, Art was seized with a sudden irrational fear. Off to Earth!

Nirgal was as blithe as ever, his dark brown eyes alight with anticipation. After saying goodbye to the others in the outer office, he sat with Art in an empty corner room of the warehouse.

'Are you sure you want to do this?' Art asked.

'Very sure. I want to see Earth.'

Art waggled a hand, uncertain what to say.

'Besides,' Nirgal added, 'someone has to go down there and show them who we are.'

'None better for that than you, my friend. But you'll have to watch out for the metanats. Who knows what they'll be up to. And for bad food – those areas affected by the flood are sure to have problems with sanitation. And disease vectors. And you'll have to be careful about sunstroke, you'll be very susceptible — '

Jackie Boone walked in. Art stopped his travel advisory; Nirgal was no longer listening in any case, but watching Jackie with a suddenly blank expression, as if he had put on a Nirgal mask. And of course no mask could do justice to Nirgal, because the mobility of his face was its essential characteristic; so he did not look like himself at all.

Jackie, of course, saw this instantly. Shut off from her old partner . . . naturally she glared at him. Something had gone awry, Art saw. Both of them had forgotten Art, who would have slipped out of the room if he could have, feeling as if he was holding a lightning rod in a storm. But Jackie was still standing in the doorway, and Art did not care to disturb her at that moment.

'So you're leaving us,' she said to Nirgal.

'It's just a visit.'

'But why? Why now? Earth means nothing to us now.'

'It's where we came from.'

'It is not. We came from Zygote.'

Nirgal shook his head. 'Earth is the home planet. We're an extension of it, here. We have to deal with it.'

Jackie waved a hand in disgust, or bafflement: 'You're leaving just when you're needed here the most!'

'Think of it as an opportunity.'

'I will,' she snapped. He had made her angry. 'And you won't like it.'

'But you'll have what you want.'

Fiercely she said, 'You don't know what I want!'

The hair on the back of Art's neck had raised; lightning was about to strike. He would have said he was an eavesdropper by nature, almost a voyeur in fact; but standing right there in the room was not the same, and he found now there were some things he did not care to witness. He cleared his throat. The other two were startled by his noise. With a waggle of the hand he sidled past Jackie and out of the door. Behind him the voices went on – bitter, accusatory, filled with pain and baffled fury.

Coyote stared gravely out of the windshield as he drove the ambassadors to Earth south to the cievator, with Art sitting beside him. They rolled slowly through the battered neighbourhoods that bordered the Socket, in the southwest part of Sheffield where the streets had been designed to handle enormous freight container gantries, so that things had an ominous Speeresque quality to them, inhuman and gigantic. Sax was explaining once again to Coyote that the trip to Earth would not remove the travellers from the constitutional congress, that they would contribute by vid, that they would not end up like Thomas Jefferson in Paris, missing the whole thing. 'We'll be on Pavonis,' Sax said, 'in all the senses that matter.'

'Then everyone will be on Pavonis,' Coyote said ominously. He didn't like this trip to Earth for Sax and Maya and Michel and Nirgal; he didn't seem to like the constitutional congress; nothing these days pleased him, he was jumpy, uneasy, irritable. 'We're not out of the woods yet,' he would mutter, 'you mark my words.'

Then the Socket stood before them, the cable emerging black and glossy from the great mass of concrete, like a harpoon plunged into Mars by Earthly powers, holding it fast. After identifying themselves the travellers drove right into the complex, down a big, straight passageway to the enormous chamber at the centre where the cable came down through the Socket's collar, and hovered over a network of pistes crisscrossing the floor. The cable was so exquisitely balanced in its orbit that it never touched Mars at all, but merely hung there with its ten-metre diameter end floating in the middle of the room, the collar in the roof doing no more than stabilizing it; for the rest, its positioning was up to the rockets installed up and down the cable, and, more importantly, to the balance between centrifugal force and gravity which kept it in its areosynchronous orbit.

A row of elevator cars floated in the air like the cable itself, though for a different reason, as they were electromagnetically suspended. One of them levitated over a piste to the cable, and latched on to the track inlaid in the cable's west side, and rose up soundlessly through a valve-door in the collar.

The travellers and their escorts got out of their car. Nirgal was withdrawn, already on his way; Maya and Michel excited; Sax his usual self. One by one they hugged Art and Coyote, stretching up to Art, leaning down to Desmond. For a time they all talked at once, staring at each other, trying to comprehend the moment; it was just a trip, but it felt like more than that. Then the four travellers crossed the floor, and disappeared into a jetway leading up into the next elevator car.

After that Coyote and Art stood there, and watched the car float over to the cable and rise through the valve-door and disappear. Coyote's asymmetrical face clenched into a most uncharacteristic expression of worry, even fear. That was his son, of course, and three of his closest friends, going to a very dangerous place. Well, it was just Earth; but it felt dangerous, Art had to admit. 'They'll be okay,' Art said, giving the little man a squeeze on the shoulder. 'They'll be stars down there. It'll go fine.' No doubt true. In fact he felt better himself at his own reassurances. It was the home planet, after all. Humans were made for it. They would be fine. It was the home planet. But still . . .

Back in East Pavonis the congress had begun.

It was Nadia's doing, really. She simply started working in the main warehouse on draft passages, and people started joining her, and things snowballed. Once the meetings were going people had to attend or risk losing a say. Nadia shrugged if anyone complained that they weren't ready, that things had to be regularized, that they needed to know more, etc; 'Come on,' she said impatiently. 'Here we are, we might as well get to it.'

So a fluctuating group of about three hundred people began meeting daily in the industrial complex of East Pavonis. The main warehouse, designed to hold piste parts and train cars, was huge, and scores of mobile-walled offices were set up against its walls, leaving the central space open, and available for a roughly circular collection of mismatched tables. 'Ah,' Art said when he saw it, 'the table of tables.'

Of course there were people who wanted a list of delegates, so that they knew who could vote, who could speak, and so on. Nadia, who was quickly taking on the role of chairperson, suggested they accept all requests to become a delegation from any Martian group, as long as the group had had some tangible existence before the conference began. 'We might as well be inclusive.'

The constitutional scholars from Dorsa Brevia agreed that the congress should be conducted by members of voting delegations, and the final result then voted on by the populace at large. Charlotte, who had helped to draft the Dorsa Brevia document twelve M-years before, had led a group since then in working up plans for a government, in anticipation of a successful revolution. They were not the only ones to have done this; schools in South Fossa and at the university in Sabishii had taught courses in the matter, and many of the young natives in the warehouse were well versed in the issues they were tackling. 'It's kind of scary,' Art remarked to Nadia. 'Win a revolution and a bunch of lawyers pop out of the woodwork.'

'Always.'

Charlotte's group had made a list of potential delegates to a constitutional congress, including all Martian settlements with populations over five hundred. Quite a few people would therefore be represented twice, Nadia pointed out, once by location and again by political affiliation. The few groups not on the list complained to a new committee, which allowed almost all petitioners to join. And Art made a call to Donald Hastings, and extended an invitation to UNTA to join as a delegation as well; the surprised Hastings got back to them a few days later, with a positive response. He would come down the cable himself.

And so after about a week's jockeying, with many other matters being worked on at the same time, they had enough agreement to call for a vote of approval of the delegate list; and because it had been so inclusive, it passed almost unanimously. And suddenly they had a real congress. It was made up of the following delegations, with anywhere from one to ten people in each delegation:

Towns

Acheron	Sheffield
Nicosia	Senzeni Na
Cairo	Echus Overlook
Odessa	Dorsa Brevia
Harmakhis Vallis	Dao Vallis
Sabishii	South Fossa
Christianopolis	Rumi
Bogdanov Vishniac	New Vanuatu
Hiranyagarbha	Prometheus
Mauss Hyde	Gramsci
New Clarke	Mareotis
Bradbury Point	Burroughs refugees organization
Sergei Korolyov	Libya Station
Dumartheray Crater	Tharsis Tholus
South Station	Overhangs
Reull Vallis	Margaritifer Plinth
southern caravanserai	Great Escarpment caravanserai
Nuova Bologna	Da Vinci
Nirgal Vallis	The Elysian League
Montepulciano	Hell's Gate

Political Parties and Other Organizations

Booneans	Ka Kaze
Reds	Editorial Board of *The Journal of*
Bogdanovists	*Areological Studies*
Schnellingistas	Space Elevator Authority
Marsfirst	Christian Democrats
Free Mars	The Metanational Economic
The Ka	Activity Co-ordination
Praxis	Committee
Qahiran Majarhi	Bolognan Neomarxists
League	Friends of the Earth
Green Mars	Biotique
United Nations	Séparation de L'Atmosphère
Transitional	
Authority	

General meetings began in the morning around the table of tables, then moved out in many small working groups to offices in the warehouse, or buildings nearby. Every morning Art showed up early and brewed great pots of coffee, kava and kavajava, his favourite. It perhaps was not much of a job, given the significance of the enterprise, but Art was happy doing it. Every day he was surprised to see a congress convening at all; and observing the size of it, he felt that helping to get it started was probably going to be his principal contribution. He was not a scholar, and he had few ideas about what a Martian constitution ought to include. Getting people together was what he was good at, and he had done that. Or rather he and Nadia had, for Nadia had stepped in and taken the lead just when they had needed her. She was the only one of the First Hundred on hand who had everyone's trust; this gave her a bit of genuine natural authority. Now, without any fuss, without seeming to notice she was doing it, she was exerting that power.

And so now it was Art's great pleasure to become, in effect, Nadia's personal assistant. He arranged her days, and did everything he could to make sure they ran smoothly. This included making a good pot of kavajava first thing every morning, for Nadia was one of many of them fond of that initial jolt toward alertness and general good will. Yes, Art thought, personal assistant and drug dispenser, that was his destiny at this point in history. And he was happy. Just watching people look at Nadia was a pleasure in itself. And the way she looked back: interested, sympathetic, sceptical, an edge developing quickly if she thought someone was wasting her time, a warmth kindling if she was impressed by their contribution. And people knew this, they wanted to please her. They tried to keep to the point, to make a contribution. They wanted that particular warm look in her eye. Very strange eyes they were, really, when you looked close: hazel, basically, but flecked with innumerable tiny patches of other colours, yellow, black, green, blue. A mesmerizing quality to them. Nadia focused her full attention on people – she was willing to believe you, to take your side, to make sure your case didn't get lost in the shuffle; even the Reds, who knew she had been fighting with Ann, trusted her to make sure they were heard. So the work coalesced around her; and all Art really had to do was watch her at work, and enjoy it, and help where he could.

And so the debates began.

In the first week many arguments concerned simply what a constitution was, what form it should take, and whether they should have one at all. Charlotte called this the metaconflict, the argument about what the argument was about – a very important matter, she said when she saw Nadia squint unhappily, 'because in settling it, we set the limits on what we can decide. If we decide to include economic and social issues in the constitution, for instance, then this is a very different kind of thing than if we stick to purely political or legal matters, or to a very general statement of principles.'

To help structure even this debate, she and the Dorsa Brevia scholars had come with a number of different 'blank constitutions', which blocked out different kinds of constitutions without actually filling in their contents. These blanks did little, however, to stop the objections of those who maintained that most aspects of social and economic life ought not to be regulated at all. Support for such a 'minimal state' came from a variety of viewpoints that otherwise made strange bedfellows: anarchists, libertarians, neotraditional capitalists, certain Greens,

126

and so on. To the most extreme of these anti-statists, writing up any government at all was a kind of defeat, and they conceived of their role in the congress as making the new government as small as possible.

Sax heard about this argument in one of the nightly calls from Nadia and Art, and he was as willing to think about it seriously as he was anything else. 'It's been found that a few simple rules can regulate very complex behaviour. There's a classic computer model for flocking birds, for instance, which only has three rules – keep an equal distance from everyone around you – don't change speed too fast – avoid stationary objects. Those will model the flight of a flock quite nicely.'

'A computer flock maybe,' Nadia scoffed. 'Have you ever seen chimney-swifts at dusk?'

After a moment Sax's reply arrived: 'No.'

'Well, take a look when you get to Earth. Meanwhile we can't be having a constitution that says only "don't change speed too fast".'

Art thought this was funny, but Nadia was not amused. In general she had little patience for the minimalist arguments. 'Isn't it the equivalent of letting the metanats run things?' she would say. 'Letting might be right?'

'No, no,' Mikhail would protest. 'That's not what we mean at all!'

'It seems very like what you are saying. And for some it's obviously a kind of cover – a pretend principle that is really about keeping the rules that protect their property and privileges, and letting the rest go to hell.'

'No, not at all.'

'Then you must prove it at the table. Everything that government might involve itself in, you have to make the case against. You have to argue it point by point.'

And she was so insistent about this, not scolding like Maya would have but simply adamant, that they had to agree: everything was at least on the table for discussion. Therefore the various blank constitutions made sense, as starting points; and therefore they should get on with it. A vote on it was taken, and the majority agreed to give it a try.

And so there they were, the first hurdle jumped. Everyone had agreed to work according to the same plan. It was amazing,

Art thought, zooming from meeting to meeting, filled with admiration for Nadia. She was not your ordinary diplomat, she by no means followed the empty vessel model that Art aspired to; but things got done nevertheless. She had the charisma of the sensible. He hugged her every time he passed her, he kissed the top of her head; he loved her. He ran around with that wealth of good feeling, and dropped in on all the sessions he could, watching to see how he could help keep things going. Often it was just a matter of supplying people with food and drink, so that they could continue through the day without getting irritable.

At all hours the table of tables was crowded; fresh-faced young Valkyries towering over sunbaked old vets; all races, all types; this was Mars, M-year 52, a kind of de facto united nations all on its own. With all the potential fractiousness of that notoriously fractious body; so that sometimes, looking at all their disparate faces and listening to the mélange of languages, English augmented by Babel, Art was nearly overwhelmed by their variety. 'Ka, Nadia,' he said as they sat eating sandwiches and going over their notes for the day, 'we're trying to write a constitution that every Terran culture could agree to!'

She waved the problem away, swallowed. 'About time,' she said.

Charlotte suggested that the Dorsa Brevia declaration made a logical starting point for discussing the content that would fill the constitutional forms. This suggestion caused more trouble than even the blanks had, for the Reds and several other delegations disliked various points of the old declaration, and they argued that using it was a way of pisting the congress from the start.

'So what?' Nadia said. 'We can change every word of it if we want, but we have to start with something.'

This view was popular among most of the old underground groups, many of whom had been at Dorsa Brevia in M-39. The declaration that had resulted remained the underground's best effort to write down what they had agreed on back when they were out of power, so it made sense to start with it; it gave them some precedent, some historical continuity.

When they pulled it out and looked at it, however, they found that the old declaration had become frighteningly radical. No private property? No appropriation of surplus value? Had they really said such things? How were things supposed to work? People pored over the bare uncompromising sentences, shaking their heads. The declaration had not bothered to say how its lofty goals were to be enacted, it had only stated them. 'The stone tablet routine,' as Art characterized it. But now the revolution had succeeded, and the time had come to do something in the real world. Could they really stick to concepts as radical as those in the Dorsa Brevia declaration?

Hard to say. 'At least the points are there to discuss,' Nadia said. And along with them, on everyone's screen, were the blank constitutions with their section headings, suggesting all by themselves the many problems they were going to have to come to grips with: 'Structure of Government, Executive; Structure of Government, Legislative; Structure of Government, Judicial; Rights of Citizens; Military and Police; Taxation; Election Procedures; Property Law; Economic Systems; Environmental Law; Amendment Procedures', and so on, in some blanks for pages on end – all being juggled on everyone's screens, scrambled, formatted, endlessly debated. 'Just filling in the blanks,' as Art sang one night, looking over Nadia's shoulder at one particularly forbidding flowchart pattern, like something out of Michel's alchemical *combinatoires*. And Nadia laughed.

The working groups focused on different parts of government as outlined in a new composite blank constitution, now being called the blank of blanks. Political parties and interest groups gravitated to the issues that most concerned them, and the many tent town delegations chose or were assigned to remaining areas. After that it was a matter of work.

For the moment, the Da Vinci Crater technical group was in control of Martian space. They were keeping all space shuttles from docking at Clarke, or aerobraking into Martian orbit. No one believed that this alone made them truly free, but it did give them a certain amount of physical and psychic space to work in – this was the gift of the revolution. They were also driven by the memory of the battle for Sheffield; the fear of civil war was strong among them. Ann was in exile with the Kakaze, and sabotage in the outback was a daily occurrence. There were also tents that had declared independence from anyone, and a few metanat holdouts; there was turmoil generally, and a sense of barely-contained confusion. They were in a bubble in history, a moment only; it could collapse at any time, and if they didn't act soon, it *would* collapse. It was, simply put, time to act.

This was the one thing everyone agreed on, but it was a very important thing. As the days passed, a core group of workers slowly emerged, people who recognized each other for their willingness to get the job done, for their desire to finish paragraphs rather than posture. Inside all the rest of the debate these people went at it, guided by Nadia, who was very quick to recognize such people and give them all the help she could.

Art meanwhile ran around in his usual manner. Up early, supply drinks and food, and information concerning the work ongoing in other rooms. It seemed to him that things were going pretty well. Most of the subgroups took the responsibility to fill in their blank seriously, writing and rewriting drafts, hammering them out concept by concept, phrase by phrase. They were happy to see Art when he came by in the course of the day, as he represented a break, some food, some jokes. One judicial group tacked foam wings on his shoes, and sent him with a caustic message along to an executive group with whom they were fighting. Pleased, Art kept the wings on; why not? What they were doing had a kind of ludicrous majesty, or majestic ludicrousness – they were rewriting the rules, he was flying around like Hermes or Puck, it was perfectly appropriate. And so he flew, through the long hours into the night, every night. And after all the sessions had closed down for the evening, he went back to the Praxis offices he shared with Nadia, and they would eat, and talk over the day's progress, and make a call to the travellers to Earth, and talk with Nirgal and Sax and Maya and Michel. And after that Nadia would go back to work at her screens, usually falling asleep there in her chair. Then Art would often go back out into the warehouse, and the buildings and rovers clustered around it. Because they were holding the congress in a warehouse tent, there was not the same party scene that had existed after hours in Dorsa Brevia; but the delegates often stayed up, sitting on the floors of their rooms drinking and talking about the day's work, or the revolution just past. Many of the people there had never met before, and they were getting to know each other. Relationships were forming, romances, friendships, feuds. It was a good time to talk, and learn more about what was going on during the daytime congress; it was the underside of the congress, the social hour, out there scattered in concrete rooms. Art enjoyed it. And then the moment would come when he would suddenly hit the wall, a wave of sleepiness would roll over him and sometimes he wouldn't even have time to stagger back to his offices, to the couch next to Nadia's; he would simply roll over on the floor and sleep there, waking cold and stiff to hurry off to their bathroom, a shower, and back to the kitchens to start up that day's kava and java. Round and round, his days a blur; it was glorious.

In sessions on many different subjects people were having to grapple with questions of scale. Without any nations, without any natural or traditional political units, who governed what? And how were they to balance the local against the global, and past versus future – the many ancestral cultures against the one Martian culture?

132

Sax, observing this recurring problem from the rocket-ship to Earth, sent back a message proposing that the tent towns and covered canyons become the principal political units: city-states, basically, with no larger political units except for the global government itself, which would regulate only truly global concerns. Thus there would be local and global, but no nation-states in between.

The reaction to this proposal was fairly positive. For one thing it had the advantage of conforming to the situation that already existed. Mikhail, leader of the Bogdanovist party, noted that it was a variant of the old commune of communes, and because Sax had been the source of the suggestion, this quickly got it called the 'lab of labs' plan. But the underlying problem still remained, as Nadia quickly pointed out; all Sax had done was to define their particular local and global. They still had to decide just how much power the proposed global confederation was going to have over the proposed semi-autonomous city-states. Too much, and it was back to a big centralized state, Mars itself as a nation, a thought which many delegations abhorred. 'But too little,' Jackie said emphatically in the human rights workshop, 'and there could be tents out there deciding slavery is okay, or female genital mutilation is okay, or any other crime based on some Terran barbarism is okay, excused in the name of "cultural values". And that is just not acceptable.'

'Jackie is right,' Nadia said, which was unusual enough to get people's attention. 'People claiming that some fundamental right is foreign to their culture – that stinks no matter who says it, fundamentalists, patriarchs, Leninists, metanats, I don't care who. They aren't going to get away with it here, not if I can help it.'

Art noticed more than a few delegates frowning at this sentiment, which no doubt struck them as a version of Western secular relativism, or perhaps John Boone's hyperamericanism. Opposition to the metanats had included many people trying to hold on to older cultures, and these often had their hierarchies pretty well intact; the ones at the top end of the hierarchies liked them that way, and so did a surprisingly large number of people farther down the ladder.

The young Martian natives, however, looked surprised that

this was even considered an issue. To them the fundamental rights were innate and irrevocable, and any challenge to that struck them as just one more of the many emotional scars that the issei were always revealing, as a result of their traumatic dysfunctional Terran upbringings. Ariadne, one of the most prominent of the young natives, stood up to say that the Dorsa Brevia group had studied many Terran human rights documents, and had written a comprehensive list of their own. The new master list of fundamental individual rights was available for discussion and, she implied, adoption wholesale. Some argued about one point or another; but it was generally agreed that a global bill of rights of some kind should be on the table. So Martian values as they existed in M-year 52 were about to be codified, and made a principal component of the constitution.

The exact nature of these rights was still a matter of controversy. The so-called 'political rights' were generally agreed to be 'self-evident' – things citizens were free to do, things governments were forbidden to do – *habeus corpus*, freedom of movement, of speech, of association, of religion, a ban on weapons – all these were approved by a vast majority of Martian natives, though there were some issei from places like Singapore, Cuba, Indonesia, Thailand, China and so on, who looked askance at so much emphasis on individual liberty. Other delegates had reservations about a different kind of right, the so-called 'social' or 'economic' rights, such as the right to housing, health care, education, employment, a share of the value generated by natural resource use, etc. Many issei delegates with actual experience in Terran government were quite worried about these, pointing out that it was dangerous to enshrine such things in the constitution; it had been done on Earth, they said, and then when it was found impossible to meet such promises, the constitution guaranteeing them was seen as a propaganda device, and flouted in other areas as well, until it became a bad joke.

'Even so,' Mikhail said sharply, 'if you can't afford housing, then it is your right to vote that is the bad joke.'

The young natives agreed, as did many others there. So economic or social rights were on the table too, and arguments over how actually to guarantee these rights in practice continued through many a long session. 'Political, social, it's all one,' Nadia said. 'Let's make all the rights work.'

So the work went on, both around the big table and in the offices where the subgroups were meeting. Even the UN was there, in the person of Donald Hastings himself, who had come down the elevator and was participating vigorously in the debates, his opinion always carrying a peculiar kind of weight. He even began to exhibit symptoms of hostage syndrome, Art thought, becoming more and more sympathetic the more he stood around in the warehouse arguing with people. And this might affect his superiors on Earth as well.

Comments and suggestions were also pouring in from all over Mars, and from Earth as well, filling several screens covering one wall of the big room. Interest in the congress was high everywhere, rivalling even Earth's great flood in the public's attention. 'The soap opera of the moment,' Art said to Nadia. Every night the two of them met in their little office suite, and put in their call to Nirgal and the rest. The delays in the travellers' responses got longer and longer, but Art and Nadia didn't really mind; there was a lot to think about while waiting for Sax and the others' part of the conversation to arrive.

'This global versus local problem is going to be hard,' Art said one night. 'It's a real contradiction, I think. I mean it's not just the result of confused thinking. We truly want some global control, and yet we want freedom for the tents as well. Two of our most essential values are in contradiction.'

'Maybe the Swiss system,' Nirgal suggested a few minutes later. 'That's what John Boone always used to say.'

But the Swiss on Pavonis were not encouraging about this idea. 'A counter-model rather,' Jurgen said, making a face. 'The reason I'm on Mars is the Swiss federal government. It stifles everything. You need a licence to breathe.'

'And the cantons have no power any more,' Priska said. 'The federal government took it away.'

'In some of the cantons,' Jurgen added, 'this was a good thing.'

Priska said, 'More interesting than Berne might be the Graubunden. That means Grey League. They were a loose

135

confederation of towns in southeast Switzerland, for hundreds of years. A very successful organization.'

'Could you call up whatever you can get on that?' Art said.

The next night he and Nadia looked over descriptions of the Graubunden that Priska had sent over. Well ... there was a certain simplicity to affairs during the Renaissance, Art thought. Maybe that was wrong, but somehow the extremely loose agreements of the little Swiss mountain towns did not seem to translate well to the densely interpenetrated economies of the Martian settlements. The Graubunden hadn't had to worry about generating unwanted changes in atmospheric pressure, for instance. No – the truth was, they were in a new situation. There was no historical analogy that would be much help to them now.

'Speaking of global versus local,' Irishka said, 'what about the land outside the tents and covered canyons?' She was emerging as the leading Red remaining on Pavonis, a moderate who could speak for almost all wings of the Red movement, therefore becoming quite a power as the weeks passed. 'That's most of the land on Mars, and all we said at Dorsa Brevia is that no individual can own it, that we are all stewards of it together. That's good as far as it goes, but as the population rises and new towns are built, it's going to be more and more of a problem figuring out who controls it.'

Art sighed. This was true, but too difficult to be welcome. Recently he had made a resolution to devote the bulk of his daily efforts to attacking what he and Nadia judged to be the worst outstanding problem they were facing, and so in theory he was happy to recognize them. But sometimes they were just too hard.

As in this case. Land use, the Red objection: more aspects of the global-local problem, but distinctively Martian. Again there was no precedent. Still, as it was probably the worst outstanding problem ...

Art went to the Reds. The three who met with him were Marion, Irishka, and Tiu, one of Nirgal and Jackie's crèche-mates from Zygote. They took Art out to their rover camp, which made him happy; it meant that despite his Praxis background he was now seen as a neutral or impartial figure, as he wanted to be. A big, empty vessel, stuffed with messages and passed along.

The Reds' encampment was west of the warehouses, on the rim of the caldera. They sat down with Art in one of their big upper-level compartments, in the glare of a late afternoon sun, talking and looking down into the giant, silhouetted country of the caldera.

'So what would you like to see in this constitution?' Art said.

He sipped the tea they had given him. His hosts looked at each other, somewhat taken aback. 'Ideally,' Marion said after a while, 'we'd like to be living on the primal planet, in caves and cliff-dwellings, or excavated crater rings. No big cities, no terraforming.'

'You'd have to stay suited all the time.'

'That's right. We don't mind that.'

'Well.' Art thought it over. 'Okay, but let's start from now. Given the situation at this moment, what would you like to see happen next?'

'No further terraforming.'

'The cable gone, and no more immigration.'

'In fact it would be nice if some people went back to Earth.'

They stopped speaking, stared at him. Art tried not to let his consternation show.

He said, 'Isn't the biosphere likely to grow on its own at this point?'

'It's not clear,' Tiu said. 'But if you stopped the industrial pumping, any further growth would certainly be very slow. It might even lose ground, as with this ice age that's starting.'

'Isn't that what some people call ecopoesis?'

'No. The ecopoets just use biological methods, but they're

137

very intensive with them. We think they all should stop, ecopoets or industrialists or whatever.'

'But especially the heavy industrial methods,' Marion said. 'And most especially the inundation of the north. That's simply criminal. We'll blow up those stations no matter what happens here, if they don't stop.'

Art gestured out at the huge, stony caldera. 'The higher elevations look pretty much the same, right?'

They weren't willing to admit that. Irishka said, 'Even the high ground shows ice deposition and plant life. The atmosphere lofts high here, remember. No place escapes when the winds are strong.'

'What if we tented the four big calderas?' Art said. 'Kept them sterile underneath, with the original atmospheric pressure and mix? Those would be huge wilderness parks, preserved in the true primal state.'

'Parks are just what they would be.'

'I know. But we have to work with what we have now, right? We can't go back to M-1 and rerun the whole thing. And given the current situation, it might be good to preserve three or four big places in the original state, or close to it.'

'It would be nice to have some canyons protected as well,' Tiu said tentatively. Clearly they had not considered this kind of possibility before; and it was not really satisfactory to them, Art could see. But the current situation could not be wished away, they had to start from there.

'Or Argyre Basin.'

'At the very least, keep Argyre dry.'

Art nodded encouragingly. 'Combine that kind of preservation with the atmosphere limits set in the Dorsa Brevia document. That's a five kilometre breathable ceiling, and there's a hell of a lot of land above five kilometres. It won't take the northern ocean away, but nothing's going to do that now. Some form of slow ecopoesis is about the best you can hope for at this point, right?'

Perhaps that was putting it too baldly. The Reds stared down into Pavonis caldera unhappily, thinking their own thoughts.

*　　*　　*

'Say the Reds come on board,' Art said to Nadia. 'What do you think the next worst problem is?'

'What?' She had been nearly asleep, listening to some tinny old jazz from her AI. 'Ah. Art.' Her voice was low and quiet, the Russian accent light but distinct. She sat slumped on the couch. A pile of paper balls lay around her feet, like pieces of some structure she was putting together. The Martian way of life. Her face was oval under a cap of straight white hair, the wrinkles of her skin somehow wearing away, as if she were a pebble in the stream of years. She opened her flecked eyes, luminous and arresting under their Cossack eyelids. A beautiful face, looking now at Art perfectly relaxed. 'The next worst problem.'

'Yes.'

She smiled. Where did that calmness come from, that relaxed smile? She wasn't worried about anything these days. Art found it surprising, given the political highwire act they were performing. But then again it was politics, not war. And just as Nadia had been terribly frightened during the revolution, always tense, always expecting disaster, she was now always relatively calm. As if to say, Nothing that happens here matters all that much – tinker with the details all you want – my friends are safe, the war is over, this that remains is a kind of game, or work like construction work, full of pleasures.

Art moved around to the back of the couch, massaged her shoulders. 'Ah,' she said. 'Problems. Well, there are a lot of problems that are about equally sticky.'

'Like what?'

'Like, I wonder if the Mahjaris will be able to adapt to democracy. I wonder if everyone will accept Vlad and Marina's eco-economics. I wonder if we can make a decent police. I wonder if Jackie will try to create a system with a strong president, and use the natives' numerical superiority to become queen.' She looked over her shoulder, laughed at Art's expression. 'I wonder about a lot of things. Should I go on?'

'Maybe not.'

She laughed. 'You go on. That feels good. These problems – they aren't so hard. We'll just keep going to the table and pounding away at them. Maybe you could talk to Zeyk.'

'Okay.'
'But now do my neck.'

Art went to talk to Zeyk and Nazik that very night, after
Nadia had fallen asleep. 'So what's the Mahjari view of all
this?' he asked.

Zeyk growled. 'Please don't ask stupid questions,' he said.
'Sunnis are fighting Shiites – Lebanon is devastated – the
oil-rich states are hated by the oil-poor states – the North
African countries are a metanat – Syria and Iraq hate each
other – Iraq and Egypt hate each other – we all hate the
Iranians, except for the Shiites – and we all hate Israel of
course, and the Palestinians too – and even though I am from
Egypt I am actually Bedouin, and we despise the Nile Egyptians, and in fact we don't get along well with the Bedouin from
Jordan. And everyone hates the Saudis, who are as corrupt as
you can get. So when you ask me what is the Arab view, what
can I say to you?' He shook his head darkly.

'I guess you say it's a stupid question,' Art said. 'Sorry.
Thinking in constituencies, it's a bad habit. How about this –
what do *you* think of it?'

Nazik laughed. 'You could ask him what the rest of the
Qahiran Mahjaris think. He knows them only too well.'

'Too well,' Zeyk repeated.

'Do you think the human rights section will go with them?'

Zeyk frowned. 'No doubt we will sign the constitution.'

'But these rights . . . I thought there were no Arab democracies still?'

'What do you mean? There's Palestine, Egypt . . . Anyway
it's Mars we are concerned with. And here every caravan has
been its own state since the very beginning.'

'Strong leaders, hereditary leaders?'

'Not hereditary. Strong leaders, yes. We don't think the
new constitution will end that, not anywhere. Why should it?
You are a strong leader yourself, yes?'

Art laughed uncomfortably. 'I'm just a messenger.'

Zeyk shook his head. 'Tell that to Antar. Now there is where
you should go, if you want to know what the Qahirans think.
He is our king now.'

He looked as if he had bitten into something sour, and Art said, 'So what does *he* want, do you think?'

'He is Jackie's creature,' Zeyk muttered, 'nothing more.'

'I should think that would be a point against him.'

Zeyk shrugged.

'It depends who you talk to,' Nazik said. 'For the older Muslim immigrants, it is a bad association, because although Jackie is very powerful, she has had more than one consort, and so Antar looks . . .'

'Compromised,' Art suggested, forestalling some other word from the glowering Zeyk.

'Yes,' Nazik said. 'But on the other hand, Jackie is powerful. And all of the people now leading the Free Mars party are in a position to become even more powerful in the new state. And the young Arabs like that. They are more native than Arab, I think. It's Mars that matters to them more than Islam. From that point of view, a close association with the Zygote ectogenes is a good thing. The ectogenes are seen as the natural leaders of the new Mars – especially Nirgal, of course, but with him off to Earth, there's a certain transfer of his influence to Jackie and the rest of her crowd. And thus to Antar.'

'I don't like him,' Zeyk said.

Nazik smiled at her husband. 'You don't like how many of the native Muslims are following him rather than you. But we are old, Zeyk. It could be time for retirement.'

'I don't see why,' Zeyk objected. 'If we're going to live a thousand years, then what difference does a hundred make?'

Art and Nazik laughed at him, and briefly Zeyk smiled. It was the first time Art had ever seen him smile.

In fact, age didn't matter. People wandered around, old or young or somewhere in between, talking and arguing, and it would have been an odd thing for the length of someone's lifetime to become a factor in such discussions.

And youth or age was not what the native movement was about anyway. If you were born on Mars your outlook was simply different, areocentric in a way that no Terran could even imagine – not just because of the whole complex of areorealities they had known from birth, but also because of

141

what they didn't know. Terrans knew just how vast Earth was, while for the Martian-born, that cultural and biological vastness was simply unimaginable. They had seen the screen images, but that wasn't enough to allow them to grasp it. This was one reason Art was glad Nirgal had chosen to join the diplomatic mission to Earth; he would learn what they were up against.

But most of the natives wouldn't. And the revolution had gone to their heads. Despite their cleverness at the table in working the constitution toward a form that would privilege them, they were in some basic sense naïve; they had no idea how unlikely their independence was, nor how possible it was for it to be taken away from them again. And so they were pressing things to the limit – led by Jackie, who floated through the warehouse just as beautiful and enthusiastic as ever, her drive to power concealed behind her love of Mars, and her devotion to her grandfather's ideals, and her essential good will, even innocence; the college girl who wanted passionately for the world to be just.

Or so it seemed. But she and her Free Mars colleagues certainly seemed to want to be in control as well. There were twelve million people on Mars now, and seven million of those had been born there; and almost every single one of these natives could be counted on to support the native political parties, usually Free Mars.

'It's dangerous,' Charlotte said when Art brought this matter up in the nightly meeting with Nadia. 'When you have a country formed out of a lot of groups that don't trust each other, with one a clear majority, then you get what they call "census voting", where politicians represent their groups, and get their votes, and election results are always just a reflection of population numbers. In that situation the same thing happens every time, so the majority group has a monopoly on power, and the minorities feel hopeless, and eventually rebel. Some of the worst civil wars in history began in those circumstances.'

'So what can we do?' Nadia asked.

'Well, some of it we're doing already, designing structures that spread the power around, and diminish the dangers of majoritarianism. Decentralization is important, because it creates a lot of small local majorities. Another strategy is to set up an array of Madisonian checks and balances, so that the government's a kind of cat's cradle of competing forces. This is called *polyarchy*, spreading power around to as many groups as you can.'

'Maybe we're a bit too polyarchic right now,' Art said.

'Perhaps. Another tactic is to deprofessionalize governing. You make some big part of the government a public obligation, like jury duty, and then draft ordinary citizens in a lottery, to serve for a short time. They get professional staff help, but make the decisions themselves.'

'I've never heard of that one,' Nadia said.

'No. It's been often proposed, but seldom enacted. But I think it's really worth considering. It tends to make power as much a burden as an advantage. You get a letter in the mail; oh no; you're drafted to do two years in congress. It's a drag, but on the other hand it's a kind of distinction too, a chance to add something to the public discourse. Citizen government.'

'I like that,' Nadia said.

'Another method to reduce majoritarianism is voting by some version of the Australian ballot, where voters vote for two or more candidates in ranked fashion, first choice, second choice, third choice. Candidates get some points for being second or third choice, so to win elections they have to appeal outside their own group. It tends to push politicians toward moderation, and in the long run it can create trust among groups where none existed before.'

'Interesting,' Nadia exclaimed. 'Like trusses in a wall.'

'Yes.' Charlotte mentioned some examples of Terran 'fractured societies' that had healed their rifts by a clever governmental structure: Azania, Cambodia, Armenia ... as she described them Art's heart sank a bit; these had been bloody, bloody lands.

'It seems like political structures can only do so much,' he said.

'True,' Nadia said, 'but we don't have all those old hatreds to deal with yet. Here the worst we have is the Reds, and they've been marginalized by the terraforming that's already happened. I bet these methods could be used to pull even them into the process.'

Clearly she was encouraged by the options Charlotte had described; they were structures, after all. Engineering of an imaginary sort, which nevertheless resembled real engineering. So Nadia was tapping away at her screen, sketching out designs as if working on a building, a small smile tugging the corners of her mouth.

'You're happy,' Art said.

She didn't hear him. But that night in their radio talk with the travellers, she said to Sax, 'It was so nice to find that political science had abstracted *something* useful in all these years.'

Eight minutes later his reply came in. 'I never understood why they call it that.'

Nadia laughed, and the sound filled Art with happiness. Nadia Cherneshevsky, laughing in delight! Suddenly Art was sure that they were going to pull it off.

So he went back to the big table, ready to tackle the next worst problem. That brought him back to Earth again. There were a hundred next worst problems, all small until you actually took them on, at which point they became insoluble. In all the squabbling it was very hard to see any signs of growing accord. In some areas, in fact, it seemed to be getting worse. The middle points of the Dorsa Brevia document were causing trouble; the more people considered them, the more radical they became. Many around the table clearly believed that Vlad and Marina's eco-economic system, while it had worked for the underground, was not something that should be codified in the constitution. Some complained because it impinged on local autonomy, others because they had more faith in traditional capitalist economics than in any new system. Antar spoke often for this last group, with Jackie sitting right next to him, obviously in support. This along with his ties to the Arab community gave his statements a kind of double weight, and people listened. 'This new economy that's being proposed,' he declared one day at the table of tables, repeating his theme, 'is a radical and unprecedented intrusion of government into business.'

Suddenly Vlad Taneev stood up. Startled, Antar stopped speaking and looked over.

Vlad glared at him. Stooped, massive-headed, shaggy-eyebrowed, Vlad rarely if ever spoke in public; he hadn't said a thing in the congress so far. Slowly the greater part of the warehouse went silent, watching him. Art felt a quiver of anticipation; of all the brilliant minds of the First Hundred, Vlad was perhaps the most brilliant — and, except for Hiroko, the most enigmatic. Old when they had left Earth, intensely private, Vlad had built the Acheron labs early on and stayed there as much as possible thereafter, living in seclusion with Ursula Kohl and Marina Tokareva, two more of the great first ones. No one knew anything for certain about the three of them, they were a limit case illustration of the insular nature of other people's relationships; but this of course did not stop gossip; on the contrary, people talked about them all the time, saying that Marina and Ursula were the real couple, that Vlad was a kind of friend, or pet; or that Ursula had done most of the work on the longevity treatment, and Marina most of the work on eco-economics; or that they were a perfectly balanced equilateral triangle, collaborating on all that emerged from Acheron; or that Vlad was a bigamist of sorts who used two wives as fronts for his work in the separate fields of biology and economics. But no one knew for sure, for none of the three ever said a word about it.

Watching him stand there at the table, however, one had to suspect that the theory about him being just a front man was wrong. He was looking around in a fiercely intent, slow glare, capturing them all before he turned his eye again on Antar.

'What you said about government and business is absurd,' he stated coldly. It was a tone of voice that had not been heard much at the congress so far, contemptuous and dismissive. 'Governments always regulate the kinds of business they allow. Economics is a legal matter, a system of laws. So far, we have been saying in the Martian underground that as a matter of law, democracy and self-government are the innate rights of every person, and that these rights are not to be suspended when a person goes to work. You—' he waved a hand to indicate he did not know Antar's name '—do you believe in democracy and self-rule?'

'Yes!' Antar said defensively.

'Do you believe in democracy and self-rule as the fundamental values that government ought to encourage?'

'Yes!' Antar repeated, looking more and more annoyed.

'Very well. If democracy and self-rule are the fundamentals, then why should people give up these rights when they enter their work place? In politics we fight like tigers for freedom, for the right to elect our leaders, for freedom of movement, choice of residence, choice of what work to pursue – control of our lives, in short. And then we wake up in the morning and go to work, and all those rights disappear. We no longer insist on them. And so for most of the day we return to feudalism. That is what capitalism is – a version of feudalism in which capital replaces land, and business leaders replace kings. But the hierarchy remains. And so we still hand over

146

our lives' labour, under duress, to feed rulers who do no real work.'

'Business leaders work,' Antar said sharply. 'And they take the financial risks —'

'The so-called risk of the capitalist is merely one of the *privileges* of capital.'

'Management —'

'Yes yes. Don't interrupt me. Management is a real thing, a technical matter. But it can be controlled by labour just as well as by capital. Capital itself is simply the useful residue of the work of past labourers, and it could belong to everyone as well as to a few. There is no reason why a tiny nobility should own the capital, and everyone else therefore be in service to them. There is no reason they should give us a living wage and take all the rest that we produce. No! The system called capitalist democracy was not really democratic at all. That's why it was able to turn so quickly into the metanational system, in which democracy grew ever weaker and capitalism ever stronger. In which one per cent of the population owned half of the wealth, and five per cent of the population owned ninety-five per cent of the wealth. History has shown which values were real in that system. And the sad thing is that the injustice and suffering caused by it were not at all necessary, in that the technical means have existed since the eighteenth century to provide the basics of life to all.

'So. We must change. It is time. If self-rule is a fundamental value, if simple justice is a value, then they are values everywhere, including in the work place where we spend so much of our lives. That was what was said in point four of the Dorsa Brevia agreement. It says everyone's work is their own, and the worth of it cannot be taken away. It says that the various modes of production belong to those who created them, and to the common good of the future generations. It says that the world is something we all steward together. That is what it says. And in our years on Mars, we have developed an economic system that can keep all those promises. That has been our work these last fifty years. In the system we have developed, all economic enterprises are to be small co-operatives, owned by their workers and by no one else. They hire their management, or manage themselves. Industry guilds

147

and co-op associations will form the larger structures necessary to regulate trade and the market, share capital, and create credit.'

Antar said scornfully, 'These are nothing but ideas. It is utopianism and nothing more.'

'Not at all.' Again Vlad waved him away. 'The system is based on models from Terran history, and its various parts have all been tested on both worlds, and have succeeded very well. You don't know about this partly because you are ignorant, and partly because metanationalism itself steadfastly ignored and denied all alternatives to it. But most of our microeconomy has been in successful operation for centuries in the Mondragon region of Spain. The different parts of the macro-economy have been used in the pseudo-metanat Praxis, in Switzerland, in India's state of Kerala, in Bhutan, in Bologna Italy, and in many other places, including the Martian underground itself. These organizations were the precursors to our economy, which will be democratic in a way capitalism never even tried to be.'

A synthesis of systems. And Vladimir Taneev was a very great synthesist; it was said that all the components of the longevity treatment had already been there, for instance, and that Vlad and Ursula had simply put them together. Now in his economic work with Marina he was claiming to have done the same kind of thing. And although he had not mentioned the longevity treatment in this discussion, nevertheless it lay there like the table itself, a big cobbled-together achievement, part of everyone's lives. Art looked around and thought he could see people thinking, well, he did it once in biology and it worked; could economics be more difficult?

Against this unspoken thought, this unthought feeling, Antar's objections did not seem like much. Metanational capitalism's track record at this point did little to support it; in the last century it had precipitated a massive war, chewed up the Earth, and torn its societies apart. Why should they not try something new, given that record?

Someone from Hiranyagarbha stood and made an objection from the opposite direction, noting that they seemed to be abandoning the gift economy by which the Mars underground had lived.

Vlad shook his head impatiently. 'I believe in the underground economy, I assure you, but it has always been a mixed economy. Pure gift exchange co-existed with a monetary exchange, in which neoclassical market rationality, that is to say the profit mechanism, was bracketed and contained by society to direct it to serve higher values, such as justice and freedom. Economic rationality is simply not the highest value. It is a tool to calculate costs and benefits, only one part of a large equation concerning human welfare. The larger equation is called a mixed economy, and that is what we are constructing here. We are proposing a complex system, with public and private spheres of economic activity. It may be that we ask people to give, throughout their lives, about a year of their work to the public good, as in Switzerland's national service. That labour pool, plus taxes on private co-ops for use of the land and its resources, will enable us to guarantee the so-called social rights we have been discussing – housing, health care, food, education – things that should not be at the mercy of market rationality. Because *la salute non si paga*, as the Italian workers used to say. Health is not for sale!'

This was especially important to Vlad, Art could see. Which made sense – for in the metanational order, health most certainly had been for sale, not only medical care and food and housing, but pre-eminently the longevity treatment itself, which so far had been going only to those who could afford it. Vlad's greatest invention, in other words, had become the property of the privileged, the ultimate class distinction – long life or early death – a physicalization of class that almost resembled divergent species. No wonder he was angry; no wonder he had turned his efforts to devising an economic system that would transform the longevity treatment from a catastrophic possession to a blessing available to all.

'So nothing will be left to the market,' Antar said.

'No no no,' Vlad said, waving at Antar more irritably than ever. 'The market will always exist. It is the mechanism by which things and services are exchanged. Competition to provide the best product at the best price, this is inevitable and healthy. But on Mars it will be directed by society in a more active way. There will be not-for-profit status to vital life support matters, and then the freest part of the market will be directed away from the basics of existence toward non-essentials, where venture enterprises can be undertaken by worker-owned co-ops, who will be free to try what they like. When the basics are secured and when the workers own their own businesses, why not? It is the process of creation we are talking about.'

Jackie, looking annoyed at Vlad's dismissals of Antar, and perhaps intending to divert the old man, or trip him up, said, 'What about the ecological aspects of this economy that you used to emphasize?'

'They are fundamental,' Vlad said. 'Point three of Dorsa Brevia states that the land, air and water of Mars belong to no one, that we are the stewards of it for all the future generations. This stewardship will be everyone's responsibility, but in case of conflicts we propose strong environmental courts, perhaps as part of the constitutional court, which will estimate the real and complete environmental costs of economic activities, and help to co-ordinate plans that impact the environment.'

'But this is simply a planned economy!' Antar cried.

'Economies are plans. Capitalism planned just as much as this, and metanationalism tried to plan everything. No, an economy *is* a plan.'

Antar, frustrated and angry, said, 'It's simply socialism returned.'

Vlad shrugged. 'Mars is a new totality. Names from earlier totalities are deceptive. They become little more than theological terms. There are elements one could call socialist in this system, of course. How else remove injustice from economy? But private enterprises will be owned by their workers rather than being nationalized, and this is not socialism, at least not socialism as it was usually attempted on Earth. And all the co-ops are businesses – small democracies devoted to some work or other, all needing capital. There will be a market, there will be capital. But in our system workers will hire capital rather than the other way around. It's more democratic that way, more just. Understand me – we have tried to evaluate each feature of this economy by how well it aids us to reach the goals of more justice and more freedom. And justice and freedom do not contradict each other as much as has been claimed, because freedom in an unjust system is no freedom at all. They both emerge together. And so it is not so impossible, really. It is only a matter of enacting a better system, by combining elements that have been tested and shown to work. This is the moment for that. We have been preparing for this opportunity for seventy years. And now that the chance has come, I see no reason to back off just because someone is afraid of some old words. If you have any *specific* suggestions for improvements, we'll be happy to hear them.'

He stared long and hard at Antar. But Antar did not speak; he had no specific suggestions.

The room was filled with a charged silence. It was the first and only time in the congress that one of the issei had stood up and trounced one of the nisei in public debate. Most of the issei liked to take a more subtle line. But now one of the ancient radicals had become angry and risen up to smite one of the neoconservative young power-mongers – who now looked as if they were advocating a new version of an old hierarchy, for purposes of their own. A thought which was conveyed very well indeed by Vlad's long look across the table at Antar, full of disgust at his reactionary selfishness, his cowardice in the face of change. Vlad sat down; Antar was dismissed.

But still they argued. Conflict, metaconflict, details, fundamentals; everything was on the table, including a magnesium kitchen sink that someone had placed on one segment of the table of tables, some three weeks into the process.

And really the delegates in the warehouse were only the tip of the iceberg, the most visible part of a gigantic two-world debate. Live transmission of every minute of the conference was available everywhere on Mars and in most places on Earth, and although the actual realtime tape had a certain documentary tediousness to it, Mangalavid concocted a daily highlights film that was shown during the timeslip every night, and sent to Earth for very wide distribution. It became 'the greatest show on Earth' as one American programme rather oddly dubbed it. 'Maybe people are tired of the same old crap on TV,' Art said to Nadia one night as they watched a brief, weirdly distorted account of the day's negotiations on American TV.

'Or in the world.'

'Yeah, true. They want something else to think about.'

'Or else they're thinking about what they might do,' Nadia suggested. 'So that we're a small-scale model. Easier to understand.'

'Maybe so.'

In any case the two worlds watched, and the congress became, along with everything else that it was, a daily soap opera — a soap opera which however held an extra attraction for its viewers, somehow, as if in some strange way it held the very key to their lives. And perhaps as a result, thousands of spectators did more than watch — comments and suggestions were pouring in, and though it seemed unlikely to most people on Pavonis that something mailed in would contain a startling truth they hadn't thought of, still all messages were read by groups of volunteers in Sheffield and South Fossa, who passed some proposals 'up to the table'. Some people even advocated including all these suggestions in the final constitution; they objected to a 'statist legal document', they wanted it to be a larger thing, a collaborative philosophical or even spiritual

153

statement, expressing their values, goals, dreams, reflections. 'That's not a constitution,' Nadia objected, 'that's a culture. We're not the damn library here.' But included or not, long communiqués continued to come in, from the tents and canyons and the drowned coastlines of Earth, signed by individuals, committees, entire town populations.

Discussions in the warehouse were just as wide-ranging as in the mail. A Chinese delegate approached Art and spoke in Mandarin to him, and when he paused for a while, his AI began to speak, in a lovely Scottish accent. 'To tell the truth I've begun to doubt that you've sufficiently consulted Adam Smith's important book *Enquiry Into the Nature and Causes of the Wealth of Nations*.'

'You may be right,' Art said, and referred the man to Charlotte.

Many people in the warehouse were speaking languages other than English, and relying on translation AIs to communicate with the rest. At any given moment there were conversations in a dozen different languages, and AI translators were heavily used. Art still found them a little distracting. He wished it were possible to know all these languages, even though the latest generations of AI translators were really pretty good: voices well-modulated, vocabularies large and accurate, grammar excellent, phrasing almost free of the errors that had made earlier translation programs such a great party game. The new ones had become so good that it seemed possible that the English-language dominance that had created an almost monoglot Martian culture might begin to recede. The issei had of course brought all languages with them, but English had been their lingua franca; the nisei had therefore used English to communicate among themselves, while their 'primary' languages were used only to speak to their parents; and so, for a while, English had become the natives' native tongue. But now with the new AIs, and a continuing stream of new immigrants speaking the full array of Terran languages, it looked as if things might broaden back out again, as new nisei stayed with their primary languages and used AIs as their lingua franca instead of English.

This linguistic matter illustrated to Art a complexity in the native population that he hadn't noticed before. Some natives were yonsei, fourth generation or younger, and very definitely children of Mars; but other natives the very same age were the nisei children of recent issei immigrants, tending to have closer ties with the Terran cultures they had come from, with all the conservatism that implied. So that there were new native 'conservatives' and old settler-family native 'radicals', one might say. And this split only occasionally correlated with ethnicity or nationality, when these still mattered to them at all. One night Art was talking with a couple of them, one a global government advocate, the other an anarchist backing all local autonomy proposals, and he asked them about their origins. The globalist's father was half Japanese, a quarter Irish, and a quarter Tanzanian; her mother had a Greek mother and a father with parents Colombian and Australian. The anarchist had a Nigerian father and a mother who was from Hawaii, and thus had a mixed ancestry of Filipino, Japanese, Polynesian and Portuguese. Art stared at them: if one were to think in terms of ethnic voting blocks, how would one categorize these people? One couldn't. They were Martian natives. Nisei, sansei, yonsei – whatever generation, they had been formed in large part by their Martian experience – areo-formed, just as Hiroko had always foretold. Many had married within their own national or ethnic background, but many more had not. And no matter what their ancestry, their political opinions tended to reflect not that background (just what would the Graeco-Colombian-Australian position be? Art wondered), but their own experience. This itself had been quite varied: some had grown up in the underground, others had been born in the UN-controlled big cities, and only come to an awareness of the underground later in life, or even at the moment of the revolution itself. These differences tended to affect them much more than where their Terran ancestors had happened to live.

Art nodded as the natives explained these things to him, in the long kava-buzzed parties running deep into the night. People at these parties were in increasingly high spirits, as the congress was, they felt, going well. They did not take the debates among the issei very seriously; they were confident that their core beliefs would prevail. Mars would be independent, it would be run by Martians, what Earth wanted did not matter; beyond that, it was detail. Thus they went about their work in the committees without much attention paid to the philosophical arguments around the table of tables. 'The old dogs keep growling,' said one message on the big message board; this seemed to express a general native opinion. And the work in the committees went on.

The big message board was a pretty good indicator of the mood of the congress. Art read it the way he read fortune cookies, and indeed one day there was one message that said, 'You like Chinese food.' Usually the messages were more political than that. Often they were things said in the previous days of the conference: 'No tent is an island'. 'If you can't afford housing then the right to vote is a bad joke.' 'Keep your distance, don't change speed, don't run into anything.' *'La salute non si paga.'* Then there were things that had not been said: 'Do unto others.' 'The Reds have Green Roots.' 'The Greatest Show on Earth.' 'No Kings No Presidents.' 'Big Man Hates Politics.' 'However: We Are The Little Red People.'

So Art was no longer surprised when he was approached by people who spoke in Arabic or Hindi or some language he did not recognize, then looked him in the eye while their AI spoke in English with an accent from the BBC or middle America or the New Delhi civil service, expressing some kind of unpredictable political sentiment. It was encouraging, really – not the translation AIs, which were just another kind of distancing, less extreme than teleparticipation but still not quite 'talking face to face' – but the political mélange, the impossibility of block-voting, or of even thinking in the normal constituencies.

It was a strange congregation, really. But it went on, and eventually everyone got used to it; it took on that always-already quality that extended events often gain over their duration. But once, very late at night, after a long bizarre translated conversation in which the AI on the wrist of the young woman he was talking to spoke in rhymed couplets (and he never knew what language she was speaking to start with), Art wandered back through the warehouse toward his office suite, around the table of tables, where work was still going on even though it was after the timeslip, and he stopped to say hi to one group; and then, momentum lost, slumped back against a side wall, half watching, half drowsing, his kavajava buzz nearly overwhelmed by exhaustion. And the strangeness came back, all at once. It was a kind of hypnogogic vision. There were shadows in the corners, innumerable flickering shadows; and eyes in the shadows. Shapes, like insubstantial bodies: all the dead, it suddenly seemed, and all the unborn, all there in the warehouse with them, to witness this moment. As if history were a tapestry, and the congress the loom upon which everything was coming together, the present moment with its miraculous thereness, its potential right in their own atoms, their own voices. Looking back at the past, able to see it all, a single, long, braided tapestry of events; looking forward at the future, able to see none of it, though presumably it branched out in an explosion of threads of potentiality, and could become anything: they were two different kinds of unreachable immensity. And all of them travelling together, from the one into the other, through that great loom the present, the now. Now was their chance, for all of them together in this present – the ghosts could watch, from before and after, but this was the moment when what wisdom they could muster had to be woven together, to be passed on to all the future generations.

They could do anything. That, however, was part of what made it difficult to bring the congress to a close. Infinite possibility was going to collapse, in the act of choosing, to the single worldline of history. The future becoming the past: there was something disappointing in this passage through the loom, this so-sudden diminution from infinity to one, the collapse from potentiality to reality which was the action of time itself. The potential was so delicious – the way they could have, potentially, all the best parts of all good governments of all time, combined magically into some superb, as yet unseen synthesis – or throw all that aside, and finally strike a new path to the heart of just government . . . To go from that to the mundane problematic of the constitution as written was an inevitable letdown, and instinctively people put it off.

On the other hand, it would certainly be a good thing if their diplomatic team were to arrive on Earth with a completed document to present to the UN and the people of Earth. Really, there was no avoiding it; they needed to finish; not just to present to Earth the united front of an established government, but also to start living their post-crisis life, whatever it might be.

Nadia felt this strongly, and so she began to exert herself. 'Time to drop the keystone into the arch,' she said to Art one morning. And from then on she was indefatigable, meeting all the delegations and committees, insisting that they finish whatever they were working on, insisting they get it on the table for a final vote on inclusion. This inexorable insistence of hers revealed something that had not been clear before, which was that most of the issues had been resolved to the satisfaction of most of the delegations. They had concocted something workable, most agreed, or at least worth trying, with amendment procedures prominent in the structure so that they could alter aspects of the system as they went along. The young natives in particular seemed happy – proud of their work, and pleased that they had managed to keep an emphasis on local semi-autonomy, institutionalizing the way most of them had lived under the Transitional Authority.

Thus the many checks against majoritarian rule did not bother them, even though they themselves were the current majority. In order not to look defeated by this development, Jackie and her circle had to pretend they had never argued for a strong presidency and central government in the first place; indeed they claimed that an executive council, elected by the legislature in the Swiss manner, had been their idea all along. A lot of that kind of thing was going on, and Art was happy to agree with all such claims: 'Yes, I remember, we were wondering what to do about that the night when we stayed up to see the sunrise, it was a good thought you had.'

Good ideas everywhere. And they began to spiral down toward closure.

The global government as they had designed it was to be a confederation, led by an executive council of seven members, elected by a two-housed legislature. One legislative branch, the duma, was composed of a large group of representatives drafted from the populace; the other, the senate, a smaller group elected one from each town or village group larger than five hundred people. The legislature was all in all fairly weak; it elected the executive council and helped select justices of the courts, and left to the towns most legislative duties. The judicial branch was more powerful; it included not only criminal courts, but also a kind of double supreme court, one half a constitutional court, and the other half an environmental court, with members to both appointed, elected and drawn by lottery. The environmental court would rule on disputes concerning terraforming and other environmental changes, while the constitutional court would rule on the constitutionality of all other issues, including challenged town laws. One arm of the environmental court would be a land commission, charged with overseeing the stewardship of the land, which was to belong to all Martians together, in keeping with point three of the Dorsa Brevia agreement; there would not be private property as such, but there would be various tenure rights established in leasing contracts, and the land commission was to work these matters out. A corresponding economic commission would function under the constitutional court, and would be partly composed of representatives from guild co-operatives which would be established for the various professions and industries. This commission was to oversee the establishment of a version of the underground's eco-economics, including both not-for-profit enterprises concentrating on the public sphere, and taxed for-profit enterprises which had legal size limits, and were by law employee-owned.

This expansion of the judiciary satisfied what desire they had for a strong global government, without giving an executive body much power; it was also a response to the heroic role played by Earth's World Court in the previous century, when almost every other Terran institution had been bought or otherwise collapsed under metanational pressures; only the World Court had held firm, issuing ruling after ruling on behalf of the disenfranchised and the land, in a mostly-ignored rearguard and indeed symbolic action against the metanats' depredations; a moral force, which if it had had more teeth, might have done more good. But from the Martian underground they had seen the battle fought, and now they remembered.

Thus the Martian global government. The constitution then also included a long list of human rights, including social rights; guidelines for the land commission and the economics commission; an Australian ballot election system for the elective offices; a system for amendments; and so on. Lastly, to the main text of the constitution they appended the huge collection of materials that had accumulated in the process, calling it Working Notes and Commentary. This was to be used to help the courts interpret the main document, and included everything the delegations had said at the table of tables, or written on the warehouse screens, or received in the mail.

So most of the sticky issues had been resolved, or at least swept under the rug; the biggest outstanding dispute was the Red objection. Art went into action here, orchestrating several late concessions to the Reds, including many early appointments to the environmental courts; these concessions were later termed the 'Grand Gesture'. In return Irishka, speaking for all the Reds still involved in the political process, agreed that the cable would stay, that UNTA would have a presence in Sheffield, that Terrans would still be able to immigrate, subject to restrictions; and lastly, that terraforming would continue, in slow non-disruptive forms, until the atmospheric pressure at six kilometres above the datum was 350 millibars, this figure to be reviewed every five years. And so the Red impasse was broken, or at least finessed.

Coyote shook his head at the way things had developed. 'After every revolution there is an interregnum, in which communities run themselves and all is well, and then the new regime comes in and screws things up. I think what you should do now is go out to the tents and canyons, and ask them very humbly how they have been running things these past two months, and then throw this fancy constitution away and say, *continue*.'

'But that's what the constitution does say,' Art joked.

Coyote would not kid about this. 'You must be very scrupulous not to gather power in to the centre just because you can do it. Power corrupts, that's the basic law of politics. Maybe the only law.'

As for UNTA, it was harder to tell what they thought, because opinions back on Earth were divided, with a loud faction calling for the retaking of Mars by force, everyone on Pavonis to be jailed or hanged. Most Terrans were more accommodating, and all of them were still distracted by the ongoing crisis at home. And at the moment, they didn't matter as much as the Reds; that was the space the revolution had given the Martians. Now they were about to fill it.

Every night of the final week, Art went to bed incoherent with cavils and kava, and though exhausted he would wake fairly often during the night, and roll under the force of some seemingly lucid thought that in the morning would be gone, or revealed as lunatic. Nadia slept just as poorly on the couch next to his, or in her chair. Sometimes they would fall asleep talking over some point or other, and wake up dressed but entangled, holding onto each other like children in a thunderstorm. The warmth of another body was a comfort like nothing else. And once in the dim predawn ultraviolet light they both woke up, and talked for hours in the cold silence of the building, in a little cocoon of warmth and companionship. Another mind to talk to. From colleagues to friends; from there to lovers, maybe; or something like lovers; Nadia did not seem inclined to romanticism of any kind. But Art was in love, no doubt about it, and there twinkled in Nadia's flecked eyes a new fondness for him, he thought. So that at the end of the long final days of the congress, they lay on their couches and talked, and she would knead his shoulders, or he hers, and then they would fall comatose, pounded by exhaustion. There was more pressure to ushering in this document than either one of them wanted to admit, except in these moments, huddling together against the cold big world. A new love: Art, despite Nadia's unsentimentality, found no other way to put it. He was happy.

And he was amused, but not surprised, when they got up one morning and she said, 'Let's put it to a vote.'

So Art talked to the Swiss and the Dorsa Brevia scholars, and the Swiss proposed to the congress that they vote on the version of the constitution currently on the table, voting point by point as they had promised in the beginning. Immediately there was a spasm of vote-trading that made Terran stock exchanges look subtle and slow. Meanwhile the Swiss set up a voting sequence, and over the course of three days they ran through it, allowing one vote to each group on each numbered paragraph of the draft constitution. All eighty-nine paragraphs passed, and the massive collection of 'explanatory material' was officially appended to the main text.

After that it was time to put it to the people of Mars for approval. So on Ls 158, 1 October 11th, M-year 52 (on Earth, February 27th, 2128), the general populace of Mars, including everyone over five M-years old, voted by wrist on the resulting document. Over ninety-five per cent of the population voted, and the constitution passed seventy-eight per cent to twenty-two per cent, garnering just over nine million votes. They had a government.

PART FOUR

Green Earth

On Earth, meanwhile, the great flood dominated everything.

The flood had been caused by a cluster of violent volcanic eruptions under the West Antarctic ice sheet. The land underneath the ice sheet, resembling North America's basin and range country, had been depressed by the weight of the ice until it lay below sea level. So when the eruptions began the lava and gases had melted the ice over the volcanoes, causing vast slippages overhead; at the same time, ocean water had started to pour in under the ice, at various points around the swiftly eroding grounding line. Destabilized and shattering, enormous islands of ice had broken off all around the edges of the Ross Sea and the Ronne Sea. As these islands of ice floated away on the ocean currents, the break-up continued to move inland, and the turbulence caused the process to accelerate. In the months following the first big breaks, the Antarctic Sea filled with immense tabular icebergs, which displaced so much water that sea level all over the world rose. Water continued to rush into the depressed basin in West Antarctica that the ice had once filled, floating out the rest of it berg by berg, until the ice sheet was entirely gone, replaced by a shallow new sea roiled by the continuing underwater eruptions, which were being compared in their severity to the Deccan Traps eruptions of the late Cretaceous.

And so, a year after the eruptions began, Antarctica was only a bit over half as big as it had been – East Antarctic like a half moon, the Antarctic peninsula like an iced-over New Zealand – in between them, a berg-clotted, bubbling, shallow sea. And around the rest of the world, sea level was seven metres higher than it had been before.

Not since the last ice age, ten thousand years before, had humanity experienced a natural catastrophe of such magnitude. And this time it affected not just a few million hunter-gatherers in nomadic tribes, but fifteen billion civilized citizens, living upon a precarious sociotechnological edifice which had already been in great danger of collapse. All the big coastal cities were inundated, whole countries like Bangladesh and Holland and Belize were awash. The unfortunates who lived in such low-lying regions usually had time to move to higher ground, for the surge was more like a tide than a tidal wave; and then there they all were, somewhere between ten and twenty per cent of the world's population – refugees.

It goes without saying that human society was not equipped to handle such a situation. Even in the best of times it would not have been easy, and the early twenty-second century had not been the best of times. Populations were still rising, resources were more and more depleted, conflicts between rich and poor, governments and metanats, had been sharpening everywhere: the catastrophe had struck in the midst of a crisis.

To a certain extent, the catastrophe cancelled the crisis. In the face of worldwide desperation, power struggles of all kinds were recontextualized, many rendered fantasmagorical; there were whole populations in need, and legalities of ownership and profit paled in comparison to the problem. The United Nations rose like some aquatic phoenix out of the chaos, and became the clearing house for the vast number of emergency relief efforts: migrations inland across national borders, construction of emergency accommodations, distribution of emergency food and supplies. Because of the nature of this work, with its emphasis on rescue and relief, Switzerland and Praxis were in the forefront of helping the UN. UNESCO returned from the dead, along with the World Health Organization. India and China, as the largest of the badly devastated countries, were also extremely influential in the current situation, because how they chose to cope made a big difference everywhere. They made alliances with each other, and with the UN and its new allies; they refused all help from the Group of Eleven, and the metanationals that were now fully intertwined into the affairs of most of the G-11 governments.

In other ways, however, the catastrophe only exacerbated the crisis. The metanationals themselves were cast into a very curious position by the flood. Before its onset they had been absorbed in what commentators had been calling the metanatricide, fighting among themselves for final control of the world economy. A few big metanational superclusters had been jockeying for ultimate control of the largest industrial countries, and attempting to subsume the few entities still out of their control: Switzerland, India, China, Praxis, the so-called World Court countries, and so on. Now, with much of the population of Earth occupied in dealing with the flood, the metanats were mostly struggling to regain what control they had had of affairs. In the popular mind they were often linked to the flood, as cause, or as punished sinners — a very convenient bit of magical thinking for Mars and the other anti-metanational forces, all of whom were doing their best to seize this chance to beat the metanats to pieces while they were down. The Group of Eleven and the other industrial governments previously associated with the metanats were scrambling to keep their own populations alive, and so could spare little effort to help the great conglomerates. And people everywhere were abandoning their previous jobs to join the various relief efforts; Praxis-style employee-owned enterprises were gaining in popularity as they took on the emergency, at the same time offering all their members the longevity treatment. Some of the metanats held onto their workforce by reconfiguring along these same lines. And so the struggle for power continued on many levels, but everywhere rearranged by the catastrophe.

In that context, Mars to most Terrans was completely irrelevant. Oh it made for an interesting story, of course, and many cursed the Martians as ungrateful children, abandoning their parents in the parents' hour of need; it was one example among many of bad responses to the flood, to be contrasted to the equally plentiful good responses. There were heroes and villains all over these days, and most regarded the Martians as villains, rats escaping a sinking ship. Others regarded them as potential saviours, in some ill-defined way: another bit of magical thinking, by and large; but there was something hopeful in the notion of a new society forming on the next world out.

Meanwhile, no matter what happened on Mars, the people of Earth struggled to cope with the flood. The damage now began to include rapid climatic changes: more cloud cover, reflecting more sunlight and causing temperatures to drop, also creating torrential rainstorms, which often wrecked much-needed crops, and sometimes fell where rain had seldom fallen before, in the Sahara, the Mojave, northern Chile — bringing the great flood far inland, in effect, bringing its *impact everywhere. And with agriculture hammered by these new severe storms, hunger itself became an issue; any general sense of co-operation was therefore threatened, as it seemed that perhaps not everyone could be fed, and the cowardly spoke of triage. And so every part of Terra was in turmoil, like an anthill stirred by a stick.*

So that was Earth in the summer of 2128: an unprecedented catastrophe, an ongoing universal crisis. The antediluvian world already seemed like no more than a bad dream from which they had all been rudely awakened, cast into an even more dangerous reality. From the frying pan into the fire, yes; and some people tried to get them back into the frying pan, while others struggled to get them off the stove; and no one could say what would happen next.

An invisible vice clamped down on Nirgal, each day more crushing than the last. Maya moaned and groaned about it, Michel and Sax did not seem to care; Michel was very happy to be making this trip, and Sax was absorbed in watching reports from the congress on Pavonis Mons. They lived in the rotating chamber of the spaceship *Atlantis*, and over the five months of the trip the chamber would accelerate until the centrifugal force shifted from Mars equivalent to Earth equivalent, remaining there for almost half the voyage. This was a method that had been worked out over the years, to accommodate emigrants who decided they wanted to return home, diplomats travelling back and forth, and the few Martian natives who had made the voyage to Earth. For everyone it was hard. Quite a few of the natives had fallen sick on Earth; some had died. It was important to stay in the gravity chamber, do one's exercises, take one's inoculations.

Sax and Michel worked out on exercise machines; Nirgal and Maya sat in the blessed baths, commiserating. Of course Maya enjoyed her misery, as she seemed to enjoy all her emotions, including rage and melancholy; while Nirgal was truly miserable, spacetime bending him in an ever more tortuous torque, until every cell of him cried out with the pain of it. It frightened him – the effort it took just to breathe, the idea of a planet so massive. Hard to believe!

He tried to talk to Michel about it, but Michel was distracted by his anticipation, his preparation; Sax by the events on Mars. Nirgal didn't care about the meeting back on Pavonis, it would not matter much in the long run, he judged. The natives in the outback had lived the way they wanted to under UNTA, and they would do the same under the new government. Jackie might succeed in making a presidency for herself, and that would be too bad; but no matter what happened, their relationship had gone strange, become a kind of telepathy which sometimes resembled the old passionate love affair but just as often felt like a vicious sibling rivalry, or even the internal arguments of a schizoid self. Perhaps they were twins – who knew what kind of alchemy Hiroko had performed in the ectogene tanks – but no – Jackie had been born of Esther. He knew that. If it proved anything. For to his dismay, she felt like his other self; he did not want that, he did not want the sudden speeding of his heart whenever he saw her. It was one of the reasons he had decided to join the expedition to Earth. And now he was getting away from her at the rate of fifty thousand kilometres an hour, but there she still was on the screen, happy at the ongoing work of the congress, and her part in it. And she would be one of the seven on the new executive council, no doubt about it.

'She is counting on history to take its usual course,' Maya said as they sat in the baths watching the news. 'Power is like matter, it has gravity, it clumps and then starts to draw more into itself. This local power, spread out through the tents —' She shrugged cynically.

'Perhaps it's a nova,' Nirgal suggested.

She laughed. 'Yes, perhaps. But then it starts clumping again. That's the gravity of history – power drawn into centres, until there is an occasional nova. Then a new drawing in. We'll see it on Mars too, you mark my words. And Jackie will be right at the middle of it —' She stopped before adding *the bitch*, in respect for Nirgal's feelings. Regarding him with a curious, hooded gaze, as if wondering what she might do with Nirgal that would advance her never-ending war with Jackie. Little novas of the heart.

The last weeks of one g passed, and never did Nirgal begin to feel comfortable. It was frightening to feel the clamping pressure on his breath and his thinking. His joints hurt. On the screens he saw images of the little blue-and-white marble that was the Earth, with the bone button of Luna looking peculiarly flat and dead beside it. But they were just more screen images, they meant nothing to him compared to his sore feet, his beating heart. Then the blue world suddenly blossomed and filled the screens entirely, its curved limb a white line, the blue water all patterned by white cloud swirls, the continents peeking out from cloud patterns like little rebuses of half-remembered myth: Asia. Africa. Europe. America.

For the final descent and aerobraking the gravity chamber's rotation was stopped. Nirgal, floating, feeling disembodied and balloonlike, pulled to a window to see it all with his own eyes. Despite the window glass and the thousands of kilometres of distance, the detail was startling in its sharp-edged clarity. 'The eye has such power,' he said to Sax.

'Hmm,' Sax said, and came to the window to look.

They watched the Earth, blue before them.

'Are you ever afraid?' Nirgal asked.

'Afraid?'

'You know.' Sax on this voyage had not been in one of his more coherent phases; many things had to be explained to him. 'Fear. Apprehension. Fright.'

'Yes. I think so. I was afraid, yes. Recently. When I found I was . . . disoriented.'

'I'm afraid now.'

Sax looked at him curiously. Then he floated over and put a hand to Nirgal's arm, in a gentle gesture quite unlike him. 'We're here,' he said.

Dropping, dropping. There were ten space elevators stranding out from Earth now. Several of them were what they called split cables, dividing into two branching strands that touched down north and south of the equator, which was woefully short of decent socket locations. One split cable Y-ed down to Virac in the Philippines and Oobagooma in western Australia, another to Cairo and Durban. The one they were descending split some ten thousand kilometres above the Earth, the north line touching down near Port of Spain, Trinidad, while the southern one dropped into Brazil near Aripuana, a boomtown on a tributary of the Amazon called the Theodore Roosevelt River.

They were taking the north fork, down to Trinidad. From their elevator car they looked down on most of the Western Hemisphere, centred over the Amazon basin, where brown water veined through the green lungs of Earth. Down and down; in the five days of their descent the world approached until it eventually filled everything below them, and the crushing gravity of the previous month and a half once again slowly took them in its grasp and squeezed, squeezed, squeezed. What little tolerance Nirgal had developed for the weight seemed to have disappeared during the brief return to microgravity, and now he gasped. Every breath an effort. Standing foursquare before the windows, hands clenched to the rails, he looked down through clouds on the brilliant blue of the Caribbean, the intense greens of Venezuela. The Orinoco's discharge into the sea was a leafy stain. The limb of the sky was composed of curved bands of white and turquoise, with the black of space above. All so glossy. The clouds were the same as on Mars but thicker, whiter, more stuffed with themselves. The intense gravity was perhaps exerting an extra pressure on his retina or optic nerve, to make the colours push and pulse so hard. Sounds were noisier.

In the elevator with them were UN diplomats, Praxis aides, media representatives, all hoping for the Martians to give them some time, to talk to them. Nirgal found it difficult to focus on them, to listen to them. Everyone seemed so strangely unaware of their position in space, there five hundred kilometres over the surface of the Earth, and falling fast.

A long last day. Then they were in the atmosphere, and then the cable led their car down onto the green square of Trinidad, into a huge socket complex next to an abandoned airport, its runways like grey runes. The elevator car slid down into the concrete mass. It decelerated; it came to a stop.

Nirgal detached his hands from the rail, and walked carefully after all the others, plod, plod, the weight all through him, plod, plod. They plodded down a jetway. He stepped onto the floor of a building on Earth. The interior of the socket resembled the one on Pavonis Mons, an incongruous familiarity, for the air was salty, thick, hot, clangorous, heavy. Nirgal hurried as much as he could through the halls, wanting to get outside and see things at last. A whole crowd trailed him, surrounded him, but the Praxis aides understood, they made a way for him through a growing crowd. The building was huge, apparently he had missed a chance to take a subway out of it. But there was a doorway glowing with light. Slightly dizzy with the effort, he walked out into a blinding glare. Pure whiteness. It reeked of salt, fish, leaves, tar, shit, spices: like a greenhouse gone mad.

Now his eyes were adjusting. The sky was blue, a turquoise blue like the middle band of the limb as seen from space, but lighter; whiter over the hills, magnesium around the sun. Black spots swam this way and that. The cable threaded up into the sky. It was too bright to look up. Green hills in the distance.

He stumbled as they led him to an open car – an antique, small and rounded, with rubber tyres. A convertible. He stood up in the back seat between Sax and Maya, just to see better. In the glare of light there were hundreds of people, thousands, dressed in astonishing costumes, neon silks, pink purple teal gold aquamarine, jewels, feathers, headdresses —

'Carnival,' someone in the front seat of the car said up to him, 'we dress in costumes for Carnival, also for Discovery Day, when Columbus arrive on the island. That was just a week ago, so we've continued the festival for your arrival too.'

'What's the date?' Sax asked.

'Nirgal Day! August the eleventh.'

They drove slowly, down streets lined with cheering people. One group was dressed like the natives before the Europeans arrived, shouting wildly. Mouths pink and white in brown faces. Voices like music, everyone singing. The people in the car sounded like Coyote. There were people in the crowd wearing Coyote masks, Desmond Hawkins's cracked face twisted into rubbery expressions beyond what even he could achieve. And words – Nirgal had thought that on Mars he had encountered every possible distortion of English, but it was hard to follow what the Trinidadians said: accent, diction, intonation, he couldn't tell why. He was sweating freely but still felt hot.

The car, bumpy and slow, ran between the walls of people to a short bluff. Beyond it lay a harbour district, now immersed in shallow water. Buildings swamped in the water stood in patches of dirty foam, rocking on unseen waves. A whole neighbourhood now a tidepool, the houses giant exposed mussels, some broken open, water sloshing in and out of their windows, rowing boats bobbing between them. Bigger boats were tied to streetlights and power-line poles out where the buildings stopped. Farther out sailboats tilted on the sunbeaten blue, each boat with two or three taut fore-and-aft sails. Green hills rising to the right, forming a big, open bay. 'Fishing boats still coming in through the streets, but the big ships use the bauxite docks down at Point T, see out there?'

Fifty different shades of green on the hills. Fish scales and flowers scattered over the road, silver and red. Palm trees in the shallows were dead, their fronds drooping yellow. These marked the tidal zone; above it green burst out everywhere. Streets and buildings were hacked out of a vegetable world. Green and white, as in his childhood vision, but here the two primal colours were separated out, held in a blue egg of sea and sky. They were just above the waves and yet the horizon was so far away! Instant evidence of the size of this world. No wonder they had thought the Earth was flat. The whitewater sloshing through the streets below made a continuous *krrrrr* sound, as loud as the cheers of the crowd.

The rank stench was suddenly cut by the smell of tar on the wind. 'Pitch Lake down by La Brea all dug out and shipped away, nothing left but a black hole in the ground, and a little pond we use locally. See that's what you smell, new road here by the water.' Asphalt road, sweating mirages. People jammed the black roadside; they all had black hair. A young woman climbed the car to put a necklace of flowers around his neck. Their sweet scent clashed with the stinging salt haze. Perfume and incense, chased by the hot vegetable wind, tarred and spiced. Steel drums, so familiar in all the hard noise, pinging and panging, they played Martian music here! The rooftops in the drowned district to their left now supported ramshackle patios. The stench was of a greenhouse gone bad, things rotting, a hot wet press of air and everything blazing in a talcum of light. Sweat ran freely down his skin. People cheered from the flooded rooftops, from boats, the water coated with flowers floating up and down on the foam. Black hair gleaming like chitin or jewels. A floating wood dock piled with several bands, playing different tunes all at once. Fish scales and flower petals strewn underfoot, silver and red and black dots swimming. Flung flowers flashed by on the wind, streaks of pure colour, yellow, pink and red. The driver of their car turned around to talk, ignoring the road, 'Hear the duglas play soaka music, pan music, listen that cuttin' contest, the best five bands in Port a Spain.'

They passed through an old neighbourhood, visibly ancient, the buildings made of small, crumbling bricks, capped by corrugated metal roofs, or even thatch – all ancient, tiny, the people tiny too, brown-skinned, 'The countryside Hindu, the cities black. T'n'T mix them, that's dugla.' Grass covered the ground, burst out of every crack in the walls, out of roofs, out of potholes, out of everything not recently paved by tarry asphalt – an explosive surge of green, pouring out of every surface of the world. The thick air reeked!

Then they emerged from the ancient district onto a broad asphalt boulevard, flanked by big trees and large marble buildings. 'Metanat grabhighs, looked big when they first built, but nothing grab as high as the cable.' Sour sweat, sweet smoke, everything blazing green, he had to shut his eyes so that he wouldn't be sick. 'You okay?' Insects whirred, the air was so hot he couldn't guess its temperature, it had gone off his personal scale. He sat down heavily between Maya and Sax.

The car stopped. He stood again, with an effort, and got out, and had trouble walking; he almost fell, everything was swinging around. Maya held his arm hard. He gripped his temples, breathed through his mouth. 'Are you okay?' she asked sharply.

'Yes,' Nirgal said, and tried to nod.

They were in a complex of raw, new buildings. Unpainted wood, concrete, bare dirt now covered with crushed flower petals. People everywhere, almost all in carnival costume. The singe of the sun in his eyes wouldn't go away. He was led to a wooden dais, above a throng of people cheering madly.

A beautiful black-haired woman in a green sari, with a white sash belting it, introduced the four Martians to the crowd. The hills behind bent like green flames in a strong western wind; it was cooler than before, and less smelly. Maya stood before the microphones and cameras, and the years fell away from her; she spoke crisp, isolated sentences that were cheered antiphonally, call and response, call and response. A media star with the whole world watching, comfortably charismatic, laying out what sounded to Nirgal like her speech in Burroughs at the crux point of the revolution, when she had rallied and focused the crowd in Princess Park. Something like that.

Michel and Sax declined to speak, they waved Nirgal up there to face the crowd and the green hills holding them up to the sun. For a time as he stood there he could not hear himself think. White noise of cheers, thick sound in the thicker air.

'Mars is a mirror,' he said in the microphone, 'in which Terra sees its own essence. The move to Mars was a purifying voyage, stripping away all but the most important things. What arrived in the end was Terran through and through. And what has happened since there has been an expression of Terran thought and Terran genes. And so, more than any material aid in scarce metals or new genetic strains, we can most help the home planet by serving as a way for you to see yourselves. As a way to map out an unimaginable immensity. Thus in our small way we do our part to create the great civilization that trembles on the brink of becoming. We are the primitives of an unknown civilization.'

Loud cheers.

'That's what it looks like to us on Mars, anyway – a long evolution through the centuries, toward justice and peace. As people learn more, they understand better their dependence on each other and on their world. On Mars we have seen that the best way to express this interdependence is to live for giving, in a culture of compassion. Every person free and equal in the sight of all, working together for the good of all. It's that work that makes us most free. No hierarchy is worth acknowledging but this one: the more we give, the greater we become. Now in the midst of a great flood, spurred by the great flood, we see the flowering of this culture of compassion, emerging on both the two worlds at once.'

He sat in a blaze of noise. Then the speeches were over and they had shifted into some kind of public press conference, responding to questions asked by the beautiful woman in the green sari. Nirgal responded with questions of his own, asking her about the new compound of buildings surrounding them, and about the situation on the island; and she answered over a chatter of commentary and laughter from the appreciative crowd, still looking on from behind the wall of reporters and cameras. The woman turned out to be the Prime Minister of Trinidad and Tobago. The little two-island nation had been unwillingly dominated by the metanat Armscor for most of the previous century, the woman explained, and only since the flood had they severed that association, 'and every colonial

178

bond at last'. How the crowd cheered! And her smile, so full of a whole society's pleasure. She was dugla, he saw, and amazingly beautiful.

The compound they were in, she explained, was one of scores of relief hospitals that had been built on the two islands since the flood. Their construction had been the major project of the islanders in response to their new freedom; they had created relief centres that aided flood victims, giving them all at once housing, work, and medical care, including the longevity treatment.

'Everyone gets the treatment?' Nirgal asked.

'Yes,' the woman said.

'Good!' Nirgal said, surprised; he had heard it was a rare thing on Earth.

'You think so!' the Prime Minister said. 'People are saying it will create all kinds of problems.'

'Yes. It will, in fact. But I think we should do it anyway. Give everyone the treatment and then figure out what to do.'

It was a minute or two before anything more could be heard over the cheering of the crowd. The Prime Minister was trying to quieten them, but a short man dressed in a fashionable brown suit came out of the group behind the Prime Minister and proclaimed into the mike, to an uproar of cheers at every sentence, 'This Marsman Nirgal is a son of Trinidad! His papa, Desmond Hawkins the Stowaway, the Coyote of Mars, is from Port of Spain, and he still has a lot of people there! That Armscor bought the oil company and they tried to buy the island too, but they picked the wrong island to try! Your Coyote didn't get his spirit from out of the air, Maistro Nirgal, he got it from T and T! He's been wandering around up there teaching everyone the T and T way, and they're all up there dugla anyway, they understand the dugla way, and they have taken over all Mars with it! Mars is one great big Trinidad Tobago!'

The crowd went into transports at this, and impulsively Nirgal walked over to the man and hugged him, such a smile, then found the stairs and got down and walked out into the crowd, which clumped around him. A miasma of fragrances. Too loud to think. He touched people, shook hands. People touched him. The look in their eyes! Everyone was shorter than he was, they laughed at that; and every face was an entire world. Black dots swam in his vision, things went darker very abruptly – he looked around, startled – a bank of clouds had massed over a dark strip of sea to the west, and the lead edge had cut off the sun. Now, as he continued to mingle, the cloudbank came rolling over the island. The crowd broke up as people moved under the shelter of trees, or verandas, or a big tin-roofed bus stop. Maya and Sax and Michel were lost in their own crowds. The clouds were dark grey at their bases, rearing up in white roils as solid as rock but mutable, flowing continuously. A cool wind struck hard, and then big raindrops starred the dirt, and the four Martians were hustled under an open pavilion roof, where room was made for them.

Then the rain poured down like nothing Nirgal had ever seen – rain sheeting down, roaring, slamming into sudden broad rivering puddles, all starred with a million white droplet explosions, the whole world outside the pavilion blurred by falling water into patches of colour, green and brown all mixed in a wash. Maya was grinning: 'It's like the ocean is falling on us!'

'So much water!' Nirgal said.

The Prime Minister shrugged. 'It happens every day during monsoon. It's more rain than before, and we already got a lot.'

Nirgal shook his head and felt a stabbing at his temples. The pain of breathing in wet air. Half drowning.

The Prime Minister was explaining something to them, but Nirgal could barely follow, his head hurt so. Anyone in the independence movement could join a Praxis affiliate, and during their first year's work they were building relief centres like this one. The longevity treatment was an automatic part of every person's joining, administered in the newly built centres. Birth control implants could be had at the same time, reversible but permanent if left in; many took them as their contribution to the cause. 'Babies later, we say. There will be time.' People wanted to join anyway, almost everyone had. Armscor had been forced to match the Praxis arrangement to keep some of their people, and so it made little difference now which organization one was part of; on Trinidad they were all much the same. The newly treated went on to build more housing, or work in agriculture, or make more hospital equipment. Trinidad had been fairly prosperous before the flood, the combined result of vast oil reserves and metanat investment in the cable socket. There had been a progressive tradition which had formed the basis of the resistance, in the years after the unwelcome metanat arrival. Now there was a growing infrastructure dedicated to the longevity project. It was a promising situation. Every camp was a waiting list for the treatment, working on its own construction. Of course people were absolutely firm in the defence of such places. Even if Armscor had wanted to, it would be very difficult for its security forces to take over the camps. And if they did they would find nothing of value to them anyway; they already had the treatment. So they could try genocide if they wanted to, but other than that, they had few options for taking back control of the situation.

'The island just walked away from them,' the Prime Minister concluded. 'No army can stop that. It is an end to economic caste, caste of all kind. This is something new, a new dugla thing in history, like you said in your speech. Like a little Mars. So to have you here to see us, you a grandchild of the island, you who have taught us so much in your beautiful new world – oh, it is a special thing. A festival for real.' That radiant smile.

'Who was the man who spoke?'

'Oh, that was James.'

Abruptly the rain let up. The sun broke through, and the world steamed. Sweat poured down Nirgal in the white air. He could not catch his breath. White air, black spots swimming.

'I think I need to lie down.'

'Oh yes, yes, of course. You must be exhausted, overwhelmed. Come with us.'

They took him to a small outbuilding of the compound, into a bright room walled with bamboo strips, empty except for a mattress on the floor.

'I'm afraid the mattress is not long enough for you.'

'It doesn't matter.'

He was left alone. Something about the room reminded him of the interior of Hiroko's cottage, in the grove on the far side of the lake in Zygote. Not just the bamboo, but the room's size and shape – and something elusive, the green light

181

streaming in perhaps. The sensation of Hiroko's presence was so strong and so unexpected that when the others had left the room, Nirgal threw himself down on the mattress, his feet hanging far off the bottom edge, and cried. A complete confusion of feeling. His whole body hurt, but especially his head. He stopped crying and fell into a deep sleep.

He woke in a small black chamber. It smelled green. He couldn't remember where he was. He rolled onto his back and it came to him: Earth. Whispers – he sat up, frightened. A muffled laugh. Hands caught at him and pressed him down, but they were friendly hands, he could feel that immediately. 'Shh,' someone said, and then kissed him. Someone else was fumbling at his belt, his buttons. Women, two, three, no two, scented overpoweringly with jasmine and something else, two strands of perfume, both warm. Sweaty skin, so slick. The arteries in his head pounded. This kind of thing had happened to him once or twice when he was younger, when the newly-tented canyons were like new worlds, with new young women who wanted to get pregnant or just have fun. After the celibate months of the voyage it felt like heaven to squeeze women's bodies, to kiss and be kissed, and his initial fright melted away in a rush of hands and mouths, breasts and tangled legs. 'Sister Earth,' he gasped. There was music coming from somewhere far away, piano and steel drums and tablas, almost washed out by the sound of the wind in the bamboo. One of the women was on top of him, pressed down on him, and the feel of her ribs sliding under his hands would stay with him forever. He came inside her, kept on kissing. But his head still pounded painfully.

The next time he woke he was damp and naked on the mattress. It was still dark. He dressed and went out of the room, down a dim hallway to an enclosed porch. It was dusk; he had slept through a day. Maya and Michel and Sax were sitting down to a meal with a large group. Nirgal assured them he was fine, ravenous in fact.

He sat among them. Out in the clearing, in the middle of the raw, wet compound, a crowd was gathered around an outdoor kitchen. Beyond them a bonfire blazed yellow in the dusk; its flames limned the dark faces and reflected in the bright liquid whites of their eyes, their teeth. The people at the inside table all looked at him. Several of the young women smiled, their

183

jet hair like caps of jewels, and for a second Nirgal was afraid he smelled of sex and perfume; but the smoke from the bonfire, and the steamy scents of the spiced dishes on the table, made such a thing irrelevant – in such an explosion of smells, nothing could be traced to its origin – and anyway one's olfactory system was blasted by the food, hot with spices, curry and cayenne, chunks of fish on rice, with a vegetable that seared his mouth and throat, so that he spent the next half hour blinking and sniffing and drinking glasses of water, his head burning. Someone gave him a slice of candied orange, which cooled his mouth somewhat. He ate several slices of bittersweet candied orange.

When the meal was over they all cleared the tables together, as in Zygote or Hiranyagarbha. Outside, dancers began to circle the bonfire, dressed in their surreal carnival costumes, with masks of beasts and demons over their heads, as during Fassnacht in Nicosia, although the masks were heavier and stranger: demons with multiple eyes and big teeth, elephants, goddesses. The trees were black against the blurry black of the sky, the stars all fat and swinging around, the fronds and leaves up there green black black green, and then fire-coloured as the flames leaped higher, seeming to provide the rhythm of the dance. A small young woman with six arms, all moving together to the dance, stepped behind Nirgal and Maya. 'This is the dance of Ramayana,' she told them. 'It is as old as civilization, and in it they speak of Mangala.'

She gave Nirgal a familiar squeeze on the shoulder, and suddenly he recognized her jasmine scent. Without smiling she went back out to the bonfire. The tabla drums were following the leaping flames to a crescendo, and the dancers cried out. Nirgal's head throbbed at every beat, and despite the candied orange his eyes were still watering from the burning pepper. And his lids were heavy. 'I know it's strange,' he said, 'but I think I have to sleep again.'

He woke before dawn, and went out on a veranda to watch the sky lighten in a quite Martian sequence, black to purple to rose to pink, before turning the startling cyanic blue of a tropical Terran morning. His head was still sore, as if stuffed, but he felt rested at last, and ready to take on the world again. After a breakfast of green-brown bananas, he and Sax joined some of their hosts for a drive around the island.

Everywhere they went there were always several hundred people in his field of vision. The people were all small: brown-skinned like him in the countryside, darker in the towns. There were big vans that moved around together, providing mobile shops to villages too small to have them. Nirgal was surprised to see how lean people were, their limbs wiry with labour or else as thin as reeds. In this context the curves of the young women were like the blooms of flowers, not long for this world.

When people saw who he was they rushed up to greet him and shake his hand. Sax shook his head at the sight of Nirgal among them. 'Bimodal distribution,' he said. 'Not speciation exactly – but perhaps if enough time passed. Island divergence, it's very Darwinian.'

'I'm a Martian,' Nirgal agreed.

Their buildings were placed in holes hacked into the green jungle, which then tried to take the space back. The older buildings were all made of mud bricks black with age, melting back into the earth. Rice fields were terraced so finely that the hills looked further away than they really were. The light green of rice shoots was a colour never seen on Mars. In general the greens were brilliant and glowing beyond anything Nirgal could recall seeing; they pressed on him, so various and intense, the sun plating his back: 'It's because of the sky's colour,' Sax said when Nirgal mentioned it. 'The reds in the Martian sky mute the greens just a bit.'

The air was thick, wet, rancid. The shimmering sea settled on a distant horizon. Nirgal coughed, breathed through his mouth, struggled to ignore his throbbing temples and fore-head.

'You have low altitude sickness,' Sax speculated. 'I've read claims that it happens to Himalayans and Andeans who come down to sea level. Acidity levels in the blood. We ought to have landed you somewhere higher.'

'Why didn't we?'

'They wanted you here because Desmond came from here. This is your homeland. Actually there seems to be a bit of conflict over who should host us next.'

'Even here?'

'More here than on Mars, I should think.'

Nirgal groaned. The weight of the world, the stifling air — 'I'm going running,' he said, and took off.

At first it was its usual release; the habitual motions and responses poured through him, reminding him that he was still himself. But as he thumped along he did not ascend into that *lung-gom-pa* zone where running was like breathing, something he could do indefinitely; instead he began to feel the press of the thick air in his lungs, and the pressure of eyes from the little people he passed, and most of all the pressure of his own weight, hurting his joints. He weighed more than twice what he was used to, and it was like carrying an invisible person on his back, except no – the weight was inside him. As if his bones had turned to lead inside him. His lungs burned and drowned at the same time, and no cough would get them clear. There were taller people in Western clothes behind him now, on little three-wheeled bicycles that splashed through every puddle. But locals were stepping into the road behind him, crowds of them blocking off the tricyclers, their eyes and teeth gleaming in their dark faces as they talked and laughed. The men on the tricycles had blank faces, and they were looking at Nirgal. But they did not challenge the crowd. Nirgal headed back toward the camp, turning down a new road. Now the green hills were blazing to his right. The road jarred up through his legs with every step, until his legs were like tree trunks aflame. That running should hurt! And his head was like a giant balloon. All the wet green plants seemed to be reaching out for him, a hundred shades of green flame melding to one dominant colour band, pouring into the world. Black dots swimming. 'Hiroko,' he gasped, and ran on with the tears streaming down his face; no one would be able to tell them from sweat. Hiroko, it isn't the way you said it would be!

He stumbled into the ochre soil of the compound, and scores of people followed him to Maya. Soaking as he was, he still threw his arms around her and put his head down on her shoulder, sobbing.

'We should get to Europe,' Maya said angrily to someone over his back. 'This is stupid, to bring him right to the tropics like this.'

Nirgal shifted to look back. It was the Prime Minister. 'This is how we always live,' she said, and pierced Nirgal with a resentful, proud look.

But Maya was unimpressed. 'We have to go to Berne,' she said.

They flew to Switzerland in a small spaceplane provided by Praxis. As they travelled, they looked down on the Earth from thirty thousand metres: the blue Atlantic, the rugged mountains of Spain, somewhat like the Hellespontus Montes; then France; then the white wall of the Alps, unlike any mountains he had ever seen. The cool ventilation of the spaceplane felt like home to Nirgal, and he was chagrined to think that he could not tolerate the open air of Earth.

'You'll do better in Europe,' Maya told him.

Nirgal thought about the reception they had got. 'They love you here,' he said. Overwhelmed as he had been, he had still noticed that the welcome of the duglas had been as enthusiastic for the other three ambassadors as for him; and Maya had been particularly cherished.

'They're happy we survived,' Maya said, dismissing it. 'We came back from the dead as far as they're concerned, like magic. They thought we were dead, do you see? From '61 until just last year, they thought all the First Hundred were dead. Sixty-seven years! And all that time part of them was dead too. To have us come back like we have, and in this flood, with everything changing – yes. It's like a myth. The return from underground.'

'But not all of you.'

'No.' She almost smiled. 'They still have to sort that out. They think Frank is alive, and Arkady – and John too, even though John was killed years before '61, and everyone knew it! For a while, anyway. But people are forgetting things. That was a long time ago. And so much has happened since. And people want John Boone to be alive. And so they forget Nicosia, and say that he is part of the underground still.' She laughed shortly, unsettled by this.

'As with Hiroko,' Nirgal said, feeling his throat constrict. A wave of sadness like the one in Trinidad washed through

187

him, leaving him bleached and aching. He believed, he had always believed, that Hiroko was alive, and hiding with her people somewhere in the southern highlands. This was how he had coped with the shock of the news of her disappearance – by being quite certain that she had slipped out of Sabishii, and would turn up again when she felt the time was right. He had been sure of it. Now, for some reason he could not tell, he was no longer sure.

In the seat on the other side of Maya, Michel sat with a pinched expression on his face. Suddenly Nirgal felt as if he were looking in a mirror; he knew his face held the same expression, he could feel it in his muscles. He and Michel both had doubts – perhaps about Hiroko, perhaps about other things. No way of telling. Michel did not seem inclined to speak.

And from across the plane Sax watched them both, with his usual birdlike gaze.

They dropped out of the sky paralleling the great north wall of the Alps, and landed on a runway among green fields. They were escorted through a cool Marslike building, downstairs and onto a train, which slid metallically up and out of the building, and across green fields; and in an hour they were in Berne.

In Berne the streets were mobbed by diplomats and reporters, everyone with an ID badge on their chest, everyone with a mission to speak to them. The city was small and pristine and rock-solid: the feeling of gathered power was palpable. Narrow stone-flagged streets were flanked by thickly arcaded stone buildings, everything as permanent as a mountain, with the swift river Aare S-ing through it, holding the main part of town in one big oxbow. The people crowding that quarter were mostly Europeans: meticulous-looking white people, not as short as most Terrans, milling around, absorbed in their talk, and always a good number of them clustering around the Martians and their escorts, who now were blue-uniformed Swiss military police.

Nirgal and Sax and Michel and Maya were given rooms in the Praxis headquarters, in a small stone building just above the Aare River. It amazed Nirgal how close to water the Swiss were willing to build; a rise in the river of even two metres would spell disaster, but they did not care; apparently they had the river under control that tight, even though it came out of the steepest mountain range Nirgal had ever seen! Terraforming, indeed; it was no wonder the Swiss were good on Mars.

The Praxis building was just a few streets from the old centre of the city. The World Court occupied a scattering of offices next to the Swiss federal buildings, near the middle of the peninsula. So every morning they walked down the cobbled main street, the *Kramgasse*, which was incredibly clean, bare and underpopulated compared with any street in Port of Spain. They passed under the medieval clock tower, with its ornate face and mechanical figures, like one of Michel's alchemical diagrams made into a three-dimensional object; then into the World Court offices, where they talked to group after group about the situations on Mars and Earth: UN officials, national government representatives, metanational executives, relief organizations, media groups. Everyone wanted to know what was happening on Mars, what Mars planned to do next, what they thought of the situation on Earth, what Mars could offer Earth in the way of help. Nirgal found most of the people he was introduced to fairly easy to talk to; they seemed to understand the respective situations on the two worlds, they were not unrealistic about Mars's ability somehow to 'save Earth'; they did not seem to expect to control Mars ever again, nor did they expect the meta-national world order of the antediluvian years to return.

It was likely, however, that the Martians were being screened from people who had a more hostile attitude toward them. Maya was quite certain this was the case. She pointed out how often the negotiators and interviewers revealed what she called their 'terracentricity'. Nothing mattered to them, really, but things Earthly; Mars was interesting in some ways, but not actually important. Once this attitude was pointed out to Nirgal, he saw it again and again. And in fact he found it comforting. The corresponding attitude existed on Mars, certainly, as the natives were inevitably areocentric; and it made sense, it was a kind of realism.

Indeed it began to seem to him that it was precisely the Terrans who showed an intense interest in Mars who were the most troubling to contemplate: certain metanat executives whose corporations had invested heavily in Martian terraformation; also certain national representatives from heavily populated countries, who would no doubt be very happy to have a place to send large numbers of their people. So he sat in meetings with people from Armscor, Subarashii, China, Indonesia, Ammex, India, Japan and the Japanese metanat council; and he listened most carefully, and did his best to ask questions rather than talk overmuch; and he saw that some of their staunchest allies up to that point, especially India and China, were likely in the new dispensation to become their most serious problem. Maya nodded emphatically when he made this observation to her, her face grim. 'We can only hope that sheer distance will save us,' she said. 'How lucky we are that it takes space travel to reach us. That should be a bottleneck for emigration no matter how advanced transport methods become. But we will have to keep our guard up, forever. In fact, don't speak much of these things here. Don't speak much at all.'

During lunch breaks Nirgal asked his escort group – a dozen or more Swiss who stayed with him every waking hour – to walk with him over to the cathedral, which someone told Nirgal was called in Swiss *the monster*. It had a tower at one end, containing a tight spiral staircase one could ascend, and almost every day Nirgal took several deep breaths and then pushed on up this staircase, gasping and sweating as he neared the top. On clear days, which were not frequent, he could see out the open arches of the top room to the distant abrupt wall of the Alps, a wall he had learned to call the Berner Oberland. This jagged white wall ran from horizon to horizon, like one of the great Martian escarpments, only covered everywhere with snow, everywhere except for on triangular north faces of exposed rock, rock of a light grey colour, unlike anything on Mars: granite. Granite mountains, raised by tectonic plate collision. And the violence of these origins showed.

Between this majestic white range and Berne lay a number

of lower ranges of green hills, the grassy alps similar to the greens in Trinidad, the conifer forests a darker green. So much green – again Nirgal was astounded by how much of Earth was covered with plant life, the lithosphere smothered in a thick ancient blanket of biosphere. 'Yes,' Michel said, along one day to view the prospect with him. 'The biosphere at this point has even formed a great deal of the upper layer of rock. Everywhere life teems, it *teems*.'

Michel was dying to get to Provence. They were near it, an hour's flight or a night's train; and everything that was going on in Berne seemed to Michel only the endless wrangling of politics. 'Flood or revolution or the sun going nova, it will still go on! You and Sax can deal with it, you can do what needs doing better than I.'

'And Maya even more so.'

'Well, yes. But I want her to come with me. She has to see it, or she won't understand.'

Maya, however, was absorbed in the negotiations with the UN, which were getting serious now that the Martians back home had approved the new constitution. The UN was turning out still to be very much a metanat mouthpiece, just as the World Court continued to support the new 'co-op democracies'; and so the arguments in the various meeting-rooms, and via video transmission, were vigorous, volatile, sometimes hostile. Important, in a word, and Maya went out to do battle every day; so she had no patience at all for the idea of Provence. She had visited the south of France in her youth, she said, and was not greatly interested in seeing it again, even with Michel. 'She says the beaches are all gone!' Michel complained. 'As if the beaches were what mattered to Provence!'

In any case, she wouldn't go. Finally, after a few weeks had passed, Michel shrugged and gave up, unhappily, and decided to visit Provence on his own.

On the day he left, Nirgal walked him down to the railway station at the end of the main street, and stood waving at the slowly accelerating train as it left the station. At the last moment Michel stuck his head out of a window, waving back at Nirgal with a huge grin. Nirgal was shocked to see this unprecedented expression, so quickly replacing the discouragement at Maya's absence; then he felt happy for his friend;

then he felt a flash of envy. There was no place that would make him feel so good to be going to, not anywhere in the two worlds.

After the train disappeared, Nirgal walked back down *Kramgasse* in the usual cloud of escorts and media eyes, and hauled his two-and-a-half bodies up the two hundred and fifty-four spiral stairs of the Monster, to stare south at the wall of the Berner Oberland. He was spending a lot of time up there; sometimes he missed early afternoon meetings, let Sax and Maya take care of it. The Swiss were running things in their usual businesslike fashion. The meetings had agendas, and started on time, and if they didn't get through the agenda, it wasn't because of the Swiss in the room. They were just like the Swiss on Mars, like Jurgen and Max and Priska and Sibilla, with their sense of order, of appropriate action well performed, with a tough, unsentimental love of comfort, of predictable decency. It was an attitude that Coyote laughed at, or disdained as life-threatening; but seeing the results in the elegant stone city below him, overflowing with flowers and people as prosperous as flowers, Nirgal thought there must be something to be said for it. He had been homeless for so long. Michel had his Provence to go to, but for Nirgal no place endured. His home town was crushed under a polar cap, his mother had disappeared without a trace, and every place since then had been just a place, and everything everywhere always changing. Mutability was his home. And looking over Switzerland, it was a hard thing to realize. He wanted a home place that had something like these tile roofs, these stone walls, here and solid these last thousand years.

He tried to focus on the meetings in the World Court, and in the Swiss Bundeshaus. Praxis was still leading the way in the response to the flood, it was good at working without plans, and it had already been a co-operative concentrating on the production of basic goods and services, including the longevity treatment. So it only had to accelerate that process to take the lead in showing what could be done in the emergency. The four travellers had seen the results in Trinidad; local movements did most of it, but Praxis was helping projects like that all over the world. William Fort was said to have been critical in leading the fluid response of the 'collective transnat', as he called Praxis. And his mutant metanational was only one of hundreds of services agencies that had come to the fore. All over the world they were taking on the problem of relocating the coastal populations, and building or relocating a new coastal infrastructure on higher ground.

This loose network of reconstruction efforts, however, was running into some resistance from the metanats, who complained that a good deal of their infrastructure, capital and labour were being nationalized, localized, appropriated, salvaged, or stolen outright. Fighting was not infrequent, especially where fights had already been ongoing; the flood, after all, had arrived right in the middle of one of the world's paroxysms of breakdown and reordering, and although it had altered everything, that struggle was often still happening, sometimes under the cover of the relief efforts.

Sax Russell was particularly aware of this context, convinced as he was that the global wars of 2061 had never resolved the basic inequities of the Terran economic system. In his own peculiar fashion he was insistent on this point in the meetings, and over time it seemed to Nirgal that he was managing to convince the sceptical listeners of the UN and the metanats that they all needed to pursue something like the Praxis method if they wanted themselves and civilization to survive. It did not matter much which of the two they really cared about, he said to Nirgal in private, themselves or civilization; it didn't matter if they only instituted some Machiavellian simulacrum of the Praxis programme; the effect would be much the same in the short term, and everyone needed that grace period of peaceful co-operation.

So in every meeting he was painfully focused, and fairly coherent and engaged, especially compared to his deep abstraction during the voyage to Earth. And Sax Russell was after all the Terraformer of Mars, the current living avatar of the Great Scientist, a very powerful position in Terran culture, Nirgal thought – something like the Dalai Lama of science, a continuing reincarnation of the embodiment of the spirit of science, created for a culture that only seemed to be able to handle one scientist at a time. Also, to the metanats Sax was the principal creator of the biggest new market in history – not an inconsiderable part of his aura. And, as Maya had pointed out, he was one of that group that had returned from the dead, one of the leaders of the First Hundred.

As with all these things, his odd halting style actually helped to build the Terrans' image of him. Simple verbal difficulty turned him into a kind of oracle; the Terrans seemed to believe that he thought on such a lofty plane that he could only speak in riddles. This was what they wanted, perhaps. This was what science meant to them – after all, current physical theory spoke of ultimate reality as ultramicroscopic loops of string, moving supersymmetrically in ten dimensions. That kind of thing had inured people to strangeness from physicists. And the increasing use of translation AIs was getting everyone used to odd locutions of all types; almost everyone Nirgal met spoke English, but they were all slightly different Englishes, so that Earth seemed to Nirgal an explosion of idiolects, no two people employing the same tongue.

In that context, Sax was listened to with the utmost seriousness. 'The flood marks a break point in history,' he said one morning, to a large general meeting in the Bundeshaus's National Council Chamber. 'It was a natural revolution. Weather on Earth is changed, also the land, the sea's currents. The distribution of human and animal populations. There is no reason, in this situation, to try to reinstate the antediluvian world. It's not possible. And there are many reasons to institute an improved social order. The old one was – flawed. Resulting in bloodshed, hunger, servitude and war. Suffering. Unnecessary death. There will always be death. But it should come for every person as late as possible. At the end of a good life. This is the goal of any rational social order. So we see the flood as an opportunity – here as it was on Mars – to – break the mould.'

The UN officials and the metanat advisers frowned at this, but they listened. And the whole world was watching; so that what a cadre of leaders in a European city thought was not as important, Nirgal judged, as the people in their villages, watching the man from Mars on the vid. And as Praxis and the Swiss and their allies worldwide had thrown all their resources into refugee aid and the longevity treatments, people everywhere were joining up. If you could make a living while saving the world – if it represented your best chance for stability and

194

long life and your children's chances – then why not? Why not? What did most people have to lose? The late metanational period had benefited some, but billions had been left out, in an ever-worsening situation.

So the metanats were losing their workers en masse. They couldn't imprison them; it was getting hard to scare them; the only way they could keep them was to institute the same sorts of programmes that Praxis had started. And this they were doing, or so they said. Maya was sure they were instituting superficial changes meant to resemble Praxis's only in order to keep their workers and their profits too. But it was possible that Sax was right, and that they would be unable to keep control of the situation, and would usher in a new order despite themselves.

Which is what Nirgal decided to say, during one of his chances to speak, in a press conference in a big side room of the Bundeshaus. Standing at the podium, looking out at a room full of reporters and delegates – so unlike the improvised table in the Pavonis warehouse, so unlike the compound hacked out of the jungle in Trinidad, so unlike the stage in the sea of people during that wild night in Burroughs – Nirgal saw suddenly that his role was to be the young Martian, the voice of the new world. He could leave being reasonable to Maya and Sax, and provide the alien point of view.

'It's going to be all right,' he said, looking at as many of them as he could. 'Every moment in history contains a mix of archaic elements, things from all over the past, right back into prehistory itself. The present is always a mélange of these variously archaic elements. There are still knights coming through on horseback and taking the crops of peasants. There are still guilds, and tribes. Now we see so many people leaving their jobs to work in the flood relief efforts. That's a new thing, but it's also a pilgrimage. They want to be pilgrims, they want to have a spiritual purpose, they want to do real work – meaningful work. There is no reason to keep being stolen from. Those of you here who represent the aristocracy look worried. Perhaps you will have to work for yourselves, and live off that. Live at the same level as anyone else. And it's true – that will happen. But it's going to be all right, even for you. Enough is as good as a feast. And it's when everyone is equal that your kids are safest. This universal distribution of the longevity treatment that we are now seeing is the ultimate meaning of the democratic movement. It's the physical manifestation of democracy, here at last. Health for all. And when that happens the explosion of positive human energy is going to transform the Earth in just a matter of years.'

Someone in the crowd stood and asked him about the possibility of a population explosion, and he nodded. 'Yes of course. This is a real problem. You don't have to be a demographer to see that if new ones continue being born while the elderly are not dying, population will quickly soar to incredible levels. Unsustainable levels, until there will be a crash. So. This has to be faced now. The birth rate simply has to be cut, at least for a while. It isn't a situation that has to last forever. The longevity treatments are not immortality treatments. Eventually the first generations given the treatment will die. And therein lies the solution to the problem. Say the current population on the two worlds is fifteen billion. That means we're already starting from a bad spot. Given the severity of the problem, as long as you get to be a parent at all, there is no reason to complain; it's your own longevity causing the problem after all, and parenthood is parenthood, one child or ten. So say that each person partners, and the two parents have only a single child, so that there is one child for every two people in the previous generation. Say that means seven and a half billion children out of this present generation. And they are all given the longevity treatment too, of course, and cosseted until they are the no doubt insufferable royalty of the world. And they go on to have four billion children, the new royalty, and that generation has two, and so on. All of them are alive at once, and the population is rising all the time, but at a lower rate as time passes. And then at some point, maybe a hundred years from now, maybe a thousand years from now, that first generation will die. It may happen over a fairly short period of time, but fast or slow, when the process is done, the overall population will be almost halved. At that point people can look at the situation, the infrastructure, the environments of the two worlds – the carrying capacity of the entire solar system, whatever that might be. After the biggest generations are gone, people can start having

196

two children each, perhaps, so that there is replacement, and a steady state. Or whatever. When they have that kind of choice, the population crisis will be over. It could take a thousand years.'

Nirgal stopped to look outside of himself, to stare around at the audience; people watching him rapt, silent. He gestured with a hand, to draw them all together. 'In the meantime, we have to help each other. We have to regulate ourselves, we have to take care of the land. And it's here, in this part of the project, that Mars can help Earth. First, we are an experiment in taking care of the land. Everyone learns from that, and some lessons can be applied here. Then, more importantly, though most of the population will always be located here on Earth, a goodly fraction of it can move to Mars. It will help ease the situation, and we'll be happy to take them. We have an obligation to take on as many people as we possibly can, because we on Mars are Terrans still, and we are all in this together. Earth and Mars – and there are other habitable worlds in the solar system as well, none as big as our two, but there are a lot of them. And by using them all, and cooperating, we can get through the populated years. And walk out into a golden age.'

That day's talk made quite an impression, as far as one could tell from within the eye of the media storm. Nirgal conversed for hours every day after that, with group after group, elaborating the ideas he had first expressed in that meeting. It was exhausting work, and after a few weeks of it without any let-up, he looked out of his bedroom window one cloudless morning, and went out and talked to his escort about making an expedition. And the escort agreed to tell the people in Berne he was touring privately; and they took a train up into the Alps.

The train ran south from Berne, past a long blue lake called the Thunersee, which was flanked by steep grassy alps, and ramparts and spires of grey granite. The lakeside towns were topped by slate roof tiles, dominated by ancient trees and an occasional castle, everything in perfect repair. The vast green pastures between the towns were dotted with big wooden

197

farmhouses, with red carnations in flowerboxes at every window and balcony. It was a style that had not changed in five hundred years, the escorts told him. Settling into the land, as if natural to it. The green alps had been cleared of trees and stones – in their original state they had been forests. So they were terraformed spaces, huge hilly lawns that had been created to provide forage for cattle. Such an agriculture had not made economic sense as capitalism defined it, but the Swiss had supported the high farms anyway, because they thought it was important, or beautiful, or both at once. It was Swiss. 'There are values higher than economic values,' Vlad had insisted back in the congress on Mars, and Nirgal saw now how there were people on Earth who had always believed that, at least in part. *Werteswandel*, they were saying down in Berne, mutation of values; but it could as well be evolution of values, return of values; gradual change, rather than punctuated equilibrium; benevolent residual archaisms, which endured and endured, until slowly these high isolated mountain valleys had taught the world how to live, their big farmhouses floating by on green waves. A shaft of yellow sun split the clouds and struck the hill behind one such farm, and the alp gleamed in an emerald mass, so intensely green that Nirgal felt disoriented, then actually dizzy; it was hard to focus on such a radiant green!

The heraldic hill disappeared. Others appeared in the window, wave after green wave, luminous with their own reality. At the town of Interlaken the train turned and began to ascend a valley so steep that in places the tracks entered tunnels into the rocky sides of the valley, and spiralled a full 360° inside the mountain before coming back out into the sun, the head of the train right above the tail. The train ran on tracks rather than pistes because the Swiss had not been convinced that the new technology was enough of an improvement to justify replacing what they already had. And so the train vibrated, and even rocked from side to side, as it rumbled and squealed uphill, steel on steel.

They stopped in Grindelwald, and in the station Nirgal followed his escort onto a much smaller train, which led them up and under the immense north wall of the Eiger. Underneath this wall of stone it appeared only a few hundred metres tall;

Nirgal had got a better sense of its great height fifty kilometres away, in Berne's Monster. Now, here, he waited patiently as the little train hummed into a tunnel in the mountain itself, and began to make its spirals and switchbacks in the darkness, punctuated only by the interior lights of the train, and the brief light from a single side tunnel. His escort, about ten men strong, spoke among themselves in low, guttural Swiss German.

When they emerged into the light again they were in a little station called the Jungfraujoch, 'the highest train station in Europe' as a sign in six languages said – and no wonder, as it was located in an icy pass between the two great peaks, the Monch and the Jungfrau, at 3,454 metres above sea level, with no point or destination but its own.

Nirgal got off the train, trailed by his escort, and went out of the station onto a narrow terrace outside the building. The air was thin, clean, crisp, about 270° K – the best air Nirgal had breathed since he left Mars, it brought tears to his eyes it felt so familiar! Ah, now this was a place!

Even with sunglasses on the light was extremely bright. The sky was a dark cobalt. Snow covered most of the mountainsides, but granite thrust through the snow everywhere, especially on the north sides of the great masses, where the cliffs were too steep to hold snow. Up here, the Alps no longer resembled an escarpment at all; each mass of rock had its own look and presence, separated from the rest by deep expanses of empty air, including glacial valleys that were enormously deep U gaps. To the north these macro-trenches were very far below, and green, or even filled with lakes. To the south however they were high, and filled only with snow and ice and rock. On this day the wind was pouring up from this south side, bringing the chill of the ice with it.

Down the ice valley directly south of the pass, Nirgal could see a huge, crumpled white plateau, where glaciers poured in from the surrounding high basins to meet in a great confluence. This was Concordiaplatz, they told him. Four big glaciers met, then poured south in the Grosser Aletschgletscher, the longest glacier in Switzerland.

Nirgal moved down the terrace to its end, to see farther into this wilderness of ice. At the far end he found that there was a staircase trail, hacked into the hard snow of the south wall where it rose to the pass. It was a path down to the glacier below them, and from there to Concordiaplatz.

Nirgal asked his escorts to stay in the station and wait for him; he wanted to hike alone. They protested, but the glacier in summer was free of snow, the crevasses all obvious, and the trail well clear of them. And no one else was down there on this cold summer day. Nevertheless the members of the escort were uncertain, and two insisted on coming with him, at least part of the way, and at a distance behind — 'just in case'.

Finally Nirgal nodded at the compromise, pulled on his hood and hiked down the ice stairs, thumping down painfully until he was on the flatter expanse of the Jungfraufirn. The ridges that walled this snow valley ran south from the Jungfrau and the Monch respectively, then after a few high kilometres dropped abruptly to Concordiaplatz. From the trail their rock looked black, perhaps in contrast to the whiteness of the snow. Here and there were patches of faint pinkness in the white snow – algae. Life even here – but barely. It was for the most part a pure expanse of white and black, and the overarching dome of Prussian blue, with a cold wind funnelling up the canyon from Concordiaplatz. He wanted to make it down to Concordiaplatz and have a look around, but he couldn't tell whether the day would give him enough time or not; it was very difficult to judge how far away things were; it could easily have been further than it looked. But he could go until the sun was halfway to the western horizon, and then turn back; and so he hiked swiftly downhill over the firn, from orange wand to orange wand, feeling the extra person inside him, feeling also the two members of the escort who were tagging along some two hundred metres behind.

For a long time he just walked. It wasn't so hard. The crenellated ice surface crunched under his brown boots. The sun had softened the top layer, despite the cool wind. The surface was too bright to see properly, even with sunglasses; the ice joggled as he walked, and glowed blackly.

The ridges to left and right began their drop. He came out into Concordiaplatz. He could see up glaciers into other high canyons, as if up ice fingers of a hand held up to the sun. The wrist ran down to the south, the Grosser Aletschgletscher. He was standing in the white palm, offered to the sun, next to a lifeline of rubble. The ice out here was pitted and gnarly and bluish in tone.

A wind picked at him, and swirled through his heart; he turned around slowly, like a little planet, like a top about to fall, trying to take it in, to face it. So big, so bright, so windy and vast, so crushingly heavy – the sheer mass of the white world! – and yet with a kind of darkness behind it, as of space's vacuum, there visible behind the sky. He took off his sunglasses to see what it really looked like, and the glare was so immediate and violent that he had to close his eyes, to cover his face in the crook of his arm; still great white bars pulsed in his vision, and even the afterimage hurt in its blinding intensity. 'Wow!' he shouted, and laughed, determined to try it again as soon as the afterimages lessened, but before his pupils had again expanded. So he did, but the second attempt was as bad as the first. How dare you try to look on me as I really am! the world shouted silently. 'My God.' With feeling. 'Ka wow.'

He put his sunglasses back on his closed eyes, looked out through the bounding afterimages; gradually the primeval landscape of ice and rock restabilized out of the pulsing bars of black and white and neon green. The white and the green; and this was the white. The blank world of the inanimate universe. This place had precisely the same import as the primal Martian landscape. Just as big as it was on Mars, yes, and even bigger, because of the distant horizons, and the crushing gravity; and steeper; and whiter; and windier, ka, it pierced so chill through his parka, even windier, even colder – ah God, like a wind lancing through his heart: the sudden knowledge that Earth was so vast that in its variety it had regions that even out-Marsed Mars itself – that among all the ways that it was greater, *it was greater even at being Martian.*

He was brought still by this thought. He only stood and stared, tried to face it. The wind died for the moment. The world too was still. No movement, no sound.

When he noticed the silence he began paying attention to it, listening for something, hearing nothing, so that the silence itself somehow became more and more palpable. It was unlike anything he had ever heard before. He thought about it; on Mars he had always been in tents or in suits – always in machinery, except for during the rare walks on the surface he had made in recent years. But then there had always been the wind, or machines nearby. Or he simply hadn't noticed. Now there was only the great silence, the silence of the universe itself. No dream could imagine it.

And then he began to hear sounds again. The blood in his ears. His breath in his nose. The quiet whirr of his thinking – it seemed to have a sound. His own support system this time, his body, with its organic pumps and ventilators and generators. The mechanisms were all still there, provided inside him, making their noises. But now he was free of anything more, in a great silence where he could actually hear himself quite well, just himself on this world alone, a free body standing on its mother earth, free in the rock and ice where it had all begun. Mother Earth – he thought of Hiroko – and this time without the tearing grief that he had felt in Trinidad. When he returned to Mars, he could live like this. He could walk out in the silence a free being, live outdoors in the wind, in something like this pure vast lifeless whiteness, with something like this dark blue dome overhead, the blue a visible exhalation of life itself – oxygen, life's own colour. Up there doming the whiteness. A sign, somehow. The white and the green, except here the green was blue.

With shadows. Among the faint lingering afterimages lay long shadows, running from the west. He was a long way from Jungfraujoch, and considerably lower as well. He turned and began hiking up the Jungfraufirn. In the distance, up the trail, his two companions nodded and turned uphill themselves, hiking fast.

Soon enough they were in the shadow of the ridge to the west, the sun now out of sight for good on this day, and the wind swirling over his back, helping on. Cold indeed. But it was his kind of temperature, after all, and his kind of air, just a nice touch of extra thickness to it; and so despite the weight inside him he began to trudge on up the crunchy hardpack in a little jog, leaning into it, feeling his thigh muscles respond to the challenge, fall into their old *lung-gom-pa* rhythm, with his lungs pumping hard and his heart as well, to handle the extra weight. But he was strong, strong, and this was one of Earth's little high regions of Marsness; and so he crunched up the firn feeling stronger by the minute, also appalled, exhilarated – awed – it was a most astonishing planet, that could have so much of the white and so much of the green as well, its orbit so exquisitely situated that at sea level the green burst out and at three thousand metres the white blanketed it utterly – the natural zone of life just that three thousand metres wide, more or less. And Earth rolled right in the middle of that filmy bubble biosphere, in the right few thousand metres out of an orbit a hundred and fifty million kilometres wide. It was too lucky to be believed.

His skin began to tingle with the effort, he was warm all over, even his toes. Beginning to sweat. The cold air was deliciously invigorating, he felt he was in a pace that he could sustain for hours; but alas, he would not need to; ahead and a bit above lay the snow staircase, with its rope-and-stanchion railing. His guides were making good time ahead of him, hurrying up the final slope. Soon he too would be there, in the little train station/space station. These Swiss, what they thought to build! To be able to visit the stupendous Concordiaplatz, on a day trip from the nation's capital! No wonder they were so sympathetic to Mars – they were Earth's closest thing to Martians, truly – builders, terraformers, inhabitants of the thin, cold air.

So he was feeling very benevolent toward them when he stepped onto the terrace and then burst into the station, where he began immediately steaming; and when he walked over to his group of escorts and the other passengers who were waiting next to the little train, he was beaming so completely, he was so high, that the impatient frowns of the group (he saw that they had been kept waiting) cracked, and they looked at each other and laughed, shaking their heads as if to say to each other, What can you do? You could only grin and let it happen – they had all been young in the high Alps for the first time, one sunny summer day, and had felt that same enthusiasm – they remembered what it was like. And so they shook his hand, they embraced him – they led him onto the little train and got going, for no matter the event, it was not good to keep a train waiting – and once under way they remarked on his hot hands and face, and asked him where he had gone, and told him how many kilometres that was, and how many vertical metres. They passed him a little hip flask of schnapps. And then as the train went by the little side tunnel that ran out onto the north face of the Eiger, they told him the story of the failed rescue attempt of the doomed Nazi climbers, excited, moved that he was so impressed. And after that they settled into the lit compartments of the train, squealing down through its rough granite tunnel.

Nirgal stood at the end of one car, looking out at the dynamited rock as it flashed past, and then as they burst back into sunlight, up at the looming wall of the Eiger overhead. A passenger walked past him on the way to the next car, then stopped and stared: 'Amazing to see you here, I must say.' He had a British accent of some kind. 'I just ran into your mother last week.'

Confused, Nirgal said, 'My mother?'

'Yes, Hiroko Ai. Isn't that right? She was in England, working with people at the mouth of the Thames. I saw her on my way here. Quite a coincidence running into you too, I must say. Makes me think I'll start seeing little red men any second now.'

The man laughed at the thought, began to move on into the next car.

'Hey!' Nirgal called. 'Wait!'

But the man only paused — 'No no,' he said over his shoulder, 'didn't want to intrude – all I know, anyway. You'll have to look her up – in Sheerness perhaps —'

And then the train was squealing into the station at Klein Scheidegg, and the man hopped out of an opening door in the next car, and as Nirgal went to follow him other people got in the way, and his escorts came to explain to him that he needed to descend to Grindelwald immediately if he wanted to get home that night. Nirgal couldn't deny them. But looking out of the window as they rolled out of the station, he saw the British man who had spoken to him, walking briskly down a trail into the dusky valley below.

He landed at a big airport in southern England, and was driven north and east to a town the escorts called Faversham, beyond which the roads and bridges were flooded. He had arranged to come unannounced, and his escort here was a police team that reminded him more of UNTA security units back home than of his Swiss escort: eight men and two women, silent, staring, full of themselves. At first they wanted to hunt for Hiroko by bringing people in to ask about her; Nirgal was sure that would put her in hiding, and he insisted on going out without fanfare to look for her. Eventually he convinced them.

They drove in a grey dawn, down to a new seafront, right there among buildings: in some places there were lines of stacked sandbags between soggy walls, in other places just wet streets, running off under dark water that spread for as far as he could see. Some planks were thrown here and there over mud and puddles.

Then on the far side of one line of sandbags was brown water without any buildings beyond, and a number of rowing boats tied to a grill covering a window half-awash in dirty foam. Nirgal followed one of the escorts into one big rowing boat, and greeted a wiry, red-faced man, wearing a grimy cap pulled low over his forehead. A kind of water policeman, apparently. The man shook his hand limply and then they were off, rowing over opaque water, followed by three more boats containing the rest of Nirgal's worried-looking guards. Nirgal's oarsman said something, and Nirgal had to ask him to repeat it; it was as if the man only had half his tongue. 'Is that Cockney, your dialect?'

'Cockney.' The man laughed.

Nirgal laughed too, shrugged. It was a word he remembered from a book, he didn't know what it meant really. He had heard a thousand different kinds of English before, but this was the real thing, presumably, and he could hardly understand it. The man spoke more slowly, which didn't help. He was describing the neighbourhood they were rowing away from, pointing; the buildings were inundated nearly to their rooflines. 'Brents,' he said several times, pointing with his oar tips.

They came to a floating dock, tied to what looked like a highway sign, saying 'OARE'. Several larger boats were tied to the dock, or swinging from anchor ropes nearby. The water policeman rowed to one of these boats, and indicated the metal ladder welded to its rusty side. 'Go on.'

Nirgal climbed the side of the boat. On the deck stood a man so short he had to reach up to shake Nirgal's hand, which he did with a crushing grip. 'So you're a Martian,' he said, in a voice that lilted like the oarsman's, but was somehow much easier to understand. 'Welcome aboard our little research vessel. Come to hunt for the old Asian lady, I hear?'

'Yes,' Nirgal said, his pulse quickening. 'She's Japanese.'

'Hmm.' The man frowned. 'I only saw her the once, but I would have said she was Asian, Bangladeshi maybe. They're everywhere since the flood. But who can tell, eh?'

Four of Nirgal's escorts climbed aboard, and the boat's owner pushed a button that started an engine, then spun the wheel in the wheelhouse, and watched forward closely as the boat's rear pushed down in the water, and they vibrated, then moved away from the drowned line of buildings. It was overcast, the clouds very low, sea and sky both a brownish grey.

'We'll go out over the wharf,' the little captain said.

Nirgal nodded. 'What's your name?'

'Bly's the name. Bee ell why.'

'I'm Nirgal.'

The man nodded once.

'So this used to be the docks?' Nirgal asked.

'This was Faversham. Out here were the marshes – Ham, Magden – it was mostly marsh, all the way to the Isle of Sheppey. The Swale, this was. More fen than flow, if you know what I mean. Now you get out here on a windy day and it's like the North Sea itself. And Sheppey is no more than that hill you see out there. A proper island now.'

'And that's where you saw . . .' He didn't know what to call her.

'Your Asian grandma came in on the ferry from Vlissingen to Sheerness, other side of that island. Sheerness and Minster have the Thames for streets these days, and at high tide they have it for their roofs too. We're over Magden Marsh now. We'll go out around Shell Ness, the Swale's too clotted.'

The mud-coloured water around them sloshed this way and that. It was lined by long, curving trails of yellowing foam. On the horizon the water greyed. Bly spun the wheel and they slapped over short, steep waves. The boat rocked, and in its entirety moved up and down, up and down. Nirgal had never been in one before. Grey cloud hung over them: there was only a wedge of air between the cloud bottoms and the choppy water. The boat jostled this way and that, bobbing corklike. A liquid world.

'It's a lot shorter around than it used to be,' Captain Bly said from the wheel. 'If the water were clearer you could see Sayes Court, underneath us.'

'How deep is it?' Nirgal asked.

'Depends on the tide. This whole island was about an inch above sea level before the flood, so however much sea level has gone up, that's how deep it is. What are they saying now, twenty-five feet? More than this old girl needs, that's sure. She's got a very shallow draught.'

He spun the wheel left, and the swells hit the boat from the side, so that it rolled in quick, uneven jerks. He pointed at one gauge: 'There, five metres. Harty Marsh. See that potato patch, the rough water there? That'll come up at midtide, looks like a drowned giant buried in the mud.'

'What's the tide now?'

'Near full. It'll turn in half an hour.'

'It's hard to believe Luna can pull the ocean around that much.'

'What, you don't believe in gravity?'

'Oh, I believe in it – it's crushing me right now. It's just hard to believe something so far away has that much pull.'

'Hmm,' the captain said, looking out into a bank of mist blocking the view ahead. 'I'll tell you what's hard to believe, it's hard to believe that a bunch of icebergs can displace so much water that all the oceans of the world have gone up this far.'

'That is hard to believe.'

'It's amazing it is. But the proof's right here floating us. Ah, the mist has arrived.'

'Do you get more bad weather than you used to?'

The captain laughed. 'That'd be comparing absolutes, I'd say.'

The mist blew past them in wet long veils, and the choppy waves smoked and hissed. It was dim. Suddenly Nirgal felt happy, despite the unease in his stomach during the deceleration at the bottom of every wave trough. He was boating on a water world, and the light was at a tolerable level at last. He could stop squinting for the first time since he had arrived on Earth.

The captain spun his big wheel again, and they ran with the waves directly behind them, northwest into the mouth of the Thames. Off to their left a brownish green ridge emerged wetly out of greenish brown water, buildings crowding its slope. 'That's Minster, or what's left of it. It was the only high ground on the island. Sheerness is over there, you can see where the water is all shattered over it.'

Under the low ceiling of streaming mist Nirgal saw what looked like a reef of foaming whitewater, sloshing in every direction at once, black under the white foam. 'That's Sheerness?'

'Yeah.'

'Did they all move to Minster?'

'Or somewhere. Most of them. There's some very stubborn people in Sheerness.'

Then the captain was absorbed in bringing the boat in through the drowned seafront of Minster. Where the line of rooftops emerged from the waves, a large building had had its roof and sea-facing wall removed, and now it functioned as a little marina, its three remaining walls sheltering a patch of water and the upper floors at the back serving as the dock. Three other fishing boats were moored there, and as they coasted in, some men on them looked up and waved.

'Who's this?' one of them said as Bly nosed his boat into the dock.

'One of the Martians. We're trying to find the Asian lady who was helping in Sheerness the other week, have you seen her?'

'Not lately. Couple of months actually. I heard she crossed to Southend. They'll know down in the sub.'

Bly nodded. 'Do you want to see Minster?' he said to Nirgal.

Nirgal frowned. 'I'd rather see the people who might know where she is.'

'Yeah.' Bly backed the boat out of the gap, turned it around; Nirgal looked in at boarded windows, stained plaster, the shelves of an office wall, some notes tacked to a beam. As they motored over the drowned portion of Minster, Bly picked up a radio microphone on a corkscrewed cord, and punched buttons. He had a number of short conversations very hard for Nirgal to follow — 'ah jack!' and the like, with all the answers emerging from explosive static.

'We'll try Sheerness then. Tide's right.'

And so they motored right into the whitewater and foam sloshing over the submerged town, following streets very slowly. In the centre of the foam the water was calmer. Chimneys and telephone poles stuck out of the grey liquid, and Nirgal caught occasional glimpses of the houses and buildings below, but the water was so foamy on top, and so murky below, that very little was visible – the slope of a roof, a glimpse down into a street, the blind window of a house.

On the far side of the town was a floating dock, anchored to a concrete pillar sticking out of the surf. 'This is the old ferry dock. They cut off one section and floated it, and now they've pumped out the ferry offices down below and reoccupied them.'

'Reoccupied them?'

'You'll see.'

Bly hopped from the rocking gunwale to the dock, and held out a hand to help Nirgal across; nevertheless Nirgal crashed to one knee when he hit.

'Come on, Spiderman. Down we go.'

The concrete pillar anchoring the dock stood chest high; it turned out to be hollow, and a metal ladder had been bolted down its inner side. Electric bulbs hung from sockets on a rubber-coated wire, twisted around one post of the ladder. The concrete cylinder ended some three metres down, but the ladder continued, down into a big chamber, warm, humid, fishy, and humming with the noise of several generators in another room or building. The building's walls, the floor, the ceilings and windows were all covered by what appeared to be a sheet of clear plastic. They were inside a bubble of some kind of clear material; outside the bubble was water, murky and brown, bubbling like dishwater in a sink.

Nirgal's face no doubt revealed his surprise; Bly, smiling briefly at the sight, said, 'It was a good strong building. The what you might call sheetrock is something like the tent fabrics you use on Mars, only it hardens. People have been reoccupying quite a few buildings like this, if they're the right size and depth. Set a tube and poof, it's like blowing glass. So a lot of Sheerness folk are moving back out here, and sailing off the dock or off their roof. Tide people we call them. They figure it's better than begging for charity in England, eh?'

'What do they do for work?'

'Fish, like they always have. And salvage. Eh, Karna! Here's my Martian, say hello. He's short where he comes from, eh? Call him Spiderman.'

'But it's Nirgal, innit? I'll be fucked if I call Nirgal Spiderman when I got him visiting in me home.' And the man, black-haired and dark-skinned, an 'Asian' in appearance if not accent, shook Nirgal's right hand gently.

The room was brightly lit by a pair of giant spotlights pointed at the ceiling. The shiny floor was crowded: tables, benches, machinery in all stages of assembly: boat engines, pumps, generators, reels, things Nirgal didn't recognize. The working generators were down a hall, though they didn't seem any quieter for that. Nirgal went to one wall to inspect the bubble material. It was only a few molecules thick, Bly's friends told him, and yet would hold thousands of pounds of pressure. Nirgal thought of each pound as a blow with a fist, thousands all at once. 'These bubbles will be here when the concrete's worn away.'

Nirgal asked about Hiroko. Karna shrugged. 'I never knew her name. I thought she was a Tamil, from the south of India. She's gone over to Southend I hear.'

'She helped to set this up?'

'Yeah. She brought the bubbles in from Vlissingen, her and a bunch like her. Great what they did here, we were grovelling in High Halstow before they came.'

'Why did they come?'

'Don't know. Some kind of coastal support group, no doubt.'

He laughed. 'Though they didn't come on like that. Just moving around the coasts, building stuff out of the wreckage for the fun of it, what it looked like. Intertidal civilization, they called it. Joking as usual.'

'Eh, Karnasingh, eh, Bly. Lovely day out innit?'

'Yeah.'

'Care for some scrod?'

The next big room was a kitchen, and a dining area jammed with tables and benches. Perhaps fifty people had sat down to eat, and Karna cried, 'Hey!' and loudly introduced Nirgal. Indistinct murmurs greeted him. People were busy eating: big bowls of fish stew, ladled out of enormous black pots that looked as if they had been in use continuously for centuries. Nirgal sat to eat; the stew was good. The bread was as hard as the tabletop. The faces were rough, pocked, salted, reddened when not brown; Nirgal had never seen such vivid, ugly countenances, banged and pulled by the harsh existence in Earth's heavy drag. Loud chatter, waves of laughter, shouts; the generators could scarcely be heard. Afterwards people came up to shake his hand and look at him. Several had met the Asian woman and her friends, and they described her enthusiastically. She hadn't ever given them a name. Her English was good, slow and clear. 'I thought she were Paki. Her eyes dint look quite Oriental if you know what I mean. Not like yours, you know, no little fold in there next to the nose.'

'Epicanthic fold, you ignorant bugger.'

Nirgal felt his heart beating hard. It was hot in the room, hot and steamy and heavy. 'What about the people with her?'

Some of those had been Oriental. Asians, except for one or two whites.

'Any tall ones?' Nirgal asked. 'Like me?'

None. Still . . . if Hiroko's group had come back to Earth, it seemed possible the younger ones would have stayed behind. Even Hiroko couldn't have talked all of them into such a move. Would Frantz leave Mars, would Nanedi? Nirgal doubted it. Return to Earth in its hour of need . . . the older ones would go. Yes, it sounded like Hiroko; he could imagine her doing it, sailing the new coasts of Terra, organizing a reinhabitation . . .

'They went over to Southend. They were going to work their way up the coast.'

Nirgal looked at Bly, who nodded; they could cross too.

But Nirgal's escorts wanted to check on things first. They wanted a day to arrange things. Meanwhile Bly and his friends were talking about underwater salvage projects, and when Bly heard about the bodyguards' proposed delay, he asked Nirgal if he wanted to see one such operation, taking place the next morning — 'though it's not a pretty business of course.' Nirgal agreed; the escorts didn't object, as long as some of them came along. They agreed to do it.

So they spent the evening in the clammy, noisy, submarine warehouse, Bly and his friends rummaging for equipment Nirgal could use. And spent the night on short, narrow beds in Bly's boat, rocking as if in a big, clumsy cradle.

The next morning they puttered through a light mist the colour of Mars, pinks and oranges floating this way and that over slack, glassy mauve water. The tide was near ebb, and the salvage crew and three of Nirgal's escorts followed Bly's larger craft in a trio of small, open motorboats, manoeuvring between chimney tops and traffic signs and power-line poles, conferring frequently. Bly had taken out a tattered book of maps, and he called out the street names of Sheerness, navigating to specific warehouses or shops. Many of the warehouses in the wharf area had already been salvaged, apparently, but there were more warehouses and shops scattered through the blocks of flats behind the seafront, and one of these was their morning's target: 'Here we go; 2 Carleton Lane.' It had been a jewellery shop, next to a small market. 'We'll try for jewels and canned food, a good balance you might say.'

They moored to the top of a billboard and stopped their engines. Bly threw a small object on a cord overboard, and he and three of the other men gathered around a small AI screen set on Bly's bridge dash. A thin cable paid out over the side, its reel creaking woefully. On the screen, the murky colour image changed from brown to black to brown.

'How do you know what you're seeing?' Nirgal asked.

'We don't.'

'But look, there's a door, see?'

'No.'

Bly tapped at a small keypad under the screen. 'In you go, thing. There. Now we're inside. This should be the market.'

'Didn't they have time to get their things out?' Nirgal asked.

'Not entirely. Everyone on the east coast of England had to move at once, almost, so there wasn't enough transport to take more than what you could carry in your car. If that. A lot of people left their homes intact. So we pull the stuff worth pulling.'

'What about the owners?'

'Oh there's a register. We contact the register and find people when we can, and charge them a salvage fee if they want the stuff. If they're not on the register, we sell it on the island. People are wanting furniture and such. Here, look – we'll see what that is.'

He pushed a key, and the screen got brighter. 'Ah yeah. Refrigerator. We could use it, but it's hell getting it up.'

'What about the house?'

'Oh we blow that up. Clean shot if we set the charges right. But not this morning. We'll tag this and move on.'

They puttered away. Bly and another man continued to watch the screen, arguing mildly about where to go next. 'This town wasn't much even before the flood,' Bly explained to Nirgal. 'Falling into the drink for a couple of hundred years, ever since the empire ended.'

'Since the end of sail you mean,' the other man said.

'Same thing. The old Thames was used less and less after that, and all the little ports on the estuary began to go seedy. And that was a long time ago.'

Finally Bly killed the engine, looked at the others. In their whiskery faces Nirgal saw a curious mix of grim resignation and happy anticipation. 'There, then.'

The other men started getting out underwater gear: full wetsuits, tanks, facemasks, some full helmets. 'We thought Eric's'd fit you,' Bly said. 'He was a giant.' He pulled a long black wetsuit out of the crowded locker, one without feet or gloves, and only a hood and facemask rather than a complete helmet. 'There's bootees of his too.'

'Let me try them on.'

So he and two of the men took off their clothes and pulled on the wetsuits, sweating and puffing as they yanked the

213

fabrics on and zipped up the tight collars. Nirgal's wetsuit turned out to have a triangular rip across the left side of the torso, which was lucky, as otherwise it might not have fitted; it was very tight around the chest, though loose on his legs. One of the other divers, named Kev, taped up the V split with duct tape. 'That'll be all right then, for one dive anyway. But you see what happened to Eric, eh?' Tapping him on the side. 'See you don't get caught up in any of our cable.'

'I will.'

Nirgal felt his flesh crawl under the taped rip, which suddenly felt huge. Caught on a moving cable, pulled into concrete or metal, ka, what an agony – a fatal blow – how long would he have stayed conscious after that, a minute, two? Rolling in agony, in the dark . . .

He pulled himself out of an intense re-creation of Eric's end, feeling shaken. They got a breathing rig attached to his upper arm and facemask, and abruptly he was breathing cold, dry air, pure oxygen they said. Bly asked again about going down, as Nirgal was shivering slightly. 'No no,' said Nirgal. 'I'm good with cold, this water isn't that cold. Besides I've already filled the suit with sweat.'

The other divers nodded, sweating themselves. Getting ready was hard work. The actual swimming was easier; down a ladder and, ah, yes, out of the crush of the g, into something very like Martian g, or lighter still; such a relief! Nirgal breathed in the cold bottled oxygen happily, almost weeping at the sudden freedom of his body, floating down through a comfortable dimness. Ah yes – his world on Earth was underwater.

Down deeper, things were as dark and amorphous as they had been on the screen, except for within the cones of light emanating from the other two men's headlamps, which were obviously very strong. Nirgal followed above and behind them, getting the best view of all. The estuary water was cool, about 285° K Nirgal judged, but very little of it seeped in at the wrists and around the hood, and the water trapped inside the suit was soon so hot with his exertions that his cold hands and face (and left ribs) actually served to keep him from overheating.

The two cones of light shot this way and that as the two

divers looked around. They were swimming along a narrow street. Seeing the buildings and the kerbs, the pavements and streets, made the murky grey water look uncannily like the mist up on the surface.

Then they were floating before a three-storey brick building, filling a narrow triangular space that pointed into an angled intersection of streets. Kev gestured for Nirgal to stay outside, and Nirgal was happy to oblige. The other diver had been holding a cable so thin it was scarcely visible, and now he swam into a doorway, pulling it behind him. He went to work attaching a small pulley to the doorway, and lining the cable through it. Time passed; Nirgal swam slowly around the wedge-shaped building, looking in second-storey windows at offices, empty rooms, flats. Some furniture floated against the ceilings. A movement inside one of these rooms caused him to jerk away; he was afraid of the cable; but it was on the other side of the building. Some water seeped into his mouthpiece, and he swallowed it to get it out of the way. It tasted of salt and mud and plant life, and something unpleasant. He swam on.

Back at the doorway Kev and the other man were helping a small metal safe through the doorway. When it was clear they kicked upright, in place, waiting, until the cable rose almost directly overhead. Then they swam around the intersection like a clumsy ballet team, and the safe floated up to the surface and disappeared. Kev swam back inside, and came out kicking hard, holding two small bags. Nirgal kicked over and took one, and with big luxurious kicks pulsed up toward the boat. He surfaced into the bright light of the mist. He would have loved to go back down, but Bly did not want them in any longer, and so Nirgal threw his fins in the boat and climbed the ladder over the side. He was sweating as he sat on one bench, and it was a relief to strip the hood off his head, despite the way his hair was yanked back. The clammy air felt good against his skin as they helped him peel the wetsuit off.

'Look at his chest will you, he's like a greyhound.'

'Breathing vapours all his life.'

The mist almost cleared, dissipating to reveal a white sky, the sun a brighter white swathe across it. The weight had come back into him, and he breathed deeply a few times to get his body back into that work rhythm. His stomach was queasy, and his lungs hurt a little at the peak of each inhalation. Things rocked a bit more than the slosh of the ocean surface would account for. The sky turned to zinc, the sun's quadrant a harsh blinding glare. Nirgal stayed sitting, breathed faster and shallower.

'Did you like it?'

'Yes!' he said. 'I wish it felt like that everywhere.'

They laughed at the thought. 'Here, have a cup.'

Perhaps going underwater had been a mistake. After that the g never felt right again. It was hard to breathe. The air down in the warehouse was so wet that he felt he could clench a fist and drink water from his hand. His throat hurt, and his lungs. He drank cup after cup of tea, and still he was thirsty. The gleaming walls dripped, and nothing the people said was comprehensible, it was all *av* and *eh* and *lor* and *da*, nothing like Martian English. A different language. Now they all spoke different languages. Shakespeare's plays had not prepared him for it.

He slept again in the little bed on Bly's boat. The next day the escort gave the okay, and they motored out of Sheerness, and north across the Thames estuary, in a pink mist even thicker than the day before.

Out in the estuary there was nothing visible but mist and the sea. Nirgal had been in clouds before, especially on the west slope of Tharsis, where fronts ran up the rise of the bulge; but never of course while on water. And every time before the temperatures had been well below freezing, the clouds a kind of flying snow, very white and dry and fine, rolling over the land and coating it in white dust. Nothing at all like this liquid world, where there was very little difference between the choppy water and the mist gusting over it, the liquid and the gaseous phasing back and forth endlessly. The boat rocked in a violent irregular rhythm. Dark objects appeared in the margins of the mist, but Bly paid them no attention, keeping a sharp eye ahead through a window beaded with water to the point of opacity, and also watching a number of screens under the window.

Suddenly Bly killed the engine, and the boat's rocking changed to a vicious side-to-side yaw. Nirgal held the side of the cabin and peered through the watery window, trying to see what had caused Bly to stop. 'That's a big ship for Southend,' Bly remarked, motoring on very slowly.

'Where?'

'Port beam.' He pointed to a screen, then off to the left. Nirgal saw nothing.

Bly brought them into a long low pier, with many boats moored to it on both sides. The pier ran north through the mist to the town of Southend-on-Sea, which ran up and disappeared in the mist covering a slope of buildings.

A number of men greeted Bly — 'Lovely day eh?' 'Brilliant' — and began to unload boxes from his hold.

Bly inquired about the Asian woman from Vlissingen, but the men shook their heads. 'The Jap? She ain't here, mate.'

'They're saying in Sheerness she and her group came to Southend.'

'Why would they say that?'

'Because that's what they think happened.'

'That's what you get listening to people who live underwater.'

'The Paki grandma?' they said at the diesel fuel pump on the other side of the pier. 'She went over to Shoeburyness, some time back.'

Bly glanced at Nirgal. 'It's just a few miles east. If she were here, these men would know.'

'Let's try it then,' Nirgal said.

So after refuelling they left the pier, and puttered east through the mist. From time to time the building-covered hillside was visible to their left. They rounded a point, turned north. Bly brought them in to another floating dock, with many fewer boats than had been moored at Southend pier.

'That Chinese gang?' a toothless old man cried. 'Gone up to Pig's Bay they have! Gave us a greenhouse! Some kind of church.'

'Pig's Bay's just the next pier,' Bly said, looking thoughtful as he wheeled them away from the dock.

So they motored north. The coastline here was entirely composed of drowned buildings. They had built so close to the

217

sea! Clearly there had been no reason to fear any change in sea level. And then it had happened; and now this strange amphibious zone, an intertidal civilization, wet and rocking in the mist.

A cluster of buildings gleamed at their windows. They had been filled by the clear bubble material, pumped out and occupied, their upstairs just above the foamy waves, their downstairs just below. Bly brought the boat in to a set of linked floating docks, greeted a group of women in smocks and yellow oilskins mending a big black net. He cut his engine: 'Has the Asian lady been to see you too, then?'

'Oh yeah. She's down inside, there, the building at the end.'

Nirgal felt his pulse jarring through him. His balance had left him, he had to hold onto the rail. Over the side, onto the dock. Down to the last building, a seafront boarding house or something like, now much broken up and glimmering in all the cracks; air inside; filled by a bubble. Green plants, vague and blurry seen through sloshing grey water. He had a hand on Bly's shoulder. The little man led him in through a door and down narrow stairs, into a room with one whole wall exposed to the sea, like a dirty aquarium.

A diminutive woman in a rust-coloured jumpsuit came through the far door. White-haired, black-eyed, quick and precise; birdlike. Not Hiroko. She stared at them.

'Are you the one came over from Vlissingen?' Bly asked, after glancing up at Nirgal. 'The one that's been building these submariners?'

'Yes,' the woman said. 'May I help you?' She had a high voice, a British accent. She stared at Nirgal without expression. There were other people in the room, more coming in. She looked like the face he had seen in the cliffside, in Medusa Vallis. Perhaps there was another Hiroko, a different one, wandering the two planets building things . . .

Nirgal shook his head. The air was like a greenhouse gone bad. The light, so dim. He could barely get back up the stairs. Bly had made their farewells. Back into the bright mist. Back onto the boat. Chasing wisps. A ruse, to get him out of Berne. Or an honest mistake. Or a simple fool's errand.

Bly sat him down in the boat's cabin, next to a rail. 'Ah well.'

Pitching and yawing, through the mist, which closed back down. Dark, dim day on the water, sloshing through the phase change where water and mist turned into each other, sandwiched between them. Nirgal got a little drowsy. No doubt she was back on Mars. Doing her work there in her usual secrecy, yes. It had been absurd to think otherwise. When he got back he would find her. Yes: it was a goal, a task he gave himself. He would find her and make her come back out into the open. Make sure she had survived. It was the only way to be sure, the only way to remove this horrible weight from his heart. Yes: he would find her.

Then as they motored on over the choppy water, the mist lifted. Low grey clouds rushed overhead, dropping swirls of rain into the waves. The tide was ebbing now, and as they crossed the great estuary the flow of the Thames was released full force. The grey-brown surface of the water was broken to mush, waves coming from all directions at once, a wild bouncing surface of foamy dark water, all carried rapidly east, out into the North Sea. And then the wind turned and poured over the tide, and all the waves were suddenly rushing out to sea together. Among the long cakes of foam were floating objects of all kinds: boxes, furniture, roofs, entire houses, capsized boats, pieces of wood. Flotsam and jetsam. Bly's crew stood on the deck, leaning over the rails with grapnels and binoculars, calling back to him to avoid things or to try to approach them. They were absorbed in the work. 'What is all of this stuff?' Nirgal asked Bly.

'It's London,' Bly said. 'It's fucking London, washing out to sea.'

The cloud bottoms rushed east over their heads. Looking around Nirgal saw many other small boats on the tossing water of the great rivermouth, salvaging the flotsam or just fishing. Bly waved to some as they passed through, tooted at others. Horn blasts floated on the wind over the grey speckled estuary, apparently signalling messages, as Bly's crews commented on each.

Then Kev exclaimed, 'Hey, what's that now!' pointing upstream.

Out of a fogbank covering the mouth of the Thames had emerged a ship with sails, many sails, sails square-rigged on

219

three masts in the archetypal configuration, deeply familiar to Nirgal even though he had never seen it before. A chorus of horn blasts greeted this apparition – mad toots, long sustained blasts, all joining together and sustaining longer and longer, like a neighbourhood of dogs roused and baying at night, warming to their task. Above them exploded the sharp penetrating blast of Bly's airhorn, joining the chorus – Nirgal had never heard such a shattering sound, it hurt his ears! Thicker air, denser sound – Bly was grinning, his fist shoved against the airhorn button – the men of the crew all standing at the rail or on it, Nirgal's escorts as well, screaming soundlessly at the sudden vision.

Finally Bly let off. 'What is it?' Nirgal shouted.

'It's the *Cutty Sark*!' Bly said, and threw his head back and laughed. 'It was bolted down in Greenwich! Stuck in a park! Some mad bastards must have liberated it. What a brilliant idea. They must have towed it around the flood barrier. Look at her sail!'

The old clipper ship had four or five sails unfurled on each of the three masts, and a few triangular ones between the masts as well, and extending forward to the bowsprit. It was sailing in the midst of the ebb flow, and there was a strong wind behind it, so that it sliced through the foam and flotsam, splitting water away from its sharp bow in a quick succession of white waves. There were men standing in its rigging, Nirgal saw, most of them leaning out over the yardarms, waving one-armed at the ragged flotilla of motorboats as they passed through it. Pennants extended from the mast tops, a big blue flag with red crosses – when it came abreast of Bly's boat, Bly hit the airhorn trigger again and again, and the men roared. A sailor out at the end of the *Cutty Sark*'s mainsail yard waved at them with both hands, leaning his chest forward against the big polished cylinder of wood. Then he lost his balance, they all saw it happen, as if in slow motion; and with his mouth a round little O the sailor fell backwards, dropping into the whitewater that foamed away from the ship's side. The men on Bly's boat shouted all together: 'NO!' Bly cursed loudly and gunned his engine, which was suddenly loud in the absence of the airhorn. The rear of the boat dug deep into the water, and then they were grumbling toward the man overboard, now one black dot among the rest, a raised arm waving frantically.

Boats everywhere were tooting, honking, blasting their horns; but the *Cutty Sark* never slowed. It sailed away at full speed, sails all taut-bellied when seen from behind, a beautiful sight. By the time they reached the fallen sailor, the stern of the clipper was low on the water to the east, its masts a cluster of white sail and black rigging, until it disappeared abruptly into another wall of mist.

'*What* a glorious sight,' one of the men was still repeating. '*What* a glorious sight.'

'Yeah yeah, glorious, here, fish this poor bastard in.'

Bly threw the engine in reverse, then idled. They threw a ladder over the side, leaned over to help the wet sailor up the steps. Finally he made it over the rail, stood bent over in his soaking clothes, holding onto the rail, shivering. 'Ah thanks,' he said between retches over the side. Kev and the other crew members got his wet clothes off him, wrapped him in thick dirty blankets.

'You're a stupid fucking idiot,' Bly shouted down from the wheelhouse. 'There you were about to sail the world on the *Cutty Sark*, and now here you are on *The Bride of Faversham*. You're a stupid fucking idiot.'

'I know,' the man said between retches.

The men threw jackets over his back, laughing. 'Silly fool, waving at us like that!' All the way back to Sheerness they proclaimed his ineptitude, while getting the bereft man dried and into the wind protection of the wheelhouse, dressed in spare clothes much too small for him. He laughed with them, cursed his luck, described the fall, re-enacted coming loose. Back in Sheerness they helped him down into the submerged warehouse, and fed him hot stew, and pint after pint of bitter, meanwhile telling the people inside, and everyone who came down the ladder, all about his fall from grace. 'Look here, this silly wanker fell off the *Cutty Sark* this afternoon, the clumsy bastard, when it was running down the tide under full sail to Tahiti!'

'To Pitcairn,' Bly corrected.

The sailor himself, extremely drunk, told his tale as often as his rescuers. 'Just took me hands off for a second, and it

221

gave a little lurch and I was flying. Flying in space. Didn't think it would matter, I didn't. Took me hands off all the time up the Thames. Oh one mo here, 'scuse me, I've got to go spew.'

'Ah God, she was a glorious sight she was, brilliant, really. More sail than they needed of course, it was just to go out in style, but God bless 'em for that. Such a sight.'

Nirgal felt dizzy and bleak. The whole big room had gone a glossy dark, except in the exact spots where there were streaks of bright glare. Everything a chiaroscuro of jumbled objects, Brueghel in black-and-white, and so loud. 'I remember the spring flood of '13, the North Sea in me living room —'

'Ah no, not the flood of '13 again, will you not go on about that again!'

He went to a partitioned room at one corner of the chamber, the men's room, thinking he would feel better if he relieved himself. Inside the rescued sailor was on the floor of one of the stalls, retching violently. Nirgal retreated, sat down on the nearest bench to wait. A young woman passed him by, and reached out to touch him on the top of the head. 'You're hot!'

Nirgal held a palm to his forehead, tried to think about it. '310° K,' he ventured. 'Shit.'

'You've caught a fever,' she said.

One of his bodyguards sat beside him. Nirgal told him about his temperature, and the man said, 'Will you ask your wristpad?'

Nirgal nodded, asked for a readout. *309° K.* 'Shit.'

'How do you feel?'

'Hot. Heavy.'

'We'd better get you to see someone.'

Nirgal shook his head, but a wave of dizziness came over him as he did. He watched the bodyguards calling to make arrangements. Bly came over, and they asked him questions.

'At night?' Bly said. More quiet talk. Bly shrugged; not a good idea, the shrug said, but possible. The bodyguards went on, and Bly tossed down the last of his pint and stood. His head was still at the same level as Nirgal's, although Nirgal had slid down to rest his back against the table. A different species, a squat powerful amphibian. Had they known that, before the flood? Did they know it now?

People said goodbye, crushed or coddled his hand. Climbing the conning tower ladder was painful work. Then they were out in the cool wet night, fog shrouding everything. Without a word Bly led them onto his boat, and he remained silent as he started the engines and unmoored the boat. Off they puttered over a low swell. For the first time the rocking over the waves made Nirgal really queasy. Nausea was worse than pain. He sat down beside Bly on a stool, and watched the grey cone of illuminated water and fog before their bow. When dark objects loomed out of the fog Bly would slow, even shove the engines into reverse. Once he hissed. This went on for a long time. By the time they docked in the streets of Faversham, Nirgal was too sick to say goodbye properly; he could only grasp Bly's hand and look down briefly into the man's blue eyes. Such faces. You could see people's souls right there in their faces. Had they known that before? Then Bly was gone and they were in a car, humming through the night. Nirgal's weight was increasing as it had during the descent in the elevator. Onto a plane, ascending in darkness, descending in darkness, ears popping painfully, nausea; they were in Berne and Sax was there by his side, a great comfort.

He was in a bed, very hot, his breathing wet and painful. Out of one window, the Alps. The white breaking up out of the green, like death itself rearing up out of life, crashing through to remind him that viriditas was a green fuse that would someday explode back into nova whiteness, returning to the same array of elements it had been before the pattern dustdevil had picked it up. The white and the green; it felt as if the Jungfrau were shoving up his throat. He wanted to sleep, to get away from that feeling.

Sax sat at his side, holding his hand. 'I think he needs to be in Martian gravity,' he was saying to someone who did not seem to be in the room. 'It could be a form of altitude sickness. Or a disease vector. Or allergies. A systemic response. Œdema, anyway. Let's take him up immediately in a ground-to-space plane, and get him into a g ring at Martian g. If I'm right it will help, if not it won't hurt.'

Nirgal tried to speak, but couldn't catch his breath. This

world had infected him – crushed him – cooked him in steam and bacteria. A blow to the ribs: he was allergic to Earth. He squeezed Sax's hand, pulled in a breath like a knife to the heart. 'Yes,' he gasped, and saw Sax squint. 'Home, yes.'

PART FIVE

Home at Last

Practical Tips

An old man sitting at a sickbed. Hospital rooms are all the same. Clean, white, cool, humming, fluorescent. On the sickbed lies a man, tall, dark-skinned, thick black eyebrows. Sleeping fitfully. The old man is hunched at his head. One finger touches the skull behind the ear. Under his breath the old man is muttering. 'If it's an allergic response, then your own immune system has to be convinced that the allergen isn't really a problem. They haven't identified an allergen. Pulmonary œdema is usually high altitude sickness, but maybe the mix of gases caused it, or maybe it was low altitude sickness. You need to get water out of your lungs. They've done pretty well with that. The fever and chills might be amenable to biofeedback. A really high fever is dangerous, you must remember that. I remember the time you came into the baths after falling into the lake. You were blue. Jackie jumped right in – no, maybe she stopped to watch. You held Hiroko and me by the arms, and we all saw you warm up. Nonshivering thermogenesis, everyone does it, but you did it voluntarily, and very powerfully as well. I've never seen anything like it. I still don't know how you did it. You were a wonderful boy. People can shiver at will if they want, so maybe it's like that, only inside. It doesn't really matter, you don't need to know how, you just need to do it. If you can do it in the other direction. Bring your temperature down. Give it a try. Give it a try. You were such a wonderful boy.'

The old man reaches out and grabs the young man by the wrist. He holds it and squeezes.

'You used to ask questions. You were very curious, very good-natured. You would say, Why, Sax, why? Why, Sax, why? It was fun to try to keep answering. The world is like a tree, from every leaf you can work back to the roots. I'm sure Hiroko felt that way, she probably was the one who first told me that. Listen, it wasn't a bad thing to go looking for Hiroko. I've done the same thing myself. And I will again. Because I saw her once, on Daedalia. She helped me when I got caught out in a storm. She held my wrist. Just like this. She's alive, Nirgal. Hiroko is alive. She's out there. You'll

find her someday. Put that internal thermostat to work, get that temperature down, and someday you'll find her . . .'

The old man lets go the wrist. He slumps over, half asleep, muttering still. 'You would say, Why, Sax, why?'

If the mistral hadn't been blowing he might have cried, for nothing looked the same, nothing. He came into a Marseilles station that hadn't existed when he left, next to a little new town that hadn't existed when he left, and all of it built according to a dripping bulbous Gaudi architecture which also had a kind of Bogdanovist circularity to it, so that Michel was reminded of Christianopolis or Hiranyagarbha, if they had melted. No, nothing looked familiar in the slightest. The land was strangely flattened, green, deprived of its rock, deprived of that *je ne sais quoi* that had made it Provence. He had been gone for a hundred and two years.

But blowing over all this unfamiliar landscape was the mistral, pouring down off the Massif Central – cold, dry, musty and electric, flushed with negative ions or whatever it was that gave it its characteristic katabatic exhilaration. The mistral! No matter what it looked like, it had to be Provence.

Praxis locals spoke French to him, and he could barely understand them. He had to listen hard, hoping his native tongue would come back to him, that the *franglaisation* and *frarabization* he had heard about had not changed things too much; it was shocking to fumble in his native tongue, shocking too that the French Academy had not done its job and kept the language frozen in the seventeenth century as it was supposed to. A young woman leading the Praxis aides seemed to be saying that they could take a drive around and see the region, go down to the new coast and so on.

'Fine,' Michel said.

Already he was understanding them better. It was possibly just a matter of Provençal accents. He followed them around through the concentric circles of the buildings, then out into a car park like all other car parks. The young woman aide helped him into the passenger seat of a little car, then she got in on the other side, behind the steering wheel. Her name was Sylvie; she was small, attractive, stylish and smelled nice, so that her strange French continuously surprised Michel. She started the car and drove them out of the airport. And then they were running noisily over a black road across a flat landscape, green with grass and trees. No, there were some hills in the distance; so small! And the horizon so far away!

Sylvie drove to the nearest coast. From a hilltop turn-out they could see far over the Mediterranean, on this day mottled brown and grey, gleaming in the sun.

After a few minutes' silent observation, Sylvie drove on, cutting inland over flat land again. Then they were stopped on a levée, and looking over the Camargue, she said. Michel would not have recognized it. The delta of the Rhône River had been a broad triangular fan of many thousands of hectares, filled by salt marshes and grass; now it was part of the Mediterranean again. The water was brown, and dotted with buildings, but it was water nevertheless, the flow of the Rhône a bluish line out there crossing the middle of it. Arles, Sylvie said, up at the tip of the fan, was a functioning seaport again. Although they were still securing the channel. Everything in the delta south of Arles, Sylvie said proudly, from Martigues in the east to Aigue-Mortes in the west, was covered by water. Aigues-Mortes was dead indeed, its industrial buildings drowned. Its port facilities, Sylvie said, were being floated and moved to Arles, or Marseilles. They were working hard to make safe navigational routes for ships; both the Camargue and the Plaine de la Crau, farther east, had been littered with structures of all kinds, many still sticking out of the water, but not all; and the water was too opaque with silt to see into. 'See, there's the station – you can see the granaries, but not the outbuildings. And there's one of the levée-banked canals. The levées are like reefs now. See the line of grey water? The levées are still breaking, when the current from the Rhône runs over them.'

'Lucky the tides aren't big,' Michel said.

'True. If they were it would be too treacherous for ships to reach Arles.'

In the Mediterranean tides were negligible, and fishermen and coastal freighters were discovering day by day what could be safely negotiated; attempts were being made to re-secure the Rhône's main channel through the new lagoon, and to re-establish the flanking canals as well, so that boats wouldn't have to challenge the flow of the Rhône when returning upstream. Sylvie pointed out at features Michel couldn't see, and told him of sudden shifts of the Rhône's channel, of ships grounding, loose buoys, ripped hulls, rescues by night, oil spills, confusing new lighthouses – false lighthouses, set by moonlighters for the unwary – even ordinary piracy on the high seas. Life sounded exciting at the new mouth of the Rhône.

After a while they got back in the little car, and Sylvie drove them south and east, until they hit the coast, the true coast, between Marseilles and Cassis. This part of the Mediterranean littoral, like the Côte d'Azur farther east, consisted of a range of steep hills dropping abruptly into the sea. The hills still stood well above the water, of course, and at first glance it seemed to Michel that this section of the coast had changed much less than the drowned Camargue. But after a few minutes of silent observation, he changed his mind. The Camargue had always been a delta, and now it was a delta still, and so nothing essential had changed. Here, however: 'The beaches are gone.'

'Yes.'

It was only to be expected. But the beaches had been the essence of this coast, the beaches with their long, tawny summers all jammed with sun-worshipping, naked human animals, with swimmers and sailboats and carnival colours, and long, warm, thrilling nights. All that had vanished. 'They'll never come back.'

Sylvie nodded. 'It's the same everywhere,' she said matter-of-factly.

Michel looked eastward; hills dropped into the brown sea all the way to a distant horizon; it looked as if he might be seeing as far as Cap Sicié. Beyond that were all the big resorts, St Tropez, Cannes, Antibes, Nice, his own little Villefranche-sur-mer, and all the fashionable beach resorts in between, big and small, all drowned like the stretch under them: the sea mud-brown, lapping against a fringe of pale, broken rock and dead yellow trees, with the beach roads dipping into dirty white surf. Dirty surf, washing up into the streets of deserted towns.

Green trees above the new sealine tossed over whitish rock. Michel had not remembered how white the rock was. The foliage was low and dusty, deforestation had been a problem

231

in recent years, Sylvie said, as people had cut trees for fire-wood. But Michel barely heard her; he was staring down at the drowned beaches, trying to recall their sandy, hot, erotic beauty. Gone. And he found, as he stared at the dirty surf, that in his mind he couldn't remember them very well – nor his days on them, the many lazy days now blurs, as of a dead friend's face. He couldn't remember.

Marseilles however had of course survived – the only part of the coast one could not care about, the ugliest part, the city. Of course. Its docks were inundated, and the neighbourhoods immediately behind them; but the land rose quickly here, and the higher neighbourhoods had gone on living their tough, sordid existence, big ships still anchored in the harbour, long floating docks manoeuvred out to them to empty their holds, while their sailors flooded the town and went mad in time-honoured fashion. Sylvie said that Marseilles was where she had heard most of the hair-raising tales of adventure from the mouth of the Rhône and elsewhere around the Med, where the charts meant nothing any more: houses of the dead between Malta and Tunisia, attacks by Barbary corsairs . . . 'Marseilles is more itself than it has been for centuries,' she said, and grinned, and Michel got a sudden sense of her night life, wild and perhaps a bit dangerous. She liked Marseilles. The car lurched in one of the road's many potholes and it felt like his pulse, he and the mistral rushing around ugly old Marseilles, stricken by the thought of a wild young woman.

More itself than it had been for centuries. Perhaps that was true of the entire coast. There were no tourists any more; with the beaches gone, the whole concept of tourism had taken a knife to the heart. The big pastel hotels and apartments now stood in the surf half-drowned, like children's building-blocks left at low tide. As they drove out of Marseilles, Michel noted that many of these buildings appeared to have been reoccupied in their upper storeys, by fishermen Sylvie said; no doubt they kept their boats in rooms downstairs, like the Lake People of prehistoric Europe. The old ways, returning.

So Michel kept looking out of the window, trying to rethink the new Provence, doing his best to deal with the shock of so much change. Certainly it was all very interesting, even if it was not as he remembered it. New beaches would eventually form, he reassured himself, as the waves cut away at the feet of seacliffs, and the charged rivers and streams carried soil downstream. It was possible they might even appear fairly quickly, although they would be dirt or stones, at first. That tawny sand – well, currents might bring some of the drowned sand up onto the new strand, who knew. But surely most of it was gone for good.

Sylvie brought the car to another windy turn-out overlooking the sea. It was brown right to the horizon, the offshore wind causing them to be looking at the back sides of waves moving away from the strand, an odd effect. Michel tried to recall the old sunbeaten blue. There had been varieties of Mediterranean blue, the clear purity of the Adriatic, the Aegean with its Homeric touch of wine . . . now all brown. Brown sea, beachless seacliffs, the pale hills rocky, desertlike, deserted. A wasteland. No, nothing was the same, nothing.

Eventually Sylvie noticed his silence. She drove him west to Arles, to a small hotel in the heart of the town. Michel had never lived in Arles, or had much to do there, but there were Praxis offices next to this hotel, and he had no other compelling idea concerning where to stay. They got out; the g felt heavy. Sylvie waited downstairs while he took his bag up; and there he was, standing uncertainly in a small hotel room, his bag thrown on the bed, his body tense with the desire to find his land, to return to his home. This wasn't it.

He went downstairs and then next door, where Sylvie was tending to other business.

'I have a place I want to see,' he said to her.

'Anywhere you like.'

'It's near Vallabrix. North of Uzès.'

She said she knew where that was.

It was late afternoon by the time they reached the place: a clearing by the side of a narrow old road, next to an olive grove on a slope, with the mistral raking over it. Michel asked Sylvie to stay at the car, and got out in the wind and walked up the slope between the trees, alone with the past.

His old *mas* had been set at the north end of the grove, on the edge of a tableland overlooking a ravine. The olive trees were gnarled with age. The *mas* itself was nothing but a shell of masonry, almost buried under long, tangled thorny blackberry vines growing against the outer walls.

Looking down into the ruin, Michel found he could just remember its interior. Or parts of it. There had been a kitchen and dining table near the door, and then, after passing under a massive roof beam, a living room with couches and a low coffee table, and a door back to the bedroom. He had lived there for two or three years, with a woman named Eve. He hadn't thought of the place in over a century. He would have said it was all gone from his mind. But with the ruins before him, fragments of that time leaped to the eye, ruins of another kind: a blue lamp had stood in that corner now filled with broken plaster. A Van Gogh print had been tacked to that wall, where now there were only blocks of masonry, roof tiles, drifts of leaves. The massive roof beam was gone, its supports in the walls gone as well. Someone must have hauled it out; hard to believe anyone would make the effort, it must have weighed hundreds of kilos. Strange what people would do. Then again, deforestation; there were few trees left big enough to provide a beam that large. The centuries people had lived on this land.

Eventually deforestation might cease to be a problem. During the drive Sylvie had spoken of the violent flood winter, rains, wind; this mistral had lasted a month. Some said it would never end. Looking into the ruined house, Michel was not sorry. He needed the wind to orient himself. It was strange how the memory worked, or didn't. He stepped up onto the broken wall of the *mas*, tried to remember more of the place, of his life here with Eve. Deliberate recall, a hunt for the past . . . Instead scenes came to him of the life he had shared with Maya in Odessa, with Spencer down the hall. Probably the two lives had shared enough aspects to create the confusion. Eve had been hot-tempered like Maya, and as for the rest, *la vie quotidienne* was *la vie quotidienne*, in all times and all places, especially for a specific individual no doubt, settling into his habits as if into furniture, taken along from one place to the next. Perhaps.

The inside walls of this house had been clean beige plaster, tacked with prints. Now the patches of plaster left were rough and discoloured, like the exterior walls of an old church. Eve had worked in the kitchen like a dancer in a routine, her back and legs long and powerful. Looking over her shoulder at him to laugh, her chestnut hair tossing with every turn. Yes, he remembered that repeated moment. An image without context. He had been in love. Although he had made her angry. Eventually she had left him for someone else, ah yes, a teacher in Uzès. What pain! He remembered it, but it meant nothing to him now, he felt not a pinch of it. A previous life. These ruins could not make him feel it. They scarcely brought back even the images. It was frightening – as if reincarnation were real, and had happened to him, so that he was experiencing minute flashbacks of a life separated from him by several subsequent deaths. How odd it would be if such reincarnation were real, speaking in languages one did not know, like Bridey Murphy; feeling the swirl of the past through the mind, feeling previous existences . . . well. It would feel just like this, in fact. But to re-experience nothing of those past feelings, to feel nothing except the sensation that one was not feeling . . .

He left the ruins, and walked back among the old olive trees.

It looked as if the grove was still being worked by someone. The branches overhead were all cut to a certain level, and the ground underfoot was smooth and covered by short, dry, pale grass, growing between thousands of old grey olive pits. The trees were in ranks and files but looked natural anyway, as if they had simply grown at that distance from each other. The wind blew its lightly percussive *shoosh* in the leaves. Standing midgrove, where he could see little but olive trees and sky, he noticed again how the leaves' two colours flashed back and forth in the wind, green then grey, grey then green . . .

He reached up to pull down a twig and inspect the leaves. He remembered; up close the two sides of an olive leaf weren't all that different in colour; a flat medium green, a pale khaki. But a hillside full of them, flailing in the wind, had those two distinct colours, in moonlight shifting to black and silver. If

235

one were looking toward the sun at them it became more a matter of texture, flat or shiny.

He walked up to a tree, put his hands on its trunk. It felt like an olive tree's bark: rough, broken rectangles. A grey-green colour, somewhat like the undersides of the leaves, but darker, and often covered by yet another green, the yellow-green of lichen, yellow-green or battleship grey. There were hardly any olive trees on Mars; no Mediterraneans yet. No, it felt as if he was on Earth. About ten years old. Carrying that heavy child inside himself. Some of the rectangles of bark were peeling down. The fissures between the rectangles were shallow. The true colour of the bark, clean of all lichen, appeared to be a pale, woody beige. There was so little of it that it was hard to tell. Trees coated with lichen; Michel had not realized that before. The branches above his head were smoother, the fissures flesh-coloured lines only, the lichen smoother as well, like green dust on the branches and twigs.

The roots were big and strong. The trunks spread outward as they approached the ground, spreading in fingerlike protrusions with holes and gaps between, like knobby fists thrust into the ground. No mistral would ever uproot these trees. Not even a Martian wind could knock one down.

The ground was covered with old olive pits, and shrivelled black olives on the way to becoming pits. He picked up one with its black skin still smooth, ripped away the skin with his thumb and fingernails. The purple juice stained his skin, and when he licked it, the taste was not like cured olives at all. Sour. He bit into the flesh, which resembled plum flesh, and the taste of it, sour and bitter, un-olivelike except for a hint of the oily aftertaste, bolted through his mind – like Maya's *déjà vu* – he had done this before! As a child they had tried it often, always hoping the taste would come round to the table taste, and so give them food in their playfield, manna in their own little wilderness. But the olive flesh (paler the further one cut in toward the pit) stubbornly remained as unpalatable as ever – the taste as embedded in his mind as any person, bitter and sour. Now pleasant, because of the memory evoked. Perhaps he had been cured.

The leaves flailed in the gusty north wind. Smell of dust. A haze of brown light, the western sky brassy. The branches rose to twice or three times his height; the underbranches drooped down where they could brush his face. Human scale. The Mediterranean tree, the tree of the Greeks, who had seen so many things so clearly, seen things in their proper proportion, everything in a gauge symmetry to the human scale – the trees, the towns, their whole physical world, the rocky islands in the Aegean, the rocky hills of the Peloponnese – a universe you could walk across in a few days. Perhaps home was the place of human scale, wherever it was. Usually childhood.

Each tree was like an animal holding its plumage up into the wind, its knobby legs thrust into the ground. A hillside of plumage flashing under the wind's onslaught, under its fluctuating gusts and knocks and unexpected stillnesses, all perfectly revealed by the feathering leaves. This was Provence, the heart of Provence; his whole underbrain seemed to be humming at the edge of every moment of his childhood, a vast *presque vu* filling him up and brimming over, a life in a landscape, humming with its own weight and balance. He no longer felt heavy. The sky's blue itself was a voice from that previous incarnation, saying, Provence, Provence.

But out over the ravine a flock of black crows swirled, crying, *Ka, ka, ka!*

Ka. Who had made up that story, of the little red people and their name for Mars? No way of telling. No beginnings to such stories. In Mediterranean antiquity the Ka had been a weird double of a pharaoh, pictured as descending on the pharaoh in the form of a hawk or a dove, or a crow.

Now the Ka of Mars was descending on him, here in Provence. Black crows – on Mars under the clear tents these same birds flew, just as carelessly powerful in the aerators' blasts as in the mistral. They didn't care that they were on Mars, it was home to them, their world as much as any other, and the people below what they always had been, dangerous ground animals who would kill you or take you on strange voyages. But no bird on Mars remembered the voyage there, or Earth either. Nothing bridged the two worlds but the human mind. The birds only flew and searched for food, and cawed, on Earth or Mars, as they always had and always would. They were at home anywhere, wheeling in the hard gusts of the wind, coping with the mistral and calling to each other, Mars, Mars, Mars! But Michel Duval, ah, Michel – a mind residing in two worlds at once, or lost in the nowhere between them. The noösphere was so huge. Where was he, who was he? How was he to live?

Olive grove. Wind. Bright sun in a brass sky. The weight of his body, the sour taste in his mouth: he felt himself soar. This was his home, this and no other. It had changed and yet it would never change – not this grove, not he himself. Home at last. Home at last. He could live on Mars for ten thousand years and still this place would be his home.

Back in the hotel room in Arles, he called up Maya. 'Please come down, Maya. I want you to see this.'

'I'm working on the agreement, Michel. The UN-Mars agreement.'

'I know.'

'It's important!'

'I know.'

'Well. It's why I came here, and I'm part of it, in the middle of it. I can't just go off on vacation.'

'Okay, okay. But look, that work will never end. Politics will never end. You *can* take a vacation, and then come back to it, and it will still be going. But this – this is my home, Maya. I want you to see it. Don't you want to show me Moscow, don't you want to go there?'

'Not if it was the last place above the flood.'

Michel sighed. 'Well, it's different for me. Please, come see what I mean.'

'Maybe in a while, when we've finished this stage of the negotiations. This is a critical time, Michel! Really it's you who ought to be here, not me who ought to be there.'

'I can watch on the wrist. There's no reason to be there in person. *Please*, Maya.'

She paused, caught finally by something in his tone of voice. 'Okay, I'll try. It won't be for a while though, no matter what.'

'As long as you come.'

After that he spent his days waiting for Maya, though he tried not to think of it like that. He occupied every waking moment travelling about in a rented car, sometimes with Sylvie, sometimes on his own. Despite the evocative moment in the olive grove, perhaps because of it too, he felt deeply dislocated. He was drawn to the new coastline for some reason, fascinated by the adjustment to the new sea level that the local people were making. He drove down to it often, following back roads that led to abrupt cliffs, to sudden valley marshes. Many of the coastal fishing people had Algerian ancestry. The fishing wasn't going well, they said. The Camargue was polluted by drowned industrial sites, and in the Med the fish were for the most part staying outside the brown water, out in the blue which was a good morning's voyage away, with many dangers en route.

Hearing and speaking French, even this strange new French, was like touching an electrode to parts of his brain that hadn't been visited in over a century. Coelacanths exploded regularly: memories of women's kindnesses to him, his cruelties to them. Perhaps that was why he had gone to Mars – to escape himself, an unpleasant fellow it seemed.

Well, if escaping himself had been his desire, he had succeeded. Now he was someone else. And a helpful man, a sympathetic man; he could look in a mirror. He could return home and face it, face what he had been, because of what he had become. Mars had done that, anyway.

It was so strange how the memory worked. The fragments were so small and sharp, they were like those furry, minute cactus needles that hurt far out of proportion to their minuscule size. What he remembered best was his life on Mars. Odessa, Burroughs, the underground shelters in the south, the hidden outposts in the chaos. Even Underhill.

If he had returned to Earth during the Underhill years, he would have been swamped with media crowds. But he had been out of contact since disappearing with Hiroko, and though he had not attempted to conceal himself since the revolution, few in France seemed to have noticed his reappearance. The enormity of recent events on Earth had included a partial fracturing of the media culture – or perhaps it was simply the passage of time; most of the population of France had been born after his disappearance, and the First Hundred were ancient history to them – not ancient enough, however, to be truly interesting. If Voltaire or Louis XIV or Charlemagne had appeared, there might be a bit of attention – perhaps – but a psychologist of the previous century who had emigrated to Mars, which was a sort of America when all was said and done? No, that was of very little interest to anyone. He got some calls, some people came by the Arlesian hotel to interview him down in the lobby or the courtyard, and after that one or two of the Paris shows came down as well; but they all were much more interested in what he could tell them about Nirgal than in anything about himself. Nirgal was the one people were fascinated by, he was their charismatic.

No doubt it was better that way. Although as Michel sat in cafés eating his meals, feeling as alone as if he were in a solo rover in the far outback of the southern highlands, it was a bit disappointing to be entirely ignored – just one *vieux* among all the rest, another one of those whose unnaturally long life was creating more logistical problems than *la fleuve blanche*, if the truth were told . . .

It was better this way. He could stop in little villages around Vallabrix, like St Quentin-la-Poterie, or St Victor-des-Quies, or St Hippolyte-de-Montaigu, and chat with the shopkeepers, who looked identical to the ones who had been running the shops when he had left, and were probably their descendants, or even possibly the same people; they spoke in an older, more stable French, careless of him, absorbed in their own conversations, their own lives. He was nothing to them, and so he could see them clearly. It was the same out in the narrow streets, where many people looked like gypsies – North African blood no doubt, spreading into the populace as it had after the Saracen invasion a thousand years before. Africans pouring in every thousand years or so; this too was Provence. The young women were beautiful: gracefully flowing through the streets in gangs, their black tresses still glossy and bright in the dust of the mistral. These had been his villages. Dusty plastic signs, everything tattered and run-down . . .

Back and forth he oscillated, between familiarity and alienation, memory and forgetfulness. But ever more lonely. In one café he ordered cassis, and at the first sip he remembered sitting in that very same café, *at that very same table*. Across from Eve. Proust had been perfectly correct to identify taste as the principle agent of involuntary memory, for one's long-term memories settled or at least were organized in the amygdala, just over the area in the brain concerned with taste and smell – and so smells were intensely intertwined with memories, and also with the emotional network of the limbic system, twisting through both areas; thus the neurological sequence, smell triggering memory triggering nostalgia. Nostalgia, the intense ache for one's past, *desire* for one's past – not because it had been so wonderful but simply because it had *been*, and now was gone. He recalled Eve's face, talking in this crowded room across from him. But not what she had said, or why they were there. Of course not. Simply an isolated moment, a cactus needle, an image seen as if by lightning bolt, then gone; and no knowing the rest of it, no matter how hard he tried to recollect. And they were all like that, his memories; that was what memories were when they got old enough, flashes in the dark, incoherent, almost meaningless, and yet sometimes filled with a vague ache.

He stumbled out of the café from his past to his car, and drove home, through Vallabrix, under the big plane trees of Grand Planas, out to the ruined *mas*, all without thinking; and he walked out to it again helplessly, as if the house might have sprung back into being. But it was still the same dusty ruin by the olive grove. And he sat on the wall, feeling blank.

That Michel Duval was gone. This one would go too. He would live into yet further incarnations and forget this moment, yes even this sharp painful moment, just as he had forgotten all the moments that had passed here the first time. Flashes, images – a man sitting on a broken wall, no feeling involved. Nothing more than that. So this Michel, too, would go.

The olive trees waved their arms, grey-green, green-grey. Goodbye, goodbye. They were no help this time, they gave him no euphoric connection with lost time; that moment too was past.

In a flickering grey-green he drove back to Arles. The clerk in the hotel's lobby was telling someone that the mistral would never stop. 'Yes it will,' Michel said as he passed.

He went up to his room and called Maya again. Please, he said. Please come soon. It was making him angry that he was reduced to such begging. Soon, she kept saying. A few more days and they would have an agreement hammered out, a bona fide written agreement between the UN and an independent Martian government. History in the making. After that she would see about coming.

Michel did not care about history in the making. He walked around Arles, waiting for her. He went back to his room to wait. He went out to walk again.

*   *   *

The Romans had used Arles for a port as much as they had Marseilles – in fact Caesar had razed Marseilles for backing Pompey, and had given Arles his favour as the local capital. Three strategic Roman roads had been constructed to meet at the town, all used for hundreds of years after the Romans had gone, and so for those centuries it had been lively, prosperous, important. But the Rhône had silted its lagoons, and the Camargue had become a pestilential swamp, and the roads had fallen into disuse. The town dwindled. The Camargue's windswept salt grasses and their famous herds of wild white horses were eventually joined by oil refineries, nuclear power plants, chemical works.

Now with the flood the lagoons were back, and flushing clean. Arles was again a seaport. Michel continued to wait for Maya there precisely because he had never lived there before. It did not remind him of anything but the moment; and he spent his days watching the people of the moment live their lives. In this new foreign country.

He received a call at the hotel, from a Francis Duval. Sylvie had contacted him. He was Michel's nephew, Michel's dead brother's son, still alive and living on Rue du 4 Septembre, just north of the Roman arena, a few blocks from the swollen Rhône, a few blocks from Michel's hotel. He invited Michel to come over.

After a moment's hesitation, Michel agreed. By the time he had walked across town, stopping briefly to peer into the Roman theatre and arena, his nephew appeared to have con-vened the entire quartier: an instant celebration, champagne corks popping like strings of firecrackers as Michel was pulled in the door and embraced by everyone there, three kisses to the cheeks, in the Provençal manner. It took him a while to get to Francis, who hugged him long and hard, talking all the while as people's camera fibres pointed at them. 'You look just like my father!' Francis said.

'So do you!' said Michel, trying to remember if it were true or not, trying to remember his brother's face. Francis was elderly, Michel had never seen his brother that old. It was hard to say.

But all the faces were familiar, somehow, and the language comprehensible, mostly, the phrases sparking image after image in him; the smells of cheese and wine sparking more; the taste of the wine yet more again. Francis it turned out was a connoisseur, and happily he uncorked a number of dusty bottles, Châteauneuf du Papes, then a century-old sauterne from Château d'Yquem, and his speciality, red premier crus from Bordeaux called Pauillacs, two each from from Châteaux Latour and Lafite, and a 2064 Château Mouton-Rothschild with a label by Pougnadoresse. These aged wonders had metamorphosed over the years into something more than mere wine, tastes thick with overtones and harmonics. They spilled down Michel's throat like his own youth.

It could have been a party for some popular town politician, say; and though Michel concluded that Francis did not much resemble Michel's brother, he sounded *exactly* like him. Michel had forgotten that voice, he would have said, but it was absolutely clear in his mind, shockingly so. The way Francis drawled 'normalement', in this case meaning the way things had been before the flood, whereas for Michel's brother it had meant that hypothetical state of smooth operation that never occurred in the real Provence – but exactly the same lilt and drawl, *nor–male–ment* . . .

Everyone wanted to speak with Michel, or at least to hear him, and so he stood with a glass in his hand and gave a quick speech in the style of a town politician, complimenting the women on their beauty, managing to make it clear how pleased he was to be in their company without getting sentimental, or revealing just how disoriented he was feeling: a slick, competent performance, which was just what the sophisticates of Provence liked, their rhetoric quick and humorous like the local bullfighting. 'And how is Mars? What is it like? What will you do now? Are there Jacobins yet?'

'Mars is Mars,' Michel said, dismissing it. 'The ground is the colour of Arlesian roof tiles. You know.'

They partied right through the afternoon, and then called in a feast. Innumerable women kissed his cheeks, he was drunk on their perfume and skin and hair, their smiling, liquid dark eyes, looking at him with friendly curiosity. Native Martian girls one always had to look up to, inspecting their chins and necks and the insides of their nostrils. Such a pleasure to look down on a straight parting in glossy black hair.

In the late evening people dispersed. Francis walked with Michel over to the Roman arena, and they climbed the bowed stone steps of the medieval towers that had fortified the arena. From the little stone chamber at the top of the stairs they looked out of small windows at the tile roofs, and the treeless streets, and the Rhône. Out of the south windows they could see a portion of the speckled sheet of water which was the Camargue.

'Back on the Med,' Francis said, deeply satisfied. 'The flood may have been a disaster for most places, but for Arles it has been a veritable coup. The rice farmers are all coming into town ready to fish, or take any work they can get. And many of the boats that survived have been docked right here in town. They've been bringing fruit in from Corsica and Mallorca, trade with Barcelona and Sicily. We've taken a good bit of Marseilles's business, although they're recovering quickly, it has to be said. But what life has come back! Before, you know, Aix had the university, Marseilles had the sea, and we had only these ruins, and the tourists who came for a day to see them. And tourism is an ugly business. It's not fit work for human beings. It's hosting parasites. But now we're living again!' He was a little bit drunk. 'Here, you must come out on the boat with me and see the lagoon.'

'I'd like that.'

That night Michel called Maya again. 'You must come. I've found my nephew, my family.'

Maya wasn't impressed. 'Nirgal went to England looking for Hiroko,' she said sharply. 'Someone told him she was there, and he left just like that.'

'What's this?' Michel exclaimed, shocked by the sudden intrusion of the idea of Hiroko.

'Oh, Michel. You know it can't be true. Someone said it to Nirgal, that's all it was. It can't be true, but he ran right off.'

'As would I!'

'Please, Michel, don't be stupid. One fool is enough. If Hiroko is alive at all, then she's on Mars. Someone just said this to Nirgal to get him away from the negotiations. I only hope it was for nothing worse. He was having too much of

245

an effect on people. And he wasn't watching his tongue. You should call him and tell him to come back. Maybe he would listen to you.'

'I wouldn't if I were him.'

Michel was lost in thought, trying to crush the sudden hope that Hiroko was alive. And in England of all places. Alive anywhere. Hiroko and therefore Iwao, Gene, Rya – the whole group – his family. His real family. He shuddered, hard; and when he tried to tell the impatient Maya about his family in Arles, the words stuck in his throat. His real family had all disappeared four years before, and that was the truth. Finally, sick at heart, he could only say, 'Please, Maya. Please come.'

'Soon. I've told Sax I'll go as soon as we're finished here. That will leave all the rest of it to him, and he can barely talk. It's ridiculous.' She was exaggerating, they had a full diplomatic team there, and Sax was perfectly competent, in his way. 'But okay, okay, I'm going to do it. So stop pestering me.'

She came the next week.

Michel drove to the new train station and met her, feeling nervous. He had lived with Maya, in Odessa and Burroughs, for almost thirty years; but now, driving her to Avignon, she seemed like a stranger sitting there beside him, an ancient beauty with hooded eyes and an expression hard to read, speaking English in harsh rapid sentences, telling him everything that had happened in Berne. They had a treaty with the UN, which had agreed to their independence. In return they were to allow some emigration, but no more than ten per cent of the Martian population per year; some transfer of mineral resources; some consultation on diplomatic issues. 'That's good, really good.' Michel tried to concentrate on her news, but it was hard. Occasionally as she spoke she glanced at the buildings shooting past their car, but in the dusty windy sunlight they looked tawdry enough in all truth. She did not seem impressed.

With a sinking feeling Michel drove as close as he could to the Pope's palace in Avignon, parked, and took her for a walk along the swollen river, past the bridge that did not reach to the other side, then to the wide promenade leading south from the palace, where pavement cafés nestled in the shade of the ancient plane trees. There they ate lunch, and Michel tasted the olive oil and the cassis, running them luxuriously over his tongue as he watched his companion relax into her metal chair like a cat. 'This is nice,' she said, and he smiled. It *was* nice: cool, relaxed, civilized, the food and drink very fine. But for him the taste of cassis was unleashing its flood of memories, emotions from previous incarnations blended with the emotions he felt now, heightening everything, colours, textures, the feel of metal chairs and wind. While for Maya cassis was just a tart berry drink.

It occurred to him as he watched her that fate had led him to a companion even more attractive than the beautiful Frenchwomen he had consorted with in that earlier life. A woman somehow *greater*. In that too he had done well on Mars. He taken on a bigger life. This feeling and his nostalgia clashed in his heart, and all the while Maya swallowed mouthfuls of cassoulet, wine, cheeses, cassis, coffee, oblivious to the interference pattern of his lives, moving in and out of phase inside him.

They talked desultorily. Maya was relaxed, enjoying herself. Happy at her accomplishment in Berne. In no hurry to go anywhere. Michel felt a glow like omegandorph all through him. Watching her he was slowly becoming happy himself; simply happy. Past, future – neither was ever real. Just lunch under plane trees, in Avignon. No need to think of anything but that. 'So civilized,' Maya said. 'I haven't felt so calm in years. I can see why you like it.' And then she was laughing at him, and he could feel an idiot grin plastering his face.

'Would you not like to see Moscow again?' he asked curiously.

'Ah no. I would not.'

She dismissed the idea as an intrusion on the moment. He wondered what she felt about this return to Earth. Surely one could not be completely without feelings about such a thing?

But to some people home was home, a complex of feeling far beyond rationality, a sort of grid or gravitational field in which the personality itself took its geometrical shape. While for others, a place was just a place, and the self free of all that, the same no matter where it was. One kind lived in the Einsteinian curved space of home, the other in the Newtonian absolute space of the free self. And while he was one of the former type, Maya was one of the latter. And there was no use struggling against that fact. Nevertheless he wanted her to like Provence. Or at least to see why he loved it.

And so, when they had finished eating, he drove her south through St Rémy, to Les Baux.

She slept during the drive, and he was not displeased; between Avignon and Les Baux the landscape consisted mostly of ugly industrial buildings, scattered on a dusty plain. She woke up at just the right time, when he was negotiating the narrow twisting road that wandered up a crease in the Alpilles to the old hilltop village. One parked in a car park, then walked up into the town; it was clearly a tourist arrangement, but the single curving street of the little settlement was now very quiet indeed, as if abandoned; and very picturesque. The village was shuttered for the afternoon, asleep. On the last turn to the hill's top, one crossed open ground like a rough, tilted plaza, and beyond that were the limestone knobs of the hilltop, every knob hollowed out by some eremite of the ancient hermitage, tucked above Saracens and all the other dangers of the medieval world. To the south the Mediterranean gleamed like gold plate. The rock itself was yellowish, and as a thin veil of bronzed cloud lay in the western sky, the light everywhere took on a metallic amber cast, as if they walked in a gel of years.

They clambered from one tiny chamber to the next, marvelling at how small they were. 'It's like a prairie dog nest,' Maya said, peering down into one squared-out little cave. 'It's like our trailer park in Underhill.'

Back on the tilted plaza, littered with limestone blocks, they stopped to watch the Mediterranean shine. Michel pointed out the lighter sheen of the Camargue. 'You used to see only a bit of water.' The light deepened to a dark apricot, and the hill seemed a fortress above the oh-so-spacious world, above time itself. Maya put an arm around his waist and hugged him, shivering. 'It's beautiful. But I couldn't live up here like they did, it's too exposed somehow.'

They went back to Arles. As it was a Saturday night, the town centre had become a kind of gypsy or North African festival, the alleys crowded with food and drink stands, many of them tucked into the arches of the Roman arena, which was open to all, with a band playing inside it. Maya and Michel walked around arm in arm, bathed in the smells of frying food and Arabic spices. Voices around them spoke in two or three different languages. 'It reminds me of Odessa,' Maya said as they made their promenade around the Roman arena, 'only the people are so little. It's nice not to feel dwarfed for once.'

They danced in the arena centre, drank at a table under the blurry stars. One star was red, and Michel had his suspicions, but did not voice them. They went back to his hotel room and made love on the narrow bed, and at some point it seemed to Michel that there were several people in him, all coming at once; he cried out at the strange rapture of that sensation . . . Maya fell asleep and he lay beside her awake, in a tristesse reverberating somewhere outside time, drinking in the familiar smell of her hair and listening to the slowly diminishing cacophony of the town. Home at last.

* * *

249

In the days that followed, he introduced her to his nephew and to the rest of his relatives, rounded up by Francis. That whole gang took her in, and through the use of translation AIs asked her scores of questions. They also tried to tell her everything about themselves. It happened so often, Michel thought; people wanted to seize the famous stranger whose story they knew (or thought they knew), and give them their story in return, to redress the balance of the relationship. Some kind of witnessing, or confessional. The reciprocal sharing of stories. And people were naturally drawn to Maya anyway. She listened to their stories, and laughed, and asked questions – utterly there. Time after time they told her how the flood had come, drowning their homes, their livings, throwing them out into the world, to friends and family they hadn't seen in years, forcing them into new patterns and reliances, breaking the mould of their lives and thrusting them out into the mistral. They had been exalted by this process, Michel saw, they were proud of their response, of how people had pulled together – also very indignant at any counter-examples of gouging or callousness, blots on an otherwise heroic affair: 'Can you believe it? And it did no good; he was jumped one night in the street and all that money gone.'

'It woke us up, do you see, do you see? It woke us up when we had been asleep for ever.'

They would say these things to Michel in French, watch him nod, and then watch Maya for her response as the AIs told their tale in English to her. And she would nod as well, absorbed as she had been in the young natives around Hellas Basin, focusing their stories by the look on her face, by her interest. Ah, she and Nirgal, they were two of a kind, they were charismatics – because of the way they focused on others, the way they exalted people's stories. Perhaps that was what charisma was, a kind of mirror quality.

Some of Michel's relatives took them out on their boats, and Maya marvelled at the rampaging Rhône as they ran down it, at the strangely cluttered lagoon of the Camargue, and the efforts people were making to rechannelize it. Then out onto the brown water of the Med, and further still, onto the blue water – the sunbeaten blue, the little boat bouncing over the whitecaps whipped up by the mistral. All the way out of the sight of land, on a blue sunbeaten plate of water: amazing. Michel stripped and jumped over the side, into cold water, where he sloshed the salt water down and drank some of it too, savouring the amniotic taste of his old beach swims.

Back on land they went out on drives. Once they went out to see the Pont du Gard, and there it was, same as ever, the Romans' greatest work of art – an aqueduct: three tiers of stone, the thick lower arches foursquare in the river, proud of their two thousand years' resistance to running water; lighter taller arches above, then the smallest on top of them. Form following function right into the heart of the beautiful – using stone to take water over water. The stone now pitted and honey-blond, very Martian in every respect – it looked like Nadia's Underhill arcade, standing there in the dusty green and limestone gorge of the Gard, in Provence; but now, to Michel, almost more Mars than France.

Maya loved its elegance. 'See how human it is, Michel. This is what our Martian structures lack, they are too big. But this – this was built by human hands, with tools anyone could construct and use. Block and tackle and human math, and perhaps some horses. And not our teleoperated machines and their weird materials, doing things no one can understand or even see.'

'Yes.'

'I wonder if we could build things by hand. Nadia should see this, she would love it.'

'That's what I thought.'

Michel was happy. They ate a picnic there. They visited the fountains of Aix-en-Provence. Went out to an overlook above the Grand Canyon of the Gard. Nosed around the street docks of Marseilles. Visited the Roman sites in Orange, and Nîmes. Drove past the drowned resorts of the Côte D'Azur. Walked out one evening to Michel's ruined *mas*, and into the middle of the old olive grove.

And every night of these few precious days they returned to Arles, and ate in the hotel restaurant, or if it was warm out, under the plane trees in the pavement cafés; and then went up to their room and made love; and at dawn woke and made love again, or went down directly for fresh croissants and coffee. 'It's lovely,' Maya said, standing one blue evening in the tower of the arena, looking over the tile roofs of the town; she meant all of it, all of Provence. And Michel was happy.

But a call came on the wrist. Nirgal was sick, very sick; Sax, sounding shaken, had already got him off Earth, back into Martian g and a sterile environment, inside a ship in Terran orbit. 'I'm afraid his immune system isn't up to it, and the g doesn't help. He's got an infection, pulmonary oedema, a very bad fever.'

'Allergic to Earth,' Maya said, her face grim. She made plans and ended the call with curt instructions to Sax to stay calm, then went to the room's little closet and began to throw her clothes out onto the bed.

'Come on!' she cried when she saw Michel standing there. 'We have to go!'

'We do?'

She waved him off, burrowed into the closet. 'I'm going.' She threw handfuls of underwear into her suitcase, gave him a look. 'It's time to go anyway.'

'It is?'

She didn't reply. She was tapping at her wristpad, asking the local Praxis team to arrange transport into space. There they would rendezvous with Sax and Nirgal. Her voice was cold, tense, businesslike. She had already forgotten Provence.

When she saw Michel still standing motionless, she exploded — 'Oh come on, don't be so theatrical about it! Just because we have to leave now doesn't mean we won't ever come back! We're going to live a thousand years, you can come back all the time if you want, a hundred times, my God! Besides how is this place so much better than Mars? It looks just like Odessa to me, and you were happy there, weren't you?'

Michel ignored that. He stumbled by her suitcases to the window. Outside, an ordinary Arlesian street, blue in the twilight: pastel stucco walls, cobblestones. Cypress trees. Tiles on the roof across the street were broken. Mars-coloured. Voices below shouted in French, angry about something.

'Well?' Maya exclaimed. 'Are you coming?'

'Yes.'

PART SIX

Ann in the Outback

PART SIX

Alone in the Crowbars

Look, not choosing to take the longevity treatment is suicide.
 So?
 Well. Suicide is usually considered to be a sign of psycho-
logical dysfunction.
 Usually.
 I think you'll find it's true more often than not. You're
unhappy at least.
 At least.
 And yet why? What now is lacking?
 The world.
 Every day you still walk out to see the sunset.
 Habit.
 You claim the destruction of the primal Mars is the source
of your depression. I think the philosophical reasons cited by
people suffering depression are masks protecting them from
harder, more personal hurts.
 It can all be real.
 You mean all the reasons?
 Yes. What did you accuse Sax of? Monocausotaxophilia?
 Touché. But there's usually a start to these things, among
all the real reasons – the first one that started you down your
road. Often you have to go back to that point in your journey
in order to start off in a new way.
 Time is not space. The metaphor of space lies about what
is really possible in time. You can never go back.
 No no. You can go back, metaphorically. In your mental
travelling you can journey back into the past, retrace your
steps, see where you turned and why, then proceed onward
in a direction that is different because it includes these loops
of understanding. Increased understanding increases meaning.
When you continue to insist that it is the fate of Mars that
concerns you most, I think it is a displacement so strong that
it has confused you. It too is a metaphor. Perhaps a true one,
yes. But both terms of the metaphor should be recognized.
 I see what I see.
 But the way it is, you are not even seeing. There is so much
of red Mars that remains. You should go out and look! Go

out and empty your mind and just see what is out there. Go out at low altitude and walk free in the air, a simple dust mask only. It would be good for you, good at the physiological level. Also it would be reaping a benefit of the terraforming. To experience the freedom it gives us, the bond with this world – that we can walk on its surface naked and survive. It's amazing! It makes us part of an ecology. It deserves to be rethought, this process. You should go out to consider it, to study the process as areoformation.

That's just a word. We took this planet and ploughed it under. It's melting under our feet.

Melting in native water. Not imported from Saturn or the like, it's been there from the beginning, part of the original accretion, right? Outgassed from the first lump that was Mars. Now part of our bodies. Our very bodies are patterns in Martian water. Without the trace minerals we would be transparent. We are Martian water. And water that has been on the surface of Mars before, yes? Rupturing out in artesian apocalypse. Those channels are so big!

It was permafrost for two billion years.

Then we helped it back onto the surface. The majesty of the great outbreak floods. We were there, we saw one with our own eyes, we nearly died in it —

Yes, yes —

You felt the car as that water swept it away, you were driving —

Yes! But it swept Frank away instead.

Yes.

It swept the world away. And left us on the beach.

The world is still here. You could go out and see.

I don't want to see. I've seen it already!

Not you. Some previous you. Now you're the you living now.

Yes yes.

I think you're afraid. Afraid of attempting a transmutation – a metamorphosis into something new. The alembic stands out there, all around you. The fire is hot. You'll be melted, you'll be reborn, who knows if you'll still be there afterward?

I don't want to change.

You don't want to stop loving Mars.

Yes. No.

You will never stop loving Mars. After metamorphosis the rock still exists. It's usually harder than the parent rock, yes? You will always love Mars. Your task becomes seeing the Mars that always endures, under thick or thin, hot or cold, wet or dry. Those are ephemeral, but Mars endures. These floods happened before, isn't it true?

Yes.

Mars's own water. All these volatiles are Mars's own volatiles.

Except the nitrogen from Titan.

Yes yes. You sound like Sax.

Come on.

You two are more alike than you think. And all we volatiles are Mars's own.

But the destruction of the surface. It's wrecked. Everything's changed.

That's areology. Or the areophany.

It's destruction. We should have tried living here as it was.

But we didn't. And so now being Red means working to keep conditions as much like the primal conditions as possible, within the framework of the areophany — the project of biosphere creation that allows humans the freedom of the surface, below a certain altitude. That's all being a Red can mean now. And there are a lot of Reds like that. I think you worry that if you ever change in even the slightest degree, then that will be the end of redness everywhere. But redness is bigger than you. You helped start it and define it, but you were never the only one. If you had been no one would ever have listened to you.

They didn't!

Some did. Many did. Redness will go on no matter what you do. You could retire, you could become someone entirely different, you could become lime green, and redness would always go on. It might even become something more red than you ever imagined.

I've imagined it as red as it can get.

All those alternatives. We'll live one of them and then go on. The process of co-adaptation with this planet will go on for thousands of years. But here we are now. At every moment

257

you should ask, what now is lacking? and work at some acceptance of your current reality. This is sanity, this is life. You have to imagine your life from here on out.

I can't. I've tried and I can't.

You should go have a look around, really. A walkabout. Look very closely. Take a look even at the ice seas, a close look. But not just that. That is in the nature of a confrontation. Confrontation is not necessarily bad, but first just a look, eh? A recognition. Then you should think about going up into the hills. Tharsis, Elysium. A rise in altitude is a voyage into the past. Your task is to find the Mars that endures through all. It's wonderful, really. So many people don't have such a wonderful task as that, you can't imagine. You're lucky to have it.

And you?

What?

What is your task?

My task?

Yes. Your task.

. . . I'm not sure. I told you, I envy you having that. My tasks are . . . confused. To help Maya, and me. And the rest of us. Reconciliation . . . I would like to find Hiroko . . .

You've been our shrink for a long time.

Yes.

Over a hundred years.

Yes.

And never any results at all.

Well. I like to think I have helped a little.

But it doesn't come naturally to you.

Perhaps not.

Do you think people get interested in studying psychology because they're troubled in the mind?

It's a common theory.

But no one has ever been shrink to you.

Oh I've had my therapists.

Helpful?

Yes! Quite helpful. Fairly helpful. I mean – they did what they could.

But you don't know your task.

No. Or, I . . . I want to go home.

What home?

That's the problem. Hard when you don't know where home is, eh?

Yes. I thought you would stay in Provence.

No, no. I mean, Provence is my home, but . . .

But now you're on your way back to Mars.

Yes.

You decided to come back.

. . . Yes.

You don't know what you're doing, do you?

No. But you do. You know where your home is. You have that, and it's precious! You should remember that, you shouldn't be throwing away such a gift, or thinking it's a burden! You're a fool to think that! It's a gift, damn you, a precious, precious gift, do you understand me?

I'll have to think about that.

She left the refuge in a meteorological rover from the previous century, a high, square thing with a luxurious windowbox driver's compartment up top. It was not unlike the front half of the expedition rover in which she had first travelled to the North Pole, with Nadia and Phyllis and Edmund and George. And because she had spent thousands of days since then in such machines, she at first had the impression that what she was doing was ordinary, contiguous with the rest of her life.

But she drove northeast, downcanyon, until she was in the bed of the little unnamed channel at 60° longitude, 53° north. This valley had been carved by a small aquifer outbreak during the late Amazonian, running in an earlier graben fault, down the lower slopes of the Great Escarpment. The scoring effects of the flood were still visible on the rims of the canyon walls, and in the lenticular islands of bedrock on the floor of the channel.

Which now ran north into a sea of ice.

She got out of the car wearing a fibrefilled windsuit, a CO_2 mask, goggles, and heated boots. The air was thin and cold, though it was spring now in the north – Ls 10, M-53. Cold and windy, ragged lines of low puffy clouds racing east. It was either going to be an ice age or, if the Greens' manipulations forestalled it, then a year-without-summer, like 1810 on Earth, when the explosion of the volcano Tambori had chilled the world.

She walked the shore of the new sea. It was at the foot of the Great Escarpment, in Tempe Terra, a lobe of ancient highlands extending into the north. Tempe had probably escaped the general stripping of the northern hemisphere by being roughly opposite the impact point of the Big Hit, which most areologists now agreed had struck near Hrad Vallis, above Elysium. So; battered hills, overlooking an ice-covered sea. The rock looked like a red sea's surface in a wild cross-chop; the ice looked like a prairie in the depths of winter. Native water, as

Michel had said – there from the beginning, on the surface before. It was a hard thing to grasp. Her thoughts were scattered and confused, darting this way and that, all at the same time – it was like madness, but not. She knew the difference. The hum and keen of the wind did not speak to her in the tones of the MIT lecturer; she suffered no choking sensations when she tried to breathe. It was not like that. Rather her thinking was accelerated, fractured, unpredictable – like that flock of birds over the ice, zigzagging across the sky in a hard wind from the west. Ah, the feel of that same wind against her body, shoving at it, the new thick air like a great animal paw . . .

The birds struggled in it with reckless skill. She stood for a while and watched: they were skuas, out hunting over dark streaks of open water. These polnyaps were just the surface signs of immense pods of liquid water under the ice; she had heard that a continuous channel of under-ice water now wrapped the globe, winding east over old Vastitas, tearing frequent polnyaps in the surface, gaps which then stayed liquid for an hour or a week. Even with the air so cold, the underwater temperatures were warmed by the drowned Vastitas moholes, and rising heat from the thousands of thermonuclear explosions set off by the metanats around the turn of the century. These bombs had been placed deep enough in the megaregolith to trap their radioactive fallout, supposedly, but not their heat, which rose in a thermal pulse through the rock, a pulse that would continue for years and years. No; Michel could talk about it being Mars's water, but there was little else that was natural about this new sea.

Ann hiked up a ridge to get a wider view. There it lay: ice, mostly flat, sometimes shattered. All as still as a butterfly on a twig, as if the whiteness might suddenly lift off and fly away. The birds' wheeling and the clouds' scudding showed how hard the wind blew, everything in the air pouring east; but the ice remained still. The wind's voice was deep and huge, scraping over a billion cold edges. A strip of grey water was striated by windchop, the strength of each gust precisely registered by the flayed cat's paws, each brush of harder wind feathering the larger waves with exquisite sensitivity. Water. And below that brushed surface, plankton, krill, fish, squid;

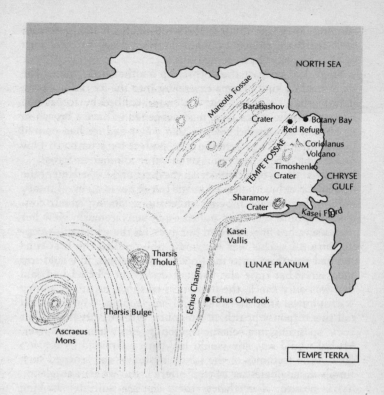

NORTH SEA

Mareotis Fossae

Barabashov
Crater

● Botany Bay

● Red Refuge

△ Coriolanus
Volcano

TEMPE FOSSAE

Timoshenko
Crater

CHRYSE
GULF

Sharamov
Crater

Kasei Fjord

Kasei
Vallis

LUNAE PLANUM

Tharsis
Tholus

Echus Chasma

● Echus Overlook

Tharsis Bulge

Ascraeus
Mons

TEMPE TERRA

she had heard they were producing in hatcheries all the creatures of the extremely short Antarctic food chain, and then
releasing them to the sea. Teeming water.

The skuas wheeled overhead. One cloud of them whirlpooled
down onto something along on the shore, behind some rocks.
Ann hiked toward them. Suddenly she saw the birds' target,
lying in a cleft at the edge of the ice: the mostly-eaten remains
of a seal. Seals! The corpse lay on tundra grass, in the lee
of a patch of sand dunes, sheltered by another rocky ridge

running down into the ice. The white skeleton emerged from dark red flesh, ringed by white blubber, black fur. All torn open to the sky. Eyes pecked out.

She hiked on past the corpse, up another little ridge. The ridge made a kind of cape extending into the ice, and beyond it was a bay. A round bay – a crater, infilled by ice. It had happened to lie at sea level, had happened to have a breach in its rim on its seaward side, so that water and ice had poured in and filled it. Now a round bay, perfect for a harbour. One day it would be a harbour. About three kilometres across.

Ann sat down on a boulder on the cape, and looked out at the new bay. Her breath heaved in and out of her in an involuntary motion, her ribcage moving violently, as during labour contractions. Sobs, yes. She pulled aside her facemask, blew her nose using her finger, wiped her eyes, all the while still weeping furiously. This was her body. She recalled the first time she had stumbled onto the flooding of Vastitas, in a solo trip ages ago. That time she had not cried, but Michel had said that was only shock, the numbness of shock, as in any injury – withdrawal from her body and her feelings. Michel would call this response healthier, no doubt, but why? It hurt – her body, spasming in a seismic trembling. But when it was over, Michel would say, she would feel better. Drained. A tension gone – the tectonics of the limbic system – she scorned such simplistic analogies as Michel offered, the woman as planet, it was absurd. Nevertheless there she sat, sniffling, looking out at the ice bay under scudding clouds, feeling drained.

Nothing moved except for clouds overhead, and cat's paws on a patch of open water, gust after gust, shimmering grey, mauve, grey. Water moved but the land was still.

Finally Ann stood and walked down a rib of hard old shishovite, now forming a narrow divide between two long beaches. To tell the truth, above the ice there was not that much that had changed from the primal state. Down at the waterline it was a different story. Here the daily trade winds over the open water of the summer bay had created waves large enough to break the remaining chunks of ice into what they called brash ice. Lines of this flotsam were now beached above the current ice level, like ice sculptures depicting drift-wood. But in the summer this ice had helped to rip up the sand of the new beaches, tearing it into a slurry of ice and mud and sand, now frozen in place like brown cake frosting.

Ann walked slowly across this mess. Beyond it there was a little inlet, crowded with ice boulders that had grounded in the shallows and then been frozen into the sea surface. Exposure to sun and wind had rendered these boulders into baroque fantasias of clear blue ice and opaque red ice, like aggregates of sapphire and bloodstone. The south sides of the blocks had melted preferentially, the meltwater frozen in icicles, ice beards, ice sheets, ice columns.

Looking back at the shore she saw again how the sand was furrowed and torn; the damage was terrific, the gouges sometimes two metres deep – incredible force, to plough such trenches! The sand drifts must have been loess, made of loose, light aeolian deposits. Now a no-man's land of frozen mud and dirty ice, as if bombs had devastated some sad army's trenches.

She continued outward, stepping on opaque ice. On the surface of the bay. Like a world covered in semen. Once the ice cracked under her boot.

When she was well out on the bay she stopped and had a look around. Tight horizons indeed; she climbed a flat-topped berg, which gave her a larger view over the expanse of ice, out to the circle of the crater rim, just under the running clouds. Though cracked and jumbled and lined by pressure ridges, the ice nevertheless clearly conveyed the flatness of the water beneath it. To the north the gap to the sea was obvious. Tabular bergs stuck out from the ice like deformed castles. A white waste.

After struggling to come to grips with the scene, and failing, she clambered off the berg and hiked back to the shore, then back toward her car. As she was crossing the little ridge cape, movement down at the edge of the ice caught her eye. A white thing moved – a person in a white walker, on all fours – no. A bear. A polar bear. Walking along the edge of the ice.

It spotted the dustdevil of skuas over the dead seal. Ann crouched behind a boulder, went prone on a patch of frosty sand. Cold all along the front of her body. She looked over the boulder.

The bear's ivory fur yellowed on its flanks and legs. It raised a heavy head, sniffed like a dog, looked around curiously. It shambled to the corpse of the seal, ignoring the column of squealing birds. It ate from the seal like a dog from a bowl. It raised its head, muzzle dark red. Ann's heart pounded. The bear sat on its haunches and licked a paw, rubbed its face until it was clean, catlike in its fastidiousness. Then without warning it dropped to all fours and started up the slope of rock and sand, toward Ann's hiding place behind the boulder. It trotted, moving both the legs on one side of its body in the same motion, left, right, left.

Ann rolled down the other side of the little cape and got up and ran up the trough of a shallow fracture, leading her southwest. Her rover was almost directly west of her, she reckoned, but the bear was coming from the northwest. She clambered up the short steep side of the southwest-trending canyon, ran over a strip of high ground to another little fracture canyon, trending a bit more to the west than the previous one. Up again, onto the next strip of high ground between these shallow fossae. She looked back. Already she was panting, and her rover was still at least two kilometres away, to the west and a little south. It was still out of sight, behind ragged hillocks. The bear was north and east of her; if it made directly for the rover it would be almost as close to it now as she was. Did it hunt by sight or by smell? Could it plot the course of its prey, and move to cut it off?

No doubt it could. She was sweating inside her windsuit. She hustled down into the next canyon and ran in it for a while, west-southwest. Then she saw an easy ramp and ran up to the next inter-canyon strip, a kind of wide high road between the shallow canyons on both sides. Looking back she found herself staring at the polar bear. It stood on all fours, behind and two canyons over, looking like a very big dog, or a cross between a dog and a person, draped in straw-white fur. It amazed her to see such a creature out there, the food chain couldn't possibly support such a large predator, could it? They must surely be feeding it at feed stations. Hopefully so, or else it would be very hungry. Now it dropped into the canyon two over, out of sight, and Ann started to run down the strip toward her rover. Despite her running around, and the tight rugged horizon, she was confident of her sense of the car's location.

She kept to a pace she thought she could sustain for the whole distance. It was hard not to let loose and sprint at full speed, but no, no, that would lead to a collapse eventually. Pace yourself, she thought, panting in short gasps. Get down off the high ground into a graben so you're out of sight. Keep oriented, are you passing south of the rover? Back up to the higher ground, for just a moment to look. There behind that low flat-topped hill, which was a small crater, with a hump on the south end of the rim – she was certain – though the rover was still out of sight, and the jumbled land was easy to get confused in. A thousand times she had briefly got semi-lost, unsure of her exact location in relation to some fixed point, usually her parked rover – not a big deal usually, as her wrist's APS could always lead her back. As it could now too, but she was sure it was over there behind that bump of a crater.

The cold air burned in her lungs. She recalled the emergency facemask in her backpack, and stopped and yanked off the backpack and dug, pulled off the CO_2 mask and put on the air mask; it contained a short supply of compressed oxygen in its frame, and with it pulled over her mouth and nose and turned on, she was suddenly stronger, faster, could hold a better pace. She ran along a strip of high ground between canyons, hoping to get a sighting of the rover round the slope of the crater apron. Ah, there it was! Panting triumphantly she sucked down the cool oxygen; it tasted lovely, but was not enough to stop her gasping. If she went down into the trough to her right it looked as if it would run straight to the rover.

She glanced back and saw the polar bear running too, legs now in a shambling kind of gallop – lumbering – but it ate up the ground with that run, and the shallow canyon walls seemed no impediment to it, it flowed over them like a white nightmare, a thing beautiful and terrifying, the liquid flow of its muscles loose under thick yellow-tipped white fur. All this she saw in a single moment of the utmost clarity, everything in her field of vision distinct and acute and luminous, as if lit from within. Even running as hard as she could, focusing on the ground to make sure she didn't trip over anything, she still saw the bear flowing over the red slope, like an afterimage.

Pounding, running hard, boulder ballet; the bear was fast and the terrain nothing to it, but she too was an animal, she too had spent years in the back country of Mars, many more years in fact than this young bear, and she could run like an ibex over the terrain, from bedrock to boulder to sand to rubble, pushing hard but perfectly balanced, in control of the dash and running for her life. And besides the rover was near. Just up one last canyon side, and the slope of the apron, and there it was, she almost ran into it, stopped, reared up and pounded the curved metal side with a hard triumphant *wham*, as if it were the bear's snout, and then with a second more controlled punch to the lock door console she was inside, inside, and the outer lock door closed behind her.

She hurried upstairs to the driver's eyrie to look back. Through the glass she saw the polar bear below, inspecting her vehicle from a respectful distance. Out of dart gun range, sniffing thoughtfully. Ann was sweating hard, still gasping hard for air, in and out, in and out – what violent paroxysms the ribcage could go through! And there she was, sitting safe in the driver's seat! She only had to close her eyes and she saw again that heraldic image of the bear flowing over the rock; but open them and there the dashboard gleamed, bright and artificial and familiar. Ah so strange!

She was still in a kind of shock a couple of days later, able to see the polar bear if she closed her eyes and thought about it; distracted. By night the ice in the bay boomed and groaned, sometimes cracked explosively, so that she dreamed of the assault on Sheffield, groaning herself. By day she drove so carelessly that she had to put the rover on automatic pilot, instructing it to make its way along the shore of the crater bay.

While it rolled she wandered around the driver's compartment, her mind racing. Out of control. Nothing to be done but laugh and endure it. Strike the walls, stare out of the windows. The bear was gone but it wasn't. She looked it up: *ursus maritimus*, ocean bear; the Inuit called it *Tôrnâssuk*, 'the one who gives power'. It was like the landslide that had almost caught her in Melas Chasma, now a part of her life forever. Facing the landslide she had not moved a muscle; this

268

time she had run like hell. Mars could kill her, no doubt it would kill her, but no big zoo creature from Earth was going to kill her, not if she could help it. Not that she was so enamoured of life, far from it; but one should be free to choose one's death. As she had chosen in the past, twice at least. But Simon and then Sax – like little brown bears – had snatched her death away from her. She still didn't know what to make of that, how to feel about it. Her mind was racing so fast. She held onto the back of the driver's seat. Finally she reached forward and punched Sax's old First Hundred number on the rover's screen keyboard, XY23, and waited for the AI to route the call to the shuttle returning Sax and the others to Mars; and after a while there he was, with his new face, staring into a screen.

'Why did you do it?' she shouted. 'It's my death to choose as I please!'

She waited for the message to reach him. Then it did and he jumped, the image of him jiggled. 'Because — ' he said, and stopped.

Ann felt a chill. That was just what Simon had said, after he had pulled her back in out of the chaos. They never had a reason, only life's idiot *because*.

Sax went on: 'I didn't want – it seemed like such a waste – what a surprise to hear from you. I'm glad.'

'To hell with that,' Ann said.

She was about to cut the connection when he started speaking again – they were in simultaneous transmission now, alternating messages, 'It was so I could talk to you, Ann. I mean it was for myself – I didn't want to be missing you. I wanted you to forgive me. I wanted to argue with you more and – and make you see why I've done what I've done.'

His chatter stopped as abruptly as it had started, and then he looked confused, even frightened. Perhaps he had just heard 'To hell with that.' She could scare him, no doubt of that.

'What crap,' she said.

After a while: 'Yes. Um – how are you doing? You look . . .'

She cut the connection. I just outran a polar bear! she shouted in her mind. I was almost eaten by your stupid games!

No. She wouldn't tell him. The meddler. He had needed a good referee for his submissions to *The Metajournal of*

Martian History, that was what it came down to. Making sure his science was properly peer reviewed – for that he would crash around in a person's most inward desires, in her essential freedom to choose life or death, to be a free human being!

At least he hadn't tried to lie about it.

And – well – here she was. Rage; remorse without cause; inexplicable anguish; a strangely painful exhilaration: all this filled her at once. The limbic system, vibrating madly, spiking every thought with contradictory wild emotions, disconnected from the thoughts' content: Sax had saved her, she hated him, she felt a fierce joy, Kasei was dead, Peter wasn't, no bear could kill her, etc – on and on and on. Oh so strange!

She spotted a little green rover, perched on a bluff over the ice bay. Impulsively she took over the wheel and drove up to it. A little face peered out at her; she waved through the windshields at it. Black eyes – spectacles – bald. Like her step-father. She parked her rover next to his. The man gestured for her to come over, holding up a wooden spoon. He looked vague, only half pulled out of his own thoughts.

Ann put on a down jacket and went through the lock doors and walked between the cars, feeling the shock of the frigid air like a dousing in cold water. It was nice to be able to walk between one rover and another without suiting up, or, to get to the crux of the matter, risking death. Amazing that more people hadn't been killed by carelessness or lock malfunction. Some had been, of course. Scores, probably, if you added them all up. Now it was just a dash of cold air.

The bald man opened his inner lock door. 'Hello,' he said, and offered a hand.

'Hello,' Ann said, and shook it. 'I'm Ann.'

'I'm Harry. Harry Whitebook.'

'Ah. I've heard of you. You design animals.'

He smiled gently. 'Yes.' No shame; no defensiveness.

'I was just chased by one of your polar bears today.'

'Were you!' His eyes opened round. 'Those are fast!'

'So they are. But they're not just polar bears, are they?'

'They've got some grizzly genes, for altitude. But mostly it's just *ursus maritimus*. They're very tough creatures.'

'A lot of creatures are.'

'Yes, isn't it marvellous? Oh excuse me, have you eaten? Would you like some soup? I was just making soup, leek soup, I guess it must be obvious.'

It was. 'Sure,' Ann said.

Over soup and bread she asked him questions about the polar bear. 'Surely there can't be a whole food chain here for something that huge?'

'Oh yes. In this area there is. It's well known for that – the first bioregion robust enough for bears. The bay is liquid to the bottom, you see. The Ap mohole is at the centre of the crater, so it's like a bottomless lake. Iced over in winter of course, but the bears are used to that from the Arctic.'

'The winters are long.'

'Yes. The female bears make dens in the snow, near some caves in dyke outcroppings to the west. They don't truly hibernate, their body temperatures drop just a few degrees, and they can wake up in a minute or two, if they need to adjust the den for heat. So they den for as much of the winters as they can, then live in there and forage out till spring. Then in spring we tow some of the ice plates through the mouth of the bay out to sea, and things develop from there, bottom to top. The basic chains are Antarctic in the water, Arctic on the land. Plankton, krill, fish and squid, Weddell seals, and on land rabbits and hares, lemmings, marmots, mice, lynx, bobcat. And the bears. We're trying with caribou and reindeer and wolves, but there isn't the forage for ungulates yet. The bears have been out just a few years, the air pressure hasn't been adequate until recently. But it's a four thousand metre equivalent here now, and the bears do very well with that, we find. They adapt very quickly.'

'Humans too.'

'Well, we haven't seen too much at the four thousand metre level yet.' He meant four thousand metres above sea level on Earth. Higher than any permanent human settlement, as she recalled.

He was going on: '. . . eventually see thoracic cavity expansion, bound to happen . . .' A man who talked to himself. Big, bulky; white fur in a fringe around his bald pate. Black eyes swimming behind round spectacles.

'Did you ever meet Hiroko?' she said.

'Hiroko Ai? I did, once. Lovely woman. I hear she's gone back to Earth, to help them adapt to the flood. Did you know her?'

'Yes. I'm Ann Clayborne.'

'I thought so. Peter Clayborne's mother, isn't that right?'

'Yes.'

'He's been in Boone recently.'

'Boone?'

'That's the little station across the bay. This is Botany Bay, and the station is Boone Harbour. A kind of joke. Apparently there was a similar pairing in Australia.'

'Indeed.' She shook her head. John would be with them forever. And by no means the worst of the ghosts haunting them.

As, for instance, this man, the famous animal designer. He clattered about the kitchen, pawing at things short-sightedly. He put the soup before her and she ate, watching him furtively as she did. He knew who she was, but he did not seem uncomfortable. He did not try to justify himself. She was a Red areologist, he designed new Martian animals. They worked on the same planet. But that did not mean they were enemies, not to him. He would eat her without malice. There was something chilling in that, overbearing despite his gentle manner. Obliviousness was so brutal. And yet she liked him; that dispassionate power, vagueness – something. He bumbled around his kitchen, sat and ate with her, quickly and noisily, his muzzle wet with the clear soup stock. Afterward they broke pieces of bread from a long loaf. Ann asked questions about Boone Harbour.

'It has a good bakery,' Whitebook said, indicating the loaf. 'And a good lab. The rest is just an ordinary outpost. But we took the tent down last year, and now it is very cold, especially in the winter. Only 46° latitude, but we feel it as a northern place. So much so that there is some talk of putting the tent back up, in winter at least. And there are people who say we should leave it on until things warm up.'

'Till the ice age is over?'

'I don't think there will be an ice age. This first year without the soletta was bad, of course, but various compensations ought to be possible. A cold couple of years, that's all it will be.'

He waggled a paw: it could go either way. Ann almost threw her chunk of bread at him. But best not to startle him. She controlled herself with a shudder.

'Is Peter still in Boone?' she asked.

'I think so. He was a few days ago.'

They talked some more about the Botany Bay ecosystem. Without a fuller array of plant life, animal designers were sharply limited; it was still more like the Antarctic than the Arctic in that respect. Possibly new soil enhancement methods could speed the arrival of higher plants. Right now it was a land of lichen, for the most part. The tundra plants would follow.

'But this displeases you,' he observed.

'I liked it the way it was before. All Vastitas Borealis was barchan dunes, made of black garnet sand.'

'Won't some remain, up next to the polar cap?'

'The ice cap will go right down to the sealine in most places. As you say, kind of like Antarctica. No, the dunes and the laminate terrain will be underwater, one way or another. The whole northern hemisphere will be gone.'

'This is the nothern hemisphere.'

'A highland peninsula. And it's gone too, in a way. Botany Bay was Arcadia Crater Ap.'

He looked at her through the spectacles, peering. 'Perhaps if you lived at high altitude, it might seem like the old days. The old days, with air.'

'Perhaps,' she said cautiously. He was circling the chamber, shambling about with heavy steps, cleaning big kitchen knives at the sink. His fingers ended in short blunt claws; even clipped they made it hard for him to work with small objects.

She stood up carefully. 'Thanks for dinner,' she said, backing toward the lock door. She grabbed her jacket on the way out and slammed the door on his look of surprise. Out into the hard cold slap of the night, into her jacket. Never run away from a predator. She walked back to her car and climbed in without looking back.

The ancient highland of Tempe Terra was dotted by a number of small volcanoes, so there were lava plains and channels everywhere; also viscous creep features caused by ground ice, and the occasional small outflow channel that had run down the side of the Great Escarpment; all this along with the usual collection of Noachian impact and deformational features, so that on the areological maps Tempe looked like an artist's palette, colours splashed everywhere to indicate the different aspects of the region's long history. Too many colours, in Ann's opinion; for her the smallest divisions into different areological units were artificial, remnants of sky areology, attempting to distinguish between regions that were more cratered or more dissected or more etched than the rest, when in the field it was all one, with all of the signature features visible everywhere. It was simply rough country – the Noachian landscape, none rougher.

Even the floors of the long straight canyons called the Tempe Fossae were too broken to drive over, so Ann made her way indirectly, on higher land. The most recent lava flows (a billion years old) were harder than the disaggregated ejecta they had run over, and now they stood on the land as long dykes or berms. On the softer land between there were a lot of splosh craters, their aprons clearly the remnants of liquid flow, like drip castles at the beach. Occasional islands of worn bedrock stuck up out of all this debris, but by and large it was regolith, with signs everywhere of water in the land, of the permafrost underfoot, causing slow slumps and creeps. And now, with the increase in temperatures, and perhaps the heat coming up from the Vastitas underground explosions, all that creep had speeded up. There were new landslides all over the place: a well-known Red trail had been wiped out when a ramp into Tempe 12 had been buried; the walls of Tempe 18 had collapsed on both sides, making a U-shaped canyon into a V-shaped one; Tempe 21 was gone, covered by the collapse of its high west wall. Everywhere the land was melting. She even saw some *taliks*, which were liquefied zones on top of permafrost, basically icy swamps. And many of the oval pits of the great alases were filled with ponds, which melted by day and froze by night, an action that tore the land apart even faster.

She passed the lobate apron of Timushenko Crater, buried on its northern flank by the southernmost waves of lava from Coriolanus Volcano, the largest of the many little volcanoes in Tempe. Here the land was extensively pitted, and snow had fallen, melted and then refrozen in myriad catchment basins. The land was slumping in all the characteristic permafrost patterns: polygonal pebble ridges, concentric crater fill, pingos, solifluction ridges on hillsides. In every depression an ice-choked pond or puddle. The land was melting.

On sunny south-facing slopes, wherever there was a bit of protection from the wind, trees were growing, over under-storeys of moss and grass and shrub. In the sunfilled hollows were krummholz dwarf trees, gnarled over their matted needles; in the shaded hollows, dirty snow and firn. The ruin-ation of so much land. Broken land, empty but not empty, rock and ice and boggy meadow all lined by shattered, low ridges. Clouds puffed out of nothing in the afternoon heat, and their shadows were another set of patches on things, a crazy quilt of red and black, green and white. No one would ever complain of homogeneity on Tempe Terra. Everything perfectly still under the rapidly moving shadows of the clouds. And yet there, one evening in the dusk, a white bulk slipping behind a boulder. Her heart jumped, but there was nothing further to see.

But she had seen something; because just before full dark-ness, there was a knocking at the door. Her heart shuddered like the rover on its shock absorbers, she ran to a window, looked out. Figures the colour of the rock, waving hands. Human beings.

It was a little group of Red ecoteurs. They had recognized her rover, they said after she let them inside, from the descrip-tion given by the people at the Tempe refuge. They had been hoping they might run into her, and so they were happy; laughing, chattering, moving around the cabin to touch her, young tall natives with stone eye-teeth and gleaming young eyes, some of them Orientals, some white, some black. All happy. She recognized them from Pavonis Mons, not individu-ally, but as a group; the young fanatics. Again she felt a chill.

'Where are you going?' she asked.

'To Botany Bay,' a young woman replied. 'We're going to take out the Whitebook labs.'

'And Boone Station,' another added.

'Ah no,' Ann said.

They went still, looked at her carefully. Like Kasei and Dao in Lastflow.

'What do you mean?' the young woman said.

Ann took a breath, tried to figure that out. They were watching her closely.

'Were you there in Sheffield?' she asked.

They nodded; they knew what she meant.

'Then you should know already,' she said slowly. 'It's pointless to achieve a Red Mars by pouring blood over the planet. We have to find another way. We can't do it by killing people. Not even by killing animals or plants, or blowing up machines. It won't work. It's destructive. It doesn't appeal to people, do you understand? No one is won over. In fact they're put off. The more we do things like that, the more Green they become. So we defeat our purpose. If we know that and do it anyway, then we're betraying the purpose. Do you understand? We aren't doing it for anything but our own feelings. Because we're angry. Or for thrills. We have to find another way.'

They stared at her, uncomprehending, annoyed, shocked, contemptuous. But riveted. This was Ann Clayborne, after all.

'I don't know for sure what that other way is,' she went on. 'I can't tell you that. I think . . . that's what I think we have to start working on. It has to be something like a Red areophany. The areophany has always been understood as a Green thing, right from the start. I suppose because of Hiroko, because she took the lead in defining it. And in bringing it into being. So the areophany has always been mixed up with viriditas. But there's no reason that should be. We have to change that, or we'll never accomplish anything. There has to be a Red worship of this place that people can learn to feel. The redness of the primal planet has to become a counterforce to viriditas. We have to stain that green until it turns some other colour. Some colour like you see in certain stones, like jasper, or ferric serpentine. You see what I mean. It will mean taking people out onto the land, maybe, up into the highlands, so they can see what it is. It will mean moving there, all over the place, and establishing tenure and stewardship rights, so that we can speak for the land and they will have to listen. Wanderers' rights as well, areologists' rights, nomads' rights. That's what areoformation might mean. Do you understand?'

She stopped. The young natives were still attentive, now looking perhaps concerned for her, or concerned at what she had said.

'We've talked about this kind of thing before,' one young man said. 'And there are people doing it. Sometimes we do it. But we think an active resistance is a necessary part of the struggle. Otherwise we'll just get steamrollered. They'll green everything.'

'Not if we stain it all. Right from the inside, right from their hearts too. But sabotage, murder; it's green that springs out of all that, believe me I've seen it. I've been fighting just as long as you and I've seen it. You stamp on life and it just comes back stronger.'

The young man wasn't convinced. 'They gave us the six kilometre limit because they were scared of us, because we were the driving force behind the revolution. If it weren't for us fighting, the metanats would still rule everything here.'

'That was a different opponent. When we fought the Terrans, then the Martian Greens were impressed. When we fight the Martian Greens they're not impressed, they're angry. And they get more Green than ever.'

The group sat in silence, thoughtful, perhaps disheartened.

'But what do we *do*?' a grey-haired woman said.

'Go to some land that's endangered,' Ann suggested. She gestured out of the window. 'Right here wouldn't be bad. Or somewhere near the six k border. Settle, incorporate a town, make it a primal refuge, make it a wonderful place. We'll creep back down from the highlands.'

They considered this glumly.

'Or go into the cities and start a tour group, and a legal fund. Show people the land. Sue every change they propose.'

'Shit,' the young man said, shaking his head. 'That sounds awful.'

'Yes it does,' Ann said. 'There's ugly work to be done. But

we have to get them from the inside too. And that's where they live.'

Long faces. They sat around and talked about it some more; the way they lived now, the way they wanted to live. What they might do to get from one to the other. The impossibility of the guerrilla life after the war was over. And so on. There were lots of big sighs, some tears, recriminations, encouragements.

'Come with me tomorrow and take a straight look at this ice sea,' Ann suggested.

The next day the guerrilla group travelled south with her along the sixtieth longitude, kilometre by difficult kilometre. *Khala*, the Arabs called it; the empty land. On the one hand it was beautiful, a Noachian desolation of rockscapes, and their hearts were full. On the other hand the ecoteurs were quiet, subdued, as if on a pilgrimage in some uncertain funereal mode. Together they came to the big canyon called Nilokeras Scopulus, and dropped into it on a broad, rough natural ramp. To the east lay Chryse Planitia, covered by ice: another arm of the northern sea. They had not escaped it. Ahead to the south lay the Nilokeras Fossae, the terminal end of a canyon complex that began far to the south, in the enormous pit of Hebes Chasma. Hebes Chasma had no exit, but its subsidence was now understood to have been caused by the aquifer outbreak just to the west, at the top of Echus Chasma. A very great amount of water had gushed down Echus against the hard western side of Lunae Planum, carving the steep, high cliff at Echus Overlook; then it had come to a break in that stupendous cliff, and had rushed down and through, tearing the big bend of Kasei Vallis, and cutting a deep channel out onto the lowlands of Chryse. It had been one of the biggest aquifer outbreaks in Martian history.

Now the northern sea had flowed back into Chryse, and water was filling back into the lower end of Nilokeras and Kasei. The flat-topped hill that was Sharanov Crater stood like a giant castle keep on the high promontory over the mouth of this new fjord. Out in the middle of the fjord lay a long narrow island, one of the lemniscate islands of the ancient flood, now islanded again, stubbornly red in the sea of white ice. Eventually this fjord would make an even better harbour than Botany Bay: it was steep-walled, but there were benches tucked here and there that could become harbour towns. There would of course be the west wind funnelling down Kasei to worry about, katabatic onslaughts holding the sailing ships out in the Chryse Gulf . . .

So strange. She led the group of silent Reds to a ramp that got them down onto a broad bench to the west of the ice fjord. By then it was evening, and she led them out of the rovers and down to the shore for a sunset walk.

At the moment of sunset itself, they found themselves standing in a tight, unhappy cluster before a solitary ice block some four metres tall, its melted convexities as smooth as muscles. They stood so that the sun was behind the ice block and shining through it. To both sides of the block brilliant light gleamed off the glassy, wet sand. An admonition of light. Undeniable, blazingly real; what were they to make of it? They stood and stared in silence.

When the sun blinked out over the black horizon, Ann walked away from the group and went alone up to her rover. She looked back down the slope; the Reds were still there by the beached iceberg. It looked like a white god among them, tinted orange like the crumpled white sheet of the ice bay. White god, bear, bay, a dolmen of Martian ice: the ocean would be there with them forever, as real as the rock.

The next day she drove up Kasei Vallis to the west, toward Echus Chasma. Up and up she drove, on broad bench after bench, making easy progress, until she came to where Kasei curved left and up onto the floor of Echus. The curve was one of the biggest, most obvious water-carved features on the planet. But now she found that the flat arroyo floor was covered by dwarf trees, so small they were almost shrubs: black-barked, thorny, the dark green leaves as glossy and razor-edged as holly leaves. Moss blanketed the ground underneath these black trees, but very little else; it was a single-species forest, covering Kasei Vallis from canyon wall to canyon wall, filling the great curve like some oversized smut.

By necessity Ann drove right over the top of the low forest, and the rover tilted this way and that as the branches, tough as manzanita, stubbornly gave under its wheels and then whipped back into place when they were freed. It would be nearly impossible to walk through this canyon any more, Ann thought, this deep-walled canyon so narrow and rounded, a kind of Utah of the imagination – or so it had been – now like the black forest of a fairy tale, inescapable, filled with flying black things, and a white shape seen scuttling in the dusk . . . There was no sign of the UNTA security complex that had once occupied the turn of the valley. A curse on your house to the seventh generation, a curse on the innocent land as well. Sax had been tortured here, and so he had sown fireseed in the ground and torched the place, causing a thorn forest to sprout and cover it. And they called scientists rational creatures! A curse on their house too, Ann thought with teeth clenched, to the seventh generation and seven after that.

She hissed and drove on, up Echus, toward the steep volcanic cone of Tharsis Tholis. There was a town there, tucked on the side of the volcano where the slope levelled off. The bear had told her Peter was headed there, and so she avoided it. Peter, the land drowned; Sax, the land burned. Once he had been hers. On this rock I will build. Peter Tempe Terra, the Rock of the Land of Time. The new man, *homo martial*. Who had betrayed them. Remember.

On she drove south, up the slope of the Tharsis bulge, until the cone of Ascraeus hove into view. A mountain continent, puncturing the horizon. Pavonis had been infested and overgrown because of its equatorial position, and the little advantage that that gave the elevator cable. But Ascraeus, just five hundred kilometres northeast of Pavonis, had been left alone. No one lived there; very few people had ever even ascended it. Just a few areologists now and then, to study its lava and occasional pyroclastic ash flows, which were both coloured the red nearest black.

She drove onto its lower slopes, gentle and wavy. Ascraeus had been one of the classic albedo feature names, as it was a mountain so big it was easily visible from Earth. Ascraeus Lacus. This was during the canal mania, and so they had decided it was a lake. Pavonis in that era had been called Phoenicus Lacus, Phoenix Lake. Ascra, she read, was the birthplace of Hesiod, 'situated on the right of Mount Helicon, on a high and rugged place'. So though they had thought it a lake, they had named it after a mountain place. Perhaps their subconscious minds had understood the telescope images after all. 'Ascraeus' was in general a poetic name for the pastoral, Helicon being the Boeotian mountain sacred to Apollo and the muses. Hesiod had looked up from his plough one day and seen the mountain, and found he had a story to tell. Strange, the birth of myths, strange the old names that they lived among and ignored, while they continued to tell the old stories over and over again with their lives.

It was the steepest of the big four volcanoes, but there was no encircling escarpment, as around Olympus Mons; so she could put the rover in low gear and grind on up, as if taking off into space, in slow motion. Lean back in her seat and take a nap. Head on the headrest; relax. Wake up on arrival, up at twenty-seven kilometres above sea level, the same height as all the other three big ones; that was as high as a mountain could get on Mars, basically, it was the isostatic limit, at which point the lithosphere began to sag under the weight of all that rock; all of the big four had maxed out, they could grow no higher. A sign of their size and their great age.

Very old, yes, but at the same time the surface lava of Ascraeus was among the youngest igneous rock on Mars, weathered only slightly by wind and sun. As the lava sheets had cooled they had stiffened in their descent, leaving low curved bulges to ascend or bypass. A distinct trail of rover tracks zigzagged up the slope, avoiding steep sections at the bottoms of these flows, taking advantage of a big loose network of ramps and flowbacks. In any permanent shade, spindrift had settled into banks of dirty, hardpacked snow; shadows were now a filmy, blackened white, as if she drove through a photographic negative, her spirits plummeting inexplicably as she drove ever higher. Behind her she could see more and more of the conical northern flank of the volcano, and North Tharsis beyond that, all the way to the Echus wall, a low line over a hundred kilometres away. Much of what she could see was patchy with snowdrifts, windslab, firn. Freckled white. The shady sides of volcanic cones often became heavily glaciated.

There on a rockface, bright emerald moss. Everything was turning green.

But as she continued to ascend, day after day, up and up beyond all imagining, the snow patches became thinner, less frequent. Eventually she was twenty kilometres above the datum – twenty-one above sea level – nearly seventy thousand feet above the ice – more than twice as high as Everest was above Earth's oceans; and still the cone of the volcano rose above her, a full seven thousand metres more! Right up into the darkening sky, right up into space.

Far below scrolled a smooth, flat layer of cloud, obscuring Tharsis. As if the white sea were chasing her up the slope. Up at this level there were no clouds, at least on this day; sometimes thunderheads would tower up beside the mountain, other days cirrus clouds could be seen overhead, slashing the sky with a dozen thin sickles. Today the sky above was a clear purple indigo suffused with black, pricked with a few daytime stars at the zenith, Orion standing faint and alone. Out to the east of the volcano's summit streamed a thin cloud, a peak banner, so faint she could see the dark sky through it. There wasn't much moisture up here, nor much atmosphere either. There would always be a tenfold difference between the air pressure at sea level and up here on the big volcanoes; pressure up here must therefore be about 35 millibars, very little more than what had existed when they had arrived.

Nevertheless she spotted tiny flecks of lichen in hollows on the tops of rocks, in pits that caught some snow and then a lot of sun. They were almost too small to see. Lichen: a symbiotic team of algae and fungus, working together to survive, even in 30 millibars. It was hard to believe what life would endure. So strange.

So strange, in fact, that she suited up and went out to look at them. Up here one had to employ all the old careful habits: secure walker, lock doors; out into the bright glare of low space.

The rocks that harboured the lichen were the kind of flat sunporches on which marmots would have sunbathed, if they could have lived so high. Instead, only little pinheads of yellow-green, or battleship grey. Flake lichen, the wristpad guide said. Bits of it torn away in storms, blown up here, falling on rocks, sticking like little vegetable limpets. The kind of thing only Hiroko could explain.

Living things. Michel had said that she loved stones and not men because she had been mistreated, her mind damaged. Hippocampus significantly smaller, strong startle reaction, a tendency toward dissociation. And so she had found a man as much like a stone as she could. Michel too had loved that quality in Simon, he told her – such a relief in the Underhill years to have even one such charge, a man you could trust, quiet and solid, that you could heft in your hand and feel the weight of.

But Simon wasn't the only one in the world like that, Michel had pointed out. That quality rested in the others as well, intermixed and less pure, but still there. Why could she not love that quality of obdurate endurance in other people, in every living thing? They were only trying to exist, like any rock or planet. There was a mineral stubbornness in all of them.

Wind keened past her helmet and over the shards of lava, humming in her air hose, drowning out the sound of her breath. The sky more black than indigo here, except low on the horizon, where it was a hazy purple violet, topped by a band of clear dark blue ... oh who could believe it would ever change, up here on the slope of Ascraeus Mons, why hadn't they settled up here to remind themselves of what they had come to, of what they had been given by Mars and then so profligately thrown away?

Back to the rover. She continued on up.

She was above silver cirrus clouds, just west of the volcano's diaphanous summit banner. In the lee of the jetstream. To ascend was to travel into the past, above all lichen and bacteria. Though she had no doubt they were still there, hiding inside the first layers of the rock. Chasmoendolithic life, like the mythic little red people, the microscopic gods who had spoken to John Boone, their own local Hesiod. So people said.

Life everywhere. The world was turning green. But if you couldn't see the greenness – if it made no difference to the land – surely it was welcome to the task? Living creatures. Michel had said to her, you love stones because of the stony quality that life has! It all comes back to life. Simon, Peter; on this rock I will build my church. Why could she not love that stony quality in every thing?

The rover rolled up the last concentric terraces of lava, working less strenuously now as it curved over the asymptotic flattening of the broad circular rim. Only slightly uphill, and less so every metre; and then onto the rim itself. Then to the inner edge of the rim.

Overlooking the caldera. She got out of the car, her thoughts flicking about like skuas.

Ascraeus's nested caldera complex consisted of eight overlapping craters, the newer ones collapsing down across the circumferences of the older ones. The largest and youngest caldera lay out near the centre of the complex, and the older higher-floored calderas embayed its circumference like the petals of a flower design. Each caldera floor was at a slightly different elevation, and marked by a pattern of circular fractures. Walking along the rim changed perspective so that distances shifted, and the floors' heights seemed to change, as if they were floating in a dream. Taken all in all, a beautiful thing to witness. And eighty kilometres across.

Like a lesson in volcano-throat mechanics. Eruptions down on the outer flanks of the volcano had emptied the magma from the active throat of the caldera, and so the caldera floor had slumped; thus all the circular shapes, as the active throat moved around over the eons. Arcing cliffs: few places on Mars exhibited such vertical slopes, they were almost true verticals. Basalt ringworlds. It should have been a climbers' Mecca, but as far as she knew it was not. Someday they would come.

The complexity of Ascraeus was so unlike the single great hole of Pavonis. Why had Pavonis's caldera collapsed in the same circumference every time? Could its last drop have erased and levelled all the other rings? Had its magma chamber been smaller, or vented to the sides less? Had Ascraeus's throat wandered more? She picked up loose rocks on the rim's edge, stared at them. Lava bombs, late meteor ejecta, ventifacts in the ceaseless winds ... These were all questions that could still be studied. Nothing they did would ever disturb the vulcanology up here, not enough to impede the study. Indeed the *Journal of Areological Studies* published many articles on these topics, as she had seen and still occasionally saw. It was as Michel had said to her; the high places would look like this forever. Climbing the great slopes would be like travel into the prehuman past, into pure areology, into the areophany itself perhaps, with Hiroko or not. With the lichen or not. People had talked of securing a dome or a tent over these calderas, to keep them completely sterile; but that would only make them zoos, wilderness parks, garden spaces with their walls and their roofs. Empty greenhouses. No. She straightened up, looked out over the vast round landscape, held up and offering itself to space. To the chasmoendolithic life that might be struggling up here, she waved a hand. Live, thing. She said the word and it sounded odd: 'Live.'

Mars forever, stony in the sunlight. But then she glimpsed the white bear in the corner of her eye, slipping behind a jagged rim boulder. She jumped; nothing there. She returned to the rover, feeling that she needed its protection. She climbed inside; but then all afternoon on the screen of the rover's AI, the vague spectacled eyes seemed to be looking out at her, about to call any second. A kind bear of a man, though he would eat her if he could catch her. If he could catch her – but they none of them could catch her, she could hide in these high rock fastnesses forever – free she was and free she would be, to be or not to be if she chose that, for as long as this rock held. But there again, right at the lock door, that white flash in the corner of her eye. Ah, so hard.

PART SEVEN

Making Things Work

*An ice-choked sea now covered much of the north. Vastitas
Borealis had lain a kilometre or two below the datum, in some
places three; now with sea level stabilizing at the minus-one
contour, most of it was underwater. If an ocean of similar
shape had existed on Earth, it would have been a bigger Arctic
Ocean, covering most of Russia, Canada, Alaska, Greenland
and Scandinavia, and then making two deeper incursions farther south, narrows seas that extended all the way to the
equator; on Earth these would have made for a narrow north
Atlantic, and a north Pacific occupied in its centre by a big
squarish island.*

*This Oceanus Borealis was dotted by several large icy
islands, and a long, low peninsula that broke its circumnavigation of the globe, connecting the mainland north of Syrtis
with the tail of a polar island. The north pole was actually
on the ice of Olympia Gulf, some kilometres offshore from
this polar island.*

*And that was it. On Mars there would be no equivalent of
the South Pacific or the South Atlantic, or the Indian Ocean,
or the Antarctic Ocean. In its south there was only desert,
except for the Hellas Sea, a circular body of water about the
size of the Caribbean. So while ocean covered seventy per
cent of the Earth, it covered about twenty-five per cent of
Mars.*

*In the year 2130, most of Oceanus Borealis was covered by
ice. There were large pods of liquid water under the surface,
however, and in the summer, melt lakes scattered on top of
the surface; there were also many polnyaps, leads and cracks.
Because most of the water had been pumped or otherwise
driven out of the permafrost, it had deep groundwater's
purity, meaning it was nearly distilled: the Borealis was a
freshwater ocean. It was expected to become salty fairly soon,
however, as rivers ran through the very salty regolith and
carried their loads into the sea, then evaporated, precipitated
and repeated the process — moving salts from the regolith into
the water until a balance was reached — a process which had
the oceanographers transfixed with interest, for the degree of*

saltiness of Earth's oceans, stable for many millions of years, was not well understood.

The coastlines were wild. The polar island, formally nameless, was called variously the polar peninsula, or the polar island, or the Seahorse, for its shape on maps. In actuality its coastline was still overrun in many places by the ice of the old polar cap, and everywhere it was blanketed by snow, blown into patterns of giant sastrugi. This corrugated white surface extended out over the sea for many kilometres, until underwater currents fractured it and one came on a 'coastline' of leads and pressure ridges and the chaotic edges of big tabular bergs, as well as larger and larger stretches of open water. Several large volcanic or meteoric islands rose up out of the shatter of this ice coast, including a few pedestal craters, sticking up out of the whiteness like great black tabular bergs.

The southern shores of the Borealis were much more exposed and various. Where the ice lapped against the foot of the Great Escarpment there were several mensae and colles regions that had become offshore archipelagos, and these, as well as the mainland coastline proper, sported many beetling seacliffs, bluffs, crater bays, fossa fjords and long stretches of low, smooth strand. The water in the two big southern gulfs was extensively melted below the surface, and, in the summers, on the surface as well. Chryse Gulf had perhaps the most dramatic coastline of all: eight big outbreak channels dropping into Chryse had partly filled with ice, and as it melted they were becoming steep-sided fjords. At the southern end of the gulf four of these fjords braided, weaving together several big cliff-walled islands to make the most spectacular seascapes of all.

Over all this water great flocks of birds flew daily. Clouds bloomed in the air and rushed off on the wind, dappling the white and red with their shadows. Icebergs floated across the melt seas, and crashed against the shore. Storms dropped off the Great Escarpment with terrifying force, dashing hail and lightning onto the rock. There were now approximately forty thousand kilometres of coastline on Mars. And in the rapid freeze and thaw of the days and the seasons, under the brush of the constant wind, every part of it was coming alive.

When the congress ended Nadia made plans to get off Pavonis Mons immediately. She was sick of the bickering in the warehouse, of arguments, of politics; sick of violence and the threat of violence; sick of revolution, sabotage, the constitution, the elevator, Earth, and the threat of war. Earth and death, that was Pavonis Mons – Peacock Mountain, with all the peacocks preening and strutting and crying *Me Me Me*. It was the last place on Mars Nadia wanted to be.

She wanted to get off the mountain and breathe the open air. She wanted to work on tangible things; she wanted to build, with her nine fingers and her back and her mind, build anything and everything, not just structures, although those would be wonderful of course, but also things like air or dirt, parts of a construction project new to her, which was simply terraforming itself. Ever since her first walk in the open air down at Dumartheray Crater, free of everything but a little CO_2 filter mask, Sax's obsession had finally made sense to her. She was ready to join him and the rest of them in that project, and more than ever now, as the removal of the orbiting mirrors had kicked off a long winter and threatened a full ice age. Build air, build soil, move water, introduce plants and animals: all that kind of work sounded fascinating to her now. And of course the more conventional construction projects beckoned as well. When the new north sea melted and its shoreline stabilized, there would be harbour towns to be inlaid everywhere, scores of them no doubt, each with jetties and seafronts, channels, wharves and docks, and the towns behind them rising into the hills. At the higher altitudes there would be more tent towns to be erected, and covered canyons. There was even talk of covering some of the big calderas, and of running cable cars between the three prince volcanoes, or bridging the narrows south of Elysium; there was talk of inhabiting the polar island continent; there were new concepts in biohousing, plans to grow homes and buildings directly out of engineered trees, as Hiroko had used bamboo, but on a bigger scale. Yes, a builder ready to learn some of the latest techniques had a thousand years of lovely projects ahead of her. It was a dream come true.

Then a small group came to her and said they were exploring possibilities for the first executive council of the new global government.

Nadia stared at them. She could see their import like a big slow-moving trap, and she tried her best to run out of it before it snapped shut. 'There are lots of possibilities,' she said. 'About ten times more good people than council positions.'

Yes, they said, looking thoughtful. But we were wondering if you had ever thought about it.

'No,' she said.

Art was grinning, and seeing that she began to get worried. 'I plan to build things,' she said firmly.

'You could do that too,' Art said. 'The council is a part-time job.'

'The hell it is.'

'No, really.'

It was true that the concept of citizen government was written everywhere into the new constitution, from the global legislature to the courts to the tents. People would presumably do a good deal of this work part-time. Nadia was quite sure, however, that the executive council was not going to be in that category. 'Don't executive council members have to be elected out of the legislature?' she asked.

Elected *by* the legislature, they told her happily. Usually fellow legislators would be elected, but not necessarily. 'Well there's a mistake in the constitution for you!' Nadia said. 'Good thing that you caught it so soon. Restrict it to elected legislators and you'll cut your pool way down—'

Way down—

'And still have lots of good people,' she backpedalled.

But they were persistent. They kept coming back, in different combinations, and Nadia kept running toward that narrowing gap between the teeth of the trap. In the end they begged. A whole little delegation of them. This was *the* crucial time for the new government, they needed an executive council trusted by all, it would be the one to get things started, etc

etc. The senate had been elected, the duma had been drafted. Now the two houses were electing the seven executive council members. People mentioned as candidates included Mikhail, Zeyk, Peter, Marina, Etsu, Nanao, Ariadne, Marion, Irishka, Antar, Rashid, Jackie, Charlotte, the four ambassadors to Earth and several others Nadia had first met in the warehouse. '*Lots* of good people,' Nadia reminded them. This was the polycephalous revolution.

But people were uneasy at the list, they told Nadia repeatedly. They had become used to her providing a balanced centre, both during the congress and during the revolution, and before that at Dorsa Brevia, and for that matter throughout the underground years, and right back to the beginning. People wanted her on the council as a moderating influence, a calm head, a neutral party, etc etc.

'Get out,' she said, suddenly angry, though she did not know why. They were concerned to see her anger, upset by it. 'I'll think about it,' she said as she shooed them out, to keep them moving.

Eventually only Charlotte and Art were left, looking serious, looking as if they had not conspired to bring all this about.

'They seem to want you on the executive council,' Art said.

'Oh shut up.'

'But they do. They want someone they can trust.'

'They want someone they're not afraid of, you mean. They want an old babushka who won't try to do anything, so they can keep their opponents off the council and pursue their own agendas.'

Art frowned; he had not considered this, he was too naïve.

'You know a constitution is kind of like a blueprint,' Charlotte said thoughtfully. 'Getting a real working government out of it is the true act of construction.'

'Out,' Nadia said.

But in the end she agreed to stand. They were relentless, there were a surprisingly large number of them, and they would not give up. She didn't want to seem like a shirker. And so she let the trap close down on her leg.

The legislatures met, the ballots were cast. Nadia was elected one of the seven, along with Zeyk, Ariadne, Marion, Peter, Mikhail and Jackie. That same day Irishka was elected the first chief justice of the Global Environmental Court, a real coup for her personally and the Reds generally; this was part of the 'grand gesture' Art had brokered at the congress's end, to gain the Reds' support. About half the new justices were Reds of one shade or another, making for a gesture just a bit too grand, in Nadia's opinion.

Immediately after these elections another delegation came to her, led this time by her fellow councillors. She had received the highest ballot total in the two houses, they told her, and so the others wanted to elect her president of the council.

'Oh no,' she said.

They nodded gravely. The presidency was just another member of the council, they told her, one among equals. A ceremonial position only. This arm of the government was modelled on Switzerland's, and the Swiss didn't usually even know who their president was. And so on. Though of course they would need her permission (Jackie's eyes glittered slightly at this), her acceptance of the post.

'Out,' she said.

After they had left Nadia sat slumped in her chair, feeling stunned.

'You're the only one on Mars that everyone trusts,' Art said gently. He shrugged, as if to say he hadn't been involved, which she knew was a lie. 'What can you do?' he said, rolling his eyes with a child's exaggerated theatricality. 'Give it three years and then things'll be on track, and you can say you did your part and retire. Besides, the first president of Mars! How could you resist?'

'Easy.'

Art waited. Nadia glared at him.

Finally he said, 'But you'll do it anyway, right?'

'You'll help me?'

'Oh yes.' He put a hand on her clenched fist. 'All you want. I mean – I'm at your disposal.'

'Is that an official Praxis position?'

'Why yes, I'm sure it could be. Praxis adviser to the Martian president? You bet.'

So possibly she could make him do it.

She heaved a big sigh. Tried to feel less tight in her stomach. She could take the job, and then turn most of the work over to Art, and to whatever staff they gave her. She wouldn't be the first president to do that, nor the last.

'Praxis adviser to the Martian president,' Art was announcing, looking pleased.

'Oh shut up!' she said.

'Of course.'

He left her alone to get used to it, came back with a steaming pot of kava and two little cups. He poured; she took one from him, and sipped the bitter fluid.

He said, 'Anyway I'm yours, Nadia. You know that.'

'Mm hmm.'

She regarded him as he slurped his kava. He meant it more than politically, she knew. He was fond of her. All that time working together, living together, travelling together; sharing space. And she liked him. A bear of a man, graceful on his feet, full of high spirits. Fond of kava, as was obvious in his slurping, in his squinched face. He had carried the whole congress, she felt, on the strength of those high spirits, spreading like an epidemic – the feeling that there was nothing so fun as writing a constitution – absurd! But it had worked. And during the congress they had become a kind of couple. Yes, she had to admit it.

But she was now one hundred and fifty-nine years old. Another absurdity, but it was true. And Art was, she wasn't sure, somewhere in his seventies or eighties, although he looked fifty, as they often did when they got the treatment early. 'I'm old enough to be your great-grandmother,' she said.

Art shrugged, embarrassed. He knew what she was talking about. 'I'm old enough to be that woman's great-grandfather,' he said, pointing at a tall native girl passing by their office door. 'And she's old enough to have kids. So, you know. At some point it just doesn't matter.'

'Maybe not to you.'

'Well, yeah. But that's half of the opinions that count.'

Nadia said nothing.

'Look,' Art said, 'we're going to live a long time. At some point the numbers have to stop mattering. I mean, I wasn't with you in the first years, but we've been together a long time now, and gone through a lot.'

'I know.' Nadia looked down at the table, remembering some of those times. There was the stump of her long-lost finger. All that life was gone. Now she was president of Mars. 'Shit.'

Art slurped his kava, watched her sympathetically. He liked her, she liked him. They were already a kind of couple. 'You help me with this damned council stuff!' she said, feeling bleak as all her technofantasies slipped away.

'Oh I will.'

'And then, well. We'll see.'

'We'll see,' he said, and smiled.

So there she was, stuck on Pavonis Mons. The new government was assembling up there, moving from the warehouses into Sheffield proper, occupying the blocky, polished, stone-faced buildings abandoned by the metanats; there was an argument of course over whether they were going to be compensated for these buildings and the rest of their infrastructure, or whether it had all been 'globalized' or 'co-opted' by independence and the new order. 'Compensate them,' Nadia growled at Charlotte, glowering. But it did not appear that the presidency of Mars was the kind of presidency that caused people to jump at her word.

In any case the government was moving in, Sheffield becoming, if not the capital, then at least the temporary seat of the global government. With Burroughs drowned and Sabishii burned, there was no other obvious place to put it, and in truth it didn't look to Nadia as if any of the other tent towns wanted to have it. People spoke of building a new capital city, but that would take time, and meanwhile they had to meet somewhere. So around the piste to Sheffield they retired, inside its tent, under its dark sky. In the shadow of the elevator cable, rising from its eastern neighbourhood straight and black, like a flaw in reality.

Nadia found an apartment in the westernmost tent, behind the rim park, up on the fourth floor where she had a fine view down into Pavonis's awesome caldera. Art took an apartment in the ground floor of the same building, at the back; apparently the caldera gave him vertigo. But there he was, and the Praxis office was in a nearby office building, a cube of polished jasper as big as a city block, lined with chrome blue windows.

Fine. She was there. Time to take a deep breath and do the work asked of her. It was like a bad dream in which the constitutional congress had suddenly been extended for three years, three M-years.

She began with the intention of getting off the mountain occasionally and joining some construction project or other. Of course she would perform her duties on the council, but working on an increase in greenhouse gas output, for instance, looked good, combining as it did technical problems and the politics of conforming to the new environmental regulatory regime. It would get her out into the back country, where a lot of the feedstocks for the greenhouse gases were located. From there she could do her council business over the wrist.

But events conspired to keep her in Sheffield. It was one thing after another − nothing particularly important or interesting, compared to the congress itself, but the details necessary to get things rolling. It was somewhat as Charlotte had said; after the design phase, the endless minutiae of construction. Detail after detail.

She had to expect this, she had to be patient. She would work through the first rush and then get away. In the meantime, along with the start-up process, the media wanted her, the new UN Martian Office wanted her, very interested in the new immigration policies and procedures; the other council members wanted her. Where would the council meet? How often? What were its rules of operation? Nadia convinced the other six councillors to hire Charlotte to be council secretary and protocol chief, and after that Charlotte hired a big crew of assistants from Dorsa Brevia. So they had the start of a staff. And Mikhail also had a great fund of practical experience in government from Bogdanov Vishniac. So there were people better suited than Nadia to do this work; but still she was called in a million times a day to confer, discuss, decide, appoint, adjudicate, arbitrate, administrate. It was endless.

And then when Nadia did clear time for herself, forcibly, it turned out that being president made it very difficult to join any particular project. Everything going on was now part of a tent or a co-op; very often they were commercial enterprises, involved in transactions that were part non-profit public works, part competitive market. So to have the president of Mars join any given co-op would be a sign of official patronage, and couldn't be allowed if one wanted to be fair. It was a conflict of interest.

'Shit!' she said to Art, accusingly.

He shrugged, tried to pretend he hadn't known.

But there was no way out. She was a prisoner of power. She had to study the situation as if it were an engineering problem, like trying to exert force in some difficult medium. Say she wanted to build greenhouse gas factories. She was constrained from joining any factory co-op in particular. Therefore she had to do it some other way. Emergence at a higher level: she could perhaps co-ordinate co-ops.

There seemed to her good reasons to promote the building of greenhouse gas factories. The Year-Without-Summer had extended to include a series of violent storms that had dropped off the Great Escarpment into the north, and most meteorologists agreed these 'Hadley cross-equatorial storms' had been caused by the orbital mirrors' removal, and the resulting sudden drop in insolation. A full ice age was deemed a distinct possibility; and pumping up greenhouse gases seemed to be one of the best ways to counter it. So Nadia asked Charlotte to initiate a conference to come back with recommendations for forestalling an ice age. Charlotte contacted people in Da Vinci and Sabishii and elsewhere, and soon she had a conference scheduled to take place in Sabishii, named, by some Da Vinci saxaclone no doubt, the 'Insolation Loss Effects Abatement Meeting M-53'.

Nadia, however, never made it to this conference. She got caught up by affairs in Sheffield instead, mostly instituting the new economic system, which she thought important enough to keep her there. The legislature was passing the law of eco-economics, fleshing out the bones drawn up in the constitution. They directed co-ops that had existed before the revolution to help the newly independent metanat local subsidiaries to transform themselves into similar co-operative organizations. This process, called horizontalization, had very wide support, especially from the young natives, and so it was proceeding fairly smoothly. Every Martian business now had to be owned by its employees only. No co-op could exceed one thousand people; larger enterprises had to be made of co-op associations, working together. For their internal structures most of the firms chose variants of the Bogdanovist models, which themselves were based on the co-operative Basque community of Mondragon, Spain. In these firms all employees were co-owners, and they bought into their positions by paying the equivalent of about a year's wages to the firm's equity fund. This became the starter of their share in the firm, which grew every year they stayed, until it was given back to them as pension or departure payment. Councils elected from the work-force hired management, usually from outside, and this management then had the power to make executive decisions, but was subject to a yearly review by the councils. Credit and capital were obtained from central co-operative banks, or the global government's start-up fund, or helper organizations such as Praxis and the Swiss. On the next level up, co-ops in the same industries or services were associating for larger projects, and also sending representatives to industry guilds, which established professional practice boards, arbitration and mediation centres, and trade associations.

The economic commission was also establishing a Martian currency, for internal use and for exchanges with Terran currencies. The commission wanted a currency that was resistant to Terran speculation, but in the absence of a Martian stock market, the full force of Terran investment tended to fall on the currency itself, as the only investment game being offered. This tended to inflate the value of the Martian sequin in Terran money markets, and in the old days it would probably have blown the sequin's value right through the roof, to Mars's disadvantage in trade balances; but as the fracturing metanats continued to struggle against co-operativization back on Earth, Terran finance remained in some disarray, and did not have its old house-on-fire intensity. So the sequin ended up strong on Earth, but not too strong; and on Mars it was just money. Praxis was very helpful in this process, as they became a kind of federal bank for the new economy, providing interest-free loans and serving as a mediated exchange with Terran currencies.

So given all this, the executive council was meeting for long hours every day to discuss legislation and other government programmes. It was so time-consuming that Nadia almost forgot there was a conference she had initiated going on at the same time in Sabishii. On good nights, however, she spent a last hour or two onscreen with friends in Sabishii, and it looked as if things were going fairly well there too. Many of Mars's environmental scientists were on hand, and they were in agreement that massively increasing greenhouse gas emissions would ease the effects of the mirror loss. Or course CO_2 was the easiest greenhouse gas to emit, but even without using it – as they were still trying to reduce it in the atmosphere to breathable levels – the consensus was that the more complex and powerful gases could be created and released in the quantities needed. And at first they did not think this would be a problem, politically; the constitution legislated an atmosphere no thicker than 350 millibars at the six kilometre contour, but said nothing about what gases could be used to create this pressure. If the halocarbons and other greenhouse gases in the Russell cocktail were pumped out until they formed one hundred parts per million of the atmosphere, rather than the twenty-seven parts per million that were currently up there, then heat retention would rise by several degrees Kelvin, they calculated, and an ice age would be forestalled, or at least greatly shortened. So the plan called for production and release of tons of carbon tetrafluoride, hexafluoroethane, sulphur hex-afluoride, methane, nitrous oxide and trace elements of other chemicals which helped to decrease the rate at which UV radiation destroyed these halocarbons.

Completing the melting of the north sea ice was the other obvious abatement strategy most often mentioned at the conference. Until it was all liquid, the albedo of the ice was bouncing a lot of energy back into space, and a truly lively water cycle was somewhat capped off. If they could get a liquid ocean, or, given how far north it was, a summer-liquid ocean, then any ice age would be done for, and terraformation essentially complete: they would have robust currents, waves, evaporation, clouds, precipitation, melting, streams, rivers, deltas – the full hydrological cycle. This was a primary goal, and so there were a variety of methods being proposed to speed the melting of the ice: feeding nuclear power plant exhaust heat into the ocean, scattering black algae on the ice, deploying microwave and ultrasound transmitters as heaters, even sailing big icebreakers through the shallow pack to aid the break-up.

Of course the increased greenhouse gases would help here as well; the ocean's surface ice would melt on its own, after all, as soon as the air stayed regularly above 273° K. But as the conference proceeded, more and more problems with the greenhouse gas plan were being pointed out. It entailed another huge industrial effort, almost the equal of the metanat monster projects, like the the nitrogen shipments from Titan, or the soletta itself. And it was not a one-time thing; the gases were constantly destroyed by UV radiation in the upper atmosphere, so they had to overproduce to reach the desired levels, and then continue producing for as long as they wanted the gases up there. Thus mining the raw materials, and constructing the factories to turn those materials into the desired gases, were enormous projects, and necessarily a largely robotic effort, with self-guided and replicating miners, self-building and regulating factories, upper atmosphere sampler drones – an entire machine enterprise.

The technical challenge of this was not the issue; as Nadia pointed out to her friends at the conference, Martian technology had been highly robotic from the very beginning. In this case, thousands of small robotic cars would wander Mars on their own, looking for good deposits of carbon, sulphur, or fluorite, migrating from source to source like the old Arab mining caravans on the Great Escarpment; then when new feedstocks were found in high concentrations, the robots could settle down and construct little processing plants out of clay, iron, magnesium and trace metals, providing the parts that could not be constructed on site, and then assembling the whole. Fleets of automated diggers and carts would be manufactured to haul the processed material in to centralized factories, where the material would be gassified and released from tall mobile stacks. It wasn't that different from the earlier mining for atmospheric gases; just a larger effort.

"But the most obvious deposits had already been mined, as people were now pointing out. And surface mining couldn't be done the way it used to be; there were plants growing almost everywhere now, and in many places a kind of desert pavement was developing on the surface, as a result of hydration, bacterial action, and chemical reactions in the clays. This crust helped greatly to cut down on dust storms, which were still a constant problem; so ripping it up to get to underlying deposits of feedstock materials was no longer acceptable, either ecologically or politically. Red members of the legislature were calling for a ban on just this kind of robotic surface mining, and for good reasons, even in terraforming terms.

It was hard, Nadia thought one night as she shut down her screen, to be faced with all the competing effects of their actions. The environmental issues were so tightly intertwined that it was hard to tease them out and decide what to do. And it was also hard to stay constrained by their own rules; individual organizations could no longer act unilaterally, because so many of their actions had global ramifications. Thus the necessity for environmental regulation, and for the Global Environmental Court, already faced with a caseload running out of control. Eventually it would have to rule on any plans coming out of this conference as well. The days of unconstrained terraforming were gone.

And as a member of the executive council, Nadia was restricted to saying that she thought increased greenhouse gases were a good idea. Other than that she had to stay out, or appear to be impinging on the environmental court's territory, which Irishka was defending very vigorously. So Nadia spent time visiting onscreen with a group designing new robot miners that would minimally disrupt the surface, or talking to a group working on dust fixatives that might be sprayed or grown over the surface, 'thin fast pavements' as they called them; but they were proving to be a knotty problem.

And that was the extent of Nadia's participation in the Sabishii conference that she herself had initiated. And since all its technical problems were enmeshed in political considerations anyway, it might have been said that she hadn't missed it at all. Not a bit of real work had been done there, by her or anyone else. Meanwhile, back in Sheffield, the council was facing any number of problems of its own: unforeseen difficulties in instituting the eco-economy; complaints that the GEC was overstepping its authority; complaints about the new police, and the criminal justice system; unruly and stupid behaviour in both houses of the legislature; Red and other types of resistance in the outback; and so on. The issues were endless, and spanned the gamut from the profoundly important to the incredibly petty, until Nadia began to lose all sense of where on that continuum any individual problem lay.

For instance, she spent a good deal of her time involved in the council's own internal struggles, which she considered trivial, but couldn't avoid. Most of these struggles involved resisting Jackie's efforts to put together a majority that would vote with Jackie every time, so that Jackie could use the council as a rubber stamp for the Free Mars party line, or in other words for Jackie herself. This meant getting to know the rest of the councillors better, and figuring out how to work with them. Zeyk was an old acquaintance; Nadia liked him, and he was a power among the Arabs, their current representative to the general culture, having defeated Antar for that position; gracious, smart, kind, he was in agreement with Nadia on many issues, including the core ones, and this made it an easy relationship, even a growing friendship. Ariadne was one of the goddesses of the Dorsa Brevian matriarchy, and acted the part to a T: imperious and rigid in her principles, she was an ideologue, probably the only thing that kept her from being a serious challenge to Jackie's prominence among the natives. Marion was the Red councillor, an ideologue also, but much changed from her early radical days, although still a long-winded arguer, not easily beaten. Peter, Ann's little boy, had grown up to be a power in several different parts of Martian society, including the space crew at Da Vinci, the Green underground, the cable crowd, and to an extent, because of Ann, the more moderate Reds. This versatility was part of his nature, and Nadia had a hard time getting a fix on him; he was private, like his parents, and seemed wary of Nadia and the rest of the First Hundred; he wanted a distance from them, he was nisei through and through. Mikhail Yangel was one of the earliest issei to follow the First Hundred to Mars, and had worked with Arkady from very early on. He had helped to start the revolt of 2061, and Nadia's impression was that he had been one of the most extreme Reds at that time — which fact sometimes made her angry at him still, which was silly, and impeded her ability to talk to him — but there it was, despite the fact that he too was much changed, a Bogdanovist willing to compromise. His presence on the council was a surprise to Nadia — a gesture toward Arkady, one might say, which she found touching.

And then there was Jackie, very possibly the most popular and powerful politician on Mars. At least until Nirgal got back.

And so Nadia dealt with these six every day, learning their ways as they made their way through item after item on their daily agendas. From the important to the trivial, the abstract to the personal — everything seemed to Nadia part of a fabric, in which everything connected to everything. Not only was the council not part-time work, it ate up the entirety of every waking day. It consumed her life. And yet at this point she had only got through two months of a three M-year term.

Art could see that it was getting to her, and he did what he could to help. He came up to her apartment every morning with breakfast, like room service. Often he had cooked it himself, and always it was good. As he came in, platter held aloft, he called up jazz on her AI to serve as the soundtrack of their morning together — not just Nadia's beloved Louis, though he sought out odd recordings by Satch to amuse her, things like 'Give Peace A Chance' or 'Stardust Memories' – but also later styles of jazz that she had never liked before, because they were so frenetic; but that seemed to be the tempo of these days. Whatever the reason, Charlie Parker now skittered and zoomed around most impressively, she thought, and Charles Mingus made his big band sound like Duke Ellington's on pandorph, which was just what Ellington and all the rest of swing needed, in her opinion – very funny, lovely music. And best of all, on many mornings Art called up Clifford Brown, a discovery Art had made during his investigations on her behalf, one he was very proud of, and advocated constantly to her as the logical successor to Armstrong – a vibrant trumpet sound joyous and positive and melodic like Satch, and also brilliantly fast and clever and difficult – like Parker, only happy. It was the perfect soundtrack for these wild times, driving and intense but as positive as one could be.

So Art would bring in breakfasts, singing 'All of Me' in a pretty good voice, and with Satchmo's basic insight that American song lyrics could only be treated as silly jokes: 'All of me, why not take all of me, Can't you see, I'm no good without you.' And call up some music, and sit with his back to the window; and the mornings were fun.

But no matter how well the days began, the council was eating her life. Nadia got more and more sick of it – the bickering, negotiating, compromising, conciliating – the dealing with people, minute after minute. She was beginning to hate it.

Art saw this, of course, and began to look worried. And one day after work he brought over Ursula and Vlad. The four of them had dinner together in her apartment, Art cooking. Nadia enjoyed her old friends' company; they were in town on business, but getting them over for dinner there had been Art's idea, and a good one. He was a sweet man, Nadia thought as she watched him moving about the kitchen. Canny diplomat as guileless simpleton, or vice versa. Like a benign Frank. Or a mix of Frank's skill and Arkady's happiness. She laughed at herself, always thinking of people in terms of the First Hundred – as if everyone was somehow a recombination of the traits of that original family. It was a bad habit of hers.

Vlad and Art were talking about Ann. Sax had apparently called Vlad from the shuttle rocket on its return to Mars, shaken by a conversation with Ann. He was wondering if Vlad and Ursula would consider offering Ann the same brain plasticity treatment that they had given him after his stroke.

'Ann would never do it,' Ursula said.

'I'm glad she won't,' Vlad said. 'That would be too much. Her brain wasn't injured. We don't know what that treatment would do in a healthy brain. And you should only undertake what you can understand, unless you are desperate.'

'Maybe Ann is desperate,' Nadia said.

'No. Sax is desperate.' Vlad smiled briefly. 'He wants a different Ann before he gets back.'

Ursula said to him, 'You didn't want Sax to try that treatment either.'

'It's true. I wouldn't have done it to myself. But Sax is a bold man. An impulsive man.' Now Vlad looked at Nadia: 'We should stick to things like your finger, Nadia. Now that we can fix.'

Surprised, Nadia said, 'What's wrong with it?'

They laughed at her. 'The one that's missing!' Ursula said. 'We could grow it back, if you wanted.'

'Ka,' Nadia exclaimed. She sat back, looked at her thin left hand, the stump of the missing little finger. 'Well. I don't need it, really.'

They laughed again. 'You could have fooled us,' Ursula said. 'You're always complaining about it when you're working.'

'I am?'

They all nodded.

'It'll help your swimming,' Ursula said.

'I don't swim much any more.'

'Maybe you stopped because of your hand.'

Nadia stared at it again. 'Ka. I don't know what to say. Are you sure it will work?'

'It might grow into an entire other hand,' Art suggested. 'Then into another Nadia. You'll be a Siamese twin.'

Nadia pushed him sideways in his chair. Ursula was shaking her head. 'No no. We've done it for some other amputees already, and a great number of experimental animals. Hands, arms, legs. We learned it from frogs. Quite wonderful, really.

The cells differentiate just like the first time the finger grew.'

'A very literal demonstration of emergence theory,' Vlad said with a small smile. Nadia saw by that smile that he had been instrumental in designing the procedure.

'It works?' she asked him directly.

'It works. We make what is in effect a new finger bud over your stump. It's a combination of embryonic stem cells with some cells from the base of your other little finger. The combination functions as the equivalent of the homeobox genes you had when you were a foetus. So you've got the developmental determiners there to make the new stem cells differentiate properly. Then you ultrasonically inject a weekly dose of fibroblast growth factor, plus a few cells from the knuckle and the nail, at the appropriate times . . . and it works.'

As he explained Nadia felt a little glow of interest spread through her. A whole person. Art was watching her with his friendly curiosity.

'Well, sure,' she said at last. 'Why not.'

So in the following week they took some biopsies from her remaining little finger, and gave her some ultrasonic shots in the stump of the missing finger, and in her arm, and gave her some pills; and that was it. After that it was only a matter of weekly shots, and waiting.

Then she forgot about it, because Charlotte called with a problem; Cairo was ignoring a GEC order concerning water pumping. 'You'd better come check it out in person. I think the Cairenes are testing the court, for a faction of Free Mars that wants to challenge the global government.'

'Jackie?' Nadia said.

'I think so.'

Cairo stood on its plateau edge, overlooking the north-westernmost U-valley of Noctis Labyrinthus. Nadia walked out of the train station with Art onto a plaza flanked by tall palm trees. She glared at the scene; some of the worst moments of her life had occurred in this city, during the assault on it in 2061. Sasha had been killed, among many others, and Nadia had blown up Phobos, she herself! – and all just a few days after finding Arkady's burned remains. She had never returned; she hated this town.

Now she saw that it had been damaged again in the recent unrest. Parts of the tent had been blown, and the physical plant heavily damaged. It was being rebuilt, and new tent segments were being tacked onto the old town, extending west and east far along the plateau's edge. It looked like a boom town, which Nadia found peculiar given its altitude, ten kilometres above the datum. They would never be able to take down the tents, or go outside without walkers on, and so Nadia had assumed it would therefore go into decline. But it lay at the intersection of the equatorial piste and the Tharsis piste running north and south, the last place one could cross the equator between here and the chaoses, a full quarter of the planet away. So unless a transMarineris bridge were built somewhere, Cairo would always be at a strategic crossroads.

And crossroads or not, they wanted more water. The Compton Aquifer, underlying lower Noctis and upper Marineris, had been breached in '61, and its water had poured down the entire length of the Marineris canyons. This was the flood that had almost killed Nadia and her companions during the flight down the canyons, after Cairo was taken. Most of the floodwater had either frozen in the canyons, creating a long, irregular glacier, or had pooled and frozen in the chaoses at the bottom of Marineris. And some water had of course remained in the aquifer. In the years since, the water in the aquifer had been pumped out for use in cities all over east Tharsis. And the Marineris glacier had slowly dropped down-canyon, receding at its upper end where there was no source to replenish it, leaving behind only devastated land and a string

311

of very shallow ice lakes. Cairo was therefore running out of a ready supply of water. Its hydrology office had responded by laying a pipeline to the northern sea's big southern arm in the Chryse depression, and pumping water up to Cairo. So far, no problem; every tent town got its water from somewhere. But the Cairenes had lately started pouring water into a reservoir in the Noctis canyon under them, and letting a stream out from this reservoir to run down into Ius Chasma, where eventually it pooled behind the upper end of the Marineris glacier, or ran by it. Essentially they had created a new river running right down the big canyon system, far away from their town; and now they were establishing a number of riverside settlements and farming communities downstream from the city. A Red legal group had gone to the Global Environmental Court to challenge this action, asserting that Valles Marineris had legal consideration as a natural wonder, being the largest canyon in the solar system; if left alone the breakout glacier would eventually have slid down into the chaos, leaving the canyons again open-floored. This was what they thought should happen, and the GEC had agreed with them, and issued an order (Charlotte called this a 'gecko') against Cairo, requiring them to halt the release of water out of the town reservoir. Cairo had refused to desist, claiming that the global government had no jurisdiction over what they called 'vital town life support issues'. Meanwhile building new downstream settlements as fast as they could.

Clearly it was a provocation, a challenge to the new system. 'This is a test,' Art muttered as they walked across the plaza, 'this is only a test. If this were a true constitutional crisis, you would hear a beep all over the planet.'

A test; exactly the kind of thing for which Nadia had lost all patience. So she crossed the city in a foul mood. No doubt it did not help that the awful days of '61 were called back so vividly to mind by the plaza, the boulevards, the city wall at the canyon rim, all just as they had been back then. They said one's memory was weakest from one's middle years, but she would have lost those memories happily if she could have; fear and rage, however, seemed to function as some kind of nightmare fixative. For it was all still there – Frank tapping madly away at his monitors, Sasha eating pizza, Maya shout-

312

ing angrily at something or other, the fraught hours of waiting to see if they would be passed over by the falling pieces of Phobos. Seeing Sasha's body, bloody at the ears. Clicking over the transmitter that had brought Phobos down.

Thus it was very hard to keep her irritation in check as she went into the first meeting with the Cairenes, and found Jackie there among them, supporting their position. Jackie was pregnant now as well, and had been for some time; she was flushed, glossy, beautiful. No one knew who the father was, it was something she was doing on her own. A Dorsa Brevia tradition, by way of Hiroko – and just one more irritant to Nadia.

The meeting took place in a building next to the city wall, overlooking the U-shaped canyon below, called Nilus Noctis. The water in dispute was actually visible downcanyon, a broad ice-sheeted reservoir stopped by a dam not visible from up here, stopped just before the Illyrian Gates and the new chaos of the Compton Break.

Charlotte stood with her back to the window, asking the Cairene officials just the questions Nadia would have asked, but without the slightest trace of Nadia's annoyance. 'You will always be in a tent. Opportunities for growth will be limited. Why flood Marineris when you won't benefit from it?'

No one seemed to care to answer this. Finally Jackie said, 'The people living down there will benefit, and they're part of greater Cairo. Water in any form is a resource at these altitudes.'

'Water running freely down Marineris is no resource at all,' Charlotte said.

The Cairenes argued for the utility of water in Marineris. There were also representatives of the downstream settlers, many of them Egyptians, claiming that they had been in Marineris for generations, that it was their right to live there, that it was the best farming land on Mars, that they would fight before they would leave, and so on. Sometimes the Cairenes and Jackie seemed to be defending these neighbours, at other times their own right to use Marineris as a reservoir. Mostly they seemed to be defending their right to do whatever they wanted. Slowly Nadia got angrier and angrier.

313

'The court made its judgment,' she said. 'We're not here to argue it again. We're here to see it enacted.' And she left the meeting before she said anything inexcusable.

That night she sat with Charlotte and Art, so irritated that she could not focus on a delicious Ethiopian meal in the station restaurant. 'What do they want?' she asked Charlotte.

Charlotte shrugged, mouth full. After swallowing: 'Have you been noticing that being president of Mars is not a particularly powerful position?'

'Fuck yes. It would be hard to miss.'

'Yes. Well, the whole executive council is the same, of course. It's looking as if the real power in this government is in the environmental court. Irishka was put in charge there as part of the grand gesture, and she's done a lot to legitimate moderate Redness by staking out a middle ground. It allows for a lot of development under the six k limit, but above that, they're very strict. That's all backed by the constitution, so they've been able to make everything stand – the legislature is laying off, they haven't overturned any judgments yet. So it's been an impressive first session for Irishka and that whole group of justices.'

'So Jackie is jealous,' Nadia said.

Charlotte shrugged. 'It's possible.'

'More than possible,' Nadia said grimly.

'And then there's the matter of the council itself. Jackie may think this is something she can get three of the others to back her on, and then the council becomes that much more hers. Cairo is an arena where she might hope that Zeyk will vote with her because of the Arab part of town. Then only two more. And both Mikhail and Ariadne are strong localists.'

'But the council can't overturn court decisions,' Nadia said, 'only the legislature, right? By legislating new laws.'

'Right, but if Cairo continues to defy the court, then it would be up to the council to order the police to go down there and physically stop them. That's what the executive branch is supposed to do. If the council didn't do that, then the court would be undermined, and Jackie would take effective control of the council. Two birds with one stone.'

Nadia threw down her bit of spongy bread. 'I'll be damned if that happens,' she said.

They sat in silence.

'I hate this stuff,' Nadia said.

Charlotte said, 'In a few years there will be a body of practices, institutions, laws, amendments to the constitution, all that. Things that the constitution never addressed, which translate it into action. Like the proper role of political parties. Right now we're in the process of working all these things out.'

'Maybe so, but I still hate it.'

'Think of it as meta-architecture. Building the culture that allows architecture to exist. Then it'll be less frustrating for you.'

Nadia snorted.

'This one should be a clear case,' Charlotte said. 'The judgment has been made, they only have to abide by it.'

'What if they don't?'

'Time for the police.'

'Civil war, in other words!'

'They won't push it that far. They signed the constitution just like everyone else, and if everyone else is abiding by it, then they become outlaws, like the Red ecoteurs. I don't think they'll go that far. They're just testing the limits.'

She did not seem annoyed by this. That was the way people were, her expression seemed to say. She did not blame anyone, she was not frustrated. A very calm woman, this Charlotte – relaxed, confident, capable. With her co-ordinating it, the executive council's work had so far been well-organized, if not easy. If that competence was what growing up in a matriarchy like Dorsa Brevia did for you, Nadia thought, then more power to them. She couldn't help but compare Charlotte to Maya, with all Maya's mood shifts, her angst and self-dramatization. Well, it was probably an individual thing in any culture. But it was going to be interesting to have more Dorsa Brevia women around to take on these jobs.

At the next morning's meeting Nadia stood and said, 'An order against dumping water in Marineris has been issued already. If you persist in the dumping, the new police powers of the global community will be exerted. I don't think anyone wants that.'

'I don't think you can speak for the executive council,' Jackie said.

'I can,' Nadia said shortly.

'No you can't,' Jackie said. 'You're only one of seven. And this isn't a council matter anyway.'

'We'll see about that,' Nadia said.

The meeting dragged on. The Cairenes were stonewalling. The more Nadia understood what they were doing the less she liked it. Their leaders were important in Free Mars; and even if this challenge failed, it might result in concessions to Free Mars in other areas; so the party would have gained more power. Charlotte agreed that this could be their ultimate motive. The cynicism of this disgusted Nadia, and she found it very hard to be civil to Jackie when Jackie spoke to her, with her easy cheerfulness, the pregnant queen cruising around among her minions like a battleship among rowing boats: 'Aunt Nadia, so sorry you felt you needed to take time for such a thing as this . . .'

That night Nadia said to Charlotte, 'I want a ruling where Free Mars gets nothing at all out of this.'

Charlotte laughed briefly. 'Been talking to Jackie, have you?'

'Yes. Why is she so popular? I don't understand it, but she is!'

'She's nice to a lot of people. She thinks she's nice to everyone.'

'She reminds me of Phyllis,' Nadia said. The First Hundred again . . . 'Maybe not. Anyway, isn't there some sort of penalty we can invoke against frivolous suits and challenges?'

'Court costs, in some cases.'

'See if you can lay that on her then.'

'First let's see if we can win.'

The meetings went on for another week. Nadia left the talking to Charlotte and Art. She spent the meetings looking out of the windows at the canyon below, and in rubbing the stump of her finger, which now had a noticeable new bump on it. So strange; despite paying close attention, she could not recall when the bump had first appeared. It was warm and pink, a delicate pink, like a child's lips. There seemed to be a bone in the middle of it; she was afraid to squeeze it very hard. Surely lobsters didn't pinch their returning limbs. All that cell proliferation was disturbing – like a cancer, only controlled, directed – the miracle of DNA's instructional abilities made manifest. Life itself, flourishing in all its emergent complexity. And a little finger was nothing compared to an eye, or an embryo. It was a strange business.

With that going on, the political meetings looked really dreadful. Nadia walked out of one having heard almost none of it, though she was sure nothing significant had happened, and she went for a long walk, out to an overlook bulging out of the western end of the tent wall. She called Sax. The four travellers were getting closer to Mars; transmission delays were down to a few minutes. Nirgal appeared to be healthy again. He was in good spirits. Michel actually looked more drained than Nirgal; it seemed that the visit to Earth had been hard on him. Nadia held up her finger to the screen to cheer him up, and it worked.

'A pinky, don't they call it that?'

'I guess so.'

'You don't seem to believe it's going to work.'

'No. I guess I don't.'

'We're in a transitional period, I think,' Michel said. 'At our age we can't really believe that we're still alive, so we act as if it will end at any minute.'

'Which it could.' Thinking of Simon. Or Tatiana Durova. Or Arkady.

'Of course. But then again it might go on for decades more, or even centuries. After a while we'll have to start believing in it.' He sounded as if he was trying to convince himself as much as her. 'You'll look at your whole hand and then you'll believe it. And that will be very interesting.'

Nadia wiggled the pink nub at the end of her hand. No fingerprint yet in the fresh translucent skin. No doubt when it came it would be the same fingerprint as the one on the other little finger. Very strange.

Art came back from one meeting looking concerned. 'I've been asking around about this,' he said, 'trying to figure out why they're doing it. I put some Praxis operatives on the case, down in the canyon and back on Earth, and inside the Free Mars leadership.'

Spies, Nadia thought. Now we have spies.

' — appears that they are making private arrangements with

317

Terran governments concerning immigration. Building settlements and giving places to people from Egypt, definitely, and probably China too. It's got to be a quid pro quo, but we don't know what they're getting in return from these countries. Money, possibly.'

Nadia growled.

In the next couple of days she met onscreen or in person with all the other members of the executive council. Marion was of course against pumping any more water into Marineris, and so Nadia only needed two more votes. But Mikhail and Ariadne and Peter were unwilling to bring the police to bear if it could be avoided in any other way; and Nadia suspected they were not much happier than Jackie at the relative weakness of the council. They seemed willing to make concessions, to avoid an awkward enforcement of a court judgment they weren't adamantly behind.

Zeyk clearly wanted to vote against Jackie, but felt constrained by the Arab constituency in Cairo, and the eyes of the Arab community on him; control of land and water were both important to them. But the Bedouin were nomadic, and besides, Zeyk was a strong supporter of the constitution. Nadia thought he would support her. That left one more to be convinced.

The relationship with Mikhail had never improved, it was as if he wanted to be closer to Arkady's memory than she was. Peter she didn't feel she understood. Ariadne she didn't like, but in a way that made it easier; and Ariadne had come to Cairo as well. So Nadia decided to work on her first.

Ariadne was as committed to the constitution as most of the Dorsa Brevians, but they were localists as well, and were no doubt thinking about keeping some independence of their own from the global government. And they too were far from any water supply. So Ariadne had been prevaricating.

'Look,' Nadia said to her in a little room across the plaza from the city offices, 'you've got to forget about Dorsa Brevia and think about Mars.'

'I am, of course.'

She was irritated that this meeting was taking place; she would rather have dismissed Nadia out of hand. The merits of the case weren't what mattered to her, it was just a matter of precedence, of not having to listen to any issei. It was power politics and hierarchy to these people now, they had forgotten the real issues involved. And in this damned city; suddenly Nadia lost her patience, and she almost shouted, 'You're not! You're not thinking at all! This is the first challenge to the constitution, and you're looking around for what you can get out of it! I won't have it!' She waved a finger under Ariadne's surprised face: 'If you don't vote to enforce the court ruling, then the next time something you really want comes up for a council you'll see reprisals, *from me*. Do you understand?'

Ariadne's eyes were like billboards: first shocked, then a moment of pure fear. Then anger. She said, 'I never said I wasn't going to vote for enforcement! What are you going ballistic for?'

Nadia returned to a more ordinary argument mode, although still hard and tense and unrelenting. Finally Ariadne threw up her hands: 'It's what most of the Dorsa Brevia council wants to do, I was going to vote for it anyway. You don't have to be so *frantic* about it.' And she hurried out of the room, very upset.

First Nadia felt a surge of triumph. But that look of fear in the young woman's eyes – it stuck with her, until she began to feel slightly sick. She remembered Coyote on Pavonis, saying, 'Power corrupts.' That was the sick feeling – that first hit of power used, or misused.

Much later that night she was still sick with repulsion, and almost weeping, she told Art about the confrontation. 'That sounds bad,' he said gravely. 'That sounds like a mistake. You still have to deal with her. When that's the case, you have to just tweak people.'

'I know, I know. *God* I hate this,' she said. 'I want to get away, I want to do something *real*.'

He nodded heavily, patted her shoulder.

Before the next meeting, Nadia went over to Jackie and told her quietly that she had the council votes to put police down at the dam to stop any further release of water. Then in the meeting itself, she reminded everyone in an offhand remark that Nirgal would be back among them very soon, along with Maya and Sax and Michel. This caused several of the Free Mars group on hand to look thoughtful, though Jackie of course showed no reaction. As they nattered on after that, Nadia rubbed her finger, distracted, still upset with herself about the meeting with Ariadne.

The next day the Cairenes agreed to accept the judgment of the Global Environmental Court. They would cease releasing water from their reservoir, and the settlements downcanyon would have to exist on piped water, which would certainly pinch their growth.

'Good,' Nadia said, still bitter. 'All that just to obey the law.'

'They're going to appeal,' Art pointed out.

'I don't care. They're done for. And even if they aren't, they've submitted to the process. Hell, they can win for all I care. It's the process that counts, so we win no matter what.'

Art smiled to hear this. A step in her political education, no doubt, a step Art and Charlotte seemed to have taken long ago. What mattered to them was not the result of any single disagreement, but the successful use of the process. If Free Mars represented the majority now – and apparently it did, as it had the allegiance of almost all the natives, young fools that they were – then submitting to the constitution meant that they could not simply push around minority groups by force of numbers. So when Free Mars won something, it would have to be on the merits of the case, judged by the full array of court justices, who came from all factions. That was quite satisfying, actually; like seeing a wall made of delicate materials bear more weight than it looked as if it could, because of a cleverly-built framework.

But she had used threats to shore up one beam, and so the whole thing left a bad taste in her mouth. 'I want to do something real.'

'Like plumbing?'

She nodded, not even close to a smile. 'Yes. Hydrology.'

'Can I come along?'

'Be a plumber's helper?'

He laughed. 'I've done it before.'

Nadia regarded him. He was making her feel better. It was peculiar, old-fashioned: to go somewhere just to be with someone. It didn't happen much any more. People went where they needed to go, and hung out with whatever friends they found there, or made new friends. It was the Martian way. Or maybe just the First Hundred's way. Or her way.

Anyway, it was clear that doing this, travelling together, was more than just a friendship, more even perhaps than an affair. But that was not so bad, she decided. In fact not bad at all. Something to get used to, perhaps. But there was always something to get used to.

A new finger, for instance. Art was holding her hand, lightly massaging the new digit. 'Does it hurt? Can you bend it?'

It did hurt, a little; and she could bend it, a little. They had injected some knuckle zone cells, and now it was just longer than the first joint of her other little finger, the skin still baby pink, unmarred by callus or scar. Every day a little bigger.

Art squeezed the tip of it ever so gently, feeling the bone inside. His eyes were round. 'You can feel that?'

'Oh yes. It's like the other fingers, only a bit more sensitive maybe.'

'Because it's new.'

'I suppose.'

Only the old lost finger was implicated, somehow; the ghost was calling again, now that there were signals coming from that end of the hand. The finger in the brain, Art called it. And no doubt there really was a cluster of brain cells devoted to that finger, which had been the ghost all along. It had faded over the years from lack of stimulus, but now it too was growing back, or being restimulated or reinforced; Vlad's explanations of the phenomenon were complex. But these days when she felt the finger, it sometimes felt just as large as the one on the other hand, even when she was looking right at it. Like feeling an invisible shell over the new one. At other times she felt the little thing at its proper size, short and skinny and weak. She could bend it at the hand knuckle, and just a little at the middle knuckle. The last kuckle, behind the fingernail, wasn't there yet. But it was on its way. Growing. Again Nadia joked about it growing on and on, though it was a creepy thought. 'That would be good,' Art said. 'You'd have to get a dog.'

But now she felt confident that wouldn't happen. The finger seemed to know what it was doing. It would be all right. It looked normal. Art was fascinated by it. But not just by it. He massaged her hand, which was a bit sore, and then her arm and shoulders too. He would massage all of her if she let him. And judging by how her finger and arm and shoulders felt, she certainly ought to. He was so relaxed. Life for him was still a daily adventure, full of marvels and hilarity. People made him laugh every day; that was a great gift. Big, round-faced, round-bodied, somewhat like Nadia herself in certain aspects of appearance; balding, unpretentious, graceful on his feet. Her friend.

Well, she loved Art, of course. She had since Dorsa Brevia at least. Something like her feeling for Nirgal, who was a most beloved nephew or student or godchild or grandchild or child; and Art, therefore, one of her child's friends. Actually he was a bit older than Nirgal, but still, those two were like brothers. That was the problem. But all these calculations were being progressively thrown off by their increasing longevity. When he was only five per cent younger than her, would it matter any more? When they had gone through thirty years of intense experience together, as they already had, as equals and collaborators, architects of a proclamation, a constitution and a government; close friends, confidants, helpers, massage partners; did it matter, the different number of years past their youths they were? No it did not. It was obvious, one only had to think about it. And then try to feel it too.

They didn't need her in Cairo any more, they didn't need her in Sheffield right that second. Nirgal would be back soon, and he would help to keep Jackie in check; not a fun job, but that was his problem, no one could help him there. It was hard when you fixed all your love on one person. As she had with Arkady, for so many years, even though he had been dead for most of them. It made no sense; but she missed him. And she still got angry at him. He had not even lived long enough to realize how much he had missed. The happy fool. Art was happy too, but he was no fool. Or not much. To Nadia all happy people were a bit foolish by definition, otherwise how could they be so happy? But she liked them anyway, she needed them. They were like her beloved Satchmo's music; and given the world, and all that it held, that happiness was a very courageous way to live – not a set of circumstances, but a set of attitudes. 'Yes, come plumbing with me,' she said to Art, and hugged him hard, hard, as if you could capture happiness by squeezing it hard enough. She pulled back and he was bug-eyed with surprise, as when holding her little finger.

But she was still president of the executive council, and despite her resolve, every day they bound her to the job a little more tightly, with 'developments' of all kinds. German immigrants wanted to build a new harbour town called Bloch's Hoffnung on the peninsula that cut the North Sea in half, and then dig a broad canal through the peninsula. Red ecoteurs objected to this plan, and blew up the piste running down the peninsula. They blew up the piste leading to the top of Biblis Patera as well, to indicate they objected to that as well. Ecopoets in Amazonia wanted to start massive forest fires. Other ecopoets in Kasei wanted to remove the fire-dependent forest that Sax had planted in the great curve of the valley (this petition was the first to receive unanimous approval from the GEC). Reds living around White Rock, an eighteen kilometre wide pure white mesa, wanted it declared a 'kami site' forbidden to human access. A Sabishii design team was recommending that they build a new capital city on the north sea coast at 0° longitude, where there was a deep bay. New Clarke was getting crowded with what looked suspiciously like metanat security snoopertroopers. The Da Vinci techs wanted to give control of Martian space over to an agency of the global government that didn't exist. Senzeni Na wanted to fill their mohole. The Chinese were requesting permission to build an entirely new space elevator tethered near Schiaparelli Crater, to accommodate their own emigration, and contract out to others. Immigration was growing every month.

Nadia dealt with all these issues in half-hour increments scheduled by Art, and so the days passed in a blur. It got very difficult to stay aware that some of these matters were much more important than others. The Chinese, for instance, would flood Mars with immigrants if they got half a chance . . . and the Red ecoteurs were getting more outrageous; there had even been death threats made against Nadia herself. She now had escorts when she left her apartment, and the apartment was discreetly guarded. Nadia ignored that, and continued to work on the issues, and to work the council to keep a majority on her side in the votes that mattered to her. She established good working relations with Zeyk and Mikhail, and even with Marion. Things never went quite right with Ariadne again, however, which was a lesson learned twice; but learned well because of that.

So she did the job. But all the time she wanted off Pavonis. Art saw her patience get shorter by the day; she knew by his look that she was becoming crotchety, crabby, dictatorial; she knew it, but could not help it. After meetings with frivolous or obstructionist people she often unleashed a torrent of vicious abuse, in a steady, low, cursing voice that Art obviously found unnerving. Delegations would come in demanding an end to the death penalty, or the right to build in the Olympus Mons caldera, or a free eighth spot on the executive council, and as soon as the door closed Nadia would say, 'Well *there's* a bunch of fucking idiots for you, *stupid* fools never even thought about tie votes, never occurred to them that taking someone else's life abrogates your own right to live,' and so on. The new police captured a group of Red ecoteurs who had tried to blow up the Socket again, and in the process killed a security guard out of his position, and she was the hardest judge they had: 'Execute them!' she exclaimed. 'Look, you kill someone, you lose your *right* to live. Execute them or else exile them from Mars for life – make them pay in a way that really gets the rest of the Reds' attention.'

'Well,' Art said uneasily. 'Well, after all.' But on she raged. She couldn't stop until she felt less angry. And Art could see that it was getting harder every time.

Flailing a bit himself, he recommended she start another conference, like the one in Sabishii she had missed; and make sure she made this one. Organizing the efforts of different organizations for a single cause; this was not really building, Nadia thought, but it looked as if it would have to do.

The fight in Cairo had started her thinking about the hydrological cycle, and what would happen when the ice began to melt. If they could set up some kind of plan for a water cycle, even only an approximation, then it might go far toward reducing conflicts over water. So she decided to see what could be done.

As often happened these days when she thought about global issues, she found herself wanting to talk to Sax about it.

The travellers to Earth were almost back now, close enough that transmission delay was insignificant, it was almost like having a normal wrist conversation. So Nadia spent evenings talking with Sax about terraforming. More than once he surprised her utterly; he did not hold the opinions she had imagined he would hold, he seemed always to be changing. 'I want to keep things wild,' he said one night.

'What do you mean?' she asked.

His face took on the puzzled expression it wore when he was thinking hard. It was considerably longer than the transmission delay before he replied: 'Many things. It's a complicated word. But – I mean – I want to maintain the primal landscape, as much as possible.'

Nadia could censor out her laughter at this; but still Sax said, 'What do you find amusing?'

'Oh nothing. It's just you sound like, I don't know, like some of the Reds. Or the people in Christianopolis, they're not Reds, but they said almost the same thing to me, last week. They want to keep the primal landscape of the far south preserved. I've helped them to set up a conference to talk about southern watersheds.'

'I thought you were working on greenhouse gases?'

'They won't let me work, I have to be president. But I am going to go to this conference.'

'Good idea.'

The Japanese settlers in Messhi Hoko (which meant, 'Self-sacrifice for the sake of the group') came to the council to demand that more land and water be dedicated to their tent high on South Tharsis. Nadia walked out on them, and flew with Art down to Christianopolis, in the far south.

The little town (and it seemed very little after Sheffield and Cairo) was set in Phillips Rim Crater Four, at latitude 67° south. During the Year-Without-Summer the far south had experienced many severe storms, dropping about four metres of new snow, an unprecedented amount; the previous record for a year had been less than one. Now it was Ls 281, just after perihelion, and high summer in the south. And the various abatement strategies for avoiding an ice age seemed to be working well; most of the new snow had melted in a hot spring, and now there were round lakes on every crater floor. The pond in the centre of Christianopolis was about three metres deep, and three hundred metres across; this was fine with the Christians, as it gave them a nice park pond. But if the same thing happened every winter – and the meteorologists believed that the coming winters would drop even more snow, and the coming summers get ever warmer – then their town would quickly be inundated by snowmelt, and Phillips Rim Crater Four become a lake full to the brim. And this was true for craters all over Mars.

The conference in Christianopolis had been convened to discuss strategies to deal with this situation. Nadia had done what she could to get influential people down to it, including meteorologists, hydrologists, and engineers, and the possibility of Sax, whose return was imminent. The problem of crater flooding was to be only the initial point of discussion for the whole question of watersheds, and the planetary hydrological cycle itself.

The crater problem specifically was to be solved as Nadia had predicted: plumbing. They would treat the craters like bathtubs, and drill drains to empty them. The brecciated pans under the dusty crater floors were extremely hard, but they could be tunnelled through robotically; then install pumps and filters and pump the water out, keeping a central pond or lake if one wanted, or draining it dry.

But what were they going to do with the water they pumped out? The southern highlands were everywhere lumpy, shattered, pocked, cracked, hillocky, scarped, slumped, fissured and fractured; when analysed as potential watersheds, they were hopeless. Nothing led anywhere; there was no downhill for long. The entire south was a plateau three to four kilometres above the old datum, with only local bumps and dips. Never had Nadia seen more clearly the difference between this highland and any continent on Earth. On Earth, tectonic movement had pushed up mountains every few score million years, and then water had run down these fresh slopes, following the paths of least resistance back to the sea, carving the fractal vein patterns of watersheds everywhere. Even the dry basin regions on Earth were seamed with arroyos and dotted with playas. In the Martian south, however, the meteoric bombardment of the Noachian had hammered the land ferociously, leaving craters and ejecta everywhere; and then the battered irregular wasteland had lain there for two billion years under the ceaseless scouring of the dusty winds, tearing at every flaw. If they poured water onto this pummelled land they would end up with a crazy quilt of short streams, running down local inclines to the nearest rimless crater. Hardly any streams would make it to the sea in the north, or even into the Hellas or Argyre basins, both of which were ringed by mountain ranges of their own ejecta.

There were, however, a few exceptions to this situation. The Noachian Age had been followed by a brief 'warm wet period' in the late Hesperian, a period perhaps as short as a hundred million years, when a thick warm CO_2 atmosphere had allowed liquid water to run on the surface, carving some river channels down the gentle tilts of the plateau, between crater aprons diverting them this way and that. And these watercourses had of course remained after the atmosphere had frozen out, empty arroyos gradually widened by the wind. These fossil riverbeds, like Nirgal Vallis, Warrego Valles, Protva Valles, Patana Valles, or Oltis Vallis, were narrow, sinuous canyons, true riverine canyons rather than grabens or fossae. Some of them even had immature tributary systems. So efforts to design a macro-watershed system for the south naturally used these canyons as primary watercourses, with water pumped to the head of every tributary. Then there were also a number of old lava channels that could easily become rivers, as the lava, like the water, had tended to follow the path of least resistance downhill. And there were a number of tilted graben fractures and fissures, as at the foot of the Eridania Scopulus, that could likewise be turned to use.

In the conference, big globes of Mars were marked up daily to display different water regimes. There were also rooms full of 3-D topo maps, with groups standing around different watershed systems, arguing their advantages and disadvantages, or simply contemplating them, or fiddling with the controls to change them, restlessly, from one pattern to another. Nadia wandered the rooms looking at these hydrographies, learning much about the southern hemisphere that she had never known. There was a six-kilometre high mountain near Richardson Crater, in the far south. The south polar cap itself was quite high. Dorsa Brevia, on the other hand, crossed a depression that looked like a ray cut out from the Hellas impact, a valley so deep that it ought to become a lake, an idea that the Dorsa Brevians naturally did not like. And certainly the area could be drained if they cared to do it. There were scores of variant plans, and every single system was strange-looking to Nadia. Never had she seen so clearly how different a gravity-driven fractal was from impact randomness. In the inchoate meteoric landscape, almost anything was possible, because nothing was obvious – nothing except for the fact that in any possible system, some canals and tunnels would have to be built. Her new finger itched with the desire to get out there and run a bulldozer or a tunnel borer.

Gradually the most efficient, or logical, or aesthetically pleasing plans began to emerge from the proposals, the best for each region being patched together, in a kind of mosaic. In the eastern quadrant of the deep south, streams would tend to run toward Hellas Basin and through a couple of gorges into the Hellas Sea, which was fine. Dorsa Brevia accepted a plan to have their town's lava tunnel ridge become a kind of dam, crossing a watershed transversely so that there was a lake above it and a river below it, coursing down to Hellas. Around the south polar cap, snowfall would remain frozen, but most of the meteorologists predicted that when things stabilized there wouldn't be much snowfall on the pole, that it would become a cold desert like Antarctica. Eventually of course they would end up with a largish ice cap, and then part of it would pool down into the huge depression under the Promethei Rupes, another partially-erased old impact basin. If they didn't want too large a southern ice cap, they would have to melt and pump some of the water back north, into the Hellas Sea perhaps. They would have to do some similar pumping in Argyre Basin, if they decided to keep Argyre dry. A group of moderate Red lawyers was even now insisting on this before the GEC, arguing that one of the two great dune-filled impact basins on the planet ought to be preserved. It seemed certain this claim would receive a favourable judgment from the court, and so all the watersheds around Argyre had to take this into account.

Sax had designed his own southern watershed plan, which he sent to the conference from their rocket as it aerobraked into orbital insertion, to be considered with all the rest. It minimized surface water, emptied most craters, used tunnels extensively, and channelized almost all drained water into the fossil river canyons. In his plan vast areas of the south would stay arid desert, making for a hemisphere of dry tableland, cut deeply by a few narrow river-bottomed canyons. 'Water is returned north,' he explained to Nadia in a call, 'and if you stay up on the plateaus, it will look as it always did, almost.'

So that Ann would like it, he was saying.

'Good idea,' Nadia said.

And indeed Sax's plan was not that much different from the consensus being hammered out by the conference. Wet north, dry south; one more dualism to add to the great dichotomy. And to have the old river canyons running with water again was satisfying. A good-looking plan, given the terrain.

But the days were long gone when Sax or anyone else could choose a terraforming project and then go out and do it. Nadia could see that Sax hadn't fully understood this. Ever since the beginning, when he had slipped algae-filled windmills into the field without the knowledge or approval of anyone but his accomplices, he had been working on his own. It was an ingrained habit of mind, and now he seemed to forget the review process that any watershed plan was going to have to go through in the environmental courts. But the process was there, inescapable now, and because of the grand gesture, half the fifty GEC justices were Reds of one shade or another. Any watershed proposal from a conference including Sax Russell, even as a teleparticipant, was going to get close and suspicious scrutiny.

But it seemed to Nadia that if the Red justices looked carefully at the proposal, they would have to be amazed at Sax's approach. Indeed it represented a kind of road-to-Damascus conversion – inexplicable, given Sax's history. Unless you knew all of it. But Nadia understood: he was trying to please Ann. Nadia doubted that was possible, but she liked to see Sax try. 'A man full of surprises,' she remarked to Art.

'Brain trauma will do that.'

In any case, when the conference was done they had designed an entire hydrography, designating all the future major lakes and rivers and streams of the southern hemisphere. The plan would eventually have to be integrated with similar plans for the northern hemisphere, which were in considerable disarray by comparison, because of the uncertainty about just how big the northern sea was going to be. Water was no longer being actively pumped up out of permafrost and aquifers – indeed many of the pumping stations had been blown up in the last year by Red ecoteurs – but some water was still rising, under the weight put on the land by the water already pumped. And summer runoff was flowing into Vastitas, more every year, both from the northern polar cap and the Great Escarpment; Vastitas was the catchment basin for huge watersheds on all sides. So a lot of water was going to pour into it every summer. On the other hand, a lot of water was always being stripped off by the arid winds, eventually precipitating elsewhere. And water would evaporate much faster than the ice currently there was subliming. So calculating how much was leaving and how much coming back was a modeller's field day, and estimates were still all over the map, literally so in that differences in prediction led to putative shorelines that were in some cases hundreds of kilometres apart.

That uncertainty would delay any GECO on the south, Nadia thought; in essence the court had to try to correlate all the current data, and evaluate the models, and then prescribe a sea level, and approve all watersheds accordingly. The fate of Argyre Basin in particular seemed impossible to decide at this point, before there was a northern plan; some plans called for pumping water up into Argyre from the northern sea if the northern sea got too full, to avoid flooding the Marineris canyons, South Fossa, and the new harbour towns being built. Radical Reds were already threatening to build 'west bank settlements' all over Argyre to forestall any such move.

So the GEC had yet another big issue to solve. Clearly it was becoming the most important political body on Mars; with the constitution and its own previous rulings to guide it, it was ruling on almost every aspect of their future on Mars.

332

Nadia thought that was probably as it should be; or at least that there was nothing wrong with it. They needed decisions with global ramifications reviewed globally, that was what it came down to.

But come what may in the courts, a provisional plan for the southern hemisphere had at least been formulated. And to everyone's surprise, the GEC gave the plan a positive preliminary judgment very soon after it was submitted – because, their ruling said, it could be activated in stages as water fell on the south, and it proceeded in much the same fashion through its first stages no matter what the eventual sea level in the north became. So there was no reason to delay beginning.

Art came in beaming with the news. 'We can begin plumbing,' he said.

But of course Nadia couldn't. There were meetings in Sheffield to go back to, decisions to be made, people to be convinced or coerced. Doggedly she did that work, stubbornly doing her duty whether she liked it or not, and as time passed she got better and better at it. She saw how she could subtly pressure other people to get her way; saw how people would do her bidding if she asked or suggested in certain ways. The constant stream of decisions honed some of her views; she found that it helped to have at least some consciously held political principles, rather than judging each case by instinct. It also helped to have reliable allies, on the council and elsewhere, rather than being a supposedly neutral and independent person. And so by degrees she found herself joining the Bogdanovists, who, to her surprise, conformed more closely to her political philosophy than anything else on Mars. Of course her reading of Bogdanovism was relatively simple: things should be just, Arkady had insisted, and everyone free and equal; the past didn't matter; they needed to invent new forms whenever the old ones looked unfair or impractical, which was often; Mars was the only reality that counted, at least to them. Using these as her guiding principles, she found it easier to make up her mind about things, to see a course and cut for it directly.

Also she became more and more ruthless. From time to time she felt freshly how power could corrupt, felt it as a slight nausea within her. But she was getting habituated. She clashed often with Ariadne, and when she recalled the remorse she had felt after her first wrangle with the young Minoan, it seemed to her ridiculously over-fastidious; she was far tougher than that every day now on people who crossed her, she showed the knives in meeting after meeting, in calculated microbursts of brutality that put people in line very effectively indeed. In fact the more she allowed herself to release little outbursts of fury and scorn, the more certainly she could control them and put them to some use. She was a power; and people knew it; and power was corrosive. Power was powerful, in more ways than one. And now Nadia felt very little remorse about that; they deserved a pop on the nose, generally; they had thought they were going to get a harmless old babushka to sit in the big chair while they worked their games on each other, but the big chair was the power seat, and she was damned if she was going to go through all this shit and not use some of that power to try to get what she wanted.

And so less and less often did she feel how ugly it was. Once when she did, after a particularly hardnosed day, she thumped down in a chair and almost cried, sick with disgust. Only seven months of her three M-years had passed. What would she become by the time her stint was done? Already she was used to power; by then she might even like it.

Art, worried by all this, squinted at her over their breakfast table. 'Well,' he said once, after she explained what was bothering her, 'power is power.' He was thinking hard. 'You're the first president of Mars. So in a way you define the office. Maybe you should declare you're only going to work the one month and not the two months, and delegate the two months to your staff. Something like that.'

She stared at him, mouth full of toast.

Later that week she abandoned Sheffield and went south again, joining a caravan of people working their way from crater to crater, installing drainage systems. Every crater had variations, but essentially it was a matter of picking the right angle to emerge from the crater apron, and then setting the robots to work. Von Karman, Du Toit, Schmidt, Agassiz, Heaviside, Bianchini, Lau, Chamberlin, Stoney, Dokuchaev,

Trumpler, Keeler, Charlier, Suess . . . they plumbed all of those craters, and many more unnamed ones, although the craters were taking on names even faster than they drilled them: 85 South, Too Dark, Fool's Hope, Shanghai, Hiroko Slept Here, Fourier, Cole, Proudhon, Bellamy, Hudson, Kaif, 47 Ronin, Makoto, Kino Doku, Ka Ko, Mondragon. The migration from one crater to the next reminded Nadia of her trips around the south polar cap during the underground years; except now everything was out in the open, and through the nearly-nightless midsummer days the team luxuriated in the sun, in the glarey light off the crater lakes. They travelled across rough, frozen bogs brilliant with sunny meltwater and meadow grass, and always of course they crossed the rust-and-black rockscape breaking out into the light, ring after ring, ridge after ridge. They plumbed craters and laid watershed pipes, and attached greenhouse gas factories to the excavators whenever the rock had any gas feedstocks in it.

But hardly any of that turned out to be work in the sense Nadia meant. She missed the old days. Of course operating a bulldozer had not been hand labour, but one's touch with the blade had been a very physical skill, and the repeated gear shifts physically taxing; and it was all around a higher level of engagement than this 'work', which consisted of talking to AIs and then walking around and watching humming and buzzing teams of waist-high robot diggers, city-block-sized mobile factory units, tunnel moles with diamond teeth that grew back like sharks' teeth – everything made of bioceramic/metallic alloys stronger than the elevator cable, all of it out there doing it all by itself. It just wasn't what she had in mind.

Try again. She went through another cycle; return to Shef-field, engagement in the council work, increasing disgust, merging with despair; look around for anything to get her out of it; notice some likely project and seize on it. Run off to check it out. Like Art had said, she could call her own shots. There was that in power too.

The next time out it was soil that drew her. 'Air, water, earth,' Art said. 'Next it'll be forest fires, eh?'

But she had heard that there were scientists in Bogdanov Vishniac trying to manufacture soil, and this interested her. So off she went, flying south to Vishniac, where she had not been for years. Art accompanied her. 'It'll be interesting to see how the old underground cities adapt, now that there's no need to hide.'

'I don't see why anyone stays down here, to tell you the truth,' Nadia said as they flew down into the rugged southern polar region. 'They're so far south their winters last forever. Six months with no sun at all. Who would stay?'

'Siberians.'

'No Siberian in his right mind would move here. They know better.'

'Laplanders, then. Inuit. People who like the poles.'

'I suppose.'

As it turned out, no one in Bogdanov Vishniac seemed to mind the winters. They had redistributed their mohole mound in a ring around the mohole itself, creating an immense circu-lar amphitheatre facing down into the hole. This terraced amphitheatre was to be the surface Vishniac. In the summers it would be a green oasis, and in the dark winters a white oasis; they planned to illuminate it with hundreds of brilliant streetlights, giving themselves a stage-set day, in a town con-templating itself across a round gap in things, or from the upper wall looking out at the frosted chaos of the polar high-lands. No, they were going to stay, no question of it. It was their place.

Nadia was greeted at the airport as a special guest, as always when she stayed with Bogdanovists. Before joining them this

337

had struck her as ridiculous, and even a bit offensive: girlfriend of the Founder! But now she accepted their offer of a guest suite located on the lip of the mohole, with a slightly overhanging window that gave one a view straight down for eighteen kilometres. The lights on the mohole's bottom looked like stars seen through the planet.

Art was petrified, not at the sight but at the very thought of the sight, and he would not go near that half of the room. Nadia laughed at him, and then when she was finished looking, closed the curtains.

The next day she went out to visit the soil scientists, who were happy at her interest. They wanted to be able to feed themselves, and as more and more settlers moved south, this was going to be impossible without more soil. But they were finding that manufacturing soil was one of the most difficult technical feats they had ever undertaken. Nadia was surprised to hear this – these were the Vishniac labs, after all, world leaders in technologically supported ecologies, having lived for decades hidden in a mohole. And topsoil was, well, soil. Dirt with additives, presumably, and additives one could add.

No doubt she conveyed some of this impression to the soil scientists, and the man named Arne leading her around told her with some exasperation that soil was in fact *very* complex. About five per cent of it by weight was made of living things, and this critical five per cent consisted of dense populations of nematodes, worms, molluscs, arthropods, insects, arachnids, small mammals, fungi, protozoa, algae and bacteria. The bacteria alone included several thousand different species, and could number as many as a hundred million individuals per gram of soil. And the other members of the microcommunity were almost as plentiful, in both number and variety.

Such complex ecologies could not be manufactured in the way Nadia had been imagining, which was basically to grow the ingredients separately and then mix them in a hopper, like a cake. But they didn't know all the ingredients, and they couldn't grow some of the ingredients, and some that they could grow died on mixing. 'Worms in particular are sensitive. Nematodes have trouble too. The whole system tends to crash, leaving us with minerals and dead organic material. That's called humus. We're very good at making humus. Topsoil, however, has to grow.'

'Which is what happens naturally?'

'Right. We can only try to grow it faster than it grows in nature. We can't assemble it, or manufacture it in bulk. And many of the living components grow best in soil itself, so there's a problem providing feedstock organisms at any faster rate than natural soil formation would provide them.'

'Hmm,' Nadia said.

Arne took her through their labs and greenhouses, which were filled with hundreds of pedons, tall cylindrical vats or tubes, in racks, all holding soil or its components. This was experimental agronomy, and from her experience with Hiroko Nadia was prepared to understand very little of it. The esoterica of science could go right off her scale. But she did understand that they were doing factorial trials, altering the conditions in each pedon and tracking what happened. There was a simple formula Arne showed her to describe the most general aspects of the problem:

$$S = f(P_M, C, R, B, T),$$

meaning that any soil property S was a factor (f) of the semi-independent variables, parent material (P_M), climate (C), topography or relief (R), biota (B), and time (T). Time, of course, was the factor they were trying to speed up; and the parent material in most of their trials was the ubiquitous Martian surface clay. Climate and topography were altered in some trials, to imitate various field conditions; but mostly they were altering the biotic and organic elements. This meant microecology of the most sophisticated kind, and the more Nadia learned about it the more difficult their task seemed – not so much construction as alchemy. Many elements had to cycle through soil to make it a growth medium for plants, and each element had its own particular cycle, driven by a different collection of agents. There were the macronutrients – carbon, oxygen, hydrogen, nitrogen, phosphorus, sulphur, potassium, calcium and magnesium – then the micronutrients, including iron, manganese, zinc, copper, molybdenum, boron and chlorine. None of these nutrient cycles was closed, as there were losses due to leaching, erosion, harvesting and outgassing; inputs

339

were just as various, including absorption, weathering, microbial action and application of fertilizers. The conditions that allowed the cycling of all these elements to proceed were varied enough that different soils encouraged or discouraged each cycle to different degrees; each kind of soil had particular pH levels, salinities, compaction and so forth; thus there were hundreds of named soils in these labs alone, and thousands more back on Earth.

Naturally in the Vishniac labs the Martian parent material formed the basis for most of the experiments. Eons of dust storms had recycled this material all over the planet, until it had everywhere much the same content: the typical Martian soil unit was made up of fine particles of mostly silicon and iron. At its top it was often loose drift. Below that, varying degrees of interparticle cementation had produced crusty, cloddy material, becoming blocky the lower one dug.

Clays, in other words; smectite clays, similar to Terra's montmorillonite and nontronite, with the addition of materials like talc, quartz, hematite, anhydrite, dieserite, clacite, beidellite, rutile, gypsum, maghemite and magnetite. And everything had been coated by amorphous iron oxyhydroxides, and other more crystallized iron oxides, which accounted for the reddish colours.

So this was their universal parent material: iron-rich smectite clay. Its loosely packed and porous structure meant it would support roots while still giving them room to grow. But there were no living things in it, and too many salts, and too little nitrogen. So in essence their task was to gather parent material, and leach out salt and aluminium, while introducing nitrogen and the biotic community, all as fast as possible. Simple, when put like that; but that phrase 'biotic community' masked a whole world of troubles. 'My God, it's like trying to get this government to work,' Nadia exclaimed to Art one evening. 'They're in big trouble!'

Out in the countryside people were simply introducing bacteria to the clay, and then algae and other micro-organisms, then lichen, and then halophyllic plants. Then they had waited for these biocommunities to transform the clay into soils, through many generations of living and dying in it. This worked, and was working even now, all over the planet; but

340

it was very slow. A group in Sabishii had estimated that when averaged over the planet's surface, about a centimetre of topsoil was being generated every century. And this had been achieved using genetically-engineered populations designed to maximize speed.

In the greenhouse farms, on the other hand, the soils used had been heavily amended by nutrients and fertilizers and inoculants of all kinds; the result was something like what these scientists were trying for, but the quantity of soil in greenhouses was minuscule compared to what they wanted to put out on the surface. Mass producing soil was their goal. But they had got into something deeper than they had expected, Nadia could tell; they had that vexed absorbed air, like a dog gnawing on a bone too big for its mouth.

The biology, chemistry, biochemistry and ecology involved in these problems were far beyond Nadia's expertise, and there was nothing she could do to make suggestions there. In many cases she couldn't even understand the processes involved. It was not construction, nor even an analogue of construction.

But they did have to incorporate some construction into whatever production methods they tried, and there Nadia was at least able to understand the issues. She began to concentrate on that aspect of things, looking at the mechanical design of the pedons, and also the holding tanks for the living constituents of the soil. She also studied the molecular structure of the parent clays, to see if it suggested anything to her about working with them. Martian smectites were aluminosilicates, she found, meaning each unit of the clay had a sheet of aluminium octahedrals sandwiched between two sheets of silicon tetrahedrals; the different kinds of smectites had different amounts of variation in this general pattern, and the more variation there was, the easier it was for water to seep into the interlayer surfaces. The most common smectite clay on Mars, montmorillonite, had a lot of variety, and so was very open to water, expanding when wet, and shrinking when dry to the point of cracking.

Nadia found this interesting. 'Look,' she said to Arne, 'what about a pedon filled with a matrix of feeder-veins, which would introduce the biota all through the parent material.' Take a batch of parent material, she went on, and get it wet, then let it dry. Insert into the crack systems the feeder-vein matrix. Then pour in whatever important bacteria and other constituents they could grow. Then if the bacteria and other creatures could eat their way out of their feeder-veins, digesting that material as they emerged, they would all suddenly be there together in the clay, interacting. That would be a tricky time, no doubt many trials would be necessary to calibrate the initial amounts of the various biota needed to avoid population booms and crashes – but if they could get them to settle into their usual communities, then they would suddenly have living soil. 'There are feeder-vein systems like this used for certain quick-setting construction materials, and now I hear that doctors feed apatite paste into broken bones the same way. The feeder-veins are made of protein gels appropriate to whatever substance they're going to contain, moulded into the appropriate tubular structures.'

A matrix for growth. Worth looking into, Arne said. Which made Nadia smile. She went around that afternoon feeling happy, and that evening when she joined Art she said, 'Hey! I did some work today.'

'Well!' Art said. 'Let's go out and celebrate.'

Easy to do, in Bogdanov Vishniac. It was a Bogdanovist city, all right, as buoyant as Arkady himself. A party every night. They had often joined the evening promenade, and Nadia loved walking along the railing of the highest terrace, feeling that Arkady was somehow there, had somehow persisted. And never more so than on this night, celebrating a bit of work done. She held Art's hand, looked down and across at the crowded lower terraces and their crops, orchards, pools, sports fields, lines of trees, arcuate plazas occupied by cafés, bars, dance pavilions – bands battling for sonic space, the crowds chugging around them, some dancing but many more simply making the night's promenade, like Nadia herself. All this still under a tent, with tenting that they hoped to remove someday; meanwhile it was warm, and the young natives wore an outlandish array of pantaloons, headdresses, sashes, vests, necklaces, so that Nadia was reminded of the video footage of

Nirgal and Maya's reception in Trinidad. Was this coincidence, or was there some supraplanetary culture coming into being among the young? And if there was, did that mean that their Coyote, the Trinidadian, had invisibly conquered the two worlds? Or her Arkady, posthumously? Arkady and Coyote, culture kings. It made her grin to think of it, and she took sips of Art's cup of scalding kavajava, the drink of choice in this cold town, and watched all the young people moving like angels, always dancing no matter what they did, flowing in graceful arcs from terrace to terrace. 'What a great little town,' Art said.

Then they came upon an old photo of Arkady himself, framed and hung on a wall next to a door. Nadia stopped and clutched Art's arm: 'That's him! That's him to the life!'

The photo had caught him talking with someone, standing just inside a tent wall and gesturing, his hair and beard lofting away from his head and blending into a landscape exactly the colour of his wild curls. A face coming out of a hillside, it seemed, blue eyes squinting in the glare of all that red glee. 'I've never seen a photo that looked so much like him. If he saw a camera pointed at him he didn't like it, and the picture came out wrong.'

She stared at the photo, feeling flushed, and strangely happy; such a lifelike encounter! Like running into someone again after years of not seeing them. 'You're like him, in some ways, I think. But more relaxed.'

'It looks as if it would be hard to get much more relaxed than that,' Art said, peering closely at the photo.

Nadia smiled. 'It was easy for him. He was always sure he was right.'

'None of the rest of us have that problem.'

She laughed. 'You're cheerful like he was.'

'And why not.'

They walked on. Nadia kept thinking of her old companion, seeing the photo in her mind's eye. There was still so much she remembered. The feelings connected to the memories were fading, however, the pain blunted – the fixative leached out, all that flesh and trauma now only a pattern of a certain kind, like a fossil. And very unlike the present moment, which, looking around, feeling her hand in Art's, was real, vivid, brief, perpetually changing – alive. Anything could happen, everything was felt.

'Shall we go back to our room?'

The four travellers to Earth returned at last, coming down the cable to Sheffield. Nirgal and Maya and Michel went their ways, but Sax flew down and joined Nadia and Art in the south, a move which pleased Nadia no end. She had come to have the feeling that wherever Sax went was the heart of the action.

He looked just as he had before the trip to Earth, and was if anything even more silent and enigmatic. He wanted to see the labs, he said. They took him through them.

'Interesting, yes,' he said. Then after a while: 'But I'm wondering what else we might do.'

'To terraform?' Art asked.

'Well . . .'

To please Ann, Nadia thought. That was what he meant. She gave him a hug, which surprised him, and she kept her hand on his bony shoulder as they talked. So good to have him there in the flesh! When had she become so fond of Sax Russell, when had she come to rely on him so much?

Art too had figured out what he meant. He said, 'You've done quite a bit already, haven't you? I mean, at this point you've dismantled all the metanats' monster methods, right? The hydrogen bombs under the permafrost, the soletta and aerial lens, the nitrogen shuttles from Titan —'

'Those are still coming,' Sax said. 'I don't even know how we could stop them. Shoot them down I guess. But we can always use nitrogen. I'm not sure I'd be happy if they were stopped.'

'But Ann?' Nadia said. 'What would Ann like?'

Sax squinted again. When uncertainty squinched his face, it reverted to precisely its old ratlike expression.

'What would you both like?' Art rephrased it.

'Hard to say.' And his face twisted into a grimace of uncertainty, indecision, split motives.

'You want wilderness,' Art suggested.

'Wilderness is a, an idea. Or an ethical position. It can't be

344

everywhere, it's not that kind of idea. But . . .' Sax waggled a hand, fell back into his own thoughts. For the first time in the century she had known him, Nadia had the sense that Sax did not know what to do. He solved the problem by sitting down before a screen and typing instructions into it. He appeared to forget their presence.

Nadia squeezed Art's arm. He enfolded her hand, and squeezed the little finger gently. It was almost three-quarters size now, but slowing down as it got closer to full size. A nail had been started, and on the pad, the delicate whorled ridges of a fingerprint. It felt good when it was squeezed. She met Art's eye briefly, then looked down. He squeezed her whole hand before letting go. After a while, when it was clear Sax was fully distracted, and going to be off in his own world for a long time, they tiptoed off to their room, to the bed.

They worked by day, went out at night. Sax was blinking around as in his lab-rat days, anxious because there was no news of Ann. Nadia and Art comforted him as best they could, which wasn't much. In the evenings they went out and joined the promenade. There was a park where parents congregated with their kids, and people walked by as if passing a little open zoo enclosure, grinning at the sight of the little primates at play. Sax spent hours in this park talking to children and parents, and then he would wander off to the dance floors, where he danced by himself for hours. Art and Nadia held hands. Her finger got stronger. It was almost full size now, and given that it was the littlest finger anyway, it looked full grown unless she held it against its opposite number. Art nibbled it gently sometimes when they were making love, and the sensation drove her wild. 'You'd better not tell people about this effect,' he muttered, 'else it could get grisly – people hacking off body parts to grow them back, you know, more sensitive.'

'Sicko.'

'You know how people are. Anything for a thrill.'

'Don't even talk about it.'

'Okay.'

*　　*　　*

But then it was time to get back to a council meeting. Sax left, to find Ann or hide from her, they couldn't be sure; they flew back up to Sheffield, and then Nadia was back into it again, every day parsed into its thirty-minute units of trivia. Except some of it was important. The Chinese application for another space elevator near Schiaparelli had come up for action, and it was only one of many immigration issues that were facing them. The UN-Mars agreement worked out in Berne stated explicitly that Mars was to take at least ten per cent of its population in immigrants every year, with the hope expressed that they would take even more – as many as possible – for as long as the hypermalthusian conditions obtained. Nirgal had made this a kind of promise, had spoken very enthusiastically (and Nadia felt unrealistically) about Mars coming to the rescue, saving Earth from overpopulation with the gift of empty land. But how many people could Mars really hold, when they couldn't even manufacture topsoil? What was the carrying capacity of Mars, anyway?

No one knew, and there was no good way to calculate it scientifically. Estimates of Terra's human-carrying capacity had ranged from one hundred million to two hundred trillion, and even the seriously defensible estimates ranged from two to thirty billion. In truth carrying capacity was a very fuzzy abstract concept, depending on an entire recombinant host of complexities such as soil biochemistry, ecology, human culture. So it was almost impossible to say how many people Mars could handle. Meanwhile Earth's population was over fifteen billion, while Mars, with almost as much land surface, had a population a thousand times as small, at right around fifteen million. The disparity was clear. Something would have to be done.

Mass transfer of people from Earth to Mars was certainly one possibility; but the speed of the transfer was limited by the size of the transport system, and the ability of Mars to absorb the immigrants. Now the Chinese, and indeed the UN generally, were arguing that as a beginning step in a process of intensified immigration, they could build up the transport system very substantially. A second space elevator on Mars would be the first step in this multistage project.

Reaction on Mars to this plan was mostly negative. The

Reds of course opposed further'immigration, and while conceding that some would have to happen, they opposed any specific development of the transfer system just to try to keep the process slowed down as much as possible. That position fitted their overall philosophy, and made sense to Nadia. The Free Mars position, however, while more important, was not so clear. Nirgal had come out of Free Mars, and had gone to Earth and issued a general invitation to Terrans to shift as many people over as they could. And historically Free Mars had always argued for strong ties with Earth, to attempt the so-called 'tail wagging dog' strategy. The current party leadership, however, no longer seemed very fond of this position. And Jackie was in the middle of this new group. They had been shifting toward a more isolationist stance even during the constitutional congress, Nadia recalled, arguing always for more independence from Earth. On the other hand, they had been apparently cutting deals in private with certain Terran countries. So the Free Mars position was ambiguous, perhaps hypocritical; and seemed designed mainly to increase its own power on the Martian scene.

Even setting aside Free Mars, though, there was a lot of isolationist sentiment out there besides the Reds – anarchists, some Bogdanovists, the Dorsa Brevian matriarchs, the Marsfirsters – all tended to side with the Reds on this issue. If millions and millions of Terrans began to pour up onto Mars, they all argued, what then of Mars – not just of the landscape itself, but of the Martian culture that had been forming over the M-years? Wouldn't that be drowned in the old ways brought up by the new influx, which might quickly outnumber the native population? Birth rates were dropping everywhere, after all, and childlessness and one-child families were as common on Mars as on Earth – so there wouldn't be any great multiplication in the native population to look forward to. They would soon be overwhelmed.

So Jackie argued, at least in public, and the Dorsa Brevians and many others agreed with her. Nirgal, just back from Earth, seemed not to be having much effect on that stance. And while Nadia could see the point of her opponents' arguments, she also felt that given the situation on Earth, they were being unrealistic to think they could close Mars down. Mars could not save Earth, as Nirgal had sometimes seemed to say during his visit there; but an agreement with the UN had been made and ratified, and they were committed to letting up at least as many Terrans as the treaty specified. So the bridge between the worlds had to be expanded if they were to meet that obligation, and keep the treaty viable. If they didn't stick to the treaty, Nadia thought, anything might happen.

So in the debate over allowing a second cable, Nadia argued for it. It increased the capacity of the transport system, as they had promised to do, if only indirectly. And it would also take some of the pressure off the towns on Tharsis, and that side of Mars generally; population density maps showed that Pavonis was like the bull's-eye of a target, with people radiating outward from it and settling as near to it as was convenient. Having a cable on the other side of the world would help to equalize things.

But this was a dubious value to the cable's opponents. They wanted the population localized, contained, slowed. The treaty didn't matter to them. So when it came to a council vote, which was only an advisory to the legislature in any case, only Zeyk voted with Nadia. It was Jackie's biggest victory so far, and put her in a temporary alliance with Irishka and the rest of the environmental courts, which were on principle resistant to all forms of swift development.

Nadia went home to her apartment that day, discouraged and worried. 'We've promised Earth we'll take lots of immigrants, then pulled up the drawbridge. It's going to lead to trouble.'

Art nodded. 'We'll have to work something out.'

Nadia blew out her breath in disgust. 'Work. We won't *work* anything out. Work isn't the word for it. We will bicker and dicker and argue and natter.' She sighed a big sigh. 'It will go on and on. I thought Nirgal being back would help, but it won't if he doesn't join in.'

'He doesn't have a position,' Art said.

'He could if he wanted one, though.'

'True.'

Nadia thought about it, her mind wandering as her spirits dropped. 'You know I've only got through ten months of my term. There's over two and a half M-years to go.'

'I know.'

'M-years are so damned long.'

'Yes. But the months are short.'

She made a noise at him. Stared out of the window of her apartment, down into Pavonis caldera. 'The trouble is that work isn't work any more. You know, we go out there and join these projects, and the work on them still isn't work. I mean I never get to go out and *do* things. I remember when I was young, in Siberia, work was really work.'

'You might be romanticizing that a bit.'

'Yeah, sure, but even on Mars. I remember putting together Underhill. That was really fun. And one day on our trip to the north pole, installing a permafrost gallery . . .' She sighed. 'What I wouldn't give for work like that again.'

'There's still a lot of construction going on,' Art pointed out.

'By robots.'

'Maybe you could go back to something more human. Build something yourself. A house in the country, or a development. Or one of the new harbour towns, hand-built to try out different things, designs, methods, whatever. It would slow the construction process down, the GEC would go for that.'

'Maybe. After my term is over, you mean.'

'Or even before. On breaks, like these other trips. They've all been analogues to construction, they haven't been construction itself. Building actual things. You have to try that, then go back and forth between the two.'

'Conflict of interest.'

'Not if it was a public works project. What about that proposal to build a global capital down at sea level?'

'Hmm,' Nadia said. She got out a map, and they pored over it. At the zero longitude line, the south shore of the northern sea bent out in a little round peninsula, with a crater bay at its centre. It was about halfway between Tharsis and Elysium. 'We'll have to go take a look.'

'Yes. Here, come to bed. We'll talk about it more later. Right now I have another idea.'

349

Some months later they were flying back from Bradbury Point to Sheffield, and Nadia remembered that conversation with Art. She asked the pilot to land at a little station north of Sklodowska Crater, on the slope of Crater Zm, called Zoom. As they descended on the airstrip they saw to the east a big bay, now covered with ice. Across the bay was the rough mountainous country of Mamers Vallis, and the Deuteronilus Mensae. The bay was an incursion into the Great Escarpment, which was here fairly gentle. Longitude 0°. Latitude 46° north, fairly far north; but the northern winters were mild compared to the south. They could see a lot of the icy sea, lying off a long shoreline. The rounded peninsula surrounding Zoom was high and smooth. The little station on the shore was home to about five hundred people, who were out there building with bulldozer and cranes and dredges and draglines. Nadia and Art got out and sent the plane on, and took a boarding-house room and spent about a week with the people there, talking about the new settlement. The locals had heard of the proposal to build a new capital city here on the bay; some of them liked the idea, some didn't. They had thought of calling their settlement Greenwich because of its longitude, but they had heard the British didn't pronounce it Green Witch, and they didn't know how they felt about spelling the town to sound that way and then calling it 'Grenich'. Maybe just London, they said. We'll think of something, they said. The bay itself, they said, had long been called Chalmers Bay.

'Really?' Nadia exclaimed. She laughed. 'How perfect.'

She was already very attracted to the landscape: Zoom's smooth conic apron, the incurve of the big bay; red rock over white ice, and presumably over blue sea, someday. On the days of their visit clouds flowed by constantly, riding the west wind and dappling both land and ice with their shadows – sometimes puffy white cumulus clouds, like galleons, other times scrolled herringbone patterns unrolling overhead, defining the dark dome of sky above them, and the curving rocky land under them. It could be a small, handsome city, encircling a bay like San Francisco or Sydney, as beautiful as those two but smaller, human scale – Bogdanovist architecture – hand-built. Well, not exactly hand-built, of course. But they could design it at a human scale. And work on it as a kind of work of art. Walking with Art on the shores of the ice bay, Nadia talked through her CO_2 mask about these ideas, while watching the parade of clouds gallop by in the low rushing air.

'Sure,' Art said. 'It would work. It's going to be a city anyway, that's the important thing. It's one of the best bays on this stretch of the coast, so it's bound to be used as a harbour. So you wouldn't get the kind of capital city that just sits in the middle of nowhere, like Canberra or Brasilia, or Washington DC. It'll have a whole other life as a seaport.'

'That's right. That would be great.' Nadia walked on, excited as she thought about it, feeling better than she had in months. The movement to establish a capital somewhere else than Sheffield was strong, supported by almost every party up there. This bay had already been proposed as a site by the Sabishiians, so it would be a matter of supporting an already existing idea, rather than forcing a new one on people. The support would be there. And as a public works project, building it would be something she could take full part in. Part of the gift economy. She might even be able to have an influence on the plan of it. The more she thought about it, the more pleased she became.

They had walked far down the shore of the bay; they turned around and began to walk back to the little settlement. Clouds tumbled over them on a stiff wind. The curve of red land made its greeting to the sea. Just under the cloud layer, a ragged V of honking geese fletched the wind, heading north.

Later that day, as they flew back to Sheffield, Art picked up her hand and held it, inspecting her new finger. He said slowly, 'You know, building a family would also be a very hands-on kind of construction.'

'What?'

'And they've got reproduction pretty much figured out.'

'What?'

'I said, as long as you're alive, you can pretty much have children, one way or another.'

'*What?*'

'That's what they say. If you wanted to, you could do it.'

'No.'

'That's what they say.'

'No.'

'It's a good idea.'

'No.'

'Well, you know, even building ... it's great, sure, but you can only go on plumbing for so long. Plumbing, hammering nails, bulldozing – it's all interesting enough, of course, I guess, but still. We have a lot of time to fill. And the only work really interesting enough to pursue over the long haul would be raising a kid, don't you think?'

'No I do not!'

'But did you ever have a kid?'

'No.'

'Well there you go.'

'Oh God.'

Her ghost finger was tingling. But now it was really there.

PART EIGHT

The Green and the White

PART EIGHT

The Government of Britain

Cadres came to the town Xiazha, in Guangzhou, and said, For the good of China we need you to re-create this village on Moon Plateau, Mars. You'll go there together, the whole village. You'll have your family and your friends and your neighbours with you. Ten thousand of you all together. In ten years if you decide you want to come back, you can, and replacements will be sent to the new Xiazha. We think you will like it. It's a few kilometres north of the harbour town of Nilokeras, near the Maumee River delta. The land is fertile. There are other Chinese villages already in that region, and Chinese sections in all the big cities. There are many hectares of empty land. The trip can begin in a month – train to Hong Kong, ferry to Manila, and then up the space elevator into orbit. Six months crossing the space between here and Mars, down their elevator to Pavonis Mons, a party train to Moon Plateau. What do you say? Let's have a unanimous vote and start things off on the right foot.

Later a clerk in the town called up the Praxis office in Hong Kong, and told an operator there what had happened. Praxis Hong Kong sent the information along to Praxis's demographic study group in Costa Rica. A planner there named Amy added the report to a long list of similar reports, and sat thinking for a morning. That afternoon she made a call to William Fort, who was surfing a new reef in El Salvador. She described the situation to him. 'The blue world is full,' he said, 'the red world is empty. There are going to be problems. Let's talk about them.'

The demographics group and part of the Praxis policy team, including many of the Eighteen Immortals, gathered in Fort's hillside surf camp. The demographers laid out the situation. 'Everyone is getting the longevity treatment now,' Amy said. 'We are fully into the hypermalthusian age.'

It was a demographically explosive situation. Naturally emigration to Mars was often seen by Terran government planners as one solution to the problem. Even with its new ocean, Mars still had almost as much land area as Earth, and hardly any people. The really populous nations, Amy told the group, were already sending up as many people as they could. Often the emigrants were members of ethnic or religious minorities who were dissatisfied with their lack of autonomy in their home countries, and so were happy to leave. In India the elevator cars of the cable that touched down at Suvadiva Atoll, south of the Maldives, were constantly at capacity, full of emigrants all day every day, a stream of Sikhs and Kashmiris and Moslems and also Hindus, ascending into space and moving to Mars. There were Zulus from South Africa. Palestinians from Israel. Kurds from Turkey. Native Americans from the United States. 'In that sense,' Amy said, 'Mars is becoming the new America.'

'And like the old America,' a woman named Elizabeth added, 'there's a native population already there to be impacted. Think about the numbers for a while. If every day the cars of all the space elevators are full, then that's a hundred people per car, therefore two thousand, four hundred per day per elevator taking off, and a different two thousand, four hundred leaving the cars at the top of each elevator, and transferring into shuttles. There are ten elevators, so that's twenty-four thousand people a day. Therefore eight million, seven hundred and sixty thousand people every year.'

'Call it ten million a year,' Amy said. 'That's a lot, but at that rate it will still take a century to transfer just one of Earth's sixteen billions to Mars. Which won't make any difference here to speak of. So it doesn't really make sense! No major relocation is possible. We can never move a significant fraction of the Terran population to Mars. We have to keep our attention on solving Earth's problems at home. Mars's presence can only help as a kind of psychological vent. In essence, we're on our own.'

William Fort said, 'It doesn't have to make sense.'

'That's right,' said Elizabeth. 'Lots of Terran governments are trying it, whether it makes sense or not. China, India, Indonesia, Brazil – they're all going for it, and if they keep emigration at the system's capacity, Mars's population will double in about two years. So nothing changes on Earth, but Mars is totally inundated.'

One of the Immortals noted that an emigration surge of a similar scale had helped to cause the first Martian revolution.

'What about the Earth-Mars treaty?' someone else asked. 'I thought it specifically forbade such overwhelming influxes.'

'It does,' Elizabeth said. 'It specifies no more than ten per cent of the Martian population to be added every Terran year. But it also states that Mars should take more if they can.'

'Besides,' Amy said, 'since when have treaties ever stopped governments from doing what they wanted to do?'

William Fort said, 'We'll have to send them somewhere else.'

The others looked at him.

'Where?' said Amy.

No one replied. Fort waved a hand vaguely.

'We'd better think of somewhere,' Elizabeth said grimly. 'The Chinese and Indians have been good allies of the Martians, so far, and even they aren't paying much attention to the treaty. I was sent a tape recording of an Indian policy meeting about this, and they spoke about running their programme at capacity for a couple of centuries, and then seeing where they stand.'

The elevator car descended and Mars grew huge beneath their feet. Finally they slowed down, low over Sheffield, and everything felt normal, Martian gravity again, without the Coriolis force pulling reality to the side. And then they were in the Socket, and back home.

Friends, reporters, delegations, Mangalavid. In Sheffield itself people hurried about their business. Occasionally Nirgal was recognized, and waved at happily; some even stopped to shake his hand, or give him a hug, inquiring about his trip or his health. 'We're glad you're back!'

Still, in most people's eyes . . . illness was so rare. Quite a few looked away. Magical thinking: Nirgal saw suddenly that for many people the longevity treatments equalled immortality. They did not want to think otherwise; they looked away.

But Nirgal had seen Simon die even though Simon's bones had been stuffed with Nirgal's young marrow. He had felt his body unravel, felt the pain in his lungs, in every cell of him. He knew death was real. Immortality had not come to them, and never would. Delayed senescence, Sax called it. Delayed senescence, that was all it was; Nirgal knew that. And people saw that knowledge in him, and recoiled. He was unclean, and they looked away. It made him angry.

He took the train down to Cairo, looking out at the vast, tilted desert of East Tharsis, so dry and ferric, the Ur landscape of red Mars: his land. His eyes felt it. His brain and body glowed with that recognition. Home.

But the faces on the train, looking at him and then looking away. He was the man who had not been able to adjust to Earth. The home world had nearly killed him. He was an alpine flower, unable to withstand the true world, an exotic to whom Earth was like Venus. This is what their eyes were saying with their darting glances. Eternal exile.

Well, that was the Martian condition. One out of every five hundred Martian natives who visited Earth died; it one of the most dangerous things a Martian could do, more dangerous

361

than cliff flying, visiting the outer solar system, childbirth. A kind of Russian roulette, with lots of empty chambers in the gun to be sure, but the full one was full.

And he had dodged it. Not by much, but he had dodged it. He was alive, he was home! These faces in the train, what did they know? They thought he had been defeated by Earth; but they also thought he was Nirgal the Hero, who had never been defeated before – they thought he was a story, an idea only. They didn't know about Simon or Jackie or Dao, or Hiroko. They didn't know anything about him. He was twenty-six M-years old now, a middle-aged man who had suffered all that any middle-aged man might suffer – death of parents, death of love, betrayal of friends, betrayal by friends. These things happen to everyone. But that wasn't the Nirgal that people wanted.

The train skirted the first curved headwalls of the Labyrinth of Night's sapped canyons, and soon it floated into Cairo's old station. Nirgal walked out into the tented town, looking around curiously. It had been a metanat stronghold, and he had never been in it before; interesting to see the little old buildings. The physical plant had been damaged by the Red Army in the revolution, and was still marked by broken black walls. People waved at him as he walked down the broad central boulevard to the city offices.

And there she was, in the concourse of the town hall, by the window walls overlooking the U of Nilus Noctis. Nirgal stopped, breath short. She had not yet seen him. Her face was rounder but otherwise she was as tall and sleek as ever, dressed in a green silk blouse and a darker green skirt of some coarser material, her black hair a shiny mane spilling down her back. He could not stop looking at her.

Then she saw him, and flinched ever so slightly. Perhaps the wrist images had not been enough to tell her how much the Terran illness had hurt him. Her hands extended on their own recognizance, and then she followed them, hands still out even while her eyes were calculating, her grimace at his appearance carefully rearranged for the cameras that were always around her. But he loved her for those hands. He could feel the warmth of his face, blushing as they kissed, cheek-to-cheek like friendly diplomats. Up close she still

362

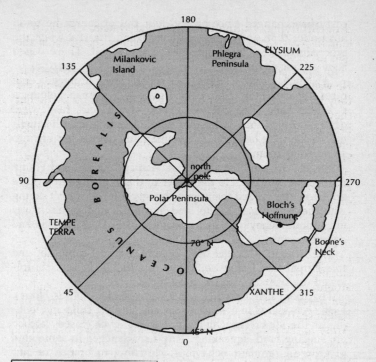

NORTH SEA POLAR PROJECTION

looked fifteen M-years old, just past the unblemished bloom of youth – at that point that is even more beautiful than youth. People said she had taken the treatment from the age of ten.

'It's true then,' she said, 'Earth almost killed you.'

'A virus, actually.'

She laughed, but her eyes kept their calculating look. She took him by the arm, led him back to her entourage like a blind man. Though he knew several of them she made introductions anyway, just to emphasize how much the inner circle of the party had changed since he had left. But of course he could not notice that, and so he was busy being cheerful when the proceedings were interrupted by a great wail. There was a baby among them.

'Ah,' Jackie said, checking her wrist. 'She's hungry. Come meet my daughter.' She walked over to a woman holding a swaddled babe. The girl was a few months old, fat-jowled, darker-skinned than Jackie, her whole face bright with squalling. Jackie took her from the woman and carried her off into an adjacent room.

Nirgal, left standing there, saw Tiu and Rachel and Frantz next to the window. He went over to them, glanced in Jackie's direction; they rolled their eyes, shrugged. Jackie wasn't saying who the father was, Rachel said in a quick undertone. It was not unique behaviour; many women from Dorsa Brevia had done the same.

The woman who had been holding the girl came out and told Nirgal that Jackie would like to speak with him. He followed the woman into the next room.

The room had a picture window overlooking Nilus Noctis. Jackie was seated in a windowseat, nursing the child and looking at the view. The child was hungry; eyes closed, latched on, sucking hard, squeaking. Tiny fists clenched in some kind of arboreal remnant behaviour, clutching to branch or fur. That was all culture, right there in that clutch.

Jackie was issuing instructions, to aides both in the room and on her wrist. 'No matter what they say in Berne, we need to have the flexibility to dampen the quotas if we need to. The Indians and Chinese will just have to get used to it.'

Some things began to clarify for Nirgal. Jackie was on the executive council, but the council was not particularly powerful. She was also still one of the leaders of the Free Mars party; and although Free Mars might have less influence on the planet, as power shifted out into the tents, in Earth-Mars relations it had the potential to become a determining body. Even if it only co-ordinated policy, it would gain all the power that a co-ordinator could command, which was considerable – it was all the power Nirgal had ever had, after all. In many situations such co-ordination could be the equivalent of making Mars's Terran policy, as all the local governments attended to their local concerns, and the global legislature was more and more dominated by a Free Mars-led supermajority. And of course there was a sense in which the Earth-Mars relationship had the potential to dwarf everything else. So that Jackie might be on the way to becoming an interplanetary power . . .

Nirgal's attention returned to the baby at her breast. The princess of Mars. 'Have a seat,' Jackie said, indicating the bench beside her with her head. 'You look tired.'

'I'm fine,' Nirgal said, but sat. Jackie looked up at one of the aides and jerked her head to the side, and very soon they were alone in the room with the infant.

'The Chinese and Indians are thinking of this as empty new land,' Jackie said. 'You can see it in everything they say. They're too damned friendly.'

'Maybe they like us,' Nirgal said. Jackie smiled, but he went on: 'We helped them get the metanats off their backs. And they can't be thinking of moving their excess population here. There's just too many of them for emigration to make any difference.'

'Maybe so, but they can dream. And with space elevators they can send a steady stream. It adds up quicker than you would think.'

Nirgal shook his head. 'It'll never be enough.'

'How do you know? You didn't go to either place.'

'A billion is a big number, Jackie. Too big a number for us to properly imagine. And Earth has got seventeen billion. They can't send a significant fraction of that number here, there aren't the shuttles to do it.'

'They might try anyway. The Chinese flooded Tibet with Han Chinese, and it didn't do a thing to relieve their population problems, but they kept doing it anyway.'

Nirgal shrugged. 'Tibet is right there. We'll keep our distance.'

'Yes,' Jackie said impatiently, 'but that's not going to be easy when there is no *we*. If they go out to Margaritifer, and cut a deal with the Arab caravans out there, who's going to stop it from happening?'

'The environmental courts?'

Jackie blew air between her lips, and the baby pulled off

and whimpered. Jackie shifted the infant to the other breast. Blue-veined olive curve. 'Antar doesn't think the environmental courts will be able to function for long. We had a fight with them while you were gone, and we only went along with them to give the process a chance, but they made no sense and they had no teeth. And everything everyone does has an environmental impact, so supposedly they should be judging everything. But tents are coming down in the lower elevations and not one in a hundred is going to the courts to ask permission for what they do once their town is part of the outside. Why should they? Everyone is an ecopoet now. No. The court system isn't going to work.'

'You can't be sure,' Nirgal said. 'So is Antar the father, then?'

Jackie shrugged.

Anyone could be the father — Antar, Dao, Nirgal himself, hell John Boone could be, if any sample of his sperm had happened to be still in storage. That would be like Jackie; except she would have told everyone. She shifted the infant's head toward her.

'Do you really think it's all right to raise a fatherless child?'

'That's how you were raised, right? And I had no mother. We were all one-parent children.'

'But was that good?'

'Who knows?'

There was a look on Jackie's face that Nirgal could not read, her mouth just slightly tight with resentment, defiance . . . impossible to say. She knew who both her parents were, but only one had stuck around, and Kasei had not been much around at that. And killed in Sheffield, in part because of the brutal response to the Red assault that Jackie herself had advocated.

She said, 'You didn't know about Coyote until you were six or seven, isn't that right?'

'True, but not right.'

'What?'

'It wasn't right.' And he looked her in the eye.

But she looked away, down at the baby. 'Better than having your parents tearing each other up in front of you.'

'Is that what you would do with the father?'

'Who knows?'

'So it's safer this way.'

'Maybe it is. Certainly there's a lot of women doing it this way.'

'In Dorsa Brevia.'

'Everywhere. The biological family isn't really a Martian institution, is it?'

'I don't know.' Nirgal considered it. 'Actually, I saw a lot of families in the canyons. We come from an unusual group in that respect.'

'In many respects.'

Her child pulled away, and Jackie tucked her breast in her bra and let down her shirt. 'Marie?' she called, and her assistant entered. 'I think her diaper needs changing.' And she handed the infant up to the woman, who left without a word.

'Servants now?' Nirgal said.

Jackie's mouth went tight again, and she stood, calling, 'Mem?'

Another woman came in, and Jackie said, 'Mem, we're going to have to meet with those environmental court people about this Chinese request. It could be that we can use it as leverage to get the Cairo water allotment reconsidered.'

Mem nodded and left the room.

'You just make the decisions?' Nirgal said.

Jackie dismissed him with a wave of the hand. 'Nice to have you back, Nirgal, but try to catch up, all right?'

Catch up. Free Mars was now a political party, the biggest on Mars. It had not always been that way; it had begun as something more like a network of friends, or the part of the underground that lived in the demi-monde. Mostly ex-students of the university in Sabishii, or, later, the members of a very loose association of communities in the tented canyons, and in clandestine clubs in the cities, and so forth. A kind of vague umbrella term for those sympathetic to the underground, but not followers of any more specific political movement or philosophy. Just something they said, in fact – 'free Mars'.

In many ways it had been Nirgal's creation. So many of the natives had been interested in autonomy, and the various issei parties, based on the thoughts of one early settler or another, did not appeal to them; they had wanted something new. And so Nirgal had travelled around the planet, and stayed with people who organized meetings or discussions, and this had gone on for so long that eventually people wanted a name. People wanted names for things.

And so, Free Mars. And in the revolution it had become a rallying point for the natives, rising up out of society as a kind of emergent phenomenon, with many more people declaring themselves members than one would have guessed possible. Millions. The native majority. The very definition of the revolution, in fact; the main reason for its success. Free Mars as a sentence, an imperative; and they had done it.

But then Nirgal had left for Earth, determined to make their case there. And while he was gone, during the constitutional congress, Free Mars had gone from a movement to an organization. That was fine, it was the normal course of events, a necessary part of institutionalizing their independence. No one could complain about it, or moan for the good old days, without revealing nostalgia for a heroic age that had not actually been heroic – or, along with heroic, had been also suppressed, limited, inconvenient and dangerous. No, Nirgal had no desire for nostalgia – the meaning of life lay not in the past but in the present, not in resistance but in expression. No – he did not want it to be like it had been before. He was happy they were in control (at least partially) of their fate. That wasn't the problem. Nor was he bothered by the tremendous growth in the numbers of supporters Free Mars had. The party seemed on the edge of becoming a super-majority, with three of the seven executive councillors coming from the party leadership, and most other global positions filled by other members. And now a fair percentage of new emigrants were joining the party – and old emigrants as well – and natives who had supported smaller parties before the revolution – and, last but not least, quite a few people who had supported the UNTA regime, and were now looking for the new power to follow. All in all, it made for a huge group. And in the first years of a new socio-economic order, this massing of political power, of opinion and belief, had some advantages, no doubt about it. They could get things done.

But Nirgal wasn't sure he wanted to be part of it.

One day walking the city wall, looking out through the tenting, he watched a group of people standing on a launchpad at the edge of the cliff, west of town. There were a number of different kinds of single-flyer craft: gliders and ultralites that were shot out of a slingshot launcher, and rose inside the thermals that formed in the mornings; smaller hang-gliders; and then a variety of new one-person aircraft, which looked like small gliders connected to the undersides of small blimps. These flyers were only a bit longer than the people who climbed into the slings or seats under the glider's wings. Clearly they were made of ultralight materials; some were transparent and nearly invisible, so that once in the sky it appeared that prone or seated people were floating around on their own. Other machines had been coloured, and were visible from kilometres away as strokes of green or blue in the air. The stubby wings had small ultralight jets attached to them, so that the pilots had control of direction and altitude; they were like planes in that respect, but with the added loft of a blimp to make them safer and more versatile; their pilots landed them almost anywhere, and it looked impossible to dive them – to crash, in other words.

The hang-gliders, on the other hand, looked as dangerous as ever.

The people who used those were the rowdiest members of the flying crowd, Nirgal could see when he went out there – thrill-seekers who ran off the edge of the cliff shouting in an adrenalated exhilaration that crackled over the intercoms – they were running off a cliff, after all, and no matter what rig they were strapped to, their bodies still saw what was happening. No wonder their shouts had that special ring!

Nirgal got on the subway and went out to the launchpad, drawn by some quality of the sight. All those people, free in the sky . . . He was recognized, of course, he shook hands; and accepted an invitation from a group of flyers to go up and see what it was like. The hang-gliders offered to teach him to fly, but he laughed and said he would try the little blimpgliders first. There was a two-person blimpglider tethered there, slightly larger than the rest, and a woman named Monica invited him up, fuelled the thing, and sat him beside her; and up the launch mast they went, to be released with a jerk into the strong downslope afternoon winds and over the city, now revealed as a small tent filled with greenery, perched on the edge of the northwesternmost of the network of canyons etching the slope of Tharsis.

Flying over Noctis Labyrinthus! The wind keened over the blimp's taut transparent material, and they bounced unpredictably up and down on the wind, while also rotating horizontally in what seemed an uncontrolled spin; but then Monica laughed and began manipulating the controls before her, and quickly they were proceeding south across the labyrinth, over canyon after canyon making their irregular X intersections. Then over the Compton Chaos, and the torn land of the Illyrian Gate, where it dropped into the upper end of the Marineris Glacier.

'These things' jets are much more powerful than they need to be,' Monica told him through their headphones. 'You can make headway into the wind until it reaches something like two hundred and fifty kilometres an hour, although you wouldn't want to try that. You also use the jets to counteract the blimp's loft, to get us back down. Here, try it. That's left jet throttle, that's right, and here are the stabilizers. The jets are dead easy, it's the stabilizer that needs some practising.'

In front of Nirgal was a complete second set of controls. He put his hands on the jet throttles, gave them pushes. The blimp veered right, then left. 'Wow.'

'It's fly by wire, so if you tell it to do something disastrous, it'll just cut out.'

'How many hours' flying time do you need to learn this?'

'You're doing it already, right?' She laughed. 'No, it takes a hundred hours or so. Depends on what you mean by knowing how to do it. There's the death mesa between a hundred hours and a thousand hours, after people have relaxed and before they're really good, so that they get into trouble. But that's mostly hang-gliders anyway. With these, the simulators are just like the real thing, so you can put in your hours on those, and then when you're actually up here you'll have it wired even though you haven't officially reached the flying time limit.'

'Interesting!'

And it was. The intersecting sapped canyons of Noctis Labyrinthus, lying under them like an enormous maze; the sudden lifts and drops as the winds tossed them; the loud keening of the wind over their partially-enclosed gondola seats . . . 'It's like becoming a bird!'

'Exactly.'

And some part of him saw it was going to be all right. The heart is pleased by one thing after another.

After that he spent time in a flight simulator in the city, and several times a week he made a date with Monica or one of her friends, and went out to the cliff's edge for another lesson. It was not a complicated business, and soon he felt that he could try a flight on his own. They cautioned him to be patient. He kept at it. The simulators felt very much like the real thing; if you tested them by doing something foolish, the seat would tilt and bounce very convincingly. More than once he was told the story of the person who had taken an ultralite into such a disastrous death spiral that the simulator had torn off its mountings and crashed through the glass wall next to it, cutting some bystanders and breaking the flyer's arm.

Nirgal avoided that kind of error, and most others as well. He went to Free Mars meetings in the city offices almost every morning, and flew every afternoon. As the days passed he discovered that he was dreading the morning meetings; he only wanted to fly. He had not founded Free Mars, no matter what they said. Whatever he had been doing in those years, it was not politics, not like this. Maybe it had had a political element to it, but mostly he had been living his life, and talking to people in the demi-monde and the surface cities about how to live theirs and still have some freedoms, some pleasures. Okay, it had been political, everything was; but it seemed he was not really interested in politics. Or perhaps it was government.

It was particularly uninteresting, of course, when dominated by Jackie and her crew. That was politics of a different kind. He had seen from his first moment back that for Jackie's inner circle, his return from Earth was no welcome thing. He had been gone for most of an M-year, and during that time a whole new group had risen to the fore, vaulted by the revolution. Nirgal to them was a threat to Jackie's control of the party, and to their influence on Jackie. They were firmly, if subtly, against him. No. For a time he had been the natives' leader, the charismatic of the tribe made up of the indigenous people of Mars – son of Hiroko and Coyote, a very potent mythic parentage – very hard to oppose. But that time had passed. Now Jackie was in control; and against him she had her own mythic parentage, her descent from John Boone, as well as their shared Zygote beginnings, and also the (partial) backing of the Minoan cult in Dorsa Brevia. Not to mention her direct power over him, in their own intense dynamic. But her advisers could not understand that, or even be fully aware of it. To them he was a threatening power, by no means finished because of his Terran illness. A threat forever to their native queen.

So he sat through morning meetings in the city offices, trying to ignore their little manoeuvrings, trying to focus on the issues coming in from all over the planet, many of them having to do with land problems or wrangles. Many tent towns wanted to take down their tents when air pressures made it possible, and hardly any of them were willing to concede that this was an operation in which the environmental courts had a say. Some areas were arid enough that water was the critical issue, and their requests for a water allotment were pouring in, until it seemed that the northern sea could be drawn down a kilometre merely by pumping it out to thirsty cities in the south. These and a thousand more matters tested the constitution's many networks for connecting local autonomy to global considerations; the debates would go on forever.

Nirgal, while fundamentally uninterested in most of these wrangles, found them yet preferable to the party politics he saw going on in Cairo. He had come back from Earth without any official position in the new government or the old party, and one thing he saw going on these days was the struggle to place him – to give him a job with limited power, or, for his backers (or rather Jackie's opponents) to put him in a position with some real power to it. Some friends advised him to wait and run for the senate when the next elections came, others mentioned the executive council, others party positions, others a post on the GEC. All these jobs sounded awful to Nirgal in one way or another, and when he talked to Nadia on the screens, he could see that he would find them a burden; though she seemed to be hammering away stolidly enough, it was obvious the executive council was distasteful to her. But he kept a straight face and listened closely as people offered their advice.

Jackie herself kept her own counsel. In meetings where people suggested that Nirgal become a kind of minister-without-portfolio, she regarded him more blankly than usual, which led Nirgal to think that she liked that possibility least of all. She wanted him pinned into some position, which given her current post could not help but be inferior to hers. But if he stayed outside the system entirely . . .

There she sat, the infant in her arms. It could be his child. And Antar watched her with the same expression, the same thought. No doubt Dao would have as well, if he were still alive. Nirgal was suddenly shaken by a spasm of grief for his half-brother, his tormentor, his friend – he and Dao had fought for as far back as he could remember, but they had been brothers for all that.

Jackie had apparently forgotten Dao already, and Kasei as well. As she would forget Nirgal, if he should happen to get killed. She had been among the Greens who had ordered the crushing of the Red assault on Sheffield, she had advocated the strong response. Perhaps she had to forget the dead.

The infant cried. Face rounded by fat, it was impossible to see any resemblance to any adult. The mouth looked like Jackie's. Other than that . . . it was frightening, this power created by anonymous parenting. Of course a man could do the same, obtain an egg, grow it by ectogenesis, raise it himself. No doubt it would begin to happen, especially if many women took Jackie's route. A world without parents. Well, friends were the real family; but he shuddered nevertheless at what Hiroko had done, what Jackie was doing.

He went flying to clear his mind of all that. One night after a glorious flight in the clouds, sitting in the launchpad pub, the conversation turned and someone mentioned Hiroko's name. 'I hear she's on Elysium,' someone said, 'working on a new commune of communes up there.'

'How did you hear?' Nirgal demanded of the woman, somewhat sharply no doubt.

Surprised, she said, 'You know those flyers who dropped in last week who are flying around the world? They were on Elysium last month, and they said they saw her there.' She shrugged. 'That's all I know. Not much by way of confirmation, I know.'

Nirgal sat back in his seat. Always third-hand information. Some of the stories, however, seemed so like Hiroko; and a few, too Hiroko-like to have been made up. Nirgal did not know what to think. Very few people seemed to think she was dead. Sightings of the rest of her group were reported as well.

'They just wish she were here,' Jackie said when Nirgal mentioned it the next day.

'Don't you wish it?'

'Of course,' (though she didn't) 'but not enough to make up stories about it.'

'You really think they're all made up? I mean, who would do that? What would they be telling themselves when they did it? It doesn't make sense.'

'People don't make sense, Nirgal. You have to learn that. People see an elderly Japanese woman somewhere, they think, that looks like Hiroko. That night they tell their room-mates, I think I saw Hiroko today. She was down in the marketplace buying plums. The room-mate goes to his construction site, says my room-mate saw Hiroko yesterday, buying plums!'

Nirgal nodded. It was no doubt true, at least for most of the stories. For the rest, though, the few that didn't fit that pattern . . .

'Meanwhile, you have to make a decision about this environmental court position,' Jackie said. It was a province court, one below the global court. 'We can arrange it so that Mem gets a position in the party that will actually be more influential, or you could take that one if you wanted, or both, I suppose. But we have to know.'

'Yeah yeah.'

People came in wanting to talk about something else, and Nirgal withdrew to the window, near the nurse and the infant.

He was not interested in what they were doing, not any of it – it was both ugly and abstract, a continuous manipulation of people devoid of any of the tangible rewards that so much work had. That's politics, Jackie would say. And it was clear she enjoyed it. But Nirgal did not. It was strange; he had worked all his life for this situation, ostensibly, and now that it was here, he did not like it.

Very possibly he could learn enough to do the work. He would have to overcome the hostility of the people who didn't want him back in the party, he would have to build his own power base, meaning collecting a group of people who would help him in their official positions; do them favours; curry their favour; play them off against each other, so that each would do his bidding in order to establish pre-eminence over the others . . . He could see all these processes at work right there in this very room, as Jackie met with one adviser after the next, discussing whatever issue happened to be their baili-wick, then working them to establish more firmly their allegi-ance to her. Of course, she would say if he pointed out this process. That was politics; they were in control of Mars now, and this work had to be done if they were to create the new world they had hoped for. One couldn't be overfastidious, one had to be realistic, you held your nose and did it. It had a certain nobility to it, really. It was the necessary work.

Nirgal didn't know if those justifications were true or not. Had they really worked all their lives to overthrow Terran domination of Mars, only in order to put in place their own local version of the same thing? Could politics ever be anything but politics, practical, cynical, compromised, ugly?

He did not know. He sat in the windowseat, looking down at Jackie's daughter's face, sleeping. Across the room Jackie was intimidating the Free Mars delegates from Elysium. Now that Elysium was an island surrounded by the northern sea, they were more determined than ever to take control of their fate, including immigration limits that would keep the massif from developing much past its current state. 'All very well,' Jackie was saying, 'but it's a very large island now, a continent really, surrounded by water so that it will be especially humid, with a coastline of thousands of kilometres, lots of fine harbour sites, fishing harbours no doubt. I can sympathize with your desire to keep a hand on development, we all feel that, but the Chinese have expressed a particular interest in developing some of these sites, and what am I supposed to say to them? That the Elysian locals don't like Chinese? That we'll take their help in a crisis, but we don't want them moving into the neighbourhood?'

'It's not that they're Chinese!' the delegate said.

'I understand. Really I do. Tell you what – you go back to South Fossa and explain the difficulties we face here, and I'll do everything I can here to help you. I can't guarantee results, but I'll do what I can.'

'Thanks,' the delegate said, and left.

Jackie turned to her assistant. 'Idiot. Who's next? Ah, naturally; the Chinese ambassador. Well, let him in.'

The Chinese, a woman, was quite tall. She spoke in Mandarin, and her AI translated into a clear British English. After an exchange of pleasantries, the woman asked about establishing some Chinese settlements, preferably somewhere in the equatorial provinces.

Nirgal stared, fascinated. This was how settlements had been started from the very beginning; groups of Terran nationals had come up, and built a tent town or a cliff dwelling, or domed a crater . . . Now, however, Jackie looked polite and said, 'It's possible. Everything of course will have to be referred to the environmental courts for judgment. However, there is a great deal of empty land on the Elysium massif. Perhaps something could be arranged there, especially if China was willing to contribute to infrastructure and mitigation and the like.'

They discussed details. After a while the ambassador left.

Jackie turned to look at Nirgal. 'Nirgal, could you get Rachel in here? And try to decide what you're going to do soon, please?'

Nirgal walked out of the building, through the city to his room. He packed his little collection of clothes and toiletries, and took the subway out to the launching pad, and asked Monica for the use of one of the single-person blimpgliders. He was ready for soloing, he had put in enough hours in simulators and with teachers. There was another flight school down in Marineris, on Candor Mensa. He talked to the school officials on the launchpad; they were willing to let him take the blimpglider down there, and have it returned by another flyer later.

It was midday. The Tharsis downslope winds had started, and would only get stronger as the afternoon progressed. Nirgal suited up, got into the pilot's seat. The little blimpglider slid up the launching mast, held by the nose; and was let free.

He rose over Noctis Labyrinthus, turned east. He flew east over the maze of interlocking canyons. A land split open by stress from below. Flight out of the labyrinth. An Icarus who had flown too close to the sun, got burned, survived the fall – and now flew again, this time down, down, down, ever down. Taking advantage of a hard tailwind. Riding a gale, shooting down over the shattered dirty icefield that marked Compton Chaos, where the great channel outbreak had begun in 2061. That immense flood had run down Ius Chasma; but Nirgal angled north, away from the glacier's flow, and then flew east again, down into the head of Tithonium Chasma, which paralleled Ius Chasma just to the north.

Tithonium was one of the deepest and narrowest of the Marineris canyons – four kilometres deep, ten wide. He could fly well below the level of the plateaux rims and still be thousands of metres over the canyon floor. Tithonium was higher than Ius, wilder, untouched by human hands, seldom travelled in, because it was a dead end to the east, where it narrowed and became rough-floored as it got shallower, then abruptly stopped. Nirgal spotted the road that switchbacked up the eastern headwall, a road he had travelled a few times in his youth, when all the planet had been his home.

The afternoon sun dipped behind him. The shadows on the land lengthened. The wind continued to blow strong, thrumming over the blimpglider, whining and whooshing and keening. It blew him over the caprock of the rim plateau again, as Tithonium became a string of oval depressions, pocking the plateau one after the next: the Tithonia Catena, each dip a giant bowl-shaped depression in the land.

And then suddenly the world dropped away again, and he flew out over the immense open canyon of Candor Chasma, Shining Canyon, the ramparts of its eastern wall in fact shining at that very moment, amber and bronze in the sunset's light. To the north was the deep entrance to Ophir Chasma, to the south the spectacular buttress-walled opening down to Melas Chasma, the central giant of the Marineris system. It was Mars's version of Concordiaplatz, he saw, but much bigger than Earth's, wilder, looking untouched, primal, gigantic beyond all human scale, as if he had flown back two centuries into the past, or two eons, to a time before the anthropogenesis. Red Mars!

And there out in the middle of broad Candor was a tall diamond mesa, a caprock island standing nearly two kilometres above the canyon floor. And in the sunset's hazy gloom Nirgal could make out a nest of lights, a tent town, at the southern-most point of the diamond. Voices welcomed him over the common band on his intercom, then guided him in to the town's landing pad. The sun was winking out over the cliffs to the west as he brought the blimpglider around and descended slowly into the wind, putting it down right on the figure of Kokopelli painted as a target on the landing pad.

Shining Mesa had a large top, more a kite shape than a diamond proper, thirty kilometres long and ten wide, standing in the middle of Candor Chasma like a Monument Valley mesa writ large. The tent town occupied only a small rise on the southern point of the kite. The mesa was just what it appeared to be, a detached fragment of the plateau that the Marineris canyons had split. It was a tremendous vantage point for viewing the great walls of Candor, with views through the deep, steep gaps into Ophir Chasma to the north and Melas Chasma to the south.

Naturally such a spectacular prospect had attracted people over the years, and the main tent was surrounded by new smaller ones. At five kilometres above the datum, the town was still tented, though there was talk of removing it. The floor of Candor Chasma, only three kilometres above the datum, was patched with growing, dark green forests. Many of the people who lived on Shining Mesa flew down into the canyons every morning to farm or botanize, floating back up to the mesa's top in the late afternoons. A few of these flying foresters were old underground acquaintances of Nirgal's, and they were pleased to take him along and show him the canyons, and what they did in them.

The Marineris canyon floors generally run down west to east. In Candor, they curved around the great central mesa, then fell precipitately down into Melas. Snow lay on the higher parts of the floor, especially under the western walls where shadows lay in the afternoon. Meltwater from this snow ran down in a faint tracery of new watersheds, made up of sandy, braided streambeds that ran together into a few shallow, muddy red rivers, which collected at a confluence just above the Candor Gap, and poured down in wild foaming rapids to the floor of Melas Chasma, where it pooled against the remnant of the '61 glacier, running redly against its northern flank.

On the banks of all these opaque red streams, forest galleries were springing up. They consisted in most places of cold-hardened balsas and other very rapidly growing tropical trees, creating new canopies over older krummholz. These days it was warm on the canyon floor, which was like a big sun-reflecting bowl, protected from the wind. The balsa canopies were allowing a great number of plant and animal species to flourish underneath them; Nirgal's acquaintances said it was the most diverse biotic community on Mars. They had to carry sedative dart guns now when they landed and walked around, because of bears, snow leopards and other predators. Walking through some of the galleries was becoming difficult because of thickets of snow bamboo and aspen.

All this growth had been aided by huge deposits of sodium nitrate that had been lying in Candor and Ophir canyons – great white bench terraces made of extremely water-soluble caliche blanco. These mineral deposits were now melting over the canyon floors and running down the streams, providing the new soils with lots of nitrogen. Unfortunately some of the biggest nitrate deposits were being buried under landslides – the water that was dissolving the sodium nitrate was also hydrating the canyon walls, destabilizing them in a radical acceleration of the mass wasting that went on all the time. No one went near the foot of the canyon walls any more, the flyers said: too dangerous. And as they soared around in their blimpgliders, Nirgal saw the scars of landslides everywhere. Several high talus plant slopes had been buried, and wall-fixing methods were one of the many topics of conversation in the mesa evenings, after the omegandorph got into the blood; in fact there was little they could do. If chunks of a ten-thousand-foot-high wall of rock wanted to give way, nothing was going to stop them. So from time to time, about once a week or so, everyone on Shining Mesa would feel the ground quiver, watch the tent shimmer, and hear in the pit of the stomach the low rumble of a collapse. Often it was possible to spot the slide, rolling across the canyon floor ahead of a sienna billow of dust. Flyers in the air nearby would come back shaken and silent, or voluble with tales of being slapped across the sky by ear-splitting roars. One day Nirgal was about halfway down to the floor when he felt one himself: it was like a sonic boom that went on for many seconds, the air quivering like a gel. Then, just as suddenly as it had began, it was over.

Mostly he explored on his own, sometimes he flew with his

old acquaintances. Blimpgliders were perfect for the canyon, slow and steady, easy to steer. More loft than was needed, more power ... the one he had rented (using money from Coyote) allowed him to drift down in the mornings to help botanize in the forests, or walk by the streams; then float back up through the afternoons, up and up and up and up. This was when one got a true sense of just how tall Candor mesa was, and the even taller canyon walls – up up and up and up, to the tent, and its long meals, its party nights. Day after day Nirgal followed this routine, exploring the various regions of the canyons below, watching the exuberant night life in the tent; but seeing everything as if through the wrong end of a telescope, a telescope consisting of the question, *is this the life I want to lead?* This distancing and somehow miniaturizing question kept returning to him, spurring him by day as he banked in the sunlight, haunting him at night in sleepless hours between the timeslip and dawn. What was he to do? The success of the revolution had left him without a task. All his life he had wandered Mars talking to people about a free Mars, about inhabitation rather than colonization, about becoming indigenous to the land. Now that task was ended, the land was theirs to live on as they chose. But in this new situation he found he did not know his part. He had to think very specifically about how to go on in this new world, no longer as the voice of the collective, but as an individual in his own private life.

He had discovered that he did not want to continue working on the collective; it was good that some people wanted to do it, but he wasn't one of them. In fact he could not think about Cairo without a stab of anger at Jackie, and of simple pain as well – pain at the loss of that public world, that whole way of life. It was hard to give up being a revolutionary. Nothing seemed to follow from it, either logically or emotionally. But something had to be done. That life was past. In the midst of a banking slow dive in his blimpglider, he suddenly understood Maya and her obsessive talk about incarnations. He was twenty-seven M-years old now, he had crisscrossed all Mars, he had been to Earth, he had returned to a free world. Time for the next metempsychosis.

So he flew around the immensities of Candor, looking for

some image of himself. The fractured, layered, scarred canyon walls were so many stupendous mineral mirrors; and indeed he saw clearly that he was a tiny creature, smaller than a gnat in a cathedral. Flying around studying each great palimpsest of facets, he scried two very strong impulses in himself, distinct and mutually exclusive yet infolded, like the green and the white. On the one hand he wanted to stay a wanderer, to fly and walk and sail over all the world, a nomad forever, wandering ceaselessly until he knew Mars better than anyone else. Ah yes; it was a familiar euphoria. On the other hand it *was* familiar, he had done that all his life. It would be the form of his previous life, without the content. And he knew already the loneliness of that life, the rootlessness that made him feel so detached, that gave him this wrong-end-of-the-telescope vision. Coming from everywhere he came from nowhere. He had no home. And so now he wanted that home, as much as the freedom or more. A home. He wanted to settle into a full human life, to pick a place and stay there, to learn it completely, in all its seasons, to grow his food, make his house and his tools, become part of a community of friends.

Both these desires existed, strongly and together – or, to be more exact, in a subtle, rapid oscillation, which jangled his emotions, and left him insomniac and restless. He could see no way to reconcile the two. They were mutually exclusive. No one he talked to had any useful suggestions as to how to resolve the difficulty. Coyote was dubious about setting down roots – but then he was a nomad, and didn't know. Art considered the wandering life impossible; but he was fond of his places now.

Nirgal's non-political training was in mesocosm engineering, but he found that little help to his thinking. At the higher elevations they were always going to be in tents, and mesocosm engineering would be needed; but it was becoming more of a science than an art, and with increasing experience the problems and their solutions would be more and more routinized. Besides, did he want to pursue a tented profession, when so much of the lower planet was becoming land they could walk on?

No. He wanted to live in the open air. To learn a patch of

land, its soil and plants and animals and weather and skies, and everything else . . . he wanted that. Part of him. Part of the time.

He began to feel, however, that whatever he chose, Candor Chasma was not the place for the kind of settlement he was thinking of. Its huge vistas made it a hard place to see as home – it was too vast, too inhuman. The canyon floors were designed and designated as wilderness, and every spring the streams surging with snowmelt would jump their banks, tear new channels, be buried under enormous landslides. Fascinating, all of it. But not home. The locals were going to stay up on Shining Mesa, and only visit the canyon floors during the day. The mesa would be their true home. It was a good plan. But the mesa – it was an island in the sky, a great tourist destination, a place for flying vacations, for partying through the nights, for expensive hotels, for the young and the in-love . . . all that was fine, wonderful. But crowded, perhaps even overrun – or else always battling the influx of visitors, and newly-settled residents enchanted by the sublime views, people who would arrive like Nirgal himself, dropping in at some dusk in their life and never going away, while the old residents looked on helplessly and grumbled about the good old days when the world had been new, and unoccupied.

No – that was not the kind of home he had in mind. Although he loved the way dawn flushed the fluted west walls of Candor, flaring all across the Martian spectrum, the sky turning indigo or mauve, or a startling earthly cerulean . . . a beautiful place, so beautiful that on some days as he flew about he felt it would be worth it to stand on Shining Mesa and hold his ground, to try to preserve it, to swoop down and learn the gnarly wilderness floor, float back up every afternoon to dinner. Would that work make him feel at home? And if wilderness was what he wanted, weren't there other places less spectacular but more remote, thus more wild?

Back and forth he went, back and forth. One day, flying over the foaming, opaque series of waterfalls and rapids in the Candor Gap, he remembered that John Boone had been through this area, in a solo rover just after the Transmarineris Highway had been built. What would that master equivocator have said about this amazing region?

Nirgal called up Boone's AI, Pauline, and asked for Candor, and found a voice diary made during a drive through the canyon in 2046. Nirgal let the tape run as he looked down on the land from above, listening to the hoarse voice with the friendly American accent, a voice unselfconscious about talking to an AI. Listening to the voice made Nirgal wish he could really talk to the man. Some people said Nirgal had filled John Boone's empty shoes, that Nirgal had done the work John would have done had he lived. If that were so, what would John have done afterward? How would he have lived?

'This is the most unbelievable country I've ever seen. Really, it's what you think of when you think of Valles Marineris. Back in Melas the canyon was so wide that out in the middle you couldn't see the walls at all, they were under the horizon! This small-planet curvature is producing effects no one ever imagined. All the old simulations lied so badly, the verticals exaggerated by factors of five or ten, as I recall, which made it look as if you were down in a slot. It's not a slot. Wow, there's a rock column just like a woman in a toga, Lot's wife I guess that would be. I wonder if it is salt, it's white, but I guess that doesn't mean much. Have to ask Ann. I wonder what those Swiss road-builders made of all this when they built this road, it's not very Alpine. Kind of like an anti-Alps, down instead of up, red instead of green, basalt instead of granite. Well, but they seemed to like it anyway. Of course they're anti-Swiss Swiss, so it makes a kind of sense. Whoa, pothole country here, the rover is bouncing around. Might try that bench there, it looks smoother than here. Yep, there we go, just like a road. Oh – it is the road. I guess I got off it a bit, I'm driving manually for the fun of it, but it's hard to keep an eye out for the transponders when there's so much else to look at. The transponders are made more for automatic pilot than the human eye. Hey, there's the break into Ophir Chasma, what a gap! That wall must be, I don't know – twenty thousand feet tall. My Lord. Since the last one was called Candor Gap, this one should be called Ophir Gap, right? Ophir Gate would be nicer. Let's check the map. Hmm, the promontory on the west side of the gap is called Candor Labes, that's lips, isn't it? Candor Throat. Or, hmm. I don't think so. It's one hell of an opening though. Steep cliffs on both sides, and twenty thousand feet tall. That's about six or seven times as tall as the cliffs in Yosemite. Sheeee-it. They don't look *that* much taller, to tell the truth. Foreshortening no doubt. They look about twice as tall, or – who knows. I can't remember what Yosemite really looked like, in terms of size anyway. This is the most amazing canyon you could ever even imagine. Ah, there's Candor Mensa, on my left. This is the first time I could see that it isn't part of the Candor Labes wall. I'll bet that mesa top has one hell of a view. Put a fly-in hotel up there, sure. I wish I could get up there and see it! This would be a fun place to fly around in. Dangerous though. I see dust-devils every now and then, vicious little things, real tight and dark. There's a shaft of sunlight there hitting the mesa through the dust. Like a bar of butter hanging in the air. Ah, God, what a beautiful world!'

Nirgal could only agree. It made him laugh to hear the man's voice, and surprised him to hear John talk about flying above. It made him understand a little bit the way the issei talked about Boone, the hurt in them that never went away. How much better it would be to have John here than just these recordings in an AI, what a great adventure it would have been to watch John Boone negotiate Mars's wild history! Saving Nirgal the burden of that role, among other things. As it was, however, they only had that friendly, happy voice. And that did not solve his problem.

Back up on Candor Mesa, the flyers met at night in a ring of pubs and restaurants placed on the high southern arc of their tent wall, where on terraces just inside the tent they could sit and look out at the long views, over the forested world of their domain. Nirgal sat among these people, eating and drinking, listening, sometimes talking, thinking his own thoughts among them, comfortably; they did not care what had happened to him on Earth, they did not care that he was there among them. This was good, as often he was distracted to the point of being oblivious to his surroundings; he would fall into reveries and come out of them, and realize that once again he had been in the steamy streets of Port of Spain, or in the refugee compound in the torrential monsoon. How often he found himself there again; everything that had happened since was so pale by comparison!

But one night he came to from a reverie, having heard some voice say 'Hiroko'.

'What's that?' he said.

'Hiroko. We met her flying around Elysium, up on its north slope.'

It was a young woman speaking, her face innocent of any knowledge of who he was.

'You saw her yourself?' he said sharply.

'Yes. She's not hiding or anything. She said she liked my flyer.'

'I don't know,' an older man said. A Mars vet, an issei immigrant from the early years, his face battered by wind and cosmic rays until it looked like leather. Voice hoarse: 'I heard she was down in the chaos where the first hidden colony used to be, working on the new harbours in the south bay.'

Other voices cut in: Hiroko had been seen here, had been seen there, had been confirmed dead, had gone to Earth; Nirgal had seen her there on Earth —

'This *here's* Nirgal,' one said to the last comment, pointing and grinning. 'He should be able to confirm or deny that one!'

Nirgal, taken aback, nodded. 'I didn't see her on Earth,' he said. 'There were rumours only.'

'Same as here, then.'

Nirgal shrugged.

The young woman, flushed now that she knew who Nirgal was, insisted she had met Hiroko herself. Nirgal watched her closely. This was different; no one had ever made such a direct claim to him (except in Switzerland). She looked worried, defensive, but was holding her ground. 'I talked with her, I say!'

Why lie about something like that? And how would it be possible for someone to get fooled about it? Impersonators? But why do that?

Despite himself Nirgal's pulse had quickened, and he was warmer. The thing was, it was possible Hiroko would do something like this; hide but not hide; live somewhere without bothering to contact the family left behind. There was no obvious motive for it, it would be weird, inhumane, inhuman;

and perfectly within Hiroko's range of possibilities. His mother was a kind of insane person, he had understood that for years – a charismatic who led people effortlessly, but was mad. Capable of almost anything.

If she was alive.

He did not want to hope again. He did not want to go chasing off after the mere mention of her name! But he was watching this girl's face as if he could read the truth from it, as if he could catch the very image of Hiroko still there in her pupils! Others were asking the questions he would have asked, so he could stay silent and listen, he did not have to make her over-selfconscious. Slowly she told the whole story; she and some friends had been flying clockwise around Elysium, and when they stopped for the night up on the new peninsula made by the Phlegra Montes, they had walked down to the icy edge of the North Sea where they had spotted a new settlement, and there in the crowd of construction workers was Hiroko; and several of the construction crew were her old associates, Gene and Rya and Iwao and the rest of the First Hundred who had followed Hiroko ever since the days of the lost colony. The flying group had been amazed, but the lost colonists had been faintly perplexed at their amazement. 'No one hides any more,' Hiroko had told the young woman, after complimenting her flyer. 'We spend most of our time near Dorsa Brevia, but we've been up here for months now.'

And there it was. The woman seemed perfectly sincere, there was no reason to believe she was lying, or subject to hallucination.

Nirgal didn't want to have to think about this. But he had been considering leaving Shining Mesa anyway and having a look around at other places. So he could. And – well – he was going to have to at least have a look. *Shikata ga nai!*

The next day the conversation seemed much less compelling. Nirgal didn't know what to think. He called Sax on the wrist, told him what he had heard. 'Is it possible, Sax? Is it possible?'

A strange look passed over Sax's face. 'It's *possible*,' he said. 'Yes, of course. I told you – when you were sick, and unconscious – that she . . .' He was picking his words, as he so often did, with a squint of concentration. '. . . that I saw her myself. In that storm I was caught out in. She led me to my car.'

Nirgal stared at the little blinking image. 'I don't remember that.'

'Ah. I'm not surprised.'

'So you . . . you think she escaped from Sabishii.'

'Yes.'

'But how likely was that?'

'I don't know the – the *likelihood*. That would be difficult to judge.'

'But *could* they have slipped away?'

'The Sabishii mohole mound is a maze.'

'So you think they escaped.'

Sax hesitated. 'I saw her. She – she grabbed my wrist. I have to believe.' Suddenly his face twisted. 'Yes, she's out there! She's out there! I have no doubt! No doubt! No doubt she's expecting us to come to her.'

And Nirgal knew he had to look.

He left Candor Mesa without a goodbye to anyone. His acquaintances there would understand; they often flew away themselves for a time. They would all be back someday, to soar over the canyons and then spend their evenings together on Shining Mesa. And so he left. Down into the immensity of Melas Chasma, then downcanyon again, east into Coprates. For many hours he floated in that world, over the '61 glacier, past embayment after embayment, buttress after buttress, until he was through the Dover Gate and out over the broadening divergence of Capri and Eos Chasmas. Then above the ice-filled chaoses, the crackled ice smoother than the drowned land below it had been. Then across the rough jumble of Margaritifer Terra, and north, following the piste toward Burroughs; then, as the piste approached Libya Station, he banked off to the northeast, toward Elysium.

The Elysium massif was now a continent in the northern sea. The narrow strait separating it from the southern mainland was a flat stretch of black water and white tabular bergs, punctuated by the stack islands which had been the Aeolis Mensa. The North Sea hydrologists wanted this strait liquid, so that currents could make their way through it from Isidis Bay to Amazonis Bay. To help achieve this liquidity they had placed a nuclear reactor complex at the west end of the strait, and pumped most of its energy into the water there, creating an artificial polynya where the surface stayed liquid year-round, and a temperate mesoclimate on the slopes on each side of the strait. The reactors' steam plumes were visible to Nirgal from far up the Great Escarpment, and as he floated down the slope he crossed over thickening forests of fir and ginko. There was a cable across the western entrance to the strait, emplaced to snag icebergs floating in on the current. He flew directly over the bergjam west of the cable, and looked down on chunks of ice like floating driftglass. Then over the black, open water of the strait – the biggest stretch of open water he had ever seen on Mars. For twenty kilometres he floated over the open water, exclaiming out loud at the sight. Then ahead, an immense airy bridge arced over the strait. The

389

black-violet water below it was dotted with sailboats, ferries, long barges, all trailing the white Vs of their wakes. Nirgal floated over them, circling the bridge twice to marvel at the sight – like nothing he had ever seen on Mars before: water, the sea, a whole future world.

He continued north, rising over the plains of Cerberus, past the volcano Albor Tholus, a steep ash cone on the side of Elysium Mons. The much bigger Elysium Mons was steep as well, with a Fujiesque profile that served as the label illustration for many agricultural co-ops in the region. Sprawled over the plain under the volcano were farms, mostly ragged at the edges, often terraced, and usually divided by strips or patches of forest. Immature orchards dotted the higher parts of the plain; closer to the sea were great fields of wheat and corn, cut by windbreaks of olive and eucalyptus. Just ten degrees north of the equator, blessed with rainy, mild winters, and then lots of hot sunny days: the people there called it the Mediterranean of Mars.

Farther north Nirgal followed the west coast as it rose up out of a line of foundered icebergs embroidering the edge of the ice sea. As he looked down at the expanse of land below, he had to agree with the general wisdom: Elysium was beautiful. This western coastal strip was the most populated region, he had heard. The coast was fractured by a number of fossae, and square harbours were being built where these canyons plunged into the ice – Tyre, Sidon, Pyriphlegethon, Hertzka, Morris. Often stone breakwaters stopped the ice, and marinas were in place behind the breakwaters, filled with fleets of small boats, all waiting for open passage.

At Hertzka Nirgal turned east and inland, and flew up the gentle slope of the Elysian massif, passing over garden belts banding the land. Here the majority of Elysium's thousands lived, in intensively cultivated agricultural-residential zones, sloping up into the higher country between Elysium Mons and its northern spur cone, Hecates Tholus. Between the great volcano and its daughter peak, Nirgal flew through the bare rock saddle of the pass, flung like a little cloud by the pass wind.

Elysium's east slope looked nothing like the west; it was bare, rough, torn rock, heavily sand-drifted, maintained in nearly its primordial condition by the rainshadow of the massif. Only near the eastern coast did Nirgal see greenery below him again, no doubt nourished by trade winds and winter fogs. The towns on the east side were like oases, strung on the thread of an island-circling piste.

At the far northeast end of the island, the ragged old hills of the Phlegra Montes ran far out into the ice, forming a spiny peninsula. Somewhere around here was where that young woman had seen Hiroko. As Nirgal flew up the western side of the Phlegras, it struck him as a likely place to find her; it was a wild and Martian place. The Phlegras, like many of the great mountain ranges of Mars, was the only remaining arc of an ancient impact basin's rim. Every other aspect of that basin had long since disappeared. But the Phlegras still stood as witness to a minute of inconceivable violence – the impact of a hundred kilometre asteroid, big pieces of the lithosphere melted and shoved sideways, other pieces tossed into the air to fall in concentric rings around the impact point, with much of the rock metamorphosed instantly into minerals much harder than their originals. After that trauma the wind had cut away at things, leaving behind only these hard hills.

There were settlements out here, of course, as there were everywhere, in the sinkholes and dead-end valleys and on the passes overlooking the sea. Isolated farms, villages of ten or twenty or a hundred. It looked like Iceland. There were always people who liked such remote land. One village perched on a flat knob a hundred metres over the sea was called Nuannaarpoq, which was Inuit for 'taking extravagant pleasure in being alive'. These villagers and all the others in the Phlegras could float to the rest of Elysium on blimps, or walk down to the circum-Elysian piste and catch a ride. For this coast in particular, the nearest town would be a shapely harbour called Firewater, on the west side of the Phlegras where they first became a peninsula. The town stood on a bench at the end of a squarish bay, and when Nirgal spotted it, he descended onto the tiny airstrip at the upper end of town, and then checked into a boarding house on the main square, behind the docks standing over the ice-sheeted marina.

In the days that followed, he flew out along the coast in both directions, visiting farm after farm. He met a lot of interesting people, but none of them was Hiroko, or anyone from the Zygote crowd – not even any of their associates. It was even a little suspicious; a fair number of issei lived in the region, but every one of them denied ever having met Hiroko or any of her group. Yet all of them were farming with great success, in rocky wilderness that did not look easy to farm – cultivating exquisite little oases of agricultural productivity – living the lives of believers in viriditas – but no, never met her. Barely remembered who she was. One ancient geezer of an American laughed in his face. 'Whachall think, we got a guru? We gonna lead ya to our guru?'

After three weeks Nirgal had found no sign of her at all. He had to give up on the Phlegra Montes. There was no other choice.

Ceaseless wandering. It did not make sense to search for a single person over the vast surface of a world. It was an impossible project. But in some villages there were rumours, and sometimes sightings. Always one more rumour, sometimes one good sighting. She was everywhere and nowhere. Many descriptions but never a photo, many stories but never a wrist message. Sax was convinced she was out there, Coyote was sure she wasn't. It didn't matter; if she was out there, she was hiding. Or leading him on a wild goose chase. It made him angry when he thought of it that way. He would not search for her.

Yet he could not stop moving. If he stayed in one place for more than a week, he began to feel nervous and fretful in a way he had never felt in his life. It was like an illness, with tension everywhere in his muscles, but concentrated in his stomach; an elevated temperature; inability to focus on his thoughts; an urge to fly. And so he would fly, from village to town to station to caravanserai. Some days he let the wind carry him where it would. He had always been a nomad: no reason to stop now. A change in the form of government, why should that make a difference in the way he lived? The winds of Mars were amazing. Strong, irregular, loud, ceaseless.

Sometimes the wind carried him out over the northern sea, and he flew all day and never saw anything but ice and water, as if Mars were an ocean planet. That was Vastitas Borealis – the Vast North, now ice. The ice was in some places flat, in others shattered; sometimes white, sometimes discoloured; the red of dust, or the black of snow algae, or the jade of ice algae, or the chill blue of clear ice. In some places big dust storms had stalled and dropped their loads, and then the wind had carved the detritus so that little dune-fields were created, looking just like old Vastitas. In some places ice carried on currents had crashed over crater-rim reefs, making circular pressure ridges; in other places ice from different currents had crashed together, creating straight pressure ridges, like dragon backs.

Open water was black, or the various purples of the sky. There was a lot of it – polynyas, leads, cracks, patches – perhaps a third of the sea's surface now. Even more common were melt lakes lying on the surface of the ice, their water both white and sky-coloured, which at times looked a brilliant light violet but other times separated out into the two colours; yes, it was another version of the green and the white, the enfolded world, two in one. As always he found the sight of a double colour disturbing, fascinating. The secret of the world.

Many of the big drilling platforms in Vastitas had been seized by Reds and blown up: black wreckage scattered over white ice. Other platforms were defended by Greens, and being used now to melt the ice: large polynyas stretched to the east of these platforms, and the open water steamed, as if clouds were pouring up out of a submarine sky.

In the clouds, in the wind. The southern shore of the northern sea was a succession of gulfs and headlands, bays and peninsulas, fjords and capes, seastacks and low archipelagos. Nirgal followed it for day after day, landing in the late afternoons at little new seaside settlements. He saw crater islands with interiors lower than the ice and water outside the rim. He saw some places where the ice seemed to be receding, so that bordering the ice were black strands, raked by parallel lines running down to ragged drift errata of jumbled rock and ice. Would these strands flood again, or would they grow wider still? No one in these seaside towns knew. No one knew where the coastline would stabilize. The settlements here were made to be moved. Dyked polders showed that some people were apparently testing the newly-exposed land's fertility. Fringing the white ice, green crop rows.

North of Utopia he passed over a low peninsula that extended from the Great Escarpment all the way to the north polar island, the only break in the world-wrapping ocean. A big settlement on this low land, called Boone's Neck, was half tented and half in the open. The settlement's occupants were engaged in cutting a canal through the peninsula.

A wind blew north and Nirgal followed it. The wind hummed, whooshed, keened. On some days it shrieked. In the sea on both sides of the long low peninsula were tabular ice shelfs. Tall mountains of jade ice broke through these white sheets. No one lived up here, but Nirgal was not searching any more – he had given up, very near despair, and was just floating, letting the winds take him like a dandelion seed: over the ice sea, shattered white; over open, purple water, lined by sunbright waves. Then the peninsula widened to become the polar island, a white bumpy land in the sea ice. No sign of the primeval swirl-pattern of melt valleys. That world was gone.

Over the other side of the world and the North Sea, over Orcas Island on the east flank of Elysium, down over Cimmeria again. Floating like a seed. Some days the world went black and white: icebergs on the sea, looking into the sun; tundra swans against black cliffs; black guillemots flying over the ice; snow geese. And nothing else in all the day.

Ceaseless wandering. He flew around the northern parts of the world two or three times, looking down at the land and the ice, at all the changes taking place everywhere, at all the little settlements huddling in their tents, or out braving the cold winds. But all the looking in the world couldn't make the sorrow go away.

One day he came on a new harbour town at the entry to the long skinny fjord of Marwth Vallis, and found his Zygote crêche-mates Rachel and Tiu had moved there. Nirgal hugged them, and over dinner and afterward he stared at their oh-so-familiar faces with intense pleasure. Hiroko was gone but his brothers and sisters remained, and that was something; proof that his childhood was real. And despite all the years they looked just as they had when they were children; there was no real difference. Rachel and he had been friends, she had had a crush on him in the early years, and they had kissed in the baths; he recalled with a little shiver a time when she had kissed him in one ear, Jackie in the other. And, though he had almost forgotten it, he had lost his virginity with Rachel, one afternoon in the baths, shortly before Jackie had taken him out into the dunes by the lake. Yes, one afternoon, almost accidentally, when their kissing had suddenly become urgent and exploratory, a matter of their bodies moving outside their own volition.

Now she regarded him fondly – a woman his age, her face a map of laugh-lines, cheery and bold. She might have recalled their early encounter as little as he did – hard to say what his siblings remembered of their shared, bizarre childhood – but she looked as if she remembered. She had always been friendly, and she was again now. He told her about his flights around the world, carried by the ceaseless winds, diving slowly against the blimp's buoyancy down to one little habitation after another, asking after Hiroko.

Rachel shook her head, smiling ironically. 'If she's out there, she's out there. But you could look forever and never find her.'

Nirgal heaved a troubled sigh, and she laughed and tousled his hair.

'Don't look for her.'

That evening he walked along the strand, just uphill from the devastated berg-strewn shoreline of the northern sea. He felt in his body that he needed to walk, to run. Flying was too easy, it was a dissociation from the world – things were small and distant – again, it was the wrong end of the telescope. He needed to walk.

Still he flew. As he flew, however, he looked more closely at the land. Heath, moor, streamside meadows. A creek falling directly into the sea over a short drop, another one crossing a beach. In some places they had planted forests, to try to cut down on dust storms that originated in this area. There were still dust storms, but the trees of the forest were saplings still.

Hiroko might be able to sort it out. Don't look for her. Look at the land.

He flew back to Sabishii. There was still a lot of work to be done there, clearing away burned buildings and then building new ones. Some construction co-ops were still accepting new members. One was doing reconstruction but was also building blimps and other flyers, including some experimental birdsuits. He talked with them about joining.

He left his blimpglider in town with them, and took long runs out onto the high moors east of Sabishii. He had run these uplands during his student years. A lot of the ridge runs were familiar still; beyond them, new ground. A high land, with its moorish life. Big kami boulders stood here and there on the rumpled land, like sentinels.

One afternoon, running an unfamiliar ridge, he looked down into a small high basin like a shallow bowl, with a break opening to lower land to the west. Like a glacial cirque, though more likely it was an eroded crater with a break in its rim, making a horseshoe ridge. About a kilometre across – quite shallow. Just a rumple among the many rumples on the Tyrrhena Massif. From the encircling ridge the horizons were far away, the land below lumpy and irregular.

It seemed familiar. Possibly he had visited it on an overnighter in his student years. He hiked slowly down into the basin, and still felt as if he were on top of the massif; something about the dark, clean indigo of the sky, the spacious long view out the gap to the west. Clouds rolled overhead like great rounded icebergs, dropping dry, granular snow, which was chased into cracks or out of the basin entirely by the hard wind. On the circling ridge, near the northwest point of the horseshoe, there was a boulder sitting like a stone hut. It stood on four points on the ridge, a dolmen worn to the smoothness of an old tooth, the sky over it lapis lazuli.

Nirgal walked back down to Sabishii and looked into the matter. The basin was untended, according to the maps and records of the Tyrrhena Massif Areography and Ecopoesis Council. They were pleased he was interested. 'The high basins are hard,' they told him. 'Very little grows. It's a long project.'

'Good.'

'You'll have to grow most of your food in greenhouses. Potatoes, however – once you get enough soil, of course — '

Nirgal nodded.

They asked him to drop into the village of Dinboche, the one nearest the basin, and make sure no one there had plans for it.

So he drove back up, in a little caravan with Tariki and Rachel and Tiu and some other friends who had gathered to help. They drove over a low ridge and found Dinboche, set on a little wadi that was now being farmed, mostly in hardscrabble potato fields. There had been a snowstorm, and all the fields were white rectangles, divided by low black walls of stacked stones. A number of long, low stone houses, with plate-rock roofs and thick, square chimneys, were scattered among the fields, with several more clustered at the village's upper end. The longest building in this cluster was a two-storeyed tea-house, with a big mattress-filled room to accommodate visitors.

In Dinboche, as in much of the southern highlands, the gift economy still predominated, and Nirgal and his companions had to endure a near potlatching when they stayed for the night. The locals were very happy when he inquired about the high basin, which they called variously 'the little horseshoe', or, 'the upper hand'. 'It needs looking after.' They offered to help him get started.

So they went up to the high cirque in a little caravan, and dumped a load of gear on the ridge near the house boulder, and stuck around long enough to clear a first little field of stones, walling it with what they cleared. A couple of them experienced in construction helped him to make the first incisions into the ridge boulder. During this noisy drilling some of the Dinboche locals cut away at the exterior of the rock, carving in Sanskrit lettering *Om Mani Padme Hum*, as seen on innumerable mani stones in the Himalayas, and now all over the southern highlands. The locals chipped away the rock between the fat, cursive letters, so that the letters stood out in raised relief against a rougher, lighter background. As for the boulder house itself, eventually he would have four rooms hacked out of the boulder, with triple-paned windows,

solar panels for heat and power, water from a snowmelt
pumped up to a tank placed higher on the ridge, and a com-
posting toilet and greywater facility.

Then they were off. Nirgal had the basin to himself.

He walked around on it for many days without doing anything but looking. Only the tiniest part of the basin would be
his farm – just some small fields inside low stone walls, and
a greenhouse for vegetables. And a cottage industry, he wasn't
sure what. It wouldn't be self-sufficient, but it would be settling in. A project.

And then there was the basin itself. A small channel already
ran down the opening out to the west, as if to suggest a
watershed. The cupped hand of rock was already a microcli-
mate, tilted to the sun, slightly sheltered from the winds. He
would be an ecopoet.

First he had to learn the land. With that as his project it
was amazing how busy every day became: there was an endless
number of things to do; but no structure, no schedule, no
rush; no one to consult; and every day, in the last hours of
summer evenings, he would walk around the ridge, and inspect
the basin in the failing light. It was already colonized by lichen
and the other first settlers; fellfields filled the hollows, and
there were small mosaics of arctic ground cover in the sunny
exposures, mounds of green moss humped on red soil less
than a centimetre thick. Snowmelt coursed down a number of
rivulet channels, pooling and dropping through any number
of potential meadow terraces, little diatom oases, falling down
the basin to meet in the gravel wadi at the gate to the land
below, a flat meadow-to-be behind the residual rim. Ribs
higher in the basin were natural dams, and after some consideration, Nirgal carried some ventifacts to these low ribs,
and assembled them with their facets touching so that the
ribs were heightened by the height of just one or two rocks.
Snow-melt would collect in meadow ponds, banked by moss.
The moors just east of Sabishii resembled what he had in
mind, and he called up ecopoets who lived on those moors,
and asked about species compatibility, growth rates, soil
amendment and the like. In his mind developed a vision of
the basin; then in second March the autumn came, the year
heading toward aphelion, and he began to see how much of
the landscaping would be done by wind and winter.

He spread seeds and spores by hand, casting them away
from bags or growth media dishes latched to his belt, feeling
like a figure from Van Gogh or the Old Testament; it was a
peculiar sensation of mixed power and helplessness, action and
fate. He arranged for loads of topsoil to be trucked up and
dumped on some of the little fields, and then he spread it out
by hand, thinly. He brought in worms from the university
farm at Sabishii. Worms in a bottle, Coyote had always called
people in cities; observing the writhing mass of moist, naked
tubules, Nirgal shuddered. He released the worms onto his
new little plots. Go little worm, prosper on the land. He

himself, walking around on the sunny mornings after a shower, was no more than moist, linked, naked tubules. Sentient worms, that's what they were, in bottles or on the land.

After the worms it would be moles and voles. Then mice. Then snow rabbits, and ermine and marmots; perhaps then some of the snow cats wandering the moors would drop in. Foxes. The basin was high, but the pressure they were hoping for at this altitude was 400 millibars, with forty per cent of that oxygen; they were already most of the way there. Conditions were somewhat as in the Himalayas. Presumably all of Earth's high-altitude flora and fauna would be viable here, and all the new engineered variants; and with so many ecopoets stewarding small patches of the upland, the problem would be mostly a matter of prepping the ground, introducing the basic ecosystem desired, and then supporting it, and watching what came in on the wind, or walked in, or flew. These arrivals could be problematic of course, and there was a lot of talk on the wrist about invasion biology and integrated microcline management; working out one's locality's connections to the larger region was a big part of the ongoing process of ecopoesis.

Nirgal got even more interested in this matter of dispersal the next spring, in first November when the snows melted, and poking out of the late slush on the flat terraces of the northern side of the basin were sprigs of snow alumroot. He hadn't planted them, he had never heard of them, indeed he wasn't even sure of his identification, until his neighbour Yoshi dropped by one week and confirmed it: *Heuchera nivalis*. Blown in on the wind, Yoshi said. There was a lot of it in Escalante Crater to the north. Not much of it in between; but that was jump dispersal for you.

Jump dispersal, spread dispersal, stream dispersal: all three were common on Mars. Mosses and bacteria were spread dispersing; hydrophilic plants were stream dispersing along the sides of glaciers, and the new coastlines; and lichen and any number of other plants were jump dispersing on the strong winds. Human dispersion showed all three patterns, Yoshi remarked as they wandered over the basin discussing the concept – spreading through Europe and Asia and Africa, streaming down the Americas and along the Australian coasts, jumping out to the Pacific Islands (or to Mars). It was common to see all three methods used by highly adaptable species. And the Tyrrhena Massif was up in the wind, catching the westerlies and also the summer trade winds, so that both sides of the massif got precipitation; nowhere more than twenty centimetres a year, which would have made it desert on Earth, but in the southern hemisphere of Mars, that was a precipitation island. In that way too a dispersion catchment, and so very invasible.

So. High, barren, rocky land, dusted with snow wherever shade predominated, so that the shadows tended to be white. Little sign of life except in basins, where the ecopoets helped along their little collections. Clouds surged in from west in the winter, east in the summer. The southern hemisphere had the seasons reinforced by the perihelion-aphelion cycle, so that they really meant something. On Tyrrhena the winters were hard.

Nirgal wandered the basin after storms, looking to see what had blown in. Usually it was only a load of icy dust, but once he found an unplanted clutch of pale blue Jacob's ladders, tucked between the splits in a breadloaf rock. Check the botanicals to see how it might interact with what was already there. Ten per cent of introduced species survived, then ten per cent of those became pests; that was invasion biology's ten-ten rule, Yoshi said, almost the first rule of the discipline. 'Ten meaning five to twenty, of course.' Once Nirgal weeded out a springtime arrival of common streetgrass, fearing it would take over everything. Same with tundra thistle. Another time a heavy dust load fell on an autumn wind. These dust storms were small compared to the old global southern-summer storms, but occasionally a hard wind would tear up the desert pavement somewhere and send the dust below flying. The atmosphere was thickening rapidly these days, 15 millibars a year on average. Each year the winds had more force, and so thicker areas of pavement were at risk of being torn away. The dust that fell was usually a very thin layer, however, and often high in nitrates; so it was like a fertilizer, to be washed into the soil by the next rain.

Nirgal bought a position in the Sabishii construction co-op he had looked into. He went in often to work on the town's buildings. Up in the basin he did some assembly and testing of solo blimpgliders. His work cottage was a small building made of stone-stacked walls, with plates of sandstone for shingles. Between that work and the farming in the greenhouse and his potato patch, and the ecopoesis in the basin, his days were full.

He flew the completed blimpgliders down to Sabishii, and stayed in a little studio above in his old teacher Tariki's rebuilt house in the old city, living there among ancient issei who looked and sounded very much like Hiroko. Art and Nadia lived there too, raising their daughter Nikki. Also in town were Vijjika, and Reull, and Annette, all old friends from his student days – and there was the university itself, no longer called the University of Mars, but simply Sabishii College – a small school that still ran in the amorphous style of the demi-monde years, so that the more ambitious students went to Elysium or Sheffield or Cairo; those who came to Sabishii were those fascinated by the mystique of those years, or interested in the work of one of the issei professors.

All these people and activities made Nirgal feel strangely, even uncomfortably at home. He put in long days as a plasterer and general labourer on various construction jobs his co-op had around town. He ate in rice bars and pubs. He slept in the loft in Tariki's garage, and looked forward to the days he returned to the basin.

One night he was walking home late from a pub, asleep on his feet, when he passed a small man sleeping on a park bench: Coyote.

Nirgal stopped short. He walked over to the bench. He stared and stared. Some nights he heard coyotes howling up in the basin. This was his father. He remembered all those days hunting for Hiroko, without a clue as to where to look. But here his father slept on a city park bench. Nirgal could call him any time, and always that bright cracked grin, Trinidad itself. Tears started to his eyes; he shook his head, composed himself. Old man lying on a park bench. One saw it fairly frequently. A lot of the issei had arrived here and gone off somehow, into the back country for good, so that when they came into a city they slept in the parks.

Nirgal went over and sat on the end of the bench, just beyond his father's head. Grey, tatty dreadlocks. Like a drunk. Nirgal just sat with him, looking at the undersides of the linden trees around the bench. It was a quiet night. Stars ticked through the leaves.

Coyote stirred, twisted his head and glanced up. 'Who dat?'

'Hey,' Nirgal said.

'Hey!' Coyote said, and sat up. He rubbed at his eyes. 'Nirgal, man. You startle me there.'

'Sorry. I was walking by and saw you. What are you doing?'

'Sleeping.'

'Ha ha.'

'Well, I was. Far as I know that was all I was doing.'

'Coyote, don't you have a home?'

'Why, no.'

'Doesn't that bother you?'

'No.' Coyote bleared a grin at him. 'I'm like that awful vid programme. The world is my home.'

Nirgal only shook his head. Coyote squinted as he saw that Nirgal was not amused. He stared at him for a long time from under half-mast eyelids, breathing deeply. 'My boy,' he said at last, dreamily. The whole city was quiet. Coyote muttered as if falling asleep. 'What does the hero do when the tale is over? Swim over the waterfall. Drift out on the tide.'

'What?'

Coyote opened his eyes fully, leaned toward Nirgal. 'Do you remember when we brought Sax into Tharsis Tholus and you sat with him, and afterwards they said you brought him back to life? That kind of thing —' He shook his head, leaned back on the bench. 'It's not right. It's just a story. Why worry about that story when it's not yours anyway. What you're doing right now is better. You can walk away from that kind of story. Sit in a park at night like any ordinary person. Go anywhere you please.'

Nirgal nodded, uncertain.

'What I like to do,' Coyote said sleepily, 'is go to a pavement café and toss down some kava and watch all the faces. Go for a walk around the streets and look at people's faces. I like to look at women's faces. So beautiful. And some of them so . . . so something. I don't know. I love them.' He was falling asleep again. 'You'll find your way to live.'

* * *

Guests who occasionally visited him in the basin included Sax, Coyote, Art and Nadia and Nikki, who got taller every year; she was taller than Nadia already, and seemed to regard Nadia like a nanny or a great-grandmother – much as Nirgal himself had regarded her, in Zygote. Nikki had inherited Art's sense of fun, and Art himself encouraged this, egging her on, conspiring with her against Nadia, watching her with the most radiant pleasure Nirgal had ever seen on an adult face. Once Nirgal saw the three of them sitting on the stone wall by his potato patch, laughing helplessly at something Art had said, and he felt a pang even as he too laughed; his old friends were now married, with a kid. Living in that most ancient pattern. Faced with that, his life on the land did not seem so substantial after all. But what could he do? Only a few people in this world were lucky enough to run into their true partners – it took outrageous luck for it to happen, then the sense to recognize it, and the courage to act. Few could be expected to have all that, and then to have things go well. The rest had to make do.

So he lived in his high basin, grew some of his food, worked on co-op projects to pay for the rest. He flew down to Sabishii once a month in a new aircraft, enjoyed his stay of a week or two, and went back home. Art and Nadia and Sax came up frequently, and much less often he hosted Maya and Michel, or Spencer, all of whom lived in Odessa – or Zeyk and Nazik, who brought news of Cairo and Mangala that he tried not to hear. When they left he went out onto the arcing ridge and sat on one of his sitting boulders, and looked at the meadows stringing through the talus, concentrating on what he had, on this world of the senses, rock and lichen and moss campion.

The basin was evolving. There were moles in the meadows, marmots in the talus. At the end of the long winters the marmots came out of hibernation early, nearly starving, their internal clocks still set to Earth. Nirgal set out food for them in the snow, and watched from his house's upper windows as they ate it. They needed help to get through the long winters to spring. They regarded his house as a source of food and warmth, and two marmot families lived in the rocks under it, whistling their warning whistle when anyone approached. Once they warned him of people from the Tyrrhena committee on the introduction of new species, asking him for a species list, and a rough census; they were beginning to formulate a local 'native inhabitant' list, which, once formed, would allow them to make judgments on any subsequent introductions of fast-spreading species. Nirgal was happy to join this effort, and apparently so was everyone else doing ecopoesis on the massif; as a precipitation island, hundreds of kilometres from the nearest others, they were developing their own mix of high-altitude fauna and flora, and there was a growing sentiment to regard this mix as 'natural' to Tyrrhena, to be altered only by consensus.

The group from the committee left, and Nirgal sat with the house marmots, feeling odd. 'Well,' he said to them, 'now we're indigenous.'

He was happy in his basin, above the world and its concerns. In the spring new plants appeared from nowhere, and some he greeted with a trowel of compost, others he plucked out and turned into compost. The greens of spring were unlike any other greens – light, electric jades and limes of bud and leaf, new blades of emerald grass, blue nettles, red leaves. And then later the flowers, that tremendous expense of a plant's energy, the push beyond survival, the reproductive urge all around him . . . sometimes when Nadia and Nikki came back from their walks holding miniature bouquets in their big hands, it seemed to Nirgal that the world made sense. He would eye them, and think about children, and feel some wild edge in him that was not usually there.

It was a feeling generally shared, apparently. Spring lasted one hundred and forty-three days in the southern hemisphere, coming all the way back from the harsh aphelion winter. More plants bloomed as the spring months passed, first early ones like promise-of-spring and snow liverwort, then later ones such as phlox and heather, then saxifrage and Tibetan rhubarb, moss campion and alpine nailwort, cornflowers and edelweiss, on and on until every patch of green carpet in the rocky palm of the basin was touched with brilliant dots of cyanic blue, dark pink, yellow, white, each colour waving in a layer at the characteristic height of the plant holding it, all of them glowing in the dusk like drips of light, welling out into the world from nowhere – a pointillist Mars, the ribbiness of the seamed basin etched in the air by this scree of colour. He stood in a cupped rock hand which tilted its snowmelt down a lifeline crease in the palm, down into the wide world so far below, a vast, shadowy world that loomed to the west under the sun, all hazy and low. The last light of day seemed to shine slightly upward.

One clear morning Jackie appeared on his house AI screen, and announced she was on the piste from Odessa to Libya, and wanted to drop in. Nirgal agreed before he had time to think.

He went down to the path by the outlet stream to greet her. Little high basin ... there were a million craters like it in the south. Little old impact. Nothing the slightest bit distinguished about it. He remembered Shining Mesa, the stupendous yellow view at dawn.

They came up in three cars, bouncing wildly over the terrain, like kids. Jackie was driving the first car, Antar the second. They were laughing hard as they got out. Antar didn't seem to mind losing the race. They had a whole group of young Arabs with them. Jackie and Antar looked young themselves, amazingly so; it had been a long time since Nirgal had seen them, but they had not changed at all. The treatments; current folk wisdom was to get it done early and often, ensuring perpetual youth and balking any of the rare diseases that still killed people from time to time. Balking death entirely, perhaps. Early, often. They still looked as if they were fifteen M-years old. But Jackie was a year older than Nirgal, and he was almost thirty-three M-years old now, and feeling older. Looking at their laughing faces, he thought, I'll have to get the treatment myself someday.

So they wandered around, stepping on the grass and oohing and ahhing at the flowers, and the basin seemed smaller and smaller with every exclamation they made. Near the end of their visit Jackie took him to one side, looking serious.

She said, 'We're having trouble holding off the Terrans, Nirgal. They're sending up almost a million a year, just like you said they never could. And these new arrivals aren't joining Free Mars like they used to. They're still supporting their home governments. Mars isn't changing them fast enough. If this goes on, then the whole idea of a free Mars will be a joke. I sometimes wonder if it was a mistake to leave the cable up.'

She frowned and twenty years jumped onto her face all at once. Nirgal suppressed a little shudder.

'It would help if you weren't hiding here,' she exclaimed with sudden anger, dismissing the basin with a wave of her hand. 'We need everyone we can get to help. People still remember you now, but in a few years . . .'

So he only had to wait a few more years, he thought. He watched her. She was beautiful, yes. But beauty was a matter of the spirit, of intelligence, vivacity, empathy. So that while Jackie grew ever more beautiful, at the same time she grew less beautiful. Another mysterious infolding. And Nirgal was not pleased by this internal loss in Jackie, not in any way; it was only one more note in the chord of his Jackie pain, really. He didn't want it to be true.

'We can't really help them by taking more immigrants,' she said. 'That was wrong, when you said that on Earth. They know it, too. They can see it better than we can, no doubt. But they send people anyway. And you know why? You know why? Just to wreck things here. Just to make sure there isn't somewhere people are doing it right. That's their only reason.'

Nirgal shrugged. He didn't know what to say; probably there was some truth to what she had said, but it was just one of a million different reasons for people to come; there was no reason to fix on it.

'So you won't come back,' she said at last. 'You don't care.'

Nirgal shook his head. How to say to her that she was not worried about Mars, but about her own power? He wasn't the one who could tell her that. She wouldn't believe him. And maybe it was only true to him anyway.

Abruptly she stopped trying to reach him. A regal glance at Antar, and Antar did the work of gathering their coterie into the cars. A final questioning look; a kiss, full on the mouth, no doubt to bother Antar, or him, or both of them; like an electric shock to the soul; and she was off.

*   *   *

407

He spent the afternoon and the next day wandering, sitting on flat rocks and watching the little rivulets bounce downstream. Once he remembered how fast water had fallen on Earth. Unnatural. No. But this was his place, known and loved, every dyad and every clump of campion, even the speed of water as it lofted off stone and plashed down in its smooth silver shapes. The way moss felt under the finger pads. His visitors were people for whom Mars was forever an idea, a nascent state, a political situation. They lived in the tents and they might as well have been in a city anywhere, and their devotion, while real, was given to some cause or idea, some Mars of the mind. Which was fine. But for Nirgal now it was the land that mattered, the places where water arrived just so, trickling over the billion-year-old rock onto pads of new moss. Leave politics to the young, he had done his part. He didn't want to do any more. Or at least he wanted to wait until Jackie was gone. Power was like Hiroko, after all – it always slipped away. Didn't it? Meanwhile, the cirque like an open hand.

But then one morning when he went out for a dawn walk, there was something different. The sky was clear, its purest morning purple, but a juniper's needles had a yellowish tinge to them, and so did the moss, and the potato leaves on their mounds.

He plucked the yellowest samples of needles and sprigs and leaves, and took them back to the workbench in his greenhouse. Two hours' work with microscope and AI did not find any problem, and he went back out and pulled up some root samples, and bagged some more needles and leaves and blades and flowers. Much of the grass had a wilted look, though it wasn't a hot day.

Heart thudding, stomach taut, he worked all day and into the night. He could discover nothing. No insects, no pathogens. But the potato leaves in particular looked yellow. That night he called Sax and explained the situation. By coincidence Sax was visiting the university in Sabishii, and he drove up the next morning in a little rover, the latest from Spencer's co-op.

'Nice,' Sax said as he got out and looked around. He checked

Nirgal's samples in the greenhouse. 'Hmm,' he said. 'I wonder.'

He had brought some instruments in his car, and they lugged them into the boulder and he went to work. At the end of a long day he said, 'I can't find anything. We'll have to take some samples down to Sabishii.'

'You can't find anything?'

'No pathogen. No bacteria, no virus.' He shrugged. 'Let's take several potatoes.'

They went out and dug potatoes from the field. Some of them were gnarled, elongated, cracked. 'What is it?' Nirgal exclaimed.

Sax was frowning a little. 'Looks like spindle tuber disease.'

'What causes it?'

'A viroid.'

'What's that?'

'A bare RNA fragment. Smallest known infectious agent. Strange.'

'Ka.' Nirgal felt his stomach clamping inward. 'How did it get here?'

'On a parasite, probably. This kind seems to be infecting grass. We need to find out.'

So they gathered samples, and drove back down to Sabishii. Nirgal sat on a futon on the floor of Tariki's living room, feeling sick. Tariki and Sax talked long after dinner, discussing the situation. Other viroids had been appearing in a rapid dispersal from Tharsis; apparently they had made it across the cordon sanitaire of space, arriving on a world that had been previously innocent of them. They were smaller than viruses, much smaller, and quite a bit simpler. Nothing but strands of RNA, Tariki said, about fifty nanometres long. Individuals had a molecular weight of about one hundred and thirty thousand, while the smallest known viruses had molecular weights of over a million. They were so small that they had to be centrifuged at over one hundred thousand g in order to be pulled out of suspension.

The potato spindle tuber viroid was well understood, Tariki told them, tapping around on his screen and pointing at the schematics called up. A chain of merely three hundred and fifty-nine nucleotides, lined out in a closed single strand with short double-strand regions braiding it. Viroids like this one caused several plant diseases, including pale cucumber disease, chrysanthemum stunt, chlorotic mottle, cadang-cadang, citrus exocortis. Viroids had also been confirmed as the agent in some animal brain diseases, like scrapie, and kuru, and Creutzfeldt-Jakob disease in humans. The viroids used host enzymes to reproduce, and then were taken to be regulatory molecules in the nuclei of infected cells, disturbing growth hormone production in particular.

The particular viroid in Nirgal's basin, Tariki said, had mutated from potato spindle tuber. They were still identifying it in the labs at the university, but the sick grass made him sure they were going to find something different, something new.

Nirgal felt ill. The names of the diseases alone were enough to do it. He stared at his hands, which had been plunged thick in infected plants. Through the skin, into the brain, some kind of spongiform encephalopathy, mushroom growths of brain blooming everywhere.

'Is there anything we can do to fight it?' he said.

Sax and Tariki looked at him.

'First,' Sax said, 'we have to find out what it is.'

That turned out to be no simple matter. After a few days, Nirgal returned to his basin. There he could at least do something; Sax had suggested removing all the potatoes from the potato fields. This was a long, dirty task, a kind of negative treasure hunt, as he turned up diseased tuber after tuber. Presumably the soil itself would still hold the viroid. It was possible he would have to abandon the field, or even the basin. At best, plant something else. No one yet understood how viroids reproduced; and the word from Sabishii was that this might not even be a viroid as previously understood.

'It's a shorter strand than usual,' Sax said. 'Either a new viroid, or something like a viroid but smaller still.' In the Sabishii labs they were calling it 'the virid'.

A long week later, Sax came back up to the basin. 'We can try to remove it physically,' he said over dinner. 'Then plant different species, ones that are resistant to viroids. That's the best we can do.'

'But will that work?'

'The plants susceptible to infection are fairly specific. You got hit by a new one, but if you change grasses, and types of potatoes – perhaps cycle out some of your potato patch soil . . .' Sax shrugged.

Nirgal ate with more appetite than he had had for the previous week. Even the suggestion of a possible solution was a great relief. He drank some wine, felt better and better. 'These things are strange, eh?' he said over an after-dinner brandy. 'What life will come up with!'

'If you call it life.'

'Well, of course.'

Sax didn't reply.

'I've been looking at the news on the net,' Nirgal said. 'There are a lot of infestations. I had never noticed before. Parasites, viruses . . .'

'Yes. Sometimes I worry about a global plague. Something we can't stop.'

'Ka! Could that happen?'

'There's all kinds of invasions going on. Population surges, sudden die-offs. All over. Things in disequilibrium. Upsetting balances we didn't even know existed. Things we don't understand.' As always this thought made Sax unhappy.

'Biomes will eventually come into equilibrium,' Nirgal suggested.

'I'm not sure there is such a thing.'

'As equilibrium?'

'Yes. It may be a matter of . . .' He waved his hands about like gulls. 'Punctuated equilibrium, without the equilibrium.'

'Punctuated change?'

'Perpetual change. Braided change – surging change — '

'Like cascading recombinance?'

'Perhaps.'

'I've heard that's a mathematics only a dozen people can really understand.'

Sax looked surprised. 'That's never true. Or else, true of every math. Depends on what you mean by understand. But I know a bit of that one. You can use it to model some of this stuff. But not predict. And I don't know how to use it to suggest any – reactions on our part. I'm not sure it can be used that way.' He talked for a while about Vlad's notion of *holons*, which were organic units that had sub-units and also were sub-units of greater holons, each level combining to create the next one up in emergent fashion, all the way up and down the great chain of being. Vlad had worked out mathematical descriptions of these emergences, which turned out to come in more than one kind, with different families of properties for each kind; so if they could get enough information about the behaviour of a level of holons and the next level up, they could try to fit them into these mathematical formulae, and see what kind of emergence they had; then perhaps find ways to disrupt it. 'That's the best approach we can take for things this little.'

The next day they called up greenhouses in Xanthe, to ask for shipments of new starts, and flats of a new strain of Himalayan-based grass. By the time they arrived, Nirgal had pulled out all the sedge in the basin, and much of the moss. The work made him feel sick, he couldn't help it; once, seeing a concerned marmot patriarch chattering at him, he sat down and burst into tears. Sax had retreated into his customary silence, which only made things worse, as it always reminded Nirgal of Simon, and of death generally. He needed Maya or some other courageous, expressive speaker of the inner life, of anguish and fortitude; but here was Sax, lost in thoughts that seemed to happen in some kind of foreign language, in a private idiolect he was now unwilling to translate.

They went to work planting new starts of Himalayan grasses throughout the basin, concentrating on the stream banks and their veinlike tracery under the trickles and ice. A hard freeze actually helped, as it killed the infected plants faster than the ones free of infection. They incinerated the infected plants in a kiln down the massif. People came from the surrounding basins to help, bringing replacement starts for planting later.

Two months passed, and the invasion surge weakened. The plants that remained seemed to be more resistant; newly-planted ones did not get infected or die. The basin looked as if it was autumn, though it was midsummer; but the dying had stopped. The marmots looked thin, and more concerned than ever; they were a worrying species. And Nirgal could see their point. The basin looked ravaged. But it seemed the biome

412

would survive. The viroid was subsiding; eventually they could hardly even find it, no matter how hard and long they centrifuged samples. It seemed to have left the basin, as mysterious in departure as in arrival.

Sax shook his head. 'If the viroids that infect animals ever get more robust . . .' He sighed. 'I wish I could talk to Hiroko about it.'

'I've heard them say she's at the north pole,' Nirgal said sourly.

'Yes.'

'But?'

'I don't think she's there. And – I don't think she wants to talk to me. But I'm still . . . I'm waiting.'

'For her to call?' Nirgal said sarcastically.

Sax nodded.

They stared into Nirgal's lamp flame glumly. Hiroko – mother, lover – she had abandoned them both.

But the basin would live. When Sax went to his rover to leave, Nirgal gave him a bearhug, lifting him and twirling him. 'Thanks.'

'My pleasure,' Sax said. 'Very interesting.'

'What will you do now?'

'I think I will talk to Ann. Try to talk to Ann.'

'Ah! Good luck.'

Sax nodded, as if to say he would need it. Then he drove off, waving once before putting both hands on the wheel. In a minute he was over the rib and gone.

So Nirgal went at the hard work of restoring the basin, doing what he could to give it more pathogen resistance. More diversity, more of an indigenous parasite load. From the chasmoendolithic rock-dwellers to the insects and microbial flyers hovering in the air. A fuller, tougher biome. He seldom went into Sabishii. He replaced all the soil in the potato patch, planted a different kind of potato.

Sax and Spencer had come back to visit him, when a big dust storm began in the Claritas region near Senzeni Na – at their latitude, but all the way around the world. They heard about it over the news, and then tracked it over the next couple

413

of days on the satellite weather photos. It came east, kept coming east; kept coming; looked as if it was going to pass to the south of them; but at the last minute it veered north.

They sat in the living room of his boulder house looking south. And there it came, a dark mass filling the sky. Dread filled Nirgal like the static electricity causing Spencer to yelp when he touched things. The dread didn't make sense, they had passed under a score of dust storms before. It was only residual dread from the viroid blight. And they had weathered that.

But this time the light of day browned and dimmed until it might as well have been night – a chocolate night, howling over the boulder and rattling the outer window. 'The winds have got so strong,' Sax remarked pensively. Then the howl lessened, while it was still dark out. Nirgal felt more and more sick the less the wind howled – until the air was still, and he was so nauseated he could scarcely stand at the window. Global dust storms sometimes did this; they ended abruptly when the wind ran into a counterwind, or a particular landform. And then the storm dropped its load of dust and fines. It was raining dust now, in fact, the boulder's windows a dirty grey, as if ash were settling over the world. In the old days, Sax was muttering uneasily, even the biggest dust storms would only have dropped a few millimetres of fines at the end of their runs. But with the atmosphere so much thicker, and the winds so much more powerful, great quantities of dust and sand were thrown aloft; and if they came down all at once, as sometimes happened, the drifts could be much deeper than a few millimetres.

As near suspension as some fines were, in an hour all but the very finest had fallen out of the air and onto them. After that it was only a hazy afternoon, windless, the air filled with something like a thin smoke, so that they could see the whole of the basin; which was covered with a lumpy blanket of dust.

Nirgal went out with his mask on as always, and dug desperately with a shovel, then with his bare hands. Sax came out, staggering through the soft drifts, to put a hand to Nirgal's shoulder. 'I don't believe there's anything that can be done.' The layer of dust was about a metre deep, or deeper.

In time, other winds would blow some of this dust away.

414

Snow would fall on the rest of it, and when the snow melted, the resulting mud would run over the spillways, and a new leaf-vein system of channels would cut a new fractal pattern, much like the old one. Water would carry the dust and fines away, down the massif and into the world. But by the time that happened, every plant and animal in the basin would be dead.

PART NINE

Natural History

Afterwards Nirgal went with Sax up to Da Vinci, and stayed with the old man in his apartment. One night Coyote dropped in, after the timeslip when no one else would have thought to visit.

Briefly Nirgal told him what had happened to the high basin.

'Yeah, so?' Coyote said.

Nirgal looked away.

Coyote went to the kitchen and started scrabbling through Sax's refrigerator, shouting back into the living room through a full mouth. 'What did you expect on a windy hillside like that? This world is not a garden, man. Some of it going to get buried every year, that's just the way it is. Another wind come in a year or ten and blow all that dust off your hill.'

'Everything will be dead by then.'

'That's life. Now it's time to do something else. What were you doing before you set in there?'

'Looking for Hiroko.'

'Shit.' Coyote appeared in the doorway, pointing a big kitchen knife right at Nirgal. 'Not you too.'

'Yes me too.'

'Oh come on. When you going to grow up? Hiroko is dead. You might as well get used to it.'

Sax came in from his office, blinking hard. 'Hiroko is alive,' he said.

'Not you too!' Coyote cried. 'You two are like children!'

'I saw her on the south flank of Arsia Mons, in a storm.'

'Join the fucking party, man.'

Sax blinked at him. 'What do you mean?'

'Fuck.'

Coyote went back into the kitchen.

'There have been other sightings,' Nirgal said to Sax. 'Reports are fairly common.'

'I know that —'

'Reports are daily!' Coyote shouted from the kitchen. He charged back into the living room. 'People see her every day! There's a spot on the wrist to report sightings! Last week I

see she appeared in two different places on the same night, in Noachis and on Olympus! Opposite sides of the world!'

'I don't see that that proves anything,' Sax said stubbornly. 'They say the same sort of thing about you, and I see you're still alive.'

Coyote shook his head violently. 'No. I am the exception that proves the rule. Anyone else, when they are reported in two places at once, that means they are dead. A sure sign.' He made a stop thrust to forestall Sax's next remark, shouted, 'She's dead! Face it! She died in the attack on Sabishii! Those UNTA storm troopers caught her and Iwao and Gene and Rya and all the rest of them, and they took them to some room and sucked the air or pulled the trigger. That's what happens! Do you think it never happens? Do you think that secret police haven't killed dissidents and then disappeared the bodies so that no one ever finds out? It happens! Fuck yes it happens, even on your precious Mars it happens, yes and more than once! You know it's true! It happened. That's how people are. They'll do anything, they'll kill people and figure they're just earning their keep or feeding their children or making the world safe. And that's what happened. They killed Hiroko and all the rest of them too.'

Nirgal and Sax stared. Coyote was quivering and looked as if he was going to stab the wall.

Sax cleared his throat. 'Desmond – what makes you so sure?'

'Because I looked! I looked. I looked like no one else could look. She's not in any of her places. She's not anywhere. She didn't get out. No one has really seen her since Sabishii. That's why you've never heard from her. She's not so inhuman she would let us go all this time without ever letting us know.'

'But I saw her,' Sax insisted.

'In a storm, you said. In a bit of trouble, I suppose. Saw her for a little while, just long enough to get you out of trouble. Then gone for good.'

Sax blinked.

Coyote laughed harshly. 'So I thought. No, that's fine. Dream about her all you want. Just don't get that confused with reality. Hiroko is dead.'

Nirgal looked back and forth between the two silent men.

420

'I've looked for her too,' he said. And then, seeing the blasted look on Sax's face: 'Anything's possible.'

Coyote shook his head. He went back into the kitchen, muttering to himself. Sax looked at Nirgal, stared right through him.

'Maybe I'll try looking for her again,' Nirgal told him.

Sax nodded.

'Beats farming,' Coyote said from the kitchen.

Recently Harry Whitebook had found a method for increasing animal tolerance to CO_2, by introducing into mammals a gene which coded for certain characteristics of crocodile hemoglobin. Crocodiles could hold their breath for a very long time underwater, and the CO_2 that should have built up in their blood actually dissolved there into bicarbonate ions, bound to amino acids in the hemoglobin, in a complex that caused the hemoglobin to release oxygen molecules. High CO_2 tolerance was thus combined with increased oxygenation efficiency, a very elegant adaptation, and as it turned out fairly easy (once Whitebook showed the way) to introduce into mammals by utilizing the latest trait transcription technology: designed strands of the DNA repair enzyme photolyase were assembled, and these would patch the descriptions for the trait into the genome during the gerontological treatments, changing slightly the hemoglobin properties of the subject.

Sax was one of the first people to have this trait administered to him. He liked the idea because it would obviate the need for a facemask in the outdoors, and he was spending a lot of his time outside. Carbon dioxide levels in the atmosphere were still at about 40 millibars of the 500 total at sea level, the rest consisting of 260 millibars nitrogen, 170 millibars oxygen, and 30 of miscellaneous noble gases. So there was still too much CO_2 for humans to tolerate without filter masks. But after trait transcription he could walk free in the air, observing the wide array of animals with similar trait transcriptions already out there. All of them monsters together, settling into their ecological niches, in a very confusing flux of surges, die-offs, invasions and retreats – everything vainly seeking a balance that could not, given the changing climate, exist. No different from the way life on Earth had ever been, in other words; but here all happening at a much faster rate, pushed by the human-driven changes, modifications, introductions, transcriptions, translations – the interventions that worked, the interventions that backfired – the effects unintended, unforeseen, unnoticed – to the point at which many thoughtful scientists were giving up any pretence of control. 'Let happen what may,' as Spencer would say when he was in his cups. This offended Michel's sense of meaning, but there was nothing to be done about that, except to alter Michel's sense of what was meaningful. Contingency, the flux of life: in a word, evolution. From the Latin, meaning the unrolling of a book. And not directed evolution either, not by a long shot. Influenced evolution perhaps, accelerated evolution certainly (in some aspects, anyway). But not managed, nor directed. They didn't know what they were doing. It took some getting used to.

So Sax wandered around on Da Vinci Peninsula, a rectangular chunk of land surrounding the round rim hill of Da Vinci Crater, and bounded by the Simud, Shalbatana, and Ravi fjords, all of which debouched onto the southern end of Chryse Gulf. Two islands, Copernicus and Galileo, lay to the west, in the mouths of the Ares and Tiu fjords. A very rich braiding of sea and land, perfect for the burgeoning of life – the Da Vinci lab techs could not have chosen a better site, although Sax was quite sure they had had no sense at all of their surroundings when they chose the crater for the underground's hidden aerospace labs. The crater had had a thick rim and was located a good distance from Burroughs and Sabishii, and that had been that. Stumbled into paradise. More than a lifetime's observations to be made, without ever leaving home.

Hydrology, invasion biology, areology, ecology, materials science, particle physics, cosmology: all these fields interested Sax extremely, but most of his daily work in these years concerned the weather. Da Vinci Peninsula got a lot of dramatic weather; wet storms swept south down the gulf, dry katabatic winds dropped off the southern highland and out of the fjord canyons, initiating big northward waves at sea. Because they were so close to the equator, the perihelion/ aphelion cycle affected them much more than the ordinary inclination seasons. Aphelion brought cold weather 20° north of the equator at least, while perihelion cooked the equator as much as the south. In the Januaries and Februaries, sun-warmed southern air lofted into the stratosphere, turned east at the tropopause and joined the jetstreams in their circum-navigations. The jetstreams were difluent around the Tharsis

424

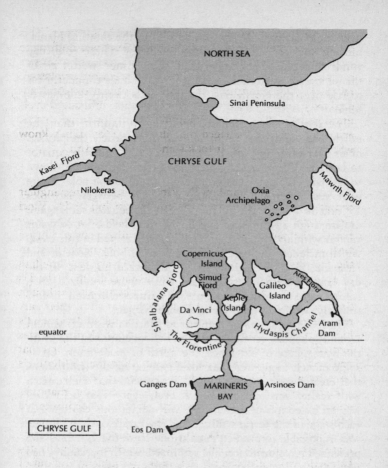

CHRYSE GULF

bulge; the southern stream carried moisture from Amazonis Bay, and dumped it on Daedalia and Icaria, sometimes even on the western wall of the Argyre Basin mountains, where glaciers were forming. The northern jetstream ran over the Tempe/Mareotis highlands, then blew over the North Sea, picking up the moisture for storm after storm. North of that, over the polar cap, air cooled and fell on the rotating planet, causing surface winds from the northeast. These cold, dry winds sometimes shot underneath the warmer, wetter air of the temperate westerlies, causing fronts of huge thunderheads to rise over the North Sea, thunderheads twenty kilometres high.

The southern hemisphere, being more uniform than the north, had winds that followed even more clearly the physics of air over a rotating sphere: southeast trades from the equator to latitude 30°; prevailing westerlies from latitude 30° down to latitude 60°; polar easterlies from there to the pole. There were vast deserts in the south, especially between latitudes 15° and 30°, where the air that rose at the equator sank again, causing high air pressure and hot air that held a lot of water vapour without condensing; it hardly ever rained in this band, which included the hyperarid provinces of Solis, Noachis and Hesperia. In these regions the winds picked up dust off the dry land, and the dust storms, while more localized than before, were also thicker, as Sax had witnessed himself, unfortunately, while up on Tyrrhena with Nirgal.

Those were the major patterns in Martian weather: violent around aphelion, gentle during the helionequinoxes; the south the hemisphere of extremes, the north of moderation. Or so some models suggested. Sax liked generating the simulations that created such models, but he was aware that their match with reality was approximate at best; every year on record was an exception of some kind, with conditions changing at each stage of the terraforming. And the future of their climate was impossible to predict, even if one froze the variables and pretended terraformation had stabilized, which it certainly had not. Over and over Sax watched a thousand years of weather, altering variables in the models, and every time a completely different millennium flitted past. Fascinating. The light gravity and the resulting scale height of the atmosphere, the vast vertical relief of the surface, the presence of the North Sea that might or might not ice over, the thickening air, the perihelion/aphelion cycle, which was an eccentricity that was slowly precessing through the inclination seasons; these had predictable effects, perhaps, but in combination they made Martian weather a very hard thing to understand, and the more he watched, the less Sax felt they knew. But it was fascinating, and he could watch the iterations play out all day long.

Or else just sit out on Simshal Point, watching clouds flow across hyacinth skies. Kasei Fjord, off to the northwest, was a wind tunnel for the strongest katabatic blows on the planet, winds pouring out of it onto Chryse Gulf at speeds that occasionally reached five hundred kilometres an hour. When these howlers struck Sax could see the cinnamon clouds marking them, over the horizon to the north. Ten or twelve hours later big swells would roll in from the north, and rise up and hammer the seacliffs, fifty-metre-high wedges of water blasting to spray against the rock, until the air all over the peninsula was a thick white mist. It was dangerous to be at sea during a howler, as he had found out once while sailing the coastal waters of the southern gulf, in a little catamaran he had learned to operate.

Nicer by far to observe storms from the seacliffs. No howler today; just a steady stiff wind, and the distant black broom of a squall on the water north of Copernicus, and the heat of sun on skin. Global average temperature changed every year, up and down, mostly up. With time as the horizontal axis, a rising mountain range. The Year-Without-Summer, now an old chasm; actually it had lasted three years, but people would not disturb such a name for a mere fact. Three-Unusually-Cold-Years – no. It didn't have what people wanted, some kind of compression of the truth, to create a strong trace in the memory, perhaps. Symbolic thinking; people needed things thrown together. Sax knew this because he spent a lot of time in Sabishii visiting Michel and Maya. People loved drama. Maya more than most, perhaps, but it served to show. Limit case demonstration of the norm. He worried about her effect on Michel. Michel seemed not to be enjoying life. Nostalgia, from the Greek *nostos*, 'a return home', and *algos*, 'pain'. Pain of the return home. A very accurate description; despite their blurs, words could sometimes be so exact. It was a paradox until you looked into how the brain worked, then it became less surprising. A model of the mind's interaction with physical reality, blurred at the edges. Even science had to admit it. Not that this meant giving up trying to explain things!

'Come out and do some field studies with me,' he would urge Michel.

'Soon.'

'Concentrate on the moment,' Sax suggested. 'Each moment is its own reality. It has its particular thisness. You can't predict, but you can explain. Or try. If you are observant, and lucky, you can say, *this* is why *this* is happening! It's very interesting!'

'Sax. When did you become such a poet?'

Sax did not know how to answer that. Michel was still stuffed with his immense nostalgia. Finally Sax said, 'Make time to come out into the field.'

In the mild winters when the winds were gentle, Sax took sailing trips around the south end of Chryse Gulf. The golden gulf. The rest of the year he stayed on the peninsula, and went out from Da Vinci Crater on foot, or in a little car for overnighters. Mostly he did meteorology, though of course he looked at everything. On the water he would sit and feel the wind in the sail as he wandered into one little convolution of the coast after another. On the land he would drive in the mornings, looking at the view until he saw a good spot. Then he would stop the car and go outside.

Trousers, shirt, windbreaker, hiking boots, his old hat; all he needed on this day of M-year 65. A fact that never ceased to amaze him. Usually it was in the 280s – bracing, but he liked it. Global averages were bouncing around the mid-270s. A good average, he felt – above freezing – sending a thermal pulse down into the permafrost. On its own this pulse would melt the permafrost in about ten thousand years. But of course it was not on its own.

He wandered over tundra moss and samphire, kedge and grass. Life on Mars. An odd business. Life anywhere, really. Not at all obvious why it should appear. This was something Sax had been thinking about recently. Why was there increasing order in any part of the cosmos, when one might expect nothing but entropy everywhere? This puzzled him greatly. He had been intrigued when Spencer had offered an offhand explanation, over beer one night on the Odessa corniche – in an expanding universe, Spencer had said, order was not really order, but merely the difference between the actual entropy exhibited and the maximum entropy possible. This difference was what humans perceived as order. Sax had been surprised to hear such an interesting cosmological notion from Spencer, but Spencer was a surprising man. Although he drank too much alcohol.

Lying on the grass looking at tundra flowers, one couldn't help thinking about life. In the sunlight the little flowers stood on their stems glowing with their anthracyins, dense with colour. Ideograms of order. They did not look like a mere difference in entropic levels. Such a fine texture to a flower petal; drenched in light, it was almost as if it were visible molecule by molecule: there a white molecule, there lavender, there clematis blue. These pointillist dots were not molecules, of course, which were well below visible resolution. And even if molecules had been visible, the ultimate building blocks of the petal were so much smaller than that that they were hard to imagine – finer than one's conceptual resolution, one might say. Although recently the theory group at Da Vinci had begun buzzing about developments in superstring theory and quantum gravity they were making; it had even got to the point of testable predictions, which historically had been string theory's great weakness. Intrigued by this reconnection with experiment, Sax had recently started trying to understand what they were doing. It meant forgoing seacliffs for seminar rooms, but in the rainy seasons he had done it, sitting in on the group's afternoon meetings, listening to the presentations and the discussions afterward, studying the scrawled math on the screens and spending his mornings working on Riemann surfaces, Lie algebras, Euler numbers, the topologies of compact six-dimensional spaces, differential geometries, Grassmannian variables, Vlad's emergence operators, and all the rest of the mathematics necessary to follow what the current generation was talking about.

Some of this math concerning superstrings he had looked into before. The theory had existed for almost two centuries now, but it had been proposed speculatively long before there was either the math or the experimental ability to investigate it properly. The theory described the smallest particles of spacetime not as geometrical points but as ultramicroscopic loops, vibrating in ten dimensions, six of which were compactified around the loops, making them somewhat exotic mathematical objects. The space they vibrated in had been quantized by twenty-first century theorists, into loop patterns called spin networks, in which lines of force in the finest grain of the gravitational field acted somewhat like the lines of magnetic force around a magnet, allowing the strings to vibrate only in certain harmonics. These supersymmetrical strings, vibrating harmonically in ten-dimensional spin networks, accounted very elegantly and plausibly for the various forces and particles as perceived at the subatomic level, all the bosons and fermions, and their gravitational effects as well. The fully elaborated theory therefore claimed to mesh successfully quantum mechanics with gravity, which had been *the* problem in physical theory for over two centuries.

All very well; indeed, exciting. But the problem, for Sax and many other sceptics, came with the difficulty of confirming any of this beautiful math by experiment, a difficulty caused by the very, very, very small sizes of the loops and spaces being theorized. These were all in the 10^{-33} centimetre range, the so-called Planck length, and this length was so much smaller than subatomic particles that it was hard to imagine. A typical atomic nucleus was about 10^{-13} centimetre in diameter, or one millionth of a billionth of a centimetre. First Sax had tried very hard to contemplate that distance for a while; hopeless, but one had to try, one had to hold that hopelessly inconceivable smallness in the mind for a moment. And then remember that in string theory they were talking about a distance twenty magnitudes smaller still – about objects one thousandth of one billionth of one billionth the size of an atomic nucleus! Sax struggled for ratio; a string, then, was to the size of an atom, as an atom was to the size of . . . the solar system. A ratio which rationality itself could scarcely comprehend.

Worse yet, it was too small to detect experimentally. This to Sax was the crux of the problem. Physicists had been managing experiments in accelerators at energy levels on the order of 100 GeV, or one hundred times the mass-energy of a proton. From these experiments they had worked up, with great effort, over many years, the so-called revised standard model of particle physics. The revised standard model explained a lot, it was really an amazing achievement, and it made predictions that could be proved or disproved by lab experiment or cosmological observations, predictions that were so varied and had been so well-fulfilled that physicists could speak with confidence about much of what had gone on in the history of the universe since the Big Bang, going as far back as the first millionth of a second of time.

String theorists, however, wanted to make a fantastic leap beyond the revised standard model, to the Planck distance which was the smallest realm possible, the minimum quantum movement, which could not be decreased without contradicting the Pauli exclusion principle. It made sense, in a way, to think about that minimum size of things; but actually seeing events at this scale would take experimental energy levels of at least 10^{19} GeV, and they could not create those. No accelerator would ever come close. The heart of a supernova would be more like it. No. A great divide, like a vast chasm or desert, separated them from the Planck realm. It was a level of reality fated to remain unknown to them in any physical sense.

Or so sceptics maintained. But those interested in the theory had never been dissuaded from studying it. They searched for indirect confirmation of the theory at the subatomic level, which from this perspective now seemed gigantic, and from cosmology. Anomalies in phenomena that the revised standard could not explain, might be explained by predictions made by string theory about the Planck realm. These predictions had been few, however, and the predicted phenomena very difficult to see. No real clinchers had been found. But as the decades passed, a few string enthusiasts had always continued to explore new mathematical structures, which might reveal more ramifications of the theory, might predict more detectable indirect results. This was all they could do; and it was a very chancy road for physics to take, Sax felt. He believed in the experimental testing of theories with all his heart. If it couldn't be tested, it remained math only, and its beauty was irrelevant; there were lots of bizarrely beautiful, exotic fields of mathematics. But if they weren't modelling the phenomenal world, Sax wasn't interested.

Now, however, after all the decades of work, they were beginning to make progress in ways that Sax found interesting. At the new supercollider in Rutherford Crater's rim, they had found the second Z particle that string theory had long predicted would be there. And a magnetic monopole detector, orbiting the sun out of the plane of the ecliptic, had captured a trace of what looked to be a fractionally-charged, unconfined particle with a mass as big as a bacterium – a very rare glimpse of a 'weakly interacting massive particle', or WIMP. String theory had predicted WIMPs would be out there, while the revised standard did not call for them. That was thought-provoking, because the shapes of galaxies showed that they had gravitational masses ten times as large as their visible light revealed; if the dark matter could be explained satisfactorily as weakly interacting massive particles, Sax thought, then the theory responsible would have to be called very interesting indeed.

Interesting in a different way was the fact that one of the leading theorists in this new stage of development was working right there in Da Vinci, part of the impressive group Sax was sitting in on. Her name was Bao Shuyo. She had been born and raised in Dorsa Brevia, her ancestry Japanese and Polynesian. She was small for one of the young natives, though still half a metre taller than Sax. Black hair, dark skin, Pacific features, very regular and somewhat plain. She was shy with Sax, shy with everyone; she even sometimes stuttered, which Sax found extremely endearing. But when she stood up in the seminar room to give a presentation, she became quite firm in hand if not in voice, writing her equations and notes on the screen very quickly, as if doing speed calligraphy. Everyone in these moments attended to her very closely, in effect mesmerized; she had been working at Da Vinci for a year now, and everyone there smart enough to recognize such a thing knew that they were watching one of the pantheon at work, discovering reality right there before their eyes.

The other young turks would interrupt her to ask questions, of course – there were many good minds in that group – and if they were lucky, off they all would all go together, mathematically modelling gravitons and gravitinos, dark matter and shadow matter – all personality and indeed all persons forgotten. Very productive, exciting sessions; and clearly Bao was the driving force in them, the one they relied on, the one they had to reckon with.

It was a bit disconcerting. Sax had met women in math and physics departments before, but this was the only female mathematical genius he had ever even heard of, in all the long history of mathematical advancement, which, now that he thought of it, had been a weirdly male affair. Was there anything in life as male as mathematics had been? And why was that?

Disconcerting in a different way was the fact that areas of Bao's work were based on the unpublished papers of a Thai mathematician of the previous century, an unstable young man named Samui, who had lived in Bangkok brothels and committed suicide at the age of twenty-three, leaving behind several 'last problems' in the manner of Fermat, and insisting to the end that all of his math had been dictated to him by telepathic aliens. Bao had ignored all that and explained some of Samui's more obscure innovations, and then used them to develop a group of expressions called advanced Rovelli-Smolin operators, which allowed her to establish a system of spin networks that meshed with superstrings very beautifully. In effect this was the complete uniting of quantum mechanics and gravity at last, the great problem solved – if it were true. And true or not, it had been powerful enough to allow Bao to make several specific predictions in the larger realms of the atom and the cosmos; and some of these had since been confirmed.

So now she was the queen of physics – the first queen of physics – and experimentalists in labs all over were online to Da Vinci, anxious to have more suggestions from her. The afternoon sessions in the seminar room were invested with a palpable sense of tension and excitement; Max Schnell would start the meeting, and at some point call on Bao; and she would stand and go to the screen at the front of the room, plain, graceful, demure, firm, pen flying over the screen as she gave them a way to calculate precisely the neutrino mass, or described very specifically the ways strings vibrated to form the different quarks, or quantized space so that gravitinos were divided into three families, and so on; and her colleagues and friends, perhaps twenty men and one other woman, would

433

interrupt to ask questions, or add equations that explained side-issues, or tell the rest of them about the latest results from Geneva or Palo Alto or Rutherford; and during that hour, they all knew they were at the centre of the world.

And in labs on Earth and Mars and in the asteroid belt, following her work, unusual gravity waves were noted, in very difficult, delicate experiments; particular geometric patterns were revealed in the fine fluctuations in the cosmic background radiation; dark matter WIMPs and shadow matter WISPs were being sought out; the various families of leptons and fermions and leptoquarks were explained; galactic clumping in the first inflation was provisionally solved; and so on. It seemed as if physics might be on the brink of the Final Theory at last. Or at least in the midst of the Next Big Step.

Given the significance of what Bao was doing, Sax felt shy about speaking to her. He did not want to waste her time on trivial things. But one afternoon at a kava party, out on one of the arc balconies overlooking Da Vinci's crater lake, she approached him – even more shy and stumbling than he was – so much so that he was forced into the very unusual position of trying to put someone else at ease, finishing sentences for her and the like. He did that as best he could, and they stumbled along, talking about his old Russell diagrams for gravitinos, useless now he would have thought, though she said they still helped her to see gravitational action. And then when he asked a question about that day's seminar, she was much more relaxed. Yes, clearly that was the way to put her at ease; he should have thought of it immediately. It was what he liked himself.

After that, they got in the habit of talking from time to time. He always had to work to draw her out, but it was interesting work. And when the dry season came, in the autumn helionequinox, and he started going out sailing again from the little harbour Alpha, he asked her haltingly if she would like to join him, and they stuttered their way through a deeply awkward interaction, which resulted in her going out with him the next nice day, sailing in one of the lab's many little catamarans.

When day sailing Sax stayed in the little bay called the Florentine, southeast of the peninsula, where Ravi Fjord widened but before it became Hydroates Bay. This was where Sax had learned to sail, and where he still felt best acquainted with the winds and currents. On longer trips he had explored the delta of fjords and bays at the bottom end of the Marineris system, and three or four times he had sailed up the eastern side of the Chryse Gulf, all the way to Mawrth Fjord and along the Sinai Peninsula.

On this special day, however, he confined himself to the Florentine. The wind was from the south, and Sax tacked down into it, enlisting Bao's help at every change of tack. Neither of them said much. Finally, to get things started, Sax was forced to ask about physics. They talked about the ways in which strings constituted the very fabric of spacetime itself, rather than being replacements for points in some absolute abstract grid.

Thinking it over, Sax said, 'Do you ever worry that work on a realm so far beyond the reach of experiment will turn out to be a kind of house of cards – knocked over by some simple discrepancy in the math, or some later, different theory that does the job better, or is more confirmable?'

'No,' Bao said. 'Something so beautiful as this has to be true.'

'Hmm,' Sax said, glancing at her. 'I must admit I'd rather have something solid crop up. Something like Einstein's Mercury – a known discrepancy in the previous theory, which the new theory resolves.'

'Some people would say that the missing shadow matter fits that bill.'

'Possibly.'

She laughed. 'You need more, I can see. Perhaps some kind of thing we can do.'

'Not necessarily,' Sax said. 'Although it would be nice, of course. Convincing, I mean. If something were better understood, so that we could manipulate it better. Like the plasmas in fusion reactors.' This was an ongoing problem in another lab at Da Vinci.

'Plasmas might very well be better understood if you modelled them as having patterns imposed by spin networks.'

'Really?'

'I think so.'

She closed her eyes – as if she could see it all written down, on the inside of her eyelids. Everything in the world. Sax felt a piercing stab of envy, of – loss. He had always wanted that kind of insight; and there it was, right in the boat beside him. Genius was a strange thing to witness.

'Do you think this theory will mean the end of physics?' he asked.

'Oh no. Although we might work out the fundamentals. You know, the basic laws. That might be possible, sure. But then every level of emergence above that creates its own problems. Taneev's work only scratches the surface there. It's like chess – we might learn all the rules, but still not be able to play very well because of emergent properties. Like, you know, pieces are stronger if they're out in the centre of the board. That's not in the rules, it's a result of all the rules put together.'

'Like weather.'

'Yes. We already understand atoms better than weather. The interactions of the elements are too complex to follow.'

'There's holonomy. Study of whole systems.'

'But it's just a bunch of speculation at this point. The start of a science, if it turns out to work.'

'And so plasmas, though?'

'Those are very homogeneous. There's only a very few factors involved, so it might be amenable to spin network analysis.'

'You should talk to the fusion group about that.'

'Yes?' She looked surprised.

'Yes.'

Then a hard gust hit, and they spent a few minutes watching the boat respond, the mast sucking in sails with a bit of humming until they were reset, and running across the strengthening breeze, into the sun. Light flaked off the fine black hair gathered at the back of Bao's neck; beyond that, the seacliffs of Da Vinci. Networks, trembling at the touch of the sun – no. He could not see it, with eyes open or closed.

Cautiously he said, 'Do you ever wonder about being, you know . . . being one of the first great women mathematicians?'

She looked startled, then turned her head away. She had

thought about it, he saw. 'The atoms in a plasma move in patterns that are big fractals of the spin network patterns,' she said.

Sax nodded, asked more questions about that. It seemed possible to him that she would be able to help Da Vinci's fusion group with the problems they were having engineering a lightweight fusion apparatus. 'Have you ever done any engineering? Or physics?'

Affronted: 'I am a physicist.'

'Well, a mathematical physicist. I was thinking of the engineering side.'

'Physics is physics.'

'True.'

Only once more did he push, and this time indirectly. 'When did you first learn math?'

'My mother gave me quadratic equations at four, and all kinds of math games. She was a statistician, very keen about it all.'

'And the Dorsa Brevia schools . . .'

She shrugged. 'They were fair. Math was mostly something I did by reading, and correspondence with the department in Sabishii.'

'I see.'

And they went back to talking about the new results from CERN; about weather; about the sailboat's ability to point to within a few degrees of the wind. And then the following week she went out with him again, on one of his walks on the peninsula's seacliffs. It was a great pleasure to show her a bit of the tundra. And over time, taking him through it step by step, she managed to convince him that they were perhaps coming close to understanding what was happening at the Planck level. A truly amazing thing, he thought, to intuit this level, and then make the speculations and deductions necessary to flesh it out and understand it, creating a very complex powerful physics, for a realm that was so very small, so very far beyond the senses. Awe-inspiring, really. The fabric of reality. Although both of them agreed that just as with all earlier theories, many fundamental questions were left unanswered. It was inevitable. So that they could lie side by side in the grass in the sun, staring as deeply into the petals of a tundra flower as ever one could, and no matter what was happening at the Planck level, in the here and now the petals glowed blue in the light with a quite mysterious power to catch the eye.

Actually, lying on the grass made it clear how much the permafrost was melting. And the melt lay on a hardpan of still-frozen ground, so that the surface became saturated and boggy. When Sax stood up, his ventral side chilled instantly in the breeze. He spread his arms to the sunlight. Photon rain, vibrating across the spin networks. In many regions heat exhaust from nuclear power plants was being directed down into capillary galleries in the permafrost, he told Bao as they walked back to the rover. This was causing trouble in some wet areas, which were tending to saturate at the surface. The land melting, so to speak. Instant wetlands. A very active biome, in fact. Though the Reds objected. But most of the land that would have been affected by permafrost melt was now under the North Sea anyway; what little remained above the sea was to be treasured as swamps and marshes.

The rest of the hydrosphere was almost equally transformative of the surface. It couldn't be helped; water was a very effective carver of rock, hard though it was to believe when watching a gossamer waterfall drift down a seacliff, turning to white mist long before it hit the ocean. Then again there was the sight of the massive giant howler waves, battering the cliffs so hard that the ground shook underfoot. A few million years of that and those cliffs would be significantly eroded.

'Have you seen the riverine canyons?' she asked.

'Yes, I saw Nirgal Vallis. Remarkable how satisfying it was to see water down at its bottom. So apt.'

'I didn't know there was so much tundra out here.'

Tundra was the dominant ecology for much of the southern highlands, he told her. Tundra and desert. In the tundra, fines were fixed very effectively to the ground; no wind could lift mud, nor quicksand, of which there was a good quantity, making it dangerous to travel in certain regions. But in the deserts the powerful winds ripped great quantities of dust into the sky, cooling temperatures while they darkened the day, and causing problems where they landed, as they had for Nirgal. Suddenly curious, he said, 'Have you ever met Nirgal?'

'No.'

The sand storms these days were nothing like the long-forgotten Great Storm of course, but still a factor that had to be considered. Desert pavement formed by microbacteria was one very promising solution, though it tended to fix only the top centimetre of deposits, and if the wind tore the edge of the pavement, what was underneath was then free to be borne away. Not an easy problem. Dust storms would be with them for centuries.

Still, an active hydrosphere. Meaning life everywhere.

As in Da Vinci Crater, in the labs and in the halls and in the dining rooms. Including social life. Bao's mother died in a small plane crash, and Bao as the youngest daughter had to go home and take care of things, including possession of the family home. Ultimogeniture in action, modelled on the Hopi matriarchy, he was told. Bao wasn't sure when she would be back; there was even a chance she wouldn't be. She was matter-of-fact about it: it was just something that had to be done. Withdrawn already into an internal world. Sax could only wave goodbye to her and walk back to his room, shaking his head. They would understand the fundamental laws of the universe before they had even the slightest handle on society. A particularly obdurate subject of study. He called Michel on screen and expressed something like this, and Michel said, 'It's because culture keeps progressing.'

Sax thought he could see what Michel meant – there were rapid changes in attitudes to many things. *Werteswandel*, as Bela called it, mutation of values. But they still lived in a society struggling with archaisms of all sorts. Primates band-ing into tribes, guarding a territory, praying to a god like a cartoon parent . . . 'Sometimes I don't think there's been any progress at all,' he said, feeling strangely disconsolate.

'But Sax,' Michel protested, 'right here on Mars we have seen both patriarchy and property brought to an end. It's one of the greatest achievements in human history.'

'If true.'

'Don't you think women have as much power as men now?'

'As far as I can tell.'

'Perhaps even more, when it comes to reproduction.'

'That would make sense.'

'And the land is in the shared stewardship of everyone. We still own personal items as property, but land as property has never happened here. That's a new social reality, we struggle with it every day.'

So they did. And Sax remembered how bitter the conflicts had been in the old days, when property and capital had been the order of the day. Yes, perhaps it was true: patriarchy and property were in the process of being dismantled. At least on Mars, at least for now. As with string theory, it might take a long time to work it into any proper state. After all, Sax himself, who had no prejudices whatsoever, had been amazed to see a woman mathematician at work. Or, to be more precise, a woman genius. By whom he had been promptly hypnotized, so to speak, along with every other man in the theory group – to the point of being rendered quite distraught by her departure. Uneasily he said, 'On Earth people seem to be fighting just as much as before.'

Even Michel had to admit it. 'Population pressures,' he said, trying to wave them away. 'There are too many people down there, and more all the time. You saw what it was like during our visit. As long as Earth is in that situation, Mars is under threat. And so we fight up here too.'

Sax took the point. In a way it was comforting; human behaviour not as irreducibly evil or stupid, but as responding, semi-rationally, to a given historical situation, a danger. Seizing what one could, with the notion that there might not be enough for all; doing everything possible to protect one's offspring; which of course endangered all offspring, by the aggregate of individual selfish actions. But at least it could be called an attempt at reason, a first approximation.

'It's not as bad as it was, anyway,' Michel was saying. 'Even on Earth people are having far fewer children. And they're reorganizing into collectives pretty well, considering the flood and all the trouble that preceded it. A lot of new social movements down there, a lot of them inspired by what we're doing here. And by what Nirgal does. They're still watching him and listening to him, even when he doesn't speak. What he said during our visit there is still having a big effect.'

'I believe it.'

'Well, there you are! It's getting better, you have to admit it. And when the longevity treatments stop working, there will come a balance of births and deaths.'

'We'll hit that time soon,' Sax predicted glumly.

'Why do you say so?'

'Signs of it cropping up. People dying from one thing or other. Senescence is not a simple matter. Staying alive when senescence should have kicked in – it's a wonder we've done as much as we have. There's probably a purpose in senescence. Avoiding overpopulation, perhaps. Making room for new genetic material.'

'That bodes poorly for us.'

'We're already over two hundred per cent the old average lifetime.'

'Granted, but even so. One doesn't want it to end just because of that.'

'No. But we have to focus on the moment. Speaking of which, why don't you come out into the field with me? I'll be as upbeat as you want out there. It's *very* interesting.'

'I'll try to free up some time. I've got a lot of clients.'

'You've got a lot of free time. You'll see.'

At this particular moment, the sun was high. Rounded white clouds were piling up in the air overhead, forming great masses that would never come again, though at the moment they were as solid as marble, and darkening at their bottoms. Cumulonimbus. He was standing on Da Vinci Peninsula's western cliff again, looking across Shalbatana Fjord to the cliff edging the east side of Lunae Planum. Behind him rose the flat-topped hill that was the rim of Da Vinci Crater. Home base. He had lived there a long time now. These days their co-op was making many of the satellites being put up into orbit, and the boosters as well, in collaboration with Spencer's lab in Odessa, and a great number of other places. A Mondragon-style co-operative, operating the ring of labs and homes in the rim, and the fields and lake filling the crater floor. Some of them chafed at restrictions imposed by the courts on projects they had in mind, involving new power plants that would put out too much heat. In the last few years the GEC had been issuing K rations, as they were called, giving communities the right to add some fraction of a degree Kelvin to the global warming. Some Red communities were doing their best to get assigned K rations and then not use them. This action, along with ongoing incidences of ecotage, kept the global temperature from rising very fast no matter what other communities did. Or so the other communities argued. But the ecocourts were still parsimonious with the K rations. Cases were judged by a provincial ecocourt, then the judgment was approved by the GEC, and that was it: no appeals, unless you could get a petition signed by fifty other communities, and even then the appeal was only dropped into the morass of the global legislature, where its fate was up to the undisciplined crowd in the duma.

Slow progress. Just as well. With the global average temperatures above freezing, Sax was content. Without the constraint of the GEC, things could easily get too warm. No, he was in no further hurry. He had become an advocate of stabilization.

Now, out in the sun of a perihelion day, it was an invigorating 281° K, and he was walking along the seacliff edge of Da Vinci, looking at alpine flowers in the cracks of the rubble, then past them to the distant quantum sheen of the fjord's sunny surface, when down the cliff-edge walking his way came a tall woman, wearing a facemask and jumper, and big hiking boots: Ann. He recognized her instantly – that stride, no doubt about it – Ann Clayborne, in the flesh.

This surprise brought a double jolt to his memory – of Hiroko, emerging out of the snow to lead him to his rover – then of Ann, in Antarctica, striding over rock to meet him – but for what?

Confused, he tried to track the thought. Double image – a fleet, single image —

Then Ann was before him and the memories were gone, forgotten like a dream.

*   *   *

He had not seen her since forcing the gerontological treatment on her in Tempe, and he was acutely uncomfortable; possibly this was a fright reaction. Of course it was unlikely she would physically assault him. Though she had before. But that was never the kind of assault that worried him. That time in Antarctica – he grasped for the elusive memory, lost it again. Memories on the edge of consciousness were certain to be lost if one made any deliberate effort to retrieve them. Why that should be was a mystery. He didn't know what to say.

'Are you immune to carbon dioxide now?' she asked through her facemask.

He explained about the new hemoglobin treatment, struggling for each word, in the way he had after his stroke. Halfway through his explanation, she laughed out loud. 'Crocodile blood now, eh?'

'Yes,' he said, guessing her thought. 'Crocodile blood, rat mind.'

'A hundred rats.'

'Yes. Special rats,' he said, striving for accuracy. Myths after all had their own rigorous logic, as Lévi-Strauss had shown. They had been genius rats, he wanted to say, a hundred of them and geniuses every one. Even his miserable graduate students had had to admit that.

'Minds altered,' she said, following his drift.

'Yes.'

'So, after your brain damage, altered twice,' she noted.

'That's right.' Depressing when you thought of it that way. Those rats were far from home. 'Plasticity enhancement. Did you . . .'

'No. I did not.'

So it was still the same old Ann. He had been hoping she would try the drugs on her own recognizance. See the light. But no. Although in fact the woman before him did not look like the same Ann, not exactly. The look in her eye; he had got used to a look from her that seemed a certain signal of hatred, ever since their arguments on the *Ares*, and perhaps before. He had had time to get used to it. Or at least to learn it.

Now, with a facemask on, and a different expression around her eyes, it was almost like a different face. She was watching him closely, but the skin around the eyes was no longer so knotted. Wrinkled, she and he were both maximally wrinkled, but the pattern of wrinkles was that of a relaxed musculature. It seemed possible the mask even hid a small smile. He didn't know what to make of it.

'You gave me the gerontological treatment,' she said.

'Yes.'

Should he say he was sorry if he wasn't? Tongue-tied, lock-jawed, he stared at her like a bird transfixed by a snake, hoping for some sign that it was all right, that he had done the right thing.

She gestured suddenly at their surroundings. 'What are you trying to do now?'

He struggled to understand her meaning, which seemed to him as gnomic as a koan. 'I'm out looking,' he said. He couldn't think what to say. Language, all those beautiful precious words, had suddenly scattered away, like a flock of startled birds. All out of reach. That kind of meaning gone. Just two animals, standing there in the sun. Look, look, look!

She was no longer smiling, if she had been. Neither was she looking daggers at him. A more evaluative look, as if he were a rock. A rock; with Ann that surely indicated progress.

But then she turned and walked away, down the seacliff toward the little seaport at Zed.

Sax returned to Da Vinci Crater feeling mildly stunned. Back inside they were having their annual Russian Roulette Party, in which they selected the year's representatives to the global legislature, and also the various co-op posts. After the ritual of names from a hat, they thanked the people who had done these jobs for the previous year, consoled those to whom the lot had fallen this year, and, for most of them, celebrated once again having been passed over.

The random selection method for Da Vinci's administrative jobs had been adapted because it was the only way to get people to do them. Ironically, after all their efforts to give every citizen the fullest measure of self-management, the Da Vinci techs had turned out to be allergic to the work involved. They only wanted to do their research. 'We should give the administration entirely to AIs,' Kouta Arai was saying, as he did every year, between sips from a foaming stein of beer. Aonia, last year's representative to the duma, was saying to this year's selection, 'You go to Mangala and sit around arguing, and the staff does what work there is. Most of it has been drained off to the council or the courts or the parties. It's Free Mars apparatchiks who are really running this planet. But it's a really pretty town, nice sailing in the bay, and iceboating in the winter.'

Sax wandered away. Someone was complaining about the many new harbour towns springing up in the south gulf, too near for comfort. Politics in its most common form: complaint. No one wanted to do it but everyone was happy to complain about it. This kind of talk would go on for about half an hour, and then they would cycle back to talking about work. There was one group doing that already, Sax could tell by the tone of their voices; he wandered over, and found they were talking about fusion. Sax stopped: it appeared they were excited by recent developments in their lab in the quest for a pulsed fusion propulsion engine. Continuous fusion had been achieved decades before, but it took extremely massive tokamaks to do it, assemblages too big and heavy and expensive to be used in many situations. This lab, however, was attempting to implode

445

small pellets of fuel many times in rapid sequence, and use the fusion results to power things.

'Did Bao talk to you about this?' Sax asked.

'Why yes, before she left she was coming over to talk with us about plasma patterns, it wasn't immediately helpful, this is really macro compared to what she does, but she's so damn smart, and afterwards something she said set Yananda off on how we could seal off the implosion and still leave a space for emission afterward.'

They needed their lasers to hit the pellets on all sides at once, but there also had to be a vent for charged particles to escape. Bao had apparently been interested in the problem, and now they returned to a lively discussion of it, which they thought they had solved at last; and when someone dropped into the circle and mentioned the day's lottery results, they brushed him off. 'Ka, no politics, please.'

As Sax wandered on, half-listening to the conversations he passed, he was struck again by the apolitical nature of most scientists and technicians. There was something about politics they were allergic to, and he felt it as well, he had to admit it. Politics was irreducibly subjective and compromised, a process that went entirely against the grain of the scientific method. Was that true? These feelings and prejudices were subjective themselves. One could try to regard politics as a kind of science – a long series of experiments in communal living, say, with all the data consistently contaminated. Thus people hypothesized a system of governance, lived under it, examined how they felt about it, then changed the system and tried again. Certain constants or principles seemed to have emerged over the centuries, as they ran through their experiments and paradigms, trying successively closer approximations of systems that promoted qualities like physical welfare, individual freedom, equality, stewardship of the land, guided markets, rule of law, compassion to all. After repeated experiments it had become clear – on Mars at least – that all these sometimes contradictory goals could be best achieved in polyarchy, a complex system in which power was distributed out to a great number of institutions. In theory this network of distributed power, partly centralized and partly decentralized, created the greatest amount of individual freedom and collective good, by maximizing the amount of control that an individual had over his or her life.

Thus political science. And fine, in theory. But it followed that if they believed in the theory, people then had to devote a fair amount of time to the exercise of their power. That was self-government, by tautology; the self governed. And that took time. 'Those who value freedom must make the effort necessary to defend it,' as Tom Paine had said, a fact which Sax knew because Bela had got into the bad habit of putting up signs in the halls with such inspirational sentiments printed on them. 'Science Is Politics By Other Means', another of his signs had announced, rather cryptically.

But in Da Vinci most people did not want to spend their time that way. 'Socialism will never succeed,' Oscar Wilde had remarked (in handwriting on yet another sign), 'it takes up too many evenings.' So it did; and the solution was to make your friends take up their evenings for you. Thus the lottery method of election, a calculated risk, for one might get stuck with the job oneself someday. But usually the risk paid off, which accounted for the gaiety of this annual party; people were pouring in and out of the French doors of the commons, onto the open terraces overlooking the crater lake, talking with great animation. Even the drafted ones were beginning to cheer up again, after the solace of kavajava and alcohol, and perhaps the thought that power after all was power; it was an imposition, but the draftees could do some little things that no doubt were occurring to them even now – make trouble for rivals, do favours for people they wanted to impress, etc. So once again the system had worked; they had warm bodies filling the whole polyarchic array, the neighbourhood boards, the ag board, the water board, the architectural review board, the project review council, the economic co-ordination group, the crater council to co-ordinate all these smaller bodies, the global delegates' advisory board – all that network of small management bodies that progressive political theorists had been suggesting in one variation or another for centuries, incorporating aspects of the almost-forgotten guild socialism of Great Britain, Yugoslavian worker management, Mondragon ownership, Kerala land tenure, and so on. An experiment in synthesis. And so far it seemed to be working, in the sense that the Da Vinci techs seemed about as self-determined and happy as they had been during the *ad hoc* underground years, when everything had been done (apparently) by instinct, or, to be more precise, by the general consensus of the (much smaller) population in Da Vinci at that time.

They certainly seemed as happy; out on the terraces they were lining up at big pots of kavajava and Irish coffee, or kegs of beer, clumped in talkative groups so that the clatter of voices was like the sound of waves, as at any cocktail party: an amazing sound, those voices all together. A chorus of talk – it was a music that no one consciously listened to but Sax, as far as he could tell; but as he listened to it he suspected strongly that the sound of it, heard unconsciously, was one of the things that made people at parties so happy and gregarious. Get two hundred people together, talking loudly so that each conversation could be heard by its small group: such a music they made!

So running Da Vinci was a successful experiment, despite the fact that the citizens showed no interest in it. If they had they might have been less happy. Maybe ignoring government was a good strategy. Maybe the definition of good government was the government you could safely ignore, 'to finally get back to my own work!' as one happily buzzed ex-water board chief was just now saying. Self-government not being considered part of one's own work!

Although of course there were those people who did like the work, something about the interplay of theory and practice, the argument, the problem-solving, the collaboration with other people, the service to others as a kind of gift, the endless talk; the power. And these people stayed on to serve two terms, or three if they were allowed, and then took on some other volunteer task that was going a-begging; indeed, most of these people did more than one task at once. Bela, for instance, had claimed not to like the chairmanship of the lab of labs, but now he was going directly into the volunteer advisory group, which always had a number of spots in danger of being unfilled. Sax wandered over to him: 'Would you agree with Aonia that Free Mars is dominating global policy?'

'Oh undoubtedly, assuredly. They are simply so big. And they have packed the courts, and rigged some things their way.

448

I think they want to control all the new asteroid colonies. And to conquer Earth too, for that matter. All the politically ambitious young natives are joining the party, like bees to the flower.'

'Trying to dominate other settlements . . .'

'Yes?'

'It sounds like trouble.'

'Yes it does.'

'Have you heard about this lightweight fusion engine they're talking about?'

'Yes, a little.'

'You might look into backing that a bit more. If we could get engines like that into spaceships . . .'

'Yes? Sax?'

'Transport that fast might have the effect of cracking domination by any one party.'

'Do you think so?'

'Well, it would make it a hard situation to control.'

'Yes, I suppose so. Hmm, well, I must think about this further.'

'Yes. Science is politics by other means, remember.'

'Indeed it is! Indeed it is.' And Bela went off to the beer kegs, muttering to himself, then greeting another group as they approached him.

So spontaneously there emerged that bureaucratic class that had been the terror of so many political theorists: the experts who took control of the polity, and supposedly would never relinquish their grip. But to whom would they relinquish it? Who else wanted it? No one, as far as Sax could tell. Bela could stay on the advisory board forever if he wanted to. Expert, from the Latin *experiri*, to try. As in experiment. So it was government by the experimenters. Trying by the tryers. In effect government by the interested. So yet another kind of oligarchy. But what other choice did they have? Once you had to draft members into the governing body, then the notion of self-government as an aspect of individual liberty became somewhat paradoxical.

Hector and Sylvia, from Bao's seminar, broke into Sax's reverie and invited him to come down and hear their music group do a selection of songs from 'Maria dos Buenos Aires'. Sax agreed and followed them.

Outside the little amphitheatre, Sax stopped at a drink table and dispensed another small cup of kava. The festival spirit was growing all around them. Hector and Sylvia hurried down to get ready, glowing with anticipation. Watching them, Sax remembered his recent encounter with Ann. If only he had been able to think! Why, he had gone completely incoherent! If only he had thought to become Stephen Lindholm again, perhaps that would have helped. Where was Ann now, what was she thinking? What had she been doing? Did she only wander the face of Mars now, like a ghost, moving from one Red station to another? What were the Reds doing now, how did they live? Had they been about to bomb Da Vinci, had his chance encounter stopped a raid? No, no. There were ecoteurs still out there monkeywrenching projects, but with the legal limits on terraforming, most Reds had rejoined society somehow; it was one mainstream political strand among the rest, vigilant, quick to litigate – indeed much more interested in taking on political work than less ideological citizens – but still, and by that very tendency, normalized. Where then would Ann fit in? With whom did she associate?

Well, he could call her and ask.

But he was afraid to call, afraid to ask. Afraid to talk to her! At least by wrist. And apparently in person as well. She had not said what she thought of him giving her the treatment against her will. No thanks, no curse; nothing. What did she think? What was she thinking?

He sighed, sipped his kava. Down below they were beginning, Hector rolling out a recitative in Spanish, his voice so musical and expressive it was almost as if Sax could understand him by tone of voice alone.

Ann, Ann, Ann. This obsessive interest in someone else's thought was so uncomfortable. So much easier to concentrate on the planet, on rock and air, on biology. It was a ploy Ann herself would understand. And there was in ecopoesis something fundamentally intriguing. The birth of a world. Out of their control. Still he wondered what she made of it. Perhaps he would run into her again.

*   *   *

Meanwhile, the world. He went back out on it again. Rumpled land under the blue dome of the sky. The ordinary sky at the equator in spring changed colour day by day, it took a colour chart even to approximate the tones; some days it was a deep violet blue – clematis blue, or hyacinth blue, or lapis lazuli, or a purplish indigo. Or Prussian blue, a pigment made from ferric ferrocyanide, interestingly, as there was certainly a lot of ferric material up there. Iron blue. Slightly more purple than Himalayan skies as seen in photographs, but otherwise like the Terran skies seen at those high altitudes. And combined with the rocky, indented landscape, it did seem like a high-altitude place. Everything: the sky colour, the crumpled rock, the cold, thin air so pure and chill. Everything so high. He walked into the wind, or across the wind, or with the wind at his back, and each felt different. In his nostrils the wind was like a mild intoxicant, flooding the brain. He stepped on lichen-crusted rocks, from slab to slab, as if walking on a personal sidepavement appearing magically out of the shatter of the land, up and down, every step just a step, wandering attentive to the thisness of each moment. Moment to moment to moment, each one discrete, like Bao's loops of timespace, like the successive positions of a finch's head, the little birds Plancking from one quantum pose to the next. It appeared on close inspection that moments were not regular units but varied in duration, depending on what was happening in them. The wind dropped, no birds in sight: everything suddenly still, and oh so silent, except for the buzzing of insects; those moments could last several seconds each. Whereas when sparrows were dogfighting a crow, the moments were nearly instantaneous. Look very closely; sometimes it was a flow, sometimes the Planck-Planck-Planck of individual stillnesses.

To know. There were different ways of knowing; but none of them was quite so satisfactory, Sax decided, as the direct knowledge of the senses. Out here in the brilliant spring light, and the cold wind, he came to the edge of a cliff, and looked down onto the ultramarine plate of Simud Fjord, silvered by myriad chips of light blazing off the water. Cliffs on the other side were banded by stratification lines, some of which had become green ledges lining the basalt. Gulls, puffins, terns, guillemots, ospreys, all wheeling in the gulfs of air below him.

As he learned the different fjords, he found he had his favourites. The Florentine, directly southeast of Da Vinci, was a pretty oval of water; a walk along the low bluffs overlooking it was continuously picturesque. Thick grass grew like a mat over these bluffs; they looked like Sax's image of the Irish coast. The land's edges were softening as soil and flora began to fill in the cracks, holding to mounds that defied the angle of repose, so that one walked over pads of ground, swelling between the sharp teeth of still-bare rocks.

Clouds poured inland from the sea to the north, and the rain fell, steady deluges that soaked everything. The day after a storm like that the air steamed, the land gurgled and dripped, and every step off bare rock was a boggy squish. Heath, moor, bog. Gnarly little forests in the low grabens. A quick brown fox, seen out of the corner of the eye as it dashed behind a sierra juniper. Away from him, after something? No way to know. On business of its own. Waves striking the seacliffs bounced back outward, creating interference patterns with the incoming waves that could have come right out of a physics wave tank: so beautiful. And so strange, that the world should conform so well to mathematical formulation. The unreasonable effectiveness of math; it was at the heart of the great inexplicable.

Every sunset was different, as a result of the residual fines in the upper atmosphere. These lofted so high that they were often illuminated by the sun long after everything else was in twilight's great shadow. So Sax would sit on the western seacliff, rapt through the setting of the sun, then stay through the hour of twilight, watching the sky colours change as the sun's shadow rose up, until all the sky was black; and then sometimes there would appear noctilucent clouds, thirty kilometres above the planet, broad streaks gleaming like abalone shells.

The pewter sky of a hazy day. The florid sunset in a hard blow. The warmth of the sun on his skin, at peace in a windless late afternoon. The patterns of waves on the sea below. The feel of the wind, the look of it.

But once in an indigo twilight, under the sparkling array of fat blurry stars, he grew uneasy. 'The snowy poles of moonless Mars,' Tennyson had written. Moonless Mars. It was in this hour that Phobos had used to shoot up over the western horizon like a flare. A moment of the areophany if ever there was one. Fear and Dread. And he had completed the desatellitization himself. They could have popped any military base built on Deimos, what had he been thinking? He couldn't remember. Some kind of desire for symmetry; down, up; but symmetry was perhaps a quality prized more by mathematicians than by other people. Up. Somewhere Deimos was still orbiting the sun. 'Hmm.' He looked it up on the wrist. A lot of new colonies were starting out there: people were hollowing out asteroids, then spinning them to create a gravity effect on their insides, then moving in. New worlds.

A word caught his eye: *Pseudophobos*. He tracked back, read; informal name for an asteroid that somewhat resembled the lost moon in size and shape. 'Hmmm.' Sax tapped around and got a photo. Well, the resemblance was superficial: a triaxial ellipsoid, but weren't they all? Potato-shaped, right size, banged hard on one end, a Stickneyesque crater. Stickney; there had been a nice little settlement tucked into it. What's in a name? Say they dropped the *Pseudo*. A couple of mass drivers and AIs, some side jets . . . that peculiar moment, when Phobos had shot up over the western horizon. 'Hmmmmm,' Sax said.

The days passed, as did the seasons. He worked at field studies and meteorology. Effects of atmospheric pressure on cloud formation, meaning drives out around the peninsula, then a walk, then out with the balloons and kites. Weather balloons these days were elegant things, instrument packages less than ten grams, lofted by a bag eight metres tall, capable of rising right into the exosphere.

Sax enjoyed arranging the bag over a smooth patch of sand or grass, the top downwind from him, then sitting and holding the delicate little payload in his fingers, then flicking the toggle that shot compressed hydrogen into the balloon, and watching it fill and yank up at the sky. If he held onto the line he was almost hauled to his feet, and without gloves on the line would cut his palm, as he had quickly learned. Release it then, thump back to the sand, watch the round, red dot shimmy up through the wind, until it was a pinprick and then could no longer be seen. That happened at around a thousand metres, depending on the haze in the air; once it had happened as low as four hundred and seventy-nine metres, once as high as 1,352 metres, a very clear day indeed. After that, he would read some of the data on his wrist, sitting in the sunshine feeling as if a little piece of him was sailing up into space. Strange what made one happy.

The kites were just as nice. They were a bit more complex than the balloons, but a special pleasure during the autumn, when the trade winds blew strong and steady every day. Go out to one of the western seacliffs, take a short run into the wind, get the kite into the air; a big orange box-kite, bobbing this way and that; then as it got up into the steadier wind it stabilized, and he reeled it out, feeling the shifts in the wind as subtle quiverings in his arms. Or else he wedged a spool pole in a crack, and set the resistance, and watched the kite soar up and away. The line was nearly invisible. When the spool ran out the line hummed, and if he held it between his fingers, the wind's fluctuations were communicated to him as a kind of music. The kite would stay up for weeks at a time, out of sight or, if he kept it low enough, just within sight, a tiny flaw in the sky. Transmitting data all the while. A square object was visible at a greater distance than a round object of the same area. The mind was a funny animal.

Michel called up to talk about nothing in particular. This was the hardest kind of conversation of all for Sax. The image of Michel would look down and to the right, and it would be very clear as he spoke that his mind was elsewhere, that he was unhappy, that Sax needed somehow to take the lead.

'Come visit and go for a walk with me,' Sax said again. 'I really think you should.' How could one emphasize that? 'I *really* think you should.' Throw things together. 'Da Vinci is like the west coast of Ireland. The end of Europe, all green seacliff over a big plate of water.'

454

Michel nodded uncertainly.

Then a couple of weeks later there he was, walking down a hall in Da Vinci. 'I wouldn't mind seeing the end of Europe.'

'Good man.'

So they went out together on a day trip. Sax drove him west to the Shalbatana cliffs, then they got out and walked north, toward Simshal Point. Such a pleasure to have his old friend with him in this beautiful place. Seeing any of the First Hundred was a welcome break in his routine, a rare event that he treasured. The weeks would pass in their comfortable round, and then suddenly one of the old family would appear, and it was like a homecoming without the home, making him think he perhaps ought to move to Sabishii or Odessa someday, so that he could experience such a wonderful feeling more often.

And no one's company pleased him more than Michel's. Although on this day Michel wandered behind, distracted, seemingly troubled. Sax observed this, and wondered what he could do to help. Michel had given him so much help in the long months of his return to speech – had taught him to think again, had taught him to see everything differently. It would be nice if he could do something to repay such a gift, even partially.

Well, it would only happen if he said something. So after they stopped, and Sax got out the kite and assembled it, he handed the spool to Michel.

'Here,' he said. 'I'll hold the kite ready. You run it up. That way, into the wind.' And he held the kite as Michel walked across the grassy mounds, until the line was taut and Sax let the kite go as Michel started running, and off it went, up up up.

Michel came back grinning. 'Here, touch the line – you can feel the wind.'

'Ah,' Sax said. 'So you can.' And the nearly-invisible line thrummed against his fingers.

They sat down and opened Sax's wicker basket, and took out the picnic lunch he had packed. Michel became quiet once again.

'Something is troubling you?' Sax ventured as they ate.

Michel waved a chunk of bread, swallowed. 'I think I want to go back to Provence.'

'For good?' Sax said, shocked.

Michel frowned. 'Not necessarily. But for a visit. I was only just beginning to enjoy my last visit there when we had to leave.'

'It's heavy on Earth.'

'True. But I found the adjustment surprisingly easy.'

'Hmm.' Sax had not liked the return to Terran gravity. Certainly evolution had adapted their bodies to it, and it was true that living in .38 g caused an array of medical problems. But he was used to the feel of Martian g now, to the point at which he never noticed it; and if he did, it felt good.

'Without Maya?' he said.

'I suppose it would have to be. She doesn't want to go. She says she will someday, but it's always later, later. She's working for the credit co-op bank in Sabishii, and thinks she's indispensable. Well, that's not fair. She just doesn't want to miss any of it.'

'Can you not make a kind of Provence where you live? Plant an olive grove?'

'It's not the same.'

'No, but . . .'

Sax didn't know what to say. He felt no nostalgia for Earth. As for living with Maya, he could no more imagine that than he could imagine living in a damaged erratic centrifuge. The effect would be much the same. Thus perhaps Michel's desire for solid ground, for the touch of the Earth.

'You should go,' Sax said. 'But wait just a little longer. If they get these pulsed fusion engines on spaceships, then you could be there fairly soon.'

'But that might cause real problems with Earth's gravity. I think you need the months of the trip to get prepared for it.'

Sax nodded. 'What you would need is a kind of exoskeleton. Inside it you'd feel somewhat supported, and therefore as if in a lighter g, perhaps. Those new birdsuits I've heard of, they must have the capacity to stiffen to something like an exoskeleton, or you'd never be able to hold the wings in position.'

'An evershifting carapace of carbon,' Michel said with a smile. 'A flowing shell.'

'Yes. You might be able to wear something like that to walk around in. It wouldn't be so bad.'

'So first we move to Mars, you're saying, where we have to wear walkers for a hundred years – then when we have changed everything, to the extent that we can sit out here in the sun only slightly freezing, then we move back to Earth, where we have to wear walkers again for another hundred years.'

'Or forever after,' Sax said. 'That's correct.'

Michel laughed. 'Well, maybe I will go then. When it gets like that.' He shook his head. 'Someday we'll be able to do everything we want, eh?'

The sun beat down on them. The wind rustled over the tips of the grass. Each blade a green stroke of light. Michel talked about Maya for a while, first complaining, then making allowances, then enumerating her good qualities, the qualities that made her indispensable, the source of all excitement in life. Sax nodded dutifully at every declaration, no matter how much they contradicted the ones that had come before. It was like listening to an addict, he imagined; but this was the way people were; and he was not so far from such contradictions himself.

After a silence had stretched out, Sax said, 'How do you think Ann sees this kind of landscape now?'

Michel shrugged. 'I don't know. I haven't seen her for years.'

'She didn't take the brain plasticity treatment.'

'No. She's stubborn, eh? She wants to stay herself. But in this world, I'm afraid . . .'

Sax nodded. If you saw all the signs of life in the landscape as contaminations, as a horrible mould encrusting the pure beauty of the mineral world, then even the oxygen blue of the sky would be implicated. It would drive one mad. Even Michel thought so: 'I'm afraid she will never be sane, not really.'

'I know.'

On the other hand, who were they to say? Was Michel insane because he was obsessively concerned with a region on another planet, or in love with a very difficult person? Was

457

Sax insane because he could no longer speak well, and had trouble with various mental operations as the result of a stroke and an experimental cure? He didn't think so, in either case. But he did believe quite firmly that he had been rescued from a storm by Hiroko, no matter what Desmond said. This some might consider a sign of, well, of purely mental events seeming to have an external reality. Which was often cited as a symptom of insanity, as Sax recalled. 'Like those people who think they've seen Hiroko,' he murmured tentatively, to see what Michel would say.

'Ah yes,' Michel said. 'Magical thinking – it's a very persistent form of thinking. Never let your rationalism blind you to the fact that most of our thinking is magical thinking. And so often following archetypal patterns, as in Hiroko's case, which is like the story of Persephone, or Christ. I suppose that when someone like that dies, the shock of the loss is nearly insupportable, and then it only takes one grieving friend or disciple to dream of the lost one's presence, and wake up crying I saw her – and within a week everyone is convinced that the prophet is back, or never died at all. And thus with Hiroko, who is spotted regularly.'

But I really did see her, Sax wanted to say. She grabbed my wrist.

And yet he was deeply troubled. Michel's explanation made good sense. And it matched up very well with Desmond's. Both these men missed Hiroko greatly, Sax presumed, and yet they were facing up to the fact of her disappearance and its most probable explanation. And unusual mental events might very understandably occur in the stress of a physical crisis. Maybe he had hallucinated her. But no, no, that wasn't right; he could remember it just as it had happened, every detail vivid!

But it was a fragment, he noticed, as when one recalled a fragment of a dream upon waking, everything else slipping out of reach with an almost tangible squirt, like something slick and elusive. He couldn't quite remember, for instance, what had come right before Hiroko's appearance, or after. Not the details.

He clicked his teeth together nervously. There were all kinds of madness, evidently. Ann wandering the old world, off on her own; the rest of them staggering on in the new world like ghosts, struggling to construct one life or another. Maybe it was true what Michel said, that they could not come to grips with their longevity, that they did not know what to do with their time, did not know how to construct a life.

Well – still. Here they were, sitting on the Da Vinci seacliffs. There was no need to get too overwrought about these matters, not really. As Nanao would have said, what now is lacking? They had eaten a good lunch, were full, not thirsty, out in the sun and wind, watching a kite soar far above in the dark velvet blue; old friends sitting in the grass, talking. What now was lacking? Peace of mind? Nanao would have laughed. The presence of other old friends? Well, there would be other days for that. Now, in this moment, they were two old brothers in arms, sitting on a seacliff. After all the years of struggle they could sit out there all afternoon if they liked, flying a kite and talking. Discussing their old friends and the weather. There had been trouble before, there would be trouble again; but here they were.

'How John would have liked this,' Sax said, haltingly. So hard to speak of these things. 'I wonder if he could have made Ann see it. How I miss him. How I want her to see it. Not to see it the way I do. Just to see it as if it were something – good. See how beautiful it is – in its own way. In itself, the way it all organizes itself. We say we manage it, but we don't. It's too complex. We just brought it here. After that it took off on its own. Now we try to push it this way or that, but the total biosphere . . . it's self-organizing. There's nothing unnatural about it.'

'Well . . .' Michel demurred.

'There isn't! We can fiddle all we want, but we're only like the sorcerer's apprentice. It's all taken on a life of its own.'

'But the life it had before,' Michel said. 'This is what Ann treasures. The life of the rocks and the ice.'

'Life?'

'Some kind of slow mineral existence. Call it what you will. An areophany of rock. Besides, who is to say that these rocks don't have their own kind of slow consciousness?'

'I think consciousness has to do with brains,' Sax said primly.

'Perhaps, but who can say? And if not consciousness as we define it, then at least existence. An intrinsic worth, simply because it exists.'

'That's a worth it still has.' Sax picked up a rock the size of a baseball. Brecciated ejecta, from the look of it: a shattercone. Common as dirt, actually much more common than dirt. He inspected it closely. Hello, rock. What are you thinking? 'I mean – here it all is. Still here.'

'But not the same.'

'But nothing is ever the same. Moment to moment everything changes. As for mineral consciousness, that's too mystical for me. Not that I'm automatically opposed to mysticism, but still . . .'

Michel laughed. 'You've changed a lot, Sax, but you are still Sax.'

'I should hope so. But I don't think Ann is much of a mystic either.'

'What, then?'

'I don't know! I don't know. Such a . . . such a pure scientist that, that she can't stand to have the data contaminated? That's a silly way to put it. An awe at the phenomena. Do you know what I mean by that? Worship of what is. Live with it, and worship it, but don't try to try to change it and mess it up, wreck it. I don't know. But I want to know.'

'You always want to know.'

'True. But this I want to know more than most things. More than anything else I can think of! Truly.'

'Ah Sax. I want Provence; you want Ann.' Michel grinned. 'We're both crazy!'

They laughed. Photons rained onto their skin, most shooting right through them. Here they were, transparent to the world.

PART TEN

Werteswandel

PART TWO

Weltewandel

It was past midnight, the offices were quiet. The head adviser went to the samovar and started dispensing coffee into tiny cups. Three of his colleagues stood around a table covered with handscreens.

From the samovar the head adviser said, 'So spheres of deuterium and helium₃ are struck by your laser array, one after the next. They implode and fusion takes places. Temperature at ignition is seven hundred million Kelvins, but this is okay because it is a local temperature, and very short-lived.'

'A matter of nanoseconds.'

'Good. I find that comforting. Then, okay, the resulting energy is released entirely as charged particles, so that they can all be contained by your electromagnetic fields — there are no neutrons to fly forward and fry your passengers. The fields serve as shield and pusher plate, and also as the collection system for the energy used to fuel the lasers. All the charged particles are directed out the back, passing through your angled mirror apparatus which is the door arc for the lasers, and the passage collimates the fusion products.'

'That's right, that's the neat part,' said the engineer.

'Very neat. How much fuel does it burn?'

'If you want Mars gravity-equivalent acceleration, that's 3·73 metres per second squared, so assume a ship of a thousand tons, three hundred and fifty tons for the people and the ship, and six-fifty for the device and fuel — then you have to burn three hundred and seventy-three grams a second.'

'Ka, that adds up fairly fast?'

'It's about thirty tons a day, but it's a lot of acceleration too. The trips are short.'

'And these spheres are how big?'

The physicist said, 'A centimetre radius, mass ·29 grams. So we burn 1,290 of them per second. That ought to give passengers in the ship a good continuous g feel.'

'I should say so. But helium₃, isn't it quite rare?'

The engineer said, 'A Galilean collective has started harvesting it out of the upper atmosphere of Jupiter. And they may be working out that surface collection method on Luna as well, though that's not been going well. But Jupiter has all we'll ever need.'

'So the ships will carry five hundred passengers.'

'That's what we've been using for our calculations. It could be adjusted, of course.'

'You accelerate halfway to your destination, turn around and decelerate for the second half of the trip.'

The physicist shook his head. 'Short trips yes, longer trips no. You only need to accelerate for a few days to be going quite fast. Longer trips you should coast through the middle, to save fuel.'

The head adviser nodded, handed the others full cups. They sipped.

The mathematician said, 'Travel times will change so radically. Three weeks from Mars to Uranus. Ten days from Mars to Jupiter. From Mars to Earth, three days. Three days!' She looked around at the others, frowning. 'It will make the solar system something like Europe in the nineteenth century. Train trips. Ocean liners.'

The others nodded. The engineer said, 'Now we're neighbours with people on Mercury, or Uranus, or Pluto.'

The head adviser shrugged. 'Or for that matter Alpha Centauri. Let's not worry about that. Contact is a good thing. Only connect, the poet says. Only connect. Now we will connect with a vengeance.' He raised his cup. 'Cheers.'

Nirgal got in a rhythm and kept it all day. *Lung-gom-pas.* The religion of running, running as meditation or prayer. Zazen, ka zen. Part of the areophany, as Martian gravity was integral to it; what the human body could achieve in two-fifths the pull it had evolved for was a euphoria of effort. One ran as a pilgrim, half worshipper, half god.

A religion with quite a few adherents these days, loners out running around. Sometimes there were organized runs, races: Thread the Labyrinth, Chaos Crawl, the Transmarineris, the Round the Worlder. And in between those, the daily discipline. Purposeless activity; art for art's sake. For Nirgal it was worship, or meditation, or oblivion. His mind wandered, or focused on his body, or on the trail; or went blank. At this moment he was running to music, Bach then Bruckner then Bonnie Tyndall, an Elysian neoclassicist whose music poured along like the day itself, tall chords shifting in steady internal modulation, somewhat like Bach or Bruckner in fact but slower and steadier, more inexorable and grand. Fine music to run by, even though for hours at a time he didn't consciously hear it. He only ran.

It was coming time for the Round the Worlder, which began every other perihelion. Starting from Sheffield the contestants could run east or west around the world, without wristpad or any other navigational aid, shorn of everything but the information of their senses, and small bags of food and drink and gear. They were allowed to choose any route that stayed within 20° of the equator (if they got outside that they would be disqualified by satellite), and all bridges were allowed, including the Ganges Strait Bridge, which made routes both north and south of Marineris competitive, and created almost as many viable routes as contestants. Nirgal had won the race in five of the nine previous runnings, because of his route-finding ability rather than his speed; the 'Nirgalweg' was considered by many fell runners to be in the nature of a mystical achievement, full of counter-intuitive extravagance, and in the last couple of races he had had trackers following him with the plan of passing him at the end. But each year he took a different route, and often he made choices that looked so bad that some of his trackers gave up and took off in more promising directions. Others couldn't keep up the pace over the two hundred days of the circumnavigation, crossing some twenty thousand kilometres – it required truly long-distance endurance, one had to be able to sustain it as a way of life. Running every day.

Nirgal liked it. He wanted to win the next Round the Worlder, to have won a majority of the first ten. He was out researching the route, checking new trails. Many new paths were being built every year: there had been a craze recently to inlay staircase trails in the sides of the canyon cliffs and dorsa and escarpments that everywhere seamed the outback. The trail he was on now had been constructed since he had last been in this area; it dropped down the steep cliff wall of Medusa 16, and there was a matching trail on the opposite wall. Going straight through the Medusas would add a fair bit of verticality to a run, but all flatter routes had to swing far to north or south, and Nirgal thought that if all the trails were as good as this one, the cost in elevation might turn out to be worth it.

The new trail occupied angled cracks in the blocky cliff wall, the steps fitted like the pieces of a jigsaw puzzle, and very regular, so that it was like running down a staircase in the ruined wall of some giant's castle. Cliffside trailmaking was an art, a lovely form of work that Nirgal had joined from time to time, helping to move cut rocks with a crane, to wedge them into position on top of the step below – hours in a belay harness, pulling on the thin green lines with gloved hands, guiding big polygons of basalt into place. The first trailbuilder Nirgal had met had been a woman constructing a trail along the finback of the Geryon Montes, the long ridge on the floor of Ius Chasma. He had helped her all of one summer, down most of the ridge. She was still in Marineris somewhere, constructing trails with her hand tools and high-powered rock saws, and pulley systems with superstrong line, and gluebolts stronger than the rock itself – painstakingly assembling a walkway or staircase from the surrounding rock; some trails like miraculously helpful natural features, others like Roman roads, others still with a Pharaonic or Incan massiveness, huge

466

blocks fitted with hairline precision across boulder slopes or large-grained chaos.

Down three hundred steps, counting, then across the canyon floor in the hour before sunset, the strip of sky a velvet violet glowing over dark cliff walls. No trail here on the shadowed sand of the canyon floor, and he focused on the rocks and plants scattered over it, running between things, his glance caught by light-coloured flowers on top of round-barrelled cacti, glowing like the sky. His body was also glowing, with the end of the day's run, and the prospect of dinner, his hunger a gnawing from within, a faintness, getting more unpleasant by the minute.

He found the staircase trail on the western cliff wall, up and up, changing gears into the uphill push stride, smooth and regular, turning left and right with the switchbacks, admiring the elegant placement of the trail in the crack system of the cliff, a placement that usually had him running with a waist-high wall of rock on the air side, except for during the ascent of one bare, sheer patch of rock, where the builders had been forced to the extremity of bolting in a solid magnesium ladder. He hurried up it, feeling his quadriceps like giant rubber bands; he was tired.

On a plinth to the left of the staircase there was a flat patch with a great view of the long, narrow canyon below. He turned off the trail, stopped running and sat down on a rock like a chair. It was windy; he popped his little mushroom tent, and it stood before him transparent in the dusk. Bedding, lamp, lectern, all pulled hastily from his bumbag in the search for food, all burnished by years of use, and as light as feathers – his gear kit altogether weighed less than three kilos. And there they were in their place at the back, stove and food bag.

The twilight passed in Himalayan majesty as he cooked a pot of powdered soup, sitting crosslegged on his sleeping pad, leaning back against the tent's clear wall. Tired muscles feeling the luxury of sitting down. Another beautiful day.

He slept poorly that night, and got up in the pre-dawn cold wind, and packed up quickly, shivering, and ran west again.

Out of the last Medusa Fossae he came to the southern shore of Amazonis Bay. The dark blue plate of the sea lay to his right as he ran. Here the long beaches were backed by wide sand dunes, covered by short grass that made for easy running. Nirgal flowed on, in his rhythm, glancing at the sea to his right, or into the taiga forest off to the left. Millions of trees had been planted along this low stretch of the Great Escarpment, in order to stabilize the ground and cut down on dust storms. The great forest was one of the least populated regions on Mars; it had been rarely visited in the earlier years of its existence, and had never been host to a tent town; deep deposits of dust and fines had discouraged travel. Now these deposits were somewhat fixed by the forest, but bordering the streams were swamps and quicksand lakes, and unstable loess bluffs that caused breaks in the lattice roof of branches and leaves. Nirgal kept to the border of forest and sea, on the dunes or among stands of smaller trees. He crossed several small bridges spanning rivermouths. He spent a night on the beach, lulled to sleep by the sound of breaking waves.

The next day at dawn he followed the trail under the canopy of green leaves, the coast having taken a curve to the northwest. The light was dim and cool. Everything at this hour looked like a shadow of itself. Faint trails branched off uphill to the left. The forest here was conifer for the most part: redwoods in tall groves, surrounded by smaller pines and junipers. The forest floor was covered by dry needles. In wet places ferns broke through this brown mat, adding their archaic fractals to the sun-dappled floor. A stream braided among narrow grassy islands. He could rarely see more than a hundred metres ahead. Green and brown were the dominant colours; the only red visible was the tint of the redwoods' hairy bark. Shafts of sunlight like slender living beings danced over the forest floor. Nirgal ran outside himself, mesmerized as he passed among these pencils of light. He skipped on rocks across a shallow creek, in a fern-floored glade. It was like crossing a room, with hallways extending to similar rooms upstream and down. A short waterfall gurgled to his left.

He stopped for a drink from the far side of the creek. Then as he straightened up he saw a marmot, waddling over moss under the waterfall. He felt a quick stab to the heart. The marmot drank and then washed its paws and face. It did not see Nirgal.

Then there was a rustle and the marmot ran, was buried in a flurry of spotted fur – white teeth – a big lynx, pinning the marmot's throat in powerful jaws, shaking the little creature hard, then pressing it still under a big paw.

Nirgal had jumped at the moment of attack, and now as the lynx stood over its prey it looked in Nirgal's direction, as if just now registering the movement. Its eyes glittered in the dim light, its mouth was bloody; Nirgal shuddered, and when the cat saw him and their gazes locked, he saw it running at him and jumping on him, its pointed teeth bright even in the dim light—

But no. It disappeared with its prey, leaving only a bobbing fern.

Nirgal ran on. The day was darker than the cloud shadow could explain, a malign dimness. He had to focus on the trail. Light flickered through the shadows, white piercing green. Hunter and hunted. Ice-rimmed ponds in the gloom. Moss on bark, fern patterns in his peripheral vision. Here a gnarly pile of bristlecone pines, there a pit of quicksand. The day was chill, the night would be frigid.

He ran all day. His pack bounced against his back, nearly empty of food. He was glad he was nearing his next cache. Sometimes on runs he took only a few handfuls of cereal and lived off the land as best he could, gathering pine nuts and fishing; but on trips of that kind half of every day had to be spent in the search for food, and there wasn't much to be found. When the fish were biting a lake was an incredible cornucopia. Lake people. But on this run he was going full tilt from cache to cache, eating seven or eight thousand calories a day, and still ravenous every evening. So when he came to the little arroyo containing his next cache, and found the arroyo's side wall collapsed in a landslide over it, he shouted with dismay and anger. He even dug for a while at the pile of loose rock; it was a small slide; but a couple of tons would have to be removed. No chance. He would have to run hard to the next cache, and go hungry. He took off in the very moment of realization, thinking to save time.

Now he looked for edible things as he ran, pine nuts,

meadow onions, anything. He ate the food left in his pack very slowly, chewing it for as long as he could, trying to imagine it to some higher level of nutrient value. Savouring every bite. Hunger kept him awake part of every night, though he slept heavily through the hours before dawn.

On the third day of this unexpected hunger run he emerged from the forest just south of Juventa Chasma, in land broken by the ancient Juventa aquifer outbreak. It was a lot of work to make his way through this land on a clean line, and he was hungrier than he could ever remember being; and his next cache still two days away. His body had eaten all its fat reserves, or so it felt, and was now feeding on the muscles themselves. This autocannibalism gave every object a sharp edge, tinged with glories – the whiteness shining out of things, as if reality itself were going translucent. Soon after this stage, as he knew from similar past experiences, the *lung-gom-pa* state would give way to hallucinations. Already there were lots of crawling worms in his eyes, and black dots, and circles of little blue mushrooms, and then green, lizardlike things scurrying along in the sand, right before the blurs of his feet, for hours at a time.

It took all the thought he could muster to navigate the broken land. He watched the rock underfoot and the land ahead equally, head up and down and up and down, in a bobbing motion that had little to do with his thinking, which browsed over near and far in an entirely different rhythm. The Juventa chaos, downhill to his right, was a shallow, jumbled depression, over which he could see to a distant horizon; it was like looking into a big shattered bowl. Ahead the land was rumpled and uneven, pits and hillocks covered with boulders and sand drifts, the shadows too dark, the sunlit highlights too bright. Dark yet glary; it was near sunset again, and his pupils were pinched by the light. Up and down, up and down; he came on an ancient dune side, and glissaded down the sand and scree, a dreamy descent, left, right, left, each step carrying him down a few metres, feet cushioned by sand and gravel shoved off the angle of repose. All too easy to get used to that; once on flat ground again it was hard work to return to honest jogging, and the next little uphill was devastating. He would have to look for a campsite soon, perhaps in the next hollow, or on the next sandy flat next to a rock bench. He was starving, faint with lack of food, and nothing in his pack but some meadow onions pulled earlier; but it would help to be so tired, he would fall asleep no matter what. Exhaustion beat hunger every time.

He stumbled across a shallow depression, over a knob, between two house-sized boulders. Then in a flash of white a naked woman was standing before him, waving a green sash; he stopped abruptly, he reeled, stunned at the sight of her, then concerned that the hallucinations had got so out of hand. But there she stood, as vivid as a flame, blood streaks spattering her breasts and legs, waving the green scarf silently. Then other human figures ran past her and over the next little knob, going where she pointed, or so it seemed. She looked at Nirgal, gestured to the south as if directing him as well, then took off running, her lean white body flowing like something visible in more than three dimensions, strong back, long legs, round bottom, already distant, the green scarf flying this way and that as she used it to point.

Suddenly he saw three antelope ahead, moving over a hillock to the west, silhouetted by the low sun. Ah; hunters. The antelope were being herded west by the humans, who were scattered in an arc behind them, waving scarves at them from behind rocks. All in silence, as if sound had disappeared from the world: no wind, no cries. For a moment, as the antelope stopped on the hillock, everyone stopped moving, everyone alert but still; hunters and hunted all frozen together, in a tableau that transfixed Nirgal. He was afraid to blink for fear the whole scene would wink away to nothing.

The antelope buck moved, breaking the tableau. He rocked forward cautiously, step by step. The woman with the green sash walked after him, upright and in the open. The other hunters popped in and out of view, moving like finches from one frozen position to the next. They were barefoot, and wore loincloths or singlets. Some of their faces and backs were painted red or black or ochre.

Nirgal followed them. They swerved, and he found himself on their left wing as they moved west. This turned out to be lucky, as the antelope buck tried to make a break around his side, and Nirgal was in position to jump in its path, waving his hands wildly. The three antelope then turned as one, dashed west again. The troop of hunters followed, running faster than Nirgal at his fastest, maintaining their arc. Nirgal had to work hard just to keep them in sight; they were very fast, barefoot or not. It was hard to see them in the long shadows, and they stayed silent; on the other wing of the arc someone yipped once, and that was their only sound, except for the squeak and clatter of sand and gravel, the harsh breath in their throats. In and out of sight they ran, the antelope keeping their distance in short bursts of flowing speed. No human would ever catch them. Still Nirgal ran, panting hard, following the hunt. Ahead he spotted their prey again. Ah – the antelope had stopped. They had come to the edge of a cliff. A canyon rim – he saw the gap and the opposite rim. A shallow fossa, pine tops sticking out of it. Had the antelope known it was there? Were they familiar with this region? The canyon had not been visible even a few hundred metres back . . .

But perhaps they did know the place, for in the pure flow of animal grace they half-trotted, half-pronged south along the cliff-edge to a little embayment. This turned out to be the top of a steep ravine, down which rubble siphoned onto the canyon floor. As the antelope disappeared down this slot all the hunters rushed to the rim, where they looked on as the three animals descended the ravine, in an astonishing display of power and balance, clacking from rock to rock in tremendous leaps down. One of the hunters howled, '*Owwwwwwwww!*' and with that cry all the hunters hurried over to the head of the ravine, yelping and grunting. Nirgal joined the others and dropped over the rim and then they were all in a mad descent, clacking and jumping, and though Nirgal's legs were rubbery his endless days of *lung-gom* now served him well, for he dropped past most of the others as he hopped down boulders and glissaded down little rockslides, jumping, holding balance, using his hands, making great desperate leaps, like everyone else utterly locked into the moment, into the striving for a quick descent without a bad fall.

Only when he was successfully on the canyon floor did Nirgal look up again, to see that the canyon was filled by the forest he had barely seen from above. Trees stood high over a needle-strewn floor of old snow, big fir and pine, and then, upcanyon to the south, the unmistakably massive trunks of giant sequoias, *big* trees, trees so huge that the canyon suddenly seemed shallow, though the descent of the ravine had taken quite a while. These were the treetops that had stuck up over the canyon rim; engineered giant sequoias two hundred metres tall, towering like great silent saints, each one extending its arms in a broad circle over daughter trees, the fir and pine, the thin patchy snow and the brown needle beds.

The antelope had trotted upcanyon into this primeval forest, headed south, and with a few happy hoots the hunters followed them, darting past one huge trunk after another. The massive cylinders of riven red bark dwarfed everything else – they all looked like little animals, like mice, dashing over a snowy forest floor in the failing light. Nirgal's skin tingled down his back and flanks, he was still adrenalated from the descent of the ravine, panting and light-headed. It was obvious that they could not catch the antelope, he didn't understand what they were doing. Nevertheless he raced between the stupendous trees, following the lead hunters. The chase itself was all he wanted.

Then the sequoia towers became more scattered, as at the edge of a skyscraper district, until there were only a few left. And looking between the trunks of the last of the behemoths, Nirgal again hauled up short: on the other side of a narrow clearing, the canyon was blocked off by a wall of water. A sheer wall of water, filling the canyon right to the rim, hanging suspended over them in a smooth transparent mass.

Reservoir dam. Recently they had begun building them out of transparent sheets of diamond lattice, sunk in a concrete foundation; Nirgal could see this one running down both canyon walls and across the canyon floor, a thick white line.

The mass of water stood over them like the side of a great aquarium, turbid near the bottom, weeds floating in dark mud. Above them, silver fish as big as the antelope flitted next to the clear wall, then receded into dark, crystalline depths.

The three antelope trotted nervously back and forth before this barrier, the doe and fawn following the quick turns of the buck. As the hunters closed on them, the buck suddenly leaped away and crashed its head against the dam with a powerful thrust of its whole body – antlers like bone knives, *thwack* –

Nirgal froze in fear, everyone froze at this violent gesture, so ferocious as to be human; but the buck bounced away, staggered. He turned and charged at them. Bola balls spun through the air and the line wrapped around his legs just above the hocks, and he crashed forward and down. Some of the hunters swarmed on him, others brought down doe and fawn in a hail of rocks and spears. A squeal cut off abruptly. Nirgal saw the doe's throat cut with an obsidian-bladed dagger, the blood pouring onto the sand next to the foundation of the dam. The big fish flashed by overhead, looking down at them.

The woman with the green scarf was nowhere to be seen. Another hunter, a man wearing only necklaces, tilted his head back and howled, shattering the strange silence of the work; he danced in a circle, then ran at the clear wall of the dam and threw his spear straight at it. The spear bounced away. The exultant hunter ran up and slammed his fist against the clear, hard membrane.

A woman hunter with blood on her hands turned her head to give the man a contemptuous look. 'Stop fooling around,' she said.

The spear-thrower laughed. 'You don't have to worry. These dams are a hundred times stronger than they need to be.'

The woman shook her head, disgusted. 'It's stupid to tempt fate.'

'It's amazing what superstitions survive in fearful minds.'

'You're a fool,' the woman said. 'Luck is as real as anything else.'

'Luck! Fate! Ka.' The spear-thrower picked up his spear and ran and threw it at the dam again; it rebounded and almost hit him, and he laughed wildly. 'How *lucky*,' he said. 'Fortune favours the bold, eh?'

'Asshole. Show some respect.'

'All honour to that buck, indeed, crashing the wall like he did.' The man laughed raucously.

The others were ignoring these two, busy butchering the animals. 'Many thanks, brother. Many thanks, sister.' Nirgal's hands shook as he watched; he could smell the blood; he was salivating. Piles of intestines steamed in the chill air. Magnesium poles were pulled from waistbags and telescoped out, and the decapitated antelope bodies were tied over them by the legs. Hunters at the ends of the poles hefted the headless carcasses into the air.

The bloody-handed woman shouted at the spear-thrower, 'You'd better help carry if you want to eat any of these.'

'Fuck you.' But he helped carry the front end of the buck.

'Come on,' the woman said to Nirgal, and then they were hurrying west across the canyon floor, between the great wall of water and the last of the massive sequoias. Nirgal followed, stomach growling.

The west wall of the canyon was marked with petroglyphs: animals, lingams, yonis, handprints, comets and spaceships, geometric designs, the hump-backed flute-player Kokopelli, all scarcely visible in the dusk. There was a staircase trail inlaid in the cliff, following a nearly perfect Z of ledges. The hunters hiked up it and Nirgal followed. Shift into the uphill rhythm one more time, his stomach eating him from within, his head swimming. A black antelope splayed across the rock beside him.

Above, a few giant sequoias stood isolated on the canyon rim. When they reached the rim, returning to the sunset's last light, he saw that these trees formed a circle, nine trees in a rough woodhenge, with a big firepit at their centre.

The band entered the circle and got to work starting a fire, skinning the antelope, cutting big venison steaks out of the haunches. Nirgal stood watching, legs in a sewing-machine tremble, mouth salivating like a fountain; he swallowed again and again as he sniffed the steak juices lofting in the smoke through the early stars. Firelight pushed like a bubble at the dusk's gloom, turning the circle of trees into a flickering roofless room. The light flickering against the needles was like seeing your own capillaries. Some of the trees had wooden staircases spiralling around their trunks, up into their branches. High above them lamps were being lit, voices like skylarks among the stars.

Three or four of the hunters bunched around him, offering him flatcakes of what tasted like barley, then a fiery liquor out of clay jars. They told him they had found the sequoia henge a few years before.

'What happened to the, the leader of the hunt?' Nirgal asked, looking around.

'Oh, the diana can't sleep with us tonight.'

'Besides she fucked up, she don't want to.'

'Yes she does. You know Zo, she always has a reason.'

They laughed and moved nearer to the fire. A woman poked out a charred steak, waved it on its stick until it cooled. 'I eat all of you, little sister.' And bit into the steak.

Nirgal ate with them, lost in the wet, hot taste of the meat, chewing hard but still bolting the food, his body all abuzz with trembling, light-headed hunger. Food, food!

He ate his second steak more slowly, watching the others. His stomach was filling quickly. He recalled the scramble down the ravine: it was amazing what the body could do in such a situation, it had been an out-of-body experience – or rather an experience so far into the body that it was like unconsciousness – diving deep into the cerebellum, presumably, into that ancient undermind that knew how to do things. A state of grace.

A resiny branch spat flames out of the blaze. His sight had not yet settled down, things jumped and blurred with afterimages. The spear-thrower and another man came up to him, 'Here, drink this,' and tilted a skin's spigot against his lips and laughed, some bitter milky drink in his mouth, 'Have some of the white brother, brother.' A group of them picked up some stones and began to hit them together in rhythm, all their different patterns meshing bass to treble. The rest of them began to dance around the bonfire, hooting or singing or chanting. 'Auqakuh, Quahira, Harmakhis, Kasei. Auqakuh, Mangala, Ma'adim, Bahram.' Nirgal danced with them, exhaustion banished. It was a cold night and one could move in or away from the heat of the fire, feel its radiance against cold bare skin, move back out into the chill. When everyone was hot and sweaty they took off into the night, stumbling back toward the canyon, south along the rim. A hand clutched at Nirgal's arm and it looked as if the diana was there beside him again, light in the dark, but it was too dark to see, and then they were crashing into the water of the reservoir, shockingly frigid, dive under, waist-deep silt and sand, heartstopping cold, stand up, wade back out all the senses pulsating wildly, gasps, laughter, a hand at his ankle and down he went again, into the shallows face-first, laughing. Through the dark wet, freez-

476

ing, toes banging 'ow! ow!' and back into the henge, into the heat. Soaking they danced again, pressed to the heat of the fire, arms extended, hugging its radiance. All the bodies ruddy in the firelight, the sequoia needles flashing against pinwheel stars, bouncing in rhythm to the rock percussion.

When they warmed back up and the fire died down, they led him up one of the sequoia staircases. On the massive upper limbs of the tree were perched small, flat sleeping platforms, low-walled and open to the sky. The floors swayed very slightly underfoot, on a cold breeze that had roused the trees' deep, airy choral voices. Nirgal was left alone on what appeared to be the highest platform. He unpacked his bedding and lay down. To the chorus of wind in sequoia needles he fell fast asleep.

In the early dawn he woke suddenly. He sat against the wall of his platform, surprised that the whole evening had not turned out to be a dream. He looked over the edge; the ground was far, far below. It was like being in the crow's nest of an enormous ship; it reminded him of his high bamboo room in Zygote, but everything here was vastly bigger, the starry dome of the sky, the horizon's distant jagged black line. All the land was a rumpled, dark blanket, with the water of the reservoir a squiggle of silver inlaid into it.

He made his way down the stairs; four hundred of them. The tree was perhaps one hundred and fifty metres tall, standing over the one hundred and fifty metre drop of the canyon cliff. In the pre-sunrise light he looked down on the wall over which they had tried to drive the antelope, saw the ravine they had crashed down, the clear dam, the mass of water behind it.

He went back to the henge. A few of the hunters were up, coaxing the fire back to life, shivering in the dawn chill. Nirgal asked them if they were moving on that day. They were; north through the Juventa Chaos, then on toward the southwest shore of the Chryse Gulf. After that they didn't know.

Nirgal asked if he could join them for a while. They looked surprised; surveyed him; spoke among themselves in a language he didn't recognize. While they talked, Nirgal wondered that he had asked. He wanted to see the diana again, yes. But it was more than that. Nothing in his *lung-gom-pa* had been like that last half hour of the hunt. Of course the running had set the stage for the experience – the hunger, the weariness – but then it had happened, something new. Snowy forest floor, the pursuit through the primeval trees – the dash down the ravine – the scene under the dam . . .

The early risers were nodding at him. He could come along.

All that day they hiked north, threading a complicated path through the Juventa Chaos. That evening they came to a small mesa, its whole cap covered by an apple orchard. A ramp road led the way up to this grove. The trees had been pruned to the shape of cocktail glasses, and now new shoots rose straight up from the gnarled older branches. Through the afternoon they pulled ladders around from tree to tree, pruning the thin shoots away and thereby harvesting some hard, tart, unripe little apples, which they saved.

In the centre of the grove was a open-walled, round-roofed structure. A disc-house, they called it. Nirgal walked through it, admiring the design. The foundation was a round slab of concrete, polished to a finish like marble. The roof was also round, held up by a simple T of interior walls, a diameter and a radius. In the open semi-circle were kitchen and living space; on the other side, bedrooms and bathroom. The circumference, now open to the air, could be closed off in inclement weather by clear walls of tenting material, drawn around the circle like curtains.

There were disc-houses all over Lunae, the woman who had butchered the antelope told Nirgal. Other groups used the same set of houses, tending the orchards when they passed through. They were all part of a loose co-op, working out a nomad life, with some agriculture, some hunting, some gathering. Now one group was cooking down the little apples, making apple-sauce for preservation; others were grilling antelope steaks over a fire outside, or working in a smokehouse.

Two round baths right next to the disc-house were now steaming, and some of the group were shedding their clothes and hopping into the smaller bath, to clean themselves before supper. They were very dirty; they had been in the back country a long time. Nirgal followed the woman (her hands still spotted with dried blood) and joined them in the bath, the hot water like another world, like the heat of the fire transmuted to liquid that one could touch, in which one could immerse one's body.

They woke at dawn and lazed around a fire, brewing coffee and kava, talking, stitching clothes, working around the disc-house. After a while they gathered their few travelling possessions, killed the fire and moved out. Everyone carried a backpack or waistpack, but most of them travelled as lightly as Nirgal or more so, with nothing but thin sleeping rolls and some food, and a few with spears or bows and arrows slung over a shoulder. They walked hard through the morning, then split into smaller groups to gather pine nuts, acorns, meadow onions, wild corn; or hunt for marmots or rabbits or frogs, or perhaps larger game. They were lean people; their ribs showed, their faces were thin. We like to stay a little hungry, the woman told him. It makes the food taste better. And indeed every night of this extended walk Nirgal bolted his food as during his runs, shaky and ravenous; and everything tasted like ambrosia. They walked a long distance every day, and during their big hunts they often ended up in terrain that would have been a disaster to run in, terrain so rough that it was often four or five days before they all managed to find each other again, at the next disc-house in its orchard. Since Nirgal didn't know where these were, he had to stick close to one or another of the group. Once they had him take the four children in the group on an easier route across Lunae Planum's cratered terrain, and the children told him what direction to take every time they had to make a choice; and they were the first to reach the next disc-house. The kids loved it. Often they were consulted by the larger group as to when they should leave a disc-house. 'Hey, you kids, is it time to go?' They would answer yes or no very firmly within seconds, in concert. Once two adults got in a fight and afterwards they had to present their cases to the four kids, who decided against one of them. The butcher woman explained to Nirgal: 'We teach them, they judge us. They're hard but fair.'

They harvested some of the yield of the orchards: peaches, pears, apricots, apples. If a crop was getting overripe they harvested everything and cooked it down and bottled it as sauces or chutneys, leaving it in big pantries under the disc-houses for other groups, or for themselves on their next time through. Then they were off again, north over Lunae until it fell down the Great Escarpment, here very dramatically, dropping from Lunae's high plateau five thousand metres down to the Chryse Gulf, in only just over a hundred horizontal kilometres.

The way was difficult across this tilted country, the land ripped and corrugated by a million small deformations. No trails had been constructed here, and there was no good way through; it was up and down and over and back and up and down again; and nothing much to hunt; and no disc-houses nearby; and not much food to be found. One of the youngsters slipped while they were crossing a line of coral cactus, seaming the land like a living barbed wire fence, and fell on one knee into a nest of spines. The magnesium poles served then as a stretcher frame, and on they went north carrying the crying boy, the best hunters out on the flanks of the group with bows and arrows, to see if they could shoot anything flushed by their passage. Nirgal saw several misses, then one long flight of an arrow that hit a running jackrabbit, which tumbled and flopped until they killed it – a tremendous shot, it had them all leaping around shrieking. They burned more calories celebrating the shot than they ever got back from eating the tiny shreds of rabbit meat that were each person's share, and the butcher woman was contemptuous. 'Ritual cannibalism of our rodent brother,' she scoffed as she ate her shred. 'Don't ever tell me there's no such thing as luck.' But the hothead spearthrower just laughed at her, and the others seemed cheered by their mouthful of meat.

Then later that same day they came on a young caribou bull, off on his own, looking disoriented. Their food problems were solved, if they could catch him. But he was wary despite his confused air, and he kept beyond the reach of even the longest bowshot, heading away from the group, down the Great Escarpment with all the hunters in view on the slope above.

Eventually everyone got on their hands and knees, and began to crawl laboriously over the hot rock of midday, trying to traverse quick enough to circle the caribou. But the wind blew from behind them, and the caribou moved skittishly downslope or traversed north, grazing as he went, and looking back at his pursuers more and more curiously, as if wondering why they continued with such a charade. Nirgal too began to wonder. And apparently he was not alone; the caribou's scepticism had infected them. A variety of subtle and not-so-subtle whistles filled the air, in what was evidently an argument over strategy. Nirgal understood then that hunting was hard, that the group failed often. That they were perhaps not very good at it. Everyone was baking on the rock, and they had not eaten properly for a couple of days. Part of life for these people; but today too miserable to be fun.

Then as they continued, the horizon below them to the east seemed to double: Chryse Gulf, gleaming blue and flat, still far below. As they continued to follow the caribou downslope, the sea covered more and more of their view of the globe; the Great Escarpment pitched so steeply here that even Mars's tight curvature did not bend fast enough to hide the long view, and they could see out over Chryse Gulf for many kilometres. The sea, the blue sea!

Perhaps they could trap the caribou against the water. But now he was trending north, traversing the slope of the escarpment. They crawled after him, over a little ridge, and suddenly had a good view down to the coastline: fringe of green forest flanking the water, small whitewashed buildings under the trees. A white lighthouse on a bluff.

As they continued north a turn in the coast hove over the horizon. Just beyond the point of the turn lay a seaside town, banked around a half-moon bay on the southern side of what they now saw was a strait, or more accurately a fjord, for across a narrow passage of water rose a wall even steeper than the slope they were on: three thousand metres of red rock rearing out of the sea, the giant cliff like the edge of a continent, its horizontal bands cut deep by a billion years of wind. Nirgal realized suddenly where they were; that massive cliff was the sea-facing escarpment of the Sharanov Peninsula; and the fjord therefore Kasei Fjord, and the harbour town therefore Nilokeras. They had come a long way.

The whistles between the hunters got very noisy and expressive. About half the group sat up – a crop of heads, sticking out over a field of stones, looking at each other as if an idea had struck them all at once – and then they stood and walked down the slope toward the town, abandoning the hunt and leaving the caribou heedlessly munching. After a while they skipped and hopped downslope, hooting and laughing, leaving the stretcher-bearers and the injured boy behind.

They waited lower down, however, under tall Hokkaido pines on the outskirts of the town. When the stretcher group caught up, they descended through the pines and orchards together, into the upper streets of the town. A loud gang, passing fine, window-fronted houses overlooking the crowded harbour, straight to a medical clinic, as if they knew where they were going. They dropped off the injured youth and then went to some public baths; and after a quick bath they went to the curve of businesses backing the docks, and invaded three or four adjacent restaurants with tables out under umbrellas, and strings of bare, incandescent lightbulbs. Nirgal sat at a table with the youngsters, in a seafood restaurant; after a while the injured boy joined them, knee and calf wrapped, and they all ate and drank in huge quantities – prawns, clams, mussels, trout, fresh bread, cheeses, peasant salad, litres of water, wine, ouzo – all in such excess that they staggered away when they had finished, drunk, their stomachs taut as drums.

Some went immediately to what the butcher woman called their usual hostel, to lie down or throw up. The rest limped on past the building to a nearby park, where a performance of Tyndall's opera 'Phyllis Boyle' was to be followed by a dance.

Nirgal lay sprawled on the grass with the park contingent, out at the back of the audience. Like the rest he was awed by the facility of the singers, the sheer lushness of orchestral sound as Tyndall used it. When the opera was over some of the group had digested their feast enough to dance, and Nirgal joined them, and after an hour of dancing joined the band as well, with many other audience sit-ins; and he drummed away until his whole body was humming like the magnesium of the pans.

But he had eaten too much, and when some of the group returned to the hostel, he decided to go back with them. On their way back, some passers-by said something – 'Look at the ferals,' or something like that – and the spear-thrower howled, and just like that he and some of the young hunters had pushed the passers-by against a wall, shoving them and shouting abuse: 'Watch your mouth or we'll beat the shit out of you,' the spear-thrower shouted happily, 'you caged rats, you drug addicts, you sleepwalkers, you fucking earthworms: you think you can take drugs and get what we get, we'll kick your ass and then you'll feel some real feeling, you'll see what we mean!' and then Nirgal was pulling him back, saying,

'Come on, come on, don't make trouble,' and the passers-by were on them with a roar, hard-fisted and -footed men who were not drunk and were not amused. The young hunters had to retreat, then let themselves be pulled away by Nirgal when the passers-by were satisfied at having driven them off; still shouting abuse, staggering up the street, holding their bruises, laughing and snarling, completely full of themselves, 'Fucking sleepwalkers, wrapped in your gift boxes, we'll kick your ass! Kick your ass right out of your dollshouse into the drink! Stupid sheep that you are!'

Nirgal cuffed them along, giggling despite himself. The ranters were very drunk, and Nirgal was not much more sober himself. When they got to their hostel he looked into the bar across the street, saw the butcher woman was sitting in there, and so went in with the rest of the rough boys. He sat back watching them while he drank a glass of cognac, swishing it over his tongue. Ferals, the passers-by had called them. The butcher woman was eyeing him, wondering what he thought. Much later he stood, with difficulty, and left the bar with the others, walking unsteadily across the cobbled street, humming along with the others as they bellowed 'Swing Low, Sweet Chariot'. On the obsidian water of Kasei Fjord the stars rode up and down. Mind and body full of feeling, sweet fatigue a state of grace.

The next morning they slept in and woke up late, dopey and hung over. They lay around for a while in their dorm room, slurping kavajava. Then they went downstairs, and even though they claimed to be still stuffed, ate a huge hostel breakfast. While they ate they decided to go flying. The winds that poured down Kasei Fjord were as powerful as any on the planet, and windsurfers and flyers of all kinds had come to Nilokeras to take advantage of them. Of course at any time howlers could take the situation 'off scale' and shut down the fun for everyone except the big wind riders; but the average day's hard blow was glorious.

The flyers' base of operations was an offshore crater-rim island, called Santorini. After breakfast the group went down to the docks together, got on a ferry, disembarked half an hour later on the little arcuate island, and trooped with the other passengers up to the gliderport.

Nirgal had not flown for years, and it was a great joy to strap into a blimpglider's gondola, raise up the mast, and let loose and soar on the powerful updraughts pushing off Santorini's steep inner rim. As Nirgal ascended he saw that most of the flyers wore birdsuits of one sort or another; it looked as if he was flying in a flock of wide-winged flying creatures, which resembled not birds but something more like flying foxes, or some mythic hybrid like the griffin or pegasus: birdhumans. The birdsuits were of several different kinds, imitating in some respects the configurations of different species – albatross, eagle, swift, lammergeier. Each suit encased its flyer in what was in effect an ever-changing exoskeleton, which responded to interior pressure from the flyer's body, to take and then hold positions, or make certain movements, all reinforced in proportion to the pressure exerted inside them, so that a human's muscles could flap the big wings, or hold them in place against the great torque of the wind's onslaughts, meanwhile keeping the streamlined helmets and tailfeathers in the proper positions. Suit-AIs helped flyers who wanted help, and they could even function as automatic pilots; but most flyers preferred to do the thinking for themselves, and controlled the suit as a waldo, exaggerating many times the strength of their own muscles.

Sitting in his blimpglider Nirgal watched with both pleasure and trepidation as these bird-people shot down past him in terrifying stoops toward the sea, then popped their wings and curved away and gyred back up again on the inner wall updraught. It looked to Nirgal as if the suits took a high level of skill to fly; they were the opposite of the blimpgliders, a few of which soared with Nirgal over the island, rising and falling in much gentler swoops, taking in the view like agile balloonists.

Then soaring up past him in a rising spiral, Nirgal spotted the face of the diana, the woman who had led the ferals' hunt. She recognized him too, raised her chin and bared her teeth in a quick smile, then pulled her wings in and tipped over, dropping away with a tearing sound. Nirgal watched her from above with fearful excitement, then a moment of terror as she dived right past the edge of Santorini's cliff; from his vantage point it had looked as if she was going to hit. Then she was back up, soaring on the updraught in tight spirals. It looked so graceful that he wanted to learn to fly in a birdsuit, even as he felt his pulse still hammering at the sight of her dive. Stoop and soar, stoop and soar; no blimpglider could fly like that, not even close. Birds were the greatest flyers, and the diana flew like a bird. Now, along with everything else, people were birds.

With him, past him, around him, as if performing one of those darting courtships that members of some species put on for each other; after about an hour of this, she smiled at him one last time and tipped away, then drifted in lazy circles down to the gliderport at Phira. Nirgal followed her down, landing half an hour later with a swoop into the wind, running and then stopping just short of her. She had been waiting, wings spread around her on the ground.

She stepped in a circle around him, as if still doing a court-ship dance. She walked toward him, pulling her hood back off her head, her black hair spilling out in the light like a crow's wing. The diana. She stretched up on her toes and kissed him full on the mouth, then stood back, watching him gravely. He remembered her running naked ahead of the hunt, a green sash bouncing from one hand.

'Breakfast?' she said.

It was mid-afternoon, and he was famished. 'Sure.'

They ate at the gliderport restaurant, looking out at the arc of the island's little bay, and the immensity of the Sharanov cliffs, and the acrobatics of the flyers still in the air. They talked about flying, and running the land; about the hunt for the three antelope, and the islands of the North Sea, and the great fjord of Kasei, pouring its wind over them. They flirted; and Nirgal felt the pleasant anticipation of where they were headed, he luxuriated in it. It had been a long time. This too was part of the descent into the city, into civilization. Flirting, seduction – how wonderful all that was when one was interested, when one saw that the other was interested! She was fairly young, he judged, but her face was sunburned, skin lined around the eyes – not a youth – she had been to the Jovian moons, she said, and had taught at the new university in Nilokeras, and was now running with the ferals for a time. Twenty M-years old, perhaps, or older – hard to tell these days. An adult, in any case; in those first twenty M-years people got most of whatever experience was ever going to give them, after that it was only a matter of repetition. He had met old fools and young sages almost as often as the reverse. They were both adults, contemporaries. And there they were, in the shared experience of the present.

Nirgal watched her face as she talked. Careless, smart, confident. A Minoan: dark-skinned, dark-eyed, aquiline nose, dramatic lower lip; Mediterranean ancestry, perhaps, Greek, Arabic, Indian; as with most of the yonsei, it was impossible to tell. She was simply a Martian woman, with Dorsa Brevia English, and that look in the eye as she watched him – ah yes – how many times in his wandering had it happened, a conversation turning at some point, and then suddenly he was flying with some woman in the long glide of seduction, the courtship leading to some bed or hidden dip in the hills . . .

'Hey Zo,' the butcher woman said in passing. 'Going with us to the ancestral neck?'

'No,' Zo said.

'The ancestral neck?' Nirgal inquired.

'Boone's Neck,' Zo said. 'The town up on the polar peninsula.'

'Ancestral?'

'She's John Boone's great granddaughter,' the butcher woman explained.

'By way of?' Nirgal asked, looking at Zo.

'Jackie Boone,' she said. 'My mother.'

'Ah,' Nirgal managed to say.

He sat back in his seat. The baby he had seen Jackie nursing, in Cairo. The similarity to her mother was obvious once he knew. His skin was goose-pimpling, the hairs lifting from the skin of his forearms. He hugged himself, shivered. 'I must be getting old,' he said.

She smiled, and he saw suddenly that she had known who he was. She had been toying with him, laying a little trap – as an experiment, perhaps, or to displease her mother, or for some other reason he could not imagine. For fun.

Now she was frowning at him, trying to look serious. 'It doesn't matter,' she said.

'No,' he said. For there were other ferals out there.

PART ELEVEN

Viriditas

It was a disordered time. Population pressures now drove everything. The general plan to get through the hypermalthusian years was obvious, and holding up fairly well; each generation got smaller; nevertheless, there were now eighteen billion people on Earth, and eighteen million on Mars; and more being born all the time; and more moving from Earth to Mars all the time; and people on both worlds crying, enough, enough!

When Terrans heard Martians crying enough, some of them became enraged. The concept of carrying capacity meant nothing before the sheer numbers, the images on the screens. Uneasily the Martian global government did what it could to deal with this anger. It explained that Mars with its thin new biosphere could not sustain as many people as the fat old Earth. It also set the Martian rocket industry into the shuttle business, and rapidly expanded a programme to turn asteroids into floating cities. This programme was an unexpected offshoot of what had been serving as part of their prison system. For many years now the punishment for conviction of serious crimes on Mars had been permanent exile from the planet, begun by some years of confinement and servitude on some new asteroid settlement. After they had served their sentence it was a matter of indifference to the Martian government where the exiles went, as long as they did not return to Mars. So inevitably a steady stream of people arrived on Hebe, shipped out and did their time, and then moved somewhere else, sometimes out to the still thinly-populated outer satellites, sometimes back into the inner system; but often to one of the many hollowed-asteroid colonies that were being established. Da Vinci and several other co-ops made and distributed shareware for starting up these settlements, and many other organizations did the same, for in truth the programme was simple. Surveying teams had found thousands of candidates in the asteroid belt for the treatment, and on the best of them they left behind the equipment to transform them. A team of self-reproducing digging robots went to work on one end of the asteroid, boring into the rock like dogs, tossing most of the rubble into space, and using the rest to make and fuel more diggers. When the rock was hollowed out, the open end was capped and the whole thing was spun, so that centrifugal force provided a gravity equivalent inside. Powerful lamps called sunlines or sunspots were fired up in the centres of these hollowed-out cylinders, and they provided light levels equivalent to the Terran or Martian day, with the g usually adjusted accordingly, so that there were little Mars-equivalent cities, and little Earth-equivalent cities, and cities all across the range in between, and beyond, at least to the light side; many of the little worlds were experimenting with quite low gs.

There were some alliances between these little new city-states, and often ties to founder organizations back on a home world, but there was no overall organization. From the independents, especially those occupied mostly by Martian exiles, there had been in the early days some fairly hostile behaviour to passers-by, including attempts to impose passage tolls on spaceships, tolls so blatant as to resemble piracy. But now shuttles passing through the belts were moving at very high speeds, and slightly above or below the plane of the ecliptic, to avoid the dust and rubble that was only getting worse with the hollowing of so many rocks. It was difficult to demand a toll from these ships without threatening their total destruction, which invited heavy retribution; and so the trend in tolls had proved to be short-lived.

Now, with both Earth and Mars feeling population pressures that were more and more intense, the Martian co-ops were doing everything they could to encourage the rapid development of new asteroid cities. They were also building large new tented settlements on the moons of Jupiter and Saturn, and most recently Uranus, with Neptune and perhaps even Pluto to follow. The big satellites of the inner gas giants were very large moons, really little planets, and all of them now had inhabitants who were beginning terraforming projects that were more or less long-range, depending on the local situation. None of them could be terraformed quickly, but all of them appeared to be possible, at least to an extent; and some offered the tantalizing opportunity of a complete new world. Titan, for instance, was beginning to come out of its nitrogen haze, as settlers living in tents on the smaller moons nearby heated and pumped the big moon's surface oxygen into its atmosphere. Titan had the right volatiles for terraformation, and though it was at great distance from the sun, receiving only one per cent the insolation that Earth did, an extensive series of mirrors was adding light, more all the time, and the locals were looking into the possibility of free-hanging deuterium fusion lanterns, orbiting Titan and illuminating it further. This would be an alternative to another device that so far the Saturnians had been averse to using, called a gas lantern. These gas lanterns were now flying through the upper atmospheres of Jupiter and Uranus, collecting and burning helium$_3$ and other gases in flares whose light was reflected outward by electromagnetic disks. But the Saturnians had refused to allow them, because they did not want to disturb the ringed planet's appearance.

So in all these outer orbits the Martian co-ops were extremely busy, helping Martians and Terrans to emigrate to one of the new little worlds. And as the process continued, and a hundred and then a thousand asteroids and moonlets were given a local habitation and a name, the process took fire, becoming what some called the explosive diaspora, others simply the Accelerando. People took to the idea, and the project gathered an energy that was felt everywhere, expressing a growing sense of humanity's power to create, its vitality and variety. And the Accelerando was also understood to be humanity's response to the supreme crisis of the population surge, a crisis so severe that it made the Terran flood of 2129 look in comparison like no more than a bad high tide. It was a crisis which could have triggered a terminal disaster, a descent into chaos and barbarity; and instead it was being met head-on by the greatest efflorescence of civilization in history, a new renaissance.

Many historians, sociologists and other social observers attempted to explain the vibrant nature of this most self-conscious age. One school of historians, called the Deluge Group, looked back to the great Terran flood, and declared that it had been the cause of the new renaissance: a forced jump to a higher level. Another school of thought put forth the so-called Technical Explanation; humanity had passed through one of the transitions to a new level of technological competence, they maintained, as it had every half-century or so right back to the first industrial revolution. The Deluge Group tended to use the term diaspora, the Technics the term Accelerando. Then in the 2170s the Martian historian Charlotte Dorsa Brevia wrote and published a dense multi-volumed analytical metahistory, as she called it, which maintained that the great flood had indeed served as a trigger point, and technical advances as the enabling mechanism, but that the specific character of the new renaissance had been caused by something much more fundamental, which was the shift from one kind of global socio-economic system to the next. She described what she called a 'residual/emergent complex of overlapping paradigms', in which each great socio-economic era was composed of roughly equal parts of the systems immediately adjacent to it in past and future. The periods immediately before and after were not the only ones involved, however; they formed the bulk of a system, and comprised its most contradictory components, but additional important features came from particularly persistent aspects of more archaic systems, and also faint hesitant intuitions of developments that would not flower until much later.

Feudalism, therefore, to take one example, was for Charlotte made up of a clash of the residual system of absolute religious monarchy, and the emergent system of capitalism – with important echoes of more archaic tribal caste, and faint foreshadowings of later individualist humanisms. The clashing of these forces shifted over time, until the Renaissance of the sixteenth century ushered in the age of capitalism. Capitalism then was composed of clashing elements of the residual feudalism, and an emergent future order that was only now being defined in their own time, which Charlotte called democracy. And now, Charlotte claimed, they were, on Mars at least, in the democratic age itself. Capitalism had therefore, like all other ages, been the combination of two systems in very sharp opposition to each other. This incompatibility of its constituent parts was underlined by the unfortunate experience of capitalism's critical shadow, socialism, which had theorized true democracy, and called for it, but in the attempt to enact it had used the methods at hand in its time, the same feudal methods so prevalent in capitalism itself; so that both versions of the mix had ended up about as destructive and unjust as their common residual parent. The feudal hierarchies in capitalism had been mirrored in the lived socialist experiments; and so the whole era had remained a highly-charged chaotic struggle, exhibiting several different versions of the dynamic struggle between feudalism and democracy.

But the democratic age had finally, on Mars, emerged from the capitalist age. And this age too, following the logic of Charlotte's paradigm, was necessarily a clash of residual and emergent – between the contentious, competitive residuals of the capitalist system, and some emergent aspects of an order beyond democracy – one that could not be fully characterized yet, as it had never existed, but which Charlotte ventured to call Harmony, or General Good Will. This speculative leap she made partly by studying closely how different co-operative economics was from capitalism, and partly by taking an even larger metahistorical perspective, and identifying a broad general movement in history which commentators called her Big See-Saw, a movement from the deep residuals of the dominance hierarchies of our primate ancestors on the savannah, toward the very slow, uncertain, difficult, unpredetermined, free emergence of a pure harmony and equality which would then characterize the very truest democracy. Both of these long-term clashing elements had always existed, Charlotte maintained, creating the Big See-Saw, with the balance between them slowly and irregularly shifting, over all human history so far: dominance hierarchies had underlain every system ever realized so far, but at the same time democratic values had been always a hope and a goal, expressed in every primate's sense of self, and resentment of hierarchies that after all had to be imposed, by force. And so as the see-saw of this meta-metahistory had shifted balance over the centuries, the noticeably imperfect attempts to institute democracy had slowly gained power. Thus a very small percentage of humans had counted as true equals in slave-holding societies like ancient Greece or revolutionary America, and the circle of true equals had only enlarged a bit more in the later 'capitalist democracies'. But as each system passed on to the next, the circle of equal citizens had bloomed wider, by a slight or great margin, until now not only were all humans (in theory, almost) equal, but consideration was being given to other animals, and even to plants, ecosystems and the elements themselves. These last extensions of 'citizenship' Charlotte considered to be among the foreshadowings of the emergent system that might come after democracy per se, Charlotte's postulated period of utopian 'harmony'. The glimmerings were faint, and Charlotte's distant, hoped-for system a vague hypothesis; when Sax Russell read the later volumes of her work, poring avidly over the endless examples and arguments, reading in an excited state at finding a general paradigm that might clarify history for him at last, he wondered if this putative age of universal harmony and good will would ever actually come about; it seemed to him possible or even likely that there was some sort of asymptotic curve in the human story – the ballast of the body, perhaps – which would keep civilization struggling there in the age of democracy, struggling always upward, also away from relapse, and never getting much further along; but it also seemed to him that this state itself would be good enough to call a successful civilization. Enough was as good as a feast, after all.

In any case, Charlotte's metahistory was very influential, providing for the explosively accelerating diaspora a kind of master narrative, by which they could orient themselves; and so she joined the small list of historians whose analyses had affected the flow of their own time, people like Plato, Plutarch, Bacon, Gibbon, Chamfort, Carlyle, Emerson, Marx, Spengler – and on Mars before Charlotte, Michel Duval. People now ordinarily understood capitalism to have been the clash of feudalism and democracy, and the present to be the democratic age, the clash of capitalism and harmony. And they also understood that their own era could still become anything else as well – Charlotte was insistent that there was no such thing as historical determinism, but only people's repeated efforts to enact their hopes; then the analyst's retroactive recognition of such hopes as came true created an illusion of determinism. Anything could have happened; they could have fallen apart into general anarchy, they could have become a universal police state to 'control' the crisis years; but as the great metanationals of Terra had in reality all mutated into Praxislike worker-owned co-operatives, with people in control of their own work – democracy it was, for the moment. They had enacted that hope.

And now their democratic civilization was accomplishing something that the previous system could never have accomplished, which was simply survival in the hypermalthusian period. Now they could begin to see that fundamental shift in systems, in this twenty-second century they were enacting; they had shifted the balance, in order to survive the new conditions. In the co-operative democratic economy, everyone saw the stakes were high; everyone felt responsible for their collective fate; and everyone benefited from the frenetic burst of co-ordinated construction that was going on everywhere in the solar system.

This flowering civilization included not only the solar system beyond Mars, but the inner planets as well. In the flush of energy and confidence humanity was working back in to areas previously considered uninhabitable, and now Venus was attracting a crowd of new terraformers, who were following up on the gesture made by Sax Russell with the relocation of Mars's great mirrors, and had elaborated a grand vision for the eventual inhabitation of that planet, the sister to Earth in so many ways.

And even Mercury had its settlement. Although it had to be admitted that for most purposes, Mercury was too close to the sun. Its day lasted fifty-nine Terran days, its year eighty-eight Terran days, so that three of its days equalled two years, a pattern that was not a coincidence but a node on the way to being tidally locked, like Luna around the Earth. The combination of these two spins gave Mercury a very slow roll through its solar day, during which the brightside hemisphere became much too hot, while the nightside hemisphere became extremely cold. The lone city currently on the planet was therefore a kind of enormous train, running around the planet on tracks set on the northern forty-fifth latitude. These tracks were made of a metalloceramic alloy that was the first of the Mercurial physicists' many alchemical tricks, a matrix that withstood the 800° K heat of mid-brightside. The city itself, called Terminator, then ran over these tracks at a speed of about three kilometres per hour, which kept it within the planet's terminator, the zone of predawn shadow that was in most terrain about twenty kilometres wide. A slight expansion of the tracks exposed to the morning sun farther to the east drove the city ever westward, as it rested on tightly-fitting sleeves shaped to slide the city away from the expansion. This motion was so inexorable that resistance to it in another part of the sleeves generated great amounts of electrical power, as did the solar collectors trailing the city, and set on the very top of the high Dawn Wall, catching the first blasting rays of sunlight. Even in a civilization where energy was cheap, Mercury was amazingly blessed. And so it joined the worlds farther out, and became one of the brightest of all. And a hundred new floating worlds opened every year – cities in flight, little city-states, each with its own charter, settler mix, landscape, style.

And yet still, with all the blossoming of human effort and confidence of the Accelerando, there was a sense of tension in the air, of danger. For despite all the building, emigration, settlement and inhabitation, there were still eighteen billion on Earth, and eighteen million on Mars; and the semipermeable membrane between the two planets was curved taut with the osmotic pressure of that demographic imbalance. Relations between the two were tense, and many feared that a prick of the taut membrane could tear everything asunder. In this pressured situation, history was little comfort; so far they had dealt with it well, but never before had humanity responded to a crisis of need with any long-term consistent, sensible sanity; mass-madness had erupted before; and they were the exact same animals that in previous centuries, faced with matters of subsistence and survival, had slaughtered each other indiscriminately. Presumably it could happen again. So people built, argued, grew furious; waited, uneasily, for signs that the oldest superelderly were dying; stared hard at every child they saw. A stressed renaissance, then, living fast, on the edge, a manic golden age: the Accelerando. And no one could say what would happen next.

Zo sat at the back of a room full of diplomats, looking out of the window at Terminator as the oval city rolled majestically over the blasted wastelands of Mercury. The hemi-ellipsoidal space under the city's high clear dome would have been a pretty airspace to fly in, but the local authorities had banned it as too dangerous – one of many fascist regulations that bound life here – the state as nanny, what Nietzsche so aptly called the slave mentality, still alive and well here at the end of the twenty-second century, in fact popping up everywhere, hierarchy re-erecting its comforting structure in all these new provincial settlements, Mercury, the asteroids, the outer systems – everywhere except on noble Mars.

Here on Mercury it was particularly bad. Meetings between the Martian delegation and the Mercurians had been going on in Terminator for weeks, and Zo was tired of them, both the meetings and the Mercurial negotiators, a secretive self-important group of oligarchic mullahs haughty and fawning at the same time, who had not yet comprehended the new order of things in the solar system. She wanted to forget them and their little world, to go home and fly.

On the other hand, in her cover as a lowly staff assistant, she had up to this point been an entirely minor figure in the proceedings, and now that negotiations were grinding to a halt, stalled on the stubborn incomprehension of these happy slaves, her turn had come at last. As the meeting broke up, she took aside an aide to the highest leader in Terminator, who was called rather picturesquely the Lion of Mercury, and asked for a private meeting. The young man, an ex-Terran, was agreeable – Zo had made sure of his interest long before – and they retired to a terrace outside the city offices.

Zo put a hand to the man's arm, said kindly, 'We're very concerned that if Mercury and Mars don't make a solid partnership, Terra will drive a wedge between us and play us off against each other. We're the two largest collections of heavy metals left in the solar system, and the more civilization spreads, the more valuable that becomes. And civilization is

501

certainly spreading. This is the *Accelerando*, after all. Metals are valuable.'

And Mercury's natural fund of metals, though hard to mine, was truly spectacular; the planet was only a little bigger than Luna and yet its gravity nearly equalled that of Mars, a very tangible sign of its heavy iron core, and its accompanying array of more precious metals, seamed all through the meteor-battered surface.

'Yes . . . ?' the young man said.

'We feel that we need to establish a more explicit . . .'

'Cartel?'

'Partnership.'

The young Mercurian smiled. 'We aren't worried about being pitted against Mars by anyone.'

'Obviously. But we are.'

For a time there, at the beginning of its colonization, Mercury had seemed to be very flush. Not only did the colonists have metals, but being so close to the sun, they had the possibility of tapping a great deal of solar energy. Just the resistance set up between the city's sleeves and the expanding tracks they slid over created enormous amounts of it, and there was even more in solar collection potential; collectors in Mercurial orbit had started lazing some of that sunlight out to the new outer solar system colonies. From the first fleet of track-laying cars, in 2142, through the rolling construction of Terminator in the 2150s, and throughout the 2160s and '70s, the Mercurians had thought they were rich.

Now it was 2181, however, and with the successful wide deployment of various kinds of fusion power, energy was cheap, and light was reasonably plentiful. The so-called lamp satellites, and the gas lanterns burning in the upper atmospheres of the gas giants, were being built and lit all over the outer system. As a result Mercury's copious solar resources had been rendered insignificant. Mercury had become once again nothing more than a metal-rich but dreadfully hot-and-cold place, a hardship assignment. And unterraformable to boot.

Quite a crash in their fortunes, as Zo reminded the young man without much subtlety. Which meant they needed to co-operate with their more conveniently located allies in the system. 'Otherwise the risk of Terran return to dominance is very real.'

'Terra is too enmeshed in its own problems to endanger anyone else,' the young man said.

Zo shook her head gently. 'The more trouble Terra is in, the worse danger for the rest of us. That's why we're worried. That's why we're thinking that, if you don't want to enter into an agreement with us, we may just have to build another city and track system on Mercury, down in the southern hemisphere, and cruise in the terminator down there. Where some of the best metal deposits are.'

The young man was shocked. 'You couldn't do that without our permission.'

'Couldn't we?'

'No city on Mercury can exist if we don't want it to.'

'Why, what will you do?'

The young man was silent.

Zo said, 'Anyone can do what they want, eh? This is true for everyone ever born.'

The young man thought it over. 'There's not enough water.'

'No.' Mercury's water supply consisted in its entirety of small ice fields lying inside craters at the two poles, where they remained in permanent shadow. These crater glaciers contained enough water for Terminator's purposes, but not much more. 'A few comets directed at the poles would add more, however.'

'Unless their impact blasted all the water on the poles away! No, that wouldn't work! The ice in those polar craters is only a tiny fraction of the water from billions of years of comets, hitting all over the planet. Most of the water was lost to space on impact, or burned off. The same thing would happen if comets struck up there now. You'd get a net loss.'

'The AI modellers suggest all kinds of possibilities. We could always try it and see.'

The young man stepped back, affronted. And rightly so; you couldn't put a threat much more explicitly than that. But in slave moralities the good and the stupid tended to become much the same, so one had to be explicit. Zo held her expression steady, though the young man's indignation had a *commedia dell'arte* quality that was quite funny. She stepped closer to him, emphasizing their difference in height; she had half a metre on him.

'I'll give the Lion your message,' he said through his teeth.

'Thanks,' Zo said, and leaned down to kiss him on the cheek.

These slaves had created for themselves a ruling caste of physicist-priests, who were a black box for those on the outside, but like all good oligarchies predictable and powerful in their exterior action. They would take the hint, and be able to act on it. An alliance would follow. So Zo left their offices, and walked happily down the stepped streets of the Dawn Wall. Her work was done, and so very likely the mission would soon return to Mars.

She entered the Martian Consulate midway down the wall and sent a call to Jackie letting her know that the next move had been made. After that she walked out onto the balcony to have a smoke.

Her colour vision surged under the impact of the chromotropics lacing her cigarette, and the little city below her became quite stunning, a Fauvist fantasia. Against the Dawn Wall the terracing rose in ever narrower strips, until the highest buildings (the offices of the city rulers, naturally) were a mere line of windows under the Great Gates and the clear dome above it. Tile roofs and balconies were nestled under the green treetops below her, the balconies all floored and walled by mosaics. Down on the oval flat that held the greater part of the city, the roofs were bigger and closer together, the greenery bunched in crops that glowed under the light that bounced down from filtered mirrors in the dome; altogether it looked like a big Fabergé egg, elaborate, colourful, pretty in the way that all cities were. But to be trapped inside one . . . well, there was nothing for it but to pass the hours in as entertaining a manner as possible, until she got the word to go home. Part of one's nobility was devotion to duty, after all.

So she strode down the Wall's staircase streets to Le Dôme, to party with Miguel and Arlene and Xerxes, and the band of composers, musicians, writers and other artists and aesthetes who hung out at the café. It was a wild bunch. Mercury's craters had all been named centuries before after the most famous artists in Terran history, and so as Terminator rolled along it passed Dürer and Mozart, Phidias and Purcell,

Turgenev and Van Dyke; and elsewhere on the planet were Beethoven, Imhotep, Mahler, Matisse, Murasaki, Milton, Mark Twain; Homer and Holbein touched rims; Ovid starred the rim of the much larger Pushkin, in one of many reversals of true importance; Goya overlapped Sophocles, Van Gogh was inside Cervantes; Chao Meng-fu was full of ice; and so on and so forth, in a most capricious manner, as if the naming committee of the International Astronomical Union had one night got hilariously drunk and started tossing named darts at a map; there was even a clue commemorating this party, a huge escarpment named Pourquoi Pas.

Zo thoroughly approved the method. But the effect on the artists currently living on Mercury had been catastrophic in the extreme. Constantly confronted as they were by Terra's unmatchable canon, an overwhelming anxiety of influence had crippled them. But their partying had taken on a corresponding greatness that Zo quite enjoyed.

On this evening, after a considerable amount of drinking in the Dôme, during which time the city rolled between Stravinsky and Vyasa, the group took off through the narrow alleyways of the city, looking for trouble. A few blocks away they barged in on a ceremony of Mithraists or Zoroastrians, sunworshippers in any case, influential in local government and indeed perhaps the heart of it, and their catcalls quickly broke up the meeting and stimulated a fistfight, and in short order they had to run to avoid arrest by the local constabulary, the spasspolizei as the Dôme crowd called them.

After that they went to the Odeon, but were kicked out for being unruly; then they cruised the alleyways of the entertainment district, and danced outside a bar where loud bad industrial was being played. But there was something missing. Forced gaiety was so pathetic, Zo thought, looking down at their sweaty faces. 'Let's go outside,' she suggested. 'Let's go out on the surface and play piper at the gates of dawn.'

No one except Miguel showed any interest. They were worms in a bottle; they had forgotten the ground existed. But Miguel had promised to take her out many times, and now, with her time on Mercury short, he was finally just bored enough to agree to go.

* * *

505

Terminator's tracks were numerous, each smooth grey cylinder held several metres off the ground by an endless row of thick pylons. As the city slid majestically westward, it passed small stationary platforms leading to underground transfer bunkers, baked Ballardian spaceplane runways, and crater-rim refuges. Leaving the city was a controlled activity (no surprise) but Miguel had a pass, and so the two of them activated the south city doors with it, and stepped into the lock and across into an underground station called Hammersmith. There they suited up, in bulky but flexible spacesuits, and went out through a lock into a tunnel, and up onto the blasted dust of Mercury.

Nothing could have been more clean and spare than this waste of black and grey. In such a context Miguel's drunken giggling bothered Zo more than usual, and she turned down her helmet intercom until it was no more than a whisper.

Walking east of the city was dangerous; even standing still was dangerous; but to see the sun's edge, that's what they had to do. Zo kicked at the rocks as they wandered southwest, to get an angle on their view of the city. She wished she could fly over this black world; presumably some kind of rocket backpack would do the trick, but no one had bothered to work it up, as far as she knew. So they trudged along instead, keeping a sharp eye to the east. Very soon the sun would rise over that horizon; above them now, in the ultrathin neon-argon atmosphere, fine dust kicked up by electron bombardment was turning to a faint white mist in the solar bombardment. Behind them the very top of the Dawn Wall was a blaze of pure white, impossible to look at even through the heavy differential filtering of their helmet facemasks.

Then the rocky flat horizon ahead of them to the east, near Stravinsky Crater, turned into a silver nitrate image of itself. Zo stared into the explosive phosphorescent dancing line, rapt: Sol's corona, like a forest fire in some silver forest just over the horizon. Zo's spirit flashed likewise; she would have flown like Icarus into the sun if she could; she felt like a moth wanting the flame, a kind of spiritual sexual hunger, and indeed she was crying out in just the same involuntary orgasmic cries, *such* a fire, *such* a beauty. The solar rapture, they called this back in the city, and well named. Miguel felt

506

it as well; he was leaping from boulder tops eastward, arms spread wide, like Icarus trying to launch himself.

Then he came down awkwardly in the dust, and Zo could hear his cry even with her intercom volume turned almost off. She ran to him and saw the impossible angle of his left knee, cried out herself and kneeled at his side. Through the suit the ground was frigid. She helped him up, his arm over her shoulder. She turned up the volume on her intercom, even though he was groaning loudly. 'Shut up,' she said. 'Concentrate, pay attention.'

They got into a rhythm, hopping west after the receding Dawn Wall, still incandescent across the top of its tall bell curve. It was receding from them; there was no time to be lost. But they kept falling. The third time, sprawled in the dust, the landscape a blinding mix of pure white and pure black, Miguel screamed in pain and then panted out, 'Go on, Zo, go save yourself! No reason both of us should die out here!'

'Oh fuck that,' Zo said, picking herself up.

'*Go!*'

'I won't! Shut up now, let me try carrying you.'

He weighed about what he would on Mars, seventy kilos with the suit, she guessed, more a matter of balance than anything else, so while he babbled on hysterically, 'Let me go, Zo, truth is beauty, beauty truth, that is all you know and all you need to know,' she leaned over and put her arms under his back and knees, which caused him to shriek. 'Shut up!' she cried. 'Right now this is the truth, and therefore beautiful.' And she laughed as she started to run with him in her arms.

He blocked her view of the ground directly before them, so she had to look forward in the blaze-and-black, with sweat in her eyes. It was hard going, and twice more she fell; but while running she thumped along at a good speed back toward the city.

Then she felt sunlight on her back. It was like the pricking of needles, even through her insulated suit. Massive surge of adrenalin; blinded by the light; some kind of valley aligned to the dawn; then back into the patchy zone of light-shot shadows, a crazy chiaroscuro; then, slowly, back into the terminator proper, everything shadowed and dim except for the

507

fiery city wall, blazing far above. She was gasping hard for air, sweating heavily, hot from exertion now rather than sunlight. And yet still the sight of the incandescent arc at the top of the city was enough to make one into a Mithraist.

Of course even when the city was directly over them, there was no immediate way of getting back up into it. She had to run past it, on to the next underground station. Complete focus on running, for minute after minute. Lactic acid pain. And there it was, up ahead on the horizon, a door in a hill beside the tracks; pound and pound over the smoothed regolith. Violent hammering on the door got the two of them let into the lock and inside, where they were arrested; but Zo just laughed at the spasspolizei, and got her helmet off, and Miguel's, and kissed the sobbing Miguel repeatedly for his clumsiness. In his pain he didn't notice, he was latched onto her as a drowning man to a lifesaver. She only succeeded in disengaging herself from his grasp by banging him gently on his hurt knee. She laughed out loud at his howl, feeling a rush pour through her; such adrenalin, so beautiful, rarer by far than any sexual orgasm, thus more precious. So she kissed Miguel again and again, kisses that he did not notice, and then she barged through the spasspolizei, claiming diplomatic status and a need for haste. 'Get him some drugs, you fools,' she said. 'A shuttle for Mars is leaving tonight, I have to go.'

'Thank you Zo!' Miguel cried. 'Thank you! You saved my life!'

'I saved my trip home,' she said, and laughed at his expression. She returned to kiss him some more. 'It's me who should be thanking you! Such an opportunity! Thank you, thank you.'

'No, thank you!'

'No, thank you!'

And even in his agony he laughed. 'I love you, Zo.'

'And I love you.'

But if she didn't hurry she would miss her shuttle.

The shuttle was a pulsed fusion rocket, and they would reach Earth the day after tomorrow. And in a decent gravity the whole time, except for during the somersault.

All manner of things were changing because of this sudden shrinkage of the solar system. One small result was that Venus was no longer needed as a gravity handle for rocket travel, and so it was coincidence only that had Zo's shuttle, the *Nike of Samothrace*, passing fairly near to the shaded planet. Zo joined the rest of the passengers in the big skylight ballroom to look at it as they passed. The clouds of the planet's superheated atmosphere were dark; the planet appeared as a grey circle against the black of space. The terraforming of Venus was proceeding apace, the whole planet in the shade of a parasol, which was Mars's old soletta with its mirrors repositioned so that they did just the opposite of what they had done in front of Mars; rather than redirect light onto the planet, they reflected it all away. Venus rolled in darkness.

This was the first step of a terraforming project that many people deemed mad. Venus had no water, a stupendously thick, superheated carbon dioxide atmosphere, a day longer than its year, and surface temperatures that would melt lead and zinc. Not a promising set of initial conditions, it was true, but people had begun to try anyway, humanity's reach continuing to exceed its grasp, even as its grasp became godlike; Zo thought it was wonderful. The people who had initiated the project were even claiming it could happen faster than the terraforming of Mars. This was because the complete removal of sunlight had profound effects; the temperature in the thick carbon dioxide atmosphere (95 'bar at the surface!) had been dropping by 5° K a year for the last half century. Soon the 'Big Rain' would begin to fall, and in just a couple of hundred years the carbon dioxide would all be on the planet, in dry-ice glaciers covering the low parts of the surface. At that point the dry ice was to be covered by an insulating layer of diamond coating or foamed rock, and once sealed off, water oceans would be introduced. The water was going to come from somewhere else, as Venus's natural inventory would cover it to a depth of a centimetre or less. The Venusian terraformers, mystics of a new kind of viriditas, were currently negotiating with the Saturnian League for the rights to the ice moon Enceledus, which they hoped to drive down into Venusian orbit and break up in successive passes through the atmosphere. This moon's water once rained onto Venus would create shallow oceans over about seventy per cent of the planet, entirely covering the wrapped carbon dioxide glaciers. An atmosphere of oxygen and hydrogen would be left in place, some light would be let through the parasol, and at that point human settlements would become possible, on the two high continents Ishtar and Aphrodite. After that, they would have all the remaining problems of terraforming that Mars had been dealing with, and they would also have the very long term, specifically Venusian projects of removing the carbon dioxide ice sheets from the planet somehow, and also imparting enough spin to the planet to give it a reasonable diurnal cycle; for the short term days and nights could be established using the parasol as a giant circular Venetian blind, but in the long run, they did not want to rely on something so fragile. Zo could understand that; could imagine a similar event some centuries hence, a biosphere and civilization on Venus, the two continents inhabited, the beautiful Diana Rift a fair valley, billions of people and animals, and then one day the parasol knocked awry, and *sssss*, a whole world roasted. Not a happy prospect. And so now, even before the massive flooding and scouring of the Big Rain, they were trying to lay metallic windings as physicalized latitude lines around the planet, windings that would, when a fleet of solar-powered generators were placed in fluctuating orbits around the planet, make the planet in effect the armature of a giant electric motor, the magnetic forces of which would create the torque that would increase the planet's spin. The system's designers claimed that, in about the same time it would take to freeze out the atmosphere and drop an ocean, the impetus of this 'Dyson motor' could speed Venus's rotation enough to give the planet a week-long day; so there they would be, in perhaps three hundred years, down on the transmogrified world, planting crops. The surface would be massively eroded of course, and still very volcanic, with carbon dioxide trapped under the seas ready to burst out and poison them, and week-long days cooking and freezing them; but there they would be nevertheless, everything stripped, raw, new.

The plan was insane. It was beautiful. Zo stared up through the ballroom ceiling at the gibbous grey globe, hopping from foot to foot in her excitement, in her horror and admiration, hoping to catch a glimpse of the little dots of the new asteroid moons that were home to the terraforming mystics, or perhaps the coronal arc of a reflection from the annular mirror that used to be Mars's. No luck there – only the grey disc of the shaded evening star, the signet of people who had taken on a task that recontextualized humanity as a kind of god-bacteria, chewing away at worlds, dying to prepare the ground for later life – dwarfed most grandiosely in the cosmic scheme of things, in an almost Calvinistic masochist-heroism – a parodic travesty of the Mars project – and yet just as magnificent. They were specks in this universe, specks! But what ideas they had. People would do anything for the sake of an idea, anything.

Even visit Earth. Steaming, clotted, infectious, a human ant-hill stuck with a stick; the panic pullulation ongoing in the dreadful mash of history; the hypermalthusian nightmare at its worst; hot, humid, and heavy; and yet still, or perhaps because of all that, a great place to visit. And Jackie wanted her to check in with a couple of people in India anyway. So Zo had taken the *Nike*, and would later catch a Mars shuttle from Earth.

Before she went to India to talk to Jackie's contacts, however, she made her regular pilgrimage to Crete, to see the ruins that here were still called Minoan, although in Dorsa Brevia she had been taught to call them Ariadnean. Minos had been the one to wreck the ancient matriarchy, after all, so it was one of the many travesties of Terran history that the destroyed civilization should now be named after the destroyer. But names could be changed.

She wore a rented exoskeleton, made for off-world visitors oppressed by the g. Gravity was destiny, as they said, and Earth had a lot of destiny. The suits were like birdsuits without wings, conformable bodysuits that moved with one's muscles while providing some under-support; body-bras. They did not entirely ease the effect of the planet's pull, for breathing was still an effort, and Zo's limbs felt heavy within the suit, so to speak, pressed down uncomfortably against the fabric. She had become used to walking around in the suits on previous trips, and it was a fascinating exercise, like weightlifting, but not one that she liked very much. Better than the alternative, however. She had tried that too, but it was a terrible distraction: it kept one from really seeing, really being there.

So she walked around the ancient site of Gournia, in the peculiar, somewhat submarine flow of the suit. Gournia was her favourite of all the Ariadnean ruins, the only ordinary village of that civilization to have been found and excavated; the other sites were all palaces. This village had probably been a satellite of the palace at Malia: now a warren of waist-high walls made of stacked stones, covering a hilltop overlooking the Aegean. All the rooms were very small, often one metre by two, with alleys running between shared walls; little labyrinths, yes, and very much like the whitewashed villages that still dotted the countryside. People said that Crete had been hard-hit by the great flood, as the Ariadneans had been by theirs following the explosion of Thera; and it was true that all the pretty little fishing harbours were flooded to one extent or another, and the Ariadnean ruins at Zakros and Malia entirely drowned. But what Zo saw on Crete was an everlasting vitality. There was no other place on Earth she had seen that had handled the population surge as well; everywhere villages clung to the land like beehives, covering hilltops, filling valleys, and surrounded by crops and orchards, with the dry knobby hills still sticking out of the cultivated land, in sculptured ridges rising to the central spine of the island. The island's population had risen to over forty million, she had heard, and yet the island still looked much the same; there were just more villages, built to match the pattern not only of the existing ones but of the ancient ones like Gournia and Itanos as well. Town planning with a continuity five thousand years old, continuity with that first peak of civilization or final peak of prehistory, so tall as to be glimpsed even by classical Greece a thousand years later, enduring by oral transmission alone as the myth of Atlantis – and then also in the shapes of all their subsequent lives, not only on Crete, but now on her Mars as well. Because of the names used in Dorsa Brevia, and that culture's valorization of the Ariadnean matriarchy, the two places had developed a relationship; many Martians came to Crete to visit the ancient sites, and there were new hotels near all of them now, built on a slightly larger scale to accommodate the tall young pilgrims, visiting the holy places station to station – Phaistos, Gournia, Itanos, Malia and Zakros under the water, even the ridiculous 'reconstruction' at Knossos. They came and saw how it had all begun, back in the morning of the world. Zo too – standing in the brilliant blue Aegean light, straddling a stone alleyway five thousand years old – felt pouring into her the reverberations of that greatness, up through the spongy, red stones underfoot and into her own heart. Nobility that would never end.

The rest of Earth, however, was Calcutta. Well, that wasn't really fair. But Calcutta itself was definitely Calcutta. Fetid humanity at its most compacted; whenever she went out of her room Zo had at least five hundred people in her field of vision, and often a few thousand. There was a frightful exhilaration in the sight of all this life in the streets, a world of dwarves and midgets and other assorted small people, all of whom saw her and clumped like baby birds to a parent who could feed them. Although Zo had to admit that the clumping was friendlier than that, composed more of curiosity than hunger – indeed they seemed more interested in her exoskeleton than her. And they seemed happy enough, thin but not emaciated, even when they were clearly permanently camped on the streets. The streets themselves were co-ops now, people had tenure, swept them, regulated the millions of little markets, grew crops in every plaza, and slept among them too. That was life on Earth in the late Holocene. After Ariadne it had been downhill all the way.

Zo went up to Prahapore, an enclave in the hills to the north of the city. This was where one of Jackie's Terran spies lived, in the midst of a jammed dorm of harried civil servants, all living at their screens and sleeping under their desks. Jackie's contact was a translator-programmer, a woman who understood Mandarin, Urdu, Dravidian and Vietnamese, as well as her Hindu and English; she also was important in an extensive eavesdropping network, and could keep Jackie informed concerning some of the Indian-Chinese conversations about Mars.

'Of course they both will send more people to Mars,' the heavyset woman said to Zo, after they were out in the compound's little herb garden. 'That's a given. But it does look as though both governments feel they have their populations in a long-term solution. No one expects to have more than one child any more. It's not only the law, it's the tradition.'

'The uterine law,' Zo said.

The woman shrugged. 'Possibly so. A very strong tradition, in any case. People look around, they see the problem. They expect to get the longevity treatment, and they expect to have a sterility implant at that time. And in India, anyway, they feel lucky if they get the permits to remove the implants. And after having one child, people expect to be sterilized for good. Even the Hindu fundamentalists have changed on this, the social pressure on them was so great. And the Chinese have been doing this for centuries. The longevity treatment only reinforced what they had already been doing.'

'So Mars has less to fear from them than Jackie thinks.'

'Well, they still want to send up emigrants, that's part of the overall strategy. And resistance to the one-child rule has been stronger in some Catholic and Moslem countries, and several of those nations would like to colonize Mars as if it were empty. The threat shifts now from India and China to the Philippines, Brazil, Pakistan.'

'Hmm,' Zo said. Talk of immigration always made her feel oppressed. Threatened by lemmings. 'What about the ex-metas?'

'The old Group of Eleven is rebanding in support of the strongest of the old metanats. They will be looking for places to develop. They're much weaker than before the flood, but they still have a lot of influence in America, Russia, Europe, South America. Tell Jackie to watch what Japan does in the next few months, she'll see what I mean.' They connected up wristpads so that the woman could make a secure transfer of detailed information for Jackie.

'Okay,' Zo said. Suddenly she was tired, as if a heavy man had crawled into the exoskeleton with her and were dragging her down. Earth, what a drag. Some people said they liked the weight, as if they needed that pressure to be convinced of their own reality. Zo wasn't like that. Earth was the very definition of exoticism, which was fine, but suddenly she longed to be home. She unplugged her wristpad from the translator's, imagining all the while that perfect middle way, that perfect test of will and flesh: the exquisite gravity of Mars.

Then it was down the space elevator from Clarke, a trip that took longer than the flight from Earth; and she was back in the world, the only real world, Mars the magnificent. 'There's no place like home,' Zo said to the train station crowd in Sheffield, and then she sat happily in the trains as they flowed over the pistes down Tharsis, then north to Echus Overlook.

The little town had grown since its early days as the terraforming headquarters, but not much; it was out of the way, and built into the steep east wall of Echus Chasma, so that there wasn't much of it to be seen – a bit on the plateau at the top of the cliff, a bit at the bottom, but with three vertical kilometres between the two, so that they were not visible one from the other – more like two separate villages, connected by a vertical subway. Indeed if it weren't for the flyers, Echus Overlook might have subsided into sleepy historic-monument status, like Underhill or Senzeni Na, or the icy hideouts in the south. But the eastern wall of Echus Chasma stood right in the path of the prevailing westerlies that came pouring down the Tharsis Bulge, causing them to shoot up in the most astonishingly powerful updraughts. Which made it a birding paradise.

Zo was supposed to check in with Jackie and the Free Mars apparatchiks working for her, but before getting embroiled in all that she wanted to fly. So she checked her old Santorini hawksuit out of storage at the gliderport, and went to the changing room and slipped into it, feeling the smooth, muscly texture of the suit's flexible exoskeleton. Then it was down the path, trailing her tail feathers, and onto the Diving Board, a natural overhang that had been artificially extended with a concrete slab. She walked to the edge of this slab and looked down, down, down, three thousand metres down, to the umber floor of Echus Chasma. With the usual burst of adrenalin she tipped forward and fell off the cliff. Headfirst, down, down, down, the wind picking up in a swift whoosh over her helmet as she reached terminal velocity, which she recognized by the pitch of the whooshing; and then she spread her arms, and felt the suit stiffen and help her muscles to hold the beautiful wings wide, and with a loud, crumping smoosh of wind she curved up into the sun, turned her head, arched her back, pointed her toes and set the tail feathers, left right left; and the wind was pulling her up, up, up. Shift her feet and arms together, turn then in a tight gyre, see the cliff then the chasm floor, around and around: flying. Zo the hawk, wild and free. She was laughing happily, and tears streamed this way and that in her goggles, dashed away by the force of the g.

The air above Echus was nearly empty this morning. After riding the updraught most flyers were peeling off to the north, soaring, or shooting down one of the clefts in the cliff wall, where the updraught was diminished and it was possible to tip and dive in stoops of great velocity. Zo too, when she reached about five thousand metres above Overlook, and was breathing the pure oxygen of her helmet's enclosed air system, turned her head right and dipped her right wing, and curved through the exhilaration of a run across the wind, feeling it keen over her body in a rapid fingering. No sound but the hard *whoosh* of wind in her wings. The somatic pressure of the wind all over her body was a subtly sensuous massage, and she felt it through the tightened suit as if the suit were not there, as if she were naked and feeling the wind directly on her skin, as she wished she could be. A good suit reinforced this impression, of course, and she had used this one for three M-years before leaving for Mercury; it fitted like a glove, it was great to be back in it.

She pulled up into a kite, then stunted forward in the manoeuvre called Jesus Falling. A thousand metres down and she pulled her wings in and began to dolphin kick to speed her stoop, until the wind was keening loudly over her, and she passed the edge of the great wall going well over terminal velocity. Passing the rim was the sign to start pulling out, because as tall as the cliff was, at full stoop the chasm floor came rushing up like a final slap in the face, and it took a while to pull out of it, even given her strength and skill and nerve, and the reinforcement of the suit. So she arched her back and popped her wings, and felt the strain in her pecs and biceps, a tremendous pressure even though the suit aided her with a logarithmically increasing percentage of the load. Tail feathers down; pike; four hard flaps; and then she was jinking across the chasm's sandy floor, she could have picked a mouse off it.

She turned and got back in the updraught, gyred back up into developing high clouds. The wind was erratic today, and it was an all-absorbing pleasure to tumble and play in it. This was the meaning of life, the purpose of the universe: pure joy, the sense of self gone, the mind become no more than a mirror of the wind. Exuberance; she flew like an angel, as they said. Sometimes one flew like a drone, sometimes one flew like a bird; and then on rare occasions one flew like an angel. It had been a long time.

She came to herself, and lofted back down the wall toward Overlook, feeling tired in her arms. Then she spotted a hawk. Like a lot of flyers, if there was a bird in sight she tracked it, watching it more closely than birders had ever before watched a bird, imitating its every twitch and flutter to try to learn the genius of its flight. Sometimes a hawk over this cliff would be innocently wheeling in a search for food and a whole squadron of flyers would be above it following its moves, or trying to. It was fun.

Now she shadowed the hawk, turning when it did, imitating the placement of the wings and tail. Its mastery of the air was like a talent that she craved but could never have. But she could try: bright sun in the racing clouds, indigo sky, the wind against her body, the little weightless gut-orgasms when she peeled over into a stoop . . . eternal moments of no-mind. The best, cleanest use of human time.

But the sun fell westward and she got thirsty, and so she left the hawk to its day and turned and coursed down in giant lazy Ss to Overlook, to nail her landing with a flap and a step, right on the green Kokopelli, just as if she had never left.

The neighbourhood behind the launching complex was called Topside, and it was a mass of cheap dorms and restaurants inhabited almost entirely by flyers, and tourists come to watch the flying, all eating and drinking and roving and talking and dancing and looking for someone with whom to tandem the night. And there, no surprise, were her flyer friends, Rose and

519

Imhotep and Ella and Estavan, all in a group at the Adler Hofbrauhaus, high already and delighted to see Zo back again among them. They had a drink at the Adler to celebrate the reunion, and then went to Overlook Overlook, and sat on the rail catching up on gossip, passing around a big spliff laced with pandorph, making ribald commentary on the passing parade below the railing, shouting at friends spotted in the crowd.

Eventually they left Overlook Overlook and went down into the crowds of Topside, and slowly made their way through the bars to one of the bathhouses. They piled into the changing room and took off their clothes, and wandered naked through the dark, warm, watery rooms, the water waist-deep, ankle-deep, chest-deep – hot, cold, lukewarm – splitting up, finding each other later, having sex with scarcely visible strangers, Zo working slowly through several partners to her own orgasm, purring happily as her body clamped down on itself and her mind went away. Sex, sex, there was nothing like sex, except for flying, which it much resembled: the rapture of the body, yet another echo of the Big Bang, that first orgasm. Joy at the sight of the stars in the skylight overhead, at the feel of warm water and of some boy who came in her and stayed in her, nearly hard, and three minutes later stiffened and started humping again, laughing at the approach of another bright orgasm. After that she sloshed into the comparative brightness of the bar and found the others there, Estavan declaring that the night's third orgasm was usually the best, with an exquisitely long approach to climax and yet still a good bit of semen left to ejaculate. 'After that it's still fine, but more of an effort: you have to be wild to get off, and then it isn't like the third anyway.' Zo and Rose and the rest of the women agreed that in this as in so many other ways, being female was superior; in a night at the baths they routinely had several wonderful orgasms, and even these were as nothing compared to the *status orgasmus*, a kind of continuous orgasm that could last half an hour if one were lucky and one's partners skilful. There was a craft to this that they studied assiduously, but it was still more art than science, as they all agreed: one had to be high but not too high, with a group but not a crowd . . . lately they had got pretty reliably good at it, they told Zo, and

happily Zo demanded proof. 'Come on, I want to be tabled.'
Estavan hooted and led her and the rest down to a room with
a big table sticking out of the water. Imhotep lay on his back
on the table, Zo's mattress man for the session; she was lifted
up by the others, lying on her back as well, and slid down
onto him, and then the whole group was on her, hands and
mouths and genitals, a tongue in each ear, in her mouth,
contact everywhere; after a while it was all an undifferentiated
mass of erotic sensation, total sex-surround, Zo purring loudly.
Then when she started to come, arching up off Imhotep with
the violence of the cramping, they all kept going, more subtly
now, teasing her, not letting her land, and then she was off
and flying, the touch of a little finger would keep her going,
until she cried out, 'No, I can't!' and they laughed and said,
'You can,' and kept her going until her stomach muscles truly
cramped, and she rolled violently off Imhotep and was caught
by Rose and Estavan. She couldn't even stand. Someone said
they had had her off for twenty minutes; it had felt like two,
or eternity. All her abdominal muscles ached, as did her thighs
and bottom. 'Cold bath,' she said, and crawled off to the cool
water in a nearby room.

But after being tabled there was little else at the baths that
could appeal. Any more orgasms would hurt. She helped to
table Estavan and Xerxes, and then a thin woman she didn't
know, all fun, but then she got bored. Flesh flesh flesh. Sometimes after being tabled one got further and further into it; at
other times it became just skin and hair and flesh, insides and
outsides, who cared?

She went to the changing room and dressed, went outside.
It was morning, the sun bright over the bare plains of Lunae.
She flowed through the empty streets to her hostel, feeling
relaxed and clean and sleepy. A big breakfast, fall into bed,
delicious sleep.

But there in the hostel restaurant was Jackie. 'If it isn't our
Zoya.' She had always hated the name, which Zo had chosen
for herself.

Zo, surprised, said, 'Did you follow me here?'

Jackie looked disgusted. 'It's my co-op too, you might recall.
Why didn't you check in when you got back?'

'I wanted to fly.'

'That's no excuse.'

'I didn't mean it as one.'

Zo went to the buffet table, piled a plate with scrambled eggs and muffins. She returned to Jackie's table, kissed her mother on the top of the head. 'You're looking good.'

Actually she looked younger than Zo, who was often sunburned and therefore wrinkled – younger but somehow *preserved*, as if she were a twin sister of Zo's who had been bottled for a time and only recently decanted. She wouldn't tell Zo how often she had had the gerontological treatments, but Rachel had said that she was always trying new variants, which were coming out at the rate of two or three a year, and that she got the basic package every three years at the most. So although she was somewhere in her fifth M-decade, she looked almost like Zo's contemporary, except for that preserved quality, which was not so much body as spirit – a look in the eye, a certain hardening, a tightness, a wariness or weariness. It was hard work being the alpha female year after year, a heroic struggle; it had worn visible tracks in her no matter how baby-smooth her skin, no matter how much a beauty she remained – and she was still quite a beauty, no doubt about it. But she was getting old. Soon her young men would unwrap themselves from around her little fingers and drop away.

Meanwhile she still had a great deal of *presence*, and at the moment she appeared considerably put out. People averted their eyes as if her look might strike them dead, which made Zo laugh. Not the politest way to greet one's beloved mother, but what else could one do? Zo was too relaxed to be irritated.

Probably a mistake to laugh at her, however. She stared coldly until Zo straightened up.

'Tell me what happened on Mercury.'

Zo shrugged. 'I told you. They still think they have the sun to give to the outer solar system, and it's gone to their heads.'

'I suppose their sunlight would still be useful out there.'

'Energy's always useful, but the outer satellites should be able to generate what they need, now.'

'So the Mercurians are left with metals.'

'That's right.'

'But what do they want for them?'

'Everyone wants to be free. None of these new little worlds are big enough to be self-sufficient, so they have to have something to trade if they want to stay free. Mercury has sunlight and metals, the asteroids have metals, the outer satellites have volatiles, if anything. So they package and trade what they have, and try to make alliances to avoid domination by Earth or Mars.'

'It isn't domination.'

'Of course not.' Zo kept a straight face. 'But the big worlds, you know —'

'Are big.' Jackie nodded. 'But add all these little ones together, and they're big too.'

'Who's going to add them?' Zo asked.

Jackie ignored the question. The answer was obvious anyway: Jackie would. Jackie was locked into a long-term battle with various forces on Earth, for what came down to the control of Mars; she was trying to keep them from being inundated by the immense home world; and as human civilization continued to spread throughout the solar system, Jackie considered the new little settlements pawns in this great struggle. And indeed if there were enough of them, they might make a difference.

'There's not much reason to worry about Mercury,' Zo reassured her. 'It's a dead end, a provincial little town, run by a cult. No one can settle very many people there, no one. So even if we do manage to bring them on board, they won't matter much.'

Jackie's face took on its world-weary look, as if Zo's analysis of the situation were the work of a child — as if there were hidden sources of political power on Mercury, of all places. It was irritating, but Zo restrained herself and did not show her irritation.

Antar came in, looking for them; he saw them and smiled, came over and gave Jackie a quick kiss, Zo a longer one. He and Jackie conferred for a while about something or other, in whispers, and then Jackie told him to leave.

There was a great deal of the will to power in Jackie, Zo saw once again. Ordering Antar around gratuitously; it was a flaunting of power that one saw in many nisei women, women who had grown up in patriarchies and therefore reacted virulently against them. They did not fully understand that patriarchy no longer mattered, and perhaps never had – that it had always been caught in the Kegel grip of uterine law, which operated outside patriarchy with a biological power that could not be controlled by any mere politics. The female hold on male sexual pleasure, on life itself – these were realities for patriarchs as much as for anyone, despite all their repression, their fear of the female which had been expressed in so many ways, purdah, clitoridectomy, foot-binding and so on – ugly stuff indeed, a desperate, ruthless last-ditch defence, successful for a time, certainly – but now blown away without a trace. Now the poor fellows had to fend for themselves, and it was hard. Women like Jackie had them whipped. And women like Jackie liked to whip them.

'I want you to go out to the Uranian system,' Jackie was saying. 'They're just settling out there, and I want to get them early. You can pass along a word to the Galileans as well; they're getting out of line.'

'I should do a co-op stint,' Zo said, 'or it will become too obvious that it's a front.'

After many years of running with a feral co-op based in Lunae, Zo had joined one of the co-ops that functioned in part as a front for Free Mars, allowing Zo and other operatives to do party work without it becoming obvious that that was their principal activity. The co-op Zo had joined built and installed crater screens, but she hadn't worked for them in any real job for over a year.

Jackie nodded. 'Put in some time, then take another leave. In a month or so.'

'Okay.'

Zo was interested in seeing the outer satellites, so it was easy to agree. But Jackie only nodded, showing no sign of awareness that Zo might not have agreed. Her mother was not a very imaginative person, when all was said and done. No doubt Zo's father was the source of that quality in Zo, ka bless him. Zo did not want to know his identity, which at this point would only have been an imposition on her freedom, but she felt a surge of gratitude to him for his genes, her salvation from pure Jackieness.

Zo stood, too tired to take her mother any longer. 'You look tired, and I'm beat,' she said. She kissed Jackie on the cheek as she went off to her room. 'I love you. Maybe you should think about getting the treatment again.'

Her co-op was based in Moreux Crater, in the Protonilus Mensae, between Mangala and Bradbury Point. It was a big crater, puncturing the long slope of the Great Escarpment as it fell down toward the Boone's Neck peninsula. The co-op was always developing new varieties of molecular netting to replace earlier nets, and the old tent fabrics; the mesh they had installed over Moreux was the latest thing, the poly-hydroxybutyrate plastic of its fibres harvested from soyabean plants, engineered to produce the PHB in the plants' chloro-plasts. The mesh held in the equivalent of a daily inversion layer, which made the air inside the crater about thirty per cent thicker and considerably warmer than the outside air. Nets like this one made it easier to get biomes through the tough transition from tent to open air, and when permanently installed, they created nice mesoclimates at higher altitudes or latitudes. Moreux extended up to 43° north, and winters outside the crater were always going to be fairly severe. With the mesh in place they were able to sustain a warm high-altitude forest, sporting an exotic array of plants engineered from the east African volcanoes, New Guinea, and the Hima-layas. Down on the crater floor in the summer the days were seriously hot, and the weird, blooming, spiky trees as fragrant as perfume.

The crater's inhabitants lived in spacious apartments dug into the northern arc of the rim, in four set-back levels of balconies and broad window walls, overlooking the green fronds of the Kilimanjaro slope forest underneath them. The balconies baked in the sun in the winter, and rested under vine-covered trellises in the summer, when daytime tempera-tures soared to 305° K, and people muttered about changing to a coarser mesh to allow more hot air to escape, or even working up a system where they could simply roll off the mesh during the summer.

Zo spent most of every day working on the outer apron or under it, grinding out as much of a full work stint as she could before it came time to leave for the outer satellites. The work this time was interesting, involving long trips underground in mining tunnels, following veins and layers in the crater's old splosh apron. The impact brecciation had created all kinds of useful metamorphic rock, and greenhouse gas minerals were a common secondary find throughout the apron. The co-op was therefore working on new methods of mining, as well as extracting some feedstocks for mesh looms, hoping to make marketable improvements in mining methods that would leave the surface undisturbed while the regolith under it was still being mined intensively. Most of the underground work was of course robotic, but there were various human-optimum tasks still, as there always would be in mining. Zo found it very satisfying to go caving in the dim subMartian world, to spend all day in the bowels of the planet between great plates of rock, with their close rough black walls gleaming with crystals, the powerful lights exploding off them; to check samples, and explore newly-cut galleries, in a forest of dull magnesium uprights jammed into place by the robot excavators; to work like a troglodyte, seeking rare treasure underground; and then to emerge from the elevator car, blinking madly at the sudden sunlight of late afternoon, the air bronze or salmon or amber as the sun blazed through the purpling sky like an old friend, warming them as they trudged up the slope of the apron to the rim gate, where the round forest of Moreux lay below them, a lost world, home to jaguars and vultures. Once inside the mesh there was a cable car that dropped on looping wires to the settlement, but Zo usually went instead to the gatehouse and got her birdsuit out of its locker, slipped into it and zipped up, ran off a flyer's platform and spread her wings, and flew in lazy spirals down to the north rim town, to dinner on one of the dining terraces, watching parrots and cockateels and lorikeets dart about trying to scavenge a meal. For work it was not bad. She slept well.

One day a group of atmospheric engineers came over to see how much air was escaping through the Moreux mesh in the midday summer heat. There were a lot of old ones in the group, people with the blasted eyes and diffuse manner of the long-time field areologist. One of these issei was Sax Russell himself, a small, bald man with a crooked nose, and skin as wrinkled as that of the tortoises clomping around the crater floor. Zo stared and stared at the old man, one of the most famous people in Martian history; it was bizarre to have such a figure out of the books saying hello to her, as if George Washington or Archimedes might dodder by next, the dead hand of the past still there living among them, perpetually dumbfounded by all the latest developments.

Russell certainly appeared dumbfounded; he looked thoroughly stunned through the whole orientation meeting, left the atmospheric inquiries to his associates, and spent his time staring down at the forest below the town. When someone at dinner introduced Zo to him, he blinked at her with a tortoise's dim cunning. 'I taught your mother once.'

'Yes,' Zo said.

'Will you show me the crater floor?' he asked.

'I usually fly over it,' Zo said, surprised.

'I was hoping to walk,' he said, and looked at her, blinking.

The novelty value was so great that she agreed to join him.

They started out in the cool of the morning, following the shade under the eastern rim. Balsa and saal trees intersected overhead, forming a high canopy through which lemurs howled and leaped. The old man walked slowly along, peering at the heedless creatures of the forest, and he spoke seldom, mostly to ask if Zo knew the names of the various ferns and trees. All she could identify for him were the birds. 'The names of plants go in one ear and out the other, I'm afraid,' she admitted cheerfully.

His forehead wrinkled at this.

'I think that helps me to see them better,' she added.

'Really.' He looked around again, as if trying it. 'Does that mean you don't see the birds as well as the plants?'

'They're different. They're my brothers and sisters, they have to have names. It's part of them. But this stuff — ' she gestured at the green fronds around them, giant ferns under spiky flowering trees, ' — this stuff is nameless, really. We make up names, but they don't really have them.'

He thought about this.

'Where do you fly?' he said a kilometre down the overgrown trail.

'Everywhere.'

'Do you have favourite places?'

'I like Echus Overlook.'

'Good updraughts?'

'Very good. I was there until Jackie descended on me and put me to work.'

'It's not your work?'

'Oh yes, yes. But my co-op is good at flex time.'

'Ah. So you will stay here for a while?'

'Only until the Galilean shuttle leaves.'

'Then you will emigrate?'

'No no. A tour, for Jackie. Diplomatic mission.'

'Ah. Will you visit Uranus?'

'Yes.'

'I'd like to see Miranda.'

'Me too. That's one reason I'm going.'

'Ah.'

They crossed a shallow creek, stepping on exposed flat stones. Birds called, insects whirred. Sunlight filled the entire crater bowl now, but under the forest canopy it was still cool, the air shot with parallel columns and wires of slanting yellow light. Russell crouched to stare into the creek they had crossed.

'What was my mother like as a child?' Zo asked.

'Jackie?'

He thought about it. A long time passed. Just as Zo was concluding with exasperation that he had forgotten the question, he said, 'She was a fast runner. She asked a lot of questions. Why why why. I liked that. She was the oldest of that generation of ectogenes, I think. The leader anyway.'

'Was she in love with Nirgal?'

'I don't know. Why, have you met Nirgal?'

'I think so, yes. With the ferals once. What about with Peter Clayborne, was she in love with him?'

'In love? Later, maybe. When they were older. In Zygote, I don't know.'

'You aren't much help.'

'No.'

'Forgotten it all?'

'Not all. But what I remember is – hard to characterize. I remember Jackie asking about John Boone one day, just in the way you're asking about her. More than once. She was pleased to be his granddaughter. Proud of him.'

'She still is. And I'm proud of her.'

'And – I remember her crying, once.'

'Why? And don't say I don't know!'

This balked him. Finally he looked up at her, with a smile almost human. 'She was sad.'

'Oh very good!'

'Because her mother had left. Esther?'

'That's right.'

'Kasei and Esther broke up, and Esther left for – I don't know. But Kasei and Jackie stayed in Zygote. And one day she got to school early, on a day I was teaching. She asked why a lot. And this time too, but about Kasei and Esther. And then she cried.'

'What did you say to her?'

'I don't . . . Nothing, I suppose. I didn't know what to say. Hmm . . . I thought she perhaps should have gone with Esther. The mother bond is crucial.'

'Come on.'

'You don't agree? I thought all you young natives were sociobiologists.'

'What's that?'

'Um – someone who believes that most cultural traits have a biological explanation.'

'Oh no. Of course not. We're much freer than that. Mothering can be any kind of thing. Sometimes mothers are nothing but incubators.'

'I suppose so — '

'Take my word for it.'

' — but Jackie cried.'

On they hiked, in silence. Like a lot of the big craters, Moreux turned out to have several pie-wedge watersheds, converging on a central marsh and lake. In this case the lake was small and kidney-shaped, curving around the rough, low knobs of a central peak complex. Zo and Russell came out from under the forest canopy on an indistinct trail that faded into elephant grass, and they would have become quickly lost except for the stream, which was oxbowing through the grass toward a meadow and then the marshy lake. Even the meadow was dominated by elephant grass, great circular clumps of it that stood well overhead, so that they often had a view of nothing but giant grasses and sky. The long blades of grass gleamed under the lilac midday zenith. Russell stumbled along well behind Zo, his round sunglasses like mirrors in his face, reflecting the grass bundles as he looked this way and that. He appeared utterly foxed, amazed at the surroundings, and he muttered into an old wristpad that hung on his wrist like a manacle.

A final oxbow into the lake had created a fine sand-and-pebble beach, and after testing with a stick for quicksand at the waterline, and finding the sand firm, Zo stripped off her sweaty singlet and walked out into the water, which got nice and cold a few metres offshore. She dived under, swam around, hit her head on the bottom. There was a beached boulder standing over some deep water, and she climbed it and dived in three or four times, doing a forward flip in the water right after entry; this forward somersault, difficult and graceless in the air, caused a quick little tug of weightless pleasure in the pit of her stomach, a feeling as close to orgasm as any non-orgasm she had ever felt. So she dived several times, until the sensation wore off and she was cooled. Then she walked out of the lake and lay on the sand, feeling its heat and the solar radiation cook both sides of her. A real orgasm would have been perfect, but despite the fact that she was laid out before him like a map of sex, Russell sat crosslegged in the shallows, absorbed apparently by the mud, naked himself except for sunglasses and wristpad. A farmer-tanned, little, bald, wizened primate, like her image of Gandhi or *homo habilis*. It was even a bit sexy how different he was, so ancient and small, like the male of some turtle-without-a-shell species. She pulled her knee to the side and shifted up her bottom in an unmistakable present posture, the sunlight hot on her exposed vulva.

'What an amazing biome,' he said. 'I've never seen anything like it.'

'Yes.'

'Do you like it?'

530

'Do I like it? I suppose so. It's a bit hot and overgrown, but interesting. It makes a change.'

'So you don't object. You're not a Red.'

'A Red?' She laughed. 'No, I'm a Whig.'

He thought that one over. 'Do you mean to say that Greens and Reds are no longer a contemporary political division?'

She gestured at the elephant grass and saal trees backing the meadow. 'How could they be?'

'Very interesting.' He cleared his throat. 'When you go to Uranus, will you invite a friend of mine?'

'Maybe,' Zo said, and shifted her hips back a bit.

He took the hint, and after a moment leaned forward and began to massage the thigh nearest him. It felt like a monkey's little hands on her skin, clever and knowing. He could lose his whole hand in her pubic hair, a phenomenon he appeared to like, as he repeated it several times and got an erection, which she held hard as she came. It was not like being tabled, of course, but any orgasm was a good thing, especially out in the sun's hot rain. And although his handling of her was basic, he did not exhibit any of that hankering for simultaneous affection which so many of the old ones had, a sentimentality which interfered with the much more acute pleasures that could be achieved one person at a time. So when her shuddering had stilled she rolled on her side, and took his erection in her mouth – like a forefinger she could wrap her tongue entirely around – while giving him a good view of her body. She stopped once to look at herself; big, rich, taut curves; and saw that the span of her hips stood nearly as high as his shoulders. Then back to it, vagina dentata, so absurd those scared patriarchal myths, teeth were entirely superfluous, did a python need teeth, did a rock stamp need teeth? Just grab the poor creatures by the cock and squeeze until they whimpered, and what were they going to do? They could try to stay out of the grip, but at the same time it was the place they most wanted to be, so that they wandered in the pathetic confusion and denial of that double bind. And put themselves at the risk of teeth anyway, any chance they got; she nipped at him, to remind him of his situation; then let him come. Men were lucky they weren't telepathic.

Afterward they took another dip in the lake, and back on

the sand he pulled a loaf of bread from his daypack. They broke the loaf in half and ate.

'Were you purring, then?' he said between swallows.

'Mm hmm.'

'You had the trait inserted?'

She nodded, swallowed. 'Last time I took the treatment.'

'The genes are from cats?'

'From tigers.'

'Ah.'

'It turns out to be a minor change in the larynx and vocal cords. You should try it, it feels really good.'

He was blinking and did not answer.

'Now who's this friend you want me to take to Uranus?'

'Ann Clayborne.'

'Ah! Your old nemesis.'

'Something like that.'

'What makes you think she would go?'

'She might not. But she might. Michel says she's trying some new things. And I think Miranda would be interesting to her. A moon knocked apart in an impact, and then reassembled, moon and impactor together. It's an image I'd ... like her to see. All that rock, you know. She's fond of rock.'

'So I've heard.'

Russell and Clayborne, the Green and the Red, two of the most famous antagonists in all the melodramatic saga of the first years of settlement. Those first years: a situation so claustrophobic Zo shuddered to think of it. Clearly the experience had brecciated the minds of all those who had suffered through it. And then Russell had had even more spectacular damage inflicted later on, as she recalled; hard to remember; all the First Hundred's stories tended to blur together for her, the Great Storm, the lost colony, Maya's betrayals – all the arguments, affairs, murders, rebellions and so on – such sordid stuff, with scarcely a moment of joy in the whole thing, as far as she could tell. As if the old ones had been anaerobic bacteria, living in poison, slowly excreting the necessary conditions for the emergence of a fully oxygenated life.

Except perhaps for Ann Clayborne, who seemed, from the stories, to have understood that to feel joy in a rock world, you had to love rock. Zo liked that attitude, and so she said,

'Sure, I'll ask her. Or you should, shouldn't you? You ask, and tell her I'm agreeable. We can make room in the diplomatic group.'

'It's a Free Mars group?'

'Yes.'

'Hmm.'

He asked her questions about Jackie's political ambitions, and she answered when she could, looking down her body and its curves, the hard muscles smoothed by the fat under the skin – hipbones flanking the belly, navel, wiry black pubic hair (she brushed bread crumbs out of it), long powerful thighs. Women's bodies were much more handsomely proportioned than men's; Michelangelo had been wrong about that, although his David made a best case for his argument, a flyer's body if ever there was one.

'I wish we could fly back up to the rim,' she said.

'I don't know how to fly the birdsuits.'

'I could have carried you on my back.'

'Really?'

She glanced at him. Another thirty or thirty-five kilos . . .

'Sure. It would depend on the suit.'

'It's amazing what those suits can do.'

'It's not just the suits.'

'No. But we weren't meant to fly. Heavy bones and all. You know.'

'I do. Certainly the suits are necessary. Just not sufficient.'

'Yes.' He was looking at her body. 'It's interesting how big people are getting.'

'Especially genitals.'

'Do you think so?'

She laughed. 'Just teasing.'

'Ah.'

'Although you would think the parts would grow that had increased use, eh?'

'Yes. Depth of chests have grown greater, I read.'

She laughed again. 'The thin air, right?'

'Presumably. It's true in the Andes, anyway. The distances from spine to sternum in Andean natives are nearly twice as large as they are in people who live at sea level.'

'Really! Like the chest cavities of birds, eh?'

533

'I suppose.'

'Then add big pecs, and big breasts . . .'

He didn't reply.

'So we're evolving into something like birds.'

He shook his head. 'It's phenotypic. If you raised your kids on Earth, their chests would shrink right back down.'

'I doubt I'll have kids.'

'Ah. Because of the population problem?'

'Yes. We need you issei to start dying. Even all these new little worlds aren't helping that much. Earth and Mars are both turning into anthills. You've taken our world from us, really. You're kleptoparasites.'

'That sounds redundant.'

'No, it's a real term, for animals that steal food from their young during exceptionally hard winters.'

'Very apt.'

'We should probably kill you all when you turn a hundred.'

'Or as soon as we have children.'

She grinned. He was so imperturbable! 'Whichever comes first.'

He nodded as if this were a sensible suggestion. She laughed, although it was vexing too: 'Of course it will never happen.'

'No. But it won't be necessary.'

'No? You're going to act like lemmings and run off cliffs?'

'No. Treatment-resistant diseases are appearing. Older people are dying. It's bound to happen.'

'Is it?'

'I think so.'

'You don't think they'll figure out ways to cure these new diseases, keep stringing things along?'

'In some cases. But senescence is complex, and sooner or later . . .' He shrugged.

'That's a bad thought,' Zo said.

She stood, pulled the dried fabric of her singlet up her legs. He stood and dressed too.

'Have you ever met Bao Shuyo?' he asked.

'No, who's she?'

'A mathematician, living in Da Vinci.'

'No. Why do you ask?'

'Just curious.'

They hiked uphill through the forest, from time to time stopping to look after the quick blur of an animal. A big jungle chicken, what looked like a lone hyena, standing looking down a wash at them . . . Zo found she was enjoying herself. This issei was unteasable, unshockable; and his opinions were unpredictable, which was an unusual trait in the old, indeed in anyone. Most of the ancient ones Zo had met seemed especially bound in the tightly warped spacetime of their values; and as the way people lived their values was in inverse proportion to how tightly they were bound in them, the old had ended up Tartuffes to a man, or so she had thought, hypocrites for whom she had no patience at all. She despised the old and their precious values. But this one didn't seem to have any. It made her want to talk more with him.

When they got back to the village she patted him on the head. 'That was fun. I'll talk to your friend.'

'Thanks.'

A few days later she gave Ann Clayborne a call. The face that appeared on the screen was as forbidding as a skull.

'Hi, I'm Zoya Boone.'

'Yes?'

'It's my name,' Zo said. 'That's how I introduce myself to strangers.'

'Boone?'

'Jackie's daughter.'

'Ah.'

Clearly she didn't like Jackie. A common reaction; Jackie was so wonderful that a lot of people hated her.

'I'm also a friend of Sax Russell's.'

'Ah.'

Impossible to read what she meant by that one.

'I was telling him that I'm on my way out to the Uranian system, and he said you might be interested in joining me.'

'He did?'

'He did. So I called. I'm going to Jupiter and then Uranus, with two weeks on Miranda.'

'Miranda!' she said. 'Who are you again?'

'I'm Zo Boone! What are you, senile?'

'Miranda, you said?'

'Yes. Two weeks, maybe more if I like it.'

'If you *like* it?'

'Yes. I don't stay in places I don't like.'

Clayborne nodded as if that were only sensible, and so Zo added mock-solemnly, as if to a child, 'There's a lot of rock there.'

'Yes, yes.'

A long pause. Zo studied the face on the screen. Gaunt and wrinkled, like Russell, only in her case almost all the wrinkles were vertical. A face hacked out of wood. Finally she said, 'I'll think about it.'

'You're supposed to be trying new things,' Zo reminded her.

'What?'

'You heard me.'

'Sax told you that?'

'No – I asked Jackie about you.'

'I'll think about it,' she said again, and cut the connection.

So much for that, Zo thought. Still she had tried, and therefore felt virtuous, a disagreeable sensation. These issei had a way of pulling one into their realities; and they were all mad.

And unpredictable as well; the next day Clayborne called back, and said she would go.

In person Ann Clayborne proved to be indeed as withered and sundried as Russell, but even more silent and strange – waspish, laconic, prone to brief ill-tempered outbursts. She showed up at the last minute with a single backpack and a slim, black wristpad, one of the latest models. Her skin was a nut brown, and marked by wens and warts and scars where skin disorders had been removed. A long life spent outdoors, and in the early days too, when UV bombardment had been intense; in short, she was fried. A bakehead, as they said in Echus. Her eyes were grey, her mouth a lizard slash, the lines from the corners of her mouth to her nostrils like deep hatchet chops. Nothing could be more severe than that face.

During the week of the voyage to Jupiter she spent her time in the little ship park, walking through the trees. Zo preferred the dining hall, or the big viewing bubble where a small group gathered in the evening watch, to eat tabs of pandorph and play Go, or smoke opium and look at the stars. So she seldom saw Ann on the trip out.

They shot over the asteroid belt, slightly out of the plane of the ecliptic, passing over several of the hollowed-out little worlds, no doubt, though it was hard to tell; inside the rock potatoes shown on the ship's screens there might be rough shells like finished mines, or towns landscaped into beautiful estates; societies anarchic and dangerous, or settled by religious groups or utopian collectives, and painfully peaceable. The existence of such a wide variety of systems, co-existing in a semi-anarchic state, made Zo doubt that Jackie's plans for organizing the outer satellites under a Martian umbrella would ever succeed; it seemed to her that the asteroid belt might serve as a model for what the entire solar system's political organization would become. But Jackie did not agree; the asteroid belt was as it was, she said, because of its particular nature, scattered through a broad band all around the sun. The outer satellites on the other hand were clumped in groups around their gas giants, and were certain to become leagues because of that; and were such large worlds, compared to the asteroids, that eventually it would make a difference with whom they allied themselves in the inner system.

Zo was not convinced. But their deceleration brought them into the Jovian system, where she would have a chance to put Jackie's theories to the test. The ship ran a cat's cradle through the Galileans to slow down further, giving them close-ups of the four big moons. All four of them had ambitious terraforming plans, and had started to put them into action. The outer three, Callisto, Ganymede and Europa, all had similar initial conditions to deal with; they were all covered by water-ice layers, Callisto and Ganymede to a depth of a thousand kilometres, Europa to a depth of a hundred kilometres. Water was not uncommon in the outer solar system, but it was by no means ubiquitous either, and so these water worlds had something to trade. All three moons had large amounts of rock scattered over their icy surfaces, the remnants of meteoric impact for the most part, carbonaeous chondrite rubble, a very useful building material. The settlers of the three moons had, on their arrival some thirty M-years before, rendered the chondrites and built tent frameworks of carbon nanotube similar to that used in Mars's space elevator, tenting spaces twenty or fifty kilometres across with multi-layered tent materials. Under their tents they had spread crushed rock to create a thin layer of ground – the ultimate permafrost – in some places surrounding lakes they had melted into the ice.

On Callisto the tent town built to this plan was called Lake Geneva; this was where the Martian delegation went to meet with the various leaders and policy groups of the Jovian League. As usual Zo accompanied the delegation as a minor functionary and observer, looking for opportunities to convey Jackie's messages to people who could discreetly do something about it.

This particular meeting was part of a biannual series the Jovians held to discuss the terraforming of the Galileans, and so a good context for Jackie's interests to be expressed. Zo sat at the back of the room next to Ann, who had decided to sit in on the meeting. The technical problems of terraforming these moons were big in scale, but simple in concept. Callisto, Ganymede and Europa were being dealt with in the same way, at least at the beginning: mobile fusion reactors were out roaming their surfaces, heating the ice and pumping gases into early hydrogen/oxygen atmospheres. Eventually they hoped to create equatorial belts in which gathered rock had been crushed to create ground over the ice; atmospheric temperatures would then be kept near freezing, so that tundra ecologies could be established around a string of equatorial lakes, in a breathable oxygen/hydrogen atmosphere.

Io, the innermost of the Galileans, was more difficult, but intriguing; rail-gun launchers were firing large missiles of ice and chaldates down to it from the other three big moons; being so close to Jupiter it had very little water, its surface made up of intermixed layers of basalt and sulphur – the sulphur spewing out onto the surface in spectacular volcanic plumes, driven by the tidal action from Jupiter and the other Galileans. The plan for Io's terraformation was more long-term than most, and was to be driven in part by an infusion of sulphur-eating bacteria into hot sulphur springs around the volcanoes.

All four of these projects were slowed by the lack of light, and space mirrors of tremendous size were being built at Jupiter's Lagrange points, where the complications of the Jovian system's gravitational fields were reduced; sunlight would be directed from these mirrors to the equators of the four Galileans. All four moons were tidally locked around Jupiter, so their solar days depended on the length of their orbits around Jupiter, ranging from forty-two hours for Io to fifteen days for Callisto; and whatever the length of their days, they all received during them only four per cent as much sunlight as the Earth. But the truth was that the amount of sunlight hitting the Earth was stupendously excessive, so that four per cent was actually a lot of light, when it came to visibility – seventeen thousand times as much as the full moon on Earth – but not much heat, if one wanted to terraform. They therefore were cadging light any way they could; Lake Geneva and all the settlements on the other moons were located facing Jupiter, to take advantage of the sunlight reflected from that giant globe in the sky; and flying 'gas lanterns' had been dropped into the upper atmosphere of Jupiter, clusters of them igniting some of the planet's helium$_3$ in points of light that were too brilliant to look directly at for more than a second; the fusion burns were suspended before electromagnetic reflecting dishes that put all the light out into the planet's plane of the ecliptic. Thus the banded monster ball was now made an even more spectacular sight by the achingly bright diamond-dots of some twenty gas lanterns wandering its face.

The space mirrors and the gas lanterns together would still leave the settlements with less than half the sunlight Mars got, but it was the best they could do. That was life in the outer solar system, a somewhat dim business all around, Zo judged. Even gathering that much light would require the manufacture of a massive infrastructure; and this was where the Martian delegation came in. Jackie had arranged to offer a lot of help, including more fusion behemoths, more gas lanterns, and also Martian experience in space mirrors and terraforming techniques generally, through an association of aerospace co-ops interested in obtaining more projects now that the situation in Martian space was largely stabilized. They would contribute capital and expertise, in return for preferential trade agreements, supplies of helium$_3$ culled from Jupiter's upper atmosphere, and the opportunity to explore, mine, and possibly join terraforming efforts on Jupiter's clutch of smaller moons, all eighteen of them.

Invested capital, expertise, trade; this was the carrot, and a big one. Clearly if the Galileans accepted it, the tendrils of association with Mars would be there, and Jackie could then follow that up with political alliances of various sorts; and pull the Jovian moons into her web. This eventuality was as clear to the Jovians as it was to anyone, however, and they were doing what they could to get what they wanted without giving too much in return. No doubt they would soon be playing the Martians off against similar offers from the Terran ex-metas and other organizations.

This was where Zo came in; she was the stick. Public carrot, private stick; this was Jackie's method, in all phases of life.

Zo revealed Jackie's threats in tiny, indirect glimpses, to make them seem even more threatening. Brief meeting with officials from Io: the ecopoetic plan, Zo said to them, casually, seemed far too slow. It would be thousands of years before their bacteria chewed the sulphur into useful gases, and meanwhile Jupiter's intense radio field, which enveloped Io and added to its problems, would mutate the bacteria beyond recognition. They needed an ionosphere, they needed water, it was possible they even needed to think about pulling the moon out into a higher orbit around their great gas god. Mars, home of terraforming expertise and the healthiest, wealthiest civilization in the solar system, could help them with all that, give them special help. Or even discuss with the other Galileans the notion of taking over the project, in order to bring it up to speed.

After that, casual conversations with various authorities from the ice Galileans: in cocktail parties after workshops, in bars after the parties, walking in groups along Lake Geneva's signature lakefront promenade, under the sonoluminescent streetlights suspended from the tent framework. The delegates from Io, she told these people, are looking into cutting a separate deal on their own. They had the situation with the most potential, when all was said and done; hard ground to stand on, heat, heavy metals; great tourist potential. Zo ventured that they seemed to be willing to use these advantages to strike out on their own, and fractionate the Jovian League.

Ann followed Zo and the others on some of these walks, and Zo let her listen in on a couple of the conversations, curious to see what she would make of them. She followed them down the waterfront promenade, which was set on the low meteor crater rim they had used to contain the lake. The slosh craters here beat any slosh crater on Mars by a long shot; the icy rim of this one was only a few metres higher than the general surface of the moon, forming a round levée from which one could look over the water of the lake, or back onto the grassy streets of the town, or beyond the streets to the rubbly ice plain outside the tent, visibly curving to the nearby horizon. The extreme flatness of the landscape outside the tent gave an indication of its nature – a glacier covering a whole world, ice a thousand kilometres deep, ice which ate every meteor impact and tidal cracking, and quickly flowed back to flatness again.

On the surface of the lake small black waves formed interference patterns on the flat sheet of water, which was white like the lake's ice bottom, tinted yellow by the great ball of Jupiter, looming gibbous overhead, all its bands of creamy yellow and orange visibly swirled at their edges and around the pinprick lanterns.

They passed a line of wooden buildings; the wood came from forested islands, floating around like rafts on the far side of the lake. Streetgrass gleamed greenly, and gardens grew in oversized planter boxes behind the buildings, under long, bright lamps. Zo showed a bit of the stick to their companions on the walk, confused functionaries from Ganymede; she reminded them of Mars's military might, mentioned again that Io was considering defection from their league.

The Ganymedans went off to get dinner, looking dismayed. 'So subtle,' Ann remarked when they were out of earshot.

'Now we're being sarcastic,' Zo said.

'You're a thug. Put it that way.'

'I will have to enrol in the Red school of diplomatic subtlety. Perhaps arrange for assistants to come along with me and blow up some of their property.'

Ann made a noise between her teeth. She continued down the promenade, and Zo kept up with her.

'Strange that the Great Red Spot is gone,' Zo remarked as they crossed a bridge over a white-bottomed canal. 'Like some kind of sign. I keep expecting it to come around into view.'

The air was chill and damp. The people they passed were mostly of Terran origin, part of the diaspora. Some flyers cut lazy spirals up near the tent frame. Zo watched them cross the face of the great planet. Ann stopped frequently to inspect cut surfaces of rock, ignoring the town on ice and its crowds, with their tiptoe grace and their rainbow clothing, a gang of young natives greyhounding past — 'You really are more interested in rocks than people,' Zo said, half-admiring, half-irritated.

Ann looked at her; such a basilisk glare! But Zo shrugged and took her by the arm, pulled her along. 'The young natives out here are less than fifteen M-years old, they've lived in ·1 g all their lives; they don't care about Earth or Mars. They believe in the Jovian moons, in water, in swimming and flying. Most of them have altered their eyes for the low light. Some of them are growing gills. They have a plan to terraform these moons that will take them five thousand years. They're the next step in evolution, for ka's sake, and here you are staring at rocks that are just the same as rocks everywhere else in this galaxy. You're just as crazy as they said.'

This bounced off Ann like a thrown pebble. She said, 'You sound like me, when I tried to get Nadia away from Underhill.'

Zo shrugged. 'Come on,' she said, 'I have another meeting.'

'Mafia work never stops, does it.' But she followed, peering around like a wizened court jester, dwarfish and oddly dressed in her old-fashioned jumper.

Some Lake Geneva council members greeted them, somewhat nervously, by the docks. They got on a small ferry, which threaded its way out through a fleet of small sailing boats. Out on the lake it was windy. They puttered to one of the forest islands. Vast specimens of balsa and teak stood over the swampy mat of the floating island's heated ground, and on the island's shore loggers were working outside a little sawmill. The mill was soundproofed, but a muffled whine of saw cuts accompanied the conversation nevertheless. Floating on a lake on a moon of Jupiter, all the colours suffused with the grey of solar distance: Zo felt little bursts of flyer's exhilaration, and she said to the locals, 'This is so beautiful. I can see why there are people on Europa who talk about making their whole world a waterworld, sail around and around. They could even ship away water to Venus and get down to some solid land for islands. I don't know if they've mentioned it to you. Maybe it's just all talk, like the idea I heard for creating a small black hole and dropping it into Jupiter's upper atmosphere. Stellarizing Jupiter! You'd have all the light you needed then.'

'Wouldn't Jupiter be consumed?' one of the locals asked.

'Oh but it would take ever so long, they said; millions of years.'

'And then a nova,' Ann pointed out.

'Yes, yes. Everything but Pluto destroyed. But by that time we'll be long gone, one way or another. Or if not, they'll figure something out.'

Ann laughed harshly. The locals, thinking hard, did not appear to notice.

Back on the lakeshore Ann and Zo walked the promenade. 'You're so blatant,' Ann said.

'On the contrary. It's very subtle. They don't know if I'm speaking for me, or for Jackie, or for Mars. It could be just talk. But it reminds them of the larger context. It's too easy for them to get wrapped up in the Jovian situation and forget all the rest. The solar system entire, as a single political body; people need help thinking about that; they can't conceptualize it.'

'You need help yourself. It's not Renaissance Italy, you know.'

'Machiavelli will always remain true, if that's what you mean. And they need to be reminded of that here.'

'You remind me of Frank.'

'Frank?'

'Frank Chalmers.'

'Now there's an issei I admire,' Zo said. 'What I've read about him, anyway. He was the only one of you who wasn't a hypocrite. And he was the one that got the most done.'

'You don't know anything about it,' Ann said.

Zo shrugged. 'The past is the same for all of us. I know as much as you do.'

A group of the Jovians walked by, pale and big-eyed, utterly absorbed by their own talk. Zo gestured: 'Look at them! They're so focused. I admire them too, really – throwing themselves so energetically into a project that won't be completed until long after their death – it's an absurd gesture, a gesture of defiance and freedom, a divine madness, as if they were sperm wiggling madly toward an unknown goal.'

'That's all of us,' Ann said. 'That's evolution. When do we go to Miranda?'

Around Uranus, four times as far from the sun as Jupiter, objects were struck by one quarter of a per cent the light that would have struck them on Earth. This was a problem for powering major terraforming projects, although as Zo found when they entered the Uranian system, it still provided quite enough illumination for visibility; the sunlight was thirteen hundred times as bright as the full moon on Earth, the sun still a blinding little chip in the black array of stars, and though things in the region were a bit dim and drained of their colour, one could see them perfectly well. Thus the great power of the human eye and spirit, functioning well so far from home.

But there were no big moons around Uranus to attract a major terraforming effort; Uranus's family consisted of fifteen very small moons, none larger than Titania and Oberon at six hundred kilometres in diameter, and most considerably smaller – a collection of little asteroids, really, named after Shakespeare's women for the most part, all circling the blandest of the gas giants, blue-green Uranus, rolling around with its poles in the plane of the ecliptic, its eleven narrow graphite rings scarcely visible fairy loops. All in all, not a promising system for inhabitation.

Nevertheless people had come, people had settled. This was no surprise to Zo; there were people exploring and starting to build on Triton, on Pluto, on Charon, and if a tenth planet were discovered and an expedition sent out to it, they would no doubt find a tent town already there, its citizens already squabbling with each other, already bristling at any suggestion of outside interference in their affairs. This was life in the *Accelerando*.

The major tent town in the Uranian system was on Oberon, the biggest and farthest out of the fifteen moons. Zo and Ann and the rest of the travellers from Mars parked in a planetary orbit just outside Oberon, and took a ferry down to the moon to make a brief visit to the main settlement.

This town, Hippolyta, spanned one of the big groove valleys that were common to all the larger Uranian moons. Because the gravity was even more meagre than the light was dim, the town had been designed as a fully three-dimensional space, with railings and glide-ropes and flying dumbbell waiters, cliffside balconies and elevators, chutes and ladders, diving boards and trampolines, hanging restaurants and plinth pavilions, all illuminated by bright, white, floating lamp-globes. Zo saw immediately that so much paraphernalia in the air made flying inside the tent impossible; but in this gravity daily life was a kind of flight, and as she bounded in the air with a flex of her foot, she decided to join those residents who treated daily life that way; she danced. And in fact very few people tried to walk in the Terran way; here human movement was naturally airborne, sinuous, full of vaulting leaps and spinning dives and long Tarzan loops. The lowest level of the city was netted.

The people who lived out here came from everywhere else in the system, although of course they were mostly Martian or Terran. At this point there were no native Uranians, except for a single crèche of young children who had been born to mothers building the settlement. Six moons were now occupied, and recently they had dropped a number of gas lanterns into the upper atmosphere of Uranus, to swim in rings around its equator; these now burned in the planet's blue-green like pinpricks of sunlight, forming a kind of diamond necklace around the middle of the giant. These lanterns had increased the system's light enough so that everyone they met in Oberon remarked on how much more colour there was in things, but Zo was not impressed. 'I'd hate to have seen it before,' she said to one of the local enthusiasts, 'it's Monochromomundos.' Actually all the buildings in the town were brightly painted in broad swathes of colour, but which colour a swathe happened to be was sometimes beyond Zo's telling. She needed a pupil dilator.

However, the locals seemed to like it. Of course some of them spoke of moving on after the Uranian towns were finished, out to Triton, 'the next great problem', or Pluto or Charon; they were builders. But others were settling in here for good, giving themselves drugs and genetic transcriptions to adapt to the low g, to increase the sensitivity of their eyes, etc. They spoke of guiding in comets from the Oort cloud to provide water, and perhaps forcing two or three of the smaller uninhabited moons to collide, to create larger and warmer bodies to work with, 'artificial Mirandas', as one person called them.

Ann walked out of that meeting, or rather pulled herself along a railing, unable to cope with the mini-g. After a while Zo followed her, onto streets covered with luxuriant, green grass. She looked up: aquamarine giant, slender, dim rings; a cold, fey sight, unappealing by any previous human standard, and perhaps untenable in the long run because of the moonlet gravity. But back in the meeting there had been Uranians praising the planet's subtle beauties, inventing an aesthetic to appreciate it, even as they planned to modify everything they could. They emphasized the subtle shades, the cool warmth of the tented air, the movement so like flight, like dance in a dream ... Some of them had even become patriots to the point of arguing against radical transformation; they were as preservationist as this inhospitable place could logically sustain.

And now some of these preservationists found Ann. They came up to Ann in a group, standing in a circle around her to shake her hand, hug her, kiss the top of her head; one got down on his knees to kiss her feet. Zo saw the look on Ann's face and laughed. 'Come on,' she said to the group, who apparently had been assigned a kind of guardian status for the moon, Miranda. The local version of Reds, sprung into existence out here where it made no sense at all, and long after Redness had ceased to be much of an issue even on Mars. But they flowed or pulled themselves into position around a table set out in the middle of the tent on a tall, slender column, and ate a meal as the discussion ranged all over the system. The table was an oasis in the dim air of the tent, with the diamond necklace in its round jade setting shining down on them; it seemed to be the centre of town, but Zo saw suspended in the air other such oases, and no doubt they seemed like the centre as well. Hippolyta was a small town, but Oberon could hold scores of towns like it, and so would Titania, Ariel, Miranda; small as they were, these satellites all had surfaces covering

547

hundreds of square kilometres. This was the attraction of these sunforsaken moons: free land, open space – a new world, a frontier, with its ever-receding chance to start anew, to found a society from scratch. For the Uranians this freedom was worth more than light or gravity. And so they had gathered the programs and the starter robots, and taken off for the high frontier with plans for a tent and a constitution, to be their own first hundred.

But these were precisely the kind of people least interested in hearing about Jackie's plans for a systemwide alliance. And already there had been local disagreements strong enough to have caused trouble; among the people sitting around the table were some serious enemies, Zo could tell. She watched their faces closely as the head of their delegation, Marie, laid out the Martian proposal in the most general terms: an alliance designed to deal with the massive historical-economic-numerical gravity well of Earth, which was huge, teeming, flooded, mired in its past like a pig in a sty, and still the dominant force in the diaspora. It was in the best interests of all the other settlements to band with Mars and present a united front, in control of their own immigration, trade, growth – in control of their destinies.

Except that none of the Uranians, despite their arguments with each other, looked at all convinced. An elderly woman who was the mayor of Hippolyta spoke, and even the Mirandan 'Reds' nodded: they would deal with Earth on their own. Earth or Mars were equally dangerous to freedom. Out here, they planned on dealing with all potential alliances or confrontations as free agents, in temporary collusion or opposition with equals, depending on circumstances. There was simply no need for any more formal arrangements to be made. 'All that alliance stuff smacks of control from above,' the woman concluded. 'You don't do it on Mars, why try it out here?'

'We do do it on Mars,' Marie said. 'That level of control is emergent from the complex of smaller systems below it, and it's useful for dealing with problems at the holistic level. And now at the interplanetary level. You're confusing totalization with totalitarianism, a very serious error.'

They did not look convinced. Reason had to be backed with

leverage; that was why Zo was along. And the application of leverage would go easier with the reasoning laid out like this beforehand.

Throughout the dinner Ann remained silent, until the general discussion ended and the Miranda group began to ask her questions. Then she came alive, as if switched on, and asked them in return about current local planetology: the classification of different regions of Miranda as parts of the two colliding planetesimals, the recent theory that identified the tiny moons Ophelia, Desdemona, Bianca and Puck as ejected pieces of the Mirandan collision, and so on. Her questions were detailed and knowledgeable; the guardians were thrilled, in transports, their eyes as big as lemurs' eyes. The rest of the Uranians were likewise pleased to see Ann's interest. She was The Red; now Zo saw what that really meant; she was one of the most famous people in history. And it seemed possible that all the Uranians had a little Red in them; unlike the settlers of the Jovian and Saturnian systems, they had no plans for large-scale terraforming, they planned to live in tents and go out on the primal rock for the rest of their lives. And they felt – at least its guardian group felt – that Miranda was so unusual that it had to be left entirely alone. That was a Red idea, of course. Nothing humans did there, one of the Uranian Reds said, would do anything but reduce what was most valuable about it. It had an intrinsic worth that transcended even its value as a planetological specimen. It had its dignity. Ann watched them carefully as they said this, and Zo saw in her eyes that she did not agree, or even quite understand. For her it was a matter of science – for these people, a matter of spirit. Zo actually sympathized more with the locals' view than with Ann's, with its cramped insistence on the object. But the result was the same, they both had the Red ethic in its pure form: no terraforming on Miranda, of course, also no domes, no tents, no mirrors; only a single visitors' station and a few rocket pads (though this too appeared to be controversial within the guardian group); a ban on anything except no-impact foot travel, and rocket-hops high enough over the surface to avoid disturbing the dust. The guardian group conceived of Miranda as wilderness, to be walked through but never lived on, never changed. A climber's world, or even better, a flyer's world. Looked at and nothing more. A natural work of art.

Ann nodded at all this. And there – there it was, something more in her than the crimping fear: a passion for rock, in a world of rock. Fetishes could fix on anything. And all these people shared the fetish. Zo found it peculiar to be among them, peculiar and intriguing. Certainly her leverage point was coming clear. The guardian group had arranged a special ferry to Miranda, to show it to Ann. No one else would be there. A private tour of the strangest moon of all, for the strangest Red. Zo laughed. 'I'd like to come along,' she said earnestly.

And the Great No said yes. That was Ann on Miranda.

It was the smallest of Uranus's five big moons, only four hundred and seventy kilometres in diameter. In its early years, some 3.5 billion years before the present, its smaller precursor had run into another moon of about the same size; the two had shattered, then clumped, then, in the heat of the collision, coalesced into a single ball. But the new moon had cooled before the coalescing was quite finished.

The result was a landscape out of a dream, violently divergent and disarranged. Some regions were as smooth as skin, others were ripped raw; some were metamorphosed surfaces of two proto-moons, others were exposed interior material. And then there were the deeply-grooved rift zones, where the fragments met, imperfectly. In these zones extensive parallel groove systems bent at acute angles, in dramatic chevron formations, a clear sign of the tremendous torques involved in the collision. The big rifts were so large that they were visible from space as hack marks, incised scores of kilometres deep into the side of the grey sphere.

They came down on a plateau next to the biggest of these hacked chasms, called Prospero's Rift. They suited up, then left the spacecraft and walked out to the rift's edge. A dim abyss, so deep that the bottom looked to be on a different world. Combined with the airy micro-g, the sight gave Zo the distinct feeling of flying, flying, however, as she sometimes did in dreams, all Martian conditions suspended in favour of some sky of the spirit. Overhead, Uranus floated full and green, giving all of Miranda a jade tinge. Zo danced along the rim, pushing off on her toes and floating, floating, coming down in little pliés, her heart full of beauty. So strange, the diamond sparks of the gas lanterns, surfing on Uranus's stratosphere; the eldritch jade. Lights hung across a round green paper lantern. The depths of the abysm only suggested. Everything glowing with its own internal greenness, viriditas bursting out of everything – and yet everything still and motionless forever, except for them, the intruders, the observers. Zo danced.

Ann hiked along much more comfortably than she had in Hippolyta, with the unconscious grace of someone who has spent a lot of time walking on rock. Boulder ballet; she carried a long, angular hammer in her thick glove, and her thigh pockets bulged with specimens. She didn't respond to the exclamations of Zo or the guardian group; she was oblivious to them. Like an actor playing the part of Ann Clayborne. Zo laughed: that one could become such a cliché!

'If they domed this "dark backward and abysm of time", it would make a beautiful place to live,' she said. 'Lots of land for the amount of tent needed, eh? And such a view. It would be a wonder.'

No response to such a blunt provocation, of course. But it would set them thinking. Zo followed the guardian group like an albatross. They had started to descend a broken staircase of rock that lined the edge of a slim buttress, extending far out from the chasm wall, like a fold of drapery in a marble statue. This feature ended in a flat swirl several kilometres out from the wall, and a kilometre or more lower than the rim. After the flat spot the buttress dropped away abruptly, in a sheer drop to the chasm floor, some twenty kilometres straight down. Twenty kilometres! Twenty thousand metres, some seventy thousand feet . . . Even great Mars itself could boast no such wall.

There were a number of buttresses and other deformations on the wall similar to the one they were hiking out on: flutings and draperies, as in a limestone cavern, but formed all at once;

the wall had been melted, molten rock had dripped into the abyss until the chill of space had frozen it forever. Everything was visible from every point of their descent. A railing had been bolted to the buttress's edge, and they were all clipped to this railing by lines, connected to harnesses in their space-suits; a good thing, as the edge of the buttress was narrow, and the slightest slip sideways could launch one out into the space of the chasm. The spidery little spacecraft that had dropped them off was going to fly down and take them off at the bottom of the staircase, from the flat spot at the end of the buttress promontory. So they could descend without a worry for the return; and descend they did, for minute after minute, in a silence that was not at all companionable. Zo had to grin; you could almost hear them thinking black thoughts at her, the grinding was palpable. Except for Ann, who was stopping every few metres to inspect the cracks between their rough stairs.

'This obsession with rock is so pathetic,' Zo said to her on a private band. 'To be so old and still so small. To limit yourself to the world of inert matter, a world that will never surprise you, never *do* a single thing. So that you won't be hurt. Areology as a kind of cowardice. Sad, really.'

A noise on the intercom: air shot between front teeth. Disgust.

Zo laughed.

'You're an impertinent girl,' Ann said.

'Yes I am.'

'And stupid as well.'

'That I am not!' Zo was surprised at her own vehemence. And then she saw Ann's face was twisted with anger behind her faceplate, and her voice hissed in the intercom over sharp heavy breaths.

'Don't ruin the walk,' Ann snapped.

'I was tired of being ignored.'

'So who's afraid now?'

'Afraid of the boredom.'

Another disgusted hiss. 'You've been very poorly brought up.'

'Whose fault is that?'

'Oh yours. Yours. But we have to suffer the results.

552

'Suffer on. I'm the one who got you here, remember.'

'Sax is the one who got me here, bless his little heart.'

'Everyone's little to you.'

'Compared to this . . .' The movement of her helmet showed she had glanced down into the rift.

'This speechless immobility that you're so safe in.'

'This is the wreckage of a collision very similar to other planetesimal collisions in the early solar system. Mars had some, Earth too. That's the matrix life emerged out of. This is a window into that time, understand?'

'I understand, but I don't care.'

'You don't think it matters.'

'Nothing matters, in the sense you mean. There is no meaning to all this. It's just an accident of the Big Bang.'

'Oh please,' Ann said. 'Nihilism is so ridiculous.'

'Look who's talking! You're a nihilist yourself! No meaning or value to life or to your senses – it's weak nihilism, nihilism for cowards, if you can imagine such a thing.'

'My brave little nihilist.'

'Yes – I face it. And then enjoy what can be enjoyed.'

'Which is?'

'Pleasure. The senses and their input. I'm a sensualist, really. It takes some courage, I think. To face pain, to risk death to get the senses really roaring . . .'

'You think you've faced pain?'

Zo remembered a stalled landing at Overlook, the pain-beyond-pain of broken legs and ribs. 'Yes. I have.'

Radio silence. The static of the Uranian magnetic field. Perhaps Ann was allowing her the experience of pain, which, given its omnipresence, was no great generosity. In fact it made Zo furious. 'Do you really think it takes centuries to become human, that no one was human until you geriatrics came along? Keats died at twenty-five; have you read *Hyperion*? Do you think this hole in a rock is as sublime as even a phrase of *Hyperion*? Really, you issei are so horrible. And you especially. For you to judge me, when you haven't changed from the moment you touched Mars . . .'

'Quite an accomplishment, eh?'

'An accomplishment in playing dead. Ann Clayborne, the greatest dead person who ever lived.'

'And an impertinent girl. But look at the grain of this rock, twisted like a pretzel.'

'Fuck the rocks.'

'I'll leave that to the sensualist. No, look. This rock hasn't changed in 3·5 billion years. And when it did change, my Lord, what a change.'

Zo looked at the jade rock under their boots. Somewhat glasslike, but otherwise utterly nondescript. 'You're obsessed,' she said.

'Yes. But I like my obsessions.'

After that they hiked down the spine of the buttress in silence. Over the course of the day they descended to Bottom's Landing. Now they were a kilometre below the rims of the chasm, and the sky was a starry band overhead. Uranus fat in the middle of it, the sun a blazing jewel just to one side. Under this gorgeous array the depth of the rift was sublime, astonishing; again Zo felt herself to be flying. 'You've located intrinsic worth in the wrong place,' she said to all of them, over the common band. 'It's like a rainbow. Without an observer at a 23° angle to the light being reflected off a cloud of spherical droplets, there is no rainbow. The whole universe is like that. Our spirits stand at a 23° angle to the universe. There is some new thing created at the contact of photon and retina, some space created between rock and mind. Without mind there is no intrinsic worth.'

'That's just saying there is no intrinsic worth,' one of the guardians replied. 'It collapses back to utilitarianism. But there's no need to include human participation. These places exist without us and before us, and that is their intrinsic worth. When we arrive we should honour that precedence, if we want to be in a right attitude to the universe, if we want to actually see it.'

'But I see it,' Zo said happily. 'Or almost see it. You people will have to sensitize your eyes with some addition to your genetic treatments. Meanwhile it's glorious, it truly is. But that glory is in our minds.'

They did not answer. After a while Zo went on:

'All these issues have been raised before, on Mars. The

whole matter of environmental ethics was raised to a new level by the experience on Mars, raised right into the heart of our actions. Now you want to protect this place as wilderness, and I can see why. But I'm a Martian, and that's why I understand. A lot of you are Martian, or your parents were. You start from that ethical position, and in the end wilderness is an ethical position. Terrans won't understand you as well as I do. They'll come out here and build a big casino right on this promontory. They'll cover this rift from rim to rim, and try terraforming it like they have everywhere else. The Chinese are still jammed into their country like sardines, and they don't give a damn about the intrinsic worth of China itself, much less a barren moonlet on the edge of the solar system. They need room and they see it's out here, and they'll come and build and look at you funny when you object, and what are you going to do? You can try sabotage like the Reds did on Mars, but they can blow you off the moons here just as easily as you can them, and they've got a million replacements for every colonist they lose. That's what we're talking about when we talk about Earth. We're like the Lilliputians with Gulliver. We've got to work together, and tie him down with as many little lines as we can devise.'

No response from the others.

Zo sighed. 'Well,' she said, 'maybe it's for the best. Spread people around out here, they won't be pressuring Mars so hard. It might be possible to work out deals whereby the Chinese are free to settle out here all they want, and we on Mars are free to cut down immigration to nearly nothing. It might work rather well.'

Again no response from the others.

Finally Ann said, 'Shut up. Let us concentrate on the land here.'

'Oh, of course.'

Then, as they were approaching the very end of the buttress, the promontory standing out in a gap of air beyond all telling, under the bejewelled jade disc and the brilliant diamond chip beyond it, the whole solar system suddenly triangulated by these celestial objects, the true size of things revealed – they saw moving stars overhead. The rocket jets of their spacecraft.

'See?' Zo said. 'It's the Chinese, coming to have a look.'

Suddenly one of the guardians was on her in a fury, striking her directly on the faceplate. Zo laughed. But she had forgotten Miranda's ultralight gravity, and was surprised when a ridiculous uppercut lifted her right off her feet. Then she hit the railing with the back of her knees, spun head over heels, twisting to catch herself, *bang* – a hard blow to the head, but the helmet protected her, she was still conscious, tumbling down the incline at the edge of the promontory – beyond it the void – fear shot through her like an electric shock, she fought for balance but was tumbling, out of control – she felt a jolt – ah yes, the end of her harness! Then the sickening sensation of a further slide down. The harness clip must have given way. Second surge of adrenal fear – she turned inward and hugged the passing rock with all her might. The same light g that had sent her flying allowed her to catch herself by her fingertips, to bring the whole weight of her falling body to a sudden halt, as in a miracle.

She was on the edge of a long drop. Sparking lights in her eyes, nausea, darkness beyond; she couldn't see the floor of the chasm, it was like a bottomless pit, a dream image, black falling . . . 'Don't move,' said Ann's voice in her ear. 'Hold on. Don't move.' Above her, a foot, then legs. Very slowly Zo turned her head up to look. A hand clutched her right wrist, hard. 'Okay. There's a hold for your left hand, above it by half a metre. Higher. There. Okay, climb. You above, pull us up.'

Human muscle in ·05 g: they were hauled up like fish on a line.

Zo sat on the ground. The little space ferry was landing soundlessly, over on a pad on the far side of the flat spot. Brief flare of light from its rockets. The concerned looks of the guardians, standing over her.

'Not such a funny joke,' Ann suggested.

'No,' Zo said, thinking hard about how she could use the incident. 'Thanks for helping me.' It was impressive how quickly Ann had jumped to her help – not impressive that she had decided to, for this was the code of nobility, one had obligations to one's peers, and enemies were just as important as friends; enemies were equals, they were necessary, they were what made it possible to be a good friend. But just as a physical manoeuvre it had been impressive. 'Very quick of you.'

On the flight back to Oberon they were all silent, until one of the ferry's crew turned to Ann and mentioned that Hiroko and some of her followers had been seen here in the Uranian system recently, on Puck.

'Oh what crap,' Ann said.

'How do you know?' Zo asked. 'Maybe she decided to get as far away from Earth and Mars as possible. I wouldn't blame her.'

'This isn't her kind of place.'

'Maybe she doesn't know that. Maybe she hasn't heard this is your private rock garden.'

But Ann simply waved her away.

physical manoeuvre to had been unnecessary. They gave up.

Our first look at Phoros was were all there watching ... and ... in the distance ... and this surprised her I think ... and peer in the hallway ... her went her on the horizon ... there is only one place ...

Over the ... Ann said

Then do you have ... said ... before she believed it, 'Do what? ...' ... and told Me, "is possible. I needed to find it ...

Then, for Her Not On's sake ...

Maybe she doesn't take us there Nat ... is more terrible ... ... what Phoros not goings ...

But Ann almost we could be sorry.

Back to Mars, the red planet, the most beautiful world in the solar system. The only real world.

Their shuttle accelerated, made its turn, floated a few days, decelerated; and in two weeks they were in the line-up for Clarke, and then on the elevator, going down, down, down. So slow, this final descent! Zo looked out at Echus, there to the northeast, between red Tharsis and the blue North Sea. So *good* to see it; Zo ate several tabs of pandorph as the elevator car made its approach into Sheffield, and when she walked out into the Socket, and then through the streets between the glossy stone buildings to the giant train station on the rim, she was in the rapture of the areophany, loving every face she saw, loving all her tall brothers and sisters with their striking beauty and their phenomenal grace, loving even the Terrans running around underfoot. The train to Echus didn't leave for a couple of hours, and so she walked the rim park restlessly for a time, looking down into the great Pavonis Mons caldera, as spectacular as anything on Miranda, even if it wasn't as deep as Prospero's Rift: infinity of horizontal banding, all the shades of red, tan, crimson, rust, umber, maroon, copper, brick, sienna, paprika, oxblood, cinnabar, vermilion, all under the dark, star-studded afternoon sky. Her world. Though Sheffield was under its tent, and would ever be; and she wanted to be back in the wind again.

So she went back to the station and got on the train for Echus, and felt the train fly down the piste, off the great cone of Pavonis, down the pure xeriscape of East Tharsis, to Cairo and a Swiss-precision exchange onto the train north to Echus Overlook. The train came in near midnight, and she checked in at the co-op's hostel and walked over to the Adler, feeling the last of the pandorph buzz through her like the feather in the cap of her happiness, and the whole gang was there as if no time had passed, and they cheered to see her, they all hugged her, singly and severally, they all kissed her, they gave her drinks and asked questions about her trip, and told her about the recent wind conditions, and caressed her in her chair, until quickly it was the hour before dawn, and they all trooped down to the ledge and suited up and took off, out into the darkness of the sky and the exhilarating lift of the wind, all of it coming back instantly like breathing or sex, the black mass of the Echus escarpment bulking to the east like the edge of a continent, the dim floor of Echus Chasma so far below – the landscape of her heart, with its dim lowland and high plateau, and the vertiginous cliff between them, and over it all the intense purples of the sky, lavender and mauve in the east, black indigo out to the west, the whole arch lightening and taking on colour each second, the stars popping out of existence – high clouds to the west flaring pink – and as several stoops had taken her well below the level of Overlook, she was able to close on the cliff and catch a hard westerly updraught and sail on it, inches over Underlook and then up in a tight gyre, motionless herself and yet cast violently up by the wind, until she burst out of the shadow of the cliff into the raw yellows of the new day, an incredibly joyful combination of the kinetic and the visual, of sense and world, and as she soared up into the clouds she thought, to hell with you, Ann Clayborne – you and the rest of your kind can go on forever about your moral imperatives, your issei ethics, values, goals, strictures, responsibilities, virtues, grand purposes of life, you can pour out those words to the end of time in all their hypocrisy and fear, and still you will never have a feeling like this one, when the grace of mind and body and world are all in perfect consort – you can rant your Calvinist rant until you are blue in the face, what humans should do with their brief lives, as if there were any way to tell for sure, as if you didn't turn out to be a bunch of cruel bastards in the end – but until you get out here and fly, surf, climb, jump, exert yourself somehow in the risk of space, in the pure grace of the body, you just don't know. You have no right to speak. You are slaves to your ideas and your hierarchies, and so can't see that there is no higher goal than this, the ultimate purpose of existence, of the cosmos itself: the free play of flight.

In the northern spring the trade winds blew, pushing against the westerlies and damping the Echus updraughts. Jackie was on the Grand Canal, distracted from her interplanetary manoeuvrings by the tedium of local politics; indeed she seemed irritated and tense at having to deal with it, and clearly she did not want Zo around. So Zo went to work in the mines at Moreux for a while, and then joined a group of flying friends on the coast of the North Sea, south of Boone's Neck, near Blochs Hoffnung, where the seacliffs reared a kilometre out of the crashing surf. Late afternoon onshore breezes hit these cliffs and sent up a small flock of flyers, wheeling through seastacks that poked out of tapestries of foam surging up and down, up and down, pure white on the wine-dark sea.

This flying group was led by a young woman Zo hadn't met before, a girl of only nine M-years, named Melka. She was the best flyer Zo had ever seen. When she was in the air leading them it was as if an angel had come into their midst, darting through them like a raptor through doves, at other times leading them through the tight manoeuvres that made flocking such fun. And so Zo worked through the days at her co-op's local partner, and flew every day after her work stint was over. And her heart was always soaring, pleased by one thing after another. Once she even called Ann Clayborne, to try to tell her about flying, about what it really meant; but the old one had nearly forgotten who she was, and did not appear interested even when Zo managed to make it clear when and how they had met.

That afternoon she flew with an ache inside. The past was a dead letter, sure; but that people could become such ghosts . . .

Nothing for such a feeling but sun and salt air, the ever-changing spill of sea foam, rising and falling against the cliffs. There was Melka, diving; Zo chased her, feeling a sudden rush of affection for such a beautiful spirit. But then Melka saw her and tipped away, and clipped the highest rock of a seastack with the end of one wing, and tumbled down like a shot bird. Shocked at the sight of the accident, Zo pulled her wings in and began dolphin kicking downward next to the seastack, until she was plummeting in a powerful stoop; she caught up the tumbling girl in her arms, she flapped one wing just over the blue waves, while Melka struggled under her; then she saw that they were going to have to swim.

PART TWELVE

It Goes So Fast

They walked down to the low bluffs overlooking the Florentine. It was night, the air still and cool, the stars bunched overhead in their thousands. They strode side by side on the bluff trail, looking down at the beaches below. The black water was smooth, pricked everywhere by reflected starlight, and the long, smeared line reflecting Phobos setting in the east, leading the eye to the dim black mass of land across the bay.

I'm worried, yes, very worried. In fact I'm scared.

Why?

It's Maya. Her mind. Her mental problems. Her emotional problems. They're getting worse.

What are the symptoms?

The same, only worse. She can't sleep at night. She hates the way she looks, sometimes. She's still in her manic-depressive cycle, but it's changing somehow, I don't know how to characterize it. As if she can't always remember where in the cycle she is. Bouncing around in it. She forgets things, a lot of things.

We all do.

I know. But Maya is forgetting things that I would have said were essentially Mayan. She doesn't seem to care. That's the worst part; she doesn't seem to care.

I find that hard to imagine.

Me too. Maybe it's just the depressive part of her mood cycle, now predominating. But there are days when she loses all affect.

What you call jamais vu?

No, not exactly. She has those incidents too, mind you. Like a certain kind of pre-stroke symptom. I know, I know — I told you, I'm scared. But I don't know what this is, not really. She has jamais vus that are like a pre-stroke symptom. She has presque vus, where she feels almost on the edge of a revelation that never comes. That often happens to people in pre-epileptic auras.

I have feelings like that myself.

Yes, I suppose we all do. Sometimes it seems as if things

will come clear, and then the feeling goes away. Yes. But for Maya these are very intense, as in everything.

Better than the loss of affect.

Oh yes. I agree. Presque vu is not so bad. It's déjà vu that is the worst, and she has periods of continuous déjà vu that can last up to a week. Those are devastating to her. They rob the world of something she can't live without.

Contingency. Free will.

Perhaps. But the net effect of all these symptoms is to drive her into a state of apathy. Almost catatonia. Tries to avoid any of them by not feeling too much. Not feeling at all.

They say one of the common issei ailments is falling into a funk.

Yes, I've been reading about that. Loss of affectual function, anomie, apathy. They've been treating it as they would catatonia, or schizophrenia – giving them a serotonin dopamine complex, limbic stimulants . . . a big cocktail, as you can imagine. Brain chemistry . . . I've been dosing her with everything I can think of, I must admit, keeping journals, running tests, sometimes with her co-operation, sometimes without her knowing much about it. I've been doing what I can, I swear I have.

I'm sure you have.

But it isn't working. She's losing it. Oh Sax —

He stopped, held onto his friend's shoulder.

I can't bear it if she goes. She was always such an airy spirit. We are earth and water, fire and air. And Maya was always in flight. Such an airy spirit, flying on her own gales up above us. I can't stand to see her falling like this!

Ah well.

They walked on.

It's nice to have Phobos back again.

Yes. That was a good idea of yours.

It was your idea, actually. You suggested it to me.

Did I? I don't remember that.

You did.

Below them the sea crunched faintly on rocks.

These four elements. Earth, water, fire, and air. One of your semantic rectangles?

It's from the Greeks.

Like the four temperaments?

Yes. Thales made the hypothesis. The first scientist.

But there were always scientists, you told me. All the way back to the savannah.

Yes, that's true.

And the Greeks – all honour to them, they were obviously great minds – but they were only part of a continuum of scientists, you know. There has been some work done since.

Yes, I know.

Yes. And some of that subsequent work might be of use to you, in these conceptual schemata of yours. In mapping the world for us. So that you might be given new ways of seeing things that might help you, even with problems like Maya's. Because there are more than four elements. A hundred and twenty, more or less. Maybe there are more than four temperaments as well. Maybe a hundred and twenty of them, eh? And the nature of these elements – well – things have become strange since the Greeks. You know subatomic particles have an attribute called spin, that comes only in multiples of one half? And you know how an object in our visible world, it spins 360°, and is back to its original position? Well, a particle with a spin designated one half, like a proton or a neutron – it has to rotate through 720° to get back to its original configuration.

What's that?

It has to go through a double rotation relative to ordinary objects, to come back to its starting state.

You're kidding.

No, no. This has been known for centuries. The geometry of space is simply different for spin one half particles. They live in a different world.

And so . . .

Well, I don't know. But it seems suggestive to me. I mean, if you are going to use physical models as analogues for our mental states, and throw them together in the patterns that you do, then perhaps you ought to be considering these somewhat newer physical models. To think of Maya as a proton, perhaps, a spin one half particle, living in a world twice as big as ours.

Ah.

And it gets stranger than that. There are ten dimensions to this world, Michel. Ten. The three of macrospace that we can perceive, the one of time, and then six more microdimensions, compactified around the fundamental particles in ways we can describe mathematically but cannot visualize. Convolutions and topologies. Differential geometries, invisible but real, down at the ultimate level of spacetime. Think about it. It could lead to whole new systems of thought for you. A vast new enlargement of your mind.

I don't care about my mind. I only care about Maya.

Yes. I know.

They stood looking over the starry water. Over them arched the dome of stars, and in the silence the air breathed over them, the sea mumbled below. The world seemed a big place, wild and free, dark and mysterious.

After a time they turned, and began walking back along the trail.

Once I was taking the train from Da Vinci to Sheffield, and there was some problem with the piste, and we stopped for a while in Underhill. I got off and took a walk through the old trailer park. And I started remembering things. Just looking around. I wasn't really trying. But things came to me.

A common phenomenon.

Yes, so I understand. But I wonder if it might not help Maya to do something like that. Not Underhill in particular, but all the places where she was happy. Where the two of you were happy. You're living in Sabishii now, but why not move back to some place like Odessa?

She didn't want to.

She might have been wrong. Why don't you try living in Odessa, and visiting Underhill from time to time, or Sheffield? Cairo. Maybe even Nicosia. The south pole cities, Dorsa Brevia. A dive into Burroughs. A train tour of the Hellas Basin. All that kind of return might help her to stitch her selves together, to see again where our story began. Where we were formed for good or ill, in the morning of the world. She might need that whether she knows it or not.

Hmm.

568

Arm in arm they walked back to the crater, following a dim track through dark bracken.

Bless you, Sax. Bless you.

The water of Isidis Bay was the colour of a bruise or a clematis petal, sparkling with sunlight that glanced off waves just on the verge of whitecapping. The swell was from the north, and the cabin cruiser pitched and yawed as they motored northwest from Dumartheray Harbour. A bright day in spring, Ls 51, M-year 79, AD 2181.

Maya sat on the upper deck of the boat, drinking in the sea

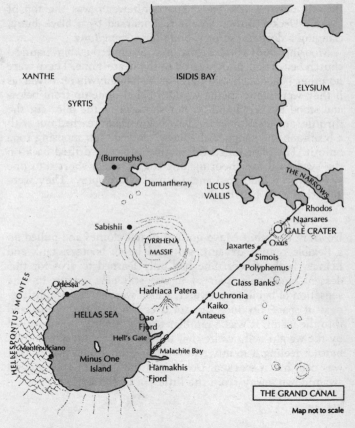

XANTHE

ISIDIS BAY

ELYSIUM

SYRTIS

(Burroughs)

Dumartheray

LICUS VALLIS

THE NARROWS

Rhodos

Naarsares

Sabishii

GALE CRATER

TYRRHENA MASSIF

Jaxartes

Oxus

Simois

Polyphemus

Glass Banks

HELLESPONTUS MONTES

Odessa

Hadriaca Patera

Uchronia

Kaiko

Antaeus

HELLAS SEA

Dao Fjord

Hell's Gate

Malachite Bay

Montepulciano

Minus One Island

Harmakhis Fjord

THE GRAND CANAL

Map not to scale

air and the flood of blue sunlight. It was a joy to be out on the water like this, away from all the haze and junk on shore. Wonderful the way the sea could not be tamed or changed in any way, wonderful how when one got out of the sight of land one rocked on blue wilderness again, always the same no matter what happened back there. She could have sailed on, all day every day, and each slide down the waves a little rollercoaster ride of the soul.

But that wasn't what they were about. There ahead whitecaps broke over a broad patch, and beside her the boat's pilot brought the wheel over a spoke or two, and knocked the throttle down a few rpm. That whitewater was the top of Double Decker Butte, now a reef marked by a black buoy, clanging a deep *bongBong, bongBong, bongBong*.

Mooring buoys were scattered around this big nautical church bell. Their pilot steered to the nearest one. There were no other boats anchored here, or visible anywhere; it was as if they were alone in the world. Michel came up from below and stood by her, hand on her shoulder as the pilot cut the throttle, and a sailor in the bow below them reached out with a boathook and snagged the buoy, clipped their mooring rope onto it. The pilot killed the engine and they drifted back on the swells till the mooring line tugged them short into one swell, with a loud slap and a fan of white spray. They were at anchor over Burroughs.

Down in the cabin Maya got out of her clothes and pulled on a flexible orange drysuit: suit and hood, bootees, tank and helmet, lastly gloves. She had only learned to dive for this descent, and every part of it was still new, except for the sensation of being underwater, which was like the weightlessness of space. So once she got over the side of the boat and into the water, it was a familiar feeling: sinking down, pulled by the weight belt, aware that the water around her was cold, but not feeling it in any real way. Breathing underwater; that was odd, but it worked. Down into the dark. She let go and swam down, away from the little pin of sunlight.

*   *   *

Down and down. Past the upper edge of Double Decker Butte, past its silvered or coppery windows, standing in rows like mineral extrusions or the one-way mirrors of observers from another dimension. Quickly gone in the murk, however, and she dream-parachuted down again, down and down. Michel and a couple of others were following her, but it was so dark that she couldn't see them. Then a robot trawl shaped like a thick bedframe sank past them all, its powerful headlights shooting forward long cones of crystalline fluidity, cones so long that they became one blurry, diffuse cylinder, flowing this way and that as the trawl dipped and bobbed, striking now a distant mesa's metallic windows, now the black muck down on the rooftops of the old Niederdorf. Somewhere down there, the Niederdorf Canal had run – there, a gleam of white teeth – the Bareiss columns, impervious white under their diamond coating, about half-buried in black sand and muck. She pulled up and kicked her fins back and forth a few times to stop descending, then pushed a button that lightened her weight belt, to stabilize herself. She floated then over the canal like a ghost. Yes; it was like Scrooge's dream, the trawl a kind of robot Christmas Past, illuminating the drowned world of lost time, the city she had loved so much. Sudden darts of pain lanced through her ribs; mostly she was numb to any feeling. It was too strange, too hard to understand or believe that this was Burroughs, her Burroughs, now Atlantis at the bottom of a Martian sea.

Bothered by her lack of feeling, she kicked hard and swam down the canal park, over the salt columns and farther west. There on the left loomed Hunt Mesa, where she and Michel had lived in hiding over a dance studio; then the broad, black upslope of Great Escarpment Boulevard. Ahead lay Princess Park, where in the second revolution she had stood on a stage and given a speech to a huge throng; the crowd had stood just below where she was floating now. Over there – that was where she and Nirgal had spoken. Now the black bottom of a bay. All of that, so long ago – her life — They had cut open the tent and walked away from the city, they had flooded it and never looked back. Yes, no doubt Michel was right, this dive was a perfect image of the murky processes of memory; and maybe it would help to see it; and yet . . . Maya felt her numbness, and doubted it. The city was drowned, sure. But it was still here. Any time they wanted to someone could rebuild the dyke and pump out this arm of the bay, and there the city would be again, drenched and steaming in the sunlight, safely enclosed in a polder as if it were some town in the Netherlands; wash down the muddy streets, plant streetgrass and trees, clean out the mesa interiors, and the houses and the shops down in the Niederdorf, and up the broad boulevards – polish the windows – and there you would have it all again – Burroughs, Mars, on the surface and gleaming. It could be done; it even made sense, almost, given how much excavation there had been in the nine mesas, given that Isidis Bay had no other good harbour. Well, no one would ever do it. But it could be done. And so it was not really like the past at all.

Numb, and feeling more and more chill, Maya shot more air into the weight belt, turned and swam back up the length of Canal Park, back toward the light trawl. Again she spotted the row of salt columns, and something about them drew her. She kicked down to them, then swam just over the black sand, disturbing the rippled surface with the downdraught from her fins. The rows of Bareiss columns had bracketed the old canal. They looked more tumbledown than ever now that their symmetricality was ruined by half-burial. She remembered taking afternoon walks in the park, west into the sun, then back, with the light pouring past them. It had been a beautiful place. Down among the great mesas it had been like being in a giant city of many cathedrals.

There beyond the columns was a row of buildings. The buildings were the anchoring point for a line of kelp; long trunks rose from their roofs into the murk, their broad leaves undulating gently in a slow current. There had been a café in the front of that end building, a pavement café, partly shaded by a trellis covered with wistaria. The last salt column served as a marker, and Maya was sure of her identification.

She swam laboriously into a standing position, and a time came back to her. Frank had shouted at her and run off, no rhyme or reason as usual with him. She had dressed and followed him, and found him here hunched over a coffee. Yes. She had confronted him and they had argued right there, she had berated him for not hurrying up to Sheffield . . . she had knocked a coffee cup off the table, and the handle had broken off and spun on the ground. Frank got up and they had walked away arguing, and gone back to Sheffield. But no, no. That wasn't how it had been. They had quarrelled, yes, but then made up. Frank had reached across the table and held her hand, and a great black weight had lifted off her heart, giving her a brief moment of grace, of being in love and being loved.

One or the other. But which had it been?

She couldn't remember. Couldn't be sure. So many fights with Frank, so many reconciliations; both could have happened. It was impossible to keep track, to remember what had happened when. It was all blurring together in her mind, into vague impressions, disconnected moments. The past, disappearing entirely. Small noises, like an animal in pain – ah – that was her throat. Mewling, sobbing. Numb and yet sobbing, it was absurd. Whatever had happened then, she just wanted it back. 'Fuh.' She couldn't say his name. It hurt, as if someone had stuck a pin in her heart. Ah – that was feeling, it was! It couldn't be denied; she was gasping with it, it hurt so. One couldn't deny it.

She pumped the fins slowly, floated off the sand, up away from the rooftops anchoring their kelp. Sitting miserably at that café table, what would they have thought if they had known that a hundred and twenty years later she would be swimming overhead, and Frank dead all that time?

End of a dream. Disorientation, of a shift from one reality to another. Floating in the dark water brought back some of the numbness. Ah but there it was, that pinprick pain, there inside, encysted – insisted – hold onto it forever, hold onto any feeling you can, any feeling you can dredge up out of all that muck, anything! Anything but the numbness; sobbing in pain was rapture compared to that.

And so Michel was proved right again, the old alchemist. She looked around for him; he had swum off on voyages of his own. Quite some time had passed, the others were making their rendezvous in the cone of light before the trawl, like tropical fish in a dark cold tank, drawn to the light in hopes of warmth. Dreamy, slow weightlessness. She thought of John, floating naked against black space and crystal stars. Ah – too much to feel. One could only stand a single shard of the past at a time; this drowned city; but she had made love to John here too, in a dorm somewhere in the first years – to John, to Frank, to that engineer whose name she could seldom recall, no doubt to others besides, all forgotten, or almost; she would have to work on that. Encyst them all, precious stabs of feeling held in her forever, till death did them part. Up, up, up, among the colourful tropical fish with their arms and their legs, back into the light of day, blue sunlight, ah, God, yes, ears popping, a giddiness perhaps of nitrogen narcosis, rapture of the deep. Or the rapture of human depth, the way they lived and lived, giants plunged through the years, yes, and what they held onto. Michel was swimming up from below, following her; she kicked then waited, waited, clasped him and squeezed hard, ah, how she loved the other's solidity in her arms, that proof of reality, she squeezed thinking, thank you, Michel, you sorcerer of my soul, thank you, Mars, for what endures in us, drowned or encysted though it may be. Up into the glorious sun, into the wind, strip off the suit with cold, clumsy fingers, pull it off and step out of it chrysalislike, careless of the power of the female nude over the male eye, then suddenly aware of it, give them that startling vision of flesh in the sunlight, sex in the afternoon, breathe deep in the wind, goosepimpling all over with the shock of being alive. 'I'm still Maya,' she insisted to Michel, teeth chattering; she hugged her breasts and towelled off, luxury of terrycloth on wet skin. She pulled on clothes, whooped at the chill of the wind. Michel's face was the image of happiness, the deification, that mask of joy, old Dionysius, laughing aloud at the success of his plan, at the rapture of his friend and companion. 'What did you see?' 'The café – the park – the canal – and you?' 'Hunt Mesa – the dance studio – Thoth Boulevard – Table Mountain.' In the cabin he had a bucket of champagne on ice, and he popped the cork and it shot off into the wind and landed lightly on the water, then floated off on the blue waves.

But she refused to say any more about it. She would not tell the story of her dive. The others did and then it was her turn, somehow, and the people on the boat were looking at her like vultures, eager to gulp down her experiences. She drank her champagne and sat silently on the upper deck, watching the broad-sloped waves. Waves looked odd on Mars, big and sloppy, impressive. She gave Michel a look to let him know she was all right, that he had done well to send her under. Beyond that, silence. Let them have their own experiences to feed on, the vultures.

The boat returned to Dumartheray Harbour, which consisted of a little crescent of marina-plaited water, curving under part of the apron of Dumartheray Crater. The slope of the apron was covered with buildings and greenery, right up to the rim.

They disembarked and walked up through the town, had dinner in a rim restaurant, watching sunset flare over the water of Isidis Bay. The evening wind fell down the escarpment and whistled offshore, holding the waves up and tearing spray off their tops, in white plumes crossed by brief rainbow arcs. Maya sat next to Michel, and kept a hand on his thigh or shoulder. 'Amazing,' someone said, 'to see the row of salt columns still gleaming down there.'

'And the rows of windows in the mesas! Did you see that broken one? I wanted to go in and look, but I was afraid.'

Maya grimaced, concentrated on the moment. People across the table were talking to Michel about a new institute concerning the First Hundred and other early colonists – some kind of museum, a repository of oral histories, committees to protect the earliest buildings from destruction, etc, also a programme to provide help for superelderly early settlers. Naturally these earnest young men (and young men could be *so* earnest) were particularly interested in Michel's help, and in finding and somehow enlisting all of the First Hundred left alive; twenty-three now, they said. Michel was of course perfectly courteous, and indeed seemed truly interested in the project.

Maya couldn't have hated the idea more. A dive into the wreckage of the past, as a kind of smelling salts, repellent but invigorating – fine. That was acceptable, even healthy. But to fix on the past, to focus on it; disgusting. She would have happily tossed the earnest young men over the rail. Meanwhile Michel was agreeing to interview all the remaining First Hundred, to help the project get started. Maya stood up and went to the rail, leaned against it. Below on the darkening water luminous plumes of spray were still blowing off the top of every wave.

A young woman came up beside her and leaned on the railing. 'My name is Vendana,' she said to Maya, while looking down at the waves. 'I'm the Green party's local political agent for the year.' She had a beautiful profile, clean and sharp in a classic Indian look: olive-skinned, black-eyebrowed, long nose, small mouth. Intelligent, subtle brown eyes. It was odd how much one could tell by faces alone; Maya was beginning to feel she knew everything essential about a person at first glance. Which was a useful ability, given that so much of what the young natives said these days baffled her. She needed that first insight.

Greenness, however, she understood, or thought she did; actually an archaic political term, she would have thought, given that Mars was fully green now, and blue as well. 'What do you want?'

Vendana said, 'Jackie Boone, and the Free Mars slate of candidates for offices from this area, are travelling around campaigning for the upcoming elections. If Jackie stays party chair again, and gets back on the executive council, then she'll continue working on the Free Mars plan to ban all new immigration from Earth. It's her idea, and she's been pushing it hard. Her contention is that Terran immigration can all be redirected elsewhere in the solar system. That isn't true, but it's a stance that goes over very well in certain quarters. The Terrans, of course, don't like it. If Free Mars wins big on an isolationist programme, we think Earth will react very badly. They've already got problems they can barely handle, they need to have what little out we provide. And they'll call it a breaking of the treaty you negotiated. They might even go to war over it.'

Maya nodded; for years she had felt a heightening tension between Earth and Mars, despite Michel's assurances. She had known this was coming, she had seen it.

'Jackie has a lot of groups lined up behind her, and Free Mars has had a supermajority in the global government for years now. They've been packing the environmental courts all the while. The courts will back her in any immigration ban she cares to propose. We want to maintain the policies as set by the treaty you negotiated, or even widen immigration quotas a bit, to give Earth as much help as we can. But Jackie's going to be hard to stop. To tell you the truth, I don't think we know quite how. So I thought I'd ask you.'

Maya was surprised: 'How to stop her?'

'Yes. Or more generally, to ask you to help us. I think it will take unpisting her personally. I thought you might be interested.'

And she turned her head to look at Maya with a knowing smile.

This was offensive, but there was something vaguely familiar in the ironic smile lifting that classic little full-lipped mouth, which, though offensive, was much preferable to the wide-eyed enthusiasm of the young historians pestering Michel. And as Maya considered it, the invitation began to look better and better; it was contemporary politics, an engagement with the present. The triviality of the current scene usually put her off, but now she supposed that the politics of the moment always looked petty and stupid; only later did it take on the look of respectable statecraft, of immutable history. And this issue could prove to be important, as the young woman had said. And it would put her back in the midst of things. And of course (she did not think this consciously) anything that balked Jackie would have its own satisfactions. 'Tell me more about it,' Maya said, moving down the balcony out of earshot of the others. And the tall, ironic young woman followed her.

Michel had always wanted to take a trip on the Grand Canal, and recently he had talked Maya into trying a move from Sabishii back to Odessa, as a way to combat Maya's various mental afflictions; they might even take an apartment in the same Praxis complex that they had lived in before the second revolution. That was the only place Maya thought of as home, apart from Underhill, which she refused even to visit. And Michel felt that coming back to some kind of home might help her. So, Odessa. Maya was agreeable; it did not matter to her. And Michel's desire to travel there by way of the Grand Canal seemed fine as well. Maya had not cared. She wasn't sure of anything these days, she had few opinions, few preferences; that was the trouble.

Now Vendana was saying that Jackie's campaign was to proceed along the Grand Canal, north to south, in a big canal cruiser that doubled as campaign headquarters. They were there now, at the canal's north end, getting ready in the Narrows.

So Maya returned to Michel on the terrace, and when the historians left them she said, 'So let's go to Odessa by the Grand Canal, like you said.'

Michel was delighted. Indeed it seemed to lift from him a certain sombreness that had followed the dive into drowned Burroughs; he had been pleased at its effect on Maya, but for himself it had perhaps not been so good. He had been uncharacteristically reticent about his experience, somehow oppressed, as if overwhelmed by all that the great sunken capital represented in his own life. Hard to tell. So that now, to see Maya responding so well to the experience, and also suddenly to be given the prospect of seeing the Grand Canal – a kind of giant joke, in Maya's opinion – it made him laugh. And that she liked to see. Michel thought that Maya needed a lot of help these days, but she knew full well that it was Michel who was struggling.

So a few days later they walked up a gangway onto the deck of a long, narrow sailing ship, whose single mast and sail were one curved unit of dull white material, shaped like a bird's wing. This ship was a kind of passenger ferry, sailing eastward around the North Sea in perpetual circumnavigations. When everyone was aboard, they motored out of Dumartheray's little harbour, and turned east, keeping within sight of land. The ship's mastsail proved to be flexible and mobile in many different directions; it shifted in its curves like a bird's wing, every moment different as its AI responded minutely to catch the fitful winds.

On the second afternoon of their voyage into the Narrows, the Elysium massif came over the horizon ahead of them, bulking alpenglow-pink against the hyacinth sky. The coast of the mainland rose to the south as well, as if to stretch up and see the great massif across the bay: bluffs alternated with marshes, and then a long, tawny reach was succeeded by an ever-higher seacliff. The horizontal red strata of this cliff were all broken by bands of black and ivory, and the ledges were lined with mats of samphire and grasses, and streaked with white guano. The waves slammed into the sheer rock at the bottom of these cliffs and rebounded, the arcs of the backwash intersecting the oncoming swells in quick points of upshot water. In short, beautiful sailing: long glides down the swells, the wind an offshore powerhouse, especially in the afternoons – the spray, the salt tang in the air – for the North Sea was becoming salty – the wind in her hair, the white V tapestry of the ship's wake, luminous over the indigo sea: beautiful days. It made Maya want to stay on board, to sail around the world and then around again, never to land and never change ... there were people doing that now, she had heard, giant greenhouse ships utterly self-sufficient, sailing the great ocean in their own thassalocracy ...

But there ahead of them were the Narrows, narrowing. The trip from Dumartheray was already almost over. Why were the good days always so short? Moment to moment, day by day – each so full, and oh so lovely – and then gone forever, gone before there was a chance to absorb them properly, really to *live* them. Sailing through life looking back at the wake, high seas, flying wind ... Now the sun was low, the light slanting across the seacliffs, accenting all their wild irregularities, their overhangs, caves, sheer, clean faces dropping

582

directly into the sea, red rock into blue water, all untouched by human hands (though the sea itself was their work). Sudden shards of splendour, splintering inside her. But the sun was disappearing, and the break in the seacliffs ahead marked the first big harbour of the Narrows, Rhodos, where they would dock and the evening would come. They would eat in a harbour café next to the water in the long twilight, and that day's glorious sail would never come again. This strange nostalgia, for the moment just gone, for the evening yet to come: 'Ah, I'm alive again,' she said to herself, and marvelled that it could have happened. Michel and his tricks – one would think that by now she would have become impervious to all that psychiatric-alchemical mumbo-jumbo. It was too much for the heart to bear. But – well – better this than the numbness, that was certain. And it had a certain painful splendour, this acute sensation – and she could endure it – she could even enjoy it, somehow, in snatches – a sublime intensity to these late afternoon colours, everything suffused with them. And under such a flood of nostalgic light, the harbour of Rhodos looked gorgeous – the big lighthouse on the western cape, the pair of clanging buoys red and green, port and starboard. Then in to the calm dark water of an anchorage, and down into rowing boats, in the failing light, across black water through a crowd of exotic ships at anchor, no two the same as ship design was going through a period of rapid innovation, new materials making almost anything possible, and all the old designs being reinvented, drastically altered, then returned to again; there a clipper ship, there a schooner, there some thing that looked to be entirely outrigger . . . finally to bang into a busy wooden dock, in the dusk.

Harbour towns at dusk were all alike. A corniche, a curving narrow park, lines of trees, an arc of ramshackle hotels and restaurants backing the wharves . . . they checked into one of these hotels, and then strolled the dock, ate under an awning just as Maya had supposed they would. She relaxed in the grounded stability of her chair, watching liquid light oxbow over the viscous black water of the harbour, listening to Michel talk to the people sitting at the next table, tasting the olive oil and bread, the cheeses and ouzo. It was strange how much beauty hurt, sometimes, and even happiness. And yet she wished the lazy postprandial sprawl in their hard chairs could go on forever.

Of course it didn't. They went up to bed, hand in hand, and she held onto Michel as hard as ever she could. And the next day they hauled their bags across town to the inner harbour, just north of the first canal lock, and up into a big canal boat, long and luxurious, like a barge become cruise ship. They were two of about a hundred passengers coming on board; and among the others were Vendana and some of her friends. And further on, on a private canal boat a few locks ahead, were Jackie and her consort of followers, about to travel south as well. On some nights they would be docked in the same canalside towns. 'Interesting,' Maya drawled, and at the word Michel looked both pleased and worried.

The Grand Canal's bed had been cut by an aerial lens, concentrating sunlight beamed down from the soletta. The lens had flown very high in the atmosphere, surfing on the thermal cloud of gases thrown up by the melted and vaporized rock; it had flown in straight lines, and burned its way across the land without the slightest regard for details of topography. Maya vaguely remembered seeing vids of the process at the time, but the photos had necessarily been taken from a distance, and they had not prepared her at all for the sheer size of the canal. Their long, low canal boat motored into the first lock; was lifted up a short distance on infilling water; motored out of an opening gate – and there they were, in a wind-rippled lake two kilometres wide, extending in a straight line directly southwest toward the Hellas Sea, two thousand kilometres away. A great number of boats large and small were proceeding in both directions, keeping to the right with the slower ones closer to the banks, in the standard rules of the road. Almost all the craft were motorized, although many also sported lines of masts in schooner rig, and some of the smallest boats had big triangular sails and no engines – 'dhows', Michel said, pointing. An Arab design, apparently.

Somewhere up ahead was Jackie's campaign ship. Maya ignored that and concentrated on the canal, gazing from bank to bank. The absent rock had not been excavated but vaporized, and looking at the banks one could tell; temperatures under the concentrated light of the aerial lens had reached 5,000° K, and the rock had simply dissociated into its constituent atoms and shot into the air. After cooling, some material had fallen back on the banks, and some back into the trench, pooling there as lava; so the canal had been left with a flat floor, and banks some hundred metres high, and each over a kilometre wide: rounded, black slag levées, on which very little could grow, so that they were nearly as bare and black now as when they had cooled forty M-years before, with only the occasional sand-filled crack bursting with greenery. The canal water appeared black under the banks, shading to sky colour out in the middle of the canal, or rather to a shade just darker than sky colour, the effect of the dark bottom no doubt; with streaks of green zigzagging across all.

The obsidian rise of the two banks, the straight gash of dark water between; boats of all sizes, but many of them long and narrow to maximize space in the locks; then every few hours a canalside town, hacked into the bankside and then spreading on top of the levée. Most of the towns had been named after one of the many canals on the classic Lowell and Antoniadi maps, and these names had been taken by the canal-besotted astronomers from the canals and rivers of classical antiquity. The first towns they passed were quite near the equator, and were bracketed by groves of palm trees, then wooden docks, backed by busy little waterside districts; pleasant terrace neighbourhoods above; then the bulk of the towns up on the flats of the levées. Of course the lens, in cutting a straight line, had carved a canal bed that rose directly up the Great Escarpment onto the high plain of Hesperia, a four kilometre rise in elevation; so every few kilometres the canal was blocked by a lock dam. These, like dams everywhere these days, were transparent walls, and looked as thin as cellophane, yet were still many magnitudes stronger than necessary to hold the water they held, or so people said. Maya found their windowpane clarity offensive, a bit of whimsical hubris that would surely be struck down one day, when one of the thin walls would pop like a balloon and wreak havoc, and people would go back to good old concrete and carbon filament.

For now, however, the approach to a lock involved sailing

toward a wall of water like the Red Sea parted for the passage of the Israelites, fish darting hither and thither overhead like primitive birds, a surreal sight, like something out of an Escher print. Then into a lock like a water-walled grave, surrounded by these bird-fish; and then up, and up, and out onto a new level of the great straight-sided river, cutting through the black land. 'Bizarre,' Maya said after the first lock, and the second and the third; and Michel could only grin and nod.

On the fourth night of the trip they docked at a small canalside town called Naarsares. Across the canal was an even smaller town called Naarmalcha. Mesopotamian names, apparently. A terrace restaurant on top of the levée gave a view far up and down the canal, and behind the canal to the arid highlands flanking it. Ahead, they could see where the canal cut through the wall of Gale Crater, floored with water: Gale was now a bulb in the canal, a holding area for ships and goods.

After dinner Maya stood on the terrace looking through the gap into Gale. Out of the inky talc of twilight Vendana and some companions approached her: 'How do you like the canal?' they asked.

'Very interesting,' Maya said curtly. She didn't like being asked questions, or being at the centre of a group; it was too much like being an exhibit in a museum. They weren't going to get anything out of her. She stared at them. One of the young men among them gave up, began to talk to the woman next to him. He had an extraordinarily beautiful face, features neatly chiselled under a shock of black hair; a sweet smile, an unselfconscious laugh; altogether captivating. Young, but not so young as to seem unformed. He looked Indian perhaps – such dark skin, such white, regular teeth – strong, lean as a whippet, a good bit taller than Maya, but not one of these new giants – human scale still, unprepossessing but solid, graceful. Sexy.

She moved toward him slowly, as the group shifted into a more relaxed, cocktail party format, people wandering around to talk and look down at the canal and the docks. Finally she got a chance to speak to him, and he did not react as if approached by Helen of Troy or Lucy the habiline fossil. It would be lovely to kiss such a mouth. Out of the question, of course, and she didn't even really want to. But she liked to think about it; and the thought gave her ideas. Faces were so powerful.

His name was Athos. He was from Licus Vallis, to the west of Rhodos. Sansei, from a seafaring family, grandparents Greek and Indian. He had helped to found this new Green party, convinced that helping Earth through its surge was the only way to stay out of the maelstrom: the controversial tail-wagging-the-dog approach, as he admitted with an easy, beautiful smile. Now he was running for representative from the Nepenthes Bay towns, and helping to co-ordinate the Green campaigns more generally.

'We'll catch up with the Free Mars campaign in a few days?' Maya asked Vendana later.

'Yes. We plan to debate them at a meeting in Gale.'

Then as they were walking up the gangplank onto their boat, the young ones turned away from her, heading together up to the foredeck to continue partying; Maya was forgotten, she wasn't part of that. She stared after them, then joined Michel in their little cabin near the stern. Seething. She couldn't help it, even though she was shocked when it occurred: sometimes she hated the young. 'I *hate* them,' she said to Michel. And simply because they were young. She might disguise it as hatred of their thoughtlessness, stupidity, callowness, utter provincialism; that was all true; but beyond that, she also hated their youth – not just their physical perfection, but simply their age – sheer chronology – the fact that they had it all in front of them. It was all best in anticipation, everything. Sometimes she woke from floating dreams in which she had been looking down on Mars from the *Ares*, after they had aerobraked, and were stabilizing their orbit in preparation for the descent; and shocked at the abrupt fall back into the present, she realized that for her that had been the best moment of all, that rush of anticipation as it all lay there below them, anything possible. That was youth.

'Think of them as fellow travellers,' Michel advised now, as he had several times before when Maya had confessed to this feeling. 'They're only going to be young for as long as

587

we were – a snap of the fingers, right? And then they're old, and then gone. We all go through it. Even a century's difference doesn't matter a damn. And of all the humans who ever existed and ever will exist, these people are the only ones alive at the same time we are. Just being alive at the same time, that makes us all contemporaries. And your contemporaries are the only ones who are ever going to really understand you.'

'Yes, yes,' Maya said. It was true. 'But I still hate them.'

The aerial lens' burn had been about equally deep everywhere, so when it had blazed across Gale Crater it had cut a wide swathe through the rim on the northeast and southwest sides; but these cuts were higher than the canal bed elsewhere, so that narrower cuts had been excavated through them, and locks installed, and the inner crater made into a high lake, a bulb in the canal's endless thermometer. The Lowellian system of ancient nomenclature was in abeyance here for some reason, and the northeastern locks were bracketed by a little divided town called Birch's Trenches, while the southwestern locks' larger town was called Banks. The town Banks covered the meltzone of the burn, and then rose in broad, bending terraces onto the unmelted rim of Gale, overlooking the interior lake. It was a wild town, crews and passengers of passing ships pounding down their gangplanks to join a more-or-less continuous festival. On this night the party was focused on the arrival of the Free Mars campaign. A big, grassy plaza, perched on a wide bench over the lake lock, was jammed with people, some attending to the speeches given from a flat rooftop stage overlooking the plaza, others ignoring the commotion and shopping, or promenading, or drinking, or sitting over the lock eating food purchased from small smoky stands, or dancing, or wandering off to explore the upper reaches of the town.

Throughout the campaign speeches Maya stood on a terrace above the stage, which gave her a view of the backstage area, where Jackie and the rest of the Free Mars leadership were milling about, talking or listening as they waited for their turn in the spotlights. Antar was there, Ariadne, some others Maya half-recognized from recent news vids. Observation from a distance could be so revealing; down there she saw all the primate dominance dynamics that Frank used to go on about. Two or three of the men were fixed on Jackie, and, in a different way, a couple of the women. One of the men, named Mikka, was on the global executive council these days, a leader of the Marsfirst party. Marsfirst was one of the oldest political parties on Mars, formed to contest terms of the renewal of the first Mars treaty; Maya had been part of that, she seemed to recall. Now Martian politics had fallen into a pattern somewhat resembling European parliamentary countries, with a broad spectrum of small parties bracketing a few centrist coalitions, in this case Free Mars, the Reds and the Dorsa Brevians, with the others latching on, or filling gaps, or running off to the sides, all of them shifting this way and that in temporary alliances, to advance their little causes. In this array Marsfirst had become something like the political wing of the Red eco-teurs still in the outback, a nasty, expedient, unscrupulous organization, folded into the Free Mars supermajority for no good ideological reason; there had to be some kind of deal going on. Or something more personal; the way that Mikka followed Jackie, the way he regarded her; a lover, or very recent ex-lover, Maya would have bet on it. Besides which she had heard rumours to that effect.

Their speeches were all about beautiful, wonderful Mars and how it was going to be ruined by overpopulation, unless they closed it to further Terran immigration. There was a strong case to be made for that point of view, actually, as could be told by the cheers and applause from the crowd. Their attitude was deeply hypocritical, as most of those applauding made their living from Terran tourists, and all of them were immigrants or the children of immigrants; but they cheered anyway. It was a good election issue. Especially if you ignored the risk of war, if you ignored the sheer immensity of Earth, and its primacy in human civilization. Defying it in this way . . . Well, it didn't matter; these people didn't give a damn about Earth, and they didn't understand it either. So defiance only made Jackie look more brave and beautiful, standing up for a free Mars. The ovation for her was loud and sustained; she had learned a lot since her maladroit speeches during the second revolution, she had got quite good. Very good.

When the Green speakers got up to take their turn, and argue for an open Mars, they tried to talk about the danger of a closed-Mars policy, but the response was of course much less enthusiastic than it had been for Jackie – their position sounded like cowardice, to tell the truth, and the desirability of an open Mars, naïve. Before arriving in Banks, Vendana had offered Maya a chance to speak, but she had declined, and now she was confirmed in her judgment; she did not envy these speakers their unpopular stance before a dwindling crowd.

Afterwards the Greens held a small party/postmortem, and Maya critiqued their performance with some severity. 'I've never seen such incompetence. You're trying to scare them, but you only sound fearful. The stick is necessary, but you need a carrot as well. The possibility of war is the stick, but you have to tell them why it would be good to keep Terrans coming up, without sounding like idiots. You have to remind them that we all have Terran origins, we are always immigrants here. For you can never leave Earth.'

They nodded at this, Athos among them looking thoughtful. After that Maya got Vendana to one side, and grilled her about Jackie's recent liaisons. Mikka was indeed a recent partner, and probably still was. Marsfirst was if anything more anti-immigration than the larger party. Maya nodded; she had begun to see the outlines of a plan.

When the postmortem was over, Maya wandered downtown with Vendana and Athos and the rest, until they passed a large band playing what they called Sheffield sound. This music was only noise to Maya: twenty different drum rhythms at once, on instruments not intended for percussion or even for musical use. But it suited her purposes, as under the clatter and pounding she was able to guide the young Greens unobtrusively toward Antar, whom she had spotted across the dance floor. When they were nearer to him she could say, 'Oh, there's Antar – hello, Antar! These are the people I'm sailing with. We're right behind you, apparently, headed to Hell's Gate and then Odessa. How's the campaign going?'

And Antar was his usual gracious, princely self, a man hard to object to even when you knew how reactionary he was, how much he had been in the pocket of Earth's Arab nations. Now he must be turning on those old allies, another dangerous

590

part of this anti-immigrant strategy. It was curious the way the Free Mars leadership had decided to defy the Terran powers, and at the same time to try to dominate all the new settlements in the outer solar system. Hubris. Or perhaps they just felt threatened; Free Mars had always been the young natives' party, and if unrestricted immigration brought in millions of new issei, then Free Mars's status would be endangered, not only its supermajority but its simple majority as well. These new hordes with all their old fanaticisms intact – churches and mosques, flags, hidden firearms, open feuds – there was definitely a case for the Free Mars position to be made, for during the intensive immigration of the past decade, the new arrivals had clearly begun to construct another Earth, just as stupid as the first one. John would have gone crazy, Frank would have laughed. Arkady would have said *I told you so*, and suggested yet another revolution.

But Earth had to be dealt with more realistically than that: it could not be banished or wished away. And here in the moment, Antar was being gracious, extra gracious, as if he thought Maya might be useful for something. And as he always followed Jackie around, Maya was not surprised at all when suddenly Jackie and some others were at his side, and everyone saying hello. Maya nodded to Jackie, who smiled back flawlessly. Maya gestured to her new companions, carefully introduced them one by one. When she came to Athos she saw Jackie watching him, and Athos, as he was introduced, gave a friendly glance to her. Swiftly but very casually Maya started asking Antar about Zeyk and Nazik, who were living on the coast of Acheron Bay, apparently. The two groups were moving slowly toward the music, and soon, if they kept going, they would be thoroughly mingled, and it would be too loud to hear any conversation but one's own. 'I like this Sheffield sound,' Maya said to Antar. 'Help me get through to the dance floor?'

An obvious ploy, as she needed no help getting through crowds. But Antar took her arm, and did not notice Jackie talking to Athos – or pretended not to. It was an old story to him anyway. But that Mikka, looking very tall and powerful up close; Scandinavian ancestry perhaps, looking a bit of a hothead; he was now trailing the group with a sour expression.

Maya pursed her lips, satisfied that the gambit had started well. If Marsfirst was even more isolationist than Free Mars, then trouble between them might be all the more useful.

So she danced with more enthusiasm than she had felt in years. Indeed if you concentrated on the bass drums only, and held to their rhythms, then it was somewhat like the knocking of an excited heart; and over that fundamental ground bass the chattering of the various woodblocks and kitchen implements and round stones was no more than the ephemera of stomach rumbling or rapid thought. It made a kind of sense; not musical sense as she understood it, but rhythmic sense, in some way. Dance, sweat, watch Antar shuffle gracefully about. He must be a fool but it didn't show. Jackie and Athos had disappeared. And so had Mikka. Perhaps he would go nova and murder them all. Maya grinned and spun in the dance.

Michel came over and Maya gave him a big smile, a sweaty hug. He liked sweaty hugs, and looked pleased but curious: 'I thought you didn't like this kind of music?'

'Sometimes I do.'

Southwest of Gale the canal rose through lock after lock, up onto the highlands of Hesperia. As it crossed the highlands, to the east of the Tyrrhena Massif, it remained at about the four kilometre elevation, now more often called five kilometres above sea level, and so there was little need for locks. For days at a time they motored along the canal, or sailed under the power of the ship's line of little mastsails, stopping in some bankside towns, passing others. Oxus, Jaxartes, Scamander, Simois, Xanthus, Steropes, Polyphemus – they stopped in each, keeping a steady pace with the Free Mars campaign, and indeed with most of the other Hellas-bound barges and yachts. Everything stretched out without change to both horizons – although occasionally in this region the lens had burned through something other than the usual basaltic regolith, so that in the vaporizing and falling out there had occurred some variation in the levées, stretches of obsidian or sideromelane, swirls of brilliant, glossy colour, of marbled porphyry greens, violent sulphuric yellows, lumpy conglomerates, even one long section of clear glass banks, clear on both sides of the canal, distorting the highlands behind them and for long stretches reflecting the sky. This stretch, called Glass Banks, was of course intensively developed. Between the canalside towns ran mosaic paths, shaded by palm trees in giant ceramic pots, and backed by villas complete with grass lawns and hedges. The Glass Banks towns were whitewashed, bright with pastel shutters and windowboxes and doors, and blue-glazed tile roofs, and long coloured neon signs over blue awnings in the waterfront restaurants. It was a kind of dream Mars, a canal cliché from the ancient dreamscape, but none the less beautiful for that, the obviousness of it indeed part of its pleasure. The days of their passage through this region were warm and windless, the canal surface as smooth as the banks, and as clear: a glass world. Maya sat on the forward deck under a green awning, watching the freight barges and the tourist paddlewheelers heading in the other direction, everyone out on deck to enjoy the sight of the glass banks and the colourful towns decorating them. This was the heart of the Martian tourist industry, the favourite destination for off-world visitors; ridiculous, but true; and one had to admit it was pretty. Gazing at the passing scene it occurred to Maya that whichever party won the next general election, and whichever way the immigration battle fell out, this world would probably go on, gleaming like a toy in the sun. Still, she hoped her gambit would work.

As they barged farther south the southern autumn put a chill in the air. Hardwood trees began to appear on the once-again basalt banks, their leaves flaring red and yellow; and one morning there was a skim of ice sheeting the smooth water against the shores. When they stood on the top of the western bank, the volcanoes Tyrrhena Patera and Hadriaca Patera loomed on the horizon like flattened Fujis, Hadriaca displaying the banded maypole of white glaciers on black rock which Maya had first seen from the other side, coming up out of Dao Vallis when she had made her tour of the flooding Hellas Basin, so long ago. With that young girl, what was her name? A relative of someone she knew.

The canal cut through the dragonback mounds of the

Hesperia Dorsa. The canalside towns grew less equatorial, more austere, more highland. Volga river towns, New England fishing villages, but with names like Astapus, Aeria, Uchronia, Apis, Eunostos, Agathadaemon, Kaiko . . . on and on the broad band of water led them, south by west, as straight as a compass bearing for day after day, until it was hard to remember that this was the only one, that such canals were not webbed everywhere, as on the maps of the ancient dream. Oh there was one other big canal, at Boone's Neck, but it was short and very wide, and getting wider every year, as draglines and the eastward current tore at it; no longer a canal, really, but rather an artificial strait. No, the dream of the canals had been enacted only here, in all the world; and while here, cruising tranquilly over the water, one's view of everything else cut off by the high banks, there was a sense of romance in the air, a sense that their political and personal squabbles had a kind of Barsoomian grandeur.

Or so it felt, strolling in the nip of an evening under the pastel neons of a canalside town. In one, called Antaeus, Maya was strolling along the canalside promenade, looking down into boats large and small, onto beautiful, big young people drinking and chatting lazily, sometimes cooking meat on braziers clamped to the railings and hung out over the water. On a wide dock extending into the canal, there was an open-air café, from which came the plaintive singing of a gypsy violin; she turned into the café instinctively, and only at the last minute saw Jackie and Athos, sitting at a canalside table alone, leaning over until their foreheads almost touched. Maya certainly did not want to interrupt such a promising scene, but the very abruptness of her halt caught Jackie's eye, so that she looked up, then started. Maya turned to leave, but saw Jackie was getting up to come over.

Another scene, Maya thought, only partly unhappy at the prospect. But Jackie was smiling, and Athos was coming with her, at her side, watching it all with wide-eyed innocence; either he had no idea of their history, or else he had good control of his expressions. Maya guessed the latter, simply because of the look in his eye, just that bit too innocent to be real. An actor.

'It's beautiful this canal, don't you think?' Jackie was saying.

594

'A tourist trap,' Maya said. 'But a pretty one. And it keeps the tourists nicely bunched.'

'Oh come now,' Jackie said, laughing. She took Athos' arm. 'Where's your sense of romance?'

'What sense of romance?' Maya said, pleased at this public display of affection. The old Jackie would not have done it. Indeed it was a shock to see that she was no longer young; stupid of Maya not to have thought of that, but her sense of time was such a mishmash that her own face in the mirror was a perpetual shock to her – every morning she woke up in the wrong century, so seeing Jackie looking matronly with Athos on her arm was only more of the same – an impossibility – this was the fresh, dangerous girl of Zygote, the young goddess of Dorsa Brevia!

'Everyone has a sense of romance,' Jackie said. The years were not making her any wiser. Another chronological discontinuity. Perhaps taking the longevity treatment so often had clogged her brain. Curious that after such assiduous use of the treatments there should be any signs of ageing left at all; in the absence of cell division error, where exactly was it coming from? There were no wrinkles on Jackie's face, in some ways she could be mistaken for twenty-five; and the look of happy Boonean confidence was as entrenched as ever, the only way really she resembled John – glowing like the neon scrim of the café overhead. But despite all that she looked her years, somehow – in her eyes, or in some gestalt at work despite all the medical manipulation.

And then one of Jackie's many assistants was there among them, panting, gasping, pulling Jackie's arm away from Athos, crying, 'Jackie, I'm so sorry, so sorry, she's killed, she's killed — ' shivering —

'Who?' Jackie said sharply, like a slap.

The young woman (but she was ageing) said miserably, 'Zo.'

'Zo?'

'A flying accident. She fell into the sea.'

This ought to slow her down, Maya thought.

'Of course,' Jackie said.

'But the birdsuits,' Athos protested. He was ageing too. 'Didn't they . . .'

595

'I don't know about that.'

'It doesn't matter,' Jackie said, shutting them up. Later Maya heard an eyewitness account of the accident, and the image stayed etched in her mind forever – the two flyers struggling in the waves like wet dragonflies, staying afloat so that they would have been okay, until one of the North Sea's big swells picked them up and slammed them into the base of a seastack. After which they had drifted in the foam.

Now Jackie was withdrawn, remote, thinking things over. She and Zo had not been close, Maya had heard; some said they hated each other. But one's child. You were not supposed to survive your children, that was something even childless Maya felt instinctively. But they had abrogated all the laws, biology meant nothing to them any more; and here they were. If Ann had lost Peter on the falling cable; if Nadia and Art ever lost Nikki . . . even Jackie, as foolish as she was, had to feel it.

And she did. She was thinking hard, trying to find the way out. But she wasn't going to; and then she would be a different person. Ageing – it had nothing to do with time, nothing. 'Oh Jackie,' Maya said, and put a hand forward. Jackie flinched, and Maya pulled the hand back. 'I'm sorry.'

But just when people most need help is when their isolation is the most extreme. Maya had learned that on the night of Hiroko's disappearance, when she had tried to comfort Michel. Nothing could be done.

Maya almost cuffed the sniffling young aide, restrained herself: 'Why don't you escort Ms Boone back to your ship? And then keep people away for a while.'

Jackie was still lost in her thoughts. Her flinch away from Maya had been instinct only, she was stunned – disbelieving – and the disbelief absorbed all her effort. All just as one would expect, from any human being. Maybe it was even worse if you hadn't got along with the child – worse than if you loved them, ah, God— 'Go,' Maya said to the aide, and with a look commanded Athos to help. He would certainly make an impression on her, one way or the other. They led her off. She still had the most beautiful back in the world, and held herself like a queen. That would change when the news sank in.

Later Maya found herself down at the southern edge of town, where the lights left off and the starry sheen of the canal was banked by black berms of slag. It looked like the scroll of a life, someone's world-line: bright neon squiggles, moving across a landscape to the black horizon. Stars overhead and underfoot. A black piste over which they glided soundlessly.

She walked back to their boat. Stumped down the gangplank. It was distressing to feel this way for an enemy, to lose an enemy to this kind of disaster. 'Who am I going to hate now?' she cried to Michel.

'Well,' Michel said, shocked. Then, in a comforting tone: 'I'm sure you'll think of someone.'

Maya laughed shortly, and Michel cracked a brief smile. Then he shrugged, looking grave. He, less than any of them, had been lulled by the treatment. Immortal stories in mortal flesh, he had always insisted. He was downright morbid about it. And here another illustration of his point.

'So the all-too-human got hers at last,' he said.

'She was an idiot with all those risks, she was asking for it.'

'She didn't believe in it.'

Maya nodded. No doubt true. Few believed in death any more, especially the young, who never had, even before the days of the treatment. And now less than ever. But believe in it or not, it was touching down more and more, mostly of course among the superelderly. New diseases, or old diseases returned, or else a rapid, holistic collapse with no apparent cause – this last had killed Helmut Bronski and Derek Hastings in recent years, people Maya had met, if not known well. Now an accident had struck someone so much younger than they were that it made no sense, fitted no pattern but youthful recklessness. An accident. Random chance.

'Do you still want to get Peter to come?' Michel asked, from out of a whole different realm of thought. What was this, *realpolitik* from Michel? Ah – he was trying to distract her. She almost laughed again.

'Let's still get in touch with him,' she said. 'See if he might come.' But this was only to reassure Michel; her heart was not in it.

That was the beginning of the string of deaths.

But she didn't know that then. Then, it was only the end of their canal journey.

The burn of the aerial lens had stopped just short of the eastern edge of the Hellas Basin watershed, between Dao and Harmakhis valleys. The final segment of the canal had been dug by conventional means, and it dropped so precipitously down the steep eastern slope of the basin that frequent locks were necessary, here functioning as dams, so that the canal no longer had the classic look it had had in the highlands, but was rather a series of reservoir lakes connected by short, broad, reddish rivers, extending out from under each clear dam. So they boated across lake after lake, down and down in a slow parade of barges and sailboats and cabin cruisers and steamers, and as they dropped in the locks they could see through their clear walls down the string of lakes like a giant staircase of blue stepping stones, down to the distant bronze plate of the Hellas Sea. Somewhere in the badlands to right and left, the Dao and Harmakhis canyons cut deeply into the redrock plateau, following their more natural courses down the great slope; but with their tents removed the two canyons were not visible until you were right on their rims, and nothing could be seen of them from the canal.

On board their ship, life went on. Apparently it was much the same on the Free Mars barge, where Jackie was said to be doing well. Still seeing Athos when the two boats were docked in the same town. Accepting sympathy graciously, and then turning the topic elsewhere, usually to the campaign business at hand. And their campaign continued to go well. Under Maya's coaching the Green campaign was being run better than before, but anti-immigrant sentiment was strong. Everywhere they went the other Free Mars councillors and candidates spoke at the rallies, and Jackie only made occasional short, dignified appearances. She was a much more powerful and intelligent speaker than she used to be. But by watching the others speak Maya got a good sense of who was at the top level of the organization, and several of these people looked very happy to have gained the limelight. One young man, another one of Jackie's young men, named Nanedi, stood out in particular. And Jackie did not seemed very pleased to see it; she became cool to him, she turned more and more to Athos, and Mikka, and even Antar. Some nights she appeared a veritable queen among the consorts. But Maya could see under that, to the truth she had witnessed in Antaeus. From a hundred metres away she could see the darkness at the heart of things.

Nevertheless, when Peter returned her call, Maya asked him to meet her for a talk about the current elections; and when Peter arrived, Maya rested, watchfully. Something would happen.

Peter looked relaxed, calm. He lived in the Charitum Montes these days, working on the Argyre wilderness project, and also with a co-op making Mars-to-space planes for people who wanted to bypass the elevator. Relaxed, calm, even a bit withdrawn. Simonlike.

Antar was already angry at Jackie, for embarrassing him more than usual by her lack of discretion with Athos. Mikka was even angrier than Antar. Now, with Peter on hand, Jackie was baffling and then angering Athos as well, as she devoted all her attention to Peter. She was as reliable as a magnet. But she was attracted to Peter, who was as inert to her as always, iron to her magnet. It was depressing how predictable they were. But useful: the Free Mars campaign was subtly losing momentum. Antar was no longer so bold as to suggest to the Qahiran Mahjaris that they forget about Arabia during its time of troubles. Mikka was intensifying the Marsfirst critique of various Free Mars positions unrelated to immigration, and pulling some of the other members of the executive council into his sphere. Yes – Peter was acting as intensifier to Jackie's impolitic side, making her erratic and ineffective. So it all was working as Maya had planned; one only had to roll men toward Jackie like bowling balls, and over she would go. And yet Maya felt no sense of triumph.

And then they were pushing out of the final lock into Malachite Bay, a funnel-shaped indentation of the Hellas Sea, its shallow water covered by a sunbeaten wind chop. Farther out they pitched gently onto the darker sea, where many of the barges and smaller craft turned north and made toward Hell's Gate, the largest deepwater harbour on the east coast of Hellas. Their barge followed this parade, and soon the great bridge crossing Dao Vallis appeared over the horizon, then the building-covered walls at the entrance to the canyon; then the masts, the long jetty, the harbour jetties.

Maya and Michel went ashore, and made their way up the cobbled and staired streets to the old Praxis dorms under the bridge. There was an autumn harvest festival the next week that Michel wanted to attend, and then they would be off to Minus One Island, and Odessa. After they had checked in and dropped their bags, Maya took off for a walk through the streets of Hell's Gate, happy to be out of the canal boat's confinement, able to get off by herself. It was near sunset, near the end of a day that had begun in the Grand Canal. That trip was over.

Maya had last visited Hell's Gate back in 2121, during her first piste-tour of the basin, working for Deep Waters, and travelling with – with Diana! that was her name! Esther's granddaughter, and a second cousin of Jackie's. That big, cheerful girl had been Maya's introduction to the young natives, really – not only by way of her contacts in the new settlements around the basin, but in herself, in her attitudes and ideas – the way Earth was just a word to her, the way her own generation absorbed all her interest, all her efforts. That had been the first time Maya had begun to feel herself slipping out of the present, into the history books. Only the most intense effort had allowed her to continue to engage the moment, to have an influence on those times. But she had made that effort, had been an influence. It had been one of the great periods of her life, perhaps the last great period of her life. The years since then had been like a stream in the southern highlands, wandering through cracks and grabens and then sinking into some unexpected pothole.

But once, sixty years before, she had stood right here, under the great bridge that carried the piste from cliff to cliff over the mouth of Dao Canyon – the famous Hell's Gate bridge, with the city falling down the steep, sunwashed slopes on both sides of the river, facing the sea. At that time there had been

601

only sand out there, except for a band of ice visible on the horizon. The town had been smaller and ruder, the stone steps of the staircase streets rough and dusty. Now their tops had been polished by feet toiling up them and the dust had been washed away by the years; everything was clean and had a dark patina; now it was a beautiful Mediterranean hillside harbour, perched in the shadow of a bridge that rendered the whole town a miniature, like something in a paperweight or a postcard from Portugal. Quite beautiful in an autumn's early sunset, all shadowed and florid to the west, everything sepia, the moment trapped in amber. But once she had passed through this way with a vibrant young Amazon, when a whole new world was opening up, the native Mars she had helped to bring into being – all of it revealed to her, while she was still a part of it.

The sun set on these memories. Maya returned to the Praxis building, still located up under the bridge, the final staircase to it as steeply pitched as a ladder. Ascending it with pushes on her thighs to help, Maya suddenly felt an overwhelming sense of *déjà vu*. She had done this before – not only climbed these steps, but climbed them with the sense that she had climbed them before – with precisely the same feeling that, in a yet earlier visit, she had been an effective part of the world.

Of course – she had been one of the first explorers of Hellas Basin, in the years right after Underhill. That had slipped her mind. She had helped to found Lowpoint, and then had driven around, exploring the basin before anyone else had, even Ann. So that later, when working for Deep Waters, and seeing the new native settlements, she had felt similarly removed from the contemporary scene. 'My *God*,' she exclaimed, appalled. Layer on layer, life after life – they had lived so long! It was like reincarnation in a way, or eternal recurrence.

There was some little kernel of hope at the middle of that feeling. Back then, in that first feeling of slipping away, she had started a new life. Yes she had – she had moved to Odessa, and made her mark on the revolution, helping it to succeed by hard work, and a lot of thought about why people support change, about how to change without engendering a bitter backlash, which though perhaps decades removed yet always seemed to smash back into any revolutionary success, wrecking what was good in it. And it looked as though they had indeed avoided that bitterness.

At least until now. Perhaps that was the best way of looking at what was happening in this election; an inevitable backlash of some kind. Perhaps she had not succeeded as well as she had thought – perhaps she had only failed less drastically than Arkady, or John, or Frank. Who could be sure; so hard to say any more what was really going on in history: it was too vast, too inchoate. So much was happening everywhere that anything might be happening anywhere. Co-ops, republics, feudal monarchies . . . no doubt there were Oriental satrapies out there in the back country, in some caravan gone wrong . . . so that any characterization one made of history would have some validity somewhere. This thing she was involved in now, the young native settlements demanding water, going off the net and outside UNTA's control – no – it wasn't that – something else . . .

But standing there at the Praxis flat door, she couldn't remember what it was. She and Diana would take a piste train south the next morning, around the southeast bend of Hellas to see the Zea Dorsa, and the lava tube tunnel they had converted to use as an aqueduct. No. She was here because . . .

She couldn't bring it back. On the tip of the tongue . . . Deep Waters. Diana – they had just finished driving up and down Dao Vallis, where on the canyon floor natives and immigrants were starting up an agrarian valley life, creating a complex biosphere under their enormous tent. Some of them spoke Russian, it had brought tears to her eyes to hear it! There – her mother's voice, sharp and sarcastic as she ironed clothes in their little apartment kitchen nook – sharp smell of cabbage —

No. It wasn't that. Look to the west, to the sea shimmering in the dusk air. Water had flooded the sand dunes of east Hellas. It was a century later at least, it had to be. She was here for some other reason . . . scores of boats, little dots down in a postage stamp harbour, behind a breakwater. It wouldn't come back to her. It wouldn't come. A horrible sense of tip-of-the-tongueism made her dizzy, then sick, as if she would get it out by vomiting. She sat down on the step. On the tip of the tongue, her whole life! Her whole life! She groaned aloud, and some kids throwing pebbles at gulls stared at her. Diana. She had met Nirgal by accident, they had had a dinner ... But Nirgal had got sick. Sick on Earth!

And it all came back with a physical snap, like a blow to her solar plexus, a wave rolling over her. The canal voyage, of course, of course, the dive down into drowned Burroughs, Jackie, poor Zo the crazy fool. Of course of course of course. She hadn't really forgotten, of course. So obvious now that it was back. It hadn't really been gone; just a momentary lapse in her thinking, while her attention had wandered elsewhere. To another life. A strong memory had its own integrity, its own dangers, just as much as a weak memory did. It was only the result of thinking that the past was more interesting than the present. Which in many ways was true. But still ...

Still, she found she preferred to sit a while longer. The little nausea persisted. And there was a bit of residual pressure in her head, as if that tongue's hard tipping had left things sore; yes, it had been a bad moment. Hard to deny when you could still feel the throbbing from that tongue's desperate thrusts.

She watched the end of dusk turn the town a deep, dark orange, then a glowing colour like light shining through a brown bottle. Hell's Gate indeed. She shivered, got up, stepped unsteadily down the stairs into the harbourside district, where the restaurants ringing the quays were bright, moth-flittering globes of tavern light. The bridge loomed overhead like a negative Milky Way. Maya walked behind the docks, toward the marina.

There was Jackie, walking toward her. There were some aides following some way back, but in front it was just Jackie, coming toward her unseeing; then seeing. At the sight of Maya a corner of her mouth tightened, no more, but it was enough to allow Maya to see that Jackie was, what, ninety years old? A hundred? She was beautiful, she was powerful; but she was no longer young. Events would soon be washing past her, the way they did everyone else; history was a wave that moved through time slightly faster than an individual life did, so that even when people had lived only to seventy or eighty, they had been behind the wave by the time they died; and how much more so now. No sailboard would keep you up with that wave, not even a birdsuit allowing you to air-surf the

wave in pelican style, like Zo. Ah, that was it; it was Zo's
death she saw on Jackie's face. Jackie had tried her best to
ignore it, to let it run off her like water off a duck's back.
But it hadn't worked, and now she stood in Hell's Gate over
star-smeared water, an old woman.

Maya, shocked by the intensity of this vision, stopped. Jackie
stopped. In the distance the clack of dishes, the loud burble of
restaurant conversations. The two women looked at each other.
This was not something Maya could remember doing with
Jackie – this fundamental act of acknowledgement, meeting
the other's eye. Yes, you are real; I am real. Here we are, the
both of us. Big sheets of glass, cracking inside. Something
freer, Maya turned and walked away.

Michel found them a passenger schooner, going to Odessa by way of Minus One Island. The boat's crew told them that Nirgal was expected to be on the island for a race, news which made Maya happy. It was always good to see Nirgal, and this time she needed his help as well. And she wanted to see Minus One; the last time she had been there it had not been an island at all, just a weather station and airstrip on a bump in the basin floor.

Their ship was a long, low schooner, with five bird's-wing mastsails. Once beyond the end of the jetty the mastsails extruded their taut triangular expanses, and then, as the wind was from behind, the crew set a big blue kite-spinnaker out front. After that the ship leaped into the clear blue swells, knocking up sheets of spray with every slam into an oncoming wave. After the confinement of the Grand Canal's black banks it felt wonderful to be out on the sea, with the wind in her face and the waves coursing by – it blew all the confusion of Hell's Gate out of her head – Jackie forgotten – the previous month now understood to be a kind of malignant carnival that she would never have to revisit – she would never return there – the open sea for her, and a life in the wind! 'Oh Michel, this is the life for me.'

'It's beautiful, isn't it?'

And at the end of the voyage they were to settle in Odessa, now a seaside town like Hell's Gate. Living there they could sail out any day they wanted when the weather was nice, and it would be just like this, windy and sunny. Bright moments in time, the living present which was the only reality they ever had; the future a vision, the past a nightmare – or vice versa – anyway only here in the moment could one feel the wind, and marvel at the waves, so big and sloppy! Maya pointed at one blue hillside rolling by in a long irregular, fluctuating line, and Michel laughed out loud; they watched more closely, laughed harder; not in years had Maya had felt so strongly the sense of being on a different world, these waves just didn't act right; they flew around and fell over and bulged and wriggled all over their surfaces much more than

607

the admittedly stiff breeze could justify, it looked odd; it was alien. Ah, Mars, Mars, Mars!

The seas were always high, the crew told them, on the Hellas Sea. The absence of tides made no difference – what mattered most when it came to waves was gravity, and the strength of the wind. Hearing that as she looked out at the heaving blue plain, Maya's spirits bounced up in the same wild way. Her g was light, and the winds were strong in her. She was a Martian, one of the first Martians, and she had surveyed this basin in the beginning, helped to fill it with water, helped to build the harbours and put free sailors at sea on it; now she sailed over it herself, and if she never did anything again but sail over it, that would be enough.

And so they sailed, and Maya stood in the bow near the bowsprit, hand on the rail to steady her, feeling the wind and the spray. Michel came and stood with her.

'*So* nice to be off the Canal,' she said.

'It's true.'

They talked about the campaign, and Michel shook his head. 'This anti-immigration campaign is so popular.'

'Are the yonsei racist, do you think?'

'That would be hard, given their own racial mix. I think they are just generally xenophobic. Contemptuous of Earth's problems – afraid of being overrun. So Jackie is articulating a real fear that everyone already has. It doesn't have to be racist.'

'But you're a good man.'

Michel blew out air. 'Well, most people are.'

'Come on,' Maya said. Sometimes Michel's optimism was too much. 'Whether it's racist or not, it still stinks. Earth is down there looking at all our open land, and if we close the door on them now they're likely to come hammer it open. People think it could never happen, but if the Terrans are desperate enough then they'll just bring people up and land them, and if we try to stop them they'll defend themselves here, and presto we'll have a war. And right here on Mars, not back on Earth or in space, but on Mars. It could happen – you can hear the threat of it in the way people in the UN are trying to warn us. But Jackie isn't listening. She doesn't care. She's fanning xenophobia for her own purposes.'

Michel was staring at her. Oh yes; she was supposed to

have stopped hating Jackie. It was a hard habit to break. She waved all that she had said away, all the malevolent hallucinatory politicking of the Grand Canal. 'Maybe her motives are good,' she said, trying to believe it. 'Maybe she only wants what's best for Mars. But she's still wrong, and she still has to be stopped.'

'It isn't just her.'

'I know, I know. We'll have to think about what we might do. But look, let's not talk about them any more. Let's see if we can spot the island before the crew.'

Two days later they did just that. And as they approached Minus One, Maya was pleased to see that the island was not at all in the style of the Grand Canal. Oh, there were whitewashed little fishing villages on the water, but these had a handmade, unelectrified look. And above them on the bluffs stood groves of treehouses, little villages in the air. Ferals and fisherfolk occupied the island, the sailors told them. The land was bare on the headlands, green with crops in the sea valleys. Umber sandstone hills broke into the sea, alternating with little bay beaches, all empty except for dunegrass flowing in the wind.

'It looks so empty,' Maya remarked as they sailed around the north point and down the western shore. 'They see the vids of this back on Earth. That's why they won't let us shut the door.'

'Yes,' Michel said. 'But look how the people here bunch their population. The Dorsa Brevians brought the pattern up from Crete. Everyone lives in the villages, and goes out into the country to work it during the days. What looks empty is being used already, to support those little villages.'

There was no proper harbour. They sailed into a shallow bay overlooked by a tiny fishing village, and dropped an anchor, which remained clearly visible on the sandy bottom, ten metres below. They ferried ashore using the schooner's dinghy, passing some big sloops and several fishing boats anchored closer to the beach.

Beyond the village, which was nearly deserted, a twisting arroyo led them up into the hills. When the arroyo ended in a box canyon, a switchbacked trail gave them access to the plateau above. On this rugged moor, with the sea in view all around, groves of big oak trees had been planted long ago. Now some of the trees were festooned with walkways and staircases, and little wooden rooms high in their branches. These treehouses reminded Maya of Zygote, and she was not at all surprised to learn that among the prominent citizens of the island were several of the Zygote ectogenes – Rachel, Tiu, Simud, Emily – they had all come to roost here, and helped to build a way of life that Hiroko presumably would have been proud to see. Indeed there were some who said that the islanders hid Hiroko and the lost colonists in one of the more remote of these oak groves, giving them an area to roam in without fear of discovery. Looking around, Maya thought it was quite possible; it made as much sense as any other Hiroko rumour, and more than most. But there was no way of knowing. And it didn't matter anyway; if Hiroko was determined to hide, as she must have been if she was alive, then where she hid was not worth worrying about. Why anyone bothered with it was beyond Maya. Which was nothing new; everything to do with Hiroko had always baffled her.

The northern end of Minus One Island was less hilly than the rest, and as they came down onto this plain they spotted most of the island's conventional buildings, clustered together. These were devoted to the island's olympiads, and they had a consciously Greek look to them: stadium, amphitheatre, a sacred grove of towering sequoia, and out on a point over the sea, a small pillared temple, made of some white stone that was not marble but looked like it – alabaster, or diamond-coated salt. Temporary yurt camps had been erected on the hills above. Several thousand people milled about this scene; much of the island's population, apparently, and a good number of visitors from around Hellas Basin – the games were still mostly a Hellas affair. So they were surprised to find Sax in the stadium, helping to do the measurements for the throwing events. He gave them a hug, nodding in his diffuse way. 'Annarita is throwing the discus today,' he said. 'It should be good.'

And so on that fine afternoon Maya and Michel joined Sax out on the track, and forgot about everything but the day at hand. They stood on the inner field, getting as close to events as they wanted. The polevault was Maya's favourite, it amazed her – more than any other event it illustrated to her the possibilities of Martian g. Although it clearly required a lot of technique to take advantage of it: the bounding yet controlled sprint, the precise planting of the extremely long pole as it jounced forward, the leap, the pull, the vault itself, feet pointing at the sky; then the catapulted flight into space, body upside down as the jumper shot above the flexing pole, and up, and up; then the neat twist over the bar (or not), and the long fall onto an airgel pad. The Martian record was fourteen metres or so, and the young man vaulting now, already winner for the day, was trying for fifteen, but failing. When he came down off the airgel pad Maya could see how very tall he was, with powerful shoulders and arms, but otherwise lean to the point of gauntness. The women vaulters waiting their turn looked much the same.

It was that way in all the events, everyone big and lean and hard-muscled – the new species, Maya thought, feeling small and weak and old. *Homo martial.* Luckily she had good bones and still carried herself well, or else she would have been ashamed to walk among such creatures. As it was she stood unconscious of her own defiant grace, and watched as the woman discus-thrower Sax had pointed out to them spun in an accelerating burst that flung the discus as if shot from a skeet-casting device. This Annarita was very tall, with a long torso, wide, rangy shoulders, and lats like wings under her arms; neat breasts, squashed by a singlet; narrow hips, but a full, strong bottom, over powerful, long thighs – yes, a real beauty among the beauties. And so strong; though it was clear that it was the swiftness of her spin that propelled her discus so far. 'One hundred and eighty metres!' Michel exclaimed, smiling. 'What joy for her.'

And the woman was pleased. They all applied themselves intensely in the moment of effort, then stood around relaxing, or trying to relax – stretching muscles, joking with each other. There were no officials, no scoreboard, only some helpers like Sax. People took turns running events other than their own. Races started with a loud bang. Times were clocked by hand, and called out and logged onto a screen. Shotputs still looked heavy, their throwing awkward. Javelins flew forever. High-jumpers were only able to clear four metres, to Maya's and Michel's surprise. Long-jumpers, twenty metres; which was a most amazing sight, the jumpers flailing their limbs through a leap that lasted four or five seconds, and crossed a big part of the field.

In the late afternoon they held the sprints. As with the rest of the events, men and women competed together, all wearing singlets. 'I wonder if sexual dimorphism itself is lessened in these people,' Michel said as he watched a group warm up. 'Everything is so much less genderized for them – they do the same work, the women only get pregnant once in their lives, or never – they do the same sports, they build up the same muscles . . .'

Maya fully believed in the reality of the new species, but at this notion she scoffed: 'Why do you always watch the women then?'

Michel grinned. 'Oh I can tell the difference, but I come from the old species. I just wonder if they can.'

Maya laughed out loud. 'Come on. I mean look there, and there,' pointing. 'Proportions, faces . . .'

'Yeah yeah. But still, it's not like, you know, Bardot and Atlas, if you know what I mean.'

'I do. These people are prettier.'

Michel nodded. It was as he had said from the start, Maya thought; on Mars it would finally become clear that they were all little gods and goddesses, and should live life in a sacred joyfulness . . . Gender, however, remained clear at first glance. Although she too came from the old species; maybe it was just her. But that runner over there . . . ah. A woman, but with short powerful legs, narrow hips, flat chest. And that one next to her? Again female – no, male! A high-jumper, as graceful as a dancer, though all the high-jumpers were having trouble: Sax muttered something about plants. Well, still; even if some of them were a bit androgynous, for most it was the usual matter of instant recognition.

'You see what I mean,' Michel said, observing her silence.

'Sort of. I wonder if these youngsters really think about it differently, though. If they have ended patriarchy, then there must necessarily be a new social balance of the sexes . . .'

'That's certainly what the Dorsa Brevians would claim.'

'Then I wonder if that's not the problem with Terran immigration. Not the numbers themselves, but the fact that so many people arriving from Earth are coming from older cultures. It's as if they're arriving out of a time machine from the middle ages, and suddenly here are all these huge Minoans, women and men much the same —'

'And a new collective unconscious.'

'Yes, I suppose. And so the newcomers can't cope. They cluster in immigrant ghettos, or new towns entire, and keep their traditions and their ties to home, and hate everything here, and all the xenophobia and misogyny in those old cultures breaks out again, against both their own women and the native girls.' She had heard of problems in the cities, in fact, in Sheffield and all over East Tharsis. Sometimes young native women beat the shit out of surprised immigrant assailants; sometimes the opposite occurred. 'And the young natives don't like it. They feel as if they're letting monsters into their midst.'

Michel grimaced. 'Terran cultures were all neurotic at their core, and when the neurotic is confronted with the sane, it usually gets more neurotic than ever. And the sane don't know what to do.'

'So they press to stop immigration. And put us at risk of another war.'

But Michel was distracted by the beginning of another race. The races were fast, but not anywhere near two and a half times as fast as Terra's, despite the gravity difference. It was the same problem as the high-jumpers' plants, but continuous through the race: the runners took off with such acceleration that they had to stay very low to keep from bounding too high away from the track. In the sprints they stayed canted forward throughout, as if desperately trying to avoid falling on their faces, their legs pumping furiously. In the longer dashes they finally straightened up near the end, and began to scull at the air as if swimming forward from an upright position, their strides longer and longer until they seemed to be leaping foward like one-leg-at-a-time kangaroos. The sight reminded Maya of Peter and Jackie, the two speedsters of Zygote, running the beach under the polar dome; on their own they had developed a similar style.

Using these techniques, the winner of the fifty metre sprint ran the race in 4.4 seconds; the winner of the one hundred in 8.3; the two hundred in 17.1; and the four hundred in 37.9; but in each case the balance problems engendered by their speeds seemed to keep them from a full sprint the way Maya remembered seeing it in her youth.

In the longer races, the running style was a graceful bounding pace, similar to what they had called the Martian lope back at Underhill, where they had tried it without much success in their tight walkers. Now it was like flight. A young woman led most of the ten thousand metre race, and she had enough in reserve to kick hard at the end, accelerating throughout the entire last lap, faster and faster until she gazelled around the track only touching down every few metres, lapping some of the other racers who seemed to toil as she flew past; it was lovely; Maya shouted herself hoarse. She held onto Michel's arm, she felt dizzy, tears sprang to her eyes even as she laughed; it was so strange and so marvellous to see these new creatures, and yet none of them knew, none of them!

She liked to see women beating men, though they themselves did not seem to remark it. Women won slightly more often in long distances and hurdles, men in the sprints. Sax said that testosterone helped with strength but caused cramping eventually, hampering long distance efforts. Clearly most of the events were a matter of technique in any case. And so one saw what one wanted, she thought. Back on Earth – but these people would have laughed if she had started a sentence with that phrase. Back on Earth, so what? There had been all sorts of bizarre and ugly behaviour back in the nest-world, but why worry about that when a hurdle was approaching and another runner advancing in your peripheral vision? Fly, fly! She shouted herself hoarse.

At the end of the day the field athletes, finished with their events, cleared a passageway into the stadium and around the track; and a single runner jogged in, to sustained applause and wild cheers. And it was Nirgal! Starting hoarse already, Maya's shouting was ragged, almost painful.

The cross-country racers had started at the southern end of Minus One that morning, barefoot and naked. They had run over a hundred kilometres, over the heavy corrugations of

Minus One's central moors, a devilish network of ravines, grabens, pingo holes, alases, escarpments and rockfalls – nothing too deep, apparently, so that many different routes were possible, making it as much an orienteering event as a run; but difficult all the way; and to come jogging in at four p.m. was apparently a phenomenal accomplishment. The next racer wouldn't be coming in until after sunset, people said. So Nirgal took a victory lap, looking dusty and exhausted, like a refugee from a disaster; then he put on track-pants, ducked his head for his laurel wreath and accepted a hundred hugs.

Maya was the last of these, and Nirgal laughed happily to see her. His skin was white with dried sweat, his lips caked and cracking, hair dust-coloured, eyes bloodshot. Ribby and wiry, almost emaciated. He gulped water from a bottle, drained it, refused another. 'Thanks, I'm not that dehydrated, I hit a reservoir there around Jiri Ki.'

'So which way did you take?' someone called.

'Don't ask!' he said with a laugh, as if it had been too ugly to own up to. Later Maya learned that people's routes were left unobserved and undescribed, a kind of secret. These cross-country races were popular in a certain group, and Nirgal was a champion, Maya knew, particularly at the longer distances; and people spoke of his routes as if they involved teleportation. This was apparently a short race for him to win, so he was especially pleased.

Now he walked over to a bench and sat down. 'Let me get myself together a bit,' he said, and sat watching the last sprints, looking distracted and happy. Maya sat next to him and stared; she couldn't get enough of him. He had been living on the land for the longest time, part of a feral farmer-and-gatherer co-op . . . it was a life Maya could scarcely imagine, and so she tended to think of Nirgal as in limbo, banished to an outback netherworld, where he survived like a rat or a plant. But here he was, exhausted but exclaiming at a four hundred metre race's photo-finish, exactly the vital Nirgal she remembered from that Hell's Gate tour so long ago – glory years for him as well as her. But looking at him, it seemed unlikely that he thought of the past in the same way she did. She felt in thrall to her past, to history; but something other than history was his fulfilment now – his destiny survived and put aside like an old book, and now here he was, in the moment, laughing in the sun, having beaten a whole pack of wild young animals at their own game, by his wits alone and his feel for Mars, and his *lung-gom-pa* technique and his hard legs. He had always been a runner, she could see in her mind Jackie and him dashing over the beach after Peter as if it were yesterday – the other two had been faster, but he had gone on all day sometimes, round and round the little lake, for no reason anyone could tell. 'Oh Nirgal.' She leaned over and kissed his dusty hair, felt him hugging her. She laughed, and looked around at all the beautiful giants around the field, the athletes ruddy in the sunset, and she felt life slipping into her again. Nirgal could do that.

Late that night, however, she took Nirgal aside, after an outdoor feast in the cool evening air, and told him all her fears about the latest conflict between Earth and Mars. Michel was off talking to people; Sax sat on the bench across from them, listening silently.

'Jackie and the Free Mars leadership are talking a hard line, but it won't work. The Terrans won't be stopped. It could lead to war, I tell you, war.'

Nirgal stared at her. He still took her seriously, God bless his beautiful soul, and Maya put her arm around him as she would have her own son, and squeezed him hard, hard.

'What do you think we should do?' he asked.

'We have to keep Mars open. We have to fight for that, and you have to be part of it. We need you more than anyone else. You were the one who had the greatest impact during our visit to Earth; in essence you're the most important Martian in Terran history, because of that visit. They still write books and articles about what you do, did you know that? There's a feral movement getting very strong in North America and Australia, and growing everywhere. The Turtle Island people have almost entirely reorganized the American West, it's scores of feral co-ops now. They're listening to you. And it's the same here. I've been doing what I can; we just fought them in the election campaign for the whole length of the Grand Canal. And I tried to counter Jackie a bit. That worked a little,

I think, but it's bigger than Jackie. She's gone to Irishka, and of course it makes sense for the Reds to oppose immigration – they think that will help protect their precious rocks. So Free Mars and the Reds may be in the same camp for the first time, because of this issue. They'll be very hard to beat. But if they aren't . . .'

Nirgal nodded. He took her point. She could have kissed him. She squeezed him across the shoulders, leaned over and kissed his cheek, nuzzled his neck. 'I love you, Nirgal.'

'And I love you,' he said with an easy laugh, looking a bit surprised. 'But look, I don't want to get involved in a political campaign. No, listen – I agree that it's important, and I agree we should keep Mars open, and help Earth out through the population surge. That's what I've always said, that's what I told them when we were there. But I won't get into the political institutions. I can't. I'll make my contribution the way I did before, do you understand? I cover a lot of ground, I see a lot of people. I'll talk to them. I'll start giving talks to meetings again. I'll do what I can at that level.'

Maya nodded. 'That would be great, Nirgal. That's the level we need to reach anyway.'

Sax cleared his throat. 'Nirgal, have you ever met the mathematician, Bao?'

'No, I don't think so.'

'Ah.'

Sax slumped back into his reverie. Maya talked for a while about the problems she and Michel had discussed that day – how immigration worked as a time machine, bringing up little islands of the past into the present. 'That was John's worry too, and now it's happening.'

Nirgal nodded. 'We have to have faith in the areophany. And in the constitution. They have to live by it once they're here, the government should insist on that.'

'Yes. But the people, the natives I mean . . .'

'Some kind of assimilationist ethic. We need to draw everyone in.'

'Yes.'

'Okay, Maya. I'll see what I can do.' He smiled at her; then suddenly he was falling asleep, right before their eyes. 'Maybe we can pull it off one more time, eh?'

'Maybe.'
'I've got to get flat. Goodnight. I love you.'

They sailed northwest from Minus One, and the island slipped under the horizon like a dream of ancient Greece, and they were on the open sea again, with its high, broad, sloppy groundswell. Hard trade winds poured out of the northeast for every hour of their passage, tearing off whitecaps that made the dark purple water look even darker. Wind and water made a continuous roar; it was hard to hear, everything had to be shouted. The crew gave up speech entirely, and worked on setting the maximum amount of sail possible, forcing the ship's AI to deal with their enthusiasm; the mastsails stretched or tightened with each gust like bird's wings, so that the wind had a visual component to match the invisible kinetics of Maya's buffeted skin, and she stood in the bow looking up and back, taking it all in.

On the third day the wind blew even harder, and the boat got up to its hydroplaning speed, the hull lifting up onto a flat section at the stern and then skipping over the waves, knocking up far more spray than was comfortable for anyone on deck; Maya retreated to the first cabin, where she could look out of the bow windows and witness the spectacle. Such speed! Occasionally crew members would come in sopping, to catch their breath and suck down some java. One of them told Maya that they were adjusting their course to take account of the Hellas Current; 'this sea's the biggest example ever of the Coriolis force on a bathtub drain, it being round, and in the latitudes where trade winds push it the same way as the Coriolis force, so it's swirling clockwise around Minus One Island like a great big whirlpool. We have to adjust for it big time or we'll make landfall halfway to Hell's Gate.'

The strong winds held, and flying along as they were, hydroplaning for most of the day, it took them only four days to sail across their radius of the Hellas Sea. On the fourth afternoon the mastsails feathered in, and the hull fell back into the water, rolling in the whitecaps. To the north land appeared over all the horizon at once: the rim of the great basin, like a mountain range without any peaks: a giant berm of a slope, looking like the inner wall of a crater, which of course it was, but so much bigger than any normal crater that one could only barely see the arcing of the circle – exactly *that* big – which struck Maya as beautiful, somehow. And as they closed on the land, and then coasted westward toward Odessa (their landfall had still been east of the town, despite their adjustment for the clockwise current), she could, by climbing up the halyards into the wind, see the beach that the sea had created: a wide strand, backed by grass-covered dunes, with creek mouths cutting through here and there. A handsome coast, and near the outskirts of Odessa; part of Odessa's handsomeness then, part of her town.

Off to the west, the rugged peaks of the Hellespontus Montes began to poke over the waves, distant and small, very different in character from the smooth northern rise. So they had to be close. Maya climbed up farther in the halyards. And there it was, on the rise of the northern slope – the topmost rows of parks and buildings, all green and white, turquoise and terracotta. And then the big, bowed middle of town, like an enormous amphitheatre looking down on the stage of the harbour, which came over the horizon white lighthouse first, then the statue of Arkady, then the breakwater, then the thousand masts of the marina, and the jumble of roofs and trees behind the stained concrete of the corniche seawall. Odessa.

She scampered down the halyard like a crew member, almost, and hugged a few of them and Michel, feeling herself grin, feeling the wind pour over them. They came into the harbour and the sails furled into their masts like touched snails. They puttered into a slip, and walked down a gangplank, along the dock, up through the marina and into the corniche park. And there they were. The blue trolley still clang-clanged on the street behind the park.

Maya and Michel walked down the corniche hand in hand, looking at all the food vendors and the small outdoor cafés across the street. All the names seemed new, not a single one the same, but that was restauranteering for you; they all looked much as they had before, and the city rising up terrace by terrace behind the seafront was just as they remembered it: 'There's the Odeon, there's the Sinter —'

'That's where I worked for Deep Waters, I wonder what they all do now?'

'I think maintaining sea level keeps a good number of them busy. There's always some kind of water work.'

'True.'

And then they came to the old Praxis apartment building, its walls now mostly ivy-covered, the white stucco discoloured, the blue shutters faded. In need of a bit of work, as Michel said, but Maya loved it that way: old. There on the third floor she spotted their old kitchen window and balcony, and Spencer's there beside it. Spencer himself was supposed to be inside.

And they went in the gate, and said hello to the new concierge, and indeed Spencer was inside, sort of: he had died that afternoon.

It shouldn't have mattered so much. Maya hadn't seen Spencer Jackson in years, she had never seen that much of him, even when he lived next door; never known him at all well. No one had. Spencer was one of the least comprehensible of the First Hundred, which was saying a lot. His own man, his own life. And he had lived as part of the surface world under an assumed identity, a spy, working for the security gestapo in Kasei Vallis for almost twenty years, until the night they had blown the town away and rescued Sax, and Spencer as well. Twenty years as someone else, with a false past, and no one to talk to; what would that do to one? But then Spencer had always been withdrawn, private, selfcontained. So maybe it hadn't mattered as much to him. He had seemed all right in their years in Odessa, always in therapy with Michel of course, and a very heavy drinker at times; but easy to have as a neighbour, a good friend, quiet, solid, reliable in his ways. And he certainly had continued to work, his production with the Bogdanovist designers had never flagged, neither during his double life or after. A great designer. And his pen sketches were beautiful. But what would twenty years of duplicity do to you? Maybe all his identities had become assumed. Maya had never thought about it; she couldn't imagine it; and now, packing Spencer's things in his empty apartment, she wondered that she had never even tried before – that somehow Spencer had managed to live in such a way that one did not even wonder about him. It was a very strange accomplishment. Crying, she said to Michel, 'You have to wonder about everybody!'

He only nodded. Spencer had been one of his best friends.

And then in the next few days an amazing number of people came to Odessa for the funeral. Sax, Nadia, Mikhail, Zeyk and Nazik, Roald, Coyote, Mary, Ursula, Marina and Vlad, Jurgen and Sibilla, Steve and Marion, George and Edvard, Samantha, really it was like a convocation of the remaining Hundred and associated issei. And Maya stared around at all their old familiar faces, and realized with a sinking heart that they would be meeting like this for a long time to come. Gathering from around the world each time one fewer, in a final game of musical chairs, until one day one of them would get a call and realize they were the last one left. A horrible fate. But not one that Maya expected to have to endure; she would die before that, surely. The quick decline would get her, or something else; she would step in front of a trolley if she had to. Anything to avoid such a fate. Well – not anything. To step in front of a trolley would be both too cowardly and too brave, at one and the same time. She trusted she would die before it came to that. Ah, never fear; death could be trusted to show up. No doubt well before she wanted it. Maybe the final survivor of the First Hundred wouldn't be such a bad thing anyway. New friends, a new life – wasn't that what she was searching for now? So that these sad old faces were just a hindrance to her?

She stood grimly through the short memorial service and the quick eulogies. Those who spoke looked somewhat perplexed as to what they could say. A big crowd of engineers had come from Da Vinci, Spencer's colleagues from his design years. Clearly a lot of people had been fond of him, it was surprising, even though Maya had been fond of him herself. Curious that such a hidden man could evoke such a response. Perhaps they had all projected onto his blankness, made their own Spencer and loved him as part of themselves. They all did that anyway; that was life.

But now he was gone. They went down to the harbour and the engineers let loose a helium balloon, and when it reached a hundred metres Spencer's ashes began to spill out, in a slow trickle. Part of the haze, the blue of the sky, the brass of sunset.

In the days that followed the crowd dispersed, and Maya wandered Odessa nosing through used furniture shops and sitting on benches on the corniche, watching the sun bounce over the water. It was lovely to be in Odessa again, but she felt the funereal chill of Spencer's death much more than she would have expected. It cast a pall over even the beauty of this most beautiful town; it reminded her that in coming back here and moving into the old building, they were attempting the impossible – trying to go back, trying to deny time's passing. Hopeless – everything was passing – everything they did was the last time they would ever do it. Habits were such lies, such lies, lulling them into the feeling that there was something that was lasting, when really nothing lasted. This was the last time she would ever sit on this bench. If she came down to the corniche tomorrow and sat on this same bench, it would again be the last time, and there would again be nothing lasting about it. Last time after last time, so it would go, on and on, always one final moment after the next, finality following finality in seamless endless succession. She could not grasp it, really. Words couldn't say it, ideas couldn't articulate it. But she could feel it, like the edge of a wave front pushing ever outward, or a constant wind in her mind, rushing things along so fast it was hard to think, hard really to feel them. In bed at night she would think, this is the last time for this night, and she would hug Michel hard, hard, as if she could stop it happening if she squeezed hard enough. Even Michel, even the little dual world they had built — 'Oh Michel,' she said, frightened. 'It goes so fast.'

He nodded, mouth pursed. He no longer tried to give her therapy, he no longer tried always and ever to put the brightest face on things; he treated her as an equal now, and her moods as some kind of truth, which was only her due. But sometimes she missed being comforted.

Michel offered no rebuttal, however, no hopeful comment. Spencer had been his friend. Before, in the Odessa years, when he and Maya had fought, he had sometimes gone to Spencer's to sleep, and no doubt to talk late into the night over glasses of whiskey. If anyone could draw out Spencer it would have been Michel. Now he sat on the bed looking out of the window, a tired old man. They never fought any more. Maya felt it would probably do her some good if they did; clear out the cobwebs, get charged again. But Michel would not respond to any provocation. He himself didn't care to fight, and as he was no longer giving her therapy, he wouldn't do it for her sake either. No. They sat side by side on the bed. If someone walked in, Maya thought, they would observe a couple so old and worn that they did not even bother to speak any more. Just sat together, alone in their own thoughts.

'Well,' Michel said after the longest time, 'but here we are.'

Maya smiled. The hopeful remark, made at last, at great

623

effort. He was a brave man. And quoting the first words spoken on Mars. John had had a knack, in a funny way, for saying things. 'Here we are.' It was stupid, really. And yet might he have meant something more than the John-obvious assertion, had it been more than the thoughtless exclamation that anyone might make? 'Here we are,' she repeated, testing the phrase on her tongue. On Mars. First an idea, then a place. And now they were in a nearly empty apartment bedroom, not the one they had lived in before but a corner apartment, with views out of big windows to south and west. The great curve of sea and mountains said Odessa, nowhere else. The old plaster walls were stained, the wood floors dark and gleaming; it had taken many years of life to achieve that patination. Living room through one door, hall to the kitchen through the other. They had a mattress on a frame, a couch, some chairs, some unopened boxes – their things from before, pulled out of storage. Odd how a few sticks of furniture hung around like that. It made her feel better to see them. They would unpack, deploy the furniture, use it until it became invisible. Habit would once again cloak the naked reality of the world. And thank God for that.

Soon after that the global elections were held, and Free Mars and its cluster of small allies were returned as a supermajority in the global legislature. Its victory was not as large as had been expected, however, and some of its allies were grumbling and looking around for better deals. Mangala was a hotbed of rumours, one could have spent days at the screen reading columnists and analysts and provocateurs hashing over the possibilities; with the immigration issue on the table the stakes were higher than they had been in years, and the kicked-anthill behaviour of Mangala proved it. The outcome of the election for the next executive council remained very much in doubt, and there were rumours that Jackie was fending off challenges from within the party.

Maya shut off her screen, thinking hard. She gave a call to Athos, who looked surprised to see her, then quickly polite. He had been elected representative from the Nepenthes Bay towns, and was in Mangala working hard for the Greens, who had made a fairly strong showing and had a solid group of representatives, and many interesting new alliances. 'You should run for the executive council,' Maya told him.

Now he was really surprised. 'Me?'

'You.' Maya wanted to tell him to go look in a mirror and think it over, but bit her tongue. 'You made the best impression in the campaign, and a lot of people want to support a pro-Earth policy, and don't know who to back. You're their best bet. You might even go talk to Marsfirst and see if you can pull them out of the Free Mars alliance. Promise them a moderate stance and a voice with a councillor, and long-range Reddish sympathies.'

Now he was looking worried. If he was still involved with Jackie and he ran for the council, then he would be in big trouble on that front. Especially if he went after Marsfirst as well. But after Peter's visit he might not be as concerned about that as he would have been during the bright nights on the canal. Maya let him go stew about it. There was only so much you could do with these people.

Although she did not want to reconstruct her previous life in Odessa, she did want to work, and at this point hydrology had overtaken ergonomics (and politics, obviously) as her primary area of expertise. And she was interested in the water cycle in the Hellas Basin, curious to see how the work was changing now that the basin was full. Michel had his practice, and was going to get involved with the first settlers' project that had been mentioned to him in Rhodos; she would have to do something; and so after they had unpacked and furnished the new apartment, she went looking for Deep Waters.

The old offices were now a seafront apartment, very smart. And the name was no longer in the directories. But Diana was, living in one of the big group houses in the upper town; and happy to see Maya at her door, happy to go out to lunch with her and tell her all about the current situation in the local waterworld, which was still her work.

'Most of the Deep Waters people moved straight into the Hellas Sea Institute.' This was an interdisciplinary group, composed of representatives from all the agricultural co-ops and water stations around the basin, as well as fisheries, the University of Odessa, the towns on the coast, and all the settlements higher in the basin's extensive rimland watersheds. The seaside towns in particular were intensely interested in stabilizing the sea's level at just above the old minus one kilometre contour, just a few score metres higher than the North Sea's current level. 'They don't want sea level to change by even a metre,' Diana said, 'if it can be helped. And the Grand Canal is useless as a runoff canal to the North Sea, because the locks need water flowing in both directions. So it's a matter of balancing the inflow from aquifers and rainfall, with evaporation loss. That's been fine so far. Evaporation loss is slightly higher than the precipitation into the watershed, so every year they draw down the aquifers a few metres. Eventually that'll be a problem, but not for a long time, because there's a good aquifer reserve left, and they're refilling a bit now, and may more in the future. We're hoping precipitation levels will also rise over time, and they have been so far, so they probably will continue to, for a while longer anyway. I don't know. That's the main worry, anyway; that the atmosphere will suck off more than the aquifers can resupply.'

'Won't the atmosphere finally hydrate fully?'

'Maybe. No one is really sure how humid it will get. Climate studies are a joke, if you ask me. The global models are just too complex, there are too many unknown variables. What we do know is that the air is still pretty arid, and it seems likely it will get more humid. So, everybody believes what they want, and goes out there and tries to please themselves, and the environmental courts keep track of it all as best they can.'

'They don't forbid anything?'

'Oh yeah, but only big heat-pumpers. The small stuff they don't mess with. Or at least they didn't used to. Lately the courts have been getting tougher, and tackling smaller projects.'

'It's exactly the smaller projects that would be most calculable, I should think.'

'Sort of. They tend to cancel each other out. There are a lot of Red projects, you know, to protect the higher altitudes, and any place they can in the south. They've got that constitutional height limit to back them, and so they're always taking their complaints right up to the global court. They win there, and do their thing, and then all the little development projects are somewhat counterbalanced. It's a nightmare legally.'

'But they're managing to hold things steady.'

'Well, I think the high altitudes are getting a bit more air and water than they're supposed to. You have to go really high to get away from it.'

'I thought you said they were winning in court?'

'In the courts, yes. In the atmosphere, no. There's too much going on.'

'You'd think they'd sue the greenhouse gas factories.'

'They have. But they've lost. Those gases have everyone else's support. Without them we'd have gone into an ice age and stayed there.'

'But a reduction in emission levels . . .'

'Yeah, I know. It's still being fought over. It'll go on forever.'

'True.'

Meanwhile the Hellas Sea's level had been agreed on; it was a legislative fact, and efforts all around the basin were co-ordinated to make sure the sea obeyed the law. The whole matter was fantastically complicated, although simple in principle: they measured the hydrological cycle, with all its storms and variations in rain and snow, melting and seeping into the ground, running over the surface in creeks and rivers, down into lakes and then into the Hellas Sea, there to freeze in the winter, then evaporate in the summer and begin the whole round again . . . and to this immense cycle they did what was necessary to stabilize the level of the sea, which was about the size of the Caribbean. If there was too much water and they wanted to draw down the sea level, there was the possibility of piping some of it back up into the emptied aquifers in the Amphitrites Mountains to the south. They were fairly limited in this, however, because the aquifers were composed of porous rock which tended to crush down when the water was first removed, making them difficult or impossible to refill. In fact spill-off possibilities were one of the main problems still facing the project. Keeping the balance . . .

And this kind of effort was going on all over Mars. It was

crazy. But they wanted to do it, and that was that. Diana was talking now about the efforts to keep the Argyre Basin dry, an effort in its way as large as the one to fill Hellas: they had built giant pipelines to evacuate water from Argyre to Hellas if Hellas needed water, or to river systems that led to the North Sea if it didn't.

'What about the North Sea itself?' Maya asked.

Diana shook her head, mouth full. Apparently the consensus was that the North Sea was beyond regulation, but basically stable. They would just have to watch and see what happened, and the seaside towns up there take their chances. Many believed that the North Sea's level would eventually fall a bit, as water returned to the permafrost or was trapped in one of the thousands of crater lakes in the southern highlands. Then again precipitation and runoff into the North Sea was substantial. The southern highlands were where the issue would be decided, Diana said; she called up a map onto her wristpad screen to show Maya. Watershed construction co-ops were still wandering around installing drainage, running water into highland creeks, reinforcing riverbeds, excavating quicksand, which in some cases revealed the ghost creekbeds of ancient watersheds below the fines; but mostly their new streams had to be based on lava features or fracture canyons, or the occasional short canal. The result was very unlike the venous clarity of Terran watersheds: a confusion of little round lakes, frozen swamps, canyon arroyos and long, straight rivers with abrupt right-angle turns, or sudden disappearances into sink-holes or pipelines. Only the refilled ancient riverbeds looked 'right'; everywhere else the terrain looked like a bomb range after a rainstorm.

Many of the Deep Waters veterans who had not directly joined the Hellas Sea Institute had started an associated co-op of their own, which was mapping the groundwater basins around Hellas, measuring the return of water to the aquifers and the underground rivers, figuring out what water could be stored and recovered, and so on. Diana was a member of this co-op, as were many of the people in Maya's old office. After their lunch Diana went to the rest of the group, and told them about Maya's return to town; when they heard that Maya was interested in joining them, they offered her a position in the co-op with a reduced joining fee. Pleased at the compliment, she decided to take them up on it.

So she worked for Aegean Water Table, as the co-op was called. She got up in the mornings and made coffee and ate some toast or a biscuit, or croissant, or muffin, or crumpet. In fine weather she ate out on their balcony; more often she ate in the bay window at the round dining table, reading the *Odessa Messenger* on the screen, noting every little incident that combined to reveal to her the darkening situation vis-à-vis Earth. The legislature in Mangala elected the new executive council, and Jackie was not one of the seven; she had been replaced by Nanedi. Maya whooped, and then read all the accounts she could find, and watched the interviews; Jackie claimed to have declined to run, she said she was tired after so many M-years, and would take a break as she had several times before, and be back (a sharp glint to her eye with that last remark). Nanedi kept a discreet silence on that topic, but he had the pleased, slightly amazed look of the man who had killed the dragon; and though Jackie declared that she would continue her work for the Free Mars party apparatus, clearly her influence there had waned, or else she would still be on the council.

So; she had bowled Jackie off the global playing field; but the anti-immigrant forces were still in power. Free Mars still held its supermajority alliance in uneasy check. Nothing important had changed; life went on; the reports from pullulating Earth were still ominous. Those people were going to come up after them someday, Maya was sure of it. They were getting along among themselves, they could rest, take a look around, make some plans, co-ordinate their efforts. Better really to eat breakfast without turning the screen on, if she wanted to keep her appetite.

So she took to going downtown and having a larger breakfast on the corniche, with Diana, or later Nadia and Art, or with visitors to town. After breakfast she would walk down to the AWT offices, near the eastern end of the seafront – a good walk, in air that each year was just the slightest bit saltier. At AWT she had an office with a window, and did what she had

629

done for Deep Waters, serving as liaison with the Hellas Sea Institute, and co-ordinating a fluctuating team of areologists and hydrologists and engineers, directing their research efforts mostly in the Hellespontus and Amphitrites mountains, where most of the aquifers were. She took trips around the curve of the coast to inspect some of their sites and facilities, going up into the hills, staying often in the little harbour town of Montepulciano, on the southwest shore of the sea. Back in Odessa she worked through the days, and quit early, and wandered around the town, shopping in used furniture stores, or for clothes; she was getting interested in the new styles and their changes through the seasons; it was a stylish town, people dressed well, and the latest styles suited her, she looked rather like a smallish, elderly native, with erect regal carriage . . . Often she arranged to be out on the corniche in the late afternoon, walking home to their apartment, or else sitting below it in the park, or having an early meal in the summer in some seaside restaurant. In the autumn a flotilla of ships docked at the wharf and threw out gangplanks between the ships and charged entry for a wine festival, with fireworks over the lake after dark. In the winter the dusk fell on the sea early, and the inshore water was sometimes sheeted with ice, and glowing with a pastel of whatever clear colour might be filling the sky that evening, dotted by iceskaters and swift, low iceboats.

One twilight hour as she was eating by herself, a theatre company put on a production of *The Caucasian Chalk Circle* in an adjoining alley, and between the dusk and the spots on the planks of the temporary stage, the quality of light was such that Maya was drawn like a moth to watch. She barely followed the play, but some moments struck her with great force, especially the black-outs when the action was supposed to stop, the actors all frozen on stage in the late light. That moment only needed some blue, she thought, to be perfect.

Afterwards the theatre company came over to the restaurant to eat, and Maya talked with the director, a middle-aged native woman named Latrobe, who was interested to meet her, to talk about the play, and about Brecht's theory of political theatre. Latrobe proved to be pro-Terran, pro-immigrationist;

she wanted to stage plays that made the case for an open Mars, and for assimilating the new immigrants into the areophany. It was frightening, she said, how few plays of the classical repertory reinforced such feelings. They needed new plays. Maya told her about Diana's political evenings in the UNTA years, how they had sometimes met in the parks. About her notion concerning the blues in the lighting of that night's production. Latrobe invited Maya to come and talk to the troupe about politics, and also to help with the lighting if she wanted, which was a weak point in the company, having had its origin in the very same parks Diana's group had used to meet in. Perhaps they could get out there again, and do some more Brechtian theatre.

And so Maya talked with the troupe, and over time, without ever really deciding to, she became one of its lighting crew, helping also with costumes, which was fashion in a different way. She also talked to them long into the nights about the concept of a political theatre, and helped them to find new plays; in effect she was a kind of political-aesthetic consultant. But she steadfastly resisted all efforts to get her on stage, not only from the company, but from Michel and Nadia as well. 'No,' she said. 'I don't want to do that. If I did they would immediately want me to be playing Maya Toitovna, in that play about John.'

'That's an opera,' Michel said. 'You'd have to be a soprano.'
'Nevertheless.'

She did not want to act. Everyday life was enough. But she did enjoy the world of the theatre. This was a new way of getting at people and changing their values, less wearing than the direct approach of politics, more entertaining, and perhaps in some ways even more effective. Theatre in Odessa was powerful; movies were a dead art, the constant incessant oversaturation of screen images had made all images equally boring; what the citizens of Odessa seemed to like was the immediacy and danger of spontaneous performance, the moment that would never return, never be the same. Theatre was the most powerful art in town, really, and the same was true in many other Martian cities as well. So as the M-years passed, the Odessa troupe mounted any number of political plays, including a complete run-through of the work of the

South African Athol Fugard, searing, passionate plays anatomizing institutionalized prejudice, the xenophobia of the soul; the best English-language plays since Shakespeare, Maya thought. And then the troupe was instrumental in discovering and making famous what was later called the Odessa Group, half a dozen young native playwrights as ferocious as Fugard, men and women who in play after play explored the wrenching problems of the new issei and nisei, and their painful assimilation into the areophany – a million little Romeos and Juliets, a million little blood knots cut or tied. It was Maya's best window into the contemporary world, and more and more her way of speaking back to it, doing her best to shape it – very satisfying indeed, as many of the plays caused talk, sometimes even a furore, as new works by the Group attacked the anti-immigrant government that was still in power in Mangala. It was politics in a new mode, the most satisfying she had yet encountered; she longed to tell Frank about it, to show him how it worked.

In those same years, as the months passed two by two, Latrobe mounted any number of vivid productions of the classics, and as Maya watched them, she got more and more snared by the power of tragedy. She liked doing the political plays, which angry or hopeful tended to contain an innate utopianism, a drive for progress; but the plays that struck her as most true, and moved her most deeply, were the old Terran tragedies. And the more tragic the better. Catharsis as described by Aristotle seemed to work very well for her; she emerged from good performances of the great tragedies shattered, cleansed – somehow happier. They were the replacement for her fights with Michel, she realized one night – a sublimation, he would have said, and a good one at that – easier on him, of course, and more dignified all around, nobler. And there was that connection to the ancient Greeks as well, a connection being made in any number of ways all around Hellas Basin, in the towns and among the ferals, a neoclassicism that Maya felt was good for them all, as they confronted and tried to measure up to the Greeks' great honesty, their unflinching look at reality. *The Oresteia, Antigone, Electra, Medea, Agamemnon* which should have been called *Clytemnestra* – those amazing women, reacting in bitter power to whatever strange fates their men inflicted on them, striking back, as when Clytemnestra murdered Agamemnon and Cassandra, first telling the audience how she had done it, and then at the end staring out into the audience, right at Maya:

'Enough of misery! Start no more. Our hands are red.
Go home and yield to fate in time,
In time before you suffer. We have acted as we had to act.'

We have acted as we had to act. So true, so true. She loved the truth of these things. Sad plays, sad music – threnodies, gypsy tangos, *Prometheus Bound*, even the Jacobean revenge plays – the darker the better, really. The truer. She did the lighting for *Titus Andronicus* and people were disgusted, appalled, they said it was just a bloodbath, and by God she certainly used a lot of red spots – but that moment when the handless and tongueless Lavinia tried to indicate who had done it to her, or knelt to carry away Titus's severed hand in her teeth, like a dog – the audience had been as if frozen; one could not say that Shakespeare had not had his sense of stagecraft right from the start, bloodbath or no. And then with every play he had grown more powerful, more electrifyingly dark and true, even as an old man; she had come out of a long, harrowing, inspired performance of *King Lear* in an elation, flushed and laughing, grabbing a young member of the lighting crew by the shoulder, shaking him, shouting, 'Was that not wonderful, magnificent?'

'Ka, Maya, I don't know, I might have preferred the Restoration version myself, the one where Cordelia is saved and marries Edgar, do you know that one?'

'Bah! Stupid child! We have told the truth tonight, that is what is important! You can go back to your lies in the morning!' Laughing harshly at him and throwing him back to his friends, 'Foolish youth!'

He explained to the friends: 'It's Maya.'

'Toitovna? The one in the opera?'

'Yes, but for real.'

'Real,' Maya scoffed, waving them away. 'You don't even know what real is.' And she felt that she did.

Friends came to town, visiting for a week or two; and then,

as the summers got warmer and warmer, they took to spending one of the Decembers out in a beach village west of the town, in a shack behind the dunes, swimming and sailing and windsurfing and lying on the sand under an umbrella, reading and sleeping through the perihelion. Then back into Odessa, to the familiar comforts of their apartment and the town, in the burnished light of the southern autumn which was the longest season of the Martian year, also the approach to aphelion, day after day dimmer and dimmer, until aphelion came, on Ls 70, and between then and the winter solstice at Ls 90 was the Ice Festival, and they iceskated on the white sea-ice right under the corniche, looking up at the town's seafront all drifted with snow, white under black clouds; or iceboating so far out on the ice that the town was just a break in the white curve of the big rim. Or eating by herself in steamy, loud restaurants, waiting for the music to start, wet snow pelting down on the street outside. Walking into a musty little theatre and its anticipatory laughter. Eating out on the balcony for the first time in the spring, sweater on against the chill, looking at the new buds on the tips of the tree twigs, a green unlike any other, like little viriditas teardrops. And so around, deep in the folds of habit and its rhythms, happy in the *déjà vu* that one made for oneself.

Then she turned on her screen one morning and checked the news and found out that a large settlement of Chinese had been discovered already ensconced in Huo Hsing Vallis (as if the name justified the intrusion); a surprised global police had ordered them to leave, but now they were calmly defying the order. And the Chinese government was warning Mars that any interference with the settlement would be regarded as an attack on Chinese citizens, with an appropriate response. 'What!' Maya shouted. 'No!'

She called up everyone in Mangala she knew; these days there weren't that many of them in positions of any importance. She asked what they knew, and demanded to be told why the settlers weren't being escorted back to the elevator and sent home, and so on; 'This is simply not acceptable, you have to stop it now!'

But incursions only a bit less blatant had been happening for some time now, as she had seen herself in occasional news

634

reports. Immigrants were being landed in cheap landing vehicles, bypassing the authorities in Sheffield. There was little that could be done about it, without provoking an interplanetary incident. People were working hard on the problem behind the scenes. The UN was backing China, so it was hard. Progress was being made, slowly but surely. She was not to worry.

She shut down the screen. Once upon a time she had suffered under the illusion that if only she exerted herself hard enough, the whole world would change. Now she knew better.

Although it was a hard thing to admit. 'It's enough to turn you Red,' she said to Michel as she left for work. 'It's enough to get us up to Mangala,' she warned him.

But in a week the crisis passed. An accommodation was reached; the settlement was allowed to remain, and the Chinese promised to send up a correspondingly smaller number of legal immigrants the following year. Very unsatisfactory, but there it was. Life went on under this new shadow.

Except that she was walking home one late spring afternoon after work, and a line of rose bushes at the back of the corniche caught her attention, and she walked over to have a closer look. Behind the bushes people were walking on Harmakhis Avenue by the cafés, most of them in a hurry. The bushes had a lot of new leaves, their brown a mixture of green and red. The new roses were a pure, dark red, their lustrous velvet petals glowing in the afternoon light. Lincoln, the tag on the trunk said. A kind of rose. Also the greatest American, a man who had been a kind of combination of John and Frank, as Maya understood him. One of the Group had written a great play about him, dark and troubling, the hero murdered senselessly, a real heartbreaker. They needed a Lincoln these days. The red of the roses was glowing brightly. Suddenly she couldn't see; for a moment everything dazzled, as if she had glanced into the sun.

Then she was looking at an array of things.

Shapes, colours – she was aware of that much, but what they were – who she was – wordlessly she struggled to recognize . . .

Then it all crashed back at once. Rose, Odessa, all of it just as if it had never been gone. But she staggered, she had to catch her balance. 'Ah no,' she said. 'My God.' She swallowed; throat dry, very dry. A physiological event. It had lasted quite some time. She hissed, choked back a cry. Stood rigid on the gravel path, the hedge brown-green before her, spotted by livid red. She would have to remember that colour effect for the next Jacobean play they did.

She had always known it was going to happen. She had always known. Habit, such a liar; she knew that. Inside her ticked a bomb. In the old days it had had three billion ticks, more or less. Now they had rigged it to have ten billion – or more – or less. The ticks kept ticking nevertheless. She had heard of a clock one could buy, which ran downward through a certain finite number of hours, presumably those you had left if you were to live to five hundred years, or whatever length of life you chose. Choose a million and relax. Choose one, and pay a little bit closer attention to the moment. Or dive into your habits and never think about it, like everyone else she knew.

She would have been perfectly happy to do that. She had done it before and would do it again. But now in this moment something had happened, and she was back in the interregnum, the stripped time between sets of habits, waiting for the next exfoliation. No, no! Why? She didn't want such a time, they were too hard – she could scarcely stand the raw sense of time passing that came to her during these periods. The sense that everything was for the last time. She hated that feeling, hated it. And this time she hadn't changed her habits at all! Nothing was different; it had struck out of the blue. Maybe it had been too long since the last time, habits notwithstanding. Maybe it would start happening now whenever it chose to, randomly, perhaps frequently.

She went home (thinking, I know where my home is) and tried to tell Michel what had happened, describing and sobbing and describing and then giving up. 'We only do things once! Do you understand?'

He was very concerned, though he tried not to show it. Blankouts or not, she had no trouble recognizing the moods of Monsieur Duval. He said that her little *jamais vu* was perhaps a small epileptic fit or a tiny stroke, but he could not be sure, and even tests might not tell them. *Jamais vu* was poorly understood; a variation on *déjà vu* essentially its reverse: 'It seems to be a kind of temporary interference in the brain's wave patterns. They go from alpha waves to delta waves, in a little dip. If you'll wear a monitor we could find out next time it happens, if it does. It's somewhat like a waking sleep, in which a lot of cognition shuts down.'

'Do people ever get stuck there?'

'No. I don't know of any cases like that. It's rare, and always temporary.'

'So far.'

He tried to act as if that were a baseless fear.

Maya knew better, and went into the kitchen to start a meal. Bang the pots, open the refrigerator, pull out vegetables, chop them and throw them in the pan. *Chop chop chop chop.* Stop to cry, stop to stop crying; even this had happened ten thousand times before. The disasters one couldn't avoid, the habit of hunger. In the kitchen, trying to ignore everything and make a meal; how many times? Well, here we are.

After that she avoided the row of rose bushes, fearful of another incident. But of course they were visible from anywhere on that stretch of the corniche, right out to the sea wall. And they were in bloom almost all the time, roses were amazing that way. And once, in that same afternoon light, pouring over the Hellespontus and making everything to the west somewhat washed out, darkened to pastel opacities, her eye caught the pinprick reds of the roses in the hedge, even though she was walking the sea wall – and seeing the tapestry of foam on the black water to one side of her, and the roses and Odessa rising up to the other side, she stopped, stilled by something in the double vision, by a realization – or the edge of an epiphany – and felt some vast truth pushing at her, just outside her – or inside her body, even, inside her skull but outside her thoughts, pushing at the dura that encased the brain – everything explained, everything come clear at last, for once.

But the epiphany never made it through the barrier. A feeling only, cloudy and huge – then the pressure on her mind passed, and the afternoon took on its ordinary pewter luminescence. She walked home feeling full, oceans of clouds in her chest, full to bursting with something like frustration, or a kind of anguished joy. Again she told Michel what had happened, and he nodded; he had a name for this too: '*Presque vu.*' Almost seen. 'I get that one a lot,' he said. With a characteristic look of secret sorrow.

But all of his symptomatic categories suddenly seemed to Maya only to mask what was really happening to her. Sometimes she got very confused; sometimes she thought she understood things that did not exist; sometimes she forgot things, forever; and sometimes she got very, very scared. And these were the things Michel was trying to contain with his names and his *combinatoires*.

Almost seen. Almost understood. And then back into the world of light and time. And there was nothing for it but to go on. And so on she went. Enough days passed and she could forget what it had felt like, forget just how frightened she had been, or how close to joy. It was a strange enough thing that it was easy to forget. Just live in *la vie quotidienne*, pay attention to daily life with its work, friends, visitors.

Among other visitors were Charlotte and Ariadne, who came down from Mangala to consult Maya about the worsening situation with Earth. They went out to breakfast on the corniche, and talked about Dorsa Brevia's concerns. Essentially, despite the fact that the Minoans had left the Free Mars coalition because they disliked its attempt to dominate the outer satellite settlements, among other things, the Dorsa Brevians had come to think Jackie had been right about immigration, at least to an extent.

'It's not that Mars is approaching its human carrying capacity,' Charlotte said, 'they're wrong about that. We could tighten our belts, densify the towns. And these new floating towns on the North Sea could accommodate a lot of people: they're a sign of how many more could live here. They have practically no impact, except on harbour towns, in some senses. But there's room for more harbour towns, on the North Sea anyway.'

'Many more,' Maya said. Despite the Terran incursions, she did not like to hear anti-immigrant talk in any form. But Charlotte was back on the executive council, and for years she had supported a close relation to Earth, so this was hard for her to say:

'It isn't the numbers. It's who they are, what they believe. The assimilation troubles are getting really severe.'

Maya nodded. 'I've read about them on the screen.'

'Yes. We've tried to integrate newcomers every way we know, but they clump, naturally, and you can't just break them up.'

'No.'

'But so many problems are rising – cases of sharia, family abuse, ethnic gangs getting in to fights, immigrants attacking natives – usually men attacking women, but not always. And young native gangs are retaliating, harassing the new settlements and so on. It's big trouble. And this with immigration already much reduced, at least legally. But the UN is angry with us about that; they want to send up even more. And if they do we'll become a kind of human disposal site, and all our work will have gone to waste.'

'Hmm.' Maya shook her head. She knew the problem, of course. But it was depressing to think that allies like these might leave and join the other side, just because the problem was getting hard. 'Still, whatever you do has to take the UN into account. If you ban immigration and they immigrate anyway, and back it up, then our work goes to waste even quicker. That's what's been happening with these incursions, right? Better to allow immigration, to keep it at the lowest level that will be satisfactory to the UN, and deal with the immigrants as they come.'

The two women nodded unhappily. They ate for a while, looking out at the fresh blue of the morning sea. Ariadne said, 'The ex-metas are a problem as well. They want to come here even more than the UN.'

'Of course.' It was no surprise to Maya that the old metanationals were still such powers on Earth. Of course they had all aped the Praxis model to survive, and so with that fundamental change in their nature, they were no longer like totalitarian fiefdoms out to conquer the world; but they were still big and strong, with a lot of people in them and a lot of capital accumulated; and they still wanted to do business, to make their members' livings. Strategies for doing that were sometimes admirable, sometimes not: one could make things that people really needed, in a new and better way; or one could play the angles, try to press advantages, try to inflate false needs. Most ex-metas pursued a mix of strategies, of course, trying to stabilize by diversification as in their old investment days. But that made fighting the bad strategies even harder in a way, because everyone was pursuing them to some extent. And now a lot of ex-metas were pursuing very active Martian programmes, working for the Terran governments and shipping people up from Earth, building cities and starting farms, mining, production, trade. Sometimes it seemed that emigration from Earth to Mars would not cease until there was an exact balance in their fullnesses; which given the hypermalthusian situation on Earth would be a disaster for Mars.

'Yes, yes,' Maya said impatiently. 'Nevertheless, we have to try to help, and we have to keep ourselves within the realm of the acceptable, vis-à-vis Earth. Or else it will be war.'

So Charlotte and Ariadne went away, both looking as worried as Maya felt. And it suddenly occurred to Maya, very grimly, that if they were coming to her for help, then they were in deep trouble indeed.

So her direct political work picked up again, although she tried to keep a limit on it. She seldom travelled away from Odessa, except for AWT business. She did not stop working with her theatre group, which in any case was now the true heart of her political work. But she started going to meetings again, and rallies, and sometimes she took the stage and spoke. *Werteswandel* took many forms. One night she even got carried away and agreed to run for Odessa's seat in the global senate, as a member of the Terran Society of Friends, if they couldn't find a more viable candidate. Later, when she had a chance to think it over, she begged them to look for someone else first, and in the end they decided to go with one of the young playwrights from the Group, who worked in the Odessa town administration; a good choice. So she escaped that, and went on doing what she could to help the Earth Quakers less actively – feeling more and more odd about it, for one could not overshoot a planet's carrying capacity without disaster following – that was what Earth's history since the nineteenth

640

century existed to prove. So they had to be careful, and not let too many people up – it was a tightrope act – but coping with a limited period of overpopulation was better than dealing with an outright invasion, and this was a point she made in meeting after meeting.

And all this time Nirgal was out there in the outback, wandering in his nomadic life and talking to the ferals and the farmers, and, she hoped, having his usual effect on the Martian world view, on what Michel called its collective unconscious. She pinned a lot of her hopes on Nirgal, and did her best to deal with this other strand in her life, to face up to history, in some ways the darkest strand of all, as it stitched its course through her life and bunched it up, in a big twisting loop, back into the foreboding that had prevailed during her previous life in Odessa.

So that was already a kind of malign *déjà vu*. And then the real *déjà vus* came back, sucking the life out of things as they aways did. Oh a single flash of the sensation was just a jolt, of course, a fearful reminder, here then gone. But a day of it was torture; and a week, hell itself. The stereotemporal state, Michel said the current medical journals were calling it. Others called it the *always-already* sensation. Apparently a problem for a certain percentage of the ancient ones. And nothing could be worse, in terms of her emotions. She would wake on these days and every moment of the day would be an exact repetition of some earlier identical day – this was how it felt – as if Nietzsche's notion of eternal recurrence, the endless repetition of all possible spacetime continuums, had become somehow transparent for her, a lived experience. Horrible, horrible! And yet there was nothing to do but stagger through the always-already of the foreseen days, zombielike, until the curse lifted, sometimes in a slow fog, sometimes in a quick snap back to the non-stereotemporal state – like double vision coming back into focus, giving things back their depth. Back to the real, with its blessed sense of newness, contingency, blind becoming, where she was free to experience each moment with surprise, and feel the ordinary rise and fall of her emotional sine wave, a roller coaster which though uncomfortable was at least movement.

'Ah good,' Michel said as she came out of one of these

spells, obviously wondering which of the drugs he had been giving her had done the trick.

'Maybe if I could just get to the other side of a *presque vu*,' Maya said weakly. 'Not *déjà* or *presque* or *jamais*, but just the *vu*.'

'A kind of enlightenment,' Michel guessed. 'Satori. Or epiphany. A mystical oneness with the universe. It's usually a short-lived phenomenon, I am told. A peak experience.'

'But with a residue?'

'Yes. Afterwards you feel better about things. But, well, it's said to usually come only if one achieves a certain . . .'

'Serenity?'

'No, well . . . yes. Stillness of mind, you might say.'

'Not my kind of thing, you mean.'

Which cracked a grin. 'But it could be cultivated. Prepared for, I mean. That's what they do in Zen Buddhism, if I understand it correctly.'

So she read some Zen texts. But they all made it clear; Zen was not information, but behaviour. If your behaviour was right, then the mystic clarity might descend; or might not. And even if it did, it was usually a brief thing, a vision.

She was too stuck in her habits for that kind of change in her mental behaviour. She was not in the kind of control of her thoughts that could prepare for a peak experience. She lived her life, and these mental breakdowns intruded on her. Thinking about the past helped to trigger them, it seemed; so she focused on the present as much as she could. That was Zen, after all, and she got fairly good at it; it had been an instinctive survival strategy for years. But a peak experience . . . sometimes she yearned for it, for the almost seen to be seen at last. A *presque vu* would descend on her, the world take on that aura of vague powerful meaning just outside her thoughts, and she would stand and push, or relax, or just try to follow it, to bring it on home; curious, fearful, hoping; and then it would fade, and pass. Still, someday . . . if only it would come clear! It might help, in the time after. And sometimes she was *so* curious; what would the insight be? What was that understanding which hovered just outside her mind, those times? It felt too real to be just an illusion . . .

So, though it didn't occur to her at first that this was what she was seeking, she accepted an invitation from Nirgal to go with him to the Olympus Mons festival. Michel thought it was a great idea. Once every M-year, in the northern spring, people met on the summit of Olympus Mons near Crater Zp, to hold a festival inside a cascade of cresent-shaped tents, over stone and tile mosaics, as during that first meeting there, the celebration of the end of the Great Storm, when the ice asteroid had blazed across the sky and John had spoken to them of the coming Martian society.

Which society, Maya thought as they ascended the great volcano in a train car, might be said to have arrived, at least in certain times and places. Now, here: here we are. On Olympus, on Ls 90 every year, to remember John's promise and celebrate its achievement. By far the greater number of celebrants were young natives, but there were a lot of new immigrants as well, come up to see what the famous festival was like, intent on partying all week long, mostly by continuously playing music or dancing to it, or both. Maya preferred dance, as she still played no other instrument than the tambourine. And she lost Michel and all their other friends there, Nadia and Art and Sax and Marina and Ursula and Mary and Nirgal and Diana and all the rest, so that she could dance with strangers, and forget. Do nothing but focus on the passing faces luminous before her, each one like a pulsar of consciousness crying, *I'm alive I'm alive I'm alive*.

Great dancing, all night long; a sign that assimilation might be happening, the areophany working its invisible spell on everyone who came to the planet, so that their toxic Terran pasts would be diluted and forgotten, and the true Martian culture achieved at last in a collective creation. Yes, and fine. But no peak experience. This was not the place for it, not for her. It was too much the dead hand of the past, perhaps; things were much the same on the peak of Olympus Mons, the sky still black and starry with a purple band around the horizon . . . There were hostels built around the immense rim, Marina said, for pilgrims to stay in as they made circumnavigations of the summit; and other shelters down in the caldera, for the Red climbers who spent their existence down in that world of overlapping, convex cliffs. Strange what people would do,

Maya thought, strange what destinies were being enacted on Mars nowadays.

But not by her. Olympus Mons was too high, therefore too stuck in the past. It was not where she was going to have the kind of experience she was seeking.

She did, however, get a chance to have a long talk with Nirgal on the train ride back to Odessa. She told him about Charlotte and Ariadne and their concerns, and he nodded and told her about some of his adventures in the outback, many illustrating progress in assimilation. 'We'll win in the end,' he predicted. 'Mars right now is the battleground of past and future, and the past has its power, but the future is where we're all going. There's a kind of inexorable power in it, like a vacuum pull forward. These days I can almost feel it.' And he looked happy.

Then he pulled their bags off the overhead racks and kissed her cheek. He was thin and hard, slipping away from her. 'We'll keep working on it, yes? I'll come visit you and Michel in Odessa. I love you.'

Which made her feel better, of course. No peak experience; but a train trip with Nirgal, a chance to talk with that most elusive native, that most beloved son.

After her return from the mountain, however, she continued to be subject to her array of 'mental events', as Michel called them. He got more worried every time one of them happened. They were beginning to scare him, Maya saw, even though he tried to hide it. And no wonder. These 'events', and others like them, were happening to a lot of his aged clients. The gerontological treatments could not seem to help people's memories hold onto their ever-lengthening pasts. And as their pasts slipped away, year by year, and their memories weakened, the incidence of 'events' grew ever higher, until some people even had to be institutionalized.

Or, alternatively, they died. The First Settlers' Institute that Michel continued to work with had a smaller group of subjects every year. Even Vlad died, one year. After that Marina and Ursula moved from Acheron to Odessa. Nadia and Art had already moved to west Odessa, after their daughter Nikki had grown up and moved there. Even Sax Russell took an apartment in town, though he spent most of the year in Da Vinci still.

For Maya these moves were both good and bad. Good because she loved all these people, and it felt as if they were clustering around her, which pleased her vanity. And it was a great pleasure to see their faces. So she helped Marina, for instance, to help Ursula to deal with Vlad's loss. It seemed that Ursula and Vlad had been the true couple, in some sense – though Marina and Ursula . . . well, there were no terms for the three points of a *ménage à trois*, no matter how it was constituted. Anyway Marina and Ursula were now the remainder, a couple very close in their grieving, otherwise much like the young native same-sex couples one saw in Odessa, men arm-in-arm on the street (a comforting sight), women hand in hand.

So she was happy to see the two of them, or Nadia, or any of the rest of the old gang. But she couldn't always remember the incidents they discussed as if unforgettable, and this was irritating. Another kind of *jamais vu*; her own life. No, it was better to focus on the moment, to go down and work on water, or the lighting for the current play, or sit chatting in the bars with new friends from work, or with complete strangers. Waiting for that enlightenment to come someday . . .

Samantha died. Then Vasili. Oh, there were two or three years between their deaths, but still, after the long decades during which none of them had died, this frequency pattern felt very fast. So they got through those funerals as best they could, and meanwhile everything was getting darker, as on the corniche when a black squall approached from over the Hellespontus – Terran nations still sending up unauthorized people and landing them, the UN still threatening, China and Indonesia suddenly at each other's throats, Red ecoteurs blowing things up more and more indiscriminately, recklessly, killing people. And then Michel came up the stairs, heavy with grief; 'Yeli died.'

'What? No – oh no.'

'Some kind of heart arrhythmia.'

'Oh my God.'

Maya hadn't seen Yeli for decades, but to lose another one

of the remaining First Hundred – lose the possibility of ever seeing again Yeli's shy smile . . . no. She didn't hear the rest of what Michel said, not so much from grief as from distraction. Or grief for herself.

'This is going to happen more and more often, isn't it?' she said at last, when she noticed Michel staring at her.

He sighed. 'Maybe.'

Again most of the surviving members of the First Hundred came to Odessa for the memorial service, organized by Michel. Maya learned a lot about Yeli in those calls, mostly from Nadia. He had left Underhill and moved to Lasswitz early on, he had helped to build the domed town, and had become an expert in aquifer hydrology. In '61 he had wandered with Nadia, trying to repair structures and stay out of trouble, but in Cairo, where Maya had seen him briefly, he had been separated from the others, and missed the escape down Marineris. At the time they had assumed he had been killed like Sasha, but in fact he had survived, as most of the people in Cairo had, and after the revolt he had moved down to Sabishii and worked again in aquifers, linking up with the underground and helping to make Sabishii into the capital of the demi-monde. He had lived for a while with Mary Dunkel, and when Sabishii was closed down by UNTA, he and Mary had come through Odessa; they had been there for the M-50 celebration, which was the last time Maya remembered seeing him, all the Russians in the group offering up the old drinking toasts. Then he and Mary broke up, Mary said, and he moved to Senzeni Na and became one of the leaders there in the second revolution. When Senzeni Na joined Nicosia and Sheffield and Cairo in the East Tharsis alliance, he had gone up to help in the Sheffield situation; after that he had returned to Senzeni Na, served on its first independent town council, and slowly become one of the grandfathers of the community there, just like so many others of the First Hundred had elsewhere. He had married a Nigerian nisei, they had had a boy; he had been back to Moscow twice, and was a popular commentator on Russian vids. Just before his death he had been working on the Argyre Basin project with Peter, siphoning off some big aquifers under the Charitum Montes without disturbing the surface. A great-granddaughter living out on Callisto was pregnant. But then one day during a picnic on the Senzeni Na mohole mound he had collapsed, and they hadn't been able to revive him.

So they were down to the First Eighteen. Although Sax, of all people, made a provisional inclusion of seven more, for the possibility that Hiroko's band was still alive somewhere. Maya regarded this as a fantasy, obvious wishful thinking, but on the other hand Sax was not prone to wishful thinking, so maybe there was something to it. Only eighteen for certain, however, and the youngest of them, Mary (unless Hiroko were alive) was now two hundred and twelve years old. The oldest, Ann, was two hundred and twenty-six. Maya herself was two hundred and twenty-one, an obvious absurdity, but there it was, year 2206 in the Terran news reports . . .

'But there are people in their two-fifties,' Michel noted, 'and the treatments may very well continue to work for a long, long time. This may just be a bad coincidence.'

'Maybe.'

Each death seemed to cut a piece from him. He was getting darker and darker, which irritated Maya. No doubt he still thought he should have stayed in Provence – that was his wish fulfilment fantasy, this imaginary home that persisted in the face of the obvious fact that Mars was his home and had been from the moment they had landed – or from the moment he had joined Hiroko – or perhaps from the moment he had first seen it in the sky as a boy! No one could say when it had happened, but Mars was his home, and it was obvious to everyone but him. And yet he pined for Provence; and considered Maya both his exiler and his country in exile, her body his replacement Provence, her breasts his hills, her belly his valley, her sex his beach and ocean. Of course it was an impossible project being someone's home as well as their partner; but as it was all nostalgia anyway, and as Michel believed in impossible projects as good things, it generally turned out all right. Part of their relationship. Though sometimes an awful burden for her. And never more than when a death of one of the First Hundred drove him to her, and thus to thoughts of home.

Sax was always vexed at a funeral or a memorial service. Clearly he felt that death was some kind of rude imposition, a flagrant bit of the great unexplainable waving its red flag in his face; he could not abide it, it was a scientific problem waiting to be solved. But even he was baffled by the various manifestations of the quick decline, which were always different except for the speed of their effect, and the lack of an obvious single cause. A wave collapse like her *jamais vu*, a kind of *jamais vivre* – theories were endless; it was a vital concern for all the old ones, and all the younger ones who expected to become old – for everyone, in other words. And so it was being intensely studied. But so far no one knew for sure what the quick decline was, or even if it was any one thing; and the deaths kept happening.

For Yeli's service they cast some portion of his ashes off in another swiftly-rising balloon, launching it from the same point of the breakwater where they had launched Spencer, standing out where they could look back and see all Odessa. Afterwards they retreated to Maya and Michel's apartment. Praxis indeed, the way they held each other then. They went through Michel's scrapbooks, talking about Olympus Mons, '61, Underhill. The past. Maya ignored all that and served them tea and cakes, until only Michel and Sax and Nadia remained in the apartment. The wake was over; she could relax. She stopped at the kitchen table, put her hand on Michel's shoulder, and looked over it at a grainy black-and-white photo, stained by what looked like spots of bolognese sauce and coffee. A faded picture of a young man grinning right at the camera, grinning with a confident, knowing smile. 'What an interesting face,' she said.

Under her hand Michel stiffened. Nadia had a stricken look. Maya knew she had said something wrong, even Sax looked somehow pinched, almost distraught. Maya stared at the young man in the photo, stared and stared. Nothing came to her.

She left the apartment. She walked up the steep streets of Odessa, past all the whitewash and the turquoise doors and shutters, the cats and the terracotta flowerboxes, until she was high in the town, and could look out over the indigo plate of the Hellas Sea for many kilometres. As she walked she cried, but without knowing why, a curious desolation. And yet this, too, had happened before.

Some time later she found herself in the west part of the upper town. There was the Paradeplatz Park, where they had staged *The Blood Knot*, or had it been *The Winter's Tale*? Yes, *The Winter's Tale*. But there would be no coming back to life for them.

Ah well. Here she was. She made her way slowly down the long staircase alleyways, down and down toward their building, thinking about plays, her spirits a bit lighter as she descended. But there was an ambulance there at the apartment gate, and feeling cold, as if iced water had been dashed over her, she veered away and continued past the building, down to the corniche.

She walked up and down the corniche, until she was too tired to walk. Then she sat on a bench. Across from her in a pavement café a man was playing a wheezy bandoneon, a bald man with a white moustache, bags under his eyes, round cheeks, red nose. His sad music was right there in his face. The sun was setting and the sea was nearly still, each broad facet glistening with the viscous, glassy lustre that liquid surfaces sometimes display, all of it as orange as the sun winking out over the mountains to the west. She sat back, relaxing, and felt the sea breeze on her skin. Gulls planed overhead. Suddenly the sea's colour looked familiar to her, and she remembered looking down from the *Ares* at the mottled orange ball that Mars had been, the untouched planet rolling below them after their arrival in orbit, symbol of every potential happiness. She had never been happier than that, in all the time since.

And then the feeling came on her again, the pre-epileptic aura of the *presque vu*, the sea glittering, a vast significance suffusing everything, immanent everywhere but just beyond reach, pressing in on things – and with a little pop she got it – that that very aspect of the phenomenon was itself the meaning – that the significance of everything always lay just out of reach, in the future, tugging them forward – that in special moments one felt this tidal tug of becoming as a sensation of sharp, happy anticipation, as she had when looking down on Mars from the *Ares*, the unconscious mind filled not with the detritus of a dead past but with the unforeseeable possibilities of the live future, ah, yes – anything could happen,

649

anything, anything. And so as the *presque vu* washed slowly away from her, unseen again and yet somehow this time comprehended, she sat back on the bench, full and glowing; here she was, after all, and the potential for happiness would always be in her.

PART THIRTEEN

Experimental Procedures

PART THREE

Experimental Program

At the last minute Nirgal went up to Sheffield. From the train station he took the subway out to the Socket, not seeing a thing. Inside the vast halls of the Socket he walked to the departure lounge. And there she was.

When she saw him she was pleased that he had come, but irritated that he had come so late. It was almost time for her to go. Up the cable, onto a shuttle, out to one of the new hollowed-out asteroids, this one particularly large and luxuriant; and then off, accelerating at a Mars gravity equivalent for a matter of months, until it could coast at several per cent of the speed of light. For this asteroid was a starship; and they were off to a star near Aldebaran, where a Marslike planet rolled in an Earthlike orbit around a sunlike sun. A new world, a new life. And Jackie was going.

Nirgal still couldn't quite believe it. He had received the message only two days before, had not slept as he tried to decide whether this mattered, whether it was part of his life, whether he ought to see her off, whether he ought to try to talk her out of it.

Seeing her now, he knew he could not talk her out of it. She was going. *I want to try something new,* she had said in her message, a voice record without a visual image. There coming from his wrist, her voice: *There's nothing for me here now any more. I've done my part. I want to try something new.*

The group in the starship asteroid were mostly from Dorsa Brevia. Nirgal had called Charlotte to try to find out why. *It's complicated,* Charlotte said. *There's a lot of reasons. This planet they're going to is relatively nearby, and it's perfect for terraforming. Humanity going there is a big step. The first step to the stars.*

I know, Nirgal had said. Quite a few starships had already left, off to other likely planets. The step had been taken.

But this planet is the best one yet. And in Dorsa Brevia, people are beginning to wonder if we don't have to get that distance from Earth to get a fresh start. The hardest part is leaving Earth behind. And now it's looking bad again. These unauthorized landings; it could be the start of an invasion. And if you think of Mars as being the new democratic society, and Earth the old feudalism, then the influx can look like the old trying to crush the new, before it gets too big. They've got us outnumbered twenty billion to two. And part of that old feudalism is patriarchy itself. So the people in Dorsa Brevia wonder if they can get a little bit more distance. It's only twenty years to Aldebaran, and they're going to live a long time. So a group of them are doing it. Families, family groups, childless couples, childless single people. It's like the First Hundred going to Mars, like the days of Boone and Chalmers.

And so Jackie sat on the carpeted floor of the departure lounge, and Nirgal sat next to her. She looked down. She was smoothing the carpet with the palm of her hand, and then drawing patterns in the nap, letters. Nirgal, she wrote.

He sat down beside her. The departure lounge was crowded but subdued. People looked grave, wan, upset, thoughtful, radiant. Some were going, some were seeing people off. Through a broad window they looked into the interior of the Socket, where elevator cars levitated in silence against the walls, and the foot of the thirty-seven thousand kilometre-long cable stood hovering ten metres over the concrete floor.

So you're going, Nirgal said.

Yes, Jackie said. I want a new start.

Nirgal said nothing.

It will be an adventure, she said.

True. He didn't know what else to say.

In the carpet she wrote Jackie Boone Went To The Moon.

It's an awesome idea when you think of it, she said. Humanity, spreading through the galaxy. Star by star, ever outward. It's our destiny. It's what we ought to be doing. In fact I've heard people say that that's where Hiroko is – that she and her people joined one of the first starships, the one to Barnard's star. To start a new world. Spread viriditas.

It's as likely as any other story, Nirgal said. And it was true; he could imagine Hiroko doing it, taking off again, joining the new diaspora, of humanity across the stars, settling the nearby planets and then on from there. A step out of the cradle. The end of prehistory.

He stared at her profile as she drew patterns on the carpet.

654

This was the last time he would ever see her. For each of them it was as if the other were dying. That was true for a lot of the couples huddled silently together in this room. That people should leave everyone they knew.

And that was the First Hundred. That was why they had all been so strange — they had been willing to leave the people they knew, and go off with ninety-nine strangers. Some of them had been famous scientists, all of them had had parents, presumably. But none of them had had children. And none of them had had spouses, except for the six married couples who had been part of the hundred. Single, childless people, middle-aged, ready for a fresh start. That was who they were. And now that was Jackie too: childless, single.

Nirgal looked away, looked back; there she was, flush in the light. Fine-grained gloss of black hair. She glanced up at him, looked back down. *Wherever you go*, she wrote, *there you are.*

She looked up at him. *What do you think happened to us?* she asked.

I don't know.

They sat looking at the carpet. Through the window, in the cable chamber, an elevator levitated across the floor, hovering upright as it moved over a piste to the cable. It latched on, and a jetway snaked out and enveloped its outer side.

Don't go, he wanted to say. *Don't go. Don't leave this world forever. Don't leave me. Remember the time the Sufis married us? Remember the time we made love by the heat of a volcano? Remember Zygote?*

He said nothing. She remembered.

I don't know.

He reached down and rubbed the nap of the carpet so that he erased the second *you*. With his forefinger he wrote *we*.

She smiled, wistfully. *Against all those years, what was a word?*

The loudspeakers announced that the elevator was ready for departure. People stood, saying things in agitated voices. Nirgal found himself standing, facing Jackie. She was looking right at him. He hugged her. That was her body in his arms, as real as rock. Her hair in his nostrils. He breathed in, held his breath. Let her go. She walked off without a word. At the entry to the jetway she looked back once; her face. And then she was gone.

Later he got a print message by radio from deep space. *Wherever you go, there we are.* It wasn't true. But it made him feel better. That was what words could do. Okay, he said as he went through his days wandering the planet. Now I am flying to Aldebaran.

The northern polar island had suffered perhaps more deformation than any other landscape on Mars; so Sax had heard, and now, walking on a bluff edging the Chasma Borealis River, he could see what they meant. The polar cap had melted by about half, and the massive ice walls of Chasma Borealis were mostly gone. Their departure had been caused by a thaw unlike any seen on Mars since the middle Hesperian, and all that water had rushed every spring and summer down the stratified sand and loess, cutting through them with great force. Declivities in the landscape had turned into deep sandwalled canyons, cutting downstream to the North Sea in very unstable watersheds, channelizing subsequent spring melts and shifting rapidly as slopes collapsed and landslides created short-lived lakes, before the dams were cut through and carried off in their turn, leaving only beach terraces and slide gates.

Sax stood looking down on one of these slide gates now, calculating how much water must have accumulated in the lake before the dam had broken. One couldn't stand too close to the edge of the overlook; the new canyon rims were by no means stable. There were few plants to be seen, only here and there a strip of pale lichen colour, providing some relief from the mineral tones. The Borealis River was a wide, shallow wash of tumbling glacial milk, some hundred and eighty metres below him. Tributaries cut hanging valleys much less deep, and dumped their loads in opaque waterfalls like spills of thin paint.

Up above the canyons, on what had been the floor of Chasma Borealis, the plateau was cut with tributary streams like the pattern of veins in a leaf. This had been laminated terrain to begin with, looking as if elevation contours had been artfully incised into the landscape, and the stream cuts revealed that the French curve laminae went down many metres, as if the map had marked the territory to a great depth.

It was near midsummer, and the sun rode the sky all day long. Clouds poured off the ice to the north. When the sun was at its lowest, the equivalent of mid-afternoon, these clouds drifted south toward the sea in thick mists, coloured bronze or purple or lilac or some other vibrant, subtle shade. A thin scattering of fellfield flowers graced the laminate plateau, reminding Sax of Arena Glacier, the landscape that had first caught his attention, back before his incident. That first encounter was very difficult for Sax to remember, but apparently it had imprinted on him in the way ducklings imprinted on the first creatures they saw as their mothers. There were great forests covering the temperate regions, where stands of giant sequoia shaded pine understoreys; there were spectacular seacliffs, home to great clouds of mewling birds; there were crater jungle terraria of all kinds, and in the winters there were the endless plains of sastrugi snow; there were escarpments like vertical worlds, vast deserts of red, shifting sands, volcano slopes of black rubble, there was every manner of biome, great and small; but for Sax this spare rock bioscape was the best.

He walked along over the rocks. His little car followed as best it could, crossing the tributaries of the Borealis upstream at the first car fords. The summertime flowering, though hard to pick out if one were more than ten metres away, was nevertheless intensely colourful, as spectacular in its way as any rainforest. The soil created by these plants in their generations was extremely thin, and would thicken only slowly. And augmenting it was difficult; all soil dropped in the canyons would wind up in the North Sea, and on the laminate terrain the winters were so harsh that soil availed little, it only became part of the permafrost. So they let the fellfields grow in their own slow course to tundra, and saved the soil for more promising regions in the south. Which was fine by Sax. It left for everyone to experience, for many centuries to come, the first areobiome, so spare and unTerran.

Trudging over the rubble, alert for any plant life underfoot, Sax veered toward his car, which was now out of sight to his right. The sun was at much the same height it had been all day, and away from the deep, narrow, new Chasma Borealis running down the broad old one, it was very hard to keep oriented; north could have been anywhere across about 180°: basically, 'behind him'. And it would not do to walk casually into the vicinity of the North Sea, somewhere ahead of him,

658

because polar bears did very well on that littoral, killing seals and raiding rookeries.

So Sax paused for a moment, and checked his wristpad maps to get a precise fix on his position and his car's. He had a very good map program in his wristpad these days. He found he was at 31·63844° longitude, 84·89926° N latitude, give or take a few metres; his car was at 31·64114°, 84·86857°; if he climbed to the top of this little breadloaf knoll to the west-northwest, up an exquisite natural staircase, he should see it. Yes. There it rolled, at a lazy walking pace. And there, in the cracks of this breadloaf (so apt, this anthropomorphic analogizing) was some small purple saxifrage, stubbornly hunkering down in the protection of broken rock.

Something in the sight was so satisfying: the laminate terrain, the saxifrage in the light – the little car moving to its dinner rendezvous with him – the delicious weariness in his feet – and then something indefinable, he had to admit it – inexplicable – in that the individual elements of the experience were insufficient to explain the pleasure of it. A kind of euphoria. He supposed this was love. Spirit of place, love of place – the areophany, not only as Hiroko had described it, but perhaps as she had experienced it as well. Ah, Hiroko – could she really have felt this good, all the time? Blessed creature! No wonder she had projected such an aura, collected such a following. To be near that bliss, to learn to feel it oneself . . . love of planet. Love of a planet's life. Certainly the biological component of the scene was a critical part of one's regard for it. Even Ann would surely have to admit that, if she were standing there beside him. An interesting hypothesis to test. Look, Ann, at this purple saxifrage. See how it catches the eye, somehow. One's regard focused, in the centre of the curvilinear landscape. And so love, spontaneously generated.

Indeed this sublime land seemed to him a kind of image of the universe itself, at least in its relation of life to nonlife. He had been following the biogenetic theories of Deleuze, an attempt to mathematicize on a cosmological scale something rather like Hiroko's viriditas. As far as Sax could tell, Deleuze was maintaining that viriditas had been a threadlike force in the Big Bang, a complex border phenomenon functioning between forces and particles, and radiating outward from the

Big Bang as a mere potentiality until second generation planetary systems had collected the full array of heavier elements, at which point life had sprung forth, bursting in 'little bangs' at the end of each thread of viriditas. There had been none too many threads, and they had been uniformly distributed through the universe, following the galactic clumping and partly shaping it; so that each little bang at the end of a thread was as far removed from the others as it was possible to be. Thus all the life-islands were widely separated in timespace, making contact between any two islands very unlikely simply because they were all late phenomena, and at a great distance from the rest; there hadn't been time for contact. This hypothesis, if true, seemed to Sax a more than adequate explanation for the failure of SETI, that silence from the stars that had been ongoing for nearly four centuries now. A blink of the eye compared to the billion light years that Deleuze estimated separated all life-islands.

So viriditas existed in the universe like this saxifrage on the great sand curves of the polar island: small, isolate, magnificent. Sax saw a curving universe before him; but Deleuze maintained that they lived in a flat universe, on the cusp between permanent expansion and the expand-contract model, in a delicate balance. And he also maintained that the turning point, when the universe would either start to shrink or else expand past all possibility of shrinking, appeared to be very close to the present time! This made Sax very suspicious, as did the implication in Deleuze that they could influence the matter one way or the other: stamp on the ground and send the universe flying outward to dissolution and heat death, or catch one's breath, and pull it all inward to the unimaginable omega point of the eskaton: no. The first law of thermodynamics, among many other considerations, made this a kind of cosmological hallucination, a small god's existentialism. The psychological result of humanity's suddenly vastly increased physical powers, perhaps. Or Deleuze's own tendencies to megalomania; he thought he could explain everything.

In fact Sax was suspicious of all the current cosmology, placing humanity as it did right at the centre of things, time after time. It suggested to Sax that all these formulations were artefacts of human perception only, the strong anthropic principle seeping into everything they saw, like colour. Although he had to admit some of the observations seemed very solid, and hard to accept as human perceptual intrusion, or coincidence. Of course it was hard to believe that the sun and Luna looked exactly the same size when seen from Earth's surface, but they did. Coincidences happened. Most of these anthropocentric features, however, seemed to Sax likely to be the mark of the limits of their understanding; very possibly there were things larger than the universe, and others smaller than strings – some even larger plenum, made of even smaller components – all beyond human perception, even mathematically. If that were true it might explain some of the inconsistencies in Bao's equations – if one allowed that the four macro-dimensions of timespace were in relation to some larger dimensions, like the six micro-dimensions were to their ordinary four, then the equations might work quite beautifully – he had a vision of one possible formulation, right there —

He stumbled, caught his balance. Another small bench of sand, about three times the size of the normal one. Okay – on and up to the car. Now what had he been thinking about?

He couldn't remember. He had been thinking something interesting, he knew that. Figuring something out, it seemed. But try as he might, he couldn't recall what it was. It bulked at the back of his mind like a rock in his shoe, a tip-of-the-tongueism that never came through. Most uncomfortable; even maddening. It had happened to him before, he seemed to recall – and more frequently recently, wasn't that true? He wasn't sure, but that felt right. He had been losing his train of thought, and then been unable to retrieve it, no matter how hard he tried.

He reached his car without seeing his walk there. Love of place, yes – but one had to be able to remember things to love them! One had to be able to remember one's thoughts! Confused, affronted, he clattered about the car getting a dinner together, then ate it without noticing.

This memory trouble would not do.

Actually, now that he thought of it, losing his train of thought had been happening a lot. Or so he seemed to remember. It was an odd problem that way. But certainly he had been aware of losing trains of thought, which seemed, in their blank aftermath, to have been good thoughts. He had even tried to talk into his wristpad when such an accelerated burst of thinking began, when he felt that sense of several different strands braiding together to make something new. But the act of talking stopped the mentation. He was not a verbal thinker, it seemed; it was a matter of images, sometimes in the languages of math, sometimes in some kind of inchoate flow that he could not characterize. So talking stopped it. Or else the lost thoughts were much less impressive than they had felt; for the wrist recordings had only a few phrases, hesitant, disconnected, and most of all slow – they were nothing like the thoughts he had hoped to record, which, especially in this particular state, were just the reverse – fast, coherent, effortless – the free play of the mind. That process could not be captured; and it struck Sax forcibly how little of anyone's thinking was ever recorded or remembered or conveyed in any way to others – the stream of one's consciousness never shared except in thimblefuls, even by the most prolific mathematician, the most diligent diarist.

So, well; these incidents were just one of the many conditions they had to adapt to in their unnaturally prolonged old age. It was very inconvenient, even irritating. No doubt the matter ought to be investigated, although memory was a notorious quagmire for brain science. And it was somewhat like the leaky roof problem; immediately after such a lost train of thought, with the absent shape of it still in his mind, and the emotional excitation, it almost drove him mad; but as the content of the thought *was* forgotten, half an hour later it did not seem much more significant than the slipping away of dreams in the minutes after waking. He had other things to worry about.

Such as the death of his friends. Yeli Zudov this time, a member of the First Hundred he had never known well; nevertheless he went down to Odessa, and after a memorial service, a lugubrious affair during which Sax was frequently distracted by thoughts of Vlad, of Spencer, of Phyllis, and then of Ann

662

– they returned to the Praxis building, and sat in Michel and Maya's apartment. It was not the same apartment they had lived in before the second revolution, but Michel had taken pains to make it look much the same, as far as Sax could recall – something about Maya's therapy, as she was having more and more mental trouble – Sax wasn't sure what the latest was. He had never been able to deal with the more melodramatic aspects of Maya, and he hadn't paid overmuch attention to Michel's talk about her when the two of them last got together – it was always different, always the same.

Now, however, he took a cup of tea from Maya, and watched her go back into the kitchen, past the table on which Michel's scrapbooks were spread. Face-up was a photo of Frank that Maya had treasured long ago; she had had it taped to the kitchen cabinet by the sink, in the apartment down the hall – Sax remembered that most clearly, it was a kind of heraldic feature of those tense years: all of them struggling while the young Frank laughed at them.

Maya stopped and looked down at the photo, stared at it closely. Remembering their earlier dead, no doubt. Those who had gone before, so very long ago.

But she said, 'What an interesting face.'

Sax felt a chill in the pit of his stomach. So distinct, the physiological manifestations of distress. To lose the substance of a speculative train of thought, a venture into the metaphysical – that was one thing. But this – her own past, their past – it was insupportable. Not to be abided. He would not abide it.

Maya saw they were shocked, though she did not know why. Nadia had tears in her eyes, not a common sight. Michel looked stricken. Maya, sensing something seriously wrong, fled the apartment. No one stopped her.

The others picked up the place. Nadia went to Michel. 'More and more like that,' Michel muttered, looking haunted. 'More and more. I feel it myself. But for Maya . . .' He shook his head, looking deeply discouraged. Even Michel could make nothing good of this, Michel who had worked his alchemy of optimism on all their previous reversals, making them part of his great story, the myth of Mars that he had somehow wrenched out of the daily morass. But this was the death of

663

story. Thus hard to mythologize. No – living on after the memory died was mere farce, pointless and awful. Something was going to have to be done.

Sax was still thinking about this, sitting in a corner absorbed in his wristpad, reading a collection of abstracts from recent experimental work on the memory, when there came a thump from the kitchen and a cry from Nadia. Sax rushed in to find Nadia and Art crouched over Michel, who lay white-faced on the floor. Sax called the concierge, and faster than he would have imagined possible an emergency crew had barged in with their equipment and shouldered Art aside, big young natives who brusquely encased Michel into their compact web of machinery, leaving the old ones as spectators only of their friend's – struggle.

Sax sat down among the medics, in their way, and put a hand to Michel's neck and shoulder. Michel's breathing had stopped, his pulse as well. White-faced. The resuscitation attempts were violent, the electrical shocks tried at a variety of strengths, the subsequent shift to machine heart-lung accomplished with a minimum of fuss; and the young medics worked in near silence, talking among themselves only when necessary, seemingly unaware of the old ones sitting against the wall. They did all they could; but Michel remained stubbornly, mysteriously dead.

Of course he had been upset by Maya's memory failure. But this did not seem an adequate explanation. He had already been aware of Maya's problem, none more so, and he had been worried; so any single display of her problem shouldn't have mattered. A coincidence. A bad one. And of course eventually – quite late that evening, actually, after the doctors had finally given up, and taken Michel downstairs, and were clearing out their equipment – Maya returned, and they had to tell her what had happened.

She was distraught, naturally. Her shock and anguish were too much for one of the young medics, who tried to comfort her (that won't work, Sax wanted to say, I've tried that myself) and got himself struck in the face for his pains, which made him angry; he went out in the hall, sat down heavily.

Sax went out and sat beside him. He was weeping.

'I can't do this any more,' the man said after a while. He shook his head, seemingly apologetic. 'It's pointless. We come and do all we can and it makes no difference. Nothing stops the quick decline.'

'Which is?' Sax said.

The young man shrugged his massive shoulders, sniffed. 'That's the problem. No one knows.'

'Surely there must be theories? Autopsies?'

'Heart arrhythmia,' said one of the other medics curtly as he passed by with some equipment.

'That's just the symptom,' the sitting man snarled, and sniffed again. 'Why does it go arrhythmic? And why doesn't CPR restart it?'

No one answered.

Another mystery to be solved. Through the door Sax could see Maya crying on the couch, Nadia beside her like a statue of Nadia. Suddenly Sax realized that even if he found an explanation, Michel would still be dead.

Art was dealing with the medics, making arrangements. Sax tapped at his wrist and looked at a list of titles for articles on quick decline: 8,361 titles in this index. There were literature reviews, and tables assembled by AIs, but nothing that looked like a definitive paradigm statement. Still at the stage of observation and initial hypothesis ... flailing. In many ways it resembled the work on memory Sax had been reading. Death and the mind; how long they had studied these problems, how long the problems had resisted! Michel himself had commented on that, implying some deeper narrative that explained their unexplainables – Michel who had brought Sax back from aphasia, who had taught him to understand parts of himself he hadn't even known existed. Michel was gone. He wouldn't be back. They had carried the last version of his body out of the apartment. He had been around Sax's age, about two hundred and twenty years old. It was an advanced age by any previous standard; why then this pain in Sax's chest, this hot blur of tears? It didn't make sense. But Michel would have understood. Better this than the death of the mind, he would have said. But Sax wasn't so sure; his memory problems seemed less important now, Maya's as well. She remembered

665

enough to be devastated, after all. Him too. He remembered what was important.

Strange to recall: he had been in her company immediately in the wake of the death of all three of her consorts. John, Frank, now Michel. Each time it got worse for her. And the same for him.

Michel's ashes, up in a balloon over the Hellas Sea. They saved a pinch for return to Provence.

The literature on longevity and senescence was so vast and specialized that Sax found it difficult at first to organize his usual assault on the material. Recent work on the quick decline was the obvious starting point, but understanding articles on the subject meant going back to their predecessors and coming to some fuller understanding of the longevity treatments themselves. This was an area Sax had never understood more than superficially, shying away from it instinctively because of its messy biological inexplicable semi-miraculous nature. A subject very near the heart of the great unexplainable, really. He had left it happily to Hiroko and to the supremely gifted Vladimir Taneev, who along with Ursula and Marina had designed and overseen the first treatments, and many major modifications since then.

Now, however, Vlad was dead. And Sax was interested. It was time to dive into viriditas, into the realm of the complex.

There was orderly behaviour, there was chaotic behaviour; and on their border, in their interplay so to speak, lay a very large and convoluted zone, the realm of the complex. This was the zone in which viriditas made its appearance, the place in which life could exist. Keeping life in the middle of the zone of complexity was, in the most general philosophical sense, what the longevity treatments had been about – keeping various incursions of chaos (like arrhythmia) or of order (like malignant cell growth) from fatally disrupting the organism.

But now something was causing the gerontologically treated individual to go from negligible senescence to extremely rapid senescence – or, even more disturbingly, straight from health to death, without senescence at all. Some heretofore unseen eruption of chaos or order, into the border zone of the complex. This was how it seemed to him, in any case, at the end of one very long session of reading the most general descriptions of the phenomenon he could find. And it suggested certain avenues of investigation as well, in the mathematical descriptions of the complexity-chaotic border, likewise the order-complexity border. But he lost this holistic vision of the problem in one of his blankouts, the train of thought concerning the substance of the math gone forever. And it had probably (he tried to console himself afterward) been too philosophical a vision to do him any good anyway. The explanation after all was not going to be obvious, or else the massive concerted effort of medical science would have searched it out by now. On the contrary; it was likely to be something very subtle in the biochemistry of the brain, an arena that had resisted five hundred years of effort to investigate it scientifically, resisted like the hydra, every new discovery only suggesting another headful of mysteries . . .

Nevertheless he persevered. And over the course of a few weeks' absorbed reading, he certainly gave himself a better orientation in the field than he had ever had before. Previously his impression had been that the longevity treatment consisted of a fairly straightforward injection of the subject's own DNA, the artificially produced strands reinforcing the ones already in the cells, so that the breaks and errors that crept in over time were repaired, and the strands generally strengthened. This much was true; but the longevity treatment was more than this, just as senescence itself was more than cell division error. It was, as one might have predicted, much more complicated than just breaking chromosomes; it was an entire complex of processes. And while some were well-understood, others were not. Senescencal action (ageing) took place on every level: molecule, cell, organ, organism. Some senescence resulted from hormonal effects that were positive for the young organism in its reproductive phase, and only later negative for the post-reproductive animal, when in evolutionary terms it no longer mattered. Some cell lines were virtually immortal; bone marrow cells and the mucus in the gut went on replicating for as long as their surroundings were alive, with no sign at all of time-related changes. Other cells, such as the non-replaced proteins in the lens of the eye, underwent change that was driven by exposure to heat or light, regular enough to function as a kind of biological chronometer. Each kind of cell line aged at a different speed, or did not age at all; thus it was not just 'a matter of time' in the sense of a kind of Newtonian absolute time, working entropically on an organism; there was no such time. Rather it was a great many trains of specific physical and chemical events, moving at different speeds, and with varying effects. There was a fantastically large number of cell-repair mechanisms inherent in any large organism, and an immune system of great and various power; the longevity treatments often supplemented these processes, or worked on them directly, or replaced them. The treatment now included supplements of the enzyme photolyase, to correct DNA damage, and supplements of the pineal hormone melatonin, and dehydroepiandrosterone, a steroid hormone produced by the adrenal glands . . . There were about two hundred components like these in the longevity treatment now.

So vast, so complex – sometimes Sax finished his day's reading and walked down to Odessa's seafront, to sit on the corniche with Maya, and he would pause in eating a burrito and stare at it – contemplate everything that went into its digestion, everything that kept them alive – feel his breath which he had never noted at all, before – and suddenly he would feel breathless – lose his appetite – lose his belief that any such complex system could exist for more than a moment before collapsing into primordial chaos and the simplicities of astrophysics. Like a house of cards a hundred storeys tall, in a wind. Tap it anywhere . . . It was lucky Maya did not require much in the way of active companionship, because often he was rendered speechless for many minutes at a time, rapt in the contemplation of his own evident impossibility.

But he persevered. This was what a scientist did, confronted with an enigma. And there were others helping in the search, working ahead of him on the frontiers, and beside him in related fields, from the small – virology, where the inquiries into tiny forms such as prions and viroids were revealing even smaller forms, almost too partial to be called life: virids, viris, virs, vis, vs, all of which might have relevance to the larger problem . . . All the way up to the large organismic issues, such as brainwave rhythms and their relationship to the heart and other organs, or the pineal gland's ever-decreasing secretions of melatonin, a hormone that seemed to regulate many aspects of ageing. Sax followed them all, trying to glean a new view by his later and hopefully larger perspective. He had to follow his intuition to what seemed important, and study that.

Of course it did not help that some of his best thoughts on the subject blanked out on him at the moment of completion. He had to be able to get these thought-flurries recorded before they disappeared! He began to talk aloud to himself, frequently, even in public situations, hoping that this would help to forestall the blanks; but again, it didn't work. It simply was not a verbal process.

In all this work the meetings with Maya were a pleasure. Every evening, if he noticed it was evening, he would stop reading and walk down the staircase streets of the town to the corniche, and there, on one of four different benches, he would often see Maya, sitting and looking out over the harbour to the sea. He would go to one of the food stands back in the park, buy a burrito or a gyro or a salad or a corndog, and walk over and sit down next to her. She would nod and they would eat without saying much. Afterwards they sat and watched the sea. 'How was your day?' 'Okay. And yours?' He did not attempt to talk much about his reading, and she didn't say much about her hydrology, or the theatre productions that she would go off to after dusk had fallen. Really they didn't have much to say to each other. But it was companionable anyway. And one evening the sunset flared to an unusual lavender brilliance, and Maya said, 'I wonder what colour that is?' and Sax had ventured, 'Lavender?'

'But lavender is usually more pastel, isn't it?'

Sax called up a large colour chart he had found long before to help him see the colours of the sky. Maya snorted at this, but he held his wrist up anyway, and compared various sample squares to the sky. 'We need a bigger screen.' And then they found one that they thought matched: *light violet*. Or somewhere between *light violet* and *pale violet*.

And after that they had a little hobby. Really it was remarkable how varied the colours of the Odessa sunsets were, affecting sky, sea, the whitewashed walls of the town; endless variation. Much more variation than there were names. The poverty of language in this area was a constant surprise to Sax. Even the poverty of the colour chart. The eye could perceive perhaps ten million different shades, he read; the colour handbook he was referring to had 1,266 samples in it; and only a very small fraction of these had names. So most evenings they held up their forearms, and tried different colours against the sky, and found a patch that matched fairly well, and it was a nondescript; no name. They made up names: 2 October, the 11th Orange, Aphelion Purple, Lemon Leaf, Almost Green, Arkady's Beard; Maya could go on forever, she was really good at it. Then sometimes they would find a named patch matching the sky (for a moment, anyway) and they would learn the real meaning of a new word, which Sax found satisfying. But in that stretch between red and blue, English had surprisingly little to offer; the language just was not equipped for Mars. One evening in the dusk, after a mauvish sunset, they went through the chart methodically, just to see: purple, magenta, lilac, amaranth, aubergine, mauve, amethyst, plum, violaceous, violet, heliotrope, clematis, lavender, indigo, hyacinth, ultramarine – and then they were into the many words for the blues. There were many, many blues. But for the red-blue span that was it, except for the many modulations of the list, royal violet, lavender grey, and so on.

One evening the sky was clear, and after the sun had gone down behind the Hellespontus, but was still illuminating the air over the sea, it turned a very familiar rusty-brown-orange; Maya seized his arm in her clawlike grip. 'That's Martian orange, look, that's the colour of the planet from space, what we saw from the *Ares*! Look! Quick, what colour is that, what colour is that?'

They looked through the charts, arms held up before them. 'Paprika red.' 'Tomato red.' 'Oxide red, now that should be right; it's oxygen's affinity for iron makes that colour after all.'

'But it's way too dark, look.'

'True.'

'Brownish red.'

'Reddish brown.'

Cinnamon, raw sienna, Persian orange, sunburn, camel, rust brown, Sahara, chrome orange . . . they began to laugh. Nothing was quite right. 'We'll call it Martian orange,' Maya decided.

'Fine. But look how many more names there are for these colours than there are for the purples, why is that?'

Maya shrugged. Sax went reading in the material accompanying the chart, to see if they said anything about it. 'Ah.

671

It appears that the rods in the retina tend to see best in the three primaries, and so colours around those three have lots of distinction, while those in between are composites.' Then in the empurpling dusk he came on a sentence that surprised him so much he read it aloud:

'Redness and greenness form another pair which cannot be perceived simultaneously as components of the same colour.'

'That's not true,' Maya said immediately. 'That's just because they're using a colour wheel, and those two are on opposite sides.'

'What do you mean? That there are more colours than these?'

'Of course. Artists' colours, theatre colours; you put a green spot and a red spot on someone and you get a colour all right, and it's not red or green.'

'But what is it? Does it have a name?'

'I don't know. Look in an artist's colour wheel.'

And so he did, and so did she. She found it first: 'Here. Burnt umber, Indian red, madder alizarin . . . those are all green-red mixes.'

'Interesting! Red-green mixes! Don't you find that suggestive?'

She gave him a look. 'We're talking about colours here, Sax, not politics.'

'I know, I know. But still . . .'

'No. Don't be silly.'

'But don't you think we need a red-green mix?'

'Politically? There's a red-green mix already, Sax. That's the trouble. Free Mars got the Reds on board to stop immigration, that's why they're having such success. They're teaming up and closing down Mars to Earth, and soon after that we'll be at war with them again. I tell you, I can see it coming. We're spiralling down into it again.'

'Hmm,' Sax said, sobered. He was not paying attention to solar systemic politics these days, but he knew that Maya, who had a very sharp eye for these things, was getting more and more worried about it – with her usual mordant Mayan dash of satisfaction at the approach of crisis. So that it was perhaps not as bad as she thought. Probably he would have to look into it again soon, pay attention. But meanwhile —

'Look, it's gone indigo, right over the mountains.' Intense saw-edge of black below, purple-blue above . . .

'That's not indigo, it's royal blue.'

'But they shouldn't call it blue if it's got some red in it.'

'Shouldn't. Look, marine blue, Prussian blue, king's blue, they all have red in them.'

'But that colour on the horizon isn't any of those.'

'No, you're right. Nondescript.'

They marked it on their charts. Ls 24, M-year 91, September 2206; a new colour. And so another evening passed.

Then one winter evening they were sitting on the western-most bench, in the hour before sunlight, everything still, the Hellas Sea like a plate of glass, the sky cloudless and clean, pure, transparent; and as the sun dropped everything drifted over the spectrum into the blue, until Maya looked up from her salade niçoise and clutched Sax by the arm, 'Oh my God, look,' and she put her paper plate aside and they both stood instinctively, like ancient veterans hearing the national anthem from an approaching parade; Sax swallowed hamburger in a lump, 'Ah,' he said, and stared. Everything was blue, sky blue, Terran sky blue, drenching everything for most of an hour, flooding their retinas and the nerve pathways in their brains, no doubt long starved for precisely that colour, the home they had left forever.

Those were pleasant evenings. By day, however, things got more and more complicated. Sax gave up studying whole-body problems, sharpened his focus to the brain alone. This was like halving infinity, but still, it cut down on the papers he had to look at, and it did seem that the brain was the heart of the problem, so to speak. There were changes in the hyperaged brain, changes visible both on autopsy and during the various scans of blood flow, electrical activity, protein use, sugar use, heat, and all the rest of the indirect tests they had managed to concoct through the centuries, studying the living brain during mental activity of every kind. Observed changes in the hyperaged brain included calcification of the pineal gland, which reduced the amount of melatonin it produced; synthetic melatonin supplements were part of the longevity treatment, but of course it would be better to stop the calcification from occurring in the first place, for it probably had other effects. Then there was a clear growth in the number of neurofibrillary tangles, which were protein filament aggregates that grew between neurons, exerting physical pressure on them, perhaps the analogue of the pressure Maya reported feeling during her *presque vus*, who could say. Then again beta-amyloid protein accumulated in the cerebral blood vessels and in the extracellular space around nerve terminals, again impeding function. And pyramidal neurons in the frontal cortex and hippocampus accumulated calpain, which meant they were vulnerable to calcium influxes, which damaged them. And these were non-dividing cells, the same age as the organism itself; damage to them was permanent, as during Sax's stroke. He had lost a lot of his brain in that incident, he didn't like to think of it. And the ability of the molecules in these non-dividing cells to replace themselves could also be damaged, a smaller but over time equally significant loss. Autopsies of people over two hundred who had died of the quick decline regularly showed serious calcification of the pineal gland, coupled with increases in calpain levels in the hippocampus. And the hippocampus and calpain levels generally were both implicated in some of the leading current models of how the memory worked. It was an interesting connection.

But all inconclusive. And no one was going to solve the mystery by literature review alone. But the experiments that might clear things up were not practical, given the inaccessibility of the living brain. You could kill chicks and mice and rats and dogs and pigs and lemurs and chimps, you could kill individuals of every species in creation, dissect the brains of their foetuses and embryos as well, and still never find what you were looking for; for it was autopsy itself that was insufficient to the task. And the various live scans were likewise insufficient to the task, as the processes involved were either more fine-grained than the scans could perceive, or more holistic, or more combinatorial, or, probably, all three at once.

Still, some of the experiments and the resultant modelling were suggestive; calpain build-up seemed to alter brainwave function, for instance; and this fact and others gave him ideas for further investigation. He began to read intensively in the literature on the effects of calcium-binding protein levels, on cortisteroids, on the calcium currents in the hippocampal pyramidal neurons, and on the calcification of the pineal gland. It appeared there were synergistic effects that might impact both memory and general brainwave function, indeed all bodily rhythms, including heart rhythms. 'Was Michel experiencing any memory troubles?' Sax asked Maya. 'Perhaps feeling that he had lost entire trains of thought – even very useful trains of thought?'

Maya shrugged. By now Michel was almost a year gone. 'I can't remember.'

It made Sax nervous. Maya seemed in retreat, her memory worse every day. Even Nadia could do nothing for her. Sax met her down on the corniche more and more frequently; it was a habit they both clearly must have enjoyed, though they never spoke of that; they simply sat, ate a kiosk meal, watched the sunset and pulled up their colour charts to see if they would catch another new one. But if it weren't for the notations they made on the charts, neither of them would have been sure whether the colours they saw were new or not. Sax himself felt that he was experiencing his blankouts more frequently, perhaps some four to eight a day, although he couldn't be sure. He took to keeping his AI running a sound recorder permanently, activated by voice; and rather than try to describe his complete train of thought, he just spoke a few words that he hoped would later key a fuller recollection of what he had been thinking. Thus at the end of the day he would sit down apprehensively or hopefully, and listen to what the AI had captured during the day: and mostly it was thought that he remembered thinking, but occasionally he would hear himself say, 'Synthetic melatonins may be a better antioxidant than natural ones, so that there aren't *enough* free radicals,' or 'Viriditas is a fundamental mystery, there will never be a grand unified theory,' without having any memory of saying such things, or, often, what they might mean. But sometimes the statements were suggestive, their meanings excavatable.

And so he struggled on. As he did, he saw it anew, as fresh as in his undergraduate days: the structure of science was so beautiful. It was surely one of the greatest achievements of the human spirit, a kind of stupendous parthenon of the mind, constantly a work in progress, like a symphonic epic poem of thousands of stanzas, being composed by them all in a giant ongoing collaboration. The language of the poem was mathematics, because this appeared to be the language of nature itself; there was no other way to explain the startling adherence of natural phenomena to mathematical expressions of great difficulty and subtlety. And so in this marvellous family of languages their songs explored the various manifestations of reality, in the different fields of science, and each science worked up its standard model to explain things, all constellating at some distance around the basics of particle physics, depending on what level or scale was being investigated, so that all the standard models hopefully interlocked in a coherent larger structure. These standard models were somewhat like Kuhnian paradigms but in reality (paradigms being a model of modelling) more supple and various, a dialogic process in which thousands of minds had participated over the previous hundreds of years; so that figures like Newton or Einstein or Vlad were not the isolate giants of public perception, but the tallest peaks of a great mountain range, as Newton himself had tried to make clear with his comment about standing on the shoulders of giants. In truth the work of science was a communal thing, extending back even beyond the birth of modern science, back all the way into prehistory, as Michel had insisted; a constant struggle to understand. Now of course it was highly structured, articulated beyond the ability of any single individual to grasp fully. But this was only because of the sheer quantity of it; the spectacular efflorescence of structure was not in any particular incomprehensible, one could still walk around anywhere inside the parthenon, so to speak, and thus comprehend at least the shape of the whole, and make choices as to where to study, where to learn the current surface, where to contribute. One could first learn the dialect of the language relevant to the study; which in itself could be a formidable task, as in superstring theory or cascading recombinant chaos; then one could survey the background literature, and hopefully find some syncretic work by someone who had worked long on the cutting edge, and was able to give a coherent account of the status of the field for outsiders; this work, disparaged by most working scientists, called the 'grey literature' and considered a vacation or a lowering of oneself on the part of the synthesist, was nevertheless often of great value for someone coming in from the outside. With a general overview (though it was better to think of it as an underview, with the actual workers up there lost in the dim rafters and entablatures of the edifice), one could then move up into the journals, the peer-reviewed 'white literature', where the current work was being recorded; and one could read the abstracts, and get a sense of who was attacking what part of the problem. So public, so explicit ... And for any given problem in science, the people who were actually out there on the edge making progress constituted a special group, of a few hundred at most – often with a core group of synthesists and innovators that was no more than a dozen people in all the worlds – inventing a new jargon of their dialect to convey their new insights, arguing over results, suggesting new avenues of investigation, giving each other jobs in labs, meeting at conferences specially devoted to the topic – talking to each other, in all the media there were. And there in the labs and the conference bars the work went forward, as a dialogue of people who understood the issues, and did the sheer hard work of experimentation, and of thinking about experiments.

And all this vast articulated structure of a culture stood out in the open sun of day, accessible to anyone who wanted to join, who was willing and able to do the work; there were no secrets, there were no closed shops, and if every lab and every specialization had its politics, that was just politics; and in the end politics could not materially affect the structure itself, the mathematical edifice of their understanding of the phenomenal world. So Sax had always believed, and no analysis by social scientists, nor even the troubling experience of the Martian terraforming process, had ever caused him to waver in that belief. Science was a social construct, but it was also and most importantly its own space, conforming to reality only; that was its beauty. Truth is beauty, as the poet had said, speaking of science. And it was; the poet had been right (they weren't always).

And so Sax moved about in the great structure, comfortable, capable, and on some levels content.

But he began to understand that as beautiful and powerful as science was, the problem of biological senescence was perhaps too difficult. Not too difficult to be solved ever, nothing was that, but simply too difficult to be solved in his lifetime. Actually it was still an open question how hard a problem it was. Their understanding of matter, space and time was incomplete, and it might be that it would always necessarily shade off into metaphysics, like the speculations about the cosmos before the Big Bang, or things smaller than strings. On the other hand the world might be amenable to progressive explanations, until it all (at least from string to cosmos) would be brought some-day within the realm of the great parthenon. Either result was possible, the court was still out, the next thousand years or so should tell the tale.

But in the meantime, he was experiencing several blankouts a day. And sometimes he was short of breath. Sometimes his heart seemed to beat so hard. Seldom did he sleep at night. And Michel was dead, so that Sax's sense of the meaning of things was becoming uncertain, and in great need of help. When he managed to think at all on the level of meaning, he found that he felt he was in a race. Him and everyone else, but especially the life scientists actually at work on the prob-lem: they were in a race with death. To win it, they had to explain one of the greatest of the great unexplainables.

And one day, sitting down on a bench with Maya after a day in front of his screen, thinking of the vastness of that growing wing of the parthenon, he realized that it was a race he couldn't win. The human species might win it, someday, but it looked to be a long way off still. It was no great surprise, really; he knew this; that is to say, he had always known it. Labelling the current largest manifestation of the problem had not disguised to him its profundity, 'the quick decline' was just a name, inaccurate, over-simple – not science, in fact, but rather an attempt (like the Big Bang) to diminish and contain the reality, as yet not understood. In this case the problem was simply death. A quick decline indeed. And given the nature of life and of time, this was a problem that no living organism would ever truly solve. Postponements, yes; solutions, no. 'Reality itself is mortal,' he said.

'Of course,' Maya said, absorbed in the sight of the sunset.

He needed a simpler problem. As a postponement, as a step toward the harder problems; or just as something he could solve. Memory, perhaps. Fighting the blankouts; it was certainly a problem that stood at hand, ready for study. His memory was in need of help. Working on it might even cast light on the quick decline. And even if it didn't, he had to try it, no matter how hard. Because they were all going to die; but they could at least die with their memories intact.

So he switched his emphasis to the memory problem, abandoning the quick decline and all the rest of the senescence issues. He was only mortal after all.

Recent memory work was fairly suggestive of avenues of approach. This particular scientific front was related in some of its aspects to the work on learning that had enabled Sax (partially) to recover from his stroke. This was not surprising, as memory was the retention of learning. All brain science tended to move together in its understanding of consciousness. But in that progression, retention and recall remained recalcitrant crux issues, still imperfectly understood.

But there were indications, and more all the time. Clinical clues; a lot of the ancient ones were experiencing memory problems of varying kinds, and behind the ancient ones came a giant generation of nisei, who could see the problems manifesting in their elders, and hoped to avoid them. So memory was a hot topic. Hundreds, indeed thousands, of labs were working on it in one way or another, and as a result many aspects of it were coming clear. Sax immersed himself in the literature in his usual style, reading intensively for several months on end; and at the end of that time he thought he could say, in general terms, how memory worked; although in the end he, like all the rest of the scientists working on the problem, ran into their insufficient understanding of the underlying basics – of consciousness, matter, time. And at this point, as detailed as their understanding was, Sax could not see how memory might be improved or reinforced. They needed something more.

The original Hebb hypothesis, first proposed by Donald Hebb in 1949, was still held to be true, because it was such a general principle; learning changed some physical feature in the brain, and after that the changed feature somehow encoded the event learned. In Hebb's time the physical feature (the engram) was conceived of as occurring somewhere on the synaptic level, and as there could be hundreds of thousands of synapses for each of the ten billion neurons in the brain, this gave researchers the impression that the brain might be capable of holding some 10^{14} data bits; at the time this seemed more than adequate to explain human consciousness. And as it was also within the realm of the possible for computers, it led to a brief vogue in the notion of strong artificial intelligence, as well as that era's version of the 'machine fallacy', an inverse of the pathetic fallacy, in which the brain was thought of as being something like the most powerful machine of the time. The work of the twenty-first and twenty-second centuries, however, had made it clear that there were no specific 'engram' sites as such. Any number of experiments failed to locate these sites, including one in which various parts of rats' brains were removed after they learned a task, with no part of the brain proving essential; the frustrated experimenters concluded that memory was 'everywhere and nowhere', leading to the analogy of brain to hologram, even sillier than all the other machine analogies; but they were stumped, they were flailing. Later experiments clarified things; it became obvious that all the actions of consciousness were taking place on a level far smaller even than that of neurons; this was associated in Sax's mind with the general miniaturization of scientific attention through the twenty-second century. In that finer-grained appraisal they had begun investigating the cytoskeletons of neuron cells, which were internal arrays of microtubules, with protein bridges between the microtubules. The microtubules' structure consisted of hollow tubes made of thirteen columns of tubulin dimers, peanut-shaped globular protein pairs, each about eight by four by four nanometres, existing in two different configurations, depending on their electrical polarization. So the dimers represented a possible on-off switch of the hoped-for engram; but they were so small that the electrical state of each dimer was influenced by the dimers around it, because of van der Waals interactions between them. So messages of all kinds could be propagated along each microtubule column, and along the protein bridges connecting them. Then most recently had come yet another step in miniaturization: each dimer contained about four hundred and fifty amino acids, which could retain information by changes in the sequences of amino acids. And contained inside the dimer columns were tiny threads of water in an ordered state, a state called vicinal water, and this vicinal water was capable of conveying quantum-coherent oscillations for the length of the tubule. A great number of experiments on living monkey brains, with miniaturized instrumentation of many different kinds, had established that while consciousness was thinking, amino acid sequences were shifting, tubulin dimers in many different places in the brain were changing configuration, in pulsed phases; microtubules were moving, sometimes growing; and on a much larger scale, dendrite spines then grew and made new connections, sometimes changing synapses permanently, sometimes not.

So now the best current model had it that memories were encoded as standing patterns of quantum-coherent oscillations, set up by changes in the microtubules and their constituent parts, all working in patterns inside the neurons. Although there were now researchers who speculated that there could be significant action at even finer ultramicroscopic levels, permanently beyond their ability to investigate (familiar refrain); some saw traces of signs that the oscillations were structured in the kind of spin network patterns that Bao's work described, in knotted nodes and networks that Sax found eerily reminiscent of the palace-of-memory plan – rooms and hallways – as if the ancient Greeks by introspection alone had intuited the very geometry of timespace.

In any case, it was sure that these ultramicroscopic actions were implicated in the brain's plasticity; they were part of how the brain learned and then remembered. So memory was happening at a far smaller level than had been previously imagined, which gave the brain a much higher computational possibility than before, up to perhaps 10^{24} operations per second – or even 10^{43} in some calculations, leading one researcher to note that every human mind was in a certain sense more complicated than all the rest of the universe (minus its other consciousnesses, of course). Sax found this suspiciously like the strong anthropic phantoms seen elsewhere in cosmological theory, but it was an interesting idea to contemplate.

So, not only was there simply more going on, it was also happening at such fine levels that quantum effects were certainly involved. Experimentation had made it clear that large-scale collective quantum phenomena were happening in every brain; there existed in the brain both global quantum coherence, and quantum entanglement between the various electrical states of the microtubules; and this meant that all the counter-intuitive phenomena and sheer paradox of quantum reality were an integral part of consciousness. Indeed it was only very recently, by including the quantum effects in the cytoskeletons, that a team of French researchers had finally managed to put forth a plausible theory as to why general anaesthetics worked, after all the centuries of blithely using them.

So they were confronted with yet another bizarre quantum world, in which there was action at a distance, in which decisions not made could affect events that really happened, in which certain events seemed to be triggered teleologically, that is to say by events that appeared to come after them in time ... Sax was not greatly surprised by this development. It supported a feeling he had had all his life, that the human mind was deeply mysterious, a black box that science could scarcely investigate. And now that science was investigating it, it was coming up hard against the great unexplainables of reality itself.

Still, one could hold to what science had learned; and admit that reality at the quantum level behaved in ways that were simply outrageous at the level of human senses and ordinary experience. They had had three hundred years to get used to that, and eventually they had somehow to incorporate this knowledge into their world views, and forge on. Sax would have indeed said that he was comfortable with the familiar quantum paradoxes; things at the microscale were bizarre but explicable, quantifiable or at least describable, using complex numbers, Riemannian geometry, and all the rest of the armatures of the appropriate branches of mathematics. Finding such stuff in the very workings of the brain should have been no surprise at all. Indeed, compared to things like human history or psychology or culture, it was even somehow comforting. It was only quantum mechanics after all, something that could be modelled by mathematics. And that was saying something.

So. At an extremely fine level of structure in the brain, much of one's past was contained, encoded in a unique complex network of synapses, microtubules, dimers and vicinal water and amino acid chains, all small enough and near enough together to have quantum effects on each other. Patterns of quantum fluctuation, diverging and collapsing; this was consciousness. And the patterns were clearly held or generated in specific parts of the brain; they were the result of a physical structure articulated on many levels. The hippocampus, for instance, was critically important, especially the dentate gyrus region and the perforant pathway nerves that led to it. And the hippocampus was extremely sensitive to action in the limbic system, directly underneath it in the brain; and the limbic system was in many ways the seat of the emotions, what the ancients would have called the heart. Thus the emotional charge of an event had much to do with how fully it was laid out in the memory. Things happened, and the consciousness witnessed or experienced them, and inevitably a great deal of this experience changed the brain, and became part of it forever; particularly the events heightened by emotion. This description seemed right to Sax; what he had felt most he remembered best – or forgot most assiduously, as certain experiments suggested, with an unconscious constant effort that was not true forgetting at all, but repression.

After that initial change in the brain, however, the slow process of degradation began. For one thing, the power of recollection was different in different people, but always less powerful than memory storage, it appeared, and very hard to direct. So much was patterned into the brain but never retrieved. And if one never remembered a pattern, never recollected and rehearsed it, then never got the reinforcement of another run-through; and after about one hundred and fifty years of storage, experiments suggested, the pattern began to degrade more and more rapidly, due apparently to the accumulated quantum effects of free radicals collecting randomly in the brain. This was apparently what was happening to the ancient ones; a breakdown process which began immediately after an event was patterned into the brain, eventually hit a cumulative level in which the effects were catastrophic for the oscillatory patterns involved, and thus for the memories. It was probably about as clocklike, Sax thought glumly, as the thermodynamic clouding of the lens of the eye.

However – if one could rehearse all one's memories, *ecphorize* them as some called it in the literature on the subject – from the Greek, meaning something like 'echo transmission'

– then it would reinforce the patterns, giving them a fresh start and setting the clock of degradation back to zero. A sort of longevity treatment for dimer patterns, in effect, sometimes referred to in the literature as *anamnesis*, or loss of forgetting. And after such treatment it would be easier to recall any given event, or at least as easy as it had been soon after the event happened. This was the general direction that work in memory reinforcement was taking. Some called the drugs and electrical devices involved in this process *nootropics*, a word which Sax read as 'acting upon mind'. There were a lot of terms for the process being bandied about in the current literature, people scrambling through their Greek and Latin lexicons in the hope of becoming the namer of the phenomenon: Sax had seen *mnemonics* and *mnemonistics*, and *mnemosynics*, after the goddess of memory; also *mimenskesthains*, from the Greek verb 'to remember'. Sax preferred *memory reinforcer*, although he also liked *anamnesis*, which seemed the most accurate term for what they were trying to do. He wanted to concoct an anamnestic.

But the practical difficulties of ecphorization – of remembering all of one's past, or even some particular part of it – were great. Not just finding the anamnestics that might stimulate such a process, but finding as well the time it would take! When one had lived two centuries, it seemed possible that it might take years to ecphorize all the significant events of one's life.

Clearly a sequential chronological run-through was impractical, in more ways than one. What would be preferable was some kind of simultaneous flushing of the system, strengthening the entire network without consciously remembering every component of it. Whether such a flushing was electrochemically possible was unclear; and what such a flushing might feel like was impossible to imagine. But if one were electrically to stimulate the perforant pathway to the hippocampus, and get a great deal of adenosine triphosphate past the blood-brain barrier, for instance, thus stimulating the long-term potentiation that aided learning in the first place; and then impose a brainwave pattern stimulating and supporting the quantum oscillations of the microtubules; and then direct one's consciousness to review the memories that felt most important to one, while the rest were being reinforced as well, unconsciously . . .

He ran through another *accelerando* of thought on this issue, then crashed blank on it. There he was, sitting in his apartment living room, blanked, cursing himself for not at least trying to mutter something into his AI. It seemed that he had been onto something – something about ATP, or was it LTP? Well. If it was a genuinely useful thought, it would come back. He had to believe that. It seemed probable.

As it did, more and more as he studied the issues, that the shock of Maya's amnesiac moment had somehow propelled Michel into the quick decline. Not that such an explanation could ever be proved, or that it even really mattered. But Michel would not have wanted to survive either his memory or hers; he had loved her as his life project, his definition of himself. The shock of Maya blanking on something so basic, so important (like the key to memory restoration) . . . And the mind-body connection was so strong – so strong that the distinction itself was probably false, a vestige of Cartesian metaphysics or earlier religious views of the soul. Mind was one's body's life. Memory was mind. And so, by a simple transitive equation, memory equalled life. So that with memory gone, life was gone. So Michel must have felt, in that final traumatic half hour, as his self tumbled into a fatal arrhythmia, under the anguish of grieving for his love's death-of-mind.

They had to remember to be truly alive. And so ecphorization, if he could figure out the appropriate anamnestic methodology, was going to have to be tried.

Of course it might be dangerous. If he did manage to work up a memory reinforcer, it would flush the system all at once, perhaps, and no one could predict what that would feel like subjectively. One would just have to try it. It would be an experiment. Self-experimentation. Well, it wouldn't be the first time. Vlad had given himself the first gerontological treatment, though it could have killed him; Jennings had inoculated himself with live smallpox vaccine; Arkady's ancestor Alexander Bogdanov had exchanged his blood for that of a young man suffering from malaria and tuberculosis, and had died while the young man had lived for thirty more years. And of course there was the story of the young physicists at Los Alamos, who had set off the first nuclear explosion wondering among themselves whether it might not burn up the entire atmosphere of the Earth, a somewhat disturbing case of self-experimentation, one had to admit. Compared to that, ingesting a few amino acids seemed no very great thing, something more like Dr Hoffman trying LSD on himself. Presumably ecphorizing would be less disorienting than an LSD experience, for if all one's memories were being reinforced at once, the consciousness would surely not be capable of being aware of it. The so-called stream of consciousness was fairly unilinear, it seemed to Sax on introspection. So that at most one might experience a quick associative train of recollections, or a random jumble – not unlike Sax's everyday mentation, to tell the truth. He could handle that. And he was willing to risk something more traumatic, if that was what it happened to take.

He flew to Acheron.

Up at Acheron a new crowd was in place in the old labs, now vastly expanded, so that the entire high, long fin of rock was excavated and occupied – it was a city now of some two hundred thousand people. At the same time it was still, of course, a spectacular fin of rock some fifteen kilometres long and six hundred metres high, while never more than a kilo- metre wide at any point; and it was still a lab, or a complex of labs, in a way that Echus Overlook had long since ceased to be – something more like Da Vinci, with a similar organization. After Praxis had renovated the infrastructure, Vlad and Ursula and Marina had led the formation of a new biological research station; now Vlad was dead, but Acheron had a life of its own, and did not seem to miss him. Ursula and Marina directed their own little labs, and lived still in the quarters they had shared with Vlad, just under the crest of the fin – a partially- walled arboreal slot, very windy. They were as private as ever, withdrawn into their own world even more than they had been with Vlad; and they were certainly taken for granted in Acheron, treated by the younger scientists as local grand- mothers or great-aunts, or simply as colleagues in the labs.

Sax, however, the younger scientists stared at, looking just as nonplussed as if they were being introduced to Archimedes. It was as disconcerting to be treated in such a way as it was to meet such an anachronism, and Sax struggled through several conversations of surpassing awkwardness as he tried to con- vince everyone that he did not know the magic secret of life, that he used words to stand for the same things as they did, that his mind was not yet altogether shattered by age, etc.

But this estrangement could also be an advantage. Young scientists as a class tended to be naïve empiricists, also ideal- istic, energetic enthusiasts. So coming in from outside, both new and old at once, Sax was able to impress them in the seminars Ursula convened to discuss the current state of memory work. Sax laid out his hypotheses concerning the creation of a possible anamnestic, with suggestions for various lines of experimental work on these possibilities, and he could see that his suggestions had for the young scientists a kind of prophetic power, even (or perhaps especially) when they were quite general comments. If these vague suggestions happened to chime with some avenue these people were already exploring, then the response could be enthusiastic in the extreme. In fact it was a case of the more gnomic the better; which was not very scientific, but there it was.

As he watched them Sax realized for the first time that the versatile, responsive, highly focused nature of science that he was getting used to in Da Vinci was not confined to Da Vinci alone, but was a feature of all the labs arranged as co-operative ventures; it was the nature of Martian science more generally. With the scientists in control of their own work, to a degree never seen in his youth on Earth, the work itself had a rapidity and power Earth had never seen, at least not in Sax's time. In his day the resources necessary to do the work would have belonged to other people, to institutions with their own interests and bureaucracies, creating a ponderous and often foolish and clumsy scattering of effort; and even the coherent efforts were often devoted to trivial things, to the monetary profits of the institution in control of the lab, very often. Here, on the other hand, Acheron was a semi-autonomous, self-contained community, answerable to the environmental courts and to the constitution of course, but to no one else. They chose among themselves what to work on, and when they were asked for help, if they were interested, they could respond immediately.

So he was not going to have to do all the work of developing a memory reinforcer himself, not by any means; the Acheron labs were highly interested, and Marina remained active in the city's lab of labs, and the city still had a close relationship with Praxis, with all its resources. And many labs there were already investigating memory. It was a big part of the longevity project now, for obvious reasons. Marina said that some twenty per cent of all human effort was now being devoted, in one form or another, to the longevity project. And longevity itself was pointless without memory lasting as long as the rest of the system. So it made sense for a complex like Acheron to focus on it.

*   *   *

690

Soon after his arrival Sax joined Marina and Ursula alone, for breakfast in the dining area of their quarters. Just the three of them, surrounded by portable walls covered by batiks from Dorsa Brevia, and trees in pots. No remembrance of Vlad. Nor did they mention him. Sax, conscious of how unusual it was to be invited into their home, had trouble focusing on the matter at hand. He had known both of these women from the beginning, and greatly respected them, Ursula especially for her great empathic qualities; but he didn't feel he knew them at all well. So he sat there in the wind, eating and looking at them, and out of the open window walls. There to the north lay a narrow strip of blue, Acheron Bay, a deep indentation in the North Sea – to the south, far beyond the first nearby horizon, the enormous bulk of Olympus Mons. In between, a devil's golf course of a land – hard, gnarled, eroded old lava flows, riven and pocked – and in each hollow a little green oasis, dotting the blackish waste of the plateau.

Marina said, 'We've been thinking about why experimental psychologists in every generation have reported a few isolated cases of truly exceptional memories, but there is never any attempt to explain them by the memory models of the period.'

'In fact they forget them as soon as they can,' Ursula said.

'Yes. And then when the reports are exhumed, no one quite believes them to be true. It's put down to the credulity of earlier times. Typically no one alive can be found who can reproduce the feats described, and so the tendency is to conclude that the earlier investigators were mistaken or fooled. But a lot of the reports were perfectly well substantiated.'

'Such as?' Sax said. It had not occurred to him to look at organism-level real-world functional accounts, anecdotal as they invariably were. But of course it made sense to do so.

Marina said, 'The conductor Toscanini knew by heart every note of every instrument for about two hundred and fifty symphonic works, and the words and music of about a hundred operas, plus a lot more shorter works.'

'They tested this?'

'Spot checks, so to speak. A bassoonist broke a key of his bassoon and told Toscanini, who thought it over and told him not to worry, he wouldn't have to play that note that night. Things like that. And he conducted without scores, and wrote down missing parts for players, and so on.'

'Uh huh . . .'

'The musicologist Tovey had a similar power,' Ursula added. 'It isn't uncommon in musicians. It's as if music is a language in which incredible memory feats are sometimes possible.'

'Hmm.'

Marina went on. 'A Professor Athens, of Cambridge University, early twenty-first century, had a vast knowledge of specifics of all sorts – again music, but also verse, facts, math, his own past on a daily basis. "Interest is the thing," he was reported to have said. "Interest focuses the attention."'

'True,' Sax said.

'He mostly used his memory for what he found interesting. An interest in meaning, he called it. But in 2060 he remembered all of a list of twenty-three words he had learned for a casual test in 2032. And so on.'

'I'd like to learn more about him.'

'Yes,' Ursula said. 'He was less of a freak than some of the others. The so-called "calendar calculators" or the ones who can recall visual images presented to them in great detail – they're often impaired in other parts of their lives.'

Marina nodded. 'Like the Latvians Shereskevskii and VP, who remembered truly huge quantities of random fact, in tests and in general. But both of them experienced synaesthesia.'

'Hmm. Hippocampal hyperactivity, perhaps.'

'Perhaps.'

They mentioned several more. A man named Finkelstein, who could calculate the election returns for the entire United States faster than any calculators of the 1930s. Talmudic scholars who had not only memorized the Talmud, but also the location of every word on every page. Oral storytellers who knew Homeric amounts of verse by heart. Even people who were said to have used the Renaissance palace-of-memory method to great effect; Sax had tried that himself after his stroke, with fair results. And so on.

'These extraordinary abilities don't seem to be the same as ordinary memory,' Sax observed.

'Eidetic memory,' Marina said. 'Based on images that return

in great detail. It's said to be the way that most children remember. Then at puberty, the way we remember changes, at least for most of us. It's as if these people don't ever meta-morphose away from the children's way.'

'Hmm,' Sax said. 'Still, I wonder if they are the upper extremes of continuous distributions of ability, or whether they are examples of a rare bimodal distribution.'

Marina shrugged. 'We don't know. But we have one here to study.'

'You do!'

'Yes. It's Zeyk. He and Nazik have moved here so that we can study him. He's being very co-operative; she's encouraging him. There might as well be some good that comes of it, she says. He doesn't like his ability, you see. In him it doesn't have much to do with computational tricks, although he's better at that than most of us. But he can remember his past in extraordinary detail.'

'I think I remember hearing about this,' Sax said. The two women laughed, and startled, he joined in. 'I'd like to see what you're doing with him.'

'Sure. He's down in Smadar's lab. It's interesting. They view vids from events that he witnessed, and ask him questions about the events, and he talks about what he remembers while they've got all the latest scans running on his brain.'

'Sounds very interesting.'

Ursula led him down to a long, dimmed lab, in which some operating beds were occupied by subjects undergoing scans of one sort or another, coloured images flickering on screens or holographically in the air; while other beds were empty, and somehow ominous.

After all the young native subjects, when they came to Zeyk he looked to Sax like a specimen of *homo habilis*, whisked out of prehistory to be tested for mental capacity. He was wearing a helmet studded with contact points on its inner surface, and his white beard was damp, his eyes sunken and weary in bruise-coloured, withered skin. Nazik sat on the other side of his bed, holding his hand in hers. Hovering in the air over a holograph next to her was a detailed three-dimensional transparent image of some part of Zeyk's brain; through it coloured light was flickering continuously, like heat lightning, creating patterns of green and red and blue and pale gold. On the screen by the bed jiggled images of a small tent settlement, after dark. A young woman, presumably the researcher Smadar, was asking questions.

'So the Ahad attacked the Fetah?'

'Yes. Or they were fighting, and my impression was that the Ahad started it. But someone was setting them on each other, I thought. Cutting slogans in the windows.'

'Did the Moslem Brotherhood often have internal conflicts this severe?'

'At that time they did. But why on that night, I don't know. Someone set them on each other. It was as if everyone had suddenly gone crazy.'

Sax felt his stomach tighten. Then he felt chilled, as if the ventilation system had let in the air of the cold morning outside. The little tent town in the vids was Nicosia. They were talking about the night John Boone had been killed. Smadar was watching the vids, asking questions. Zeyk was being recorded. Now he looked at Sax, nodded a greeting. 'Russell was there also.'

'Were you?' Smadar said, looking at Sax speculatively.

'Yes.'

It was something Sax had not thought about in years; decades; a century, perhaps. He realized that he had never been back to Nicosia again, not even once since that night. As if he had been avoiding it. Repression, no doubt. He had been very fond of John, who had worked for him for several years before the assassination. They had been friends. 'I saw him attacked,' he said, surprising them all.

'Did you!' Smadar exclaimed. Now Zeyk and Nazik and Ursula were staring at him as well, and Marina had joined them.

'What did you see?' Smadar asked him, glancing briefly up at Zeyk's brain image, flickering away in its silent storm. This was the past, just such a silent flickering electric storm. This was the work they had embarked on.

'There was fighting,' Sax said slowly, uneasily, looking into the hologram image as if into a crystal ball. 'In a little plaza,

694

where a side street met the central boulevard. Near the medina.'

'Were they Arab?' the young woman asked.

'Possibly,' Sax said. He closed his eyes, and though he could not see it he could somehow imagine it, a kind of blind sight. 'Yes, I think so.'

He opened his eyes again, saw Zeyk staring at him. 'Did you know them?' Zeyk croaked. 'Can you tell me what they looked like?'

Sax shook his head, but this seemed to shake loose an image, black and yet there. The vid showed the dark streets of Nicosia, flickering with light like the thought in Zeyk's brain. 'A tall man with a thin face, a black moustache. They all had black moustaches, but his was longer, and he was shouting at the other men attacking Boone, rather than at Boone himself.'

Zeyk and Nazik were looking at each other. 'Yussuf,' Zeyk said. 'Yussuf and Nejm. They led the Fetah then, and they were worse about Boone than any of the Ahad. And when Selim appeared at our place later that night, dying, he said Boone killed me, Boone and Chalmers. He didn't say I killed Boone; he said Boone killed me.' He stared again at Sax: 'But what happened then? What did you do?'

Sax shuddered. This was why he had never returned to Nicosia, never thought about it: on that night, at the critical moment, he had hesitated. He had been afraid. 'I saw them from across the plaza. I was a distance away, and I didn't know what to do. They struck John down. They pulled him away. I – I watched. Then – then I was in a group running after them, I don't know who the rest were. They carried me along. But the attackers were dragging him down those side streets, and in the dark, our group . . . our group lost them.'

'There were probably friends of the assailants in your group,' Zeyk said. 'There by plan, to lead you the wrong way in the pursuit.'

'Ah,' Sax said. There had been moustachioed men among the group. 'Possibly.'

He felt sick. He had frozen, he had done nothing. The images on the screen flickered, flashes in darkness, and Zeyk's cortex was alive with microscopic coloured lightning.

'So it was not Selim,' Zeyk said to Nazik. 'Not Selim, and so not Frank Chalmers.'

'We should tell Maya,' Nazik said. 'We must tell her.'

Zeyk shrugged. 'She won't care. If Frank did set Selim on John, and yet someone else actually did the deed, does that matter?'

'But you think it was someone else?' Smadar said.

'Yes. Yussuf and Nejm. The Fetah. Or whoever it was setting people on each other. Nejm, perhaps . . .'

'Who is dead.'

'And Yussuf as well,' Zeyk said grimly. 'And whoever started the rioting that night . . .' He shook his head, and the image overhead quivered slightly.

'Tell me what happened next,' Smadar said, looking down at her screen.

'Unsi al-Khan came running into the hajr to tell us Boone had been attacked. Unsi . . . well, anyway, I went with some others to the Syrian Gate, to see if it had been used. The Arab method of execution at that time was to throw you out onto the surface. And we found that the gate had been used once and no one had come back in by it.'

'Do you remember the lock code?' Smadar asked.

Zeyk frowned, his lips moved, his eyes clamped shut. 'They were part of the Fibonacci sequence, I remember noticing that. 581321.'

Sax gaped. Smadar nodded. 'Go on.'

'Then a woman I didn't know ran past and told us Boone had been found in the farm. We followed her to the medical clinic in the medina. It was new, everything was clean and shiny, no pictures on the walls yet. Sax, you were there, and the rest of the First Hundred in the town: Chalmers and Toitovna, and Samantha Hoyle.'

Sax found he had no memory of the clinic at all. Wait . . . an image of Frank, his face flushed, and Maya, wearing a white domino, her mouth a bloodless line. But that had been outside, on the glass-scattered boulevard. He had told them of the attack on Boone, and Maya had cried instantly, Didn't you stop them? Didn't you stop them? and he had realized all of a sudden that he hadn't stopped them – that he had failed to help his friend – that he had stood there frozen in shock, and watched while his friend had been assaulted and dragged off. We tried, he had said to Maya. I tried. Though he hadn't.

But at the clinic, later; nothing. Nothing came to him of the whole rest of that night, in fact. He closed his eyes like Zeyk, clamped the lids shut as if that might squeeze out another image. But nothing came. The memory was odd that way; he remembered the critical moments of trauma, when these realizations had stabbed into him; the rest had disappeared. Surely the limbic system and the emotional charge of every incident must be crucially involved in the entrainment or encoding or embedding of a memory.

And yet there was Zeyk, slowly naming every person he had known in the clinic waiting room, which must have been crowded; then describing the face of the doctor who had come out to give them the news of Boone's death. 'She said, "He's dead. Too long out there." And Maya put a hand on Frank's shoulder, and he jumped.'

'We have to tell Maya,' Nazik whispered.

'He said to her, "I'm sorry," which I thought was odd. She said something to him about how he had never liked John anyway, which was true. And Frank even agreed, but then he left. He was angry at Maya as well. He said, he said, "What do you know about what I like or don't like?" So bitter. He didn't like her presumption. The idea that she knew him.' Zeyk shook his head.

'Was I there during this?' Sax said.

'. . . Yes. You were sitting right on the other side of Maya. But you were distracted. You were crying.'

Nothing came back to Sax of that, nothing. It occurred to him with a lurch that just as there were many things that he had done that no one else would ever know about, there were also things he had done that others remembered, that he himself could not recall. So little they knew! So little!

And still Zeyk went on: the rest of that night, the next morning. The appearance of Selim, his death; then the day after that, when Zeyk and Nazik had left Nicosia. And the day after that as well. Later Ursula said that he could go on in that amount of detail for every week of his life.

But now Nazik stopped the session. 'This one is too hard,' she said to Smadar. 'Let's start again tomorrow.'

Smadar agreed, and began tapping at the console of the machine beside her. Zeyk stared at the dark ceiling like a haunted man; and Sax saw that among the many dysfunctions of the memory, one would have to include memories that worked too well. But how? What was the mechanism? That image of Zeyk's brain, replicating in another medium the patterns of quantum activity – lightning flickering around in his cortex . . . a mind that held the past far better than the rest of the ancient ones, impervious to the affliction of breaking memory, which Sax had believed to be an inexorable clocklike breakdown . . . well, they were giving that brain every test they could think of. But it was quite possible the secret would remain unsolved; there was simply too much happening of which they were completely unaware. As on that night in Nicosia.

Shaken, Sax changed into a warm jumper and went outdoors. The land around Acheron had already been providing welcome breaks from his lab time, and now he was very happy to have a place to get away.

He headed north, toward the sea. Some of his best thinking about memory had come when he was walking down to this seashore, over routes so circuitous that he could never find the same way twice, partly because the old lava plateau was so fractured by grabens and scarps, partly because he was never paying attention to the larger topography – he was either lost in his thoughts or lost in the immediate landscape, only intermittently looking around to see where he was. In fact it was a region in which one could not get lost; ascend any small ridge, and there the Acheron fin stood, like the spine of an immense dragon; and in the other direction, visible from more places as one approached it, the wide blue expanse of Acheron Bay. In between lay a million micro-environments, the rocky plateau pocked with hidden oases, and every crack filled with plants. It was very unlike the melting landscape on the polar shore across the sea; this rocky plateau and its little hidden habitats seemed immemorial, despite the gardening that was certainly being done by the Acheron ecopoets. Many of these oases were experiments, and Sax treated them as such, staying out of them, peering down into one steep-walled alas after another, wondering what the ecopoet responsible was trying to discover with his or her work. Here soil could be spread with no fear of it being washed into the sea, although the startling green of the estuaries extending back into the valleys showed that some fertile soil was making its way down the streams. These estuarine marshes would fill with eroded soils, while at the same time they were getting saltier, along with the North Sea itself . . .

This time out, however, his observations were broken repeatedly by thoughts of John. John Boone had worked for him for the last several years of John's life, and they had had many a conference as they discussed the rapidly developing Martian situation; vital years; and through them John had been always happy, cheerful, confident – trustworthy, loyal, helpful, friendly, courteous, kind, obedient, cheerful, thrifty, brave, clean and reverent – no, no, not exactly – he had also been abrupt, impatient, arrogant, lazy, slipshod, drug-dependent, proud. But how Sax had come to rely on him, how he had loved him – loved him like a big brother who had protected him out in the world at large. And then they had killed him. Those are the ones the killers always go after. They can't stand that courage. And so they had killed him and Sax had stood on watching and hadn't done a thing. Frozen in shock and personal fear. You didn't stop them? Maya had cried; he remembered it now, her sharp voice. No, I was afraid. No, I did nothing. Of course it was unlikely that there was anything he could have done at that point. Before, when the attacks on John had first started, Sax might have been able to talk him into another assignment, got him some bodyguards, or, since John would never have accepted that, hired some bodyguards to follow him in secret, to protect him while his friends froze and stared in shocked witness. But he hadn't hired anyone. And so his brother had been killed, his brother who had laughed at him but who had loved him as well, loved him before anyone else thought of him at all.

Sax wandered over the fractured plain, distraught – distraught at the loss of a friend a hundred and fifty-three years before. Sometimes it seemed there was no such thing as time.

*   *   *

699

Then he stopped short, brought back to the present by the sight of life. Small white rodents, sniffing around on the green of a sunken meadow. They were no doubt snow pika or something like, but in their whiteness they looked enough like lab rats to give Sax a start. White lab rats, yes, but tailless – mutant lab rats, yes – free at last, out of their cages and into the world, wandering over the intense green meadow grass like surreal hallucinatory objects, all ablink and sniff-whiskered as they checked out the ground between grass clumps for tasties. Munching away on seeds and nuts and flowers. John had been greatly amused at the myth of Sax as the hundred lab rats. Sax's mind, now free and scattered. This is our body.

He crouched and watched the little rodents until he got cold. There were greater creatures out on that plain, and they always stopped him short: deer, elk, moose, bighorn sheep, reindeer, caribou, black bear, grizzly bear – even packs of wolves, like swift grey shadows – and all to Sax like citizens out of a dream, so that every time he spotted even a single creature he felt startled, disconnected, even stunned; it did not seem possible; it was certainly not natural. Yet here they were. And now these little snow pika, happy in their oasis. Not nature, not culture: just Mars.

He thought of Ann. He wanted her to see them.

He often thought of her these days. So many of his friends were dead now, but Ann was alive, he could still talk to her, it was at least possible. He had looked into the matter, and found that she now lived in the caldera of Olympus Mons, as part of the small community of Red climbers that occupied it. Apparently they took turns in the caldera, to keep the population low despite the big holes' steep walls and primeval conditions, both so attractive to them. But Ann stayed as long as she liked, Sax had heard, and left only infrequently. This was what Peter had told him, although Peter had only heard it secondhand. Sad how those two were estranged; pointless; but family estrangements seemed to be the most intransigent of all.

Anyway, she was on Olympus Mons. Therefore almost in sight, just over the horizon to the south. And he wanted to talk to her. All his reflections on what happened to Mars, he thought, were framed as an internal conversation with Ann.

Not so much as an argument, or so he hoped, but as an endless persuasion. If he could be so changed by the reality of blue Mars, could not Ann as well? Was it not almost inevitable, even necessary? Might it have already happened? Sax felt he had come over the years to love what Ann loved in Mars; and now he wanted her to reciprocate, if possible. She had become for him, in a most uncomfortable way, his measure of the worth of what they had done. The worth, or the acceptability. It was a strange feeling to have settled in him, but there it was.

Another uncomfortable lump in his mind, like the suddenly rediscovered guilt about John's death, which he would try again to forget. If he could blank out on the interesting thoughts he ought to be able to blank out on the awful ones, oughtn't he? John had died, and nothing Sax could have done would have prevented it. Very probably. There was no way to say. And no way to go back. John had been killed and Sax had failed to help him; and here they were, Sax alive and John dead, nothing now but a powerful node-and-network system in the minds of all the people who had known him. And nothing to be done.

But Ann was alive, up there climbing the caldera walls of Olympus. He could talk to her if he wanted. Although she would not come out. He would have to hunt her down. But he could do it, that was the thing. The real sting of John's death lay in the death of that chance; he could no longer talk to him. But he could still talk to Ann, the chance existed.

Work on the anamnestic package continued. Acheron was a joy that way: days in the labs, talking with the lab directors about their experiments and seeing if he could help. Weekly seminars, where they got together in front of the screens and shared their results, and talked about what they meant and what they might try next. People interrupted their work to help with the farm, or do other business or go on trips; but others were there to fill in, and when people came back they often had new ideas, and always had a new charge of energy. Sax sat in the seminar rooms after the weekly round-ups, looking at the coffee cups and the rings of brown coffee and black kava stains on the battered wooden tabletops, the white, shiny blackboard screens covered with schemata and chemical diagrams and big looping arrows pointing to acronyms and alchemical symbols that Michel would have loved, and something inside him would glow till it hurt, some parasympathetic reaction spilling out of his limbic system – now *this* was science, by God, this was Martian science, in the hands of the scientists themselves, working together for some collective goal that made sense, that was for the common good; pushing at the edge of what they knew, theory and experiment bouncing back and forth like a blur of ping-pong balls, week after week finding out more, going after more, extending the great invisible parthenon right out into the uncharted territory of the human mind, into life itself. It made him so happy that he almost didn't care if they ever figured things out; the search was all.

But his short-term memory was damaged. He was experiencing blankouts and tip-of-the-tongueism every day; sometimes in the seminars he had to stop mid-sentence, almost, and sit down and wave at the others, asking them to go on; and they would nod and the person at the blackboard would continue. No, he needed the solution to this one. There would be other puzzles to pursue afterwards, without any doubt; the quick decline itself, for instance, or any of the rest of the senescence problem. No, there was no lack of the unexplainable to work on, and never would be. Meanwhile, the problem of the anamnestic was hard enough.

The outlines of it were coming clear, however. One part of it would be a drug cocktail, a mixture of protein synthesis enhancers, including even amphetamines and chemical relatives of strychnine, and then transmitters like serotonin, glutamate receptor sensitizers, cholinesterase, cyclic AMP, and so on. All of these would be there to help in different ways to reinforce the memory structures when they were rehearsed. Others would be included from the general brain plasticity treatment that Sax had received in the period following his stroke, at much smaller doses. Then it seemed from the experiments in electrical stimulation that a stimulus shock, followed by a continuous oscillation at very rapid frequencies phased with the subject's natural brainwaves, would serve to initiate the neurochemical processes augmented by the drug package. After that, subjects would have then to direct the work of remembering as best they could, perhaps moving from node to node if possible, with the idea that as each node was recalled, the network surrounding the node would then be flushed by the oscillations and reinforced accordingly. Moving from room to room in the theatre of memory, in essence. Experiments with all these various aspects of the process were being run on volunteer subjects, often the young native experimenters themselves; they were remembering a great many things, they said with a kind of stunned awe, and the overall prospect was looking more and more promising. Week by week they honed their techniques, and homed in on a process.

For the work of recollection to succeed best, it was becoming clear from the experiments that context was an important component. Lists memorized underwater in diving suits could be recalled much better when the subjects returned to the seafloor than when they tried to remember them on land. Subjects hypnotically induced to feel happy or sad during memorization of a list were better at remembering the list when again hypnotized to feel happy or sad. Congruence of items in the lists helped, as did returning to rooms of the same size or colour when remembering them. These were of course all very crude experiments, but the link between context and power of recollection was demonstrated by them strongly enough to cause Sax to think hard about where he might want to try the treatment when they finalized it; where, and with whom.

For the final work on the treatment Sax called up Bao Shuyo and asked her to come join them in Acheron for some consultations. Again, her work was much more theoretical, and very much more fine-grained, but after her work with the fusion group in Da Vinci, he had a healthy respect for her ability to help in any problem that involved quantum gravity and the ultramicrostructure of matter. Just to have her run through what they had done and comment on it would be valuable, he was sure.

Unfortunately, Bao's obligations in Da Vinci were heavy, as they had been ever since her much-heralded return from Dorsa Brevia. Sax was put in the unusual position of manipulating his home labs in order to extricate one of their best theorists, but he did it without compunction, getting Bela's help to put the arm on the current administration, to twist their arms as hard as ever he could. 'Ka, Sax,' Bela exclaimed during one call, 'I never would have guessed that you would turn out to be such a fierce headhunter.'

'It's my own head I'm hunting,' Sax replied.

Usually tracking someone down was as simple as contacting their wristpad, and looking to see where the person was. Ann's wristpad, however, had been left on the rim of the Olympus Mons caldera, at the descent station near the festival grounds at Crater Zp. This struck Sax as peculiar, since they had worn wristpads of some kind or another since the very beginning in Underhill, Ann as much as anyone, as he recalled. Hadn't she? He called Peter to ask, but Peter did not know, of course, having been born well after the Underhill years. In any case, to go without a wristpad now was to borrow a behaviour from the neoprimitive nomads wandering the canyonlands and the North Sea coast – not a lifestyle he would have expected Ann to take any interest in. One couldn't live in anything like the paleolithic style up on Olympus Mons, indeed it required the kind of continuous technological support that was no longer necessary in most places, with wristpads an integral part of it. Perhaps she only wanted to get away. Peter didn't know.

But he did know how to contact her: 'You have to go in and find her.'

At Sax's expression he laughed. 'It isn't so bad. There's only a couple of hundred people in the caldera, and when they're not staying in one of their huts, they're on the cliff walls.'

'She's become a climber?'

'Yes.'

'She climbs for – for recreation?'

'She climbs. Don't ask me why.'

'So I just go look at all the cliffs?'

'That's how I had to do it when Marian died.'

The summit of Olympus Mons had for the most part been left alone. Oh, there were a few low boulder hermitages on rim overlooks, and a piste had been built on the northeast lava flow that broke the escarpment ring surrounding the volcano, for easy access to the festival complex at Crater Zp; but other than that, there was nothing to show what had happened to the rest of Mars, which from the rim of the caldera was entirely

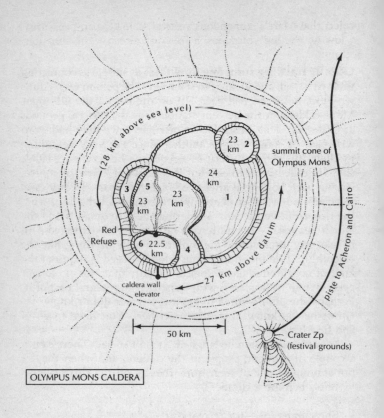

(28 km above sea level)

summit cone of
Olympus Mons

23
km 2

24
km

1

3 5

23
km 23
km

Red
Refuge

6 22.5
km

4

piste to Acheron and Cairo

caldera wall
elevator

27 km above datum

50 km

Crater Zp
(festival grounds)

OLYMPUS MONS CALDERA

invisible, under the horizon of the encircling escarpment. From
its rim Olympus Mons appeared to be the world entire. The
local Reds had decided against putting a protective molecular
dome over the caldera, something they had done over Arsia
Mons; so no doubt there were bacteria, and perhaps some
lichens that had blown over on winds and floated down into
the caldera and survived; but at pressures little higher than
the original ten millibars, they were not going to flourish.
Probably the survivors were mostly endochasmoliths, so there
would be no sign of them. It was a lucky thing for the Red

project that Mars's stupendous vertical scale kept air pressures so low on the big volcanoes; a free and effective sterilization technique.

Sax took the train up to Zp, and then a car on up to the rim, a taxi-van driven by the Reds who controlled access into the caldera. The car came to the edge of the rim, and Sax looked down.

The caldera was multi-ringed, and big: ninety kilometres by sixty, about the same size as Luxembourg, Sax recalled hearing. The main central circle, by far the largest, was marred by overlapping smaller circles to the northeast, centre and south. The southernmost circle cut in half a slightly older, higher circle to the southeast; the meeting of these three arcuate walls was considered one of the finest climbing areas on the planet, Sax was told, with the greatest height of all, a drop from twenty-six kilometres above the datum (they used the old term rather than sea level) down to 22.5 kilometres on the southernmost crater floor. A ten thousand foot cliff, the young Coloradoan in Sax mused.

The floor of the main caldera was marked by a great number of curving fault patterns, concentric with the caldera walls: arcing ridges and canyons, across which ran some straighter escarpments. These features were all explicable, they had been caused by recurrent caldera collapses following the sideslope drainage of magma from the main chamber under the volcano; but as he looked down from their perch on the rim, it seemed to Sax a mysterious mountain – a world of its own – nothing visible but the vast embayed rim, and the five thousand square kilometres of the caldera. Ring on ring of high, curved walls and flat, round floors, under a black starry sky. Nowhere were the encircling cliffs less than a thousand metres tall. As a rule they were not completely vertical; their average slope appeared to be just steeper than 45°. But there were steeper sections all over the place. No doubt the climbers flocked to the very steepest sections, given the nature of their interest. There looked to be some very vertical faces out there, even an overhang or two, as right under them, over the confluence of the three walls.

'I'm looking for Ann Clayborne,' Sax said to the drivers, who were rapt with the view. 'Do you know where I could find her?'

'You don't know where she is?' one asked.

'I've heard she's climbing in the Olympus caldera.'

'Does she know you're looking for her?'

'No. She's not answering her calls.'

'Does she know you?'

'Oh yes. We're old – friends.'

'And who are you?'

'Sax Russell.'

They stared at him. One said, 'Old friends, eh?'

Her companion elbowed her.

They called the spot they were at Three Walls, sensibly enough. Directly under their car, on a little slump terrace, there was an elevator station. Sax peered at it through binoculars: outer lock doors, reinforced roofing – it could have been a structure from the early years. The elevator was the only way down into this part of the caldera, if you did not care to abseil.

'Ann resupplies at Marian Station,' the elbower finally said, shocking her co-driver. 'See it, there? That square dot, where the lava channels from the main floor cut down into South Circle.'

This was on the opposite rim of the southernmost circle, which Sax's map named '6'. Sax had trouble making out any square dot, even with the binoculars' magnification. But then he saw it – a tiny block just a bit too regular to be natural, although it had been painted the rusty grey of the local basalt. 'I see it. How do I get there?'

'Take the elevator down, then walk on over.'

So he showed the elevator attendants the pass the elbower had given him, and took the long elevator ride down the wall of South Circle. The elevator ran on a track affixed to the cliffside, and it had windows; it was like dropping in a helicopter, or coming down the last bit of the space elevator over Sheffield. By the time he got down to the caldera floor it was late afternoon; he checked into the spartan lodge at the bottom and ate a big, leisurely dinner, thinking from time to time what he might say to Ann. It came to him, slowly: a coherent and it seemed convincing self-explication, or confession, or *cri de coeur*, piece by piece. Then to his great chagrin he blanked the whole thing. And there he was on the floor of a volcanic caldera, the blinkered circle of sky dark and starry above. On Olympus. Searching for Ann Clayborne, with nothing to say to her. Very chagrined.

The next morning after breakfast, he pushed his way into a walker. Although the materials were improved, the elastic fabric necessarily clasped the limbs and torso just as tightly as their old suits had. Strange how the kinetics of it evoked trains of thought, flashes of memory: the look of Underhill as they were building the foursquare dome; even a kind of somatic epiphany, which seemed to be a recollection of his very first walk out of the landing craft, with the surprise of the close horizons and the textured pink of the sky. Context and memory, again.

He walked out across the floor of South Circle. This morning the sky was a dark indigo very near black – marine blue, the chart said, an odd choice of name considering how dark it was. Many stars were visible. The horizon was a round cliff, rising on all sides: the southern semi-circle three kilometres tall, the northeast quadrant two kilometres, the northwest quadrant one kilometre only, and shattered. Astonishing sight, chambers, magma throats. Out in the middle the encircling walls were a dizzying sight. The walls looked much the same height in all directions, a textbook example of foreshortening's ability to telescope the perception of vertical distances.

He tramped on at a steady pace. The caldera floor was fairly smooth, pocked by occasional lava bombs and late meteor hits, and curving shallow grabens. Some of these had to be circumvented, a beautifully apt word in this case, as they *were* circumvents. But for the most part he could tramp directly toward the broken spill of cliff in the northwest quadrant of the caldera.

It took six hours of steady walking to cross the floor of South Circle, which was less than ten per cent of the caldera complex's total area – all the rest of which was invisible to him for the entire hike. No sign of life, nor of any disturbance to the caldera floor or walls; the atmosphere was visibly thin, everything equally sharp to the eye, right around the primal 10 millibars, he judged. The untouched nature of things made him feel uncertain about even his bootprints, and he tried to step on hard rock, and avoid dust patches. It was strangely satisfying to see the primal landscape – quite reddish – though the colour was mostly an overlay on dark basalt. His colour chart was not good at odd mixes.

Sax had never descended into one of the big calderas before. And even many years spent inside impact craters did not prepare one, he found – for the depth of the chambers, the steepness of the walls, the flatness of the floor. The sheer size of things.

Around mid-afternoon he approached the foot of the northwest arc of the wall. The meeting of wall and floor came up over his horizon, and to his slight relief, the block shelter appeared directly before him; his APS setting had been quite accurate. Not a complicated bit of navigation, but in such an exposed place it was pleasant to be precisely on line. Ever since his experience in the storm so long ago, he had been a bit wary about getting lost. Although there would be no storms up here.

As he approached the hut's lock doors, a group of people appeared from out of the bottom of a stupendously huge, steep gully in the vast broken cliff face, debouching onto the crater floor about a kilometre to the west of the refuge. Four figures, carrying big packs on their backs. Sax stopped, the sound of his breath loud in his helmet: he recognized the last figure immediately. Ann was coming in to resupply. Now he was going to have to think of something to say. And then remember it too.

Inside the hut Sax unclipped his helmet and took it off, feeling a familiar but most unwelcome tension in his stomach as he did. Every meeting with Ann it got worse. He turned around, and waited. Finally Ann came in, and took off her helmet, and saw him. She started as if she were seeing a ghost. 'Sax?' she cried.

He nodded. He remembered when they had last met; long ago, on Da Vinci Island; it felt like a previous life. He had lost his tongue.

Ann shook her head, smiled to herself. She crossed the room with an expression he couldn't read, and held his arms in her two hands, and leaned forward and kissed his cheek gently. When she pulled back, one of her hands continued to clutch his left arm, sliding down to the wrist. She was staring right into him, and her grip was like metal. Sax was speechless again, although he very much wanted to speak. But there was nothing to say, or too much, he couldn't even tell which it was; his tongue was again paralysed. That hand on his wrist; it was more incapacitating than any glare or cutting remark had ever been.

A wave seemed to pass through her, and she became somewhat more the Ann he knew, looking at him suspiciously, then with alarm. 'Everyone's okay?'

'Yes yes,' Sax said. 'I mean – you heard about Michel?'

'Yes.' Her mouth tightened, for a second she became the black Ann of his dreams. Then another wave passed through her, and she was this new stranger, still clutching his wrist as if trying to snip his hand off. 'But now you're just here to see me.'

'Yes. I wanted to . . .' He searched wildly for a finish to the sentence — '. . . to talk! Yes – to, to, to, to, to ask you some questions. I'm having some trouble with my memory. I wondered if I, if we could travel up here, and talk. Hike — ' he gulped — 'or climb. You could show me some of the caldera?'

She was smiling. Again it was some other Ann. 'You can climb with me if you want.'

'I'm not a climber.'

'We'll go up an easy route. Up Wang's Gully, and over the great circle to North Circle, I've wanted to get up there while it's still summer anyway.'

'It's Ls 200, actually. But I mean, it sounds good.' His heart was beating at about a hundred and fifty beats a minute.

Ann had all the equipment they needed, it turned out. The next morning, as they were suiting up, she said to him, 'Here, take that off.' Pointing at his wristpad.

'Oh dear,' Sax said. 'I – isn't it really part of the suit's system?'

It was, but she shook her head. 'The suit is autonomous.'

'Semi-autonomous, I hope.'

She smiled. 'Yes. But no wristpad is necessary. Look – that thing connects you to the whole world. It's your manacle to spacetime. Today let's just be in Wang's Gully. It will be enough.'

It was enough. Wang's Gully was a broad, weathered chute, cutting up through steeper cliff ridges like a giant, shattered culvert. Most of the day Sax followed Ann up smaller gullies within the body of this larger one, scrambling up waist-high steps, using his hands most of the time, but seldom with the feeling that a fall would kill him, or do much more than sprain an ankle. 'This isn't as dangerous as I thought it would be,' he said. 'Is this the kind of climbing you always do?'

'This isn't climbing at all.'

'Ah.'

So she went up slopes steeper than this. Taking risks that were, strictly speaking, unjustifiable.

And indeed, in the afternoon they came to a short wall, cut by horizontal fissures; Ann began to climb it, without ropes or pitons, and gritting his teeth, Sax followed. Near the top of a gecko-like ascent, with his boot tips and gloved fingers all jammed into small cracks, he looked back down Wang's Gully, which suddenly seemed very much steeper in its entirety than it had in any given section, and all his muscles began to quiver with some kind of fatigued excitation. Nothing for it but to finish the pitch; but he had to risk his position time after time as he hurried higher, the holds getting slimmer just as he was becoming of necessity hastier. The basalt was very slightly pitted, its dark grey tinged rust or sienna; he found himself hyper-focused on one crack over a metre above his eye level; he was going to have to use that crack; was it deep enough for his fingertips to gain any purchase? He had to try to be sure. So he took a deep breath and reached up and tried, and as it turned out it was not really deep enough at all; but with a quick pull, groaning involuntarily at the effort, he was up and past it, using holds he never even consciously saw; and then he was on his hands and knees next to Ann, breathing very heavily. She sat serenely on a narrow ledge.

'Try to use your legs more,' she suggested.

'Ah.'

'Got your attention, did it?'

'Yes.'

'No memory problems, I trust?'

'No.'

'That's what I like about climbing.'

Later that day, when the gully had laid back a bit, and opened up, Sax said, 'So have you been having memory problems?'

'Let's talk about that later,' Ann said. 'Pay attention to this crack here.'

'Indeed.'

That night they lay in sleeping bags, in a clear mushroom tent big enough to hold ten. At this altitude, with its superthin atmosphere, it was impressive to consider the strength of the tent fabric, holding in 450 millibars of air with no sign of untoward bulging at any point; the clear material was nice and taut, but not rock-hard; no doubt it was holding many bars of air fewer than would test its holding capacity. When Sax recalled the metres of rock and sandbags they had had to pile on their earliest habitats to keep them from exploding, he couldn't help but be impressed by the subsequent advancements in materials science.

Ann nodded when he spoke of this. 'We've moved beyond our ability to understand our technology.'

'Well. It's understandable, I think. Just hard to believe.'

'I suppose I see the distinction,' she said easily.

Feeling more comfortable, he brought up memory again. 'I've been having what I call blankouts, where I can't remember my thoughts of the previous several minutes, or up to say an hour. Short-term memory failures, having to do with brainwave fluctuations, apparently. And the long-term past is getting very uncertain as well, I'm afraid.'

For a long time she didn't reply, except to grunt that she'd heard him. Then:

'I've forgotten my whole self. I think there's someone else in me now. In partway. A kind of opposite. My shadow, or the shadow of my shadow. Seeded, and growing inside me.'

'How do you mean?' Sax said apprehensively.

'An opposite. She thinks just what I wouldn't have thought.'

713

She turned her head away, as if shy. 'I call her Counter-Ann.'

'And how would you – characterize her?'

'She is . . . I don't know. Emotional. Sentimental. Stupid. Cries at the sight of a flower. Feels that everyone is doing their best. Crap like that.'

'You weren't like that before, at all?'

'No no no. It's all crap. But I feel it as though it's real. So . . . now there's Ann and Counter-Ann. And . . . maybe a third.'

'A third?'

'I think so. Something that isn't either of the other two.'

'And what do you – I mean, do you call that one anything?'

'No. She doesn't have a name. She's elusive. Younger. Fewer ideas about things, and those ideas are – strange. Not Ann or Counter-Ann. Somewhat like that Zo, did you know her?'

'Yes,' Sax said, surprised. 'I liked her.'

'Did you? I thought she was awful. And yet . . . there's something like that in me as well. Three people.'

'It's an odd way to think of it.'

She laughed. 'Aren't you the one who had a mental lab that contained all your memories, filed by room and cabinet number or something?'

'That was a very effective system.'

She laughed again, harder. It made him grin to hear it. Though he was frightened too. Three Anns? Even one had been more than he could understand.

'But I'm losing some of those labs,' he said. 'Whole units of my past. Some people model memory as a node-and-network system, so it's possible the palace-of-memory method intuitively echoes the physical system involved. But if you somehow lose the node, the whole network around it goes too. So, I'll run across a reference in the literature to something I did, for instance, and try to recall doing it, what methodological problems we had or whatever, and the whole, the whole era will just refuse to come to me. As if it never happened.'

'A problem with the palace.'

'Yes. I didn't anticipate it. Even after my – my incident – I was sure nothing would ever happen to my ability to – to think.'

'You still seem to think okay.'

714

Sax shook his head, recalling the blankouts, the gaps in memory, the *presque vus* as Michel had called them, the confusions. Thinking was not just analytical or cognitive ability, but something more general . . . He tried to describe what had been happening to him recently, and Ann seemed to be listening closely. 'So you see, I've been looking at the recent work being done on memory. It's become interesting – pressing, really. And Ursula and Marina and the Acheron labs have been helping me. And I think they've worked out something that might help us.'

'A memory drug, you mean?'

'Yes.' He explained the action of the new anamnestic complex. 'So. My notion is to try it. But I've become convinced that it will work best if a number of the First Hundred gathered at Underhill, and took it together. Context is very important to recollection, and the sight of each other might help. Not everyone is interested, but a surprising number of the remaining First Hundred are, actually.'

'Not so surprising. Who?'

He named everyone he had contacted. It was, sad to admit, most of them left; a dozen or so. 'And all of us would like it if you were there too. I know I would like it more than anything.'

'It sounds interesting,' Ann said. 'But first we have to cross this caldera.'

Walking over the rock, Sax was amazed anew by the stony reality of their world. The fundamentals: rock, sand, dust, fines. Dark chocolate sky, on this day, and no stars. The long distances with no blurring to define them. The stretch of ten minutes. The length of an hour when one was only walking. The feeling in one's legs.

And there were the rings of the calderas around them, jutting far into the sky even when the two walkers were out in the centre of the central circle, out where the later, deeper calderas appeared as big embayments in a single wall's roundness. Out here the planet's sharp curvature had no effect on one's perspective, the curve was for once invisible, the cliffs free and clear even thirty kilometres away. The net effect, it seemed to Sax, was of a kind of enclosure. A park, a stone garden, a maze with only one wall separating it from the world beyond, the world which, though invisible, conditioned everything here. The caldera was big but not big enough. You couldn't hide here. The world poured in and overflowed the mind, no matter its hundred trillion bit capacity. No matter how big the neural array there was still just a single thread of awed mentation, consciousness itself, a living wire of thought saying *rock, cliff, sky, star*.

The rock became heavily cracked by fissures, each one an arc of a circle with its centre point back in the middle of the central circle: old cracks relative to the big new holes of the north and south circles, old cracks filled with rubble and dust. These rock crevasses made their walk into a wandering ramble – in a real maze now, a maze with crevasses rather than walls, yet just as difficult of passage as a walled one.

But they threaded it, and finally reached the rim of North Circle, number 2 on Sax's map. Looking down into it gave them a new perspective – a proper shape to the caldera and its circular embayments, a sudden drop to a heretofore hidden floor, a thousand metres below.

Apparently there was a climbing route down onto the floor of north circle; but when Ann saw the look on his face as she pointed it out – achievable only by abseiling – she laughed. They would only have to climb up out of it again, she said easily, and the main caldera wall was already tall enough. They could hike around north circle to another route instead.

Surprised by this flexibility, and thankful for it, Sax followed her around north circle on its west circumference. Under the great wall of the main caldera they stopped for the night, popped the tent, ate in silence.

After sunset Phobos shot up over the western wall of the caldera like a little grey flare. Fear and dread, what names.

'I heard that putting the moons back in orbit was your idea?' Ann said from her sleeping bag.

'Yes, it was.'

'Now that's what I call landscape restoration,' she said, sounding pleased.

Sax felt a little glow. 'I wanted to please you.'

After a silence: 'I like seeing them.'

'And how did you like Miranda?'

'Oh, it was very interesting.' She talked about some of the geological features of the odd moon. Two planetesimals, impacted, joined together imperfectly . . .

'There's a colour between red and green,' Sax said when it appeared she was done talking about Miranda. 'A mixture of the two. Madder alizarin, it's sometimes called. You see it in plants sometimes.'

'Uh huhn.'

'It makes me think of the political situation. If there couldn't be some kind of Red-Green synthesis.'

'Browns.'

'Yes. Or alizarins.'

'I thought that's what this Free Mars-Red coalition was, Irishka and the people who tossed out Jackie.'

'An anti-immigration coalition,' Sax said. 'The wrong kind of Red Green combination. In that they're embroiling us in a conflict with Earth that isn't necessary.'

'No?'

'No. The population problem is soon going to be eased. The issei – we're hitting the limit, I think. And the nisei aren't far behind.'

'Quick decline, you mean.'

'Exactly. When it gets our generation, and the one after, the human population of the solar system will be less than half what it is now.'

'Then they'll figure out a different way to screw it up.'

'No doubt. But it won't be the hypermalthusian age any more. It'll be their problem. So, worrying so much about immigration, to the point of causing conflict, threatening inter-planetary war . . . it just isn't necessary. It's short-sighted. If there was a Red movement on Mars pointing that out, offering to help Earth through the last of the surge years, it might keep people from killing each other, needlessly. It would be a new way of thinking about Mars.'

'A new areophany.'

'Yes. That's what Maya called it.'

She laughed. 'But Maya is crazy.'

'Why no,' Sax said sharply. 'She certainly is not.'

Ann said no more, and Sax did not press the issue. Phobos moved visibly across the sky, backward through the zodiac.

They slept well. The next day they made an arduous climb up a steep gully in the wall, which apparently Ann and the other Red climbers considered the walker's route out. Sax had never had such a hard day's work in his life; and even so they didn't make it all the way out, but had to pitch the tent in haste at sunset, on a narrow ledge, and finish their emergence the following day, around noon.

On the great rim of Olympus Mons, all was as before. A giant cored circle of flat land; the violet sky in a band around the horizon so far below, a black zenith above; little hermitages scattered in boulder ejecta that had been hollowed out. A separate world. Part of blue Mars, but not.

The hut they stopped at first was inhabited by very old Red mendicants of some sort, apparently living there while waiting for the quick decline to strike them, after which their bodies would be cremated, and the ashes cast into the thin jetstream.

This struck Sax as over-fatalistic. Ann apparently was likewise unimpressed: 'All right,' she said, watching them eat their meagre meal. 'Let's go try this memory treatment then.'

Many of the First Hundred argued for sites other than Underhill, arguing in a way that they didn't even recognize as part of their group nature; but Sax was adamant, shrugging off requests for Olympus Mons, low orbit, Pseudophobos, Sheffield, Odessa, Hell's Gate, Sabishii, Senzeni Na, Acheron, the south polar cap, Mangala, and on the high seas. He insisted that the setting for such a procedure was a critical factor, as experiments on context had proved. Coyote brayed most inappropriately at his description of the experiment with students in scuba gear learning word lists on the floor of the North Sea, but data were data, and given the data, why not do their experiment in the place where they would get the best results? The stakes were high enough to justify doing everything they could to get it right. After all, Sax pointed out, if their memories were returned to them intact, anything might be possible – anything – breakthroughs on other fronts, a defeat of the quick decline, health that lasted centuries more, an ever-expanding community of garden worlds, from thence perhaps up again in some emergent phase change to a higher level of progress, into some realm of wisdom that could not even be imagined at this point – they teetered on the edge of some such golden age, Sax told them. But it all depended on wholeness of mind. Nothing could continue without wholeness of mind. And so he insisted on Underhill.

'You're too sure,' Marina complained; she had been arguing for Acheron. 'You have to keep more of an open mind about things.'

'Yes, yes.' Keep an open mind. This was easy for Sax, his mind was a lab that had burned down. Now he stood in the open air. And no one could refute the logic of Underhill, not Marina nor any of the rest of them. Those who objected were afraid, he thought – afraid of the power of the past. They did not want to acknowledge that power over them, they did not want to give themselves fully over to it. But that was what they needed to do. Certainly Michel would have supported the choice of Underhill, had he been still among them. Place was crucial, that was all their lives had served to show. And even the people dubious, or sceptical, or afraid – i.e. all of them – had to admit that Underhill was the appropriate place, given what they were trying to do.

So in the end they agreed to meet there.

At this point Underhill was a kind of museum, kept in the state it had been in in 2138, the last year it had been a functioning piste stop. This meant that it did not look exactly as it had in the years of their occupancy, but the older parts were all still there, so the changes since wouldn't affect their project much, Sax judged. After his arrival with several others he took a walk around to see, and there the old buildings all were: the original four habitats, dropped whole from space; their junk heaps; Nadia's square of barrel-vault chambers, with their domed centre; Hiroko's greenhouse framework, its enclosing bubble gone; Nadia's trench arcade off to the northwest; Chernobyl; the salt pyramids; and finally the Alchemists' Quarter, where Sax ended his walk, wandering around in the warren of buildings and pipes, trying to ready himself for the next day's experience. Trying for an open mind.

Already his memory was seething, as if trying to prove that it needed no help to do its work. Here among these buildings he had first witnessed the transformative power of technology over the blank materiality of nature; they had started with just rocks and gases, really, and from that they had extracted and purified and transformed and recombined and shaped, in so many different ways that no one person could keep good track of them all, nor even imagine their effect. So he had seen but he had not understood: and they had acted perpetually in ignorance of their true powers, and with (perhaps as a result) very little sense of what they were trying for. But there in the Alchemists' Quarter, he hadn't been able to see that. He had been so sure that the world made green would be a fine place.

Now here he stood in the open, head free under a blue sky, in the heat of second August, looking around and trying to think, to remember. It was hard to direct the memory; things simply occurred to him. The objects in the old part of town felt distinctly familiar, as in the word's root meaning 'of the

720

family'. Even the individual red stones and boulders around the settlement, and all the bumps and hollows in view, were perfectly familiar, all still in their proper places on the compass flower. Prospects for the experiment seemed very good to Sax; they were in their place, in their context, situated, oriented. At home.

He returned to the square of barrel-vaults, where they were going to stay. Some cars had driven in during his walk, and some little excursion trains were parked on the sidings next to the piste. People were arriving. There were Maya and Nadia, hugging Tasha and Andrea, who had arrived together; their voices rang in the air like a Russian opera, like recitative on the edge of bursting into song. Of the hundred and one they had begun with, there were only fourteen of them going to show up: Sax, Ann, Maya, Nadia, Desmond, Ursula, Marina, Vasili, George, Edvard, Roger, Mary, Dmitri, Andrea. Not so many, but it was every one of them still alive and in contact with the world; all the rest were dead, or missing. If Hiroko and the other seven of the First Hundred who had disappeared with her were still alive, they had sent no word. Perhaps they would show up unannounced, as they had at John's first festival on Olympus. Perhaps not.

So they were fourteen. Thus reduced, Underhill seemed under-occupied; though all of it was theirs to spread out in, they yet crowded together into the south wing of the barrel-vaults. Nevertheless the emptiness of the rest of it was palpable. It was as if the place itself was an image of their failing memories, with their lost labs and lost lands and lost companions. Every single one of them was suffering from memory losses and disorders of one sort or another – between them they had experienced almost all the problems in mentation mentioned in the literature, as far as Sax could tell, and a good bit of their conversation was taken up in comparative symptomology, in the recounting of various terrifying and/ or sublime experiences that had afflicted them in the last decade. It made them jocular and sombre by turns, as they milled around that evening in the little barrel-vault kitchen in the southwest corner, with its high window looking out onto the floor of the central greenhouse, still under its thick glass dome, in its muted light. They ate a picnic dinner brought

721

in coolers, talking, catching up, then spreading along the south wing, preparing the upstairs bedrooms for an uneasy night. They stayed up as late as they could, talking and talking; but eventually they gave up, in ones and twos, and tried to sleep. Several times that night Sax woke from dreams, and heard people stumbling down to the bathrooms, or whispering conversations in the kitchen, or muttering to themselves in the troubled sleep of the aged. Each time he managed to slip back under again, into a light dream-filled sleep of his own.

Finally morning came. They were up at dawn; in the horizontal light they ate a quick breakfast, fruit and croissants and bread and coffee. Long shadows cast west from every rock and hillock. So familiar.

Then they were ready. There was nothing else to do. There was a kind of collective deep breath – uneasy laughter – an inability to meet the others' eyes.

Maya, however, was still refusing to take the treatment. She was unswayed by every argument they tried. 'I won't,' she had said over and over again the night before. 'You'll need a keeper in any case, in case you go crazy. I'll do that.'

Sax had thought she would change her mind, that she was just being Maya. Now he stood before her, baffled. 'I thought you were having the worst memory troubles of all.'

'Perhaps.'

'So it would make sense to try this treatment. Michel gave you lots of different drugs for mental trouble.'

'I don't want to,' she said, looking him in the eye.

He sighed. 'I don't understand you, Maya.'

'I know.'

And she went into the old med clinic in the corner, and took on her role as their keeper for the day. Everything in there was ready, and she called them in one by one, and took up little ultrasound injectors and put them to their necks, and with a little click-hiss administered one part of the drug package, and gave them the pills that contained the rest of it, and then helped them insert the earplugs that were custom designed for each of them, to broadcast the silent electromagnetic waves. In the kitchen they waited for everyone to finish their preparations, in a nervous silence. When they were all done Maya ushered them to the door and guided them outside. And they were off.

Sax saw and felt an image: bright lights, a feeling of his skull being crushed, choking, gasping, spitting. Chill air and his mother's voice, like an animal's yelp, 'Oh? Oh? Oh! Oh!' Then lying wet on her chest, cold.

'Oh my.'

The hippocampus was one of several specific brain regions that had been very strongly stimulated by the treatment. This meant that his limbic system, spread under the hippocampus like a net under a walnut, was likewise stimulated, as if the nut were bouncing up and down on a trampoline of nerves, causing the trampoline to resonate or even to jangle. Thus Sax felt the start of what would no doubt be a flood of emotions – registering not any single emotion, he noted, but many at once and at nearly the same intensity, and free of any cause – joy, grief, love, hate, exhilaration, melancholy, hope, fear, generosity, jealousy – many of which of course did not match with their opposite or with most of the others present in him. The result of this overcrowded mix, for Sax at any rate, sitting on a bench outside the barrel-vault, breathing hard, was a kind of adrenalized, breathstopping growth in his sensation of *significance*. A suffusion of meaning through everything – it was heartbreaking, or heartfilling – as if oceans of clouds were stuffed in his chest, so that he could scarcely breathe – a kind of nostalgia to the *nth* power, a fullness, even bliss – pure sublimity – just sitting there, just the fact that they were alive! But all of it with a sharp edge of loss, with regret for lost time, with fear of death, fear of everything, grief for Michel, for John, for all of them really. This was so unlike Sax's usual calm, steady, one might even say phlegmatic state, that he was almost incapacitated; he could not move well, and for several minutes he bitterly regretted ever initiating any such experiment as this. It was very foolish - idiotically fool-hardy – no doubt everyone would hate him forever.

Stunned, nearly overwhelmed, he decided to try to walk, to

see if that would clear his head. He found he could walk; push off the bench, stand, balance, walk, avoiding others who were wandering by in their own worlds, as oblivious to him as he was to them, everyone getting past each other like objects to be avoided. And then he was out in the open space of the Underhill environs, out in the chilly morning breeze, walking toward the salt pyramids, under a strangely blue sky.

He stopped and looked around – considered – grunted in surprise, came to a halt – could not walk. For all of a sudden he could remember *everything*.

Not everything everything. He could not recall what he had had for breakfast on 2 August 13th in 2029, for instance; that was in accord with experiments which suggested that daily habitual activities were not differentiated enough on entrainment to allow for individual recall. But as a class . . . in the late 2020s he had started his days back in the barrel-vault, at the southeast corner, where he had shared an upstairs bedroom with Hiroko, Evgenia, Rya and Iwao. Experiments, incidents, conversations flickered in his mind as he saw that bedroom in his mind's eye. A node in timespace, vibrating a whole network of days. Rya's pretty back across the room as she washed under her arms. Things people said that hurt in their carelessness. Vlad talking about clipping genes. He and Vlad had stood out here together on this very spot, in their very first minute on Mars, looking around at everything without a word for each other, just absorbing the gravity and the pink of the sky and the close horizons, looking just as they looked now, so many years later: areological time, as slow and long as the great systolis itself. In the walkers one had felt hollow. Chernobyl had required more concrete than could be cured in the thin dry cold air. Nadia had fixed it somehow, how? Heating it, that's right. Nadia had fixed a lot of things in those years – the barrel-vaults, the manufactories, the arcade – who would have suspected a person so quiet on the *Ares* would prove so competent and energetic? He hadn't remembered that *Ares* impression of her for ages. She had been so pained when Tatiana Durova was killed by a falling crane; it was a shock to them all, all except Michel, who had been revealed as amazingly dissociated by the disaster, their first death. Would Nadia remember that now? Yes, she would if she thought about it. Nothing unique about Sax, or to be more accurate, if the treatment was working on him, it would work on all of them. There was Vasili, who had fought for UNOMA in both revolutions; what was he remembering? He looked stricken, but it could have been rapture – anything or everything – very likely it was the everything emotion, the fullness, apparently one of the first effects of the treatment. Perhaps he was remembering Tatiana's death as well. Once Sax and Tatiana had gone out on a hike in Antarctica during their year there, and Tatiana had slipped on a loose boulder and sprained an ankle, and they had had to wait on Nussbaum Riegel for a helicopter from McMurdo to lift them back to camp. He had forgotten that for years, and then Phyllis had reminded him of it the night she had had him arrested, and he had promptly forgotten it again until this very moment. Two rehearsals in two hundred years; but now it was back, the low sun, the cold, the beauty of the Dry Valleys, Phyllis's jealousy of Tatiana's great dark beauty. That their beauty should die first – it was like a sign, a primal curse, Mars as Pluto, planet of fear and dread. And now that day in Antarctica, the two women long dead – he was the only carrier of that day so precious, without him it would be gone. Ah yes – what one could remember was precisely the part of the past that one had felt the most, the events spiked by emotion above a certain threshold – the great joys, the great crises, the great disasters. And the small ones as well. He had been cut from the seventh grade basketball team, had cried alone after reading the list, at a drinking fountain at the far edge of the school, thinking, You will remember this forever. And by God he had. Great beauty. The first times one did things had that special charge, first love – who had that been, though? A blank, back there in Boulder, a face – some friend of a friend – but that wasn't love; and he couldn't recall her name. No – now he was thinking of Ann Clayborne, standing before him, looking at him closely, some time long ago. What had he been trying to recall? The rush of thought was so dense and rapid he would not be able to remember some of this remembering, he was pretty sure. A paradox, but only one of many caused by the single thread of consciousness

725

in the huge field of the mind. Ten to the forty-third power, the matrix in which all big bangs flowered. Inside the skull was a universe as vast as the one outside. Ann – he had taken a walk with her in Antarctica as well. She was strong. Curious, during the walk across Olympus Mons caldera he had never once remembered this walk across Wright Valley in Antarctica, despite the similarities, a walk during which they had argued so earnestly over the fate of Mars, and he had wanted so much to take her hand, or for her to take his, why, he had had a kind of crush on her! And him in his lab rat mode, having never before risen to such feelings, now stifled for no better reason than shyness. She had looked at him curiously but had not understood his import, only wondered that he should stammer so. He had stammered a fair bit when a boy, it was a biochemical problem apparently solved by puberty, but it occasionally came back when he was nervous. Ann – Ann – he saw her face as he argued with her on the *Ares,* in Underhill, in Dorsa Brevia, in the warehouse on Pavonis. Why always this assault on a woman he had been attracted to, why? She was so strong. And yet he had seen her so depressed that she lay helplessly on the floor, in that boulder car, for many days as her red Mars died. Just laid there. But then she had pried herself off the floor and gone on. She had stopped Maya from yelling at him. She had helped bury her partner Simon. She had done all these things, and never, never, never had Sax been anything but a burden to her. Part of her pain. That was what he was for her. Angry with her in Zygote or Gamete – Gamete – both, really – her face so drawn – and then he hadn't seen her for twenty years. And then later, after he had forced the longevity treatment on her, he hadn't seen her for thirty years. All that time, wasted. If they lived for a thousand years it wouldn't be long enough to justify such waste.

Wandering in the Alchemists' Quarter. He came on Vasili again, sitting in the dust with the tears running down his face. The two of them had botched the Underhill algae experiment together, right there inside this very building, but Sax doubted very much that this was what Vasili was crying about. Something from the many years he had worked for UNOMA, perhaps, or something else – no way to know – well, he could

726

ask – but wandering around Underhill seeing faces, and then remembering in a rush everything about them that one knew, was not a situation conducive to follow-up inquiries. No – walk on, leave Vasili to his own past. Sax did not want to know what Vasili regretted. Besides, halfway to the horizon to the north a figure was striding away alone – Ann. Odd to see her head free of a helmet, white hair coursing back in the wind. It was enough to stop the flow of memories – but then he had seen her that way before, in Wright Valley, yes, her hair light then too, dishwater-blonde they called that colour, not very generously. So dangerous to develop any bond under the watchful eyes of the psychologists. They were there on business, under pressure, there was no room for personal relations which were dangerous indeed, as Natasha and Sergei had proved. But still it happened. Vlad and Ursula became a couple, solid, stable; and the same with Hiroko and Iwao, Nadia and Arkady. But the danger, the risk. Ann had looked at him across the lab table, eating lunch, and there was something in her eye, some regard – he didn't know, he couldn't read people. They were all such mysteries. The day he got his letter of acceptance, selection to the First Hundred, he had felt so sad; why was that? No way of knowing. But now he saw that letter in the fax box, the maple tree outside the window; he had called Ann to see if she had been included – she had, a bit of a surprise, her such a loner, but he had been a bit happier, but still – sad. The maple had been red-leafed; autumn in Princeton, traditionally a melancholy time, but that hadn't been it, not at all. Just *sad*. As if accomplishment were nothing but a certain number of the body's three billion heartbeats passed. And now it was ten billion, and counting. No, there was no explanation. People were mysteries. So when Ann had said, 'Do you want to hike out to Lookout Point?' in that dry valley lab, he had agreed instantly, without a stammer. And without really arranging to, they had walked out separately; she had left the camp and hiked out to Lookout Point, and he had followed, and out there – oh, yes – looking down at the cluster of huts and the greenhouse dome, a kind of proto-Underhill, he had taken her gloved hand in his, as they sat side by side arguing over terraforming in a perfectly friendly way, no stakes involved. And she had pulled her hand away as if shocked, and shuddered (it was very cold, for Terra anyway) and he had stammered just as badly as he had after his stroke. A limbic haemorrhage, killing on the spot certain elements, certain hopes, yearnings. Love dead. And he had harried her ever since. Not that these events functioned as proper causal explanations, no matter what Michel would have said! But the Antarctic cold of that walk back to the base. Even in the eidetic clarity of his current power of recollection he could not see much of that walk. Distracted. Why, why had he repelled her so? Little man. White lab coat. There was no reason. But it had happened. And left its mark forever. And even Michel had never known.

Repression. Thinking of Michel made him think of Maya. Ann was on the horizon now, he would never catch her; he wasn't sure he wanted to at that moment, still stunned by this so-surprising, so-painful memory. He went looking for Maya. Past where Arkady had laughed at their tawdriness when he came down from Phobos, past Hiroko's greenhouse where she had seduced him with her impersonal friendliness, like primates on the savannah, the alpha female grabbing one male among the others, an alpha, a beta, or that class of could-be-alpha-but-not-interested which struck him as the only decent way to behave; past the trailer park where they had all slept on the floor together, a family. With Desmond in a closet somewhere. Desmond had promised to show them how he had lived then, all his hiding places. Jumble of Desmond images, the flight over the burning canal, then the flight over burning Kasei, the fear in Kasei as the security people strapped him in to their insane device; that had been the end of Saxifrage Russell. Now he was something else, and Ann was Counter-Ann, also the third woman that was neither Ann nor Counter-Ann. He could perhaps speak to her on that basis: as two strangers, meeting. Rather than the two who had met in the Antarctic.

Maya was sitting in the barrel-vault kitchen, waiting for a big teapot to boil. She was making tea for them.

'Maya,' Sax said, feeling the words like pebbles in his mouth, 'you should try it. It's not so bad.'

She shook her head. 'I remember everything that I want to. Even now, without your drugs, even now when I hardly

728

remember anything, I still remember more than you ever will. I don't want any more than that.'

It was possible that minute quantities of the drugs had got into the air and thus onto her skin, giving her a small fraction of the hyper-emotional experience. Or perhaps this was just her ordinary state.

'Why shouldn't now be enough?' she was saying. 'I don't want my past back, I don't want it. I can't bear it.'

'Maybe later,' Sax said.

What could one say to her? She had been like this in Underhill as well – unpredictable, moody. It was amazing what eccentrics had been selected to the First Hundred. But what choice had the selection committee had? People were all like that, unless they were stupid. And they hadn't sent stupid people to Mars, or not at first, or not too many. And even the dull-witted had their complexities.   ·

'Maybe,' she said now, and patted his head, and took the teapot off the burner. 'Maybe not. I remember too much as it is.'

'Frank?' Sax said.

'Of course. Frank, John – they're all there.' She stabbed her chest with a thumb. 'It hurts enough. I don't need more.'

'Ah.'

He walked back outside, feeling stuffed, uncertain of anything, off balance. Limbic system vibrating madly under the impact of his whole life, under the impact of Maya, so beautiful and damned. How he wished her happy, but what could one do? Maya lived her unhappiness to the full, it made her happy one might say. Or complete. Perhaps she felt this acutely uncomfortable emotional overfullness all the time! Wow. So much *easier* to be phlegmatic. And yet she was so alive. The way she had flailed them onward out of the chaos, south to the refuge in Zygote . . . such strength. All these strong women. Actually to face up to life's awfulness, awe-full-ness, to face it and feel it without denial, without defences, just admit it and carry on. John, Frank, Arkady, even Michel, they had all had their great optimism, pessimism, idealism, their mythologies to mask the pain of existence, all their various sciences, and still they were dead – killed off one way or another – leaving Nadia and Maya and Ann to carry on and carry on.

No doubt he was a lucky man to have such tough sisters. Even Phyllis – yes, somehow – with the toughness of the stupid, making her way, pretty well at least, fairly well, well at least making it, for a while. Never giving up. Never admitting anything. She had protested about his torture, Spencer had told him so, Spencer and all their hours of aerodynamics together, telling him over too many whiskeys how she had gone to the security chief in Kasei and demanded his release even after he had knocked her cold, almost killed her with nitrous oxide, lied to her in her own bed. She had forgiven him apparently, and Spencer had never forgiven Maya for killing her, though he pretended he had; and Sax had forgiven her, even though for years he had acted as if he hadn't, to get some kind of hold on her. Ah the strange recombinant tangle they had made of their lives, result of the overextension, or perhaps it was that way in every village always. But so much sadness and betrayal! Perhaps memory was triggered by loss, as everything was inevitably lost. But what about joy? He tried to remember: could one cast back by emotional category, interesting idea, was that possible? Walking through the halls of the terraforming conference, for instance, and seeing the poster board that estimated the heat contribution of the Russell Cocktail at 12 Kelvins. Waking up in Echus Overlook and seeing that the great storm was gone, the pink sky radiant with sunlight. Seeing the faces on the train as they slid out of Libya Station. Being kissed in the ear by Hiroko, in the baths one winter day in Zygote, when it was evening all afternoon. Hiroko! Ah – ah – he had been huddling in the cold, quite vexed to think he would be killed by a storm just when things were getting interesting, trying to work out how he might call his car to him, as it seemed he would not be able to get to it, and then there she had appeared out of the snow, a short figure in a rust-red spacesuit, bright in the white storm of wind and horizontal snow, the wind so loud that even the intercom mike in his helmet was no more than a whisper: 'Hiroko?' he cried as he saw her face through the slush-smeared faceplate; and she said 'yes'. And pulled him up by the wrist – helped him up. That hand on his wrist! He *felt* it. And up he came, like viriditas itself, the green force pouring through him, through the white noise, the white static sleeting by, her grip warm and hard, as full as the plenum itself. Yes. Hiroko had been there. She had led him back to the car, had saved his life, had then disappeared again, and no matter how certain Desmond was of her death in Sabishii, no matter how convincing his arguments were, no matter how often second climbers had been hallucinated by solo climbers in distress, Sax knew better, because of that hand on his wrist, that visitation in the snow – Hiroko herself in the hard compact flesh, as real as rock. Alive! So that he could rest in that knowledge, he could *know* *something* – in the inexplicable seeping of the unexplainable into everything, he could rest in that known fact. Hiroko lived. Start with that and go on, build on it, the axiom of a lifetime of joy. Perhaps even convince Desmond of it, give him that peace.

He was back outside, looking for the Coyote. Not an easy task, ever. What did Desmond recall of Underhill – hiding, whispers, the lost farm crew, then the lost colony, slipping away with them – out there driving around Mars in disguised boulder cars, being loved by Hiroko, flying over the night surface in a stealthed plane, playing the demi-monde, knitting the underground together – Sax could almost remember it himself, it was so vivid to him. Telepathic transfer of all their stories to all of them; one hundred squared, in the square of barrel-vaults. No. That would be too much. Just the imagination of someone else's reality was stunning enough, was all the telepathy one required or could handle.

But where had Desmond gone? Hopeless. One could never find Coyote; one only waited for him to find you. He would show up when he chose. For now, out northwest of the pyramids and the Alchemists' Quarter, there was a very ancient lander skeleton, probably from the original pre-landing equipment drop, its metal stripped of paint and encrusted with salt. The beginning of their hopes, now a skeleton of old metal, nothing really. Hiroko had helped him unload this one.

Back into the Alchemists' Quarter, all the machines in the old buildings shut down, hopelessly outdated, even the very clever Sabatier processor. He had enjoyed watching that thing work. Nadia had fixed it one day when everyone else was baffled; little round woman humming some tune in a world of her own, communing with machinery, back when machines

731

could be understood. Thank God for Nadia, the anchor holding them all to reality, the one they could always count on. He wanted to give her a hug, this most beloved sister of his, who it appeared was over there in the vehicle yard trying to get a museum exhibit bulldozer to run.

But there on the horizon was a figure walking westward over a knoll: Ann. Had she been circling the horizon, walking and walking? He ran out toward her, stumbling just as he would have in the first week. He caught up with her, slowly, gasping.

'Ann? Ann?'

She turned and he saw the instinctive fear on her face, as on the face of a hunted animal. He was a creature to run from; this was what he had been to her. 'I made mistakes,' he said as he stopped before her. They could speak in the open air, in the air he had made over her objection. Though it was still thin enough to make one gasp. 'I didn't see the – the beauty until it was too late. I'm sorry. I'm sorry. I'm sorry. I'm sorry.' Oh he had tried to say it before, in Michel's car when the deluge poured, in Zygote, in Tempe Terra; never had it worked. Ann and Mars, all intertwined – and yet he had no apology to make to Mars, every sunset was beautiful, the sky's colour a different washed tint every minute of every day, blue sign of their power and their responsibility, their place in the cosmos and their power within it, so small and yet so important; they had brought life to Mars and it was good, he was sure of that.

But to Ann he needed to apologize. For the years of missionary fervour, the pressure applied to *make* her agree, the hunt for the wild beast of her refusal, to kill it dead. Sorry for that, so sorry – his face wet with tears, and she stared at him so – just precisely as she had on that cold rock in Antarctica, in that first refusal – which had all come back and rested inside him now. His past.

'Do you remember?' he said to her curiously, shunted onto that new train of thought. 'We walked out to Lookout Point together – I mean one after the next – but to meet, to talk in private? We went out separately, I mean – you know how it was then – that Russian couple had fought and been sent home – we all hid everything we could from the selection people!'

He laughed, choking somewhat, at the image of their deeply irrational beginnings. So apt! And everything since played out so in keeping with such a beginning! They had come out to Mars and replayed everything just as it had always been played before, it was nothing but trait recurrence, pattern repetition. 'We sat there and I thought we were getting on and I took your hand but you pulled it away, you didn't like it. I felt, I felt bad. We went back separately and didn't talk again like that, in that way, not ever. And then I hounded you through all this, I guess, and I thought it was because of the, the . . .' He waved at the blue sky.

'I remember,' she said.

She was looking cross-eyed at him. He felt the shock of it; one didn't get to do this, one never got to say to the lost love of one's youth I remember, it still hurts. And yet there she stood, looking at his face amazed.

'Yes,' she said. 'But that wasn't what happened,' she said, frowning. 'It was me. I mean, I put my hand on your shoulder, I liked you, it seemed like we might become . . . but you jumped! Ha, you jumped as if I had shocked you with a cattle prod! Static electricity was bad down there, but still — ' sharp laugh ' — no. It was you. You didn't – it wasn't your kind of thing, I figured. And it wasn't mine either! In a way it should have worked, just because of that. But it didn't. And then I forgot about it.'

'No,' Sax said.

He shook his head, in a primitive attempt to recast his thought, to re-remember. He could still see in his mental theatre that awkward instant at Lookout Point, the whole thing clear almost word for word, move for move, it's a net gain in order, he had said, trying to explain the purpose of science; and she had said, for that you would destroy the entire face of a planet. He remembered it.

But there was that look on Ann's face as she recalled the incident, that look of someone in full possession of a moment of her past, alive with the upwelling – clearly she remembered it too – and yet remembered something different than he had. One of them had to be wrong, didn't they? Didn't they?

'Could we really,' he said, and had to stop and try again. 'Could we really have been two such maladroit people as to

733

both go out – intending to – to reveal ourselves — '

Ann laughed. 'And both go away feeling rebuffed by the other?' She laughed again. 'Why sure.'

He laughed as well. They turned their faces to the sky and laughed.

But then Sax shook his head, rueful to the point of agony. Whatever had happened – well. No way of knowing, now. Even with his memory upwelling like an artesian fountain, like one of the cataclysmic outbreak floods themselves, there was still no way to be sure what had really happened.

Which gave him a sudden chill. If he could not trust these upwelling memories to be true – if one so crucial as this one was now cast in doubt – what then of the others, what about Hiroko there in the storm, leading him to his car, hand on his wrist – could that too be . . . No. That hand on his wrist. But Ann's hand *had* jerked away from him, a somatic memory just as solidly real, just as physical, a kinetic event remembered in his body, in the pattern of cells for as long as he should live. That one had to be true; they both had to be true.

And so?

So that was the past. There and not there. His whole life. If nothing was real but this moment, Planck instant after Planck instant, an unimaginably thin membrane of becoming between past and future – his life – what then was it, so thin, so without any tangible past or future: a blaze of colour. A thread of thought lost in the act of thinking. Reality so tenuous, so barely there; was there nothing they could hold to?

He tried to say some of this, stammered, failed, gave up.

'Well,' Ann said, apparently understanding him. 'At least we remember that much. I mean, we agree that we went out there. We had ideas, they didn't work out. Something happened that we probably neither understood at the time, so it's no surprise we can't remember it properly now, or that we recall it differently. We have to understand something to remember it.'

'Is that true?'

'I think so. It's why two-year-olds can't remember. They feel things like crazy, but they don't remember them because they don't really understand them.'

'Perhaps.'

He wasn't sure that was how memory worked. Early child-hood memories were eidetic images, like exposed photographic plates. But if it was true, then he was perhaps all right; for he had definitely understood Hiroko's appearance in the storm, her hand on his wrist. These things of the heart, in the violence of the storm . . .

Ann stepped forward and gave him a hug. He turned his face to the side, his ear pressed against her collarbone. She was tall. He felt her body against his, and he hugged her back, hard. You will remember this forever, he thought. She held him away from her, held him by the arms. 'That's the past,' she said. 'It doesn't explain what happened between us on Mars, I don't think. It's a different matter.'

'Perhaps.'

'We haven't agreed, but we had the same – the same terms. The same things were important to us. I remember when you tried to make me feel better, in that boulder car in Marineris, during the outbreak flood.'

'And you me. When Maya was yelling at me, after Frank died.'

'Yes,' she said, thinking back. Such power of recall they had in these amazing hours! That car had been a crucible, they had all metamorphosed in it, in their own ways. 'I suppose I did. It wasn't fair, you were just trying to help her. And that look on your face . . .'

They stood there, looking back at the scattering of low struc-tures that was Underhill.

'And here we are,' Sax said finally.

'Yes. Here we are.'

Awkward instant. Another awkward instant. This was life with the other: one awkward instant after the next. He would have to get used to it, somehow. He stepped back. He reached out and held her hand, squeezed it hard. Then let go. She wanted to walk out past Nadia's arcade, she said, into the untouched wilderness west of Underhill. She was experiencing a rush of memory too strong to concentrate on the present. She needed to walk.

He understood. Off she went, with a wave. With a wave! And there was Coyote, over there near the salt pyramids so brilliant in the afternoon light. Feeling Mars's gravity for the first time in decades, Sax hopped over to the little man. The only one of the First Hundred's men who had been shorter than Sax. His brother in arms.

Stumbling here and there through his life, step by step shocked elsewhere, it was actually quite difficult to focus on Coyote's asymmetrical face, faceted like Deimos – but there it was, most vibrantly there, pulsing it seemed with all its past shapes as well. At least Desmond had more or less resembled himself throughout. God knew what Sax looked like to the others, or what he would see if he looked in a mirror – the idea was dizzying, it might even be interesting to test it, look in a mirror while remembering something from his youth, the view might distort. Desmond, a Trinidadian of Indian descent, now saying something difficult to comprehend, something about rapture of the deep, unclear if he was referring to the memory drug or to some nautical incident from his youth. Sax wanted so much to tell him that Hiroko was alive, but just as the words were on the tip of his tongue, he stopped himself. Desmond looked so happy at this moment; and he would not believe Sax. So it would only upset him. Knowledge by experience is not always translatable into discursive knowledge, which was a shame, but there it was. Desmond would not believe him because he had not felt that hand on his wrist. And why should he, after all?

They walked out toward Chernobyl, talking about Arkady and Spencer. 'We're getting old,' Sax said.

Desmond hooted. He still had a most alarming laugh – infectious, however, and Sax laughed too. '*Getting* old? *Getting* old?'

The sight of their little Rickover put them into paroxysms. Though it was pathetic as well, and brave, and stupid, and clever. Their limbic systems were overloaded still, Sax noted, jangling with all the emotions at once. All his past was coming clearer and clearer, in a kind of simultaneous overlay of sequences, each event with its unique emotional charge, now firing all at once: so full, so full. Perhaps fuller than the, the what, the mind? the soul? Fuller than it was capable of being.

Overflowing, yes, that was the way it felt. 'Desmond, I'm overflowing.'

Desmond only laughed harder.

His life had exceeded his capacity to feel it all at once. Except what was this, then, this feeling? A limbic hum, the roaring hum of the wind in conifers high in the mountains, lying in a sleeping bag at night in the Rockies, with the wind thrumming through the pine needles ... Very interesting. Possibly an effect of the drug, which would pass, although he was hoping that there were effects of the drug that would last, and who could say if this aspect might not as well, as an integral part of the whole? Thus: if you can remember your past, and it is very long, then you will necessarily feel very full, full of experiences and emotions, perhaps to the point where it might not be easy to feel much more. Wasn't that possible? Or perhaps everything would feel more intensely than was appropriate; perhaps he had inadvertently turned them all into horribly sentimental people, stricken with grief if they stepped on an ant, weeping with joy at the sight of sunrise, etc. That would be unfortunate. Enough was enough, or more than enough. Enough was as good as a feast. In fact Sax had always believed that the amplitude of emotional response exhibited in the people around him could be turned down a fair bit with no great loss to humanity. Of course it wouldn't work to try consciously to damp one's emotions, that was repression, sublimation, with a resulting overpressure elsewhere. Curious how useful Freud's steam-engine model of the mind remained, compression, venting, the entire apparatus, as if the brain had been designed by James Watt. But reductive models were useful, they were at the heart of science. And he had needed to blow off steam for a long time.

So he and Desmond walked around Chernobyl, throwing rocks at it, laughing, talking in a halting rush and flow, not so much a conversation as a simultaneous transmission, as they were both absorbed by their own thoughts. Thus very dislocated talk, but companionable nevertheless, and reassuring to hear someone else sounding so confused. And altogether a great pleasure to feel so close to this man, so different from him in so many ways, and yet now babbling together with him about school, the snowscapes of the southern polar region,

737

the parks in the *Ares*: and they were so similar anyway.

'We all go through the same things.'

'It's true! It's true!'

Curious that this fact didn't affect people's behaviour more. Eventually they wandered back to the trailer park, slowing down as they passed through it, held by ever thickening cobwebs of past association. It was near sunset. In the barrel-vaults people were milling around, working on dinner. Most had been too distracted to eat during the day, and the drug appeared to be a mild appetite suppressant; but now people were famished. Maya had been cooking a big pot of stew, chopping and peeling potatoes and throwing them in. Borsch? Bouillabaisse? She had had the forethought to start a breadmaker in the morning, and now the yeasty smell filled the warm air of the barrel-vaults.

They congregated in the large double vault at the southwest corner, the room where Sax and Ann had had their famous debate at the beginning of the formal terraforming effort. With luck this would not occur to Ann when she came in. Except that a videotape of the debate was playing on a small screen in the corner. Oh well. She would arrive soon after dark, in her old way; this constancy was a pleasure to all of them. It made it possible in some sense to say Here we are – the others are away tonight – otherwise everything is the same. An ordinary night in Underhill. Talk about work, the various sites – food – the old familiar faces. As if Arkady or John or Tatiana might walk in any second, just as Ann was now, right on time, stamping her feet to warm them, ignoring the others – just as always.

But she came and sat beside him. Ate her meal (a Provençal stew that Michel used to make) beside him. In her customary silence. Still, people stared. Nadia watched them with tears in her eyes. Permanent sentimentality: it could be a problem.

Later, under the clatter of dishes and voices, everyone seemingly talking at once – and sometimes it seemed possible also to understand everyone all at once, even while speaking – under that noise, Ann leaned into him and said,

'Where are you going after this?'

'Well,' he said, suddenly nervous again, 'some Da Vinci colleagues invited me to, to, to – to *sail*. To try out a new

738

boat they've designed for me, for my, my sailing trips. A sailboat. On Chryse – on Chryse *Gulf*.'

'Ah.'

Terrible silence, despite all the noise.

'Can I come with you?'

Burning sensation in the skin of the face; capillary engorgement; very odd. But he must remember to speak! 'Oh yes.'

And then everyone sitting around, thinking, talking, remembering. Sipping Maya's tea. Maya looked content, taking care of them. Much later, well into the middle of the night, with almost everyone still slumped in a chair, or hunched over the heater, Sax decided he would go over to the trailer park, where they had spent their first few months. Just to see.

Nadia was already out there, lying down on one of the mattresses. Sax pulled down another one from the wall; his old mattress, yes. And then Maya was there, and then all the rest of them, pulling along the reluctant and one had to say fearful Desmond, sitting him on a mattress in the middle, gathering around him, some in their old spots, others who had slept in other trailers filling the empty mattresses, the ones that had been occupied by people now gone. A single trailer now housed them all quite easily. And some time in the depth of the night they all lay down, and slid down the slow, uneven glide into sleep. All around the room, people falling to sleep in their beds – and that too was a memory, drowsy and warm, this was how it had always felt, to drift off in a bath of one's friends, weary with the day's work, the oh-so-interesting work of building a town and a world. Sleep, memory, sleep, body; fall thankfully into the moment, and dream.

They sailed out of the Florentine on a windy, cloudless day, Ann at the rudder and Sax up in the starboard bow of the sleek new catamaran, making sure the anchor cat had secured the anchor; which reeked of anaerobic bottom mud, so much so that Sax got distracted and spent some time hanging over the rail looking at samples of the mud through his wristpad magnifying lens: a great quantity of dead algae and other bottom organisms. An interesting question whether or not this was typical of the North Sea's bottom, or was restricted for some reason to the Chryse Gulf environs, or to the Florentine, or shallows more generally —

'Sax, get back here,' Ann called. 'You're the one who knows how to sail.'

'So I am.'

Though in truth the boat's AI would do everything at the most general command; he could say for instance, 'Go to Rhodos,' and there would be nothing more to be done for the rest of the week. But he had grown fond of the feeling of a tiller under his hand. So he abandoned the anchor's muck to another time, and made his way to the wide shallow cockpit suspended between the two narrow hulls.

'Da Vinci is about to go under the horizon, look.'

'So it is.'

The outer points of the crater rim were the only parts of Da Vinci Peninsula still visible over the water, though they weren't more than twenty kilometres away. There was an intimacy to a small globe. And the boat was very fast; it hydroplaned in any wind over fifty kilometres an hour, and the hulls had underwater outrigger keels that extended and set in various dolphinlike shapes, which along with sliding counterbalance weights in the cross-struts kept the windward hull in contact with the water, and the leeward hull from driving too far under. So in even moderate winds, like the one striking their unfurled mastsail now, the boat shoved up onto the water and skated over it like an iceboat over ice, moving at a speed just a few per cent slower than the wind itself. Looking over the stern Sax could see that a very small percentage of the hulls were actually in contact with the water; it looked as if the rudder and the outrigger keels were the only things that kept them from taking flight. He saw the last bits of Da Vinci disappear, under a bouncing, serrated horizon no more than four kilometres away from them. He glanced at Ann; she was clutching the rail, looking back at the brilliant white V-tapestries of their wake. Sax said, 'Have you been at sea before?' meaning, entirely out of the sight of land.

'No.'

'Ah.'

They sailed on north, out into Chryse Gulf. Copernicus Island appeared over the water to their right, then Galileo Island behind it. Then both receded under the blue horizon again. The swells on the horizon were individually distinct, so that the horizon was not a straight blue line against the sky, but rather a shifting array of swell tops, one after another in swift succession. The groundswell was coming out of the north, almost directly ahead of them, so that looking to port or starboard the horizon line was particularly jagged, a wavy line of blue water against the blue sky, in a too-small circle surrounding the ship – as if the proper Terran distance to the horizon were stubbornly embedded in the brain's optics, so that when they saw things clearly here, they would always appear to stand on a planet too small for them. Certainly there was a look of the most extreme discomfort on Ann's face; she glared at the waves, groundswell after groundswell lifting the bow and then the stern. There was a crosschop nearly at right angles to the groundswell, pushed by the west wind and ruffling the bigger broader swells. Wavetank physics; one could see it all laid out; it reminded Sax of the physics lab on the second storey of the northeasternmost building in his high school, where hours had passed like minutes, the flat little wavetank full of marvels. Here the groundswell originated in the North Sea's perpetual eastward motion around the globe; the swell was greater or smaller depending on whether local winds reinforced it or interfered with it. The light gravity made for big, broad waves, quickly generated by strong winds; if today's wind got very much stronger, for instance, then the windchop from the west would quickly grow bigger than the groundswell from the north, and obscure it completely. Waves on the North Sea were notorious for their size and mutability, their recombinant surprises, though it was also true that they moved fairly slowly through the water; big slow hills, like the giant dunes of Vastitas far underneath them, migrating around the planet. Sometimes they could get very big indeed; in the aftermath of the typhoons that blew over the North Sea, waves seventy metres high had been reported.

This lively crosschop seemed enough for Ann, who was looking a bit distressed. Sax could not think what to say to her. He doubted that his thoughts on wave mechanics would be appropriate, though it was very interesting of course, and would be to anyone interested in the physical sciences. As Ann was. But perhaps not now. Now the sheer sensory array of water, wind, sky – it looked as if it was enough for her. Perhaps silence was in order.

Whitecaps began to roll down the faces of some of the crosschop waves, and Sax immediately checked into the ship's weather system to see what the windspeed was. The ship had it at thirty-two kilometres per hour. So this was about the speed at which the crests of waves were first knocked over. A simple matter of surface tension against windspeed, calculable, in fact . . . yes, the appropriate equation in fluid dynamics suggested they should start to collapse at a windspeed of thirty-five kilometres per hour, and here they were: whitecaps, startlingly white against the water, which was a dark blue, Prussian blue, Sax thought it might be. The sky today was almost sky blue, slightly empurpled at the zenith, and somewhat whitened around the sun, with a metallic sheen between the sun and the horizon under it.

'What are you doing?' Ann said, sounding annoyed.

Sax explained, and she listened in stony silence. He didn't know what she might be thinking. That the world was somewhat explicable – he always found that a comfort. But Ann . . . well, it could be as simple as seasickness. Or something from her past, distracting her; Sax had found in the weeks since the experiment at Underhill that he was often distracted by some past incident, rising unbidden from a great bulk of them in his mind. Involuntary memory. And for Ann, that might include negative incidents of one kind or another; Michel had said she had been mistreated as a child. It still seemed to Sax too shocking to believe. On Earth men had abused women; on Mars, never. Was that true? Sax did not know for sure, but he felt it was true. This was what it meant to live in a just and rational society, this was one of the main reasons it was a good thing, a value. Possibly Ann would know more about the reality of the situation these days. But he did not feel comfortable asking her. It was clearly contraindicated.

'You're awfully quiet,' she said.

'Enjoying the view,' he said quickly. Perhaps he had better talk about wave mechanics after all. He explained the groundswell, the crosschop, the negative and positive interference patterns that could result. But then he said, 'Did you remember much about Earth, during the Underhill experiment?'

'No.'

'Ah.'

This was probably some kind of repression, and exactly the opposite of the psychotherapeutic method that Michel would probably have recommended. But they were not steam engines. And some things were no doubt better forgotten. He would have to work on once again forgetting John's death, for instance; also on remembering better those parts of his life when he had been most social, as during the years of work for Biotique in Burroughs. So that across the cockpit from him sat Counter-Ann, or that third woman she had mentioned – while he was, at least in part, Stephen Lindholm. Strangers, despite that startling encounter at Underhill. Or because of it. Hello; nice to meet you.

Once they got out from among the fjords and islands at the bottom of Chryse Gulf, Sax turned the tiller and the boat swooped northeast, rushing across the wind and the whitecaps. Then the wind was behind them, and with a following wind the mastsail bloomed into its own splayed-wing version of a spinnaker, and the hulls surfed on the mushy crests of the waves before losing to their superior speed. The eastern shore of the Chryse Gulf appeared before them; it was less spectacular than the western shore, but in many ways prettier. Buildings, towers, bridges: it was a well-populated coast, as were most of them these days. Coming off Olympus all the towns must be a bit of a shock.

After they passed the broad mouth of the Ares Fjord, Soochow Point emerged over the horizon, and then beyond it the Oxia Islands, one by one. Before the water's arrival these had been the Oxia Colles, an array of round hills that stood at just the height to become an archipelago. Sax sailed into the narrow waterways between these islands, each a low, round, brown hump, standing forty or fifty metres out of the sea. By far the larger percentage of them were uninhabited, except perhaps by goats, but on the largest ones, especially kidney-shaped ones with bays, the stones covering the hills had been gathered up into walls, which split the slopes into fields and pastures; these islands were irrigated, green with orchards laden with fruit, or pastures dotted with white sheep or miniature cows. The ship's maritime chart named these islands – Kipini, Wahoo, Wabash, Naukan, Libertad – and reading the map Ann snorted. 'These are the names of the craters out in the middle of the gulf, underwater.'

'Ah.'

Still, they were pretty islands. The fishing villages on the bays were whitewashed, with blue shutters and doors: the Aegean model again. Indeed, on one high point bluff there stood a little Doric temple, square and proud. The boats down below in the bays were small sloops, or simply rowing boats and dories. As they sailed past Sax pointed out a hilltop windmill here, a pasture of llamas there. 'It seems a nice life.'

They talked about the natives then, easily and without hidden tension. About Zo; about the ferals and their strange hunter-gatherer, city-shopper lifestyle; about the ag nomads, moving from crop to crop like migrant labourers who owned the farms; about the cross-fertilization of all these styles; about the new Terran settlements elbowing into the landscape; about the increasing number of harbour towns. Off in the middle of the bay, they spotted one of the new big townships, a floating island of a seacraft, with a population in the thousands; it was too big to enter the Oxia archipelago, and looked to be headed across the gulf to Nilokeras, or down to the southern fjords. As the land all over Mars was becoming more crowded, and the possibility of settling on it more and more restricted by the courts, more and more people were moving onto the North Sea, making townships like these their permanent home.

'Let's go and visit it,' Ann said. 'Can we?'

'I don't see why not,' Sax said, surprised at the request. 'We can certainly catch it.'

He brought the catamaran about and tacked south and west toward the township, pushing the cat as much as he could, to impress the seafarers. In less than an hour they had reached its broad side, a rounded scarp about two kilometres long and fifty metres tall. A dock just above the waterline had a section against the township that would rise, as an open elevator, and when they had stepped across from the cat to the dock and tied their boat on, they got into this railed-off section and were lifted up to the deck of the township.

The deck was almost as broad as it was long, its central area a farm with many small trees scattered on it, so that it was hard to see the other side. But it was clear from what they could see that the circumference of the deck was a kind of rectangular street or arcade, with buildings on both sides that were two to four storeys high, the outer buildings topped by masts and windmills, the inner ones opening into broad breaks where parks and plazas led inward to the crops and groves of the farm, and a big freshwater pond. A floating town, somewhat like a walled city in Renaissance Tuscany in appearance, except that everything was extraordinarily neat and orderly, shipshape as one might say. A small group of the ship's citizens greeted them on the plaza overlooking the dock, and when they found out who their visitors were they were thrilled – they insisted the travellers stay for a meal, and a few of them guided them on a walk around the perimeter of the ship, 'or for as far as you care to go, it's a good fair walk'.

This was a small township, they were told. Population, five thousand. Since its launch it had been almost entirely self-sufficient. 'We grow most of our food, and fish for the rest. There are arguments now with other townships about overfishing certain species. We're doing perennial polyculture, growing new strains of corn, sunflower, soybean, sand plum and so on, all intermixed and harvested by robot, because harvesting is backbreaking work. We've finally got the technology to go home to gathering, that's what it comes down to. There are a lot of onboard cottage industries. We've got wineries – see the vineyards out there – and there are vintners and brandy distillers. That we do by hand. Also special function semi-conductors, and a famous bike shop.'

'Most of the time we sail around the North Sea. There are some really violent storms sometimes, but we're so big that we ride them out pretty easily. Most of us have lived here for all ten years the ship has existed. It's a great life. The ship is all you need. Although it's great fun to make landfall from time to time. We come down to Nilokeras every Ls zero for the spring festival. We sell what we've made and resupply, and party all night long. Then back out to sea.'

'We don't use anything but wind and sunlight, and some fish. The environmental courts like us, they agree we're minimum impact. The population of the North Sea's area might be even higher now than if it had stayed land. There are hundreds of townships now.'

'Thousands. And the harbour towns with the shipyards, and the seaports we visit to do business, they're doing very well indeed.'

Ann said, 'And you think this is one way we can take on some of Earth's surplus population.'

'Yes, we do. One of the best ways. It's a big ocean, it could take a lot more ships like this.'

'As long as they didn't rely too much on fishing.'

As they walked on, Sax said to Ann, 'That's another reason that it just isn't worth it to force a crisis over the immigration issue.'

Ann didn't reply. She was staring down at the sun-burnished water, then up at one of the couple of dozen masts, each with its single schooner sail. The town looked like a tabular iceberg with its surface entirely claimed by earth. A floating island.

'So many different kinds of nomads,' Sax commented. 'It seems that very few of the natives feel impelled to settle in a single place.'

'Unlike us.'

'Point taken. But I wonder if this tendency means they are inclined to a certain Redness. If you know what I mean.'

'I do not.'

Sax tried to explain. 'It seems to me that nomads in general tend to make use of the land as they find it. They move around with the seasons, and live off what they find growing at that time. And seafaring nomads of course even more so, given that the sea is impervious to most human attempts to change it.'

'Except for the people trying to regulate sea level, or salt content. Have you heard about them?'

'Yes. But they're not going to have much luck with that, I would guess. The mechanics of saltification are still very poorly understood.'

'If they succeed it will kill a lot of freshwater species.'

'True. But the saltwater species will be happy.'

They walked across the middle of the township toward the plaza over the dock, passing between long rows of grapevines pruned to the shape of waist-high Ts, the intermingled horizontal vines heavy with grape clusters of dusty indigo, bracken and clear viridine. Beyond the vineyards the ground was covered with a mix of plants, like a kind of prairie, with narrow foot-trails cutting through it.

At a restaurant fronting the plaza they were treated to a meal of pasta and prawns. The conversation ranged everywhere. But then someone came rushing out of the kitchen, pointing at his wrist: news had just come in of trouble on the space elevator. The UN troops who had been sharing the customs duties on New Clarke had taken over the whole station, and sent all the Martian police down, charging them with corruption and declaring that the UN would administer the upper end of the elevator by itself from now on. The UN's Security Council was now saying that their local officers had overstepped their instructions, but this backpedalling did not include an invitation to the Martians to come back up the cable again, so it looked like a smokescreen to Sax. 'Oh my,' he said. 'Maya will be very angry, I fear.'

Ann rolled her eyes. 'That isn't really the most important ramification, if you ask me.' She looked shocked, and for the first time since Sax had found her in Olympus caldera, fully engaged in the current situation. Drawn out of her distance. It was fairly shocking, now that he thought of it. Even these seafarers were visibly shaken, though before they like Ann had seem distanced from whatever circumstances obtained on land. He could see the news tearing through the restaurant's conversations, and throwing them all into the same space: upheaval, crisis, the threat of war. Voices were incredulous, faces were angry.

The people at their table were also watching Sax and Ann, curious as to their reaction. 'You'll have to do something about this,' one of their guides noted.

'Why us?' Ann replied tartly. 'It's you who will have to do something about it, if you ask me. You're the ones responsible now. We're just a couple of old issei.'

Their dinner companions looked startled, uncertain how to take her. One laughed. The host who had spoken shook his head. 'That's not true. But you're right, we will be watching, and talking with the other townships about how to respond. We'll do our part. I was just saying that people will be looking to you, to both of you, to see what you do. That isn't so true for us.'

Ann was silenced by this. Sax returned to his meal, thinking furiously. He found he wanted to talk to Maya.

The evening continued, the sun fell; the dinner limped on, as they all tried to return to some sense of normality. Sax repressed a little smile; there might be an interplanetary crisis and there might not, but meanwhile dinner had to be got through in style. And these seafarers were not the kind of people who looked inclined to worry about the solar system at large. So the mood rallied, and they partied over their dessert, still very pleased to have Clayborne and Russell visiting them. And then in the last light the two of them made their excuses, and were escorted down to sea level and their boat. The waves on Chryse Gulf were a lot larger than they had seemed from up above.

Sax and Ann sailed off in silence, wrapped in their own thoughts. Sax looked back up at the township, thinking about what they had seen that day. It looked like a good life. But something about . . . he chased the thought, and then at the end of the rapid steeplechase he caught it, and still held it all: no blankouts these days. Which was a great satisfaction, although the content of this particular train of thought was quite melancholy. Should he even try to share it with Ann? Was it possible to say it?

He said, 'Sometimes I regret – when I see those seafarers, and the lives they lead – it seems ironic that we – that we stand on the brink of a – of a kind of golden age —' There, he had said it; and felt foolish; ' — which will only come to pass when our generation has died. We've worked for it all our lives, and then we have to die before it will come.'

'Like Moses outside Israel.'

'Yes? Did he not get to go in?' Sax shook his head. 'These old stories —' Such a throwing together, like science at its heart, like the flashes of insight one got into an experiment when everything about it clarified, and one understood something. 'Well, I can imagine how he felt. It's – it's frustrating. I would rather see what happens then. Sometimes I get so *curious*. About the history we'll never know. The future after our death. And all the rest of it. Do you know what I mean?'

Ann was looking at him closely. Finally she said, 'Everything dies someday. Better to die thinking that you're going to miss a golden age, than to go out thinking that you had taken down your children's chances with you, that you'd left your descendants with all kinds of toxic long-term debts. Now that would be depressing. As it is, we only have to feel bad for ourselves.'

'True.'

And this was Ann Clayborne talking. Sax felt that his face was glowing. That capillary action could be quite a pleasant sensation.

They returned to the Oxia archipelago and sailed through the islands, talking about them. It was possible to talk. They ate in the cockpit, and slept each in their own hull cabin, port and starboard. One fresh morning, with the wind wafting offshore cool and fragrant, Sax said, 'I still wonder about the possibility of some kind of Browns.'

Ann glanced at him. 'And where's the Red in it?'

'Well, in the desire to hold things steady. To keep a lot of the land untouched. The areophany.'

'That's always been Green. It sounds like Green with just a little touch of Red, if you ask me. The Khakis.'

'Yes, I suppose. That would be Irishka and the Free Mars coalition, right? But also Burnt Umbers, Siennas, Madder Alizarins, Indian Reds.'

'I don't think there are any Indian Reds.' And she laughed darkly.

Indeed she laughed fairly often, though the humour expressed seemed often quite mordant. One evening he was in his cabin, and she up near the bow of her hull (she took the port, he the starboard) and he heard her laugh out loud, and coming up and looking around, he thought it must have been caused by the sight of Pseudophobos (most people just called it Phobos), rising again swiftly out of the west, in its old manner. The moons of Mars, sailing through the night again, little grey potatoes of no great distinction, but there they were. As was that dark laugh at the sight of them.

'Do you think this takeover of Clarke is serious?' Ann asked one night as they were retiring to their hulls.

'It's hard to say. Sometimes I think it must be a threatening gesture only, because if it's serious it would be so – unintelligent. They must know that Clarke is very vulnerable to – removal from the scene.'

'Kasei and Dao didn't find it that easy to remove.'

'No, but —' Sax did not want to say that their attempt had been botched, but he was afraid that she would read the comment out of his silence. 'We in Da Vinci set up an X-ray laser complex in Arsia Mons caldera, buried behind a rock curtain in the north wall, and if we set it off the cable will be melted right at about the areosynchronous point. There isn't a defensive system that could stop it.'

Ann stared at him; he shrugged. He wasn't personally responsible for Da Vinci actions, no matter what people thought.

'But bringing down the cable,' she said, and shook her head. 'It would kill a lot of people.'

Sax remembered how Peter had survived the fall of the first cable, by jumping out into space. Rescued by chance. Perhaps Ann was less likely to write off the lives that would inevitably be lost. 'It's true,' he said. 'It isn't a good solution. But it could be done, and I would think the Terrans know that.'

'So it may just be a threat.'

'Yes. Unless they're prepared to go further.'

North of the Oxia archipelago they passed McLaughlin Bay, the eastern side of a drowned crater. North of it was Mawrth Point, and behind it the inlet to Mawrth Fjord, one of the narrowest and longest fjords of all. It was a matter of constant tacking to sail up it, pushed this way and that by tricky winds, swirling between steep, convolute walls; but Sax did it anyway, because it was a pretty fjord, at the bottom of a very deep and narrow outbreak channel, widening as one sailed farther into it; and beyond and above the end of the water, the rock-floored canyon continued inland for as far as one could see, and many kilometres beyond that. He hoped to show Ann that the existence of the fjords did not necessarily mean the drowning of all the outbreak channels; Ares and Kasei also retained very long canyons above sea level, and Al Qahira and Ma'adim as well. But he said nothing of this, and Ann made no comment.

After the manoeuvring in Mawrth, he sailed them almost directly west. To get out of the Chryse Gulf into the Acidalia region of the North Sea, it was necessary to work around a long arm of land called the Sinai Peninsula, sticking out into the ocean from the west side of Arabia Terra. The strait beyond it connecting Chryse Gulf with the North Sea was five hundred kilometres wide; but it would have been fifteen hundred kilometres wide if it were not for the Sinai Peninsula.

So they sailed west into the wind, day after day, talking or not talking. Many times they came back to what it might mean to be Brown. 'Perhaps the combination should be called Blue,' Ann said one evening, looking over the side at the water. 'Brown isn't very attractive, and it reeks of compromise. Maybe we should be thinking of something entirely new.'

'Maybe we should.'

At night after dinner, and some time looking at the stars swimming over the sloppy sea surface, they said goodnight, and Sax retired to the starboard hull cabin, Ann to the port; and the AI sailed them slowly through the night, dodging the occasional icebergs that began to appear at this latitude, pushed into the gulf from the North Sea. It was quite pleasant.

One morning Sax woke early, stirred by a strong swell under the hull, which pitched his narrow bed up and down in a way that his dreaming mind had interpreted as a giant pendulum, swinging them this way and that. He dressed with some difficulty and went abovedeck, and Ann, standing at the halyards, called out, 'It seems the groundswell and the wind-chop are in a positive interference pattern!'

'Are they!' He tried to join her, and was slammed down into a cockpit seat by a sudden rise of the boat. 'Ah!'

She laughed. He grabbed the cockpit handrail, pulled himself up to her side. He saw immediately what she meant; the wind was strong, perhaps sixty-five kilometres per hour, and the whine in the boat's minimal rigging was loud and sustained. There were whitecaps everywhere on the blue sea, and the sound of the wind coursing through all that broken water was very unlike what it would be pouring over rock – there it would be a high, keening shriek – here, among the trillions of bursting bubbles, it was a deep, solid roar. Every wave was whitecapped, and the great hills of the groundswells were obscured by foam flying off the crests and rolling in the troughs. The sky was a dirty, opaque, raw umber, very ominous-looking, the sun a dim old coin, everything else dark, as if in shadow, though there were no clouds. Fines in the air: a dust storm. And now the waves were picking up, so that they spent many long seconds shooting up the side of one, then almost as many schussing down into the trough of the next one. Up and down in a long rhythm. The positive interference Ann had spoken of made some waves doubly big. The water not foaming was turning the colour of the sky, brownish and dull, dark, though there was still not a cloud to be seen – only this ominous colour; not the old pink, but more like the dust-choked air of the Great Storm. The whitecaps ceased in their area and the sound of water against the boat grew louder, a slushy rumble; the sea here was coated with frazil ice, or the thicker elastic layer of ice crystals called nilas. Then the whitecaps returned, twice as thick as before.

Sax climbed down into the cockpit and checked the weather report on the AI. A katabatic wind was pouring down Kasei Vallis and onto Chryse Gulf. A howler, as the Kasei flyers would say. The AI should have warned them. But like many katabatic storms it had come up in an hour, and was still a fairly local phenomenon. Yet strong for all that; the boat was on a roller coaster ride, shimmying under hammerblows of air as it shot up and down on the huge groundswell. To the side the waves looked as if they were being knocked over by the wind, but the boat's skittering flights up and down showed that they underlay the flying foam as big as ever. Overhead, the mastsail had contracted almost to a pole, in the shape of an aerodynamic foil. Sax leaned over to check the AI more closely; the volume knob on the beeper was turned all the way down. So perhaps it had tried to warn them after all.

A squall at sea; they came up fast. Horizons only four kilometres away didn't help matters; and the winds on Mars had never slowed down much, in all the years of thickening. Underfoot, the boat shuddered as it smashed through some invisible fragments of ice. Brash ice now, it appeared, or the broken pancake ice of a sea surface that had been about to freeze over in the night; difficult to spot in all the flying foam. Occasionally he felt the impact of a larger chunk, bergy-bergs as sailors called them. These had come through the Chryse Strait on a current from the north; now they were being pushed against the lee shore of the southern side of the Sinai Peninsula. As they were too, for that matter.

They were forced to cover the cockpit with its clear shell, rolling up out of the decking and over to the other side. Under its waterproof cover they were immediately warmer, which was a comfort. It was going to be a true howler, Kasei Vallis serving as a conduit for an extremely powerful blast of air; the AI listed windspeeds at Santorini Island fluctuating between one hundred and eighty and two hundred and twenty kilometres an hour, winds which would not diminish much in speed as they crossed the Gulf. Certainly it was still a very strong wind, one hundred and sixty kilometres an hour at the masthead; the surface of the water was disintegrating now, crests flattened by gusts, torn apart. The ship was shutting down in response to all that, mast retracting, cockpit covered, hatches battening; then the sea anchor went out, a tube of material like a windsock, dragging underwater upwind of them, slowing their drift to leeward, and mitigating the jarring impacts against small icebergs that were becoming more frequent as they all clustered against the lee shore. Now with the sea anchor in place, the brash ice and bergy-bergs were floating downwind faster than they were, and knocking against the windward hull, even as the leeward hull still slammed against a thickening ice mass. Both hulls were mostly underwater; in effect the boat was becoming a kind of submarine, lying at the surface and just under it. The strength of the materials of the boat could sustain any shock that even a howler and a lee shore of icebergs could deliver; indeed they could sustain forces several magnitudes stronger. But the weak point, as Sax reflected as he was thrown hard against his seatbelt and shoulder harness, holding grimly to the tiller and his seatback, was their bodies. The catamaran lifted on a swell, dropped with a sickening swoop, crashed to a halt against a big berg; and he slammed breathlessly into the restraints. It seemed they might be in danger of being shaken to death, an unpleasant way to go, as he was beginning to understand. Internal organs damaged by seatbelts; but if they freed themselves they would be flung around the cockpit, into each other or into something sharp, until something broke or burst. No. It was not a tenable situation. Possibly the restraints he had seen on his bed's frame would be gentler, but the decelerations when the boat struck the ice mass were so abrupt that he doubted being horizontal would help much.

'I'm going to see if the AI can get us into Arigato Bay!' he shouted in Ann's ear. She nodded that she had heard. He shouted the instruction right into the AI's pickup, and the computer heard and understood, which was good, as it would have been hard to type accurately with the boat soaring and plunging and shuddering as it slammed into the ice. In all that jarring it was not possible to feel the boat's engine, which had been running all along, but a slight change in their angle to the groundswell convinced him that it was pushing harder as the AI tried to get them farther west.

Down near the point of the Sinai Peninsula, on the southern side, a large, inundated crater called Arigato made a round bay. The entrance of the bay was about 60° of the circle of the crater, facing southwest. The wind and waves were both also from the southwest; so the mouth of the bay, quite shallow, as it was a low part of the old crater rim, was bound to be broken water, a difficult crossing no doubt. But once inside the bay the groundswell would be cut off by that same rim, and both waves and wind much reduced, especially when they got behind the western cape of the bay. There they would wait out the howler, and be on their way again when it was over. In theory it was an excellent plan, although Sax worried about conditions in the mouth of the bay; the chart showed it was only ten metres deep, which was certain to cause the groundswells to break. On the other hand, in a boat that became a kind of submarine (and yet drawing less than two metres of water for all that) negotiating broken surf might not be much of a problem; just go with it. The AI appeared to consider his instructions within the realm of the possible. And indeed the boat had pulled in the sea anchor, and with its powerful little engines was making its way across the wind and waves toward the bay, which was not visible; nothing of the lee shore could be seen through the dirty air.

So they held to the cockpit railings and waited out the reach, speechless; there was little to say, and the booming howl of the howler made it difficult to communicate. Sax's hands and arms got very tired from holding on, but there was no help for that except to abandon the cockpit and go below and strap himself into his bed, which he did not want to do. Despite the discomfort, and the nagging worry about the bay entrance, it was an extraordinary experience to watch the wind pulverize the surface of the water the way it was.

A short while later (though the AI indicated it had been seventy-two minutes), he caught sight of land, a dark ridge over the whitecaps to the lee side of them. Seeing it meant they were probably too close to it, but there ahead it disappeared, and reappeared farther west: the entrance to Arigato Bay. The tiller shifted against his knee, and he noted a shift in the boat's direction. For the first time he could hear the hum of the little engines at the sterns of the two hulls. The jarring against the ice got rougher, and they had to hold on tight. Now the groundswells were getting taller, their crests torn off, but the bulk of every wave remaining, its face surging up as it encountered the sea bottom. And now he could see in the foam rolling over the water-ice chunks, and larger, bergy bits – clear, blue, jade, aquamarine – pitted, rough, glassy. A great deal of ice must have been driven against the lee shore ahead of them. If the bay mouth was choked with ice, and waves were breaking over the bar nevertheless, it would be a nasty passage indeed. And yet that looked as if it was what the situation would be. He shouted a question or two at the AI, but its replies were unsatisfactory. It seemed to be saying that the boat could sustain any shocks the situation could inflict, but that the engines could not drive it through pack ice. And in fact the ice was thickening rapidly; they seemed to be in the process of being enveloped by a loose mass of bergy bits, driven onshore by the wind from all over the gulf. Their grinding and knocking was now a big component of the overwhelming noise of the storm. Indeed it looked as if it would now be difficult to motor out of the situation, straight offshore into the wind and waves and out to sea. Not that he really wanted to be out there, tossed up and down on waves that were growing ever larger and more unruly; capsizing would be a very real possibility; but because of the unexpected density of ice inshore, it was beginning to look as if getting offshore had been their better option. Now closed to them. They were in for a hard pummelling.

Ann was looking uncomfortable in her restraints, holding to the cockpit rail for dear life, a sight that gave part of Sax's mind satisfaction: she showed no inclination to let go, none at all. In fact she leaned over so that she could shout in his ear, and he turned his head to listen.

'We can't stay here!' she shouted. 'When we tire – the impacts are going to tear us up – ah! – like dolls!'

'We can strap ourselves to our beds,' Sax shouted.

She frowned doubtfully. And it was true that those restraints might not be any better. He had never tried them out; and there was the problem of getting secured in them by oneself to consider. Amazing how loud the wind was – shrieking wind, roaring water, thunking ice. The waves were growing larger and larger; when the boat rose on their faces, it took them ten or twelve heartstopping seconds to shoot to the crests, and now when they got up there they saw chunks of ice being thrown clear of the waves, thrown off with the flying foam to crash down into their fellows below, and sometimes into the boat's hulls and decking, and even the clear, thin cockpit shell, with a force they could feel all through their bodies.

Sax leaned over to shout again in Ann's ear. 'I believe this is one of those situations in which we are meant to use the lifeboat function!'

'. . . lifeboat?' Ann said.

Sax nodded. 'The boat is its own lifeboat!' he shouted. 'It flies!'

'What do you mean?'

'It flies!'

'You're kidding!'

'No! It becomes a – a blimp!' He leaned over and put his mouth right to her ear. 'The hulls and the keels and the bottom of the cockpit empty their ballast. They fill with helium from tanks in the bow. And balloons deploy. They told me about it back in Da Vinci, but I've never seen it! I didn't think we'd be using it!' The boat could also become a submarine, they had said in Da Vinci, quite pleased with themselves at the new craft's versatility. But the ice packing against the lee shore made that option unavailable to them, something that Sax did not regret; for no particular reason, the idea of going down in the boat didn't appeal to him.

Ann pulled back to look at him, amazed at this news. 'Do you know how to fly it?' she shouted.

'No!'

Presumably the AI would take care of that. If they could get it into the air. Just a matter of finding the emergency release, of flicking the right toggles. He pointed at the control panel to mime this thought, then leaned forward to shout in her ear; her head swung in and banged his nose and mouth hard, and then he was blinking with bright pain, the blood running out of his nose like water from a tap. Impact just like the two planetesimals; he grinned and split his lip even wider, a painful mistake. He licked and licked, tasting his blood. 'I love you!' he shouted. She didn't hear him.

'How do we launch it?' Ann cried.

He indicated the control panel again, there beside the AI, the emergency board under a protective bar.

If they chose to try an escape by air, however, it would bring about a dangerous moment. Once they were moving at the wind's speed, of course, there would be very little force brought to bear on the boat, they would simply blimp along. But at the moment of lift-off, while they were still nearly stationary, the howler would tear hard at them. They would tumble, probably, and this might disable the balloons enough to cast the boat back into the ice-choked breakers, or onto the lee shore. He could see Ann thinking this through herself. Still – whatever happened, it was likely to be preferable to the bonejarring impacts that continued to rack them. It would be a temporary thing, one way or the other.

Ann looked at him, scowled at the sight of him; presumably he was a bloody mess. 'Worth a try!' she shouted.

So Sax detached the protection bar from the emergency panel, and with a final look at Ann – their eyes meeting, a gaze with some content he could not articulate, but which warmed him – he put his fingers on the switches. With luck the altitude control would be obvious when the time came. He wished he had spent more time flying.

As the boat rose up the foamy face of each wave, there came a nearly weightless moment at the top, just before the fall down into the next icy trough. In one of these moments Sax flicked the switches on the panel. The boat fell down the wave-back anyway, hit the growlers with its usual jar – then bounced right up and away, lifted, and tilted right over on its lee hull, so that they were hanging in their restraints. Balloons entangled no doubt, the next wave would capsize them and that would be that; but then the boat was dragging away over ice and water and foam, almost free of contact, rolling them head over heels in their restraints. A wild, tumbling interval, and then the boat righted itself, and began to swing back and forth like a big pendulum, side to side, front to back – oops – then all the way over again, topsy-turvy – then righted, and swinging again. Up up up, thrown this way and that, hold on – his shoulder harness came free and his shoulder slammed against Ann's, even though he had been pressed against her.

The tiller was bashing his knee. He held onto it. Another crash together and he held onto Ann, twisted in his seat and clutched her, and after that they were like Siamese twins, arms around each other's shoulders, in danger at every slam of breaking each other's bones. They looked at each other for a second, faces centimetres apart, blood on both of them from some cut or other, or no it was probably just from his nose. She looked impassive. Up they shot into the sky.

His collarbone hurt, where Ann's forehead or elbow had struck it. But they were flying, up and up in an awkward embrace. And as the boat was accelerated to something nearer the wind's speed, the turbulence lessened greatly. The balloons seemed to be connected by rigging to the top of the mast. Then just when Sax was beginning to hope for some kind of zeppelinlike stability, even to expect it, the boat shot straight up and began its horrible tumbling again. Updraught no doubt. They were probably over land by now, and it was all too possible they were being sucked up into a thunderhead, like a hail ball. On Mars there were thunderheads ten kilometres tall, often powered by howlers from far to the south, and balls of hail flew up and down in these thunderheads for a long time. Sometimes hail the size of cannonballs had come crashing down, devastating crops and even killing people. And if they were pulled up too high they might die of altitude, like those early balloonists in France, was it the Montgolfiers themselves it had happened to? Sax couldn't remember. Up and up, tearing through wind and red haze, no chance to see very far —

BOOM! He jumped and hurt himself against his seatbelt, came down hard. Thunder. Thunder banging around them, at what had to be well over one hundred and thirty decibels. Ann seemed limp against him, and he shifted sideways, reached up awkwardly and twisted her ear, trying to turn her head so he could see her face. 'Hey!' she cried, though it sounded to him like a whisper in the roar of the wind. 'Sorry,' he said, though he was sure she couldn't hear him. It was too loud to talk. They were spinning again, but without much centrifugal force. The boat was shrieking as the wind pushed it up; then they dived, and his eardrums hurt to bursting, he wiggled his jaw back and forth, back and forth. Then up again and they popped,

760

painfully. He wondered how high they would go; very possible they would die of thin air. Though maybe the Da Vinci techs had thought to pressurize the cockpit, who knew. It behoved him to try to understand the boat as blimp, or at least to master the altitude adjustment system. Not that there was much to be done against the force of such updraughts and downdraughts. Sudden rattle of hail against the cockpit shell. There were small toggles on the emergency panel; in a moment of less violent tumbling he was able to put his face down near the bar and read the display terminal embedded in it. Altitude . . . not obvious. He tried to calculate how high the boat would go before its weight caused it to level off. Hard when he wasn't actually sure of the boat's weight, or the amount of helium deployed.

Then some kind of turbulence in the storm tossed them again. Up, down, up; then down, for many seconds in a row. Sax's stomach was in his throat, or so it felt. His collarbone was an agony. Nose running or bleeding continuously. Then up. Gasping for air, too. He wondered again how high they were, and whether they were still ascending; but there was nothing to be seen outside the shell of the cockpit, nothing but dust and cloud. He seemed to be in no danger of fainting. Ann was motionless beside him, and he wanted to tug her ear again to see if she was conscious, but couldn't move his arm. He elbowed her side. She elbowed back; if he had elbowed her as hard as that, he would have to remember to go lighter next time. He tried a very gentle elbowing, and felt a less violent prod in return. Perhaps they could resort to Morse code, he had it learned as a boy for no reason at all, and now in his reborn memory he could hear it all, every dit and dot. But perhaps Ann had not learned it, and this was no time for lessons.

The violent ride went on for so long he couldn't estimate it: an hour? Once the noise lessened to the point at which they could shout to each other, which they did just because it could be done; there actually wasn't much to say.

'We're in a thunderhead!'

'Yes!'

Then she pointed down with one finger. Pink blurs below. And they were descending rapidly, his eardrums aching again.

Being spat out of the bottom of the cloud, as hail. Pink, brown, rust, amber, umber. Ah yes – the surface of the planet, looking not very different than it ever had from the air. Descent. He and Ann had come down in the same landing vehicle, he recalled, the very first time.

Now the boat was scudding along under the cloud's bottom, in falling hail and rain; but the helium might pull them back up into the cloud. He pushed down a likely toggle on the panel, and the boat began to descend. A pair of small toggles; manipulating them seemed to dip them forward or raise them up. Attitude adjustors. He pushed them both gently down.

They seemed to be descending. After a while it was clearer below. In fact they appeared to be over jagged ridges and mesas; that would be the Cydonia Mensa, on the mainland of Arabia Terra. Not a good place to land.

But the storm continued to carry them along, and soon they were east of Cydonia, out over the flat plains of Arabia. Now they needed to descend soon, before they were flung out over the North Sea, which might very well be as wild and ice-filled as Chryse had been. Below lay a patchwork of fields, orchards – irrigation canals and curving streams, lined by trees. It looked as if it had been raining a lot, there was water all over the surface of the land, in ponds, in canals, in little craters, and covering the lower parts of fields. Farmhouses clustered in little villages, only outbuildings in the fields – barns, equipment sheds. Lovely wet countryside, quite flat. Water everywhere. They were descending, but slowly. Ann's hands were a bluish white in the dim afternoon; and so were his.

He pulled himself together, feeling very weary. The landing would be important. He pushed down the adjustors hard.

Now they were descending more swiftly. They were being blown over a line of trees, then down, rapidly over a broad field. At the far end it was inundated, brown rainwater filling the furrows. Beyond the field stood an orchard, and a water landing would be perfect anyway; but they were moving horizontally quite fast, and still perhaps ten or fifteen metres over the field. He shoved the adjustors full forward and saw the underhulls tilt down like diving dolphins, and the boat tilted as well, and then the land came right up at them, brown water, big splash, white waves winging away to both sides, and they

762

were being dragged through muddy water until the boat skated right into a line of young trees, and stopped hard. Down the line of trees a group of children and a man were running toward them, their mouths all perfect round Os in their faces.

Sax and Ann struggled to a sitting position. Sax opened the cockpit shell. Brown water spilled in over the gunwale. A windy hazy day in the Arabian countryside. The water pouring in felt distinctly warm. Ann's face was wet and her hair stood out in stiff tufts, as if she had been electrocuted. She smiled a crooked smile. 'Nicely done,' she said.

PART FOURTEEN

Phoenix Lake

A gunshot, a bell rung, a choir singing counterpoint.

The third Martian revolution was so complex and non-violent that it was hard to see it as a revolution at all, at the time; more like a shift in an ongoing argument, a change in the tide, a punctuation of equilibrium.

The takeover of the elevator was the seed of the crisis, but then a few weeks later the Terran military came down the cable and the crisis flowered everywhere at once. On the shore of the North Sea, on a small indentation of the coast of Tempe Terra, a cluster of landers dropped out of the sky, swaying under parachutes or shimmering down on plumes of pale fire: a whole new colony, an unauthorized incursion of immigrants. This particular group was from Kampuchea; elsewhere on the planet other landers were descending, with settlers from the Philippines, Pakistan, Australia, Japan, Venezuela, New York. The Martians did not know how to respond. They were a demilitarized society, with no idea that something like this could ever happen, with no way to defend themselves. Or so they thought.

Once again it was Maya who pulled them into action, playing the wrist like Frank used to, calling everyone in the open Mars coalition and many others besides, orchestrating the general response. Come on, she said to Nadia. One more time. And so through the cities and villages the word spread, and people went down into the streets, or got on trains to Mangala.

On the coast of Tempe, the new Kampuchean settlers got out of their landers and went to the little shelters that had been dropped with them, just like the First Hundred, two centuries before. And out of the hills came people wearing furs, and carrying bows and arrows. They had red stone eye-teeth, and their hair was tied in topknots. Here, they said to the settlers, who had bunched before one of their shelters. Let us help you. Put those guns down. We'll show you where you are. You don't need that kind of shelter, it's an old design. That hill you see to the west is Perepelkin Crater. There are already apple and cherry orchards on the apron, you can take what you need. Look, here are the plans for a disc-house, *that's the best design for this coast. Then you'll need a marina, and some fishing boats. If you let us use your harbour we'll show you where the truffles grow. Yes, a disc-house, see, a Sattelmeier disc-house. It's lovely to live out in the open air. You'll see.*

All branches of the Martian government had met in the assembly hall in Mungala, to deal with the crisis. The Free Mars majority in the senate, and the executive council, and the global environmental court, all agreed that the illegal incursion of Terrans was an act of aggression the equivalent of war, which had to be responded to in kind. There were suggestions from the floor of the senate that asteroids could be directed at Terra, as bombs that would be diverted only if the immigrants returned home and the elevator went back to a system of dual supervision. It would only take one strike to have a KT event, and so on. UN diplomats on the scene pointed out that this was a sword that could cut both ways.

In these tense days there came a knock on the door of the assembly hall in Mangala, and in walked Maya Toitovna. She said, 'We want to speak.' Then she ushered in a crowd waiting outside, pushing them up onto the stage like an impatient sheepdog: first Sax and Ann, walking side by side; then Nadia and Art, Tariki and Nanao, Zeyk and Nazik, Mikhail, Vasili, Ursula and Marina, even Coyote. The ancient issei, come back to haunt the present moment, come back to take the stage and say what they thought. Maya pointed to the room's screens, which showed images of the outside of the building; the group on the stage now extended in an unbroken line through the halls of the building out onto the big central plaza facing the sea, where some half a million people were assembled. The city streets were also stuffed with people, watching screens to see what was happening in the assembly hall. And out in Chalmers Bay there sailed a fleet of townships like a startling new archipelago, with flags and banners waving from their masts. And in every Martian city the crowds were out, the screens were on. Everyone could see everyone else.

Ann went to the podium and said quietly that the government of Mars in recent years had broken both the law and the spirit of human compassion, by forbidding immigration

768

from Earth to Mars. The people of Mars did not want that. They needed a new government. This was a vote of no confidence. The new incursions of Terran settlers were also illegal, and unacceptable, but understandable; the government of Mars had broken the law first. And the number of new settlers in these incursions was no greater than the number of legitimate settlers who had been illegally barred from coming by the current government. Mars, Ann said, had to be open to Terran immigration as much as could be, given the physical constraints, for as long as the population surge years might last. The surge years would not last much longer. Their duty now to their descendants was to get through the last of these packed years in peace. 'Nothing on the table now is worth war. We have seen it, and we know.'

Then she looked over her shoulder at Sax, who stepped up to her next to the microphones. He said, 'Mars has to be protected.' The biosphere was new, its carrying capacity limited. It did not have the physical resources of Earth, and much of its empty land would of physical necessity have to stay empty. Terrans had to understand that, and not overwhelm local systems; if they did, Mars would be no use to anyone at all. Clearly there was a severe population problem on Earth, but Mars alone was not the solution. 'The Earth-Mars relationship has to be renegotiated.'

They began that renegotiation. They asked a UN representative to come up and explain the incursions. They argued and debated and expostulated; and shouted in each other's faces. Out in the outback, locals confronted settlers, and some of them on both sides threatened violence; and others stepped in and started talking, cajoling, scolding, wrangling, negotiating; and shouting in each other's faces. At any point in the process, in a thousand different places, things could have turned violent; many people were furious; but cooler heads prevailed. It remained, in most places, at the level of argument. Many feared this could not continue, many did not believe it possible; but it was happening, and the people in the streets saw it happening. They kept it happening. At some point, after all, the mutation of values has to express itself; and why not here, why not now? There were very few weapons on the planet, and it was hard to strike someone in the face,

769

or stick them with a pitchfork, when they were standing there arguing with you. This was the moment of mutation, history in the making, and they could see it right before them, in the streets and on the human hillsides and on the screens, history labile right there in their hands – and so they seized the moment, and wrenched it in a new direction. They talked themselves into it. A new government. A new treaty with Earth. A polycephalous peace. The negotiations would go on for years. Like a choir in counterpoint, singing a great fugue.

Eventually that cable was going to come back to haunt us, that's what I said all along. You did not, you loved the cable. The only complaint you had was that it was too slow. You can get to Earth faster than you can get to Clarke, you said. That's true, you can, it's ridiculous. But not the same as saying the cable was going to come back and haunt us, you have to admit. Waiter, hey waiter! We'll have tequilas all around, and some lime wedges. We were working the Socket when they came down, the inner chamber didn't have a chance but the Socket is a big building, I don't know if they had a plan and it didn't work or if they didn't have a plan at all, but by the time their third car came down the Socket was sealed off and they were the proud masters of a thirty-seven-thousand kilometre dead end. It was stupid. It was a nightmare, these foxes kept coming in and at night only, so that they looked like wolves only a lot faster. And they went right for the throat. A plague of rabid foxes, man, it was a nightmare. Like 2128 all over again, I don't know if that's true or not but there they were, Terran police in Sheffield, and when people heard they all came out into the streets, the streets were packed, really packed, I'm short and sometimes my face was squished right into people's backs or women's breasts. I heard about it from a neighbour in the next apartment only about five minutes after it happened, she had heard from a friend living out near the Socket. The response of the people to the takeover of the cable's lower facility was rapid and tumultuous. Those UN storm troopers didn't know what to make of us, a detachment tried to take over Hartz Plaza and we just flowed around them, moving out from in front of them but shoving in at the sides so that it was like a kind of vacuum pull. This snarling, foam-toothed, rabid demon at my throat, *it was a fucking nightmare. Took them right out to Rim Park and these goddamned starship troopers couldn't have moved a centimetre at that point, not without slaughtering thousands of people. People in the streets, that's the only thing governments are afraid of. Well, or term limits. Or free elections! Or assassination. Or being laughed at, ah, ha ha ha! And there were hook-ups to all the other cities and giant street parties in every one of them. We were in Lasswitz and everyone went down to the river park and stood with candles in their hand, so that cameras could shoot down from the Overlook and see this sea of candles, it was great. And Sax and Ann standing there together, it was amazing. Amazing. Unbelievable. They probably scared the UN to death saying each other's lines like that! The UN probably thought we had brain transfer devices all ready to zap them. What I liked was later when Peter called for a new election for the Red party leadership, and challenged Irishka to hold it right then and there on the wrist. Those party things are basically heavyweight challenges, mano a mano, if Irishka had refused to call a vote then she would have been finished anyway, so she had to call it no matter what, you should have seen the look on her face. We were in Sabishii when we heard the call for a Red vote and when Peter won we went wild, Sabishii was an instant festival. And Senzeni Na. And Nilokeras. And Hell's Gate. And Argyre Station, you should have seen it. Well, wait a second, it was only about a sixty forty vote, in Argyre Station it went crazy because there were so many Irishka backers spoiling for a fight. It's Irishka who saved Argyre Basin and every dry, low spot on this planet if you ask me, Peter Clayborne is just an old nisei, he never did anything. Waiter, waiter! Beers all around, weiss beers, bitte. Bringing food out to these little Terrans, didn't have any idea. Nirgal shaking hands with every one of them. So the doctor says, how do you know you've got the quick decline? It was a fucking nightmare. It was a surprise Ann working with Sax, that looked like a sell-out. Not if you had paid attention, they been travelling together and everything, you must have been on Venus or something. Or something. The Browns, the Blues, it's stupid. We shoulda done something like this a long time ago. Well, why worry so much, they're goners, there won't*

771

be a single one left in ten years. Don't be too sure about that. Don't be too happy about that, you're only a few years younger than them, you idiot. Oh it was a most interesting week, we have been sleeping in the parks, and everyone was most kind. Werteswandel, the Germans call it. They've got a word for everything. Bound to happen, that's evolution. We're all mutants at this point. Speak for yourself, Jack. Speak to the waiter. Six years! That's great news, I'm surprised you're sober. Oh I'm not, ah ha ha, I'm not! Little red people charging around on red ants, think they're helping out, whoops, right over the edge of the rim, better hope they're flying ants. No wonder I've been getting so many ants. So the man says, Well, Doc — Yes, and? That's the end of the joke, asshole, he only just gets to say, Well Doc and then he dies, quick decline get it? Very funny. That's right, it is funny! All right, all right, ha ha, it's not worth getting hot over it. Any time you have to threaten people to get them to laugh at your joke you have to consider it less than successful, okay? Fuck you. Oh clever. So anyway there we were when the troops kind of make like they want to go back to the Socket. They go at it very gently, single file behind a little electric hotel cart they got their hands on, and everyone moves a little and lets them go, and they were passing through us looking nervous, and then people were shaking their hands like they were all Nirgal at the gates, and asking them to stay, leaving them alone if they couldn't handle it, kissing them on the cheeks, leis piled up till they couldn't see over them. Right back into the Socket. And why not, since they made their point and threatened us enough for the goddamned traitor government to fold without a fight? This joker doesn't seem to understand the principles of jujitsu. Of what? What? Hey, just who the hell are you? I'm a stranger in town. What? What? Excuse me miz, could you bring us another round of kava? Well, yes, we're still trying to get it into the parts per billion range, but no luck yet. Don't give me Fassnacht, I hate Fassnacht, the worst day of the year to me, they killed Boone on Fassnacht. They firebombed Dresden on Fassnacht. No end of evil to atone for. They were sailing in Chryse when a howler picked up their boat and threw it all the way over the Cydonia Mountains. That'll be the kind of experience that brings you closer

772

together. Oh please, who is this guy? It's no big deal – there's blimps every week get blown around a bit, it's no big deal. We got caught out in that same howler, but we were just outside Santorini, I mean to tell you, the water's surface was torn to smithereens to a depth of about ten metres, I'm not kidding. The boat we were in the AI got scared and took us under right down into another boat that was already down there, so we banged into this boat and it was like the end of the world, boom, everything dark, the AI went insane, scared it to death I swear. It probably just broke. Well I broke my collarbone. That'll be ten sequins please. Thanks. Those howlers are dangerous. I was in one in Echus and we all had to sit down on our butts and even then we were kind of scraping along. I had to hold onto my glasses or else they would have been torn right off my ears. Cars flipping like tiddlywinks. The whole marina cleared of every single boat, it was like some kid took his toy harbour and knocked it across the room. I too experienced this storm at its utmost fury. I was visiting the township Ascension, in the North Sea near Korolev Island. Hey that's where Will Fort surfs. Yes, here as I understand it the waves on Mars reach their greatest heights, and in this storm they towered a hundred metres from trough to crest, no, I do not jest. Waves much taller than the sides of the township, which on these dire rolling black hills appeared no larger than a lifeboat to those of us on it. We were a veritable cork. The animals were unhappy. And to compound our difficulties, we were being cast onto the south point of Korolev. The waves were breaking completely over the final cape into the sea beyond. So every time we rose up the gigantic face of each wave, the pilot of the Ascension turned the township south, and it slid across the face of the wave for some distance before losing the crest and falling back into the next trough. On each wave we moved a little faster and farther, for as we approached the point of the island the wave faces grew steeper and bigger. The very tip of the point curves off to the east, so that the waves were breaking left to right as we looked ahead, crashing onto the rocks and then onto the reef offshore. On our final wave the Ascension was pitched down the steep face of the wave. At the bottom of the face the pilot turned the township right, and the great raft made the cut at the bottom and drifted back up onto the face, moving across it at a speed we could not calculate. It was like flying. Yes – we were surfing a hundred-metre-high wave, on a raft as big as a village, just over the rocks of the reef below. For a second we flew in the tube of the breaking wave. Then we were out, onto the shoulder of the wave, which was back in deep water, and no longer breaking. And so we passed the island. So the doctor says, how do you know? How? So pretty. Yes, it was a moment to remember. I'm going to take my fund and retire, it just ain't the same any more. These people are thugs. Heard she went out on one of those starships, that's what I heard. You really saw her? You got to get you a better translator, I did not say, Never mind, Doctor, I am feeling better. What the hell kind of machine? Waiter! Villages just like the ones back home, except no caste. If they want caste they have to carry it in their heads. Some issei try but the nisei go feral. The way I heard it is that the little red people finally got sick of all the bullshit, and they were hot to do something having recently domesticated the red ant, and they started this whole campaign so that they could come charging to the rescue when the Terrans invaded. You might think they were being overconfident, but you have to remember that the biomass of red ants on this planet is closing in on a metre thick if averaged, so much damn biomass they're going to throw us out of orbit they should try ants on Mercury, and every ant has a whole tribe of the little people riding around on it in howdah cities or whatever, and so they weren't so overconfident after all. There's strength in numbers. So they deliberately made the government act stupid to spark this confrontation. I wondered what excuse those bastards had, they need an excuse, why it is that people go to Mangala and immediately turn into rapacious corrupt morons, it's a mystery to me. Went down for us. Why is it always the little red people, whatever happened to Big Man, I hate these little red people and their twee little folk tales, if you're going to be so stupid as to tell folk tales at all, the truth being much more interesting, then at least they could be big fucking tall tales, titans and gorgons duking it out with spiral galaxies like razor-edged boomerangs, zip, zip, zip! Hey, watch it there, slow down, guy, slow down. Waiter, get this motor mouth some kava, will you? He needs to mellow. Be calm, agitated sir. Be calm. Throwing nova bombs back and forth! Boom! Kapow! KA BOOM! Hey! Hey! Calm oneself, oh agitated one. I'm sick of these little people. Get your hands off me. It's a sorry excuse for a government anyway. It always gets back to the same damn thing, power-suckers sucking power. I told them to stick with tents, no global government, so there wouldn't be so much power to suck, but did they listen to me? They did not. You told them. Yeah, I told them, I was there. Nirgal, sure. Nirgal and I go way back. What do you mean, honoured old one, are you not the Stowaway? Why yes, I am. So you are Nirgal's father, you should go way back as you say. Yeah, well, in Zygote it didn't always work that way. I tell you that bitch pull the wool over your eyes your whole life if you let her. Have you living in a closet for years on end. Ah come on, you're not Coyote. Well what can I say? Not many people recognize me. And why should they? I bet he is. You can't be. If you're Nirgal's dad then why is he so tall and you're so short? I'm not short. Why are you laughing? I'm five feet five inches tall. Feet? Feet? Holy ka, here's a man measures his height in feet! In feet! Oh my God, you must be kidding, five feet? Feet? Hey, you look like it would take more feet than that, just how long were these feet? A foot was about a third of a metre, a little less. This is how they measured? A little less than a third of a metre? No wonder Earth is so fucked up. Hey, what makes you think your precious metre is so great, it's just some fraction of the distance from Earth's North Pole to its equator, Napoleon chose the fraction on a whim! It's a bar of metal in Paris France and its length was determined by the whim of a madman! Don't you be imagining you're more rational than the old ways. Oh stop, please, I'll die laughing, please. You people have very little respect for your elders, I like that. Hey, give the old Coyote another drink, what're you having? Tequila, thanks. And some kava. Oh oh! This guy knows how to live. That's right I do know how to live. These ferals got it figured out, as long as you don't take it too far. They're copying me but they've gone too far. Don't walk, drive. Don't hunt, buy. Sleep every night on a gel bed, and try to have two naked young native women as your blankets. Oh, oh, oh! Whoo! You old *lecher! Oh honoured sir. Indecent. Well, it works for me. I don't sleep that well but I'm happy. Thanks, don't mind if I do, thanks. I appreciate it. Cheers. Here's to Mars.*

She woke in a silence so still she could hear her heart. She couldn't remember where she was. Then it came back. They were at Nadia and Art's house, on the coast of the Hellas Sea, just west of Odessa. Tap tap tap. Dawn; the first nail of the day. Nadia was building outside. She and Art lived at the edge of their beach village, in their co-op's complex of intertwined houses, pavilions, gardens, paths. A community of about a hundred people, linked to a hundred more like it. Apparently Nadia was always working on the infrastructure. *Tap tap tap tap tap!* Currently building a deck to surround a Zygote bamboo tower.

In the next room someone was breathing. There was an open door between the rooms. She sat up. Hangings on the wall; she pulled them open a crack. Predawn. Grey on grey. A spare room. Sax was on a big bed in the next room, through the door. Under thick coverlets.

She was cold. She got up and padded through the door into his room. His face slack on a broad pillow. An old man. She crawled under the coverlets into bed with him. He was warm. He was shorter than she was, short and round. She knew that, she knew him: from the sauna and pool in Underhill, the baths in Zygote. Another part of their communal body. Tap tap tap tap tap. He stirred and she wrapped herself around him. He snuggled back into her, still deeply asleep.

During the memory experiment she had focused on Mars. Michel had once said it: Your task is to find the Mars that endures through all. And seeing the same hillocks and hollows around Underhill had reminded her intensely of the early years, when over each horizon had been a new thing. The land. In her mind it endured. On Earth they would never know what it was like, never. The lightness, the tight intimacy of the horizon, everything almost within touch; then the sudden immense vistas, when one of Big Man's neighbourhoods hove into view: the vast cliffs, the canyons so deep, the continent volcanoes, the wild chaos. The giant calligraphy of

777

areological time. The world-wrapping dunes. They would never know; it could not be imagined.

But she had known. And during the memory experiment she had kept her mind focused on it, throughout the entirety of a day that had seemed to last ten years. Never once thought of Earth. It was a trick, a tremendous effort; don't think of the word *elephant*! But she hadn't. It was a trick she had got good at, the singlemindedness of the great refuser, a kind of strength. Perhaps. And then Sax had come flying over the horizon, crying, Remember Earth? Remember Earth? It was almost funny.

But that had been Antarctica. Immediately her mind, so tricky, so focused, had said, That's just Antarctica, a bit of Mars on Earth, a continent transposed. The year they had lived there, a snatched glimpse of their future. In the Dry Valleys they had been on Mars without knowing it. So that she could remember it and it did not lead back to Earth, it was only an ur-Underhill, an Underhill with ice, and a different camp, but the same people, the same situation. And thinking about it, all of it had indeed come back to her, in the magic of the anamnestic enchantment: those talks with Sax; how she had liked someone as solitary in science as she was, how she had been attracted to him. No one else had understood how far you could walk out into it. And out there in that pure distance they had argued. Night after night. About Mars. Aspects technical, aspects philosophical. They had not agreed. But they were out there together.

But not quite. He had been shocked by her touch. Poor flesh. So she had thought. Apparently she had been wrong. Which was too bad, because if she had understood; if he had understood; if they had understood; perhaps all history would have changed. Perhaps not. But they had not understood. And here they were.

And in all the rush into that past, she had never once thought of the Earth farther north, the Earth before. She had stayed inside the Antarctic convergence. Indeed for the most part she had stayed on Mars, the Mars in her mind, red Mars. Now the theory was that the anamnestic treatment stimulated the memory and caused the consciousness to rehearse the associational complexes of node and network, bounding through the years. This rehearsal reinforced the memories in their physical tracery, such as it was, an evanescent field of patterns formed by quantum oscillation. Everything recalled was reinforced; and what was not recalled was perhaps not reinforced; and what was not reinforced would continue to fall prey to breakage, error, quantum collapse, decay. And be forgotten.

So she was a new Ann now. Not the Counter-Ann, nor even that shadowy third person who had haunted her for so long. A new Ann. A fully Martian Ann at last. On a brown Mars of some new kind, red, green, blue, all swirled together. And if there was a Terran Ann still in there, cowering in a lost quantum closet of her own, that was life. No scar was ever fully lost until death and the final dissolution, and that was perhaps the way it should be; one wouldn't want to lose too much, or it would be trouble of a different kind. A balance had to be kept. And here, now, on Mars, she was the Martian Ann, not issei any longer, but an elderly new native, a Terran-born yonsei. Martian Ann Clayborne, in the moment and the only moment. It felt good to lie there.

Sax stirred in her arms. She looked at his face. A different face, but still Sax. She had an arm draped over him, and she ran a cold hand down his chest. He woke up, saw who it was, smiled a sleepy little smile. He stretched, turned, pressed his face into her shoulder. Kissed her neck with a little bite. They held onto each other, as they had in the flying boat during the storm. A wild ride. It would be fun to make love in the sky. Not practical in a wind like that. Some other time. She wondered if mattresses were made the same way they used to be. This one was hard. Sax was not as soft as he looked. They hugged and hugged. Sexual congress. He was inside her, moving. She seized him and hugged him, hard, hard.

Now he was kissing her all over, nibbling at her, completely under the covers. Submarining around down there. She could feel it all over her. His teeth, occasionally, but mostly it was the licking of a tonguetip over her skin, like a cat. Lick lick lick. It felt good. He was humming, or mumbling. His chest vibrated with it, it was like purring. 'Rrrr, rrrr, rrrrrrrrrr.' A peaceful luxurious sound. It, too, felt good on her skin. Vibration, cat tongue, little licks all over her. She tented the coverlet so she could look down at him.

'Now which feels better,' he murmured. 'A?' Kissing her. 'Or B?' Kissing a different place.

She had to laugh. 'Sax, just shut up and do it.'

'Ah. Okay.'

They had breakfast with Nadia and Art, and the members of their family that were around. Their daughter Nikki was off on a feral trip into the Hellespontus Mountains, with her husband and three other couples from their co-op. They had left the previous evening in a clatter of excited anticipation, like kids themselves, leaving behind their daughter Francesca, and the friends' kids as well: Nanao, Boone and Tati. Francesca and Boone were both five, Nanao three, Tati two; all of them thrilled to be together, and with Francesca's grandparents. Today they were going to go to the beach. A big adventure. Over breakfast they worked on logistics. Sax was going to stay home with Art, and help him plant some new trees in an olive grove that Art was establishing on the hill behind the house. Sax would also be waiting to meet two visitors he had invited: Nirgal, and a mathematician from Da Vinci, a woman named Bao. Sax was excited to be introducing them, Ann saw. 'It's an experiment,' he confided to her. He was as flushed as the kids.

Nadia was going to keep working on her deck. She and Art would perhaps get down to the beach later, with Sax and his guests. For the morning the kids were to be in the care of Aunt Maya. They were so excited by this prospect they couldn't sit still; they squirmed, they bolted around the table like young dogs.

So Ann, it seemed, was needed to go to the beach with Maya and the kids. Maya could use the help. All of them eyed Ann warily. Are you up to it, Aunt Ann? She nodded. They would take the tram.

So she was off to the beach with Maya and the kids. She and Francesca and Nanao and Tati were crowded in the first seat behind the driver, with Tati on Ann's lap. Boone and Maya were sitting together in the seat behind. Maya came in this way every day; she lived on the far side of Nadia and Art's village, in a detached cottage of her own, on bluffs over the beach. She went in most days to work for her co-op, and stayed in many evenings to work with her theatre group. She was also an habituée of the café scene, and, apparently, these kids' most regular babysitter.

Now she was engaged in a ferocious tickle-fight with Boone, the two of them groping each other hard and giggling unabashedly. Something else to add to the day's store of erotic knowledge: that there could be such a sensuous encounter between a five-year-old boy and a two-hundred-and-thirty-year-old woman, the play of two humans both very experienced in the pleasures of the body. Ann and the other kids fell silent, slightly embarrassed to witness such a scene.

'What's the matter,' Maya demanded of them in a breathless break, 'cat got your tongue?'

Nanao stared up at Ann, appalled. 'A *cat* got your *tongue*?'

'No,' Ann said.

Maya and Boone shrieked with laughter. People on the tram looked up at them, some grinning, some glowering. Francesca had Nadia's curious flecked eyes, Ann saw. It was all of Nadia to be seen in her, she looked more like Art, but not much like either. A beauty.

They came to the beach stop: a little tram station, a rain shelter and kiosk, a restaurant, a parking lot for bikes, some country roads leading inland, and a broad path cutting through grassy dunes, down to the beach. They got off the tram, Maya and Ann laden by bags full of towels and toys.

It was a cloudy windy day. The beach proved to be nearly deserted. Swift, low waves came in at an angle to the strand, breaking in the shallows just offshore, in abrupt white lines. The sea was dark, the clouds pearl grey, in a herringbone pattern under a dull lavender sky. Maya dropped her bags. She and Boone ran to the water's edge. Down the beach to the east Odessa rose on its hillside, under a hole in the clouds so that all the tiny white walls glowed yellow in the sun. Gulls wheeled by looking for things to eat, feathering in the onshore wind. A pelican air-surfed over the waves, and above the pelican flew a man in a big birdsuit. The sight reminded Ann of Zo. People had died so young: in their forties, thirties, twenties; some in their teens, when they could just guess what they were going to miss; some at the age of these kids. Cut short like frogs in a frost. And it could still happen. At any moment the air itself could pick you up and kill you. Although that would be an accident. Things were different now, it had to be admitted; for barring accident, these kids would probably live a full span. A very full span. There was that to be said for the way things were now.

Nikki's friends had said it would be best to keep their daughter Tati out of the sand, as she was prone to eating it. So Ann tried to keep her back on the narrow lawn between dunes and beach, but she broke away, howling, and trundled over and plopped back on her nappy on the sand, near the others, looking satisfied. 'Okay,' Ann said, giving up and joining her, 'but don't eat any of it.'

Maya was helping Nanao and Boone and Francesca dig a hole. 'When we reach water-sand we'll start the drip castle,' Boone declared. Maya nodded, absorbed in the digging.

'Look,' Francesca shrieked at them, 'I'm running circles around you.'

Boone glanced up. 'No,' he said, 'you're running ovals around us.'

He returned to discoursing with Maya about the life cycle of sand crabs. Ann had met him before; a year ago he had scarcely been talking, just simple phrases like Tati and Nanao's, Fishie! Mine! and now he was a pedant. The way language came to children was incredible. They were all geniuses at that age, it took adults years and years to twist them down into the bonsai creatures they eventually became. Who would dare to do that, who would dare deform this natural child? No one; and yet it got done. No one did it and everyone did it. Although Nikki and her friends, packing happily for their mountain trip, had still seemed a lot like kids to Ann. And they were nearly eighty years old. So perhaps it didn't happen as much any more. There was that too to be said for things as they were.

Francesca stopped her circling or ovalling, and plucked a plastic shovel out of Nanao's hands. Nanao wailed in protest. Francesca turned away and stood on her tiptoes, as if to demonstrate how light her conscience was.

'It's my shovel,' she said over her shoulder.

'Is not!'

Maya barely glanced up. 'Give it back.'

Francesca danced off with it.

'Ignore her,' Maya instructed Nanao. Nanao wailed more furiously, his face magenta. Maya gave Francesca the eye. 'Do you want an ice cream or not?'

Francesca returned, dropped the shovel on Nanao's head. Boone and Maya, already reabsorbed in their digging, paid no attention.

'Ann, could you go get some ice creams from the kiosk?'

'Sure.'

'Take Tati with you, will you?'

'No!' Tati said.

'Ice cream,' Maya said.

Tati thought it over, worked laboriously to her feet.

She and Ann walked back to the tram stop kiosk, hand in hand. They bought six ice creams, and Ann carried five of them in a bag; Tati insisted on eating hers while they walked. She was not yet good at performing two such operations at once, and they made slow progress. Melted ice cream ran down the stick, and Tati sucked ice cream and fist indiscriminately. 'Pretty,' she said. 'Taste pretty.'

A tram came into the station and stopped, then moved on. A few minutes later, three people biked down the path: Sax, leading Nirgal and a native woman. Nirgal braked his bike next to Ann, gave her a hug. She hadn't seen him in many years. He was old. She hugged him hard. She smiled at Sax; she wanted to hug him too.

They went down and joined Maya and the kids. Maya stood to hug Nirgal, then shake hands with Bao. Sax biked back and forth on the lawn behind the sand, at one point riding with no hands and waving at the group; Boone, who was still using training wheels on his bike, saw him and shouted, flabbergasted: 'How do you *do* that!'

Sax abruptly grabbed the handlebars. He stopped the bike

and stared frowning at Boone. Boone walked awkwardly over to him, arms extended, and staggered right into his bike. 'Something wrong?' Sax inquired.

'I'm trying to walk without using my cerebellum!'

'Good idea,' Sax said.

'I'll go get more ice cream,' Ann offered, and left Tati this time, and trundled back up the sand to the grass path. It felt good to walk into the wind.

As she was returning with a second bag of ice cream bars, the air suddenly turned cold. Then she felt a kind of lurch inside her, and a faintness. The sea surface had a glittery hard purple sheen, well above the actual surface of the water. And she was very cold. Oh shit, she thought. Here it comes. Quick decline: she had read about the various symptoms, reported by people who had been somehow resuscitated. Her heart pounded madly in her chest, like a child trying to get out of a black closet. Body insubstantial, as if something had leached her of substance and left her porous; she would collapse into dust at the tap of a finger. Tap! She grunted with surprise and pain, held onto herself. Pain in her chest. She took a step toward a bench beside the path, then stopped and hunched over at a new pain. Tap tap tap! 'No!' she exclaimed, and clutched the bag of ice creams. Heart arrhythmic, yes it was bounding about, *bang bang, bang bang bang bang, bang, No,* she said without speaking. Not yet. The new Ann no doubt, but there was no time for that, Ann herself squeaked, 'No,' and then she was thoroughly absorbed in the effort to hold herself together. Heart you must beat! She held it so tightly she staggered. No. Not yet. The wind was a subzero frigidity, blowing right through her, her body ghostly; she held it together by will alone. Sun so bright, the harsh rays slanting right through her ribcage – the transparency of the world. Then everything was beating like a heart, the wind breathing right through her. She held herself together with every cramping muscle. Time stopped, everything stopped.

She took a short breath. The fit passed. The wind slowly warmed back up. The sea's aura went away, leaving plain blue water. Her heart thumped with its old *bump bump bump.*

Substance returned, pain subsided. The air was salty and damp, not cold at all. One could sweat in it.

She walked on. How forcibly the body reminded one of things. Still, she had held. She was going to live. For a while longer, at least. If it be not now ... but not now. So here she was. Tentatively she walked on, one step after another. Everything seemed to work. She had got away. Brushed only.

From the sandcastle Tati saw Ann and came trundling toward her, intent on the bag of ice creams. But she went too fast and fell right on her face. When she pulled herself up her face was coated with sand, and Ann expected her to howl. But she licked her upper lip like a connoisseur.

Ann walked over to help her. Pulled her to her feet, tried to wipe the sand off her upper lip; but she whipped her head back and forth to avoid the help. Ah well. Let her eat some sand, what harm could it do? 'There. Not too much. No, those are for Sax and Nirgal and Bao. No! Hey, look – look at the gulls! Look at the gulls!'

Tati looked up, saw seagulls overhead, tried to track them, fell on her bottom. 'Ooh!' she said. 'Pretty! Pretty! Innit pretty! Innit pretty?'

Ann hauled her back to her feet. They walked hand in hand toward the group by its widening hole, its mound of sand topped with drip castles. Nirgal and Bao were down by the waterline, talking. Gulls planed overhead. Down the beach an old Asian woman was surf-fishing. The sea was dark blue, the sky clearing, pale mauve, the remaining clouds scrolling off to the east. The air all rushing by. Some pelicans glided in a line over the rising face of a wave, and Tati dragged Ann to a halt, pointing at them. 'Innit pretty?'

Ann tried to walk on, but Tati refused to budge, tugged insistently at her hand: 'Innit pretty? Innit pretty? Innit pretty?'

'Yes.'

Tati let go of her and trundled over the sand, just managing to stay on her feet, her nappy waddling like a duck's behind, the backs of her fat knees dimpling.

But it still moves, Ann thought. She followed the child, smiling at her little joke. Galileo could have refused to recant, gone to the stake for the sake of the truth, but that would have been silly. Better to say what one had to, and go on from there. A brush reminded one what was important. Oh yes, very pretty! She admitted it and was allowed to live. Beat on, heart. And why not admit it? Nowhere on this world were people killing each other, nowhere were they desperate for shelter or food, nowhere were they scared for their kids. There was that to be said. The sand squeaked underfoot as she toed it. She looked more closely: dark grains of basalt, mixed with minute seashell fragments, and a variety of colourful pebbles, some of them no doubt brecciated fragments of the Hellas impact itself. She lifted her eyes to the hills west of the sea, black under the sun. The bones of things stuck out everywhere. Waves broke in swift lines on the beach, and she walked over the sand toward her friends, in the wind, on Mars, on Mars, on Mars, on Mars, on Mars.

CHRONOLOGY IN *BLUE MARS*

2127:	Battle for Sheffield and the cable
early 2128:	Constitutional congress
late 2128:	Ambassadors' trip to Earth
2128–2134:	Nadia's presidency
2129:	Zo Boone born
2134–2144:	Nirgal on Tyrrhena Massif
2155:	Sax meets Ann on Da Vinci
2160s:	Introduction of pulsed fusion space travel
2171:	Nirgal's run with the ferals
2180:	Zo and Ann visit Jovian and Uranian systems
2181:	Grand Canal election campaign
2190s:	Beginning of illegal immigration from Earth
2206:	Death of Michel
2211:	Underhill reunion
2212:	Sax and Ann sailing trip, cable crisis, third revolution

ACKNOWLEDGEMENTS

Thanks this time to Lou Aronica, Stuart Atkinson, Terry Baier, Kenneth Bailey, Paul Birch, Michael Carr, Bob Eckert, Peter Fitting, Karen Fowler, Patrick Michel François, Jennifer Hershey, Patsy Inouye, Calvin Johnson, Jane Johnson, Gwyneth Jones, David Kane and Ridge, Christopher McKay, Beth Meacham, Pamela Mellon, Lisa Nowell, Lowry Pei, Bill Purdy, Joel Russell, Paul Sattelmeier, Mark Tatar, Ralph Vicinanza, Bronwen Wang and Vic Webb.

A special thanks to Martyn Fogg, and, again, to Charles Sheffield.

The Broken God
David Zindell

'SF as it ought to be: challenging, imaginative, thought-provoking and well-written. Zindell has placed himself at the forefront of literary SF'   *Times Literary Supplement*

Book One of David Zindell's new epic trilogy is set in Neverness, legendary city of Light, where inner space and outer space meet . . . where the God program is up and running.

Into its maze of colour-coded streets of ice a wild boy stumbles, starving, frostbitten and grieving, a spear in his hand: Danlo the Wild, a messenger from the deep past of man. Brought up far from Neverness by the Alaloi people, neanderthal cave-dwellers, Danlo alone of his tribe has survived a plague – because he is not, as he had thought, a misshapen neanderthal, but human, with immunity engineered into his genes. He learns that the disease was created by the sinister Architects of the Universal Cybernetic Church. The Architects possess a cure which can save other Alaloi tribes. But the Architects have migrated to the region of space known as the Vild, and there they are killing stars.

All of civilization has converged on Neverness through the manifold of space travel. Beyond science, beyond decadence, sects and disciplines multiply there. Danlo, his mind shaped by primitive man, brings to Neverness a single long-lost memory that will challenge them all.

ISBN 0 586 21189 6